I0831747

KEEPER: THE GOVERNESS

Keeper

The Governess

Nicholas Adams

Cover Art by Eric LaTulippe

Map by Nicholas Adams

ISBN(s): 979-8-9992607-0-3 (hardcover) | 979-8-9992607-1-0 (e-book)

Library of Congress Control Number: 2025915709

Printed in the United States of America

First Edition: September 2025

Published by JDA Fiction, LLC

www.nicholasadamsauthor.com

To those who pushed me to finally finish writing this book over five years after the first page was put to paper.

Dead Lands

Brekkenia

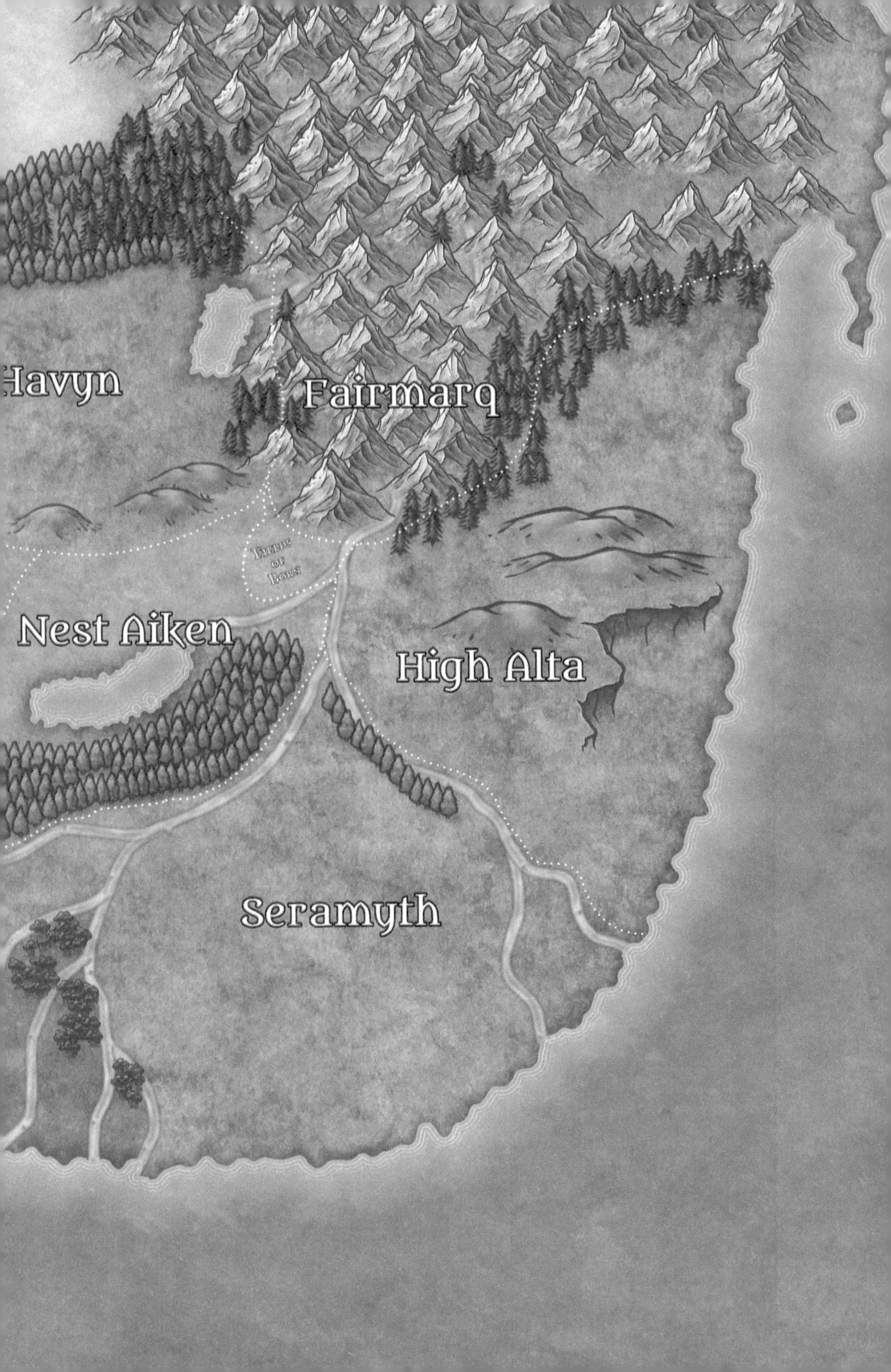

Havyn
Fairmarq
Fields of Born
Nest Aiken
High Alta
Seramyth

PROLOGUE

The mourning was quiet and gloomy. No one spoke as they lined the streets of Gabrenas, capital city of the region of Avalon, one of seven regions within the Kingdom of Havyn. A dark day indeed, for the sun could not break through the heavy fog that blanketed the city. Trumpets blared over the morning silence.

The trumpets were not a symbol of joy, not this time.

They signified demise. Death. A funeral.

The trumpets blared in a low tone once, twice. On the third bleat, the casket was lifted by the pallbearers and carried one step at a time. Drums beat off in the distance, setting the pace at which the pallbearers marched, armed guards protecting the flanks.

Guards were unnecessary, though, for the lord was loved by all. Not a soul would dare stir up trouble during the processions out of respect for their late leader. Having armed guards appeared more professional, more official.

Following behind the casket, a widowed wife walked with her eyes to the ground and a bouquet of white flowers in her hands. She wore an elegant black dress, perfect for the occasion. The citizens among the crowd knew no difference, though, for Lady Raven always dressed in black. Her long, platinum hair and pale skin were emphasized by her dark attire.

The silence was only broken by the quiet sobs from the crowd. The lord's death had seemed so surreal until they saw his wife walking alone. She had never been more than an arm's length apart from him anytime they were seen in public. The love she bore for him was unmatched by another couple in all of the country of Lynidas.

The lord had ruled with the popularity of the people in Avalon for nearly twenty-five years, one of the longest terms served by a lord in the Kingdom of Havyn. Seven lords for the seven regions that made up Havyn—the same provincial setup could be found in the other four kingdoms of Lynidas.

Raindrops gently fell on the back of Lady Raven's head as the funeral procession proceeded around the first bend of the main road leading from the capital building—the Grand Ballroom of Avalon. The procession that followed the casket was made up of the lord's closest friends and political allies, despite Raven's wishes.

She had not even wanted a public funeral. She wished to share her final moments with her late husband privately, but their allies insisted on including all of Avalon in the celebration of his life.

Some celebration this turned out to be, Lady Raven thought as the drizzle turned into a steady rain. The city guards held out umbrellas over the procession, who marched in pairs side by side. When the lady was offered one by the guard nearest her, she refused, brushing the guard away with her hand.

Let them see.

Let the people see her face the elements in the wake of her beloved husband's passing.

She would either appear stronger, or she would appear a fool. Truthfully, she didn't give a shit.

Finally, the end of the procession walked into the rain. The last pair sparked much interest in the crowd.

No one spoke as their eyes shifted from the casket to the pair moving in sync with the beat of the drums.

The City Watch did not guard these two like they had the rest of the procession. Instead, they were guarded by three very powerful individuals—two Guardians of the Faith and a Keeper.

Guardians of the Faith were only present while accompanying one important person—someone that could be seen as a deity to many. She was the Providence—the spiritual leader of Havyn, and gateway between the people and all religion and magic in the kingdom. Why was she here, many wondered? At the same time, however, they recognized the significance of being in the presence of someone so influential.

The Providence's partner in the procession was none other than the Master of Cities. The Master of Cities was the highest democratic position in all of the kingdom, requiring all of Havyn to vote for nominated candidates.

What struck people the most was the fact that the current Master of Cities was a dwarf. Dwarves were not common in the country of Lynidas, particularly in Havyn. Though he was voted for by an overwhelming majority of citizens, knowing he was a dwarf warranted strange reactions from people.

One of only two Keepers belonging to a member of the royal family held guard over the Master. The Order of the Keeper outstood all political parties and rivalries across Lynidas. Two Keepers were assigned to each immediate member of the royal family in the five kingdoms, with their master—the Librarian—overseeing them all. Keepers dedicate their lives to guarding members of the Monarchy, protecting them at all costs, and even sacrificing their lives if necessary. New Keepers are chosen by the Order and undergo decades of training before being assigned to guard a member of the royal family.

No umbrellas were held out for them, though. Instead, the Providence held a hand over her head, palm towards the sky, forming a thin ward over herself and her companions, deflecting the drops of rain as they grew heavier.

Magic...

A powerful and exquisite thing. Equally as hated as it is in rarity, though no one would dare cross the Providence, for she was the bridge between the Connections of Magic and those gifted enough to weave them.

The Providence was young. With youth usually came inexperience, but not in her case. She was the youngest Providence in Havyn's history, perhaps even in the history of all the kingdoms in Lynidas. She inherited the position, as each Providence before her had, by being the next female in the line of succession from the crown.

Some argue that her succession was questionable, but the power she possessed was both fearful and admirable enough to hold the tongues of those who may speak out against her.

Two miles of walking in the increasingly heavy rain finally ceased when the procession arrived at its destination—the Church of Avalon. Those who could fit inside the gates of the cemetery behind the church gathered around the gravesite. The granite mausoleum already opened to place the cherry casket containing the late lord's body.

The casket was lowered in front of the mausoleum. A golden Oblong Eye—symbol of the All-Seeing God—perched above the ornately carved mausoleum entrance. Muffled sobs amongst the crowd could barely be heard over the patter of the rain.

The drums stopped beating, and the trumpets bleated twice more, marking the entrance of the Master White Mage of Avalon. The Master White Mage of each region acted as the local spiritual leader, answering only to the lord or lady of the region and the Providence herself. His white robe would have dragged through the mud if not for the two lesser white mages following behind with the ends of the robe in hand.

The Master White Mage stood beneath the canopy in front of the mausoleum. A lesser white mage opened up a gilded copy of the *Paladin* and the Master White Mage turned to the marked page.

"I, Archem, Master White Mage of Avalon," the Master White Mage began his sermon, "am truly humbled and honored, though with great reluctance, to preside over the Ceremony of Life for our dearly departed Lord of Avalon. He leaves us now in a brighter world than when he first arrived. He now brings his light to the world beyond, accompanying the All-Seeing God in their prospect to save all their children from evil. Let us bow our heads for two moments of silence—one for the gods and one for our Lord."

Lady Raven's remained bowed, just as it had been during the entire procession. Her heartbeat thumped in her ears. Her breathing deep and slow. A weight pressed on her shoulders—the weight of grief.

"The All-Seeing God thanks us for our moment of silence. This day marks not only the passing of our beloved Lord, it marks the birth of a new era. The era the Lord created for us is not one to take for granted. He dedicated his life to serving the people of Avalon and has touched each one of us in some way. Whether it be his loving wife and life partner or just a common citizen, his smile and commitment has aided us all in a better life.

"The Faith recalls the moment the Lord first won the support of the people twenty-five years ago. Newly married and ambitious to campaign across all of Avalon, and the governor of Gabrenas for five years prior to his election. Such a swift succession in his career can hardly be matched by any other in all of Lynidas.

"My heart shatters saying these final goodbyes to his physical body, just as it does your own. Fear not, children of the Faith, for he is still alive in the Connections of Magic. Bear the fruits of our gods and consume their strength to aid us in this challenging time."

With that, the white mages carried around wicker baskets, handing perfectly shiny, red apples to each of the patrons in the crowd. Part of funerary tradition in Lynidas was to take a single bite from an apple and discard the remainder of the apple to the earth below. One bite to embrace the growth and harvest of the All-Seeing God and the rest to be sacrificed to the earth from which it grows, so the Faith states.

Raven would have refused the apple had it not been handed to her by Master Archem himself. She hadn't eaten in a week, and the thought of biting into the fruit made her nauseous. Looking at her dull reflection on the skin of the apple, Raven waited for the crunches of those around her taking a bite from their apples, and dropped her whole apple to the ground with their sacrifices.

Surely a sin, should anyone notice, but a grieving wife was not to be messed with. Especially not Lady Raven.

"The Connections of Magic weave through us all," Master Archem began again, "and intertwine our spiritual bodies together. Let us all focus our spirits within the Connections. Join me as we recite the *Hymn of the Paladin* and rest our lord's physical body with the earth and release his spirit to become one with the Connections."

The pallbearers took their spots next to the casket and carried it into the emptiness of the tomb. The Master White Mage chanted the hymn. Many others in the crowd joined him. Raven remained silent and held back tears as she said goodbye to her beloved husband.

Once the stone doors to the tomb were shut behind the pallbearers and the hymn was over, the funeral attendants were invited by Master Archem to join the lord's friends and family at the capital estate for a celebration of life. Food and drinks would be served all day into the evening. As pessimistic as Raven was, and however much she did *not* want to spend the entire day with people she could care less for, she could not wait to have a drink in her hand.

With a glass of wine in hand, Raven watched the partygoers laughing, smiling, and having a wonderful time. Had they forgotten why they were there? Sure, it was a Celebration of Life, but Raven hardly had time to mourn her husband's death before they buried him.

Twenty-five years... She had not spent a single day without him in twenty-five years. Reality was finally sinking in. Raven put her head into her free hand, holding back the emotions she was feeling.

"You are permitted to cry, I hope you know," a soft female voice said from behind her.

Raven whipped around to find the Providence standing behind her. Her Guardians of the Faith standing on either side of her, each holding a staff with a golden Oblong Eye mounted to the top.

Raven stood and bowed slightly, not forgetting her manners. "Providence, thank you for taking the time to attend today's events."

The Providence followed a chuckle with a sigh, "It was a funeral, Lady Raven. Your husband's, nonetheless. This was no cheerful event. Cry if you need to cry. Do not keep a stern composure simply for their amusement." She gestured a hand to the crowd of over three hundred guests on the ballroom floor. The Providence pulled out a chair and sat next to Lady Raven at the head table.

"He would want me to remain strong," Raven confided.

"If we did everything the men in our lives wanted us to do, we would never achieve success." Raven returned the Providence's comment with a confused look. "When people think of me, the *almighty* Providence," she rolled her eyes, "they consider me a 'powerful woman.' But what about the king, or even your late husband? Do they refer to them as 'powerful men?' No, simply 'powerful.' Why emphasize *our* gender but not of the men who hold power? Write your own destiny, Raven. Make your own path."

"I don't believe I have attained the title of 'powerful woman' quite yet," Raven managed to crack a smile. "My husband held the power, not I."

"*Yet*, Lady Raven," the Providence corrected. "Your husband held the power, but you went with him everywhere he went. They know your face. They know your name. Rule in your own name, not your husband's."

"Forgive me, Providence, but that is not how society works. The people will soon vote on a new lord. I cannot just keep being Lady because I want to."

"Forget the damned vote, my lady," another voice came from the other side of her. The Master of Cities approached and sat in the empty chair beside her. Raven couldn't help but stare. She had never met the dwarf in person. She forced herself to ignore the basic fact that she was nearly eye to eye with the man while remaining seated. What the dwarf lacked in stature, though, he made up for in muscle mass. Thick cords of pure muscle bulging from his arms could be seen under the tight sleeves of his tunic.

"Forget the vote," the Master of Cities repeated. "All nominations for Governor or Lord positions in any kingdom must first be approved by the Master of Cities. And as Master of Cities, *I* say you have the sole nomination."

Could he do that? Raven thought.

"No one would question anything," the dwarf elaborated. "I've spent the past four hours speaking with all the governors of Avalon and many of its citizens who attended today. They love you. None of them even mentioned the vote. They expect you to hold your position. Allow me to utilize the distraction of your husband's death to quietly move the pieces into place and ensure no one questions your place here in Avalon."

Raven's mind stirred. Part of her was excited to take up her husband's position. Another part was furious that the dwarf wanted to use her husband's death as a distraction. *That is how the game of politics is played, I suppose.*

But where did Raven fit into this political game? Why her, of all eligible people?

"Why me?" she asked out loud.

After many seconds of hesitation, the Providence responded, "I will be honest with you, Lady Raven. Your husband's death comes at a very suspicious time, under very suspicious circumstances."

"You know?" Raven whispered, eyes widening.

"I read the Master White Mage's report. When he inspected the body, he tested his blood and found light traces of—"

"Poison..." Raven finished. "It was poison."

The Master of Cities spoke, "Do not worry. You will be safe. Should you accept the position of Lady, I can offer plenty of protection from the City Watch. I will assign another thousand—fuck it, *ten* thousand—guards to Avalon for added security."

"We want to investigate this situation further," the Providence said, "and help you find out who did this to you and your husband. More importantly, *why* this happened."

"What else do you know?" Raven asked suspiciously. She was overwhelmed by the sudden burst of information and responsibility. She wanted more than anything to find her husband's killer, but she couldn't help but feel like information was being withheld by these two.

"All we know," answered the Providence, "is that there is one person who we believe might be able to help. They have experience solving crimes that even the City Watch and the Military cannot solve."

"Who?"

The Master of Cities leaned back in his chair, ran his gloved fingers through his thick, red beard. "She is young. But she is very smart, dedicated, and she does not let anyone push her around. She is the governess of a small city in the Cyprien region. Not a soul in Avalon would know who she is, allowing her to find the details we might overlook. She can help."

Raven thought for a moment. This governess certainly would be a help, if what the dwarf says about her is true. She would not draw too much attention. Finding killers was generally easy, but killers who use low traces of poison were practically invisible.

Raven took a deep breath and sighed, "Okay, okay. We have a deal. Thank you both for doing this. Finding his killer won't bring him back, but it will bring him justice. When can I expect to meet this young governess?"

"In due time, Lady Raven," the Providence placed a dainty hand over Raven's. "I am forever sorry for your loss. If you need anything, send a dove." With that, the Providence stood up and walked out, Guardians of the Faith and their Oblong Eye staves tailing her.

The Master of Cities stood, patting Raven on the shoulder, "Talk with you soon, *Lady*." The dwarf followed the same path as his counterpart, his Keeper meeting him at the base of the dais.

Only when Raven was finally alone that night did she shed a single tear for her lost love.

CHAPTER 1

Morning broke through the forest canopy. Sunlight shimmered through the rustling leaves while the birds began singing their morning chorus. A blue jay flapped its wings, launching itself from a branch. It landed on the forest floor to pick up some seeds it spotted from above. As it hopped along, it suddenly noticed something moving by a nearby tree. Curiously, it stopped and watched.

The blue jay chirped loudly.

A pile of leaves shifted slightly. The jay chirped again.

The leaf pile grunted.

The jay tipped its head and chirped a third time.

"Shut up," the pile of leaves groaned. The leaves rustled as the body beneath turned over. The bird picked up its wings and flew off, startled. A young man, maybe in his late teens or early twenties, threw the blanket of leaves from himself. The bird had woken him from a much-needed sleep. Days of travelling alone—fleeing—had exhausted him.

He cracked open an eyelid. Glancing around, he noted the amber and auburn leaves floating in the canopy above and freckling the forest floor.

It's finally autumn, he thought to himself. The young man sat up and brushed the leaves off of himself. He stood and adjusted the sword sheathed at his hip. He could just barely see his breath in the morning sunlight. *Soon to be winter...*

He had to stay hidden, but he had lost his bearings in the past day. He would have to reconnect with the main road and figure out where he should go. There was no destination, he just had to get away.

He supposed there was no difference whether he travelled through the woods or on the main road. He had avoided the roads to keep from being seen, but the crunching of the leaves under his boots could attract anyone, or anything, for a mile off. His only saving grace was the sound of the singing birds drowning out his heavy steps.

It had been a week since he fled his village. His was not the first to succumb to the same fate in recent months. The thought of the event made his knees weak and his head heavy. He couldn't think about it... He had to focus on where he was going, not what he was running from.

These roads were not travelled much. Being on the outskirts of the kingdom, there was no noise of traffic to be heard. He walked without thinking in a straight direction, only moving to avoid trees and rocks in his path. He could be walking in the opposite direction, away from the road, for all he knew.

He could find another village to stay in for a night or two, or perhaps he could find a town or city with some work. Forget this whole thing ever happened. He supposed he could find work in a scribe's services, or maybe a library, or an assistant to some kind of tradesman. Something quiet and unnoticeable. Something to stay hidden in plain sight.

The young man escaped from his thoughts to realize that the birds had stopped chirping. He stood still for a moment in the middle of a clearing.

He listened. Something wasn't right.

The brush on the outskirts of the clearing rustled. The man turned in the direction of the brush. The rustling occurred behind him. He whipped around.

Nothing...

A stick snapped, echoing off the trees.

He turned once more, slowly.

A massive wolf with salivating jaws stood at the edge of the clearing across from him. He held his breath, trying not to show fear. The beast curled back its lips, showing teeth.

The young man reached for the sword sheathed at his side. He touched the hilt.

The wolf began to growl at the threat, signaling the rest of its pack. Four other wolves equal in size and ferocity stepped out from the shadows of the trees.

Oh, fuck, he cursed under his breath.

Taking one step backwards, a stick snapped under his heel.

The wolves lunged.

The sword was drawn from its sheath, metal flashing as the wolves leaped.

He swung the sword over one shoulder, then the other. The wolves dodged away at the last moment, avoiding the blade. They circled around the clearing, preparing their next attack.

Fight or flight. A basic instinct for animals—an overwhelming thought for humans. Should he risk fighting off five full-grown wolves? There was little questioning that his skill with a sword was mediocre at best. If he stood his ground, there would be little left of him should he succeed in killing the beasts, if he survived at all. Fleeing, though... Was it possible to run from a single wolf, let alone a pack skilled in communicating and hunting down their prey?

The man let out the breath he had been holding. In a momentary flash of instinct, he turned and sprinted.

Flight.

The wolves hardly blinked. They waited a split second before bursting after him, tearing up the ground in their wake. One would think an army was marching with how the ground shuddered under the stampede of the hunters. The young man was soon to become the hunted.

He still had no idea where the nearest road or civilization was. All sense of direction was lost in the skirmish. The sword was still gripped in his hands as he flew across the forest floor. Trying to see where the wolves were was impossible. If he looked away from the path in front of him, he would surely trip over a branch or bramble or run face first into a tree.

Just run. Don't look back. Just run.

The trees began to spread out. Was he coming up to another clearing? He could hear the pounding of the wolves' paws thundering closer and closer. Less trees meant less obstacles between him and the creatures chasing after their prey. His lungs burned. He had enough strength in him for one final push.

The density of the forest continued to dissipate as he closed his eyes and gave his muscles a burst of energy. Picking up speed for a few moments, he burst through the edge of the forest, tripping over his own feet and tumbling head-over-heel.

The sword flew from his hand, landing five yards away as his face dragged through the dirt. Quickly, he flipped onto his back and shuffled backwards as the wolves sped towards him.

Two approached simultaneously and leaped, claws ready to shred. He closed his eyes and clenched his teeth, praying for a swift death.

The guttural growl was suddenly interrupted by the singing of metal. A pair of yelps squealed in the air.

The man opened his eyes to see someone clad in armor wielding a sword standing over two wolves with opened throats. The three remaining wolves ceased their attack and circled around the two humans.

A whistle in the air was followed by two arrows from afar lunging into the eyes of two of the remaining wolves. They dropped to the dirt instantly.

Behind them, two men in leather armor dismounted their horses and held bows nocked with arrows.

The final wolf did not break eye contact with the young man's rescuer as it stepped over the corpses of its departed pack. Fight or flight. And this beast intended to fight.

It lunged swiftly, latching its jowls on the sword-bearing arm of the rescuer. The rescuer grunted as they drew a dagger from their hip and plunged the blade into the beast's neck. Blood sprayed from the animal as it loosened its grip on the rescuer's arm, allowing them to slip out of its jaws. Blood pooled around the creature, dagger lodged in its throat, yet it continued to fight. Weakly, it pounced again at its attacker, who uppercut their blade just in time to slash the wolf across the chest.

The rescuer caught the dying beast in their arms, throwing the limp body to the ground. The beast twitched and blood heaved from its mouth as it struggled to breathe.

Within seconds, all life left the wolf's eyes.

The young man watched the whole scene unfold in front of him. His jaw dropped in awe.

The person who rescued him, who had stood in front of him as five wolves charged at him, cleaned the blood off of their blade with a rag. They pulled the arrows from the eye sockets of the other two wolves and tossed them back to the leather-clad horse riders.

The young man met eyes with his rescuer. *A woman! In armor?*

In fact, it *was* a woman standing before him. Shoulder-length black hair caressed a hardened, yet strangely pretty, young face. Her green eyes met his brown.

"Come on," she offered him a gauntleted hand. "Up you go."

He grasped her hand, and she hoisted him to his feet.

She was much shorter than he was, maybe a few inches over five feet. *Size clearly doesn't matter,* he thought, glancing at the hundred-and-twenty-pound wolves decorating the forest floor.

Only, they weren't in the forest anymore. He had made it to the main road.

"Are you going to stand there all day?" she asked. "Or are you going to help me move the carcasses out of the road?"

He snapped back to reality. "Yeah, sorry. I'm a bit shaken up."

"Understandable, but let us get to it. Then, we need to talk."

He did as he was told and moved the wolves' bodies to the edge of the forest with this mysterious woman. Her two companions pulled their horses to the side of the road, out of the way of any traffic. The young man and his rescuer met them at the road's edge.

"Alright," the woman sighed, "it is time to talk." She nodded to her two companions, who then gripped the young man by the shoulders and forced him to his knees.

"What in the Connections are you doing?" the young man shouted in confusion. Why were they being forceful with him?

The woman drew her sword and held the tip of the steel blade against his jugular.

"I ask the questions, you will answer. Do you understand?" the woman asked with an icy coolness.

He nodded.

"Where are you from and what are you doing out in the forest?" she asked coldly, not a single expression breaking from her face.

"I'm from one of the villages on the outskirts," he answered nervously. "You won't know it—"

"Elsaia? Spriggen's Farm? Outland?" she recited the names of many of the small villages that did not even appear on some maps. "Arolye?"

"Arolye! I'm from Arolye. How do you know of it?"

She ignored the question. "What are you doing so far from Arolye?"

"I… I don't know…"

"Cut the shit," she pressed the blade deeper. "The way I see it, there are two reasons why you would be fleeing your village. One, you are running away from something that happened to you in your village. Or two, you are running away from a crime you committed there. Which is it?"

"You wouldn't believe me if I told you..."

"You have two options right now, villager. You can either come with me back to the city and explain what happened, or you will be forced to come back to the city against your will and be tortured until you tell the truth. Either way, you are coming with me, and you are telling me what happened. How that happens is entirely up to you."

"I would prefer the option where I'm *not* held prisoner," he sighed, thinking for a moment. "My village was attacked. Burned down. I am the only survivor, that I know of."

"Attacked by who? Or by what?"

"People. People who could control fire. Mages..." he chuckled. "Sounds so ridiculous saying it out loud."

The woman withdrew the blade from his neck. She sheathed it and pulled the horses together. Her two companions mounted their own horses. She offered the reigns of a spare horse to him.

"What?" He was confused. "Just like that, I'm trusted?"

She patted the neck of the horse. "I never said I trusted you. I believe you. That is most important right now."

"You believe me about the mages?" he was astounded. Mages were legends in the villages. Myths. He told her as much.

"They are real," the woman confirmed. "Your village is not the first to be torched by them. You just happen to be the only survivor we have found so far. One of our own died during our travels, so you are lucky enough to have a horse."

"I... I'm sorry about your friend."

"It is the risk we take." She tightened the straps of the saddle and adjusted the stirrups. "Not the first to die, nor the last. Just as your village will not be the last."

Other villages have suffered the same fate. And he was the *only* survivor? Unbelievable.

He wanted to ask this woman what she was doing out here in the middle of nowhere, but intimidation overcame him. There was nothing outwardly special about her. She was of average height for a young woman, and with an athletic build, but her armor made her appear fearless and powerful. She *was* fearless and powerful, though. That was no mere appearance.

The young man was beckoned to the armored woman's side and handed the reins of the horse.

"My name is Drake, by the way," he said, holding out his hand.

The woman paused for a moment, looked at his extended hand, and replied sourly, "Perhaps it is best we do not exchange formalities just yet."

Drake dropped his hand. He meant no offense by formally introducing himself. Reading this woman was impossible. She expressed no emotion and stubbornly refused to lower her guard. In her defense, she did not know Drake at all. Anything he told her could be a lie. But that still didn't change the fact that her harsh tone was taken personally.

Seeing the perturbed look on Drake's face, the woman sighed, "Fine, the name is Ena. Get on the horse. We can make it to El Vadora by sun-high if we keep a steady pace."

El Vadora. One of the seven cities in the region of Cyprien—the smallest and least memorable of the seven.

Drake nodded and placed a foot in the stirrup, preparing to hoist his other leg over the wide body of the horse he was given. Something was off, though. He suddenly realized his sword was not at his side. It had flown from his hand in the skirmish with the wolves. He took his foot out of the stirrup and searched around.

Ena's two guards grunted impatiently. They shouted to Ena, who was mounting her own horse. "Drake, what is it?" she asked.

"My sword..." He scoured the path around them with no sword in sight. He muttered with defeat, "Shit..."

Ena made a sharp whistle with her tongue, grabbing Drake's attention out of his scattered thoughts. She unbuckled a large sack hanging from her horse's side and drew the large, black blade from the saddlebag.

"My sword!" Drake sped towards Ena.

"Ah! No." Ena's guards immediately drew arrows pointed at Drake's head. "I will hold onto this until I can be sure to trust you. Scabbard, please." Ena inspected the blade in her hand while Drake frustratingly gave up, unclipped the sheathe from his belt, handing it to Ena, and mounted the horse.

There was more to Drake than he cared to reveal. She watched his every movement like a hawk hunting a field mouse and instructed her two companions to do the same.

One of her companions took the lead while the other led their horse behind Ena and Drake, who travelled side-by-side. Anxiety and zeal washed over Drake knowing he was being brought into the city. The uncertainty of Ena's plan for him left a lump in his throat. Perhaps he could manage to break off from her once inside the city walls and find honest work. Curiosity surrounded Ena, though. Who was she? What was she doing out here? How did she know about the mages and why did she care?

All would soon be revealed.

CHAPTER 2

Drake's skill on horseback, or lack thereof, was obvious. Ena lost count of how many times Drake's horse bumped into hers. Or the number of times his horse drifted off the side of the road.

"I thought these things basically controlled themselves," Drake finally vocalized his frustrations an hour into their journey.

Ena had laughed, emotion breaking through her stoic composure for the first time. "Not exactly. It takes months to master one horse. Years to master them all."

Ena was right. She was raised riding horses. *Every beast is different,* her father used to say. *Each has a mind of their own. Only* you *can learn to control them.* Almost anyone, imbecile or genius, could learn to ride a horse that is given to them. But the ability to get atop any horse and master it—make them an extension of oneself—requires many years of training. Some may even argue that the ability is inherited, not learned.

From the age of five, Ena's father had her on top of a new horse every week with one task in mind—make it obey you. Most of the time, she was successful. The times she wasn't, she had bruises and scars to replace her success.

She grew up with hundreds of horses. Being the daughter of an esteemed horse salesman in a wealthy city had its perks. They were rich beyond Ena's comprehension as a child. Her father's name was known by every aristocrat, politician, and merchant from Cyprien to Havana. He sold horses to every lord and lady, governor and governess, and even the royal family.

The rarest, most beautiful, and most expensive horses came in and out of her father's stable just as often as the cheaper, more common breeds. Ena had seen them all, raised them all, ridden them all, and broken them all.

She could not help but laugh as Drake struggled to walk in a straight line with his easy-tempered horse.

As great of a teacher as her father was, and as smart of a man as he could be, he was a horrible parent. Ena was thankful for her equine mastery, but that was as far as her affection for the man went. If she wasn't being thrown from untamed, unbroken horses, she was being beaten by the man who claimed to love her. Of course, he never told *her* that—only the people who came to purchase his horses would ever hear how wonderful his daughter was.

Once she reached her fourteenth birthday, she grew into a woman's body enough for her to pass off for the legal age of sixteen to enlist in the City Watch. Many of the guards and officers knew her from frequenting her father's shop for their own horses, yet no one questioned it as she forged her age on the enlistment paperwork. She never even told her father she was leaving. He never came looking for her either. He must have known where she was, for the City Watch continued going to him for their horses right up until his death.

It came unexpectedly, but not surprisingly.

He was sick for years and most of the fortune he amassed from his business was spent on medical bills. He also did not have the free labor of his daughter any longer to assist him, and he was too frugal and indebted to the white mages for their healing capabilities to hire a new stable hand. The work overload, the debt creeping higher and higher, and his illness became the death of him.

Ena was in her third year of enlistment when she got word of his death. She attended the funeral and was the only family member or friend to show. The rest were all business associates and customers who were even more aggrieved by his passing due to their loss of good quality merchandise. Ena immediately sold her father's business, paid off his debts, and broke even with nothing to show for his hard work, or hers. The remaining horses at the stable were given away for free to the City Watch. She buried her father with everything he had, including any respect or love his own daughter had for him.

"You need to hold the reins tighter," Ena instructed. Her arrogant tone came off more judgmental than educational. "If you do not keep her head from wandering, *she* will keep wandering. When turning, pull the reins and tap your heel into the hip on the opposite side. Keep your damned eyes on the road where you want to go. She cannot follow your direction if you are not giving her any."

Drake took a deep breath and straightened his back, focusing on the road before him. He did as Ena told him and pulled the left side of the reins and jerked his right heel into the horse's side. As Ena predicted, the horse listed to the left until she was back on the road by Ena's side. "It is not that hard, more so with a horse broken from birth like the morgan you now ride. She is a sweet one, an obedient one. Perfect for someone who has never been on horseback."

Drake opened his mouth to argue, but realized it was pointless. After all, she wasn't wrong. "Is it really that obvious?"

A slight smile snuck from Ena's hardened face, "You were from a farming village. Horses are not necessary for that line of work, and they are growing more and more expensive as the years pass." No business could compete with the high demand like her father's did. Even now, seven years after his passing, he haunted the horse and stable business like a plague.

Drake didn't need an interpreter to understand what she was saying—he was a poor farmer who could not afford a mule, let alone a fully broken and trained horse.

"How did you learn so much about horses?" Drake asked, breaking the momentary silence.

Each step Ena's horse took was felt throughout her entire body. A horse is an extension of oneself, Ena always told herself. Each step the horse took, she took. Wherever she looked, the horse looked. Any slight movement by Ena was felt by the horse beneath her, just as the horse's movements were felt by Ena. The uncertainty in Ena's thoughts translated into anxiety that the horse felt, snorting and jerking her head, tugging the reins. How much could she tell this total stranger?

"Being part of the City Watch in El Vadora has its advantages," she attempted to keep her answer simple.

City Watch? Drake thought. *That explains the armor.* "I thought the Watch only trained the guards to use horses for war and battle. You have a different understanding of them, something more personal."

"The Watch does not train for war and battle," Ena retorted. "They train for protection and order. That is the difference between us and the Military."

"However," she rolled her eyes and continued, knowing he would keep asking questions if she didn't give him a worthy answer, "you are not wrong. I was raised on a stable and rode hundreds of horses throughout childhood. You can say I have a 'different understanding' of them."

Ena had been away from her home at El Vadora too long. She was eager to get back.

Sun-high was approaching. The crispness in the air had ebbed for the day. Any breeze broke leaves from their branches. Ena watched them fall to the forest floor like rain. Though they were on what was considered by many to be the main road, they still remained in the middle of a forest. Cyprien was the smallest of the seven regions in the Kingdom of Havyn in terms of population and economy. However, in terms of land, Cyprien was one of the largest. The total number of farms and villages was unknown. These farms are what fed the people of Havyn—something most did not realize.

Cyprien was the furthest region from Havana, the region which housed the capital city of Havyn, Havana City; therefore, Cyprien tends to be easily forgotten. The city of El Vadora did not even appear on some maps. Its relevance was not apparent to the rest of the kingdom.

Ena knew the importance of El Vadora. Being on the outskirts of the kingdom bordering open farmland and an endless forest, they were occasionally attacked by bands of thugs, packs of wolves and other dangerous creatures, and, most recently, mages.

Could they rely on the king of Havyn to send an army to fight off these attackers? Of course not. Despite that job falling under the jurisdiction of the king and the Military, it was the City Watch that handled the protection of the Cyprien region from outside invaders.

A shame that half the kingdom would starve if these farms were all destroyed, Ena thought to herself. *Maybe that would finally get El Vadora the recognition it deserves.*

The red and gold canopy opened to clear skies as the walls of El Vadora appeared on the horizon. The dirt path that served as a road widened, allowing Ena's companions to flank her and Drake. In a single row, their horses walked up to the large wooden gate. City Watch guards mounted the ramparts and saw the them approaching. Without a word, one of the guards nodded to someone below on the inside of the wall.

A sound of clattering chains could be heard as the wooden gates creaked open slowly. A single City Watch guard on horseback trotted to meet them.

"You're back," was all the guard said.

Ena walked her horse forward a step and replied, "Yes, Commander Veto, I am back. We have much to discuss."

"I'm sure we do, Governess Athenia," Commander Veto turned his horse and led them into the city.

Governess Athenia?! Drake was speechless... Everyone in the villages outside of El Vadora knew Governess Athenia by name. She was the youngest person in Havyn's history to hold the office of Governor. She had the reputation of being unbreakable, incorruptible. During her three years as Governess, she had solved more "unsolvable" crimes single-handedly than the whole of the City Watch has in the past decade.

Fearless. That was the first impression Drake got from her. Now the pieces all started falling together.

"Why didn't you tell me you were Governess Athenia?" Drake asked quietly, leaning over into Ena's ear.

Ena shot him warning glance, fire shooting from her eyes, "Keep your mouth shut, if you want to keep yourself alive, Drake. I prefer 'Ena' over 'Athenia.'"

Together, they walked their horses through the gates. Creaking wood sounded as the gates were shut behind them. On either side of the gate behind the wall, massive cranks connecting a chain to the two doors of the gate were being turned by guards. The walls and the gate were not extraordinarily high. Anyone with a tall enough ladder could scale them. The defense of the city clearly rested with the guards, not the fortifications. Guards were positioned atop the ramparts every twenty feet, armed with a sword and a bow.

Their horses were led by guards on foot to a nearby stable, where the governess, her two companions, and Drake dismounted. Ena made certain to carry the saddlebag containing Drake's strange blade. Her own sword hung from the belt at her side. She walked closely with Commander Veto as they strolled through the streets.

Drake hadn't a clue where they would be going. Athenia did not want to tip him off, so she gestured for her two companions to walk far behind her with Drake between them.

"You were gone three months, Athenia," Veto said. Not a question, just a simple comment.

"I, too, can keep track of time, Veto," she retorted. Veto silently asked why she had been gone so long. "I was doing what you couldn't do, per usual."

They turned onto a bustling cobblestone street lined with businesses and cart vendors. The citizens of El Vadora knew Athenia's face and they all waved and shouted to her upon recognition. The governess smiled stiffly and waved back.

Veto, a man twice the height of the governess and twice as armored, was one of few people who did not back down to Ena's blunt remarks. "It is my job to protect the people of El Vadora. Not to run around through the woods chasing ghosts."

"Those villages and farms fall within our city's jurisdiction. Where is your protection for them?" Athenia demanded, still managing to smile and shake a few hands as she passed.

"Your job is here within the city, not out there," Veto would not accept her degrading comments.

A little girl ran up and took Athenia into a hug and squeezed her abdomen. Veto shouted at the girl to get off the governess and unsheathed half of his sword as a threat.

"Enough of that, Veto," Ena snapped. "She is a child." Ena rubbed her gloved hand on the top of the girl's head, disheveling her hair. The girl smiled up at Ena from ear-to-ear before returning to her parents.

"They miss you because you were absent for three months." Another dig towards her.

"You may not approve of how I handle my time or my position, Commander," Ena bit back, "but it is *my* time and *my* position to do with as I please. The people of my city approve of me and my absences because of what I get done during that time. How many times now have you exhausted the resources of these taxpayers attempting to solve crimes within the city that remain unsolved? How many times do I venture out alone and solve the same cases within a fraction of the time and a fraction of the cost? The numbers are equivalent, Veto. I should have removed you from your position after the first dozen cases. I chose otherwise. Why? Because you are a valuable asset in other regards and the people support you as well. However, even you would not be equipped to handle the situation outside of our walls."

"My men and I can handle anything that you and your *personal guard detail* can." Veto spat.

"Go bring me the heads of some fire mages, then, Commander," Ena stopped and faced the commander. Drake and her guard detail stopped ten feet behind them.

"Fire mages?" Veto's demeanor shifted "Are you certain?"

"I spent three months ensuring my certainty."

The commander held his tongue for the remainder of their walk. At the end of the business quarter, they took a right turn down an even wider cobblestone street. The buildings were not tall or extravagant. Simple homes made from wood or stone. Down the middle of the street, trees were planted every fifty-or-so feet, as if separating the sides of the road. At the end of the street was their destination.

A domed stone building three stories high rested stop a set of stone steps, like a dais in a throne room. A statue of a person stood at the foot of the steps with a plaque at the foot. Which read *"El Vadora House of the Governor."* The city was governed entirely from behind the walls of this magnificent structure. Well, not entirely—Governess Athenia saw to that when she sought a more hands-on method for administrating the city she acquired.

Drake was awestruck. This was the first time he was outside of his tiny village in the middle of nowhere since birth, and here he was in what seemed to be the most extravagant, luxurious environment he could ever imagine. They climbed the handful of steps and entered the House of the Governor through stone doors held open by two City Watch guards.

Drake's world had been shaken to its core in the best possible way, so he believed. This city was a new start for him. For Governess Athenia, though, the city was soon to be left behind. For what she did not yet know, marching along the southern road and approaching the southern gates of El Vadora, were six Guardians of the Faith, armed with their Oblong Eye staves, mounted on white stallions carrying a letter stamped with an Oblong Eye, seal of the Providence.

CHAPTER 3

"Where is she?" asked the king of Havyn. He stood at the railing of the balcony overlooking Havana City. When his predecessors built the Spire of the New King, they ensured a way for all future kings to keep watch over their kingdom. Havyn was meant to be a place safe from all judgement—equality for all, rich or poor—yet the palace that served as the symbol of the monarchy stood high and mighty atop the peak of the hill on which Havana City was built, casting judgement down on its subjects.

Havana City, capital of the Havana region of Havyn, was perched at the southernmost edge of the Kingdom of Havyn. Outside of the massive walls surrounding the city, open grassland spread for miles over the horizon not belonging to any kingdom of Lynidas. According to the Concordat, signed over a thousand years ago, all land to the southwest of Havyn belonged to the forty-nine kingdoms of the Brekken Alliance. To the very east of Havyn, lay the Kingdom of Fairmarq, the largest territory with the largest royal family of all of the Five Kingdoms of Lynidas. To the south of Havyn, lay the Kingdom of Nest Aiken, which shared a border with the Brekken kingdoms to the west, just as Havyn did.

A thousand years ago, with the signing of the Concordat, Fairmarq and Nest Aiken gave up a significant portion of each of their kingdoms to the first king of Havyn to serve as the newly founded kingdom. Even the Brekkens agreed to hand over a sliver of land bordering the forest and farmland to the north for Havyn's creation.

The establishment of Havyn gave many a sense of hope and freedom. The first king of Havyn was said to have fought for its creation to give people a promised land of peace and equality. For the people of Havyn, the Concordat meant safety. For the other four kingdoms and the Brekkens to the west, the Concordat meant the end of political strife and created a system of checks-and-balances. It took power solely from the hands of the kings and divided their responsibilities between the Monarchy, the Faith, and the People—the King, the Providence, and the Master of Cities. One existed in each of the Five Kingdoms, and no one branch of government could become stronger than another.

Havyn's current king, though, was much less a player in the game of politics and more of an enemy of himself. His position was merely symbolic. Was it always this way? No, absolutely not—the Concordat prevented as much. However, royal blood was waning, and the king's sanity began to falter years ago. The Providence and the Master of Cities took it upon themselves to rule in his stead.

Did the king realize this? No, absolutely not.

He did not realize much these days.

"Where is she?!" the king asked again. This time, much angrier. He whipped around on his heels to face his two counterparts, his two Keepers at both of his sides.

Sheridan, the Master of Cities, and the only dwarf in the palace, spoke up, "Your Highness, she is gone."

"Gone? Gone where?" the king's frustration grew. His arms flailed with each word he spoke, nearly knocking the elaborate crown from his brow.

"Dead, Your Highness," Sheridan spoke again, crossing his hands in front of him. He withheld a sigh. This was not the first time this conversation had occurred, nor would it likely be the last.

"Dead?" the king's face morphed into utter sorrow. "How... how is she dead? Who killed her?!" He strode forward, stomping, and lowered his stance until he was face-to-face with the red-bearded dwarf.

The Providence cleared her throat, "Typhus, your wife was not killed by anyone." She looked at him, he looked at her. "She died of the plague. Five years ago. We have spoken about this before."

"That's impossible..." King Typhus whispered, more to himself than he was responding to the Providence. He stood up straight and paced back and forth, his cloak levitating behind him each time he rotated. "I just saw her last evening... She is not dead. She can't be! You!" He charged at the Providence, halting mere inches from her face. He held a finger to her collar bone and jabbed his long, unkempt fingernail into her flesh with each syllable, "You. Killed. Her. You are jealous!"

The Providence lifted her porcelain hand, gently brushing the king's finger away from her. The Keepers lifted their spears and took a single step forward. No one was to lay a hand on the king. Thankfully, the Providence and Sheridan held a good reputation with the Keepers to prevent them from immediately attacking. They also knew if they struck the Providence, her two Guardians of the Faith were waiting not even five yards behind her. The Guardians dropped into an attack stance and their staves lowered, the center of the Oblong Eyes glowing and spinning like a gold coin on a tabletop.

The Providence lifted a hand. The Guardians returned to attention and held the staves at their sides. "Typhus, what could I be jealous of? You know what I speak is the truth. We have discussed this before, many times."

"Jealous!" King Typhus threw his cloak behind him, exaggerating his movements, as usual. "Jealous that I have always loved her and *never* loved you!"

The Providence sighed, her shoulders drooping with grief. Not grief because the king was correct, but grief because his mind was not processing things clearly at all. "Typhus, I am not jealous of you and Helena. I am your cousin. We share the same blood, as is necessary for our positions." The king returned to the edge of the balcony looking over his city. She looked to the Keepers. "Why don't you take him to bed? The king is clearly distressed."

The Keepers exchanged a glance. "We will retire the king when the king commands, unfortunately. My apologies, Providence."

"We will leave him be, then," Sheridan said. The Providence and the Master of Cities dipped their heads with respect before turning and walking back into the palace. The Guardians of the Faith turned inboard and marched behind them.

Returning inside from the balcony, the Providence and Sheridan strode down one of the parallel set of stone steps leading down a level into the throne room. Once in front of the throne, the two conversed about the state of the king's health.

"I need not run tests on him," the Providence spoke in a whisper. "I have already witnessed enough to know he is not of sound mind. I need only to convince him to willingly allow me to heal him. At least enough to get him to realize what is happening within him."

"First off," Sheridan matched her whisper, "he is not going to go willingly. Not at this point. Second, what even is wrong with him?"

The Providence held a hand to her face, pinching her brow in thought, "I have never personally taken on a case such as this, but I know of others who have. His mind is rotting. Similar to the rot that the plague caused within Helena, but rather within one's mind instead of their body. Only, the reported cases I have knowledge of indicate patients of a much older age."

"Perhaps the stress of losing Helena has induced this sickness on him?"

"My thoughts exactly," the Providence pulled a lock of her golden hair and tucked it behind her ear. The porcelain skin of her hands, face, and chest illuminated red, gold, and blue as the sun broke through the clouds and burst through the stained-glass window behind the throne. "If he will not allow me to try and heal him by his own resolve, then my white magic will not work."

The light coming through the stained-glass equally illuminated the red in Sheridan's beard. He nodded agreeably. King Typhus had momentary lapses in his illness, during which his thoughts were clear. Those lapses were far and few between lately, though. Catching His Highness in a lapse was the only possible way to get him to agree to be healed, and even then, would it work?

To become a basic healer, all one needed was to acquire the knowledge of the healing arts and to study the Connections of Magic with the teachings of the All-Seeing God. These healers relied on salves, poultices, and other holistic approaches to health and wellness. No city in Havyn was short of healers.

White magic was a powerful ability that few possessed, though. Those with basic or advanced skills with white magic were able to heal a variety of ailments beyond that of salves and poultices, and in a fraction of the time. The mastery of white magic and its healing and protective abilities was vital to lead the white mages of a particular city or region. Those who mastered these skills could be granted the chance to become Master White Mage of an entire region. No promotion to Master White Mage could occur without the Providence's approval and the passing of the Trials of the Connections.

A similar rule applies to all Providences. While the position was inherited by blood, the woman selected by birthright had to undergo the Trials as well. Only a handful of Providence in history failed the Trials, requiring another to be selected. Failing the Trials guaranteed death, for one must give up all sense of being to enter the Trials—removing their mind from their physical body and transmitting it spiritually to the Connections of Magic. If one failed the Trials, their mind simply did not return, and their physical body would rot.

With white magic being a rarity, not every Providence possesses it prior to the Trials. Upon passing the Trials, the Connections of Magic grant the proper mechanisms within their blood and they are reborn as a mage, giving up their birthname and only taking the title of *Providence* until death.

The current Providence of Havyn, though, was born with a strong affinity for the Connections of Magic, mastering the white mage ability by her eighth birthday. Facing the Trials of the Connections only strengthened her abilities, making her revered, yet feared, by many.

Part of the Providence wanted desperately to help the king overcome his illness. He was the king and only his blood could continue the dynasty as rulers of Havyn. That included the Providence's position. By the law of the Concordat and the Connections of Magic, the Monarchy is inherited by the eldest male in the bloodline. If no male is present to assume the position, it passes to the eldest female. The position of the Providence, though, passes to the eldest daughter of the current living monarch. The one and only heir to both the Monarchy and the Faith was currently set to be inherited by King Typhus's daughter, Lia. If the king passed away first, Lia would assume the role of queen and forgo her rights to the Providency. If the Providence passed before the king, that position instead would pass to Lia, forgoing her inheritance of the Monarchy instead.

The royal bloodline in Havyn had exhausted itself. The king was in no state of mind to marry again and sire another child. That reason alone demanded the Providence's attention to the king's treatment.

Other than that, the Providence could care less whether the king lived or died. Related by blood or not—sick or not—Typhus had always been cruel to her. He blamed her for the death of the previous Providence, their great aunt, and for assuming the position merely days before the previous king, Typhus's grandfather, King Tytan, also perished. If the

Providence's health held out until after Tytan's death, then Typhus would have become king and Lia would have been granted the position of the Providence by birthright.

According to Typhus, the Providence stole his daughter's birthright.

His accusations grew worse upon the death of Queen Helena. Following the queen's untimely death from the plague, insanity soon overtook the grieving king and solidified the fate of the Havyn bloodline.

"Providence," Sheridan tugged her pale-blue dress, pulling her from her thoughts. "We have company." She followed the Master of Cities's eyes to the arched doorway leading from the foyer into the throne room.

"Friends! Family! Business associates!" As the grand doors of the throne room creaked open, a dwarf slightly shorter than Sheridan with salt-and-pepper hair ambled to the center of the throne room. A cloak fit for a human tacked onto his leather pauldrons trailed behind him like the train of a dress. A beautiful woman with ebony skin tailed him. The Guardians of the Faith crossed their staves as the dwarf approached, defending the Providence. "Easy fellas, I'm a friend!"

"An overstatement," Sheridan sighed under his breath. "Mida, what could you possibly be doing here on this fine day?" Sarcasm, at its finest.

Mida raised a thick, stumpy finger, "Ah, it's *Lord* Mida now!"

Sheridan coughed to suppress a laugh, "Who granted you a lordship, Mida? Considering that I am the Master of Cities, I would have needed to approve your appointment to lordship of one of the seven regions."

"Bah, keep your regions, *Master*," Mida ran his hand along his salt-and-pepper beard. "I am Mida, Lord of Steel, according to the Merchant's Guild of Fairmarq!"

The Providence had little patience for the man before them. His skill as a merchant, particularly in the steel trade, was doubtlessly exceptional. As a person, he was equivalent to a gnat in the Providence's eyes.

"Seeing as the Merchant's Guild does not extend beyond the borders of Fairmarq," the Providence started, managing to maintain an expressionless face despite her strong dislike for the dwarf, "that position remains on their side of the wall that separates us. You are no 'lord' here."

"Not yet!" Mida bolstered. "Upon hearing me out, you may think differently. I come with a proposition."

"You *always* come with propositions," the Providence stepped down from the dais, her Guardians at her side, "that never bring any benefit for us. Why bother proposing at all, Mida?"

"Providence," Mida held out a hand, seeking the common formality that one kisses the top of the Providence's hand upon introduction. The Providence obliged, turning her head to hide a gag as Mida took her hand and placed his sloppy lips on her knuckles. "I am pleased to introduce my beautiful paramour to you and the court." He gestured for the woman behind him to approach. The Providence nodded to her Guardians, signaling the okay. The woman exchanged the same formality as Mida, though much more gracefully. "This is Arahs, the love of my life and my future queen!"

Queen? Now he seeks a kingship? Sheridan thought.

"A pleasure, Arahs. I must say, Arahs sounds like a Brekken name. Am I correct?" the Providence asked.

The dark-skinned beauty lowered herself into a bow. "Yes, Your Faithfulness."

"I met her," Mida spoke proudly, "during my most recent journey to Brekkenia. I must say, they have the *finest* silver there!"

"Get on with it, Mida!" Sheridan impatiently shouted as he descended the dais steps.

"Right!" Mida pulled back part of his cloak and pulled a small sack from his belt. He emptied the contents to the stone floor of the throne room. Nuggets of an unrefined metallic substance. "Do you know what this is?" They both shook their heads. "*This,*" he picked up one of the nuggets and held it to the light, "is unrefined Aconyte steel—one of the strongest substances on earth. Once refined and smithed properly, it can be transformed into the sharpest of blades and the strongest of armors without ever losing their sharpness, shape, or shine."

"Yeah, we know of *refined* Aconyte. Keepers are donned with it from head to toe, and are the *only* warriors permitted to wield it. What do you want *us* for?" Sheridan was practically begging for Mida to cut to the chase.

"This substance is in high demand across the entire country, as it is a rarity that can only be mined with specific equipment deep in the tunnels of Garmoire. To mine it is expensive, to refine it is expensive, to smith it is expensive, but *selling* it should *not* be. Selling anything should be a profit. I humbly request that the tariffs on my products be reduced so that I may supply your wonderous people with a product so fine that they will be dropping silver and gold like feed for a hog. What do you say?"

The Providence and Sheridan conversed secretly for barely a minute before turning back to the steel merchant. The high demand for such a product would greatly influence the tax revenue if sold freely, that was unquestionable. The Military and City Watch could benefit from stronger weapons and armor as well, reducing costs of armor repairs and costs of new equipment. Intriguing, yes. Smart, perhaps. But those tariffs were set for a reason.

"Mida," Sheridan spoke up, "do you know about the horse merchant and stablemaster from Havana who died several years back?" Mida nodded. "He was considered, if you will, the 'lord' of the horse trade, as you like to call yourself 'lord' of the steel trade. He was *so* good at what he did, in fact, that his death and the termination of his business caused a rift in the economy and corrupted the economic value of horses as a whole. No one could compete. The economy is still struggling to correct itself from this incident."

Mida clasped his hands together and shook his head, chuckling, "No offense, Master of Cities, but you were not even in Havyn when all that occurred. More so, you were not in a position to observe the economic behavior of this kingdom like you are now. Helping me will *only* help you collect revenue to boost the economy."

"I do not doubt you," the Providence's usually sweet voice turned scratchy with frustration, "or your ability to create and sell a popular and useful product as this. Nor do I doubt for a moment that this would lead to a successful economic era. Our concerns are about you. You control the trade, you control the product, you control the profits. You play the part of the horselord, and if something were to happen to you, the economy would collapse. Those tariffs are in place to prevent merchants like you from using your product as a volatile power that the kingdom cannot prevent or influence. Our Master of Cities may not have been present during the deterioration of the horse market, but I was. It was a pleasure to meet you Arahs and I wish you the best with Mida. Mida, I respectfully decline your proposition and ask that you take your business endeavors elsewhere."

The Providence lifted her chin, sending her Guardians of the Faith towards the steel merchant. They gripped their staves and escorted

Mida and Arahs to the foyer. Mida shouted again and again that they were making a mistake. That helping them would help the kingdom. Pleading for a second opportunity to present his case.

It was not silent until the doors at the end of the throne room slammed and a squad of City Watch guards escorted the dwarf the rest of the way down the spiraling stairs to the base of the palace. Words need not be exchanged between the Providence and the Master of Cities. That encounter had wiped them both of their patience.

"When is she coming?" Sheridan asked, finally breaking the silence.

The Providence collected her thoughts and spoke, "My Guardians were sent to escort her a week ago. By my calculations, they should be arriving in El Vadora as we speak. She should be set to arrive in Havana City within the week."

They separated and went towards opposite sides of the throne room. One passage led to the Master of Cities's wing of the palace, the other led to the Providence's study.

CHAPTER 4

May I ask who the boy is?" Commander Veto leaned back in a chair at the small table within Governess Athenia's chambers. Veto was adamant that Ena's personal guard detail waited outside the room while they spoke privately. Damian, one of Ena's guards, insisted otherwise, until Ena herself asked him to give them privacy. Ena admired her guards' loyalty, but she knew exactly why Veto requested a private audience with her.

"He is... different," Ena popped the cork on a bottle of red wine, serving Veto a glass. She poured herself one and sat opposite Veto at the table. "A farmer from Arolye, a small good-for-nothing village deep in the forest. They pay a tithe each year, so they fall under El Vadora's watch. Or *did* pay a tithe." Commander Veto asked her to clarify. "The mages I spoke of burned his entire village to the ground. From what I understand, he is the sole survivor. I believe him, considering Arolye was only one of many villages on the outskirts to suffer the same fate. No survivors were found at those other villages."

"Why him? Unskilled, untrained, unimportant. Should he have survived while many others could have also escaped?" Veto sipped his wine. The wooden chairs creaked uncomfortably, likely struggling under the weight of the armor Veto wore.

The governess's chambers were simple. A bed in one corner with several bookshelves against the walls and a wooden table and chairs set in a small breakfast nook by a window overlooking the street they arrived from. Her life has led her to appreciate the simple things and not indulge in the extravagancies one in her office might, despite the grand paycheck it came with.

"He had this on him," Ena opened the saddlebag that rested on the floor next to the table. She pulled out the sword Drake was carrying on him and placed it gently on the table.

Veto took off his helm and studied the blade intently. Never before had he seen a weapon with a similar color, design, or intensity. Something about the blade gave off an internal power in his hands. He could have sworn the sword was humming with the power it emanated. "Is it magical?"

Ena took the sword from him. She stood and spun the sword around in her hand, swinging it and practicing different maneuvers. With each stroke, the blade's hum intensified. "Perhaps, but even a magic such as this is nothing like I have seen. The magic this sword possesses can only be either so ancient that there is no knowledge recorded of it or so new that it has yet to be recorded. Drake claims it is an heirloom that has been passed through his family. My guess is ancient versus new."

Veto nodded in agreement.

Even the sunlight beaming in from the window touched the sword differently. Both blade and hilt were fabricated from an unknown black metal. A black so deep that the sun was absorbed by it. Silver flecks shone when the sword caught the eye a certain way, almost like stars in the night sky. The blade was sharpened and curved on one side. Though the blade came to an incredibly sharp point at the end, the curve indicated the sword was meant for cleaving, not for stabbing.

"I will have to take the scabbard off of the boy if I intend to carry this around," Ena commented, running her fingers along the flat of the blade. "The shape is too unique to fit in any standard one we may have on hand.

"You intend to carry it around?" Veto asked.

Ena raised her eyebrows. "Do you intend for me to let it go unguarded? I will hold onto it until we can learn more about it."

Suddenly, trumpets from outside blasted thrice. The City Watch guards positioned outside the House of the Governor utilized trumpets to signal when diplomats were arriving with the desire to speak with the governor or governess. Ena had no idea who could have been here for her. She looked to Veto, who would have handled any diplomacy in her absence these past few months. He only shrugged his shoulders.

"What in the Connections?" Ena went to the window.

"Who is it?" Veto asked.

"Guardians of the Faith..." Ena hooked the ancient sword onto her belt and marched out the door of her chambers. Veto followed closely behind. Immediately, Damian and Klaus, the governess's personal detail, guarded her rear. They dragged Drake along, who had no clue as to what was happening.

Ena made her way to the entrance of the House and waited on the landing at the top of the steps from the street. Approaching from the main road were six Guardians of the Faith, clad in their white armor accented with gold atop their white stallions. Each held an ornate staff topped with an Oblong Eye, symbol of the All-Seeing God.

"Governess," a City Watch guard ran up to meet her. "They arrived through the southern gates about an hour ago. They won't tell us why they are here. They only have a letter addressed to you."

Of course they would not tell them why they were here—the Guardians of the Faith took vows of silence, so the legends said. Any that stood in the way of their goal would have the All-Seeing God to answer to.

Ena assumed the Guardians would dismount as they reached the steps. She assumed wrong.

The stallions climbed the steps to the top until all six Guardians and their horses stood side by side. The one closest to Ena lowered its staff and placed it horizontally in a hook on the side of the saddle. A Guardian of the Faith lowering its staff was symbolic of peace. The Guardian reached into a pocket on the saddlebag and produced a small, sealed letter and handed it to Ena.

She had to stand on her toes to reach the letter hanging high above her head. The envelope read *Athenia, Governess of El Vadora, Cyprien.* She flipped the envelope and recognized the golden Oblong Eye wax seal as the Providence's seal.

What does the Providence want with me? She thought to herself. Curiously and nervously, she cracked the seal and unfolded the letter within.

Governess Athenia,

I request an audience with you to discuss a rather confidential task that you, and only you, may have the ability to assist with. Your flawless résumé as the Governor of El Vadora these past three years, along with your investigative skills and attention to detail in the solving of nearly two dozen crimes single-handedly, have brought your name to the offices of the Faith, the Monarchy, and the People.

A grievous crime has recently been committed, and the minimal evidence presenting itself in this case proves over the heads of all chief investigators. I desire to speak with you regarding the crime and all exhibits collected in response to the investigations which have been conducted thus far. Including the collaboration of information in this letter proved dangerous, should the letter fall into the wrong hands.

The Guardians of the Faith will escort you to the Spire of the New King in Havana City immediately.

Sincerely,

The Providence

For the first time in years, Ena felt overwhelmed. Years of torment and forced labor from her father and years in the City Watch could not compare to this moment. The Providence, one of the most powerful beings in the kingdom, wanted to speak with *her*? She was nothing more than one of nearly fifty other governors and governesses across Havyn. El Vadora was not a significant city, either. How had the Providence even learned her name or any of her accomplishments?

"What does it say?" Veto asked.

"At least someone appreciates my hard work doing *your* job, Commander." She thrusted the letter into Veto's chest. Turning her attention to her guard detail, she ordered, "Damian, prepare my horse. And the three of yours, as well, Klaus."

"Three?" Drake asked.

Ena nodded. "Welcome to my personal guard detail, Drake. Now, get used to riding, because this journey will be longer than a few hours." Damian brought over the governess's personal horse, which was stabled near the House for convenience.

Once Klaus returned with the three morgans, Drake and Damian mounted. Ena was unsure if making Drake a member of her personal guard detail was a wise decision. She still could not trust him—she hardly knew him—but she refused to let him fall out of her sight, along with the sword.

As the saying goes, keep your enemies close.

Maybe someone in Havana City would know more about artifacts like the sword and could explain how a simple farmer could have acquired it.

Before departing, Ena made Veto begrudgingly promise her that he would send squads of guards into the forest should there be any reports of disturbances or fires. She hated leaving during such a delicate time, but the summons from the Providence could not be ignored.

Within the hour, the governess, her guard detail, and the Guardians of the Faith rode off from the southern gates of El Vadora with Havana City in their sights. Ena hadn't been to Havana City since her father's death. She couldn't tell if she was excited or dreading it already...

CHAPTER 5

Havana City was the largest city in all of Havyn. It served as the capital of the entire kingdom, seating the king inside of the Spire of the New King. Hills rolled through the region of Havana, with Havana City built atop the highest of them. From miles away, the Spire, constructed in the very center of Havana City, was noticeable on the horizon. It was a common rumor that King Typhus could see his entire kingdom from the top of the Spire.

As Governess Athenia and the Guardians of the Faith approached from the northern road, they traversed between the hills until the Spire of the New King was spotted on the horizon. Ena knew they would reach their destination in a few hours. A massive wall, built high and thick enough to withstand a hundred sieges, towered over them with an open archway constructed over the road. City Watch guards stood at attention, shoulder-to-shoulder. Any typical traveler would be interrogated by the guards as to their business in the city. Upon seeing the Guardians of the Faith, though, they parted and allowed the white-armored Guardians to pass with their convoy.

The road began blending with artisan villages on the outskirts of the city, which was so massive that they were still several miles from the base of the hill on which the inner city was settled. The outer city was familiar to Ena.

As the settlement thickened the closer to the inner city they led their horses, memories distracted Ena. She had walked these streets as a child, she had ridden her horses through the surrounding hills, she grew up here. Though she never had a chance to experience a normal childhood, this was still her home.

Joining the City Watch was the best decision she ever made, especially when they allowed her to choose her assignment after her promotion to

Guard Captain and she chose to get as far from Havana City as possible. Although, she had to admit that a part of her was sad to leave. She had only returned to bury her father and sell the business, travelling back to El Vadora by the end of the week following the funeral.

How many years ago was that? Ena thought. *Five? Six?*

That may not seem like a long stretch of time, but considering how much she has accomplished in her career, half a decade felt like a hundred years. She joined the City Watch at age fourteen, became a captain at age sixteen, and then governess of El Vadora at age nineteen, the youngest in Havyn's history to achieve these feats, and perhaps the youngest in the country of Lynidas.

"Hold the entourage a moment," Ena stopped her horse. The Guardians of the Faith halted in their tracks. Ena pulled her horse off the road and dismounted, the ancient black blade in its scabbard Drake had reluctantly turned over to her upon her demand clattering metallically against her thigh plate. She tied the reins to a hitching post outside of a small inn. Two of the Guardians dismounted and armed their staves. "Damian, Klaus, watch my horse. Drake, with me."

Damian and Klaus nodded. Drake dismounted his horse and handed the reins to Klaus. Drake followed behind Ena as she turned down a side street. The two Guardians marched behind them side-by-side.

"Where are we going?" Drake asked.

"You will find out shortly," Ena responded vaguely. She continued walking along the street, observing the buildings as they passed.

"This city is marvelous," Drake commented. El Vadora had been a wonder to him, but even the outskirts of Havana City were breathtaking. Each structure was made using the finest craftsmanship, unlike the poorly hand-crafted cottages from his home village.

Ena turned her head and raised her brow. "You've seen nothing yet."

"In a good way or a bad way?"

Ena hesitated. "Let us simply answer 'yes' to that question."

Confused, Drake ignored her reply and continued to follow her down another side street. The main road had been bustling with small businesses, artisans, restaurants, and inns. These side streets, however, were residential. Drake did not know enough about Ena to even begin to guess where they were going, or why she asked only him to go with her.

The end of the street suddenly opened onto a wide-open field. An enormous, uninhabited stable sat on the opposite side of the field with a small ranch home situated next to it. The grass in the field was shriveled and dry. The fence surrounding the field was broken in several spots, the wood rotting. Ena was solemn as she walked through the field to the run-down stable. The roof had begun to cave in on one side and the barn doors were ripped from their hinges. Drake remained quiet while Ena ran her hand along the splintered wood on the stable wall.

"This," Ena finally spoke, "is my home. The stable I was raised on." The stable and its land was the size of Drake's entire village, Arolye. Ena led him inside. Sunlight beaming through the broken roof illuminated the interior enough for Drake to see the dozens of empty stalls. "My father was a *very* successful horseman and merchant. In his prime, we sold fifty horses per week. It got to the point where the merchant portion of the business became too demanding, and I was left responsible for raising the foals and training them once they were fully grown."

Drake couldn't read Ena's expression. Couldn't tell if she was sad, happy, or angry. "What happened?" he asked.

"My father died."

"I'm so sorry," Drake put a hand on Ena's shoulder. She shrugged it off, clearly turning down his affectionate display of empathy.

"I'm not," Ena snarked. Drake seemed shocked. "He was an asshole. He was a *brilliant* businessman, and his equine knowledge was far beyond mine. He amassed a small fortune before his death." Drake again asked what happened. "I left for the City Watch and he was stubbornly left alone to run the business himself. He exhausted and overworked himself to death. I sold the business and wiped my hands clean of it. And him."

"What did he do for you to hate him so much?" Drake was mortified that she could speak of her own father in such a way. He would give anything for his father to be alive with him right now.

"I still have scars all over my body from the abuse I endured from him. I miss the horses. I miss the people I knew because of his success. I miss my home. But fuck him. He is rotting in the ground now."

Ena looked through the stables. She noted the blemishes in its structure. What once was beautiful was now broken. Sorrow welled up inside her. Was she to blame for the property's dilapidated state? Of course not. She was a City Watch guard at the time. She could not simply uproot herself and return home to continue her father's business. She had no choice but to sell the horses and walk away from it all. She was happy now, despite what others say about her.

She took Drake by the hand and rushed out of the stable where the two Guardians waited for them. Ena wanted to be away from here, unsure of why she had the urge to come here in the first place. *If I did not see it,* Ena justified, *then I would never have believed it. I am glad it is all gone.*

Damian and Klaus must have known where she went, for they gave her a clap on the back before handing her horse back to her.

"Alright, let's keep moving," Ena said, turning her horse behind the Guardians of as they continued to approach the inner city.

◆◆◆◆◆◆◆◆◆

The Guardians of the Faith led their white stallions through the thickening city and up the slowly inclining hill where the Spire of the New King loomed over. For the first time, Ena observed the Spire up close. She analyzed its structure like a soldier would analyze a battlefield. The central tower was home to Havyn's king and royal family, while the two keeps constructed on opposite sides of the spire housed the Providence, the Master of Cities, and the business they each conducted.

As they neared the base of the Spire, the economic difference of the city's residents became prominent. The top of the hill was home to every aristocrat and nobleman, rich merchant, and banker in their stone and brick mansions. Halfway up the hill were smaller houses and structures that house the families of the highest-ranking City Watch guards and Military soldiers.

Towards the base of the hill, middle class workers and small business owners lived mostly in peace. Other than the artisan districts developed along the main roads, the remainder of the city was filled with lower class exploited workers living in shambles where criminals thrived.

Ena was lucky enough to grow up living right off of the main roads in a good part of the city, so crime was never much of an issue. She was certain that every criminal in the city knew who she and her father were and would not think twice about messing with their business. Having the Military and City Watch of the entire kingdom at their backs had its advantage.

Upon seeing the excessive prosperity of the upper class atop Havana City's hill made Ena question who the real criminals in the city were...

The sun peaked in the sky by the time they reached the steps to the palace. The Guardians of the Faith dismounted from their stallions. The governess and her guards did the same. Drake, Damian, and Klaus walked to Ena, but were halted when one of the Guardians raised a palm to them. Ena looked to them, unable to make eye contact through their golden visors that covered their entire faces. She didn't need them to explain.

"I must go alone," Ena elaborated. She nodded her head to Damian and Klaus. "Watch him." Meaning Drake. She had made him part of her personal guard to keep a closer eye on him, not because she trusted him. Not yet.

She was flanked by four Guardians of the Faith. Together, they marched up the marble steps into the palace doors. They continued straight across the circular entrance hall to the steps that curved sharply to the left, following the curve of the wall to the top of the Spire.

At the top of the steps was a set of massive, gilded doors. She assumed that led to the throne room, as they banked immediately to the left, following the curved hall towards what Ena knew was the tower of the Providence's section of the palace.

The narrow corridor eventually led to a straight hallway with two large, gold-engraved wooden doors at the end with two Guardians of the Faith standing guard. The Guardians did not speak. Their sole purpose was to defend the Providence at all costs, even if it meant their death. No one alive was certain of the abilities of the Guardians of the Faith. Some say they have magical abilities. Others say they are simply normal, non-magical people in an expensive set of armor to appear threatening.

A powerful magical aura in the air was so strong that Ena swore she could physically feel it, as if she were wading through water. This strange atmosphere grew stronger the closer to the gold-engraved doors she approached. *This must be the Providence's study.*

When she was face-to-face with the two Guardians outside the door, they turned inboard and stepped backwards. Ena knocked lightly on the door.

"Enter," said the Providence upon hearing the knock.

Ena walked in, flanked on both sides by two Guardians. Their white and gold armor seemed to glow in the softly lit room. The Providence's study was circular and open with a botanical garden in the center of the room. Flora of all colors, shapes, and sizes decorated the garden. The Providence watered a blue fire-lily as the governess approached.

"Life is all around us, Governess," she did not look up as she poured the contents of the tin watering can onto the azure petals. "Life is what I know best. How to protect it and make it thrive."

Ena gently caressed a frond hanging from the palm nearby. She asked, "Can you create it?"

The Providence looked up, locking her blue eyes with the governess's green ones. "Create life?" She huffed a laugh. "Impossible. The origins of life are for the gods. The All-Seeing God produces the life all around us, and mastering that life is where I come in."

Her blonde hair was hardly noticeable in the dim sapphire light from the crystals that hung from the walls surrounding the room. She took a few steps closer to the governess and placed her fingertips against the same palm frond. "Possessing the gift of life is accompanied by the curse of death." Suddenly, a soft glow illuminated from the Providence's fingers, causing the frond to shrivel and blacken. What little matter remained broke off from the stem and crumbled to the soil beneath their feet. "Death. Death is created, Governess. Life is given."

The blonde-haired beauty smiled at Ena before turning to water the next plant in her path. Ena opened her mouth to speak, but the Providence must have known what she would ask, for she answered for her, "You wonder why I have summoned you here so far from your home. Just like the leaf, death has been created, yet in one of the strangest places, and in the strangest of ways." Ena was now more confused than ever. "I am certain you received word somewhere throughout your travels of the death of the Lord of Avalon?"

"No," Ena shook her head. "I was away on an errand for some time. My condolences. How did he pass?"

"The true reason," the Providence placed down her watering can and beckoned for Ena to follow her, "has been justly hidden from the public."

The Providence led Ena to a desk against the far wall of the circular room. On the wall, the Providence pulled a lever, causing a metallic clunking and churning that echoed through the room. Suddenly, the dome in the center of the ceiling high above them began to split down the middle and open. A beam of sunlight erupted from the ceiling into the botanical garden at the center of the chambers. The flowers and leaves exploded with color once exposed to the sun.

The remainder of the room became visible with light. The walls were lined with bookshelves compiled with tomes of all sizes and ages.

"Wow..." Ena had never seen so many books in her life.

The Providence followed Ena's daunted gaze, "Welcome to my study, Athenia." Ena finally caught a good look at the Providence. They were roughly the same age and height. But where the governess was dark-haired and green-eyed, the Providence's hair was golden-blonde and her eyes as blue as the ocean. The Providence's white dress with its tightly fitted bodice and loose, flowing skirt that touched the floor was the complete opposite of Ena's steel armor. "Do know, I allow very few individuals into this room."

"Why me?" Ena still had no idea why she had been summoned here. Or what made her so special that the Providence allowed her into her private study.

"The Lord of Avalon was murdered. I have faith that you are capable of finding the killer, or killers, and bringing them to justice." Ena once again asked why. "It is no mystery that you have operated outside the boundaries of the City Watch to unravel a multitude of unsolved crimes within El Vadora and the surrounding towns and villages within your jurisdiction. Others may not know your name, but I do. The Lady of Avalon fears that others may be targeted if the speculation becomes publicized. I fear this as well. You see, Governess, the lord was very well-liked. He ruled as lord for twenty-five years and never once received as much as a complaint, never mind a death threat. Yet suddenly he dies in his youth with no explanation, or so we thought."

"What was the cause of death?" Ena asked, running her fingertips along the spines of the books on a nearby bookshelf.

"Poison," the Providence whispered. Ena's head whipped around. *Poison?!* "It is my understanding that you have experience with poisons." She did. Three of the murder cases in El Vadora she investigated had been caused by poison. While one was a suicide pact with a group of eight victims in a religious cult, the other two were victims of a crazed sociopath who was experimenting with different toxic plants.

"The annual Lordship Ball is being held in Avalon next week," the Providence continued. "You are to go and introduce yourself to Lady Raven. Find out what you can. You are not known in Avalon, so anonymity will be your ally."

"No offense, Providence," Ena shook her head, "but I have not even agreed to this. I have my own city to manage. You are asking me to spend possibly several months away from my home to take care of someone else's problem."

The sound of the wooden door behind her creaking open startled Ena. She instinctively placed a hand on the ancient blade that hung at her belt to draw it from its scabbard. The two Guardians of the Faith took this for a threat and instantly dropped into an attack stance, their Oblong Eye staves pointed at Ena. The pupil in the center of the Eyes began to spin and glow. A low droning sound filled the quiet of the room, coming from whatever magical power was churning from the center of each staff.

"Easy, easy!" A dwarf with red-orange hair and matching beard charged into the study. "She isn't going to hurt the Providence!" The dwarf scampered over to Ena. "Hopefully you won't hurt me either. I'm Sheridan, Master of Cities," he extended a hand to Ena. She lowered her chin to meet his gaze and clasped his right hand in hers.

Ena jumped back once she caught the feeling of his hand. It was as cold and hard like ice under the glove he wore. "Ah, shit, sorry. That's just my prosthetic arm." Sheridan took off his glove and rolled up his sleeve. His arm was mechanical—gold-plated steel joined together with bolts and pins from his shoulder to his fingers. "It surprises people who aren't used to it. I had an injury a number of years ago. Lost my entire arm. Dwarves have an excellent skill for mechanics, so they threw together this make-shift arm for me. It works great."

"Anyway," the Master of Cities continued, "do not worry about El Vadora, Governess. I will have extra guards sent to protect it should anything happen. I trust that Commander Veto will rule soundly in your stead, as is his job when the Governor, or Governess in this case, is called elsewhere for duty. Providence," Sheridan shot her a glance of annoyance, "call off your Guardians, please. I don't need them killing Governess Athenia before she agrees to help us."

The Providence nodded to her Guardians, who returned to attention and brought their staves back to their sides. Ena returned the courtesy by removing her hand from the hilt of Drake's blade. Sheridan's eyes were drawn to the sword once Ena's hand was free from it.

"Providence," Sheridan said. "Do you mind if I escort the governess to the balcony? I would like to have a word with her."

The Providence nodded, "Yes, of course. It has been a pleasure to meet you, Governess Athenia. I do hope that Sheridan can help explain our desperation for your assistance."

"A pleasure, indeed, Providence," Ena dipped her head. She was inclined to shake the Providence's hand, but her Guardians were already on edge. Best not test her luck.

◆◆◆◆◆◆◆◆◆

The balcony wrapped around the entire cylindrical expanse of the Spire of the New King. Sheridan and Ena did laps around the balcony as they spoke. All of Havana City could be seen from there. The wall surrounded all of the city; from the archway they had entered through to the southernmost edge of the Kingdom of Havyn. Havana City bordered Brekken territory to the southwest, Fairmarq to the east, and Nest Aiken to the southeast; therefore, its walls were built tall and strong.

The land outside of Havyn was vacant. The barren grasslands were waves of green in the daytime breeze. The Brekken Alliance kept their civilization far from the borders of Havyn. Though the Concordat deemed the grasslands a territory of Brekkenia, the Brekken kings wanted to remain as separate from the Five Kingdoms as possible. It had been decades since Havyn had needed to communicate with the nearest Brekken kingdom. Both parties were satisfied with that arrangement. Brekkenia had been an ally of Hayn's during the creation of the Concordat, but their people were too stubborn and proud to maintain a friendship after the signing was complete.

"You will send guards to El Vadora in my absence?" Ena asked. "I've had a mage problem on the outskirts."

"So I've heard," Sheridan confirmed. "I already sent a message to Commander Veto telling him you will be assisting us with something confidential. Hearing it from me will hopefully withhold his scorn for you."

"You know how he feels about me?"

"He is a very old-school City Watch guard. He has also been Commander of the City Watch in El Vadora for most of his life and has been under the command of countless governors. You scare the living hell out of him because you are unconventional for any governor he has worked beside. He steps out of line and you put him right back in his place."

It was true. They had clashed from the moment she set foot in the House of the Governor her first day on duty. Veto pushed his influence on everyone and acted as if he were governor. Previous governors may have let him do so, believing they could rest and relax while Veto did all the work. Athenia was different. She took her position seriously, but not seriously enough to fear from stepping outside of the lines if it meant the good of her people.

This was precisely why Sheridan knew he could rely on her. She would operate in ways that the City Watch as a whole simply could not. She could navigate Gabrenas alone much swifter and more inconspicuously than groups of armored guards.

"Lady Raven will be able to explain things better than I," Sheridan talked about the business at hand. "She is the one who discovered his body. She immediately had the Master White Mage check his vitals and perform an autopsy once he was declared dead. Poison was in his system, almost unnoticeably. No one in Havyn knows much about poisons."

"No one except me?" Ena asked. Sheridan nodded. "Why do you trust me? You know nothing about me besides my career accomplishments. Who is to say I will not leave here today and spread this news across all of Avalon and spark a demand for a murder investigation? You and I both know a spouse is always the primary suspect. That would not bode well for Lady Raven."

Sheridan's bushy red eyebrows raised, "You certainly have fire within you, don't you, Athenia? I suppose I can ask you the same question about trust. I hear your new personal guard is a complete stranger, yet he is meant to lay down his life protecting you?"

"If your ears heard about my personal guard, then maybe your eyes also told you he is unarmed and unarmored. I do not trust him. I am keeping a potential enemy close."

Sheridan stopped walking and pointed to the sword at Ena's hip. "I'll venture a guess and say he has something to do with that weapon?"

Ena looked down. She drew the sword from its scabbard and held it out. "You noticed it right away." Sheridan nodded. He was staring at the night-black blade with awe. "It has magical potential, I believe." She demonstrated the natural hum it released as the blade cut through the air.

"I have a theory about this blade, Athenia," Sheridan scratched his beard in thought. He took the blade from Ena by the hilt and waved it around, experiencing the restricted magical aura. "Allow me to do some further research and I will explain at another point. For now, please travel to Avalon and prepare for the Lordship Ball. Introduce yourself to Raven. She will be expecting you."

Sheridan handed the blade back to Ena. He turned to walk away, but Ena caught his shoulder, "Fine, I will do this. First tell me what you think this is." She sheathed the sword.

Sheridan sighed, "You are a smart woman. Much smarter than most. That sword may be an ancient faerie artifact. Before you think I'm crazy, give me time to find some evidence."

A faerie artifact? What? How?! Ena couldn't find words to respond. She simply nodded.

"Consider this," Sheridan took Ena's hand in his metal one, "our first step towards earning one another's trust. Send my regards to Lady Raven."

Sheridan left Ena alone on the balcony overlooking the plains beyond Havyn.

Faeries once existed alongside humans, elves, and dwarves. A thousand years ago, they were all terminated during the Mage Wars. The Concordat, and Havyn, was born from the ashes of the Mage War. No faeries, nor their magical artifacts, have existed since then. Why, a millennia later, did the governess of a small, forgotten city have one at her side?

CHAPTER 6

Sheridan shifted through the piles and piles of books, scrolls, and maps on the table in his office. A light breeze brushed the white curtains leading out to a small outdoor balcony along the stone floor. Light from the afternoon sun snuck through the crack in the curtains each time they gusted open, flashing orange on his rugged face. *Where did I put it?*

Moving from the table, he walked up the steps to the mezzanine above the desk in the corner of the office. Up here, a pile of pelts made up a makeshift bed. He tore the pelts apart searching and searching with no luck. He had spent days fingering through the stacks of books in the library and the Providence's study. It had been three years since he first laid eyes on the book, never thinking it would come in handy until now. But what had he done with it?

He rose to his feet, bracing himself against the wall next to his bed with his metal arm. Sheridan scratched his beard with his one good hand, thinking deeply and digging through his vault of memories. He may have only been Master of Cities for three years, but those three years were full of information that he held onto. He certainly would not remember where he placed one simple book.

Suddenly, the brick beneath his metallic palm loosened, stone scraping against stone. *Huh...* Sheridan managed to grasp his fingers on the edge of the brick and wiggled it loose. He pulled it free, followed by a cloud of dust. A hand went inside the dark space between the bricks until it found something organic. Excitement pulsed inside him.

He pulled the book from between the stones and blew off the thick layer of dust.

Encantorum. "*Book of Magic*," Sheridan translated the cover. The faerie language had been lost over the last millennium, but the Master of Cities had read a few translated, old maps of the faerie kingdom to understand some of the basic words.

He lifted the cover, the leather screeching with obduracy. The pages had yellowed over the years, but they were still legible. Though there were many words Sheridan could not identify on the first cover page, he filled in the blanks with context clues that seemed fit. "*The history and understanding of the faerie race. A narration by every king and queen, prince and princess, and leader of the faerie world. Where life and magic first began. Where love and altruism first encountered greed and wrath. By the Connections of Magic, we seek eternal life and everlasting strength.*"

The language grew increasingly more complex as he flipped through the brittle pages. Frustration set in as Sheridan admitted to himself that he would not be able to read this book. How was he supposed to learn the language of the faeries when no one else in the world could understand it?!

Fuck this! He hurled the book over his shoulder onto the floor below the mezzanine and collapsed onto the pelts.

"You know, Sheridan," came a soft female voice from the lower level, "this book is very old and delicate... The knowledge it contains would certainly not appreciate being abused this way."

Sheridan stood up and walked to the edge of the mezzanine. The Providence held the *Encantorum* in her porcelain hands. She wore a beige gown, and her golden hair was tied back.

"I wondered what happened to this tome," the Providence gracefully flipped the pages as the Master of Cities came down the steps to meet her. "That spot on my shelf has been empty conveniently since you took office, Master." She closed the book and looked at him. "May I ask why?"

"Providence," Sheridan almost couldn't find the words. He looked up and met her blue eyes. "The book called to me when I first entered your study. That first day we met. This book is interweaved with the Connections of Magic in ways even you cannot understand..."

"You underestimate my abilities, Sheridan." She narrowed her eyes. "What would you know of the Connections? You are but a dwarf."

Sheridan sighed, "A dwarf with an unnatural perception for the Connections. Listen, I will explain more in due time. Right now, I need that book. Well, I need to learn to *read* the damned book..."

The Providence stared at the dwarf curiously. Dwarves were not known for having the ability to weave the Connections. It was unheard of—impossible, some might say. The Providence's magical ability was stronger than most, and she knew the world of magic originated with the faeries.

Faeries, supposedly crafted in the gods' image, were practically gods themselves. They could master all magical types and abilities, including elemental magic, arcane magic, kinetic magic, and white magic.

Elemental mages had the potential to wield fire, earth, and water. Faeries could master all three, if properly trained.

Arcane magic dealt in warping and mastering the mind. One who mastered the arcane arts could read minds, control minds, and even communicate with others through their minds from very long distances. They were of the most dangerous, most scrutinized, and mistrusted of the mage classes.

Kinetic mages, while the rarest, were the most powerful. Kinetic mages had the ability to move, warp, and control anything physical with a simple wave of their hand. Faeries with strong kinetic abilities were trained under the Order of the Dymund Auryx, who could warp the molecules around them into an impenetrable armor, making them nearly invincible.

White mages were, like the Providence, masters of life. They could heal and protect with wards, among their many abilities. White mages were cherished, while the other mage classes were ostracized, one of the major causes of the Mage Wars over a thousand years ago.

Elves were the closest in ancestry to the faeries. Most elves had a natural white mage ability, while few others were able to master one of the other types of magic. Having the same holy link to the Connections of Magic as the faeries, their lives exceeded those of humans or dwarves. The average lifespan for an elf was six hundred years, with the oldest known elves exceeding seven hundred and fifty years.

Humans were next in the ancestral line. Before the Mage Wars, it was not uncommon for human beings to weave at least one form of magic, with the most powerful of human mages weaving two. Though, the king of the mages, at the time of the Mage Wars, was said to have mastered all four classes. However, much about the king of the mages has been lost over time.

Following the Mage Wars, which turned all non-magic humans against the magic-wielding ones, mages were made nearly extinct. Now, should any human in the Five Kingdoms of Lynidas, or anywhere else around the world, begin to show signs of talent from the Connections, they were monitored closely. White mages were utilized as healers and priests. Anyone showing the abilities of any other magical class was typically scrutinized.

Theorists believed that dwarves were the deformed, unworthy faerie descendants. They looked much different than any other race, being drastically shorter and stockier, and were known to have no magical ability. They were scorned by many and lived their lives in different kingdoms far from all humans and elves. The Dwarven Kingdom of Garmoire lay far underground. Very few humans or elves have ventured deep enough below the surface to see the kingdom with their own eyes. Branching off from the kingdom were clans of Tunnel Dwarves. They guarded the tunnels that led from the surface world to the underground kingdom of the dwarves. Those who broke away from the life of an kingdom or tunnel dwarf resided in separate kingdoms of Surface Dwarves. The Surface Dwarves were not considered "real" dwarves by the Tunnel and Garmoire Dwarves. Those who lived in the sunlight were not welcome in the dark. The Surface Dwarves thought of themselves as external guards of the Dwarven Kingdom, keeping back enemies before even the Tunnel Dwarves had to encounter them. Though dwarves were the runts of the faerie and magical world, their life expectancy measured about three hundred years with the eldest known dwarves living past four hundred.

The purpose of Havyn's formation had been to give ostracized mages a home. Havyn also claimed to be tolerant of all religions and races. Everything written into the Concordat about Havyn sounded great on paper, but the reality was far different.

With all the Providence's knowledge of the races of the world, she was confused why a dwarf would be so entuned with knowledge of the Connections of Magic.

"I will explain, Providence," Sheridan repeated. "I just need to be able to decipher that book. You have to have *something* else on those shelves of yours about the faerie language."

The Providence continued to flip through the pages of the *Encanto-*

rum until something caught her eye. She stopped and tilted the book to show the dwarf. "This is the same sword that Athenia was carrying, was it not?"

She wasn't wrong. On the page was a detailed sketch of a blade identical to the governess's. "You know about the blade?"

"Yes," the Providence nodded. "I could feel its energy the moment she led her horse inside the walls of the city. A possible faerie artifact?"

"Well?" Sheridan tilted his head. "Will you help me learn to read this language?"

"Of course, Sheridan," the Providence nodded, her blond bun bouncing. "I will search through my library for anything related to the faerie language. Then, you must reveal whatever secrets you are withholding."

"Of course, Providence."

CHAPTER 7

Ballgowns and parties were never Athenia's taste for fun. Maybe that was because she never had the opportunity to experience such things growing up. There was never any time for fun, only for work. The horses would not take care of themselves if she went off partying and playing dress-up with the other girls her age.

The reflection in the mirror looking back at Ena was something out of a nightmare. A tight, violet satin dress was being buttoned behind her back by one of the Providence's hired handmaidens. Her shoulder-length black hair was curled into magnificent waves. A layer of ivory makeup hiding away her blemishes. A rose petal blush on her cheeks to breathe life into her pale face.

Ena may have been able to handle all of that, but when the handmaiden forced her to sit with her fingers and toes spread wide, taking a file to her nails, Ena nearly lost her patience. Even more so when the handmaiden began decorating her toes and fingertips with a deep indigo paint. Her nails shined like the hyacinths the dyes had derived from.

Ena closed her eyes and took a deep breath to settle her irritation. That is, until she opened her eyes to the sight of the handmaiden coming at her face with a pair of tweezers.

"No!" Ena shot up from the divan waving her hands in the handmaiden's face. "No! I've had enough of this. Have you not already tortured me enough with all this embellishment?!" She reached behind her back and released the top two buttons. "I cannot breathe in this godsdamned thing."

Hearing Ena shouting, Damian and Klaus ran into the room with weapons drawn. Drake walked in shortly behind them, still weaponless.

The handmaiden looked at Ena with a look of disappointment. She pursed her lips, "Sorry, Governess. I will be done."

Seeing the look on the handmaiden's face made Ena realize she may have overreacted. "I am the one who is sorry, maiden. This is your job, and you are doing excellently. I am not used to this whole... beauty thing. Can you give me a moment and we can continue later?"

The handmaiden dipped her chin and curtsied before exiting the room behind Ena's guards. "I am fine. Thank you for your concern. You may go. I need a few minutes to myself."

Damian and Klaus retired their swords into their sheaths, bowed, and left the room. Drake remained. He took two steps closer before Ena's head turned to face him.

"I said I am fine," Ena grunted. "Please go."

Drake scanned her from head to toe, "You look beautiful, Governess."

"You *really* do not enjoy following orders, do you, Drake?" She was ready to hit the next person who approached her. That person might be Drake, if he kept pressing his luck.

"I mean it, Ena." He still stepped closer. "You're stunning. You already looked gorgeous in your armor. This is another beautiful side of you."

She turned her whole body towards him, looking down at the dress. She hated to admit it fit her figure rather well. "Beautiful" was not typically a word she heard used to describe her—"hardened," "impenetrable," "focused," even "miserable," on occasion, were the regular adjectives often used.

What was beauty if not subjective, anyway?

Drake was now standing within her reach. She could take a swing at him, tell him one last time to leave her *alone*. But she was vulnerable. *Vulnerable?* No, she didn't get vulnerable. Hadn't she already been vulnerable with Drake once before? Taking him to her father's stable was a moment to show her strength, to explain the trials she endured as a child and how she could face any challenge because of it. She thought it was a moment of power, but in reality, she opened up about something personal. She had let Drake sneak through the wall she had worked so hard to build.

Fuck. Ena was angry with herself for not realizing it. Drake must have realized it as well, for he now took the point of her chin cusped between his thumb and index finger and lifted her head. They locked eyes and

Ena felt her stomach fluttering.

"Ena," Drake spoke just above a whisper, "I have spent my entire life in a village of less than a hundred people. The only girls I've seen were covered in dirt from tilling the fields or animal shit from working in the barns. You saved my life that day with the wolves, which I am still in your debt for, but you were also a fresh of breath air standing above me with your armor gleaming." Ena tried to break his gaze. He leaned in, eyes resting on her pink lips. "Look, I know you don't particularly trust me—"

"Exactly, Drake," she came to her senses, finally. She smacked his hand from her chin and pushed him back. "I *don't* trust you. I don't know you." She tapped her hand on the bare skin above the low neckline of the dress, "You don't know *me*. You are not part of my personal guard because I trust you to watch my fucking back. You are here because I keep my enemies close. You are here because you mysteriously show up in the middle of a forest with a weapon of *unbelievable* power as the one and only survivor from any of these onslaughts that have occurred at the villages on the outskirts of Cyprien." Her eyebrows ached from being scrunched together with fury. She jabbed her decorated finger into Drake's chest. "Tell me how, Drake! How did you survive? How did you come by that sword? How the *fuck* did you manage to trick your way into my company?"

Ena was looking for a fight. Looking for any reason to tell Drake off or, better yet, kill him and be done with it. She could not allow herself to get attached to anyone else. But Drake would not give in. He said, "Ena, give me a chance to prove myself to you. I'll leave you be for now."

With that, Drake walked out, shutting the door behind him. Moments later, her handmaiden returned with a tuxedo draped over her arm. When Ena asked what it was for, the handmaiden replied, "You will need someone to accompany you to the ball, Governess. The young man who came with you volunteered when we first arrived in Gabrenas."

Are you fucking kidding me? Ena was certain she would kill Drake with her own bare hands before the ball was done and over with. She was on a mission, though, and she would do whatever necessary to complete the task. Maybe Drake really was simply a villager who happened to escape fate. Maybe the sword was really an ornament of his family or his home, unknowing what power it truly contained. Trust was built by experiences and actions, not words. Drake clearly trusted her since her actions showed she would protect him.

"Let me see those eyebrows, Governess," the handmaiden smiled with those godsdamned tweezers in her hand once more...

◆◆◆◆◆◆◆◆◆

Should she apologize to Drake for how she reacted earlier? Probably. Apologies could wait, though. Her goal at the moment was to survive this insufferable party and introduce herself to Raven, the Lady of Avalon.

Drake stood beside her in his sleek, black tuxedo. His dark brown hair combed back in a typical formal fashion. He looked at her, and she met his gaze. The idiot was smiling, as if he expected her to enjoy this... Why him? Why couldn't Damian or Klaus have attended this thing with her?

According to the handmaiden, she needed to look less threatening, as to not draw unneeded attention to herself, and Drake had a personal touch to him that her other two guards did not. Damian and Klaus were gruff and battle-worn—even Ena admitted to herself that they could not blend in wearing a tux like Drake was.

Drake extended his elbow. Ena rolled her eyes and locked arms with him. Together, they stepped off of the carriage Sheridan organized to deliver them and entered the Grand Ballroom through a set of gilded doors. Standing at the top of a shallow staircase leading into the belly of the beast, Ena took a moment to read her surroundings. The floors were carpeted with the finest fabrics, a compilation of colors and patterns that screamed royalty. The oak floor in the center of the ballroom, serving as the dance floor, was polished to reflect the light that refracted through the glass crystals and fragments of the overexaggerated and extravagant chandelier that hung from the arched ceilings. Frost-white tablecloths draped over sets of tables and cushioned chairs decorated the edges of the dance floor. If Ena didn't know any better, she would have assumed Gabrenas was the seat of the Havyn monarchy. The Spire of the New King was not nearly as regal as the Grand Ballroom of Avalon.

"Wow..." Ena gasped.

"I become starstruck each year when I enter this room, as well!" came an excited female voice from behind her. The woman approached on her left side. She was older, perhaps in her late fifties, and wore her curly light-brown hair up with her carnation pink dress touching the floor. "I have attended this gala each year since I was a child. It never fails to leave me breathless!"

Ena gave the woman a very fake smile. Better to seem interested enough to not offend her, but not interested enough to continue the conversation.

It didn't work. The woman continued, "I have never seen you here before. What is your name?"

"Kate," Ena recited the fake identity provided to her by the Providence. Best to not have her name fall upon public ears. "Representative of the City of Lothol's court. This is my... husband." She almost choked on that last word. She also had never been to Lothol, another of Avalon's seven cities. Hopefully, this woman would not try to pick her brain any further and catch her in a lie.

"A pleasure, Kate," she extended a gloved hand and shook Ena's. "I represent the Lord of Cyprien." *Cyprien? Shit... This could complicate things.* "Lady Marie, wife of Lord Gregor. My poor old husband was too ill to make it, so I came alone. 'Cyprien must always have a voice,' as Gregor would say." Ena remained quiet. Marie kept talking anyway. "We are quite far apart in age, though, so I am not surprised that he has weakened in his old age. Gregor has been Lord of Cyprien for fifteen years, but we have been involved in the royal courts for our entire lives."

During Ena's short stint as Governess of El Vadora, she had yet to meet Lord Gregor. After her years of studying the civics of Havyn, she knew more about Marie's life with Gregor than she cared to admit.

Gregor is ten years Marie's senior. They met when Marie accompanied her father, a court representative of a small city in the region of Estera, to a ball similar to the one Ena now attended. They hit it off famously and were married within the year. Marie had been sixteen. Gregor had always been involved in the politics of Cyprien one way or another. After many years as a simple court representative, he attained the office of Governor of the Cyprien city of Benest, where he served for twenty or so years before being elected Lord. Marie was by his side through every moment of it.

Sad to think that she would soon be alone for the first time in her life, if the rumors surrounding Gregor's health were true.

"I am sorry to hear about Lord Gregor's condition." Ena sympathy was real, even if her persona in that moment was not.

Marie dipped her head, acknowledging Ena's concern.

"If I might make a suggestion, Kate," Marie leaned into Ena's ear. "Switch arms with your husband. A woman should always be on the right side of her man, because women are always right." She winked. "It's your first time to an event like this. I can tell. Just breathe, sweetie! Enjoy yourself, have a few glasses of champagne, dance!" Ena couldn't help but feel embarrassed. Something so small as which side of Drake she stood on already placed a target on her back as the "new girl" in the crowd. What else would she do wrong? *I can't do this.*

"I see friends of mine," Marie waved across the room. "I am grateful to have been introduced to you, Kate. Remember what I said about having fun. Don't take life for granted!" And with that, Marie was off to the other side of the ballroom.

Ena felt foolish as she switched positions with Drake. At least her companion for the night was supportive in this endeavor. It could not have been easy for him either. Surrounded by all of these extravagancies were intimidating. If Drake felt overwhelmed, he did a wonderful job of hiding it.

"Now to find Lady Raven," Ena said. They began walking through the ballroom, hoping to find Raven and have a subtle conversation with her. "I do not even know what she looks like."

"Neither do I," Drake said.

As they slowly paced through the room, couples began dancing on the oak wood floor to the string quartet performing on the dais against the far wall across from the gilded doors. Ena held her rigid stance with Drake along the edge of the dance floor, scanning the room for any sign of the lady.

Dress skirts were swaying and shined dress shoes illuminated as the rich couples waltzed. Something nudged Ena in the small of her back. She turned her head to see Marie mouthing *Get out there!* Urging her to dance. When Ena shook her head no, Marie nudged Drake. Drake grinned at Ena and pulled her to the dance floor.

"No! Drake, stop!" she hissed.

Ena took a deep breath as she watched the other dancers around her.

Drake placed a hand on Ena's hip and took her hand with his other. Discomfort shone on her face. They mimicked the footwork of their counterparts and began swaying and stepping with the rhythm of the quartet.

Around and around they spun on the dancefloor. Ena kept her eyes sharp, perusing the audience. As they circled the center of the room, something caught Ena's eye.

"Drake," she whispered, "I found her."

Drake nodded. At the end of the song, they finished their dance and stepped off the floor.

Ena pointed at the stage.

Climbing the steps to the stage was someone out of a fairytale. The woman's black, lace ballgown absorbed all the light that touched it. Her flesh, paler than moonlight, and her platinum blonde hair offsetting the darkness of her attire. She approached the front of the stage and tapped a silver knife against the rim of her champagne glass, ringing to collect the crowd's attention. She placed her champagne glass on the floor, her platinum waves cascading as she brushed her locks behind her ears.

"Lords and ladies, governors and governesses," Lady Raven's cold, firm voice began, "and all other distinguished guests. I will first begin by thanking you all for attending tonight's Lordship Ball. This annual event was near and dear to my late husband, as he always made an apparent effort to build relationships with other representatives of the people. Everyone here has been touched by my husband's influence over the past twenty-five years in some way. Tonight is for him. He will always be the Lord of Avalon to me and its people. I know he would have given anything to be here with you all tonight, but instead, he watches over us all from the Connections.

"In honor of his name and everything he stood for, I will donate any proceeds from tonight's gala to feed, clothe, and house those without. We are all lucky. We have been granted the opportunity to do right by the people we serve, which comes with great reward and an overabundance of benefits. I ask that we all take this moment to consider our wealth a burden, not on ourselves, but as a vacuum—a void—on those who could use it most. From this day forwards, I am recycling all of my personal income as Lady of Avalon back into the economy. That wealth will be distributed amongst the neediest of families and I urge you all to do the same." Raven paused, then sighed deeply before finishing. "Thank you again for your attendance tonight. It is most appreciated."

The heavy weight of silence hung over them like fog. Had the Lady of Avalon truly just asked—no, *urged*—the richest individuals in Havyn to give up their wealth? Ena wasn't certain how to read the crowd's reaction. Were they angry? Had Lady Raven touched them? It was unimaginable that they would all hand over their gold and silver like it was spare change.

Lady Raven's husband built their wealth from the ground up. They fell in love young, and both came from working-class families. Raven's husband decided it was time to fight back for the working-class families and ran for the office of Governor of Gabrenas first without any prior political experience. Soon after, to the surprise of many, he defeated two governors and was inaugurated into the office of Lord when the open position presented itself.

Twenty-five years of service to the people made them a powerful couple.

This is a display of that power. Ena was figuring out the game Raven was playing. *She just showed every other powerful person in this room that she is above them. It is a threat to not mess with her.*

The other patrons of the Lordship Ball parted as Lady Raven descended from the stage and strode across the dance floor holding her empty champagne glass in one hand and the skirt of her ballgown lifted in the other. She kept her chin down as she marched through the crowd, refusing to look anyone in the eye.

That is, until she passed Ena and Drake.

Eye contact was made, though briefly. Time seemed to slow as Lady Raven took two massive strides before disappearing into the ensemble of colored dresses and black suits. During that fleeting moment, Raven's icy irises slashed through Ena. The lady knew exactly whose gaze she met, there was no denying that.

As the other attendees broke the awkward silence, the string quartet bowed their instruments once more, setting a more pleasant mood. Ena and Drake simultaneously spun on their heels and headed after the Lady of Avalon. They navigated their way to the gilded doors, assuming the lady had left the party. As they met the first step leading up to the doorway out, a sharp whistle sounded behind them. They whipped around to find Lady Raven leaning against a nearby marble column having her glass filled by one of the servants.

"Representative *Kate*, is it?" The sarcastic sound of her fake identity pierced Ena. She nodded in response.

Raven delicately stepped closer. "*You're* what they send me? You're no more than a child." Raven towered over Ena by a head in her stiletto heels. Raven circled Ena like a predator hunting its prey.

"I apologize, Lady Raven," Ena squinted as she met Raven's predatory gaze. Raven could speak every thought of hers through her cyan eyes. At this moment, they were studying Ena, curious if the governess could be trusted. Ena continued, "I cannot deny that I am young. However, was your husband not as young as I when he was elected Lord?"

Raven pressed her forehead against Ena and hissed through her unnaturally white teeth, "You dare speak of my husband? The nerve of you! The nerve of a child!" She tossed her free hand in the air, emphasizing her frustration.

"No offense, Lady," Ena would not show fear, "but this *child* was recruited to help *you* find your husband's killer! You should be showing me more respect!"

Raven hushed, "Keep your voice down! It cannot start going around that he was killed. It would cause too much unrest."

"How in the Connections," Drake spoke for the first time, "are you hiding his cause of death? Wasn't he young and healthy?"

Ena raised her eyebrows as she glared at him. *Keep quiet!*

Raven swirled the champagne in her fluted glass, "You tell the people he was 'sick' for some time and did not want to burden his loyal supporters with the imminence of his death." She sipped her drink. "Knowing his selfless nature, they believed it without question."

"Not one single person believes otherwise?" Ena asked.

"Five people know of his... murder," she whispered the last word. "The Providence, the Master of Cities, you, your *pet*, and that disgraceful excuse for a white mage."

Disgraceful? The Master White Mage? "What is the issue with Archem?" Ena had learned as many names as she could during their carriage ride to Avalon. Her efforts were paying off.

"He grew angry when the Providence ordered him to leave his research on the poison be and have you essentially replace him and his efforts," Raven rolled her eyes. "There was some disdain against me personally when the Master of Cities made me Lady without a proper election, as well. He was too old and his faith too controlling. I wanted to be rid of him for years, but my late husband insisted otherwise."

"Where is he now? Are you not afraid of him speaking the truth?"

"Not without a tongue," said the lady ominously subtle. Ena was stunned. She had studied enough history books to recognize the qualities of a tyrant. First came the lies and withholding of information from the public, then came the dismissal of the Faith. Followed shortly by the prevention of those who know the truth from speaking such truths. What would occur next?

"You know, Lady Raven," Ena knew she was testing her luck, "the spouse is always a primary suspect in murder cases such as these..." The look of pure disdain Raven replied with could kill thousands. "You seem so keen on hiding the truth and playing as if you do not know what killed him. How much knowledge of poisons do you truly have?"

That icy glare sent shivers down Ena's spine. She could feel Drake swallow in fear behind her.

"Governess," Lady Raven's tone was calm. Clearly a trap. "You are in my home as a guest. Avalon is a place of peace." *Funny, I didn't realize places of peace cut out tongues of those who talked too much...* "A death by poison would create chaos outside the walls of the Grand Ballroom. Business would shut down. People would lock themselves in their homes. The City Watch would be demanded to patrol the streets day and night."

"Fear is a tyrant's weapon, Raven," Ena spoke sternly. "How ambitious are you? Your husband's death left a vacancy in the lordship of Avalon. Avalon is a large, powerful region of Havyn. No doubt you would be nominated next for Master of Cities should Sheridan leave his post someday. You are still young—what, mid-forties at most?—you could be ruling Havyn by the time your first wrinkles appear on your face."

Ena half-expected Raven to smack her, or order guards to remove her from the ball, at least. Instead, Raven relaxed the scowl on her face and laughed.

"You are a force to be reckoned with, Governess Athenia. You talk of *my* ambition. Let's someday talk of yours. After you find my husband's killer. What will you need for the job?"

Surprised at Raven's sudden change in temperament, Ena was thrown off. Was this the behavior she could expect from Lady Raven's hospitality? Maybe she was in over her head.

"I will need a temporary residence at an inn downtown, for starters," Ena began to list her requirements. "If I am to remain inconspicuous, I cannot be traversing to and from your palace each day. We will either need food and supplies for a minimum of three months, or roughly ten thousand gold to purchase supplies myself. I will also need consistent access to a private courier to exchange messages with you in secret."

Raven remained speechless for several seconds, thinking, before bursting out with laughter. "You are insane, *Kate*. How am I supposed to 'inconspicuously' contribute all that to you on such short notice? Even if you were to purchase that all yourself, ten thousand gold is a significant amount to hand over to a young girl I only just met. How in the Connections would I explain this to inquisitive minds?"

Ena shrugged, "I am not sure, Lady Raven, but my guard detail and I will be finding ourselves an accommodating room at an inn this evening. I will have a courier bring you the bill for our next three months' stay. Could you have those supplies to me by sun high tomorrow?"

Raven threw back her head, letting the remnants in her champagne glass fall down her throat. She handed the empty glass to a passing servant.

"Three months?" Raven asked. Ena nodded. "Are you certain?"

"I will need the first few weeks to acclimate myself within Gabrenas and mingle with its people," Ena explained. "After that, I will ask subtle questions and listen around the city for any talk of strange activity. I understand we have only now been introduced, but you must trust me, Raven."

Lady Raven bit her lower lip, deep in thought. Her trust was running short these days. The governess was right, though she hated to admit it. Whatever little hope she had left would need to be placed in Athenia's hands.

Raven bowed slightly, "It has been a pleasure to make your acquaintance, Representative Kate. I do hope you enjoy your stay in Gabrenas." She winked at Ena and marched out of the ballroom on her jet-black stilettos.

CHAPTER 8

Havana City was bustling with commerce on the morning Sheridan accompanied the lord of Havana on his monthly walkthrough of the capital city. Though Havana City was the seat of the Kingdom of Havyn, the Havana region still required a lord and Havana City still required a governor. Complications tended to arise with the city being home to the governor, lord, and the kingdom concurrently. Sheridan happened to be skilled at diffusing these tensions by playing the part of an unbiased party when concerns developed.

Lord Elmar had been a strong supporter of Sheridan's during his campaign for the open Master of Cities position three years prior. The Lord of Havana had refused the nomination when his name peaked on the people's tongues as to who was best suited for the role. However, with supporters came rivals.

Elmar's heritage stemmed back to the Elf Nation to the far west of Lynidas. Though Elmar did not resemble much of an elf, besides, perhaps, his tall stature and inability to grow facial hair, prejudice was against him.

Seven years of his life up to this point had been dedicated to his lordship. Seven years he has worked to correct the malpractice of his predecessors. The economy in Havana was unstable for so long that Elmar had to prolong his efforts of recovering commerce to a healthy level to prevent it from rebounding in the opposite direction. That is, to rapidly shift from everyone being poor and struggling to everyone being rich and prospering could have an adverse effect. A middle class must always exist, Elmar was a strong believer in that. Wealth distribution was the key to a successful economy.

That same principle further increased the number of enemies in Elmar's wake. The abundantly rich were stripped of their superfluity. The rich were too stubborn to give up a spare slice of bread to the poor, never mind their coffers.

If Elmar had placed his name in for the candidacy, he likely would not have lived to see election night.

Instead, he supported a dwarf with no reputation in politics. A dwarf with no friends or allies in Havyn. A dwarf with nothing but the clothes on his back and a vision for reform. Lord Elmar's inclinations of the dwarf did not disappoint.

Under Sheridan's short term as Master of Cities, he reformed the City Watch by recognizing the corruption, removing those corrupted from their positions, and distributing the patrols of guards among the upper-class and lower-class districts of the cities. A direct opposition of the former practice of only patrolling the wealthy areas to make the rich feel protected from the "scum" and allowing crime in the impoverished sections of the city run rampant. Sheridan also greatly reduced tariffs between the regions and cities, allowing trade to prosper and for the working and lower classes to share in the commodities that they could not previously afford. That particular motion was a shot in the dark, even Sheridan could admit that. Reducing tariffs could have crippled the trade industry with the same effect that it had made it flourish.

Sheridan was smart, though—he would not have risked odds like that without having a failsafe in place.

"The topic of tariffs is common amongst the citizens these past few weeks, Master," Lord Elmar led Sheridan through the mercantile district of Havana City. "Something about the steel trade being in uproar recently."

The lord towered far above Sheridan's head. The Master of Cities could double in stature and still not be at eye level with Elmar, thanks to his elven ancestry. Sheridan, like most dwarfs, were not exactly nimble, so forcing himself to lift his chin straight up to meet Lord Elmar's eyes would cause an unbearable strain in his neck later in the day, therefore, both walked side by side without making eye contact. To others, this would be considered a sign of disrespect, but the understanding was mutual between these two.

"The steel trade, huh?" Sheridan knew exactly what the problem was. "Has there also been talk of a dwarf with greying hair attending market with a Brekken woman?"

Elmar snickered slightly and nodded. His long, dark hair flowed behind him as he walked.

Mida...

"I will have to gently escort him from the city if he is causing trouble," Sheridan walked along the cobblestone roads that made up the market. To the Keeper that accompanied him, he said, "Make note of that for me, Keeper."

The Keepers were assigned to protect the royal family, yet Sheridan typically had one accompanying him whenever he left the Spire of the New King. The idea had supposedly been King Typhus's to offer the Master of Cities "extra protection." Sheridan couldn't understand why, seeing as he had the entire City Watch in the palm of his hand if he truly desired extra protection. Understanding finally came when Typhus announced his distrust of the dwarf. Typhus never wanted Sheridan to win the election to begin with, but after winning by a landslide, Typhus bit his tongue and allowed the dwarf to conduct his business with little restriction, at first.

As Typhus grew sicker and his mind began to wander, he freely vocalized his feelings of Sheridan. Most often, these feelings were vocalized to Sheridan's face, unbeknown to the king that he was speaking to the very one he was speaking about. Typhus occasionally recognized the Providence, having grown up with her in the royal family, but Sheridan was never the same person twice whenever they spoke. The Keepers accompanied Sheridan because the king wanted a spy to watch over his every move.

Spies were only useful when their intentions remained hidden. Though the Keepers were bound by law to take orders from the royal family only, they were not mindless soldiers, and they understood the king was ill and not always in his right mind. They entertained Typhus's delusions, to an extent, but respected Sheridan and the Providence for their efforts ruling the kingdom themselves.

"This is that Mida fellow again, is it not?" the Keeper asked. Keepers were armed with spears in one hand, kite shields in the other, gladiuses buckled at their hips, and thick Aconyte steel armor with crested helms. "What is his purpose in Havyn?"

This particular Keeper belonged to Princess Lia. She often spared one of hers, knowing Sheridan was skeptical of what Typhus's Keepers reported back to him.

"He wishes for me to lower the taxes at the border for him specifically," Sheridan sighed. "The steel trade is under his thumb in Fairmarq. According to him, the Merchant's Guild named him Mida, the *Lord* of Steel."

Elmar asked, "What makes his steel so special to grant him such a title?"

"It's Aconyte steel..."

"*What?!*" disbelief shown on the Keeper's face. "Aconyte steel is one of the rarest metals in Lynidas, if not the world. Keeper armor and weapons are constructed with Aconyte and the product is nearly impossible to come by. How has he established an entire trade with it?"

Sheridan pulled a scroll from the canvas pouch he carried at his side and began reading it as he walked, "He has a deal with the Tunnel Dwarves of Garmoire who mine it. I don't know details. I try not entertaining his fantasies if I can help it." To a passing guard captain and their platoon, he pointed to the scroll and ordered, "New itinerary, men. Stay near the markets. If anyone so much as breathes about Aconyte steel, I want to know." The guards nodded and turned down the next street. To Elmar and the Keeper, he added, "Last time Mida was here, he tried selling me on some kind of secret combination of herbs that could make you younger. I had him escorted back to Nest Aiken, where he was setting up his shop at the time. I would do the same now, but Fairmarq's Merchant's Guild has a nasty reputation. I would much rather he leave on his own accord after failing to make a profit."

"You think he is dangerous?" Elmar asked.

"Not him, per se, but the Merchant's Guild is for sure."

Sheridan had spent a period of time in Fairmarq, serving as King Henree Grey's personal advisor, before coming to Havyn a few years ago. If there is anything Sheridan learned during his travels, it was to stay clear of the Merchant's Guild and its business. Fairmarq's king, Henree Grey, had been at political war with the Merchant's Guild since his coronation over thirty years ago. Though Farimarq's economy soared far above the other four kingdoms of Lynidas, the lack of control over the Merchant's Guild was a danger. The amount of influence the Guild had in the political affairs of Fairmarq scared the hell out of King Grey. Thankfully, the royal family was powerful enough to withstand any diplomatic attack.

"I do not trust him bringing Aconyte into Havyn..." the Keeper expressed his concern. "We do not need private citizens gaining access to weapons of Aconyte. Too dangerous."

"Agreed," Elmar said. "Besides, if we let Mida have free reign over the steel trade in Havyn, who's to say that he will not bring the Guild with him?"

"Exactly," Sheridan agreed.

"Last thing we need is for a third competitor for the throne," Elmar half whispered.

Sheridan stopped in his tracks, looking up at Elmar for the first time today, "What is that comment supposed to mean, Lord?"

Elmar returned his glare, "Oh, nothing, Master." But seeing Sheridan's scowl, he continued, "It is no mystery that the king has not exactly been in the prime of his life since Queen Helena's passing. It is also no secret that since your inauguration as Master of Cities that you have taken on many of King Typhus's tasks and responsibilities."

"Governing a kingdom does not simply pause whenever its ruler is having a bad day," Sheridan defended. "The Providence and I do what we can to keep things in check."

Before Elmar could respond, around the corner marched a pair of Guardians of the Faith. They gripped their staves at their sides and approached Sheridan in step with one another. Sheridan pushed through Elmar and the Keeper and met the Guardians on their approach. One of the Guardians held out a hand with a sealed note addressed to *Master of Cities*.

Sheridan took the note, cracked the seal, and read the few handwritten words to himself. It read, *I have something for you if you have something for me*.

Sheridan turned to Lord of Havana. "If you would excuse me, Lord Elmar. Duty calls."

◆◆◆◆◆◆◆◆◆

Sheridan entered the Providence's study alone. No Guardians of the Faith followed him inside, likely on the Providence's orders. Though the Guardians of the Faith did not speak and were solely loyal to the Providence, some discussions were best had in complete privacy.

The door shut behind him. The Providence waited for him at her desk on the opposite wall. She did not look up as he approached. She was scribbling a letter to be sealed and sent. Her desk work consisted mostly of reading and replying to letters from the Master White Mages across the kingdom. Keeping the Faith in line was tasking, though the Providence would never admit it.

There was a curriculum to be followed. Most teachings by the white mages derived from the religious tomes *The Paladin*, *Weaving the Connections of Magic*, and *The Oblong Eye*. The first of these, *The Paladin*, contained verses utilized in various ceremonies and events, such as funerals or weddings. *Weaving the Connections of Magic* was strictly used for white mages to hone their abilities and master the art of healing. Just as the Providence had demonstrated upon her introduction with Governess Athenia, healing magic could also be used for the opposite effect. Her primary concern was ensuring that the lessons were being responsibly taught from *Weaving*, since an irresponsible practice of magic could lead to unexpected deaths. *The Oblong Eye* was the most widely used tome during the daily religious services held within the cathedrals in each city. For decades, the number of attendees during the daily services had progressively dropped. Due to the current Providence's rigorous restructuring of the religious curriculum, numbers have significantly improved.

Sheridan pulled up a chair in front of the Providence's desk and waited until she signed and sealed the letter, placing it in a pile with dozens of others.

"Apologies, Sheridan," she brushed a lock of golden hair from her face. "I expected to finish sending my weekly letters before you arrived."

"Not to worry, Providence," Sheridan put his hands behind his head and leaned back in his chair. "Normally, I would not have rushed over as swiftly as I did, but I needed the break."

Her pink lips curled in a smile, "Understandable."

"You had something for me?"

"Indeed," she pushed a stack of books in front of Sheridan. "These are all I found on my shelves containing knowledge of the faerie language. They are *very* old and brittle."

Sheridan reached for the top book before the Providence placed her own hand on the book, stopping him.

"Now would be a good time for a look into your own past, if you would not mind," she said sternly.

Sheridan dropped his hand onto the desk. His fingers on his metallic hand tapping the wood rapidly. *Where to begin?*

The Providence continued, "Your interest in the long-since extinct faeries is an interest of mine. You must understand why, do you not?" Sheridan remained silent. "If we do not have trust, Sheridan, then all we have strived for will be for naught."

"Fine," Sheridan grumbled. "Better to *show* you than to tell you."

The Providence tilted her head curiously. Show her what?

Sheridan inhaled deeply, closing his eyes. The Providence could feel the air around them still—eerily soundless—as if time had frozen. Suddenly, one by one, the books between them lifted in the air and began circling Sheridan. The dwarf raised both hands in front of him and the pages of the books flipped back and forth like the crescendo of a piano. The books stopped, levitating motionlessly, and Sheridan opened his eyes to find a shocked look on the Providence's face. Shock and awe.

"You're..." The Providence was amazed at what she beheld, "you're... a kinetic mage!"

Sheridan smirked under his thick, red beard. *She hasn't seen anything yet.*

The dwarf made another motion with his hands. The large desk between them slowly lifted above their heads and started rotating. Before the Providence could react, the chair she was seated in also lifted from the floor. She hung far above Sheridan's head as she nervously trembled.

"Do you trust me, Providence?" he called to her.

She nodded apprehensively and gripped the edges of her chair. Her knuckles turned white from her tight grasp. Before she could blink, she was being turned upside down and right-side up over and over, twirled head over heels in a somersault.

Slowly, Sheridan lowered the Providence and the desk back to the floor. As the legs of her chair met the stone beneath her feet, she let loose the breath she had been holding.

The faerie books neatly rearranged back into their stack on the desk, which also slowly descended back into its place on the floor.

"Sheridan..." The Providence whispered. "How in the world..."

Sheridan shrugged, "I was born with it. Not sure why or how."

"But," she was speechless, "you are a dwarf... Dwarves cannot use magic..."

"Not to correct you, Providence," Sheridan laughed, "but no dwarf has ever been known to use magic. That doesn't mean one *cannot* use magic."

"This is impossible. I must be dreaming."

Sheridan threw his hands up, "You asked for the truth, Providence. Now you have it."

"Why are you here, Sheridan? Who even are you? You appear from nowhere three years ago and get elected as Master of Cities, and yet each time I learn more about you, the more of a mystery you become."

His secret was already out, he might as well tell her everything.

Sheridan heaved a sigh, "I was born a tunnel dwarf in Garmoire and orphaned very young. I always knew of my ability, but I also knew other dwarves did not have the same skill, so I kept it to myself. The Tunnel Dwarves went to war very briefly with the Surface Dwarves in the Garmoire Mountains. Sure, it was a short war, but many tunnel dwarves were captured as prisoners and held for ransom. I happened to be one of them, but I was a child. Instead of fighting them, I joined them. Why not? I was hungry, homeless, and had no one to turn to.

"I joined the Surface Dwarf army and helped defend the borders for many years. Not much ever happened besides a skirmish or two here and there. One day, though, we were unexpectedly attacked and the area of the border I was stationed at was lost and many of my fellow soldiers died. I was brutally hit in the arm during the attack and when the retreat order was issued, I ran until I was seeing spots. I didn't realize how far I ran, but I was completely lost.

"I was losing blood and had lost most mobility in my arm. Finally, I found an empty hunting camp to rest in. By the time I would find help, an infection would have started and spread and likely killed me. So, I cut it off." The Providence grimaced.

Sheridan continued, "I cauterized the stump and passed out from the pain. The hunters had returned while I was unconscious. They patched me up as best they could and brought me back to the town they were from. Little did I realize, I had strayed so far from Garmoire that I ended up in Fairmarq. I had managed to get my hands on some scrap metal and shaped it to look like an arm. Before you ask, my arm is not the typical dwarven prosthetic like I always said it was. I use my magic to move my arm. My magic is an extension of myself, literally."

"After leaving Fairmarq," the Providence was starting to make sense of it all, "you came to Havyn? What, you heard about the Master of Cities vacancy and decided to become a candidate? Why?"

"I quickly saw the flaws in the system," Sheridan explained, "and I believed I could fix them. While in Fairmarq, I worked my way into the graces of King Henree Grey, becoming his personal advisor, and he endorsed by nomination for Master of Cities here."

The Providence squinted, "You still are not telling me the whole truth."

"I have my reservations with telling my entire truth, yes," Sheridan snapped, "but I have told and shown you more just now than I have with anyone else in my entire life. I have only the best of intentions for Havyn, just as you do."

The Providence huffed, "I suppose I can accept that for now. Kinetic mages have been nearly extinct since the Mage Wars. Yet one sits before me. A *dwarf*, nonetheless..."

Sheridan had a hard time believing it himself some days. He grew up with dwarves. He fought alongside them for decades, and no one had anything close to a touch of magic except him. His was more than a simple "touch." He had a command over the Connections of Magic. A command that only the most skilled of mages could possess. Perhaps evenly matched with that of the Providence's own skill? Sheridan was not about to challenge that.

"What are your 'best of intentions' for Havyn anyhow?" the Providence asked.

Sheridan scratched his chin under his beard, "To make it stronger. To have the kingdom survive the turmoil of the world outside of its walls. Tensions are rising, whether or not you know or believe it. Nest Aiken has been struggling to maintain relations with the Brekken Alliance, the Greys and the High King of High Alta are sending idle threats to one another, and Athenia tells me that fire mages have been burning down villages on the outskirts of Cyprien. The people will look to the Faith during a time of need, that is where you come in. But even The

All-Seeing God cannot protect against an army."

The rising tensions were no mystery to the Providence. She had her own sources who provided her with information, as well. Havyn was stronger than Sheridan gave it credit for, she firmly believed. But would Havyn be able to survive if the bloodline of the monarchy ceased to exist?

Lord Elmar was not incorrect in their suspicions against Sheridan. He and the Providence have spoken on this topic many times. If the king dies, Princess Lia would become Queen. However, if Lia became Queen, then the position of the Providence would no longer have a successor. The Concordat demanded that, if such situation occurred, then the Monarchy and the Master of Cities would nominate a new Providence, should the nominee successfully complete the Trials of the Connections.

If Lia became the queen, then Sheridan, as Master of Cities, would be her primary influence ruling the kingdom. If the Providence died and a new one needed to be nominated, others may wonder if Sheridan would be the one swaying that decision. Governors and lords would likely see Sheridan's actions as a coup to seize the crown for himself. Rebellion would soon follow.

They wanted to avoid that outcome at all cost. However, they were at a loss for any possible solution. The end of the royal bloodline was inevitable.

"What do you intend to find by deciphering the *Encantorum*?" the Providence asked finally.

"To be quite honest," Sheridan shook his head, "I am not even sure. There are too many coincidences lately for comfort. First, the Lord of Avalon is mysteriously poisoned. Simultaneously, mages are burning down villages in El Vadora. Then, a random farmer is found with an ancient faerie weapon. Not to mention that it was Athenia who discovered him. The same person who has been cursed with discovering far too much than she ever cared to about various poisons."

It all tied together *too* coincidentally.

What could the *Encantorum* reveal that their own common sense could not? The Providence reserved her belief that Sheridan may be too suspicious of some deeper conspiracy. All would be revealed soon. She had to believe that for her own peace of mind.

Athenia would soon bring to justice the Lord of Avalon's killer. Doing so would then build a greater alliance between Avalon, the Providence, and the Master of Cities. They needed any alliance they could get if what Sheridan spoke was true. Havyn, as a whole, needed to remain united should the hostilities in its neighboring kingdoms spill over the borders.

Sheridan thanked the Providence for her assistance. He collected the books and brought them back to his section of the Spire and began studying them immediately. The words were foreign. They were hardly even *words*. Maybe he was in over his head, maybe he was entirely wrong, but the knowledge contained in the *Encantorum* had to be worth his time and effort. And now that the Providence knew his secret, could she be trusted to keep it?

CHAPTER 9

I need to see the body," Ena demanded the following morning.

After the Lordship Ball, Ena stripped herself of the uncomfortable dress and donned a tunic and a pair of trousers. She promised herself she would never attend another stupid ball again. Not even a full twenty-four hours in Avalon and a strong contempt for the entire region grew within the governess. She could not wait for this to be over so she could return to El Vadora. That wouldn't be for another three months, though. Ena hadn't been bluffing when she requested rooms at an inn for three months. She knew nothing of Avalon, or its capital city of Gabrenas, and an investigation would take time.

Three months may not be enough time, but Ena refused to admit that to herself just yet.

The first thing she needed to do was to see the Lord of Avalon's body. All she knew of the poison that ultimately killed the lord was from Master Archem's report, which was already deemed faulty and inconclusive. Contrary to everyone's belief, Ena was no poison expert, but she had uncovered enough knowledge regarding various toxins during her gubernatorial experience to at least begin a formal investigation.

"*Representative Kate*," Lady Raven spat. "My late husband has been locked within his mausoleum for well over a month now. I am not allowing you to traipse in there and disturb his tomb by *dissecting* him. You know everything you need to know!"

Ena had played the role of her alter ego in order to enter the Grand Ballroom of Avalon inconspicuously. The guards had not questioned her presence there, having seen Lady Raven speaking to her at the Lordship Ball the evening prior. Though she was not dressed as formal in her violet dress, she emitted a professional exuberance in her form-fitting black silk tunic. Representative Kate was everything Governess Athenia was not, and she played the part better than she cared to admit.

Ena took the report from the lady's cherry desk between them. She flipped through it delicately, scanning the words written by the former Master White Mage. She stopped on one of the pages and pointed to the words, reciting them, "'...possibility of a strange toxin located within the bloodstream...', '...no known symptoms prior to death... the Lord was in excellent health.', 'Final report for Cause of Death: Unknown; only possible approach is death by untraceable poisoning.'" Ena snickered, closing the report. "*That* is what your Master White Mage wrote. There is no single piece of evidence of a cause of death, Raven. You are all *so* convinced that he was poisoned, and the only way I can prove that for certain is by seeing his body."

Lady Raven stood from her desk and glided towards the open window overlooking Gabrenas. She silhouetted against the morning sun in her midnight black dress. Only the lady's ivory hands, carefully clasped behind the small of her back, could be seen. The light manifesting on the eastern-facing walls of the buildings had always brought Raven peace. When lost in thought, this was her therapy.

"Allow me to speak with Governor Josef for permission to enter the cemetery," Raven responded softly.

Ask for permission? Ena thought to herself.

As if hearing her thoughts, Raven continued, "The cemetery in which my husband was buried is sacred ground belonging to Gabrenas. It remains locked except during the burial of a lord, governor, or other esteemed member of the government. Could I enter it whenever I wish? Absolutely, Gabrenas and its governor answer to me, but I try to be as courteous as I can."

"How much does the governor know?" Ena asked.

"Nothing," Raven turned her face from the window. "However, a grieving widow wishing to visit her husband's tomb should be a simple enough reason to get done whatever sickening act it is you wish to conduct on his body."

Ena rolled her eyes, "Raven, you must trust me. If poison truly is the cause of death, I will be able to prove it to you without being too invasive with his body."

Raven hesitated for a moment, once again facing the glistening sunrise over the horizon. Finally, she rotated on her heels, invisible under her floor-length dress, and nodded.

◆◆◆◆◆◆◆◆◆

The door to the tomb was sealed tight. It took the might of both Ena and Raven to pry it open. These mausoleums were not intended to be opened frequently. Raven assumed the next time it would be opened was when placing her own corpse in there after her death.

Much to their disapproval, Ena traveled to the cemetery with Raven without the company of her guard detail. Only a handful of guards accompanied the pair. Ena agreed to leave her own guards aside for the sake of maintaining some level of secrecy.

A strange ominous essence hung in the air as they entered the darkened tomb. Only the dull, natural light seeping in from the vent carved at the top of the back wall gave them any vision.

Raven had insisted on coming at night when they were less likely to be spotted, but using a torch for light may have given away their position easier. They faced no trouble arriving just before dawn, though. Two guards escorted them to the gates of the cemetery, which they were ordered to guard while the lady "grieved" with her new friend, Kate. Governor Josef respectfully told Lady Raven she did not need his permission to visit the lord's grave ever, which put a genuine smile on the lady's face for the first time since the last conversation she had with her husband.

The cherry casket lay on a stone tablet in the center of the mausoleum. A thick layer of dust already settled on the surface. The essence grew stronger as they approached the casket.

"Do you smell that?" Ena asked.

Raven gave her a sharp scowl, "My husband's body is rotting beneath the lid of this casket. That is probably what you smell."

"Relax, Raven," Ena said. "A rotting body is much more pungent. This smells almost earthy. Even a hint of sweetness."

"I can't smell a thing."

Ena knew that smell—so subtle that one without a trained nose could detect the odor. The governess had a strong feeling of what they would see when the casket opened.

She urged Raven to help her open the lid. As reluctant as Lady Raven was, she wanted answers. If this helped to reach a conclusion, she felt obligated to continue.

The hinges creaked and the layer of dust plumed around them. The women choked as they fanned the dust from their faces. As the cloud settled, tears welled up in Raven's eyes. She feared seeing her husband's face after so long would make her emotional, but seeing him like *this* was too much to bear.

"*What's wrong with him?*" Lady Raven cried out hysterically.

"Shhhh," Ena calmed her. "There was no way to know how far along it would be. I'm so sorry, Raven."

Raven covered her face as she wept. She peaked between her fingers and the gruesome sight only worsened. "What's wrong with him?"

Ena approached the body. The odor was now significant.

"Do you smell it now?" Raven's lip trembled as she nodded. "And do you see the blue foam coming from his eyes, nose, and mouth? I understand this is difficult, but this is what I hoped for."

"'*Hoped for?*'" Raven repeated with disgust.

Ena explained, "Most untraceable toxins only remain untraceable for so long. They begin to show in the body in a variety of ways as the body decays. The blue foam and that nutty smell—that is bluebite."

Ena's first and only encounter with the deadly poison, bluebite, was during her first year as governess. Upon assuming the position, one of the first unsolved murder cases she found interest in involved a series of serial murders in which groups of people were mysteriously found dead. Nearly identical to the Lord of Avalon's death, without any clear indication of foul play, the bodies were buried, and the cases were left unsolved. Ena combined the cases into one, connecting the similarities between them.

After months of examining the bodies and discovering that subtle smell and blue foam, she determined the victims must have been poisoned. She tracked down the source of the poison to a black-market dealer who sold large quantities of bluebite to one person—a cult leader who tricked his followers into taking the poison as a way meeting the All-Seeing God.

Ena has never been an advocate for the death penalty, but as her first major act as governess, she swung the sword herself. Sending the cultist's head rolling, and helping the families of twenty poor souls find closure, gave her the outstanding reputation that now proceeded her.

"Bluebite?" Raven asked.

"Yes, highly untraceable in the body until weeks or months after death," Ena clarified. "The effects are almost instant. Within seconds of touching the tongue, the body has a negative reaction within the bloodstream. Within mere minutes, the heart stops entirely."

Raven shook her head neurotically. "How could this have happened? Who would want him dead like this? He had no enemies... Who would want him to end up like *that?*" She pointed a shaky finger at the corpse. She could not even recognize him anymore.

Ena wrapped her fingers over Lady Raven's hand, lowering her pointing finger. "That is what I intend to find out. This is an exceedingly rare toxin. Very few know of it, but those who do will not keep it secret for long. Three months, Raven. I requested three months, and I intend to use every second of my time solving this."

Ena's curiosity was at its peak. If she wasn't solving this murder for Lady Raven, then she was solving it for herself. This was not a common event. At least, she did not think it was. How many others have perished from bluebite poisoning whose families will never know? She feared this would open a bigger event that she was incapable of stopping on her own...

"Come on," Ena urged, "I found what I needed. Let's get you back to the Grand Ballroom, and I will get to work."

Raven composed herself, just barely. If the governess could bring justice to her husband's killer, she would owe her the world. Raven has always been strong, competent, and unbreakable. How much longer could she keep up this façade? She was broken. Now was the time to start admitting that to herself.

◆◆◆◆◆◆◆◆◆

Ena led Drake, Damian, and Klaus to the inn towards the outskirts of the city. The inn was called *Dragonfly & the Fruit* and was located in a very precarious section of the city. The carriage driver helped unload their few articles of luggage and saw them inside. As soon as they were within the walls of the inn, the carriage driver sped to his carriage and led the horses in a gallop.

"He was in a rush, huh?" Drake quipped.

The driver could not be blamed for his quick exit. The inn was a diamond among a sea of coal. Although, "diamond" may be an exaggeration. The inn had stable walls, decent food, and beds to sleep in. Less could be said about the surrounding residences on the street.

"You must be the surveyors from the city," called a voice from above them. From the second-floor balcony overhanging the common room, a short, heavyset woman wearing an apron called out to them. "Hold on a minute. I'll be right down."

"We're surveyors from the city?" Damian whispered to Ena.

"Raven said she would acquire us lodging," Ena answered, "but she never exactly said how."

Heavy footsteps thudded down the wooden steps from upstairs. The woman trudged towards them. She unenthusiastically introduced herself as if she was reading it from a script, "I'm Inga, the innkeeper. Welcome to *Dragonfly & the Fruit*. If you need anything, do not hesitate to ask. Allow me to take you to your rooms. You can choose a complimentary item from our dinner menu."

Before Ena or her detail could respond, Inga was walking back towards the steps leading to the second floor. They each grabbed their luggage and followed. Inga led them up to the third floor where two rooms were available across the narrow hallway from one another. Inga unlocked the doors with the keys on her oversized keyring hanging from her belt and threw the doors wide open. The rooms were small, hardly large enough to fit two small beds against either wall. The pitch from the roof cut out much of their standing headspace. The rooms' best features were the singular windows in each cut from the narrow dormers.

"Sorry they aren't much to look at, but here they are," Inga grumbled. "Three months is a long stay for two rooms, so I had to give you what I had available. Tell your boss I did the best I could."

Ena glanced into the rooms. "Yes, we will extend your regrets."

"What was it you're doing here these next few months again? Something about evaluating the neighborhood for reconstruction?" Inga asked.

"Yes," Ena improvised. "Our goal is to investigate the infrastructure and architecture of this area of the city and determine what is up to code or not. The parts not up to code will be offered assistance from the city to get the structures updated."

"Well?" Inga winked. "What about my inn? Am I all up to code? I should be. I'm the only place around here that has managed to stay open long enough to afford repairs."

"Yeah, why is that?" Drake asked. Ena glared at him. Whenever he opened his mouth, she shook with anger. He was a wildcard—never knowing what he was going to say at the most inappropriate times. "Doesn't seem like any business could survive here."

Inga shrugged, "People need a place to sleep and eat, I suppose." She began her heavy march back down the steps. "Bring down your orders when you are ready. First night's dinner is on the house. After that, it comes from your pocket."

Ena nodded with gratitude. Once Inga was out of sight, she grabbed Drake by the collar of his shirt and threw him into the room behind her. He stumbled, catching himself on the slant of the ceiling.

Before Drake could react, Ena pulled a dagger on him, placing it against his jugular.

"Stop fucking talking!" she spat. "You are going to give us away with your stupid comments and questions. *I* do the talking. You will stay with me, where I can keep a close eye on you. Got it? Damian and Klaus will be across the hall." She lowered the blade.

Drake rubbed his neck where the blade was. "What if I don't want to stay in your room with you?"

"It wasn't a fucking question, Drake. We are going to scope out the neighborhood. Hopefully we will have a warm dinner when we get back. Choose what you want from the menu and then we will leave."

Reluctantly, Ena hid the faerie sword under her mattress. She did not want to paint a target on her back for any common thugs thinking they could rob her. She kept two daggers hidden at her sides. Damian and Klaus did the same. Blending in was most important at this stage in the investigation.

The common room on the first floor of the inn was filled with patrons. Each had a beer in their hands as a fire burned in the center of the room. A bard was playing a tune on his lute and Inga and a few barmaids were delivering food to each of the tables. Now was their time to leave unnoticed.

As they left the inn, they turned left and walked down the cobblestone road. The first few weeks would be only listening and observing. Eventually, someone would accidentally slip up and say something they shouldn't. They were in the belly of the city where the skeletons in the closet would come alive.

Avalon, in general, was a peaceful region free of corruption. Though, in Ena's experience, no such place of peace existed. There would always be corruption, crime, and chaos waiting to burst from the seams. Time was the only factor. The city supposedly has not had a murder in many years, until the death of the Lord, but the governess doubted it. As Ena has proven to Raven, there were ways to cover up a murder. More would likely be uncovered.

They carefully walked by run down homes and structures, dark alleyways, and gruff individuals. Conditions only worsened the deeper into the belly of the city they traversed. There wasn't anything that stood out to Ena, though. Not until they saw a woman glance over her shoulder conspicuously and glue a small paper flyer to the wall of a crumbling stone house.

Ena held out a hand, ordering the detail to stop. She ducked into an alley between two apartment buildings across the street. The others followed. She peaked an eye around the corner, watching the woman carefully. After the flyer was hung, the woman stepped inside the crumbled stone house and disappeared.

"We wait here," Ena stated. "Damian, can you find out what that paper on the wall says?"

Damian gave a faint grunt and snuck around the back of the building behind them. Ena, Drake, and Klaus watched as Damian walked back into the street a block down the road, blending in with a crowd of drunks leaving a bar a few buildings down. As they walked by the stone house, Damian tripped one of the drunk men, causing him to tumble to the ground. The rest of the crowd stopped in front of the house to help him up. While everyone's attention was on the tipsy drunk, Damian studied the paper flyer.

As the tipsy man stabilized himself, the crowd continued walking. Damian snuck down another alleyway and came back around behind

Ena and the two others.

"The sign says 'Auction is here' in a very careless handwritten script," Damian said. "Auction... that's interesting."

"Mmm, very," Ena agreed. "Alright, here's the plan. She is either going to come out or others are going to meet her there for this 'auction.' Either way, I want to be in there to see what she has to hide."

Damian and Klaus nodded. Drake was more wary of the situation, "Are you sure we should be going in there?"

Ena faced him and spoke softly, "Yes. It could have absolutely nothing to do with why we are here, but we will not know unless we explore every hunch we have. There is no room for coincidences in my line of work."

"Your line of work is to govern your city," Drake retorted. "Not to sneak around a random city under a pseudonym to find a killer."

"Remind yourself why you are here, Drake."

If she hadn't been playing investigator, she would never have stumbled across him being mauled by wolves in the forest. Was Drake wrong? Absolutely not. The danger she puts herself in *was* out of character, but she did it for her people. In this case, though, she was doing it for people she hardly knew. For what?

The most influential factor in this whole situation still remains with the faerie weapon found on Drake and why he survived the onslaught of his village. If anything, she was doing this as a favor for the Master of Cities. If she solved this murder mystery, perhaps Sheridan could find out more about the sword and would be willing to assist her in hunting down the mages killing her people. She usually didn't admit when she needed help, but mages were far above her paygrade.

Ena refused to peel her eyes from that stone structure. Hours went by before something caught her eye. She tapped Klaus behind her. Klaus looked at Drake and Damian and signaled for them to look as well.

Two hooded men slowed as they approached the house, glancing up and down the silent street. All foot traffic had died out an hour ago once the sun retired for the day. The two men waited a moment before stepping inside the house and pulling up on a hidden door in the floor. Once they disappeared beneath the floor, the wooden door shut.

So that *is where the woman disappeared to...*

Ena held up a hand, *Hold.* She needed a larger group to blend in with. This could not work if only a handful show up. Within minutes, another pair arrived and entered through the secret hatch. Then another. And another.

Finally.

She counted fifty people in total.

Ena pointed at the stone house and flicked her wrist. Damian and Klaus slid around her and approached the house. Mimicking the others they witnessed, they suspiciously scanned up and down the street before quietly stepping inside the house, lifting the wooden hatch, and disappearing from sight.

"What now?" Drake whispered.

After a moment, Ena answered, "We follow. Stay close to me."

Ena stood up and led Drake from the alley. She, too, looked up the street once. After seeing nothing besides some stray animals scurrying around, she looked down the other end of the street. *Empty.* She tiptoed up the cracked steps and into the fractured house.

It was completely empty. No shelves, no furniture, not a creature or speck of dust stirred.

Ena studied the floor in the darkness of night, only a streetlamp across from them a hundred feet away giving any sense of light. Finally, she found the seams in the hardwood floor of a small, square hatch. She slid her fingers into the small crack along the seam and lifted upwards, slowly. Inaudibly, the hatch lifted to reveal a shallow shaft wide enough for one body. Slats of wood were nailed unsteadily down the walls of the shaft, imitating a ladder.

"Drake," she hushed, "you will go first. Do not make a sound. Step gently." She could not trust him to refrain from fleeing his captives if she entered the shaft first. But she also couldn't trust him to not mess this up and remain silent.

Drake sighed and swung himself into the shaft. Stepping slowly and silently, he descended into the dark shaft. Once the darkness absorbed him, Ena looked around once more for any eyes in the distance. Confirming she was alone, she stepped into the hole, closing the hatch over her head.

The shaft was not too deep. Within moments, her feet found solid dirt. She dropped into a crouch with her hand on the hilt of the dagger at her side. A narrow tunnel lay before her. Her guard detail waiting up ahead for her. In the darkness, only hazy torchlight could be seen at the far end of the tunnel.

A dull roar of voices talking among one another sounded in the distance.

One voice, a female's, proclaimed over the rest, "If I could have everyone's attention! If we are all here, allow us to begin."

Damian and Klaus looked at Ena. The governess nodded.

They remained crouched as they silently scurried down the tunnel.

The tunnel opened into an underground amphitheater with a stage against the far wall. Attendees were seated in the sloped rows in a semicircle around the front of the stage.

There are far more than fifty people here... Ena never miscounted. Even if she had, it may have been by one or two people, not an additional hundred. *There must be multiple entrances.*

Klaus tapped her shoulder and signaled to the eastern and western walls. Two other openings, likely leading to similar tunnels. Unfortunately, it was too risky to explore further. They waited in the shadows of the tunnel for the auction to begin.

The stage lit as an elf male walked to a podium at stage right. The stands applauded.

"Thank you, everyone," the man embraced the applause, "thank you! The hour is one-hour past midnight. We have something quite special for you tonight. We'll save the best for last, of course. Let us begin!"

Ena watched from the shadows as a cart was wheeled out by the first woman they saw. On the cart was an object she could not quite make out.

"Ah," the auctioneer began, "I see many of you salivating over this delicacy. Yes, it's been some time since we've had a batch of these to auction off. Behold, basilisk tongue!" The audience clapped and cheered. "This luxurious meal comes to you from deep within Brekkenia and cannot be found anywhere in the Five Kingdoms of Lynidas. Five hundred pounds, my friends! Five hundred pounds of basilisk tongue can be yours tonight. Let us start the bid at five-hundred gold. Do I have a bid for five hundred?"

Members of the audience started raising their hands and cheering. With each bid, the auctioneer raised the price incrementally.

"Basilisk tongue?" Damian's voice was hardly audible below the roar of the crowd. "Kate," he was smart to use her fake name, in the case anyone overheard them. "Basilisk tongue is not even served in the royal courts. How could they have acquired this?"

Ena was dumbfounded, "I'm not sure... Whoever these people are must have connections in Brekkenia, if that is where this truly originated."

"Five hundred pounds of it, though?" Damian shook his head in disbelief. "Only an unimaginably skilled smuggler could manage this."

"Sold!" The auctioneer announced. "Five hundred pounds of basilisk tongue to the gentleman in the third row for the fair price of thirteen-thousand gold! That's a steal in today's market. Tough crowd tonight!"

The next few items sold included more exquisite, and illegal, delicacies, such as jackrabbit tusk powder, thespian tiger flank, and elfinscence leaf. The elfinscence stood out to Ena, for she knew that the Elf Nation far to the west of Lyndias was strict about the exporting of the product. It was used in all kinds of elven dishes and herbal teas. The small batch on the auction block sold for seventy-five-thousand gold.

"Seventy-five-thousand gold is a small fortune," Damian said. "A small fortune spent on a kilo of leaves. This is insane!"

"Shhh, voice down," Ena hushed him. "The black market in Gabrenas goes deeper than anything I have come across. Even the gentleman I arrested for selling the bluebite in El Vadora could not get his hands on these products."

"Do you think we'll see some bluebite cross that stage?" Damian asked.

"I... I do not think so..." Ena pulled a lock of her dark hair behind her ear. "Not tonight. These people are here for luxury items, not means to harm others."

Ena was proven wrong when the next item was brought on stage.

"And now," the auctioneer exclaimed, "what you have all been waiting for!" He left the podium and picked up the object on the cart. A highly decorated longsword. "Ladies and gentlemen. Allow me to introduce you to Aconyte steel. The hardest steel known to mankind, the most difficult to acquire, and only a few of the most skilled smiths in the world can mold a beauty such as this! This blade will not dull. This blade will not break. This blade will pierce the thickest of armors and cut through the most rigid of shields." He swung the sword and performed a variety of choreographed swordplay movements. The sword glowed bright under the lights of the stage. "Bidding will begin at one-hundred thousand gold."

The audience lifted from their seats and ignited in cheer. Bids were placed every thirty seconds.

"I don't like this at all, Kate," Damian displayed physical discomfort. "You do know what Aconyte steel is used for, don't you?"

"Yes," Ena admitted. "Keepers are decorated with Aconyte."

Klaus spoke up, "That does not look like a Keeper's sword to me."

"No, it doesn't," Ena agreed, "because it's not. That sword was newly forged and for a different purpose than arming a Keeper."

"Sold!" the auctioneer finally shouted after nearly an hour of bidding. "One truly rare and one-of-a-kind Aconyte steel blade sold to the gentleman in the back row for two and a half million gold! Truly a record to behold, ladies and gentlemen. This is our highest selling item ever sold at our auction. There are more where that came from! Next week's auction will be bigger and better!"

Ena watched from the shadows as the man in the back row walked down to the stage to claim his prize. He handed over a banknote for two and a half million gold, and, in exchange, he walked away with a sword and scabbard of the highest caliber. As the man mounted the steps back up to his seat, he came face-to-face with the darkened tunnel and spotted the whites of four sets of eyes staring back at him. He stopped.

The man's emerald green eyes met Ena's. He smiled sharply before turning towards his seat.

"Fuck," Ena shouted under her breath. "He saw us. We have to go."

They shifted on their heels and sped back to the makeshift ladder.

They flew out the hatch and stuck to the shadows as they made their way through the city. *Dragonfly & the Fruit* appeared just over the horizon and a wave of safety washed over them.

"Head inside and go straight to your rooms," Ena ordered. "Our food is probably cold by now, but I will grab it and bring it up."

Inga was kind enough to reheat their meals over a fire before handing them to Ena. Ena thanked Inga for her hospitality and carried the meals up two flights to their small rooms. The four of them huddled on the floor of Ena's and Drake's room and ate in silence.

Drake swallowed a piece of overcooked fish before breaking the silence, "Should we talk about what we witnessed tonight?"

"No," Ena snapped.

"But," Drake continued, "I feel like it's important that we understand what we saw."

Damian spoke for Ena, "*We* understand what we saw. *You* are not privy to that information."

Drake dipped his head, "All due respect, Athenia, but if I am forced to be here with you, I deserve to know what I'm getting into."

The governess collected their dishes and left them on a tray table just outside the door. Before responding, she excused Damian and Klaus to their room and closed the door, locking it.

She stood face-to-face with Drake. Drake could feel her warm breath on his neck as she said gently, "Sometimes, being ignorant to dangers you face will make the inevitable that much easier. You cannot be surprised by something you know is coming."

"Do you know what is coming?"

Ena looked into Drake's eyes, speechless.

Finally, she broke his sight and said, smiling, "Best get some sleep, village boy. We will be hunting for Gabrenas's black market in the morning."

CHAPTER 10

The following evening, the governess and her guard detail travelled back to the crumbling stone house, only to find that the tunnel beneath the hatch had caved in. Ena had cursed aloud when the discovery was made. The insane thought crossed her mind to start digging it out by hand, but she estimated that would have taken weeks to accomplish. And all for what? To make their way back into that amphitheater and find that the other two tunnels were also caved in?

This certainly was no accident, Ena decided. The governess did not believe in coincidences. No, this was done on purpose to prevent them from snooping around.

Ena was more furious at herself for allowing them to get caught. How could she be so careless? Her curiosity had made her lose focus on her surroundings. Had she noticed that the bidder who purchased the elaborate Aconyte blade was sitting at the far back seat on the aisle leading down to the stage, she would have urged her guards to fall back farther into the shadows.

She would not forget the eyes that spotted her. Green as emeralds, and a smile that could cut steel. No doubting that she would recall those eyes if she encountered the man again.

"He must have tipped off the auctioneers," Damian had assumed.

Their only lead was now buried under tons of rubble. They were back to square one.

"Look on the bright side," Drake started, "we only just began our search. This one setback won't throw us off."

Ena had scowled, despite having to admire his positive attitude towards the situation. She did not give up, no matter how difficult things got. Knowing this was because of her own doing, though, she couldn't help criticizing herself.

A fortnight had passed since that night and they were still no closer to setting themselves on the right track. They scoured every inch of the city within twenty blocks of the stone house without a single whisper of evidence. No talk of the black market or Aconyte steel. It was as if they imagined the whole event.

Ena needed to speak with Lady Raven. They were wasting too much time.

Frustratingly, Ena scripted a letter and handed it off to Lady Raven's undercover courier, who delivered the letter promptly. The next day, the courier slipped a response letter to Ena in passing. She cracked the letter's seal and read it quietly to her guards,

Representative Kate –

Why, yes! Of course, I would love nothing more than to meet for tea and discuss the happenings of Lothol. Meet me by the church on East Street in the Upper District at sun high.

– Raven

Without hesitation, they turned down the nearest street bringing them back to the Upper District. The golden dome of the Grand Ballroom loomed over them as they entered the church.

The church clearly had not been tended to in quite some time. Vines were overgrowing the mortar between the stones, sending cracks up the walls. Dust settled on every surface and the tapestries on the walls were torn and stained.

"Welcome," Lady Raven said from the altar. She lit each candle on the altar individually with a match. Four guards accompanied her, two at the doors and two at the crossing. She wore her typical black garb, though her platinum hair reflected rainbows of color streaming in through the stained glass.

"I expected to meet some place nicer," Ena glanced around the room.

She could feel Raven's smug smile, though Raven had yet to face her, "Master Archem shut down this church ten years ago with the hope of repairing it to bring in more of a crowd. Just one of his many projects he never followed through with."

"Your feelings of Archem have not improved much in the past couple of weeks, I take it?"

"He has fled Gabrenas," Raven blew out the match and inhaled the aromas of the lit candles. "My new Master White Mage wished to bring him up on corruption charges after taking office and unmasking the skeletons Archem had tucked away."

"So," Raven turned to face the governess, "what is it you had to discuss so urgently? By your letter, it did not sound as though you solved the crime."

Ena sighed. "We discovered evidence of a black market operating in Gabrenas. Unfortunately, by the time we returned to investigate further, the evidence had been... destroyed."

"Black market?" Raven's brows scrunched. "What of it?"

"*What of it?*" Ena repeated. "You know of it?"

Raven stepped down from the altar and slowly approached Ena, "Yes, I know about the black market. Black markets exist all across Havyn. We could waste thousands of hours and gold hunting down smugglers and dealers, and someone would eventually start it back up again. We've always kept an eye on it, but so long as it remains 'regulated' and no one is being harmed, we try not getting involved."

Ena shook her head, "No black market is regulated."

"An oxymoron," the Lady of Avalon shrugged.

"What if the evidence we discovered could lead to harm being caused on others?"

That caught Raven's attention. She perked up. "What kind of harm?"

"What do you know of..." Ena lowered her voice. "Aconyte steel?"

"Aren't the Keepers armed with Aconyte?"

Ena nodded. "So, why would a freshly smithed sword crafted from Aconyte be sold at auction for two and a half million gold?"

She thought Raven was about to drop unconscious to the floor. All color left the lady's already-pale face. Raven's proper posture was replaced with heavy shoulders and weak knees. Two questions instantly came to her mind—how did that sword get smuggled into the city without warning, and how did someone come by that much gold and go unnoticed?

Gabrenas, like most cities, flooded with gossip whenever something new or exciting happened. Facts were rooted in most rumors. Any rumor of something new spreading through the black market usually got to Raven's ear by the end of the day. Not this time, though.

"You found nothing else?" Raven asked.

"As I said, all evidence was destroyed when we went back to the scene," Ena said. "I am hoping you might know of some way something of that magnitude could pass through the city without raising alarm. If anyone knows this city's secrets, it would be you."

"What does this have to do with my husband's death?" Raven avoided the request.

"If someone could smuggle in a sword worth two and a half million gold, who is to say they did not smuggle in the bluebite that killed your husband?"

Raven took a deep breath and exhaled, "You don't realize the amount of trust you are asking for. To give up my city's secrets is a tremendous burden."

"Raven," Ena pleaded, "all I need is a name, a location, *something*–"

"The Shipmaster." Ena's eyes narrowed. Raven sighed and explained, "The last bend in the river, you will find a shipyard. Ask for the Shipmaster."

No river ran through or near Gabrenas, though... Raven knew this, of course. The coded message was all the governess would get from her.

Before Ena could question her any further, Lady Raven wished her luck and walked briskly down the aisle, leaving Ena and her guards alone in the abandoned church. They all looked to one another, scratching their heads.

"Better to figure this out now while we have privacy to speak aloud," Klaus suggested.

Ena agreed.

Damian pulled a map from his pocket, "There is not a single body of water in all of Gabrenas." He pointed to different spots on the map of the city and traced the roads coming to and from the city with his finger. "The city's trade routes are all by land. She's playing tricks with us, Ena."

Ena studied the map herself, "What goal would she have for giving us false information? She needs us to solve this murder."

"Unless she did it herself," Damian muttered.

"I haven't ruled that out just yet. There was truth in her words, though. I understand her desire to hide her city's secrets. El Vadora has plenty of its own that I would not want strangers knowing. Let us find this shipyard."

Upon glancing at the map briefly, Drake pointed to a small road in the Lower District, "River Street. Could that be our river?"

Ena smiled at Drake. "Good eye."

Damian rolled up the map. "Let's get going."

For the first time, Drake actually helped rather than hinder their progress. As they exited the church, Ena clapped him on the shoulder, thanking him.

◆◆◆◆◆◆◆◆◆

River Street was in the belly of the Lower District, far beyond *Dragonfly & the Fruit* and with far sketchier people. The winding street was no longer than a half mile, but it bustled with people of all races—elves, dwarves, and humans alike. Stores and vendor stalls lined each side of the street. As Ena and her guard detail walked precariously down the street, she witnessed at least a dozen people get their pockets picked and purses cut. A fight broke out between a dwarf and a human, to which the poor human ended with his head stomped into the cobblestones by the dwarf's stumpy, yet muscular, leg.

Guards were called to the scene. Their attempt at arresting the dwarf for murder led to an all-out brawl among everyone down the road. Blood was being shed as most of the brawlers drew their weapons. More guards were called to break up the conflict to no avail.

"We have to get through this!" Ena shouted over the screaming. "Raven's riddle said the shipyard was at the last bend in the river. We must keep moving!"

Ena unsheathed the dagger at her thigh and Damian and Klaus followed suit. Drake, unarmed, stuck to the middle of them and lowered his head as they pushed through the erupting crowd.

The governess slashed her dagger at any unlucky fool who attempted to cross her. Her blows were not fatal, but they were enough to send her victims fleeing in pain. An elf grabbed her hood on her cloak and yanked her back, causing her to stumble to the ground. As the elf stood over her, about to plunge a rusty sword into her gut, Damian and Klaus attacked from the left and right, slicing off his swordhand at the wrist and killing him with a series of quick jabs to his intestines.

Drake held out his hand and helped Ena to her feet. They rushed down the street further, keeping their eyes open and sharp.

"There!" Drake pointed. As the street curved before them, a sign on a two-story storefront hung over their heads. *Shipyard Tavern*. "Run!"

They plowed through the bloodshed towards the tavern and burst through the door. The sitting room was empty, and a waitress was nonchalantly washing down the tables.

"We are closed until the fighting stops outside," the waitress said. "Please leave."

"We," Ena panted, "are looking for the Shipmaster."

The waitress stopped scrubbing the table, glanced at Ena, and nodded. The young woman walked behind the counter at the back wall and into a back room.

Klaus took a chair and wedged it under the door handle of the entrance, holding back any others who may try coming in.

A few minutes later, the waitress came into the sitting room and returned to scrubbing her tables. Following her from the back room, a large man came to the counter. His grey hair touched his shoulders, and he held one of his eyes shut, the flesh around the socket was scarred and discolored. He beckoned for them to approach.

"How can I help ye?" the man's yellow teeth shown as he spoke.

"We are looking for the Shipmaster," Ena repeated herself.

"In tha flesh," the man responded.

Ena looked at the waitress, who was clearly listening in on their conversation. She rested her hands on the counter as she leaned in closer, "Could we speak some place more private?"

Metal flashed as the Shipmaster took a large cleaver from behind the counter and chopped the blade into the wooden counter inches from Ena's pinky. The governess did not even flinch.

"One mer time, I'll ask ye," the Shipmaster growled. "How can I help ye?"

Damian and Klaus held out their daggers. The Shipmaster chuckled with a deep, hearty laugh. He was not a man to be messed with.

Ena instructed them to lower their weapons. They obeyed.

"Aconyte steel," Ena stated bluntly. "One of the recent auctions had a blade forged from it."

The Shipmaster squinted with his good eye, "Who sent ye?"

"I'm a customer," Ena lied. "Or I could be. If you have what I am looking for."

He huffed a warm, rancid breath, "Tha steel ain't mine. But I can take ye to whose 'tis." He opened the door to the back room. "Follow me. *Only* ye."

Ena knew Damian and Klaus would not like that idea. She never went far without them at her side. She would be walking into the unknown alone.

With a stern look from Ena, telling them to stand down, and her guards sat down at the nearest table. She walked around the counter and followed the Shipmaster.

In the back was a simple kitchen. A fire stove roared in the back of the room. A cutting table in the center of the kitchen was decorated with slabs of cut meat and hundreds of herbs and spices hung from the ceiling, drying. The Shipmaster moved a crate of vegetables out from the corner of the kitchen, revealing a wooden hatch in the floor.

Just like the one in the stone house.

Once the hatch opened, the Shipmaster beckoned Ena to climb down, "I'll be behind ye."

Every instinct drilled into Ena's mind from her City Watch training screamed at her to not go down the hatch. She could not trust the Shipmaster any more than she could trust being locked in a cell with a murderer and rapist, but what choice did she have? If Lady Raven sent her here, she had to ignore her feelings and see what lay ahead.

Ena stepped down the ladder leading underground. She estimated her descent at about twenty feet before her toes met solid ground. Above, the Shipmaster followed. As his feet hit the ground heavily, he took the torch from a nearby sconce on the wall and lit it.

From the torchlight, Ena saw a room expand before them. Crates were spread along the floor, some stacked to the ceiling. *This could be where he stores all of those exotic foods...* On the far wall of the room, a doorway led out into a hall. The Shipmaster nudged her to keep walking.

They walked in silence down the vacant hallway for a quarter of an hour before Ena could hear something besides the crackling of the torch.

Is that water? The babbling of a slow-moving stream came from the very end of the hall. As they approached the stream, the hallway opened into a hand-carved landing along the edge of the water. A small rowboat was tied up at the edge of the water. Someone was standing next to the boat unloading crates onto the landing. Torches lined the walls of the landing. *This must be the river.*

The Shipmaster pushed in front of Ena and met the person standing by the boat, instructing Ena to wait in the shadows.

"Ah, Shipmaster!" a gruff voice said. "I was just about to come get you. Here are your goods."

"Thank ye. Thar's someun here for ye."

"Someone for me? That's interesting."

"Came lookin' for tha Shipmaster fer some a yer steel."

"Is that so? Let them approach."

Ena saw the Shipmaster look in her direction. She stepped forwards into the torchlight. As Ena came into the light, she saw the Shipmaster was speaking to a dwarf with a salt-and-pepper beard.

"Well, aren't you a dame," the dwarf checked Ena out from head to toe. "You don't seem like the type who would be looking for steel." Ena put her hands on her hips, brushing aside her cloak and revealing the dagger at her thigh. "I stand corrected. How can I help you?"

"I'm looking for Aconyte steel," Ena's nerves almost caused her voice to shake. "I heard there was a sword sold at one of the last auctions. Where can I find one?"

The dwarf nudged the Shipmaster, "Why don't you take your goods back to your cellar? I'd like to speak with our friend alone."

The Shipmaster picked up the crates like they were weightless and disappeared back down the hall.

"Who are you?" the dwarf looked up at Ena.

"I could ask you the same thing," Ena retorted. "We both know, though, that you giving me your name puts you at risk. The prison time for illegal weapons dealing is a twenty-five year minimum."

"Let's say the sword was mine, and it was stolen from me or given away. That someone could easily resell the sword at auction legally, correct?" Ena nodded reluctantly. The dwarf smiled, "Names are just as dangerous as a blade. We can refer to me as the Lord of Steel. How does that sound?"

Ena crossed her arms and paced to the edge of the water, "So this underground river is how all of the market materials make their way to auction?"

"This river is the sewer system for the entire city. Gross, I understand. But sewers get a bad reputation. This is not the exit sewer. These pipes bring fresh water into the city. Jump in and bathe in it. You'll be cleaner than you are now, guaranteed."

"The steel," Ena pushed. "If I asked you for a sword, could you get it for me?"

"Ha!" the Lord of Steel laughed. "You couldn't afford my prices. Besides, I'm not a dealer, remember?"

"What if I 'stole' one from you?" Ena's lip curled up in a grin. "Or if you gave one away to me?"

The Lord of Steel dipped his head and paced back and forth, "You would need to gain my loyalty to receive such a gift. My loyalty also comes at a steep price."

"What will it cost?"

"First, answer a question for me," the Lord of Steel hesitated. "Why do you want an Aconyte steel sword?"

Ena had to play her cards right. She was not here for the Aconyte. She was here for bluebite. But this was the only lead she had to follow. This Lord of Steel had more authority over the black market than the Shipmaster, from what it seemed. To gain the trust of a black market dealer... That hung on the edge of insanity.

Let us play his game, Ena thought. "I want to kill the Lady of Avalon."

The dwarf smiled from ear to ear. The type of smile that told the governess they had similar goals in mind. That scared the hell out of her...

"Very well, dame," he held out a muscular hand. Ena shook it. "Let us begin this test of loyalty. One week from today, you will come to this address at noon." He handed her a slip of paper.

Ena read the address and carefully tucked the slip of paper into her pocket. "Can I bring friends?"

"One," the dwarf said sternly. "No need for an army."

She nodded, "Very well. See you in one week."

She returned to her guards, who waited impatiently where she left them. She knew they would be looking for answers, and she would give them. Though, she was afraid for their reactions. Testing limits was a normality for the governess, despite Damian's and Klaus's occasional disapproval.

What if she failed to gain the dwarf's loyalty? Would he dispose of her for knowing too much?

What if she succeeded? How deep undercover will she have to go to find the answers she seeks?

CHAPTER 11

The Faerie language was easier to decipher than Sheridan thought. The books the Providence had given him helped him to understand the random symbols and words he came across. Many of the Providence's books were written right before or immediately following the collapse of the Faerie Kingdom by faerie sympathizers; therefore, many of the pages were written in both languages for future historians to understand. These books, however, were not historical or provided any in-depth information on the faeries. They were simply popular fiction novels translated for faerie children to read.

The *Encantorum*, though, contained the entire history of the faeries leading up to their demise. Sheridan was able to decipher the first few pages, giving him an introduction into what the thick book contained. Over fifteen hundred pages of pure knowledge and information, most of which was unknown to any living being in the world today.

Sheridan was not sure what he expected to find in the book. He only hoped to uncover more information about the sword that Athenia now carried. Faerie weapons were rumored to have magical properties imbued within the metals, but what kind of magical properties?

And how in the world did a simple farming villager end up with it? It made no sense to Athenia and it made no sense to Sheridan.

Upon reading the introduction, Sheridan learned that the Faerie Kingdom, like most other kingdoms, was originally comprised of many smaller kingdoms. After thousands of years of brutal warfare, the many kingdoms were unified under one ruler. The *Encantorum* had yet to touch on any other races or groups of people existing beyond their walls, though.

As Sheridan flipped gently through the ancient pages, he heard the door to his chambers burst open.

“Sheridan!” the Providence’s voice sounded anxious. “Sheridan, I need your help!”

Sheridan looked up from his desk as the Providence ran to him with the train of her cream-colored dress pulling over everything that caught against it.

“What is it?” Sheridan quickly stood up to meet the Providence.

“It’s Princess Lia!” she was breathless. She must have run straight from her chambers on the other side of the palace. “High Alta is here demanding her.”

“Demanding her? What? Why>”

The Providence shook her head vigorously. “I… I don’t know! Something about Typhus owing something to High Alta and now they are demanding *Lia* as payment.”

“For the love of the All-Seeing God! What in the Connections could Typhus have gotten us into now?”

Without another word, the two made their way quickly to the throne room. Along the way, the Providence ensured Lia was safe and surrounded by her Keepers and Guardians of the Faith. Sheridan could tell the severity of the situation in the Providence’s words. She was not giving up the princess without a fight.

Upon entering the throne room, King Typhus sat in his throne atop the dais. Princess Lia stood, shaking with fear, at the bottom of the dais, protected by her Keepers.

In the center of the room stood Prince Salmeides, the eldest son of High King Eriputes, two Keepers from High Alta, and a platoon of armed soldiers. A man in his mid-twenties, Salmeides’s air of confidence and regal demeanor made him the textbook definition of an arrogant prince.

“What is the meaning of this, Sal?” Sheridan stood between the prince and King Typhus. “You dare to threaten the princess in her own palace!”

Prince Sal gleamed in his elegant golden armor with his short, wavy silver hair combed back to reveal a deep widow’s peak. He wore a heavy white cape hooked on his pauldrons that hung down to his heels. What terrified Sheridan the most was the unsheathed greatsword in his hand, the point of which was resting on the ground with his palm wrapped around the pommel.

“Your king owes my father *a lot* of money, Master Sheridan,” Sal was practically growling with rage. "He has dodged every letter demanding for repayment, yet the fool consistently takes and takes from High Alta's coffers. Repayment is due, and if what your king says is true, that Havyn has not the money, then we need collateral."

Sheridan stepped closer to the prince. Though the prince towered over him at nearly six-and-a-half feet tall, the Master of Cities attempted to intimidate him, "A young girl is *not*, and *will* not, be collateral for your father's demands! How much does Havyn owe? I'm sure we can come up with something."

"No, dwarf," Typhus huffed from his throne, "we can't."

Sal answered the question anyway, "Two hundred and forty million gold."

Sheridan swallowed so hard his throat dropped into his stomach. Typhus was right—they could not afford to pay that all at once.

"Certainly we could come up with some kind of repayment plan," Sheridan began before Sal cut him off by pounding the tip of his sword against the marble floor, the clash reverberating off of the walls.

"No! That time has passed. Ask your lackadaisical king how many chances we have given him."

The Providence walked up to Typhus and whispered with him for a few moments. One of his Keepers handed her a stack of letters. She flipped through them as she met Sheridan in the center of the room.

"There are probably fifty letters, if not more," she said to Sheridan, showing him the letters. The most recent one was received a month prior, stating that an answer must be received by Typhus directly, not from one of his other "subjects," assumedly meaning the Providence or himself. Typhus has not attended a single meeting of Lynidas's biannual Court of Kings since Sheridan assumed his office. Sheridan and the Providence always went in his place, claiming he was ill or had other matters to attend to.

"Fifty-seven, to be exact," Sal calmed himself enough to talk reasonably. "The letters were addressed to him directly, and he reads them and tosses them aside. By the Connections, I do not believe he has even listened to a word that has been said since I arrived!"

Sheridan looked at the king. Typhus lay back in his throne and examined his cracked, yellow nails, ignoring everything around him.

"Typhus," Sheridan confronted the king at his throne. "What is the meaning of this? How could you borrow that much money without any of us knowing? What on earth did that money go towards?"

Typhus looked up from his nails and raised his brows. "What money? I don't have the slightest idea what you are talking about. Who are you?"

Not now... If he had one of his lapses in memory episodes in front of Prince Sal, he would instantly report that back to High King Eriputes. The last thing they needed right now was to appear vulnerable.

Hearing Typhus's response to Sheridan, the Providence rushed to his side, muttering to him, "Typhus, Your Majesty, High Alta says you owe them millions of gold. Think hard. Where did that money go?"

Typhus stared at the Providence with a blank face until he broke his silence, "Helena! My love, when did you get home from your trip? How are your parents doing? Did you send them my love?"

"Fuck," Sheridan scoffed. He turned back to face Sal, "Can *we* make a deal with you?"

"No can do, Master," Sal shook his head. "You read the letters. My father needs to hear it from him."

"Please," Sheridan met the prince at the center of the room once more, "let's talk about this. Havyn would be bankrupt if it delivered the full balance right now. We can set up payments."

Sal crouched down to meet the dwarf face-to-face, a very disrespectful gesture in dwarven culture. "No offense, Master Sheridan, but you cannot even name where the money was spent. How can I trust that your payments will remain consistent? No more. My father demands the full payment right now, or the young princess can return to High Alta with me as collateral until it *can* be paid in full."

"You and I both know that would mean a life sentence for the princess..." Sheridan said with panic in his throat.

Sal ran his gloved fingers through his silver hair. "There is one other option. If repayment cannot be made, my father is *generously* willing to write off the entire debt in exchange for a marriage vow between Princess Lia and my brother, Prince Edacles."

Sheridan's heart sank in his chest. They were stuck without options, all at the fault of King Typhus.

"How much time do we have to decide?"

"There is no more time!" Sal stood and lifted his sword with one hand, the blade nearly resting on Sheridan's shoulder. "Fifty-seven letters, Master Sheridan. Time is up! What will it be?"

The Providence spoke up, "Prince Salmeides, give us one week. Before you deny us that, understand this request is coming from me, the Providence of Havyn. I know High Alta's Providence very well—your aunt. You are very entuned with the Faith, are you not? Take my word from the Faith. Please. We will give you and your men lodging for the week."

Sal thought for a moment, then grunted in frustration, "All other living expenses paid in full. Food, drink, and lodging. One week! Not a day more!"

The prince turned with his Keepers and bolted from the throne room, his platoon at his heels. By this point, Princess Lia was sobbing. Her entire world was about to be flipped upside down. King Typhus would not get away with this discrepancy.

CHAPTER 12

Sheridan was so furious he was certain his face matched the color of his beard. Two hundred and forty million gold was a significant amount. A single gold piece could feed a single person for a week, if spent sparingly. A new recruit City Watch guard's income was a hundred gold per week, which was considered a generous rate of pay. Two hundred and forty million gold was unthinkable.

The moment Prince Sal exited the Spire of the New King, tensions rose. Sheridan observed as Princess Lia broke down on the cold, marble floor and the Providence attempted to console her. Even the Keepers held a defeated look on their faces.

Sheridan could hold his tongue no longer.

"You!" he threw a thick finger in the king's face. "You pitiful excuse for a *king!* You better damn well remember where that money went or there will be worse consequences than losing your daughter!"

Typhus scowled and spit on the floor at Sheridan's feet, "Get away from me, you vile creature! Who let in this *dwarf*?" Sheridan felt the venom in his words.

"I am your fucking Master of Cities, you fool!"

"Since when?!" his mouth gaped.

Seeing Sheridan's growing frustration and thinning patience, one of the king's Keepers stepped forwards.

"Your Majesty," the Keeper said, "the dwarf, Sheridan, was elected as Havyn's Master of Cities over three years ago."

The king was dumbfounded, "Is that so? My apologies, dwarf. I didn't know. Nor do I know about this money you speak of."

Sheridan calmed down just enough to entertain Typhus's memory lapse. "It's a pleasure to meet you, Your Highness. My apologies for yelling. But please, think hard. If we don't pay back that money, you will lose your daughter. Your only child..."

"Daughter?" Typhus scratched his head. "I don't have a daughter. Maybe you should be directing this question to my grandfather, the king. He handles most of the finances of the kingdom." He directed his attention to the Providence, "Helena, my dear, would you please fetch the king?"

Gods... Sheridan was shocked. The king's mind was set back over twenty years when he was just a young prince. Lia had yet to be born. He and Helena must have been newlyweds, wherever his mind was trapped.

Upon hearing her father not even recognize the existence of a daughter, Lia's sobbing intensified. Typhus seemed to pay no mind to it.

"Typhus," the Providence left Lia's side and stepped up the dais, "Helena is not here. I am your cousin, the Providence."

"Helena, quit your quipping!" Typhus laughed. "My cousin is hardly more than an infant! Please, if you wouldn't mind, fetch my grandfather. This dwarf here is enquiring about some money."

The Providence got on her knees and pleaded quietly with her cousin, "Please, Typhus. Look into my eyes. I am not Helena. Even if you do not believe I am your cousin, you *must* realize that I am not your wife."

He looked deep into the Providence's blue eyes for a minute. Suddenly, his pupils widened and understanding blinked into his eyes.

"You..." he struggled to match the words to his thoughts. "You are not Helena? Then where is she? Helena!" He called for her.

"Typhus..." the Providence touched his arm gently. "We have had this conversation before. You know where she is."

"Helena!" he shouted out once more. Then, softer, "Helena? Is she...? Is she gone?"

The Providence gently nodded.

"Gone where? She is at her parents' estate in Estera, isn't she? She's leaving me... Isn't she?"

The Providence was not certain what Typhus meant. As far as she knew, there was nothing wrong in their marriage that would cause Helena to move back in with her parents. But Typhus clearly had this obsession in his mind.

"No, no, Typhus... Helena is dead," the Providence explained, yet again. She couldn't keep count any longer. Typhus's face turned white. "She died here in the palace. Almost five years ago."

"No, that can't be..." The king could not process what he was hearing, for the hundredth time. "She is with her parents. In Estera. She... She said she needed time on her own to think, so she went to her parents' estate. She'll be back. She always comes back."

Sheridan and the Providence heard the light steps of Princess Lia walking up behind them. Her wide, hazel eyes were red and glistening with tears. She had calmed down enough to soothe her sobbing.

"Father, they are telling you the truth," the princess' soft voice seemed to alert something in Typhus's mind. "Please remember."

Typhus smiled and leaned forward with his arms out wide, "Lia, my dear! How are you today? Come sit on daddy's lap!"

Princess Lia understood what was happening with her father. She was kept from her father most of the time, for her own protection. The king was prone to violent outbursts, and Sheridan and the Providence feared for her safety if he had access to his daughter's whereabouts. Lia knew the man she was speaking to right now was from a decade ago, when she was only a little girl.

"Father, I am not a little girl anymore," Lia explained calmly. "I am a young woman now."

"Oh," Typhus blinked, not fully understanding. "You look an awful lot like your mother. So beautiful. Speaking of your mother, do you know where she is?"

Lia reached under the seam of her pale blue dress at her neckline and pulled out a folded piece of parchment. A silver necklace—an heirloom of her mother's—resting around her collar shifted with each movement. Her unsteady hands made it difficult to open up the note. As it crinkled open, tears rolled down her cheeks.

"Lia, what is that?" Sheridan asked.

Lia, ignoring Sheridan, began to read the words on the paper.

My Beautiful Lia,

You have always been a strong and beautiful girl. I ask you to be strong for me while I am gone. You are too young to understand, but your father and I are having some problems getting along and we think it would be best if I spent some time with Grandma and Grandpa while we figure things out. I will write to you while I am away. Maybe you can come visit sometime! Grandma and Grandpa would love to see their little girl soon. Never forget that I will always love you and I promise to see you again.

–Mom

The air stilled as Lia folded the letter and tucked it back into her breast. No one spoke. No one even breathed. This was the first time anyone else in the room had read that letter from Helena.

Lia broke the silence, "Mom left you. She went home to Estera."

"No!" Typhus was upset. "She came back! I remember!"

"Father, she went home to Estera and got really sick."

"That's right!" The Providence was beginning to recall the events from five years ago, connecting the dots. "Estera was corrupted by the plague back then. Of course, it all makes sense now."

Lia continued, "White mages brought her home after Grandma and Grandpa died of the plague and mom got infected."

"By the time she got back to the palace, there was no hope to save her..." the Providence finished. "I struggled for weeks to keep her alive. Keeping her alive as long as we did only prolonged the inevitable and infected many in the palace."

Typhus took Lia's hand and pulled her close. He wiped a tear from his daughter's eye and gave her a longing hug. "I'm sorry, Lia. I am *so* sorry, sweetheart."

Lia threw her arms around her father for the first time in years. "I'm sorry, too, Father. I should have showed you that letter from the night she left a long time ago."

Typhus opened his eyes and peered at the Providence from over Lia's shoulder. "I'm sorry I let her kill your mother."

Lia sniffled, "What?"

Typhus threw Lia from his grasp, sending her tumbling down the dais. Her Keepers rushed to her aid.

Typhus stood from his throne and roared with ferocity, "Keepers! Arrest the Providence for the murder of Queen Helena!"

The two Keepers standing on either side of the throne looked to one another and hesitated.

"Keepers!" King Typhus roared once more. "Arrest the Providence!" Spit flew from his lips as he barked the order.

The Keepers reluctantly stepped forwards with their pikes. In the distance, the metallic clank of footsteps drew near. A dozen Guardians of the Faith formed a semicircle at the base of the dais behind the Providence. Lia's Keepers lifted her off the floor and carried her off to the side of the room, out of danger.

The king's Keepers took one more step towards the Providence. In response, the Guardians pointed their staves and the pupil of their Oblong Eyes began to hum, glow, and spin aggressively.

Stepping between them, Sheridan shouted, "Keepers, stop! Don't do anything stupid."

One of the Keepers spoke up, "Apologies, sir. Orders are orders. We serve the king. Providence, come with us peacefully. There is no need for bloodshed."

"No!" Typhus screamed. "I want her dragged out of here in rags by the roots of her hair!"

"Typhus!" Sheridan shouted over him. "Shut the fuck up! Do you want civil war to erupt? Tell your men to stand down!"

"I want her pretty blonde head on a *fucking* pike, dwarf! Get out of my sight or I'll do the same to you." Typhus drew his sword and pointed it at the Providence. "Kill her!"

Sheridan swore he could hear the Keepers gulp with fear as they took another step forward. He had to do something to stop this. If the Keepers touched a single hair on the Providence's head, the Guardians of the Faith would attack relentlessly. Two Keepers against a dozen Guardians. The results would not end well.

Without a single selfish thought, Sheridan drew the war axe from behind his back and swung the flat head of the axe with all his might against the king's knee. He heard a bloodcurdling crunch as the bones of Typhus's kneecap shattered and he collapsed to the ground. Instantly, seeing the king fall, the Keepers turned their attention away from the Providence.

"You son of a bitch!" Sheridan threw his axe to the side, jumped on top of the king, and punched him three times in the jaw with his metal fist. The king's crown rolled off his head and clattered on the floor. The Keepers grabbed Sheridan's shoulders and yanked him off of Typhus. "Fuck you!"

"Sir!" the Keeper yelled. "That's enough! He's unconscious."

The Guardians of the Faith raised their staves once the Keepers' attention fell from the Providence.

They held Sheridan tight as he tried throwing himself at Typhus again. He pointed at Typhus's unconscious body and yelled, "He should be rotting in a cell! He doesn't deserve to wear that crown!"

"How the hell are we supposed to *not* arrest and behead you for this?" the Keeper shook Sheridan, trying to get him to see sense.

"You would've started a civil war if you crossed blades with the Guardians! I just did everyone a fucking favor."

"That may be so... but—"

"'Orders are orders,'" Sheridan mocked. "Yes, I know." He yanked his shoulder from the Keeper's hard grip. "To the gods with him. I'm taking that crown. He isn't fit to wear it any longer."

Sheridan reached for the crown, only to have it scooped up by a Keeper, who stated coldly, "The crown belongs to the king."

"Bah!" Sheridan turned away and swatted his hand in the air, as if shooing away a fly. "You're both useless. You are sworn to protect the royal family, yet the princess is thrown down a flight of marble steps and you still defend the perpetrator."

"I'm okay, Sheridan," Lia released herself from her Keeper's hold. Purple bruises were already forming on her arms and legs from her fall.

Sheridan gave a slight dip of his bearded chin in acknowledgement. Rage burned within him still. The Providence ordered a pair of her Guardians to fetch white mages for the king and ordered Lia to return to her chambers with her Keepers. The princess looked at the floor, rubbing her bruised arms, as she was escorted from the throne room.

"The way I see it, sir," the Keeper spoke, "you should be in chains right now. He is going to wake up and wonder why you are still walking free."

The Providence stepped forwards. She had observed most of the events without raising her voice, but her time for silence was over, "The way *I* see it, Keeper, the king may not remember the events that befell this afternoon when he wakes. After today's conversation, his mind has evidently regressed much further than I realized. That being said, when he regains consciousness, you will tell him he sustained those injuries in a horseback riding accident. Do you understand me?"

"Unfortunately," the Keeper shook his head, "I do not take orders from you. If the king asks about his injuries, I will be obliged to tell the truth."

"Be sure to tell him the truth about how he attacked his own daughter, too," Sheridan retorted.

"Perhaps," the Providence responded, "by the time the king wakes, he will no longer be king." She met Sheridan's eyes, entertaining his thoughts of removing the crown from Typhus' possession.

The Keepers pointed their sharp pikes, "Careful! You speak treason."

The Providence heard the humming of the Guardians' staves behind her.

"Careful!" she mocked. "You threaten the Faith."

"It seems we're at an impasse." Sheridan smiled grimly at the Keepers. "We should *all* choose our next course of action carefully. Listen, the very last thing I want to be known for is deposing my king, but these actions are inexcusable! He endangers the entire kingdom. High Alta demands for his only heir's hand in a joint marriage. Do you understand what that means? When Lia's time comes to rule, she will be accompanied by a High Altan prince, who would then become King of Havyn."

The Keepers stood their ground, "Keepers are not permitted to engage in political affairs. Stand down. Please, sir."

Sheridan observed the Guardians behind the Providence. They were ready to unleash whatever power they held in those weapons of theirs. Only the Providence could order them to stand down, and that did not seem like an option by the fire growing in her eyes. Two Keepers could hold their own against a room full of trained warriors, but have they ever tested their mettle against Guardians of the Faith?

Sheridan did not want to find out, especially caught in the middle of that fight.

"Providence," he urged. She glanced at him momentarily and sighed. Her Guardians instantly returned to attention with their staves at their sides. The Master of Cities turned his attention back to the Keepers. "I want full access to the king's private coffers and all bank statements. Wherever this money came and went, it was not through the kingdom's accounts. With your assistance, Keepers, we can save Lia from an awful fate."

The Keeper nodded and looked at the Master of Cities suspiciously from under his Aconyte helm, "Very well. The king will be watched more closely in your presence, so you are aware." He assured the Providence, "I will inform the king of his horseback riding accident when he comes to."

Without a word, the Providence turned on her heels and marched off in the direction of her chambers with her Guardians at her back. Sheridan picked up his axe from the floor before falling in behind them. The conversation may have been over with the Keepers, but it would continue with the Providence.

While the white mages worked on healing the king's injuries in the royal chambers, the Providence called on Lia to report to her study. She waited for the princess' arrival as she discussed with Sheridan the possible outcomes of the current situation with the king.

Sheridan did not trust the Keepers. They agreed to maintain the fragile status quo for the time being, but for how long? They knew Sheridan and the Providence desired to remove the king from power, and Sheridan and the Providence knew the Keepers would defend the king's crown with their lives. This stalemate would not last forever. Not with Typhus's actions growing more volatile by the day.

Princess Lia meant everything to Sheridan and the Providence. She was the key to Havyn's royal bloodline *or* the succession of the Providence.

"The problem is," the Providence explained, "that Lia is only sixteen years old. If Typhus is no longer the acting monarch, Lia is not old enough to assume the throne without a regent."

"And as the Concordat would have it..." Sheridan scratched his thick beard.

"*You*, as Master of Cities, would serve as the King Regent until Lia's eighteenth birthday," the Providence tapped her fingers on the surface of her desk.

Sheridan leaned back in the chair across from her and asked, "How many would believe the rumor that I overthrew the king to take the throne for myself?"

"That is my gravest concern."

Sheridan slammed his fist down in frustration. "Either way we will have a civil war on our hands! Too many lords and governors blindly support the Monarchy. Armies would be at the Spire's doorstep the day following my coronation."

"The kingdom is not stable enough to handle stress at that magnitude," the Providence agreed. "Let's begin first by reviewing Typhus's bank statements once we are granted access to them."

"Best case, all of the money is in his account unspent and we can return it all to High Alta."

The two looked at one another and burst out laughing. The Providence cried, "As if we could be so lucky!"

While they laughed hysterically at the irony of the situation, the Guardians of the Faith opened the doors to the study, escorting Lia with them. She came alone. Her Keepers must have been ordered to remain behind.

Smart girl, Sheridan thought as he let out his last few chuckles.

The Providence greeted Lia halfway at her terrarium and led her to one of the medical beds along the wall adjacent from her desk. She examined the princess's bruises and, after finding a bump on her head, checked her for any signs of concussion. The princess was strong-willed and would not admit if she was in pain, though.

"I am fine, don't worry about me," she boasted.

The Providence spent her entire life studying the body and medicine. She also learned over the years to ignore the pleas or the obstinacy of her patients and focus on the ailment and its function within the body. Though the princess declared that she was unharmed, the Providence used her magic to search deep under the bruised outer skin and discovered the periosteum of Lia's bones were damaged in her fall down the dais.

"Unfortunately," the Providence concluded, "you are *not* fine. Your arm and your hip are in danger of fracturing. The protective surface covering your bones is weak and, if you sustain a similar injury, your bones will fracture or break entirely."

Lia looked at her with wide hazel eyes, "You can heal that, right?"

The Providence stood up. She paced back and forth deep in thought. Finally, she glanced at Sheridan and smirked.

Returning to Lia, she said, "I *could* heal you, and your bruises would be better by morning. Or, an injury like this could potentially take four to six weeks to heal on its own. You could *never* travel all the way back to High Alta with injuries like this!" She winked. "Prince Sal would have to wait until you are fit to travel, or return home on his own and retrieve you in a month."

"Hmm," Sheridan played along, "do you believe in a month we would be able to collect the money to pay back High Alta?"

"Certainly a possibility," the Providence crossed her arms. "That all depends, though, on what our princess would rather do."

Lia smiled humbly, "If it means not having to marry a prince I don't even know, then I will do whatever I need to."

"Smart," the Providence curled a lock of the princess' brunette hair around her finger. "We will find out what your father did with that money soon enough and, hopefully, get it back. You will be okay."

Lia stood from the medical bed and shared a worried look with Sheridan and the Providence, "And in a month, if you *don't* get the money, what happens to me?"

Sheridan and the Providence exchanged a grave look. Admittedly, they knew giving up Lia would be the only option to prevent conflict with High Alta. High Alta was crowned the capital kingdom of Lynidas as part of the Concordat. History would have it that High Alta, known simply as Alta at the time, remained neutral during all negotiations for the Concordat in exchange for becoming the seat of the country. The idea behind this decree was for High Alta to maintain neutrality, strictly following the laws instilled by the Concordat, during any and all conflicts that arise as to not play favorites for one kingdom over another.

High Alta collected heavy taxes each year from the other four kingdoms to store in hefty coffers to be utilized as emergency funds. Assumably, this emergency fund is where King Typhus requested a loan from and has since misplaced the gold.

"What will happen to the king?" Lia asked. "You are right, Providence, he is no longer in a right state of mind."

She may be a child by age, Sheridan thought, *but she is mature enough to handle the truth.* The Providence must have thought the same, for she shared the conversation that took place in the throne room after Lia was escorted out.

"Will he be removed from power?" Lia questioned.

"Not without the Keepers' intervention, I fear," the Providence answered honestly.

While the Providence was explaining the situation to the princess, Sheridan had pulled the massive book of the Concordat's laws from the nearby bookshelf and cycled through the pages. Sheridan knew the Concordat well. He studied it during his campaign for Master of Cities and could recite a majority of the laws detailing his position's duties and the restrictions that accompanied them.

One area he had not touched on much was the Concordat's monarchial branch of government. As he flipped the pages one after another, he stumbled across a very interesting page regarding the reduction of a monarch's power should they overstep their boundaries.

The three branches of government—the Monarchy, the Faith, and the People—coexisted together to prevent one branch from achieving more power than another by splitting the duties of the kingdom equally. However, what would happen if one of the branches *did* achieve more power than another? Or, in Havyn's case, if the power of one branch was being abused by an ill-fit ruler?

"There may be a way," Sheridan announced, "but it will be a difficult process."

The Providence urged him to continue.

"According to the Concordat,

Addendum Four, Chapter Twenty-Seven, Section Fourteen—Deposition of a Ruling Monarch Due to Ill Health Preventing Supplementary Concordat Laws from Transpiring:

If the ruling monarch falls ill by any of the following—severe injury, disease, caducity, or by any means which renders the monarch unable to carry out the tasks demanded of them—the monarch may relinquish their crown and throne to an existing heir. Relinquishment of said monarchial birthrights must be voluntary and contractually signed with the Providence, Master of Cities, rightful heir, and Keeper Librarian as witness to such signature.

If the ruling monarch is unable to voluntarily relinquish monarchial rights by the mandatory means due to any illness, as described above, the Providence, Master of Cities, and rightful heir must appear before a Court of Kings to present the justifications for forced elimination of the ruling monarch from their position as the seat of the Branch of the Monarchy. The Court of Kings must review the evidence and approve the emergency removal of the ruling monarch's birthright. If approval is granted, the ruling monarch would thenceforth be considered 'deposed' and the rightful heir will be granted the title of King or Queen.

If approval is denied due to false claim, the Providence, Master of Cities, and rightful heir will be brought up on treason charges and will be removed from their positions of power, relinquishing all democratic rights or birthrights, until said charges are proven untrue. If said charges are proven true, criminal punishment must be endured to the effect of, but not limited to, exile or execution."

Princess Lia took in all of the information and responded, "So, we would have to prove that the king is unfit to rule and the other kings of Lynidas would need to approve?"

"In theory, it sounds that easy," the Providence hesitated.

With High Alta's current demands of Havyn, it was unlikely High King Eriputes would welcome a new ruler unless he was paid back the gold owed to him.

Admitting to a Court of Kings that Havyn was in a weakened state sat uncomfortably with Sheridan. High Alta may not be seeking blood yet, but they knew to strike where it hurts by forcing Havyn to sacrifice Lia to them. As was explained to the Keepers, sending Lia to High Alta will advertently allow High Alta to rule Havyn through Lia's future husband.

Nothing existed in the Concordat to prevent such a power play from being executed by High Alta. Eriputes knew the Concordat by heart—he was well aware of the advantage he would be taking from Havyn without the return of his money.

"I would say," Sherida conversed, "we could trick your father into signing a contract that would relinquish his rights, but his Keepers would tip off the Librarian as soon as he arrives to witness the signing."

"He is not my father," Lia declared, much to the Providence's and Sheridan's surprise. "That man is no longer my father. He hasn't been since my mother died."

The Providence placed a gentle palm on Lia's forearm to comfort her. Though Lia's stubbornness would not show the sorrow behind her words, the Providence could see it in her eyes. Lia was right—she lost both of her parents the day her mother passed away.

"There are still some questions we have to answer before we can move forward with any of this," Sheridan pointed out. "Where is the money, and can we pay it back? And if you, Lia, were to be coronated as Queen of Havyn, would you be ready for that responsibility?"

Lia tipped her head, "Isn't that why you would rule as my regent until I come of age?"

Sheridan laughed, "That is precisely the other question we need to answer. How many would approve of a dwarf as their regent for the next two years?"

"I don't care what others would think!" the princess stood her ground. "I would be Queen! I may not be the 'ruling monarch,' but I would still have some authority. Isn't that what the Concordat says?" Sheridan knew enough about regency in the Concordat to nod in approval. "Then *fuck* what the disapprovers say! They can question your word all they want, but they cannot question mine."

Princess Lia's fervor was exactly what they needed to move forward with a plan of action. They needed her total support as the future queen if this was to go smoothly. Or, as smoothly as it could go, given their current state of affairs.

By the morning, Sheridan will have access to King Typhus's bank records. He promised to report back with any news he found. The Providence, in the meantime, drafted an official physician's notice describing the nature of Lia's injuries, with the fib that they were sustained during a horseback riding accident, preventing her from traveling for the next four to six weeks. The notice would only be used if all else failed. The Providence also compiled all of her reports on Typhus's health. Any piece of evidence they could use against Typhus in the Court of Kings would be helpful to prove their case.

Sheridan also decided it would be helpful to win Prince Sal over to their case, after having witnessed the king's delusion himself. If the prince would testify at the Court of Kings, there was hope that the deposition would be a success.

CHAPTER 13

Damian and Klaus typically held their tongues and followed orders as Ena gave them, but this time, they were fervently disputing what the governess demanded of them. The Lord of Steel only allowed her to bring one companion to the test he had prepared for her. That one companion, Ena decided, would be Drake.

"How could you trust him over us?" they had demanded.

"This isn't about trust," Ena answered. "This is about keeping a potential enemy close."

She viewed the paper the Lord of Steel had given her. A set of coordinates. The map was sprawled out on the floor, and she marked the point on the map with a small *X*. She was unsure where the location was. Her guards said she was being far too trusting of a dwarf dealing black market weapons. She could not disagree, the possibility of walking into a trap was high.

Before departing, she strapped her daggers to her thighs and sheathed two more into a harness behind her back. Blades were Ena's lifeline. She never felt comfortable without a hilt in her hand.

Lifting the edge of her mattress, Ena observed the faerie blade she tucked away. The temptation to wield that beauty in battle hung over her head, but the risk of exposing the weapon was not worth it. She wondered how much it would go for on the black market.

She tucked the sword back under her mattress and met Drake outside the front of *Dragonfly & the Fruit*. Drake, as usual, was weaponless, which he argued adamantly about. Ena's trust was hard to gain, though.

"Drake," Ena explained, "You must see it from my point of view. There has been no good explanation as to why you survived the onslaught of your village, or why you had that sword in your possession. How can you ensure me that you will not use a weapon against me if one was put in your hands?"

Drake huffed, "You could have left me in El Vadora. Things would have been better without coming with you. That was my plan. To find a city to work in and start a new life."

"For what? To hide? To plot your next move? I apologize for my skepticism, Drake, but I find it hard to believe the mages let you slip away after the destruction they caused. Bodies that were not killed in the blazes were hung. From tree branches. I cut down a dozen myself. Why would they hunt down and hang all survivors, but leave you to run free?"

"I don't know!" Drake yelled. "And I am tired of being interrogated over it and treated as if this was *my* choice!"

Ena smacked him gently on the arm with the back of her hand. "Keep it down! Do not forget where we are and the mission at hand. You want to earn my trust and prove that this was all a happy coincidence? Then stop acting like a fool."

Drake reluctantly gave up his argument and looked at her as they walked. "How are you going to convince this Lord of Steel that you *aren't* here to spy on him and possibly arrest him?"

"That is exactly what I intend to find out today."

Before continuing further towards their destination, Ena stopped at a postal office. She figured she should thank Lady Raven for her subtle tip that led her on her current path. The letter she drafted was simple, but it would keep communications with Raven open.

Raven –

Found the shipyard. What do you know of the Lord of Steel?

– Kate

"Make sure this letter gets there today." Ena placed two gold pieces into the postmaster's hand. "There is more where that came from."

The postmaster was captivated by the shiny gold in his palm. He nodded and pocketed the coins.

She continued with Drake down the main road leading into the eastern section of the city. The cluster of buildings began to spread and reveal beautiful landscapes. Grasslands and fields of flowers spread between each homestead, and the road transitioned from gravel and dirt to cobblestone and brick.

What part of the city is this? Ena wondered.

Their current place of residence was located in the lower-class section of the city. All low-income households were clustered together, and many residents shared walls, water, and toilets. During her stay so far in that section of Gabrenas, Ena could see the division in social classes and how awful the lower class lived compared to those living near the Grand Ballroom. Raven boasted about the fairness and equality of all of Avalon's people, but how often did she actually set foot in the crumbling backwash of her own capital city?

The strangest part, Ena found, was that no one complained about their social status. The poor were happy being poor, the rich were happy being rich. Not once did she hear anyone in the past month say anything negative about their ramshackle homes or the daily crime—it was their way of life. Perhaps Raven was not wrong about her people being happy, in a strange sort of way.

Coming from her point of view as a governess, and having grown up in Havana City, where social classes were literally divided geographically by how high up the hill one lived, she feared the status quo in Gabrenas. It is expected to have minimal tension between the classes. The rich get richer, the poor get poorer, the poor hate the rich for being rich and vice versa. But not here. Not in Gabrenas.

Ena saw the type of people who poured into that black market auction. Most wore rags and appeared homeless, yet they were the ones bidding over and over for luxury items. Weeks later and Ena was still calculating in her head just how much gold was in that underground amphitheater that night. There was only one individual who did not appear to be lower class.

The man with the emerald eyes.

He remained the greatest threat in this undercover operation, and Ena didn't even know who he was. But that foxlike grin when he spotted her in the shadows that night made her wonder if he knew who *she* was. Even if he had no idea who Ena was, he still got a look at her face and certainly would not forget it.

Uncertainty was growing like wildfire, and Ena feared she was going in too deep to get out if the mission grew too dangerous.

As they moved farther from the center of the city into the countryside, platoons of City Watch guards passed them on the road. None of the guards paid them any mind, likely thinking they were travelers.

"Wow," Drake stopped a moment, observing the view before them as the clouds broke.

The sun ignited the grasslands ahead. Rolling waves of green as a breeze captured every blade of grass in the countryside. The main road kept on straight for miles into the horizon and teams of wild horses galloped through the sea of green. Ena flooded with emotion and nostalgia watching the muscular equines run free.

"It seems endless," Drake noted. "What's out there?"

"Lothol," Ena knew this part of Avalon well. Though she had never been here in person, her father gathered many of his wild horses from this span of grassland between Gabrenas and Lothol. By the time Ena started working on her father's horse farm, he had begun transitioning from taming wild horses to breeding his own, so Ena never made the trip with him.

Years ago, Ena helped her father break two dozen Avalonian steeds from Lothol as black as midnight for the Avalonian City Watch. Avalonian steeds were massive, measuring seventeen hands on average, and even some of the tallest riders needed a step stool to swing their legs over the saddle. The steeds were broken to handle any terrain and any combat environment. Perfect for the City Watch platoon in the Avalonian city of Saw known as the Dread Watch. Specialized in warfare, the Dread Watch requested mounts that could handle being ridden hard and would not flinch if struck with an arrow during combat.

Saw was a crime-ridden prison city where all of Havyn's worst criminals were detained. The Dread Watch was tasked with hunting down these criminals and bringing them to justice.

Ena would never forget how difficult training those two dozen horses was, or how delighted her father was when he got his paycheck once the job was complete.

She made a mental note to return here on her own time and ride with the stallions. Without her father's constant belittling and abuse, she may actually enjoy herself.

Ena followed the directions on the map off of the main road. A small trodden footpath between two farmhouses led up a small knoll to a broken-down windmill perched overlooking the farmhouses and the grassy plains.

This must be the place, Ena guessed.

As they approached, two hooded figures in black, with masks covering their noses and mouths, came from inside the doorway to the mill. Ena and Drake stopped. Ena's hands rested on her hips, ready to draw her daggers at her sides in less than a moment's notice. Was this the trap that was set for her? Two unarmed rogues?

Pathetic, the governess rolled her eyes. She stepped forward dauntingly, not sure what to expect.

The two rogues turned inboard to one another and pointed into the doorway, "This way, please."

Ena cautiously padded between them, Drake at her back. The mill inside was empty except for a spiraling wooden staircase built into the stone walls circling up to the top above them. Once again, the rogues gestured for her to continue.

The splintered steps creaked under her feet. She gracefully climbed the spiral, dizzying her towards the top.

She stepped into the sunlight at the peak of the mill. The roof was a sheltered lookout nest overlooking the surrounding horizon. Here, the Lord of Steel stood on the far side from the stairs looking out at something. Next to him, a man with bound hands and feet was blindfolded and gagged with rags. Two more rogues stood on either side of the prisoner.

"Ah! You're here right on time," the dwarf said without turning around. "Come, join me."

As Ena walked towards him, he turned and studied Drake, "You brought a friend."

"As you said I could," Ena retorted. "Just one, remember?"

"Well, yes," he laughed, "but I expected you to bring some defense. The lad is unarmed. What good would that have done you if I decided to kill you for being intrusive?"

Ena looked down and met the Lord of Steel's narrowed eyes. "I am not sure if you noticed, Lord of Steel, but your men are unarmed as well."

"You and I have different definitions of unarmed, lass," he chuckled solemnly. He shifted his focus to what lay in the distance about half of a mile away.

Ena followed his gaze and met it at a group of buildings clustered together with a fenced-in field. She focused closely.

A City Watch barracks? She was right. In the field, guards were training, some swinging swords against practice dummies and others using wooden swords and shields to spar. She then shot a glance at the bound prisoner behind the dwarf.

He wore the same light leather spaulders and breastplate as the guards training below.

"He's..."

"A City Watch guard," the Lord of Steel finished. "Yes, indeed."

He turned to face Ena and looked up to meet her gaze. "Are you ready for your first loyalty test?"

She was afraid to acknowledge his question. She nodded anyway.

"This young man here," the Lord of Steel lifted the prisoner's head up by his hair and yanked off the blindfold, "happened to stumble across one of my private meetings with an investor in the black market. As he ran off to report his findings, one of my *unarmed* guards stopped him from advancing."

The young man, not much older than Drake, was sweating profusely and trembling with fear. His pupils were wide and could not refrain from shifting back and forth between them. He mumbled from beneath the rag stuffed halfway down his throat. The dwarf forcibly tore it from the guard's mouth and backhanded him, breaking skin on his cheekbone.

The young guard tried to speak, but every word was inaudible. As he picked up his head, Ena noticed blood pooling and dribbling down the corners of his mouth.

His teeth are missing... Not just missing—ripped out. One by one.

The guard started weeping and fell forwards with his face pressed in the wood of the roof, his hands bound tightly behind his back. "Please let me go!" were the only words Ena could make out amongst the mumbled speech.

The governess herself had undergone many months of psychological and physical endurance training in the City Watch. She knew firsthand how intensely guards exercised physical and mental resolution, so to see this guard broken down to tears... It upset her greatly, though, she couldn't show it. Whatever torture the Lord of Steel put this man through was unforgivable.

He's a fucking monster, Ena scowled.

"And now," the dwarf continued, "he has seen your face. If he goes back to the barracks, not only am I discovered, but you are as well, my dear." He pointed to the dagger at Ena's hip. "Kill him."

"What?" Ena was taken back.

"Your first test. Kill the guard," the Lord of Steel smiled cruelly as the words left his lips.

Ena hesitated, unmoving.

"If you want what I offer, girl, you must be willing to do what it takes to protect yourself."

Ena opened her mouth to speak.

The Lord of Steel cut her off and spat, "I *hate* murderers. Absolutely fucking hate them. Taking another innocent life is the worst sin we can commit in the gods' eyes. However, in my line of work, sometimes the law may not agree and we have to watch our backs. Besides, this bastard has probably killed enough innocent people to forgive your actions for taking his life."

He was speaking of the man as if he was already dead. Ena was certain if she did not kill the guard herself, the dwarf would do it himself and then turn his blade on her and Drake for failing his test.

She was conflicted. She could never forgive herself if she went through with it.

"You have five seconds, girl," the dwarf said ominously.

Ena's head spun, *Shit. What do I do?*

"Five."

She looked around for any way of getting out of this mess, but the Lord's rogues stood around them.

"Four."

If I kill him, everything I believe in and everything I have stood for would be lost!

"Three."

The dwarf was tapping him foot, growing impatient.

"Two!"

Ena couldn't do it. She couldn't bring herself to kill him...

"ONE!"

As the dwarf unsheathed his own dagger and moved in towards the guard, Ena removed all emotion from her mind and acted entirely on instinct. Metal sung as she drew her sharp dagger from its sheath on her thigh. She lunged forwards, taking the guard by the back of the head, holding his chin high, and brought the blade deep into his throat. With one swift motion, she brought the edge of the blade from the left side of his neck to the right.

Blood sprayed onto the wooden floor in front of the guard. A blood-curdling gargle emanated from his throat as he grew limp and dropped to the floor, blood pooling around him.

Ena dropped to her knees in disbelief. Her crimson dagger rolled from her palm and clattered to the ground beside her.

The Lord of Steel snapped his fingers, and his four rogues walked him over to the stairs.

"Next time," he snarled at Ena, "You don't wait for me to start counting. You passed your first test. Barely."

He trotted down the stairs with his guards at his back and disappeared.

Once Drake was certain the dwarf was gone, he rushed to Ena's side.

"Are you okay? Gods, I can't believe he made you do that!"

Ena barely comprehended Drake was speaking to her. All her focus was pressed on the poor man in front of her. Her murder victim.

Has she ever taken a life before this moment? Yes, numerous times. She was doing her job, protecting people from greater harm by ending the life of one who can end the lives of dozens of others. With each kill, the final swing of a sword or loosing of an arrow grew easier. More mindless. Requiring less thought and effort. However, that doesn't mean that their faces don't haunt Ena at night. She remembered each face, each name.

But she always told herself it was the right thing to do to protect the greater good.

How much truth was behind the Lord of Steel's words? Was senseless murder justified in the eyes of the All-Seeing God? Were the City Watch just murderers paid to kill without legal conviction?

The victim that lay before her would never leave her memory. The look on his fearful face as she drove her blade across his throat...

"His death cannot be in vain..." Ena said softly to herself, her bottom lip quivering.

Drake tilted his head, not hearing her quiet voice.

"Promise me, Drake. Promise me his life will not have been taken in vain." Ena turned her head, staring into Drake's dark brown irises. She was not a vulnerable woman. She *hated* Drake seeing her like this.

For once, Athenia, just let your godsdamned guard down, she told herself as she took a deep breath.

"I promise," Drake held up a hand and gently caressed her cheek. "We will get to the bottom of this. Even if we never find out who killed the Lord of Avalon, we have to stop this dwarf."

Tears welled up in Ena's eyes. She took Drake's hand in hers and squeezed it, acknowledging his kind words.

Together, they stood up and descended the stairs. As they walked out of the windmill, they noticed a man on horseback approaching from the footpath. Five yards away, his horse came to a halt. He hopped off his horse and grabbed a letter from the saddlebag.

A courier?

The courier read the back of the letter, "Are you... 'Pretty Lass?'"

Ena dried her tear-filled eyes and rolled them. "Yes, I believe that would be me."

The courier handed off the letter and returned to his horse and rode off.

The letter had no return address or name. She flipped it open and read the scribbled script.

Pretty Lass –

If you're receiving this letter, it means you passed the first test. Your second test awaits you at the address below. Return to me an item of great value that was taken from my possession. I hate thieves, almost as much as I hate murderers. Leave this one alive. Just get me what was stolen from me.

– You Know Who

Drake, reading the letter over her shoulder, said to her, "Ena, do you think you should be continuing with this?"

Ena squeezed Drake's hand again, "You said it yourself, Drake. We need to stop this monster."

She tucked the letter into the waist of her trousers. Continuing down the footpath, the two made their way back to *Dragonfly & the Fruit* by nightfall.

As they entered the inn, Drake turned towards the stairs, probably assuming they were immediately going back to their rooms. Ena didn't even look in the direction of the stairs before she sat at the bar and asked for a shot of whiskey from Inga.

CHAPTER 14

Shot after shot after shot and Ena still maintained a stable resolution. Drake was amazed. If he drank half of what was in her body at that moment, he would be on the floor unconscious.

Ena waved for him to keep her company. He looked up the stairs, wondering if it would be wise to get Damian and Klaus to help calm her down.

"Forget them," Ena said, clearly understanding his thoughts. "Come sit. Inga," she slapped a gold coin onto the rugged bartop, "three more shots of whiskey, please. Two of them are for him."

Inga saluted her, "You got it, hun."

Drake casually approached the barstool and sat down. Inga returned with an unlabeled bottle of dark liquor and aggressively filled the three small glasses to the brim, whiskey spilling over the edges. Ena lifted up a glass and tilted her head towards the glass in front of Drake, instructing him to pick it up. She clanked her glass against his, causing whiskey to splash all over Drake, and threw back the shot like it was water.

Drake took one look at the shot and held back a gag. The pungent aroma of spice and earth wafted into his olfactory nerves as he brought the glass closer to his face. He was convinced his nose hairs were burning off. He grimaced.

"Just do it!" Ena yelled playfully.

Drake pressed his lips to the edge of the glass and slowly tilted it back, drinking the alcohol in multiple small sips. He only drank about half before he started choking. The burning sensation in his gullet caught him by surprise. As he coughed and struggled to catch his breath, Drake felt the liquor hit his stomach and warm his insides in a pulsating euphoric wave.

Ena broke out in a hearty laugh Drake had never heard before. The smile spreading from ear to ear may have been influenced by the booze, but her laugh was real. The governess kept a strong composure so often, Drake wondered if she even knew *how* to laugh.

"Your face is hilarious!" she burst out. "Have you never touched a sip of whiskey to your tongue before?"

Drake heaved one final cough, clearing his windpipe. He rasped, "No. Nothing beyond a glass of wine or mug of beer."

Ena raised her brow, glancing at the half-drank shot glass, "You are going to finish that. *And* you are going to have another!"

Drake sneered, "Can it *please* be something other than this putrid crap?"

"Fine," Ena agreed. She flagged down Inga from the other end of the bar. "Inga, do you have any rum?"

Inga leaned on the bar with her meaty arm. "Do I have rum? What in the Connections do you think this place is, girl? *Of course* I have rum! Only the best watering holes this side of the city do. What kind would you like? We have *Siwa's Own*, *Brightfirst*, and *Brekken Special No. 62*, to name a few."

Ena's eyes lit up, "The *Brekken Special*, for sure!" Down came three more shot glasses and another alcoholic waterfall splashing over the bar. Ena slid two of the shots in front of Drake. "This time, do both of them." She picked up his remaining shot of whiskey and tossed it down her gullet, followed by the rum.

Drake picked up the rum and cautiously observed it. This dark liquor smelled almost sweet. He touched the glass to his lips. The taste was much better than the whiskey, though his lips still burned. Drake took a deep breath, then exhaled. In one swift motion, copying Ena, he let his head fall back and his throat open as the rum poured down.

That euphoric rush and burn hit all at once and Drake slammed his forehead down into his palms, holding back the urge to vomit, choke, or cry.

"You're evil!" he teased Ena. "This isn't fun! How do people do this all the time?"

Ena laughed and jokingly shoved him, "Give it a few minutes and you will be feeling differently."

The playful energy Ena exuberated was unlike her typical characteristic. Drake hoped he was breaking through her guarded exterior enough to actually get to know her. They had shared a close conversation upon their arrival in Havana City at her father's old stable, but it was still met with resistance. It had not been the right time to ask questions and get to know her.

Maybe now would be different.

"Hey, Athenia," Drake took the risk. "Tell me about yourself." Ena gave him a stern look. "I mean, other than everything you went through with your father. Your friends, family, career. If I'm going to be with you for a while, I should probably get to know you better."

Ena squinted at him, contemplating his intentions. She slid the other full shot glass towards him. "Take another shot." Drake squinted back at her. "Another shot and I will tell you something about myself. Also, my name is *Kate*, remember? Don't call me Athenia."

"Why can't I call you by your full name? It's a wonderful name."

Ena called Inga back over. As Inga poured more shots, Ena tossed five more gold coins on the bar, instructing her to leave the bottle. Ena slid a shot in front of Drake.

"Drink and I'll tell you." Drake reluctantly swallowed the shot whole. It went down easier this time. "Good," Ena continued. "I do not like being referred to by the name my father gave me. Simple as that."

"What about your mother?"

Ena poured him another shot from the bottle.

"I could die from drinking all of this," Drake sighed.

"You won't know your limits until you reach them," Ena grinned slyly.

Drake groaned and drank the shot. By the time he slammed the empty glass back onto the bar, the room was spinning.

"My mother," Ena explained, "died during childbirth. Those who knew my father best always told me he lost a piece of himself when she died. He always used to say I looked just like her. Reminded him of her." She lowered her chin. "And then he would beat me. Or throw me onto the back of a wild stallion and would not let me off until it was broken. If I fell off, he threw me right back on."

"That's torture... How did you survive?" He already knew her story—she left for the City Watch and never returned until after his death. But she could have died long before she went off on her own.

"I always wanted to join the City Watch. I met so many guards of varying ranks as a child, they became role models of mine. I was not even of age to join when I snuck out in the middle of the night, stole my father's favorite horse, and fled to the barracks. To sign on before the age of sixteen, I would have needed a parent's signature. Luckily, I had a guard captain friend who willingly forged the paperwork for me and backed up my story."

"You never went back, except for your father's funeral, right?" Drake asked.

Ena nodded, "I completed my six months of intensive training for the City Watch, donned my armor, carried my sword, served in Havana City for another year or so, then off to Cyprien I went."

Ena popped off the cork of the rum and poured another glass for herself and another for Drake.

Drake stared at the glass and said, "But I didn't ask a question."

Ena's nose wrinkled as she chuckled. "No, but I want to keep talking. And this," she tapped the glass, "is the price for listening."

Drake lifted the glass, grimaced, and replied, "You're lucky I find you so interesting, otherwise I wouldn't be indulging like this."

Ena turned on her barstool and faced Drake. Her leg brushed against his. She smirked, "Oh, you find me interesting, do you?"

Drake felt his cheeks flush. He turned and met her and drank the glass, *Yes, I do.*

Ena continued her story, "No one knew me in Cyprien. I was a clean slate. I had worked my way to the top of my squad in Havana City and was raised to the rank of Guard Captain. When looking at open captain assignments, I saw an opening in El Vadora and took it."

"Where you ran for Governess and won," Drake said.

"That is the simple version," Ena began twirling the ends of her dark locks. She was in desperate need of a haircut. She kept it short for easy maneuverability, but it had been several months without trimming it and it began to cascade down her shoulders. "As a captain, I had to pay attention to the political agenda of the city. In doing so, my job of assigning the squads of my platoon to certain high-risk areas of the city became easier. My interest in politics grew and once the elderly governor passed away peacefully in his sleep at eighty years old, I threw my name onto the ballot."

"Did you have much competition?"

Ena snarked, "Uh, yes. The former governor held that position for twenty years—a long term for most governors. It was like wolves pouncing on a piece of prey." She winked, "Or a lonely young man in the woods."

Drake sighed and ignored her joke. "You won, though. That's what matters most."

Ena modded. "El Vadora's citizens wanted young blood. The former governor was limited by his age. He hadn't seen the sides of his city that I saw. Confined to the House of the Governor for his own safety."

"And here you are," Drake poured himself more rum and swirled it around, "hundreds of miles away from your city solving a case for someone else that you don't want to solve."

Ena poured herself another shot, "I *desire* to solve this case. After today, I questioned whether the underlying situation is becoming more than I can handle, but I could not leave now. Raven's heart would shatter if she does not get an answer. Furthermore, the Master of Cities is relying on me."

"Why is that?" Drake asked.

"I believe he understands there is something bigger here than we realize," Ena tossed back yet another shot. "Besides, he is sending guards into El Vadora to hopefully warn off any more mage attacks. I am thankful for him."

That caught Drake's attention, "Really? Does he think he can put a stop to them?"

"He didn't say," Ena shrugged. "He knows about the situation, though, and more guards means more patrols to protect those at risk. Hopefully, he will find more information about that sword," Ena realized she was speaking out loud. She hadn't wanted to bring attention to the sword around Drake.

Drake stared intently at Ena, "The Master of Cities knows about the sword?"

The liquor was clearly causing her to lose her filter. Ena sighed, "Yes, he spotted the blade when I was at the palace. He believes it contains magical properties. Truth is, we know nothing about it and it will paint a target on our backs if the wrong person discovers we have it." Ena rested her hand on Drake's thigh. "It's your turn. Tell me more about yourself."

"What's there to know?" Drake could feel the liquor coursing through his veins now. He felt elated. "I'm just a kid from a farming village who was dragged into a mess of trouble. I'm now an orphan with no home."

"Hey," Ena grabbed Drake's chin and turned his head, catching his brown eyes. "Earlier you said that you wish you could have stayed in El Vadora and worked, starting fresh. Did you mean that?"

"I *could* have stayed in El Vadora and started a life," Drake clarified. He felt a sudden burst of courage, taking Ena's hand from his chin and holding it. "But I wouldn't want to be anywhere else."

Ena began to blush, her cheeks turning hot. She gently pulled her hand back and cupped her palms together in her lap.

Avoiding Drake's comment, she asked, "What would you have done for work in the city, if you had the chance?"

Drake cleared his throat, "Um, I guess I never thought ahead that far. All I ever knew was farming—livestock, crops, understanding weather patterns—and those skills aren't entirely useful in city life..."

"This may not be the life you wanted," Ena spoke softly, "but I will pay you handsomely for your service."

"Ena, stop!" Drake slammed his glass on the bar top. "This isn't about money. This is about you. I'm here for *you!* I was captivated by you the moment we met."

"Oh, gods..." Ena ran a hand through her hair. Her hot cheeks brightened more. "Drake, stop, we cannot keep talking like this." Drake fervently asked why they couldn't. "It is not appropriate. Boundaries must exist between us."

"Fuck boundaries," adrenaline pumped through Drake as he quickly leaned in and pressed his lips against Ena's. She pressed a palm against his chest, trying feebly to push him away. Drake felt the slight pressure against his chest and met Ena's hand with his own, interlocking his fingers with hers.

Against Ena's best judgement, she gave in to the butterflies in her stomach and allowed herself to kiss Drake back. Their soft lips played tug-of-war. Ena found her free hand finding a place behind Drake's head, fingering through his rough hair. She pulled his face closer to hers.

The other patrons at the bar, hearing their lips smacking together, turned and cheered them on. Liquor and beer sprayed in the air as the gruff men sitting at the bar slammed their mugs against the bar, whistling at them.

Embarrassed, Ena pulled herself away from Drake and bit her lower lip.

"Come," she stood from the barstool and took Drake's hand. She led him towards the stairs, wobbling from the alcohol throwing a tantrum in her bloodstream. The bar patrons clapped Drake on his back and shoulders as they stumbled by, applauding him.

Ena gripped the wooden banister tightly as she climbed the mountain of stairs. Her other arm was twisted behind her back, clutching Drake's hand as he tailed her. Finally, at the top of the stairs on the tiny third floor, Drake spun Ena around and pressed her against the wall. Ena threw her arms around his broad shoulders and met his tongue with hers.

She moaned lightly as he pressed his hips into hers.

Drake pulled away and pressed his index finger to her lips, "Shhh, we don't want to wake the others."

Around the corner, they quietly opened their room's door and entered. Drake quietly pressed the door shut. Behind him, Ena began stripping off her less-than-flattering boots and tunic.

Drake admired her as he watched her undress. Ena could feel his eyes spying on each curve of her body, and every scar. She instinctively tried to cover them with her hands, especially the massive scar on her right hip. Drake approached her slowly and touched the scar. "How did you get this one?"

Ena shuddered in her skin at his touch, memories of receiving the wound that caused the scar flooding back to her. "I was nine years old on the back of a thoroughbred. My father kept urging me to ride faster and faster. The poor horse was heaving under me, exhausted. As I turned her, she slipped and fell through the wooden pen. The shattered wood shred right through my pants into my flesh. White mages worked on me for weeks to repair the torn muscle. This is what remains."

She expected the sour sight to turn Drake off or distract him. Instead, much to Ena's surprise, Drake got onto his knees and kissed the scar. He made a trail of kisses from her scarred hip, slowly over her hip bone, and onto her lower abdomen. A tingle of pleasure rained down her back.

Drake got back to his feet and kissed Ena's lips. As they kissed, Ena unbuttoned his shirt and pushed it back over his shoulders. She pulled her lips away and admired his toned shoulders and chest, gliding her fingertips along his skin.

"Wow," Ena gazed at him, "Farming is a good look on you."

Drake laughed and continued kissing Ena's jaw and neck. Ena let out another soft moan.

Ena turned Drake around and pushed him back onto the bed. She straddled him and grinded her hips against his as she kissed down his pectorals and traced the outline of his abs with her lips. She reached over to the side table and snuffed the flame of the lantern.

◆◆◆◆◆◆◆◆◆

The following morning, Ena woke up with her head resting on Drake's chest and her leg wrapped over his waist. She winced as she picked up her leg to roll onto her back. Her hips ached extraordinarily, but in a good way, she supposed. Sunlight pooled into the room from the window behind them.

"Good morning," the voice next to her groaned. She picked her head up and saw Drake open one eye, looking at her.

Ena smirked, "Morning."

Drake flipped onto his side, leaning on his arm and supporting his head in his hand. He said, "You did a number on me last night. I think I have bruises."

"*You* have bruises?" Ena raised her brows. "I am going to have hand marks all up and down my legs from you grabbing me."

Drake leaned over and kissed her, "I had fun. I don't do that very often, so I apologize if you expected better."

She kissed him back, "It's been quite some time for me, as well."

Now that she was sober, Ena took a moment to recall last night's activities. This was not the outcome she predicted, or even wanted, but she could not go back on her drunken decision now. It *was* a fun night, though. She released all of her inhibitions and allowed herself to act entirely on emotion, something she never had the freedom to do. Drake saw a side of her she showed to no one, and he embraced it through intimacy. She understood their relationship had now changed forever, all boundaries were now nonexistent, but she reminded herself to keep some distance between them emotionally.

"Drake, listen," Ena began.

Drake pressed a finger against her lips, "I know, Athenia. You're about to say that we can't get too attached because we are all still at risk and attachments will only endanger one another." Ena nodded. "I understand. When this is all over and we're back in El Vadora, maybe we could talk more about this?"

Ena bit her lower lip and nodded, "Yes, I think we could do that."

Suddenly, a footstep sounded from the hall. The door flew open as Damian and Klaus walked in to see Ena and Drake laying naked with one another.

"You're fucking kidding me," Damian burst out.

CHAPTER 15

The National Bank of Havyn was centered in the business district of Havana City. Rumor had it, more money cycled in and out of this bank in one day than all other banks in the Kingdom of Havyn combined in one year. Only the high rollers, government officials, and family money stored their vast wealth in the National Bank.

Family money referred to those members of the most ancient and wealthiest families in Havyn. Seeing as Havyn is the youngest of the five kingdoms of Lynidas, these ancient families were still considered "young blood" among the other kingdoms. The National Bank secured their wealth and insured that it could not be touched or destroyed.

King Typhus and Queen Helena were both family money. The king's family was the third dynasty of Havyn's rulers, and by far the one with the lengthiest reign. Six-hundred years had passed since Typhus' ancestor assumed the throne after marrying the step-daughter and closest heir of the former dynasty's last king.

Queen Helena's wealth and status stemmed from the housing market. Considered "young blood," even in the eyes of Havyn's family money, Helena's great-great-grandmother struck gold when she got into the business of designing and selling high-class, expensive abodes to the governors of Havyn's cities. All of which now known as Houses of the Governor, all political operations occurred behind the walls of the magnificent structures Helena and her family maintained for over a century.

Not any longer, though.

When Helena and her parents died of the plague, the family wealth passed to Princess Lia. The princess, however, was unaware that this exchange ever occurred. Being underage, the wealth was placed in a trust with her father as the trustee.

Her father never informed her of this.

It was unlikely the king even remembered.

That massive wealth was stored here, in the National Bank.

Sheridan rarely set foot in the National Bank since he first assumed his role as Master of Cities. His signature was required on hundreds of pieces of documentation to transfer just as many bank accounts belonging to the kingdom into his name. Sheridan knew of every piece of copper that moved in and out of those accounts, with armlength paper statements privately delivered to him each month.

His personal agreement with the president of the bank stated that all transactions would be handled confidentially through the bank's secret courier service. It had worked flawlessly up to this point.

Unfortunate for Sheridan, when he requested the statements on the king's personal accounts, he was denied.

Knowing full well this was the only way to get the access he needed, Sheridan walked up the limestone steps of the National Bank of Havyn. He stopped a moment, raising his chin to admire the pantheon that housed the moneys of hundreds of very important, very rich people. Six marble columns, three to each side of the open doorway, stood forty feet high, gleaming in the midmorning sun.

Glancing over his shoulder, Sheridan spotted the four City Watch captains he instructed to remain ten paces behind him at all times.

Sheridan rolled up his sleeves, exposing his metallic arm, and continued for the doorway.

The National Bank's personal guards watched skillfully as he walked through the threshold. Alabaster tiles inlaid with gold trim decorated the floors of the foyer. Knowing how much money the bank generated, Sheridan doubted they spared any expense—the gold was real.

An azure area rug consumed the center of the foyer with a dozen armchairs set evenly spaced apart. Several patrons sat talking with one another, likely waiting for their bankers to be available.

One of the women Sheridan recognized. A famous interior decorator who frequented the homes of many others with accounts at this very bank. A simple paint job recommended by her would grant her a commission of tens of thousands of gold. To decorate or design an entire interior, especially of the elaborate, multi-story homes of the upper class, could earn her a paycheck upwards of half a million gold.

"The Master of Cities himself!" she called out once she spotted Sheridan's arrival and waved. The woman stood from the chair and walked over to him on too-tall stilettos. She reached down and shook his hand. "I have not seen you since I practically *begged* you to update the tapestries in your chambers."

"Charlaia," Sheridan bowed his head respectfully. He gave her a big smile. Even Sheridan could not ignore the beauty and sexuality that this woman exuded. Her regal blue bodycon dress gripped her slim body and was short enough for a dwarf as tall, or as short, as Sheridan to perfectly see her black lace thong at eye level. Her bronze-tinted legs gave note to her Brekken heritage, though very distant.

She crossed her arms, perking her breasts up. "You better be here to take out a hefty down payment for my services. Trust me, the tapestries are not the only area you need my tasteful eye."

"I do not doubt that for a moment, Char," the Master of Cities joked. "However, that's not why I am here. Do you happen to know if President Aroy is here?"

Charlaia tossed her brunette hair over her shoulder. "Yes, my fiancé is here. He promised to take me for lunch, though, so please do not occupy too much of his time!" Sheridan nodded, promising to only take a few moments. Charlaia snickered and started back towards her chair. "Good! On a side note, you could not afford me anyway." She followed with a seductive wink.

It was no wonder she was so successful in her career. Any man with money would bend over backwards for a woman of her magnitude.

Sheridan continued to the counter. The teller situated herself behind a thick layer of glass, thick enough to hold back the power of any cross-bow bolt or swing of a mace. An older woman Sheridan remembers from his first, and only, time here.

"Hi there," the dwarf introduced himself. "Could you please let the president know I am here for him, if he has a moment?"

The teller went into the room behind the counter and returned a minute later. She said, "President Aroy can see you now, Master. Please, this way."

To the far right of the teller booths, a massive iron door inlaid with three separate combination locks and two keyholes grunted as it opened from the inside. One of the bank's guards held it open as the dwarf entered, shutting and turning the lever, locking it behind them.

The guard led Sheridan through the door the teller had disappeared through. A short hallway appeared with two doors on either wall with another iron multi-lock door at the far end. The door to the left, Sheridan knew, led to the bank staff's quarters. The door to the right was Aroy's office.

The President himself waited at his door. He wore a charcoal suit with a royal blue tie, clearly trying to match his fiancée; though, Sheridan was sure that was Charlaia's idea, not his.

Aroy's thin mustache curled upwards at the ends when he smiled at the dwarf.

"Master Sheridan! To what do I owe this unexpected pleasure?"

Sheridan entered the president's office, similarly decorated as the foyer in the front of the building. An espresso desk pressed against the far wall was cluttered with piles of paper and bank statements, and hundreds of small filing drawers built into the wall behind it from floor to ceiling. Aroy pulled out the armchair for Sheridan at the front of his desk. The president sat adjacent to him in the sister armchair.

Sheridan began, "I think we both know why I'm here. The letter you replied with stated you could not provide me those statements by courier. How about in person?"

Aroy leaned back and crossed his legs. The shine of his dress shoes mirrored Sheridan's bushy red beard. "I am glad you are as smart as your reputation has me believe. Yes, our agreement works fine for your own accounts, or any with your name on them. My private couriers are sworn to secrecy and instructed to burn all messages if they should be caught in a bind. My concern was not security. My concern was appropriation. If King Typhus wanted you to see his records, he would have requested them himself and provided you with them."

"I understand that." Sheridan cleared his throat. "My problem is that the king would probably not want me seeing his bank statements. But I need them."

"Assuming you cannot inform me as to *why* you need them because the security clearance is above my paygrade," Aroy worded carefully, "I can perhaps allow you to glance at the records in question. For one reason in particular... And for a price."

Sheridan's eyes narrowed, "It's illegal for you to take bribes, Aroy."

"Consider it," Aroy twirled his hand in the air, "an early wedding gift. Besides, I have no love for the king, otherwise I would be thinking twice about this offer."

Sheridan took a banknote from the desk before him. With a pen, he scribbled his personal account information and a hefty value of twenty-five thousand gold signed to Aroy's personal account.

He handed the president the banknote, who observed it cautiously.

"All right," Aroy sighed, probably expecting more. However, Sheridan wasn't incorrect—Aroy legally could not accept bribes, so he refrained from arguing for a higher value. "Your one and only saving grace, Master, is Princess Lia. Lia's name was placed on all of Typhus' accounts after Helena's death. Helena's will detailed that carefully. However, Lia being not yet eighteen, access to any accounts rests in the hands of a trustee."

Sheridan opened his mouth to respond, but was interrupted.

"I know what you're going to say," Aroy held up a hand. "Wouldn't Typhus be her trustee? Yes, but in this case, since the accounts are Typhus's own, acting as her trustee becomes what we call a 'conflict of interest.' Well, according to the Concordat, if the ruling monarch passes and the heir is not yet of age, then the Master of Cities acts as regent until they come of age." Aroy shrugged. "I figured, if that is the case with ruling an entire kingdom, then surely the same can be thought of when viewing a simple bank account."

"Let me get this straight," Sheridan chuckled. "Because Lia is not old enough to access the account herself, and because her trustee is the other name on the account, I become an indirect trustee?" Sheridan could not help but laugh at the loose interpretation of the rule, but President Aroy had clearly put some thought into this in order to essentially create a loophole on his own.

Aroy nodded, "Now, don't get me wrong, this account is still in Typhus's name. While Typhus lives, you cannot touch this account. Not the money, not the names on the account, nothing. You can simply view it here within the walls of the bank."

Sheridan couldn't hold back his victorious smirk. Asking to see the statements, Aroy stood and instructed the dwarf to wait. Aroy left the room and turned right down the hall, heading for the iron door in the back of the bank.

Sheridan sat in silence for five minutes, twiddling his thumbs, before Aroy appeared again. Shutting and locking the deadbolt to his office door, Aroy proceeded to hand over a stack of papers to the Master of Cities.

The account number had been blacked out for privacy and security purposes, but the name *Typhus Casalvania* read loudly at the top.

Sheridan scanned each line of the account carefully. He quickly counted the pages—thirty-nine in total. Clearly the account had been touched frequently, for most accounts, even ones with the kind of money that this bank held, a handful of pages was the max.

Besides Typhus' salary deposits for being king, the only influx of wealth came from an account number Sheridan did not recognize.

When Sheridan asked Aroy what that account number was, Aroy replied, "The first seven digits relate to a High Alta account. The same seven digits can be seen on the kingdom's tax account as a payout."

That's right! Sheridan thought. *Our tax we pay towards High Alta each month has a similar account number. This must be what I'm looking for.*

Indeed, it was. Sheridan spotted the same account number about a dozen times in the past few years. All of which were valued in the tens of millions.

Sheridan did some quick math. *Two hundred and forty million gold...*

"Fuck," Sheridan huffed. "That son of a bitch."

What Sheridan found odd, though, was that the total moneys in the account was miniscule compared to the borrowed value. Where had the money gone?

Sheridan spied the values once more, tracking every payment and expense in Typhus's account since that first multi-million gold deposit.

Suddenly, Sheridan noticed a pattern. After each excessively large payment from High Alta, there were about a dozen expenses tallying close to the same large value.

Typhus's mind may not be as sharp as it once was, but he was not a stupid man, by any means. Each transaction was entirely blank besides the value and account number. Not a single note was written on any transaction.

Typhus covered his tracks well.

"Some of these are Havyn accounts," Sheridan pointed out. "Could you tell me what they are?"

Aroy stood from his chair, "It will take me a few moments to search for the exact accounts, but I can inform you that this one," he pointed, "is one of the kingdom accounts."

Sheridan shook his head, "That's impossible. I have every kingdom account number by memory."

"Only the ones you have access to, Master. There are a handful that only the king himself has knowledge of."

Aroy walked behind his desk and began fingering through the files in one of the built-in drawers on the wall. Each drawer was five-by-three inches in dimension and extended out from the wall by at least a foot-and-a-half. Thousands of small note cards containing the account numbers and names were organized in alphabetical order in each drawer.

Gods, Sheridan calculated, *there must be millions of accounts housed in this bank.*

Seeing Sheridan's jaw hitting the floor, the president responded, "The National Bank contains account from all over Havyn. Do not forget that each governor and lord is mandated to bank with us, whether personal or for their city or region. Many cannot take the time to travel here to access their accounts, so each city has a bank of our choosing to make their transactions. The transactions are written on a bank note and mailed to us, at which time we send armed couriers with the money owed to the banks to pay them for the money expended, or they provide us with the money deposited."

The use of account numbers versus names maintained the essential anonymity that the bank's valued customers required. Their money was insured up to a certain amount per account; therefore, when that insurance limit was reached, they simply created a new account and filled the new one to the brim. Considering the amount of money some of these people possessed, it was no wonder they had dozens of accounts ensuring their money was protected.

The kingdom alone had hundreds of accounts, each divvying the funds to whatever department, program, or investment opportunity required for managing Havyn.

But Aroy pulled out the small note cards containing the account information of five private accounts for the kingdom that Sheridan had never seen before.

"These are all military accounts..." Sheridan read the account information carefully upon being handed the cards. "Typhus's name is the only one on them!"

"Well, with two exceptions," President Aroy leaned forward in his own chair after taking his seat. He placed his finger on one spot at the bottom of the card in Sheridan's hand. "One is Princess Lia's, listed as a beneficiary should anything happen to the king. Same as Typhus's own personal account. There is another, though—a cosigner. Does that name look familiar?"

Braxon, Sheridan read the name. *The General of Havyn's Military?*

"Any account pertaining to the use of the kingdom's funds," Aroy explained, "as you are aware, must have a secondary signer for checks and balances. That individual," he made a careful effort not to speak the name out loud, "is entrusted by the king to utilize the funds, within reason. Statements are sent to the king alone, to monitor the expenditure, but the cosigner has a limited spending access, as well."

Sheridan compared the king's personal account statement with the military account numbers in his hands. He stated, mostly to himself, "That bastard has been funding his godsdamned military with this money..."

Aroy, understanding the Master of Cities's concern, commented, "Master, I tend to stay away from politics, as I prefer to keep my head on my shoulders and not on a pike, but may I offer some advice?" Sheridan grunted his approval. Aroy leaned in close. "Speak with the alternative individual on these accounts. The king himself has performed most of this spending. The general, I fear, is simply following the orders of a madman."

Sheridan glanced at Aroy ominously. *The orders of a madman,* he repeated to himself. How much of the king's illness was the bank's president aware of? Had he gossiped with others about it?

Sheridan's mistrust was shaken from him when he thought about that possibility once more. Aroy was a respectable man with the ability to view millions of individuals' personal bank records, to which he was sworn to secrecy at the cost of his life. If he kept those private, surely he will have kept his knowledge of the king's degenerative mind private, Sheridan hoped

"Can I ask you for another favor, Aroy?" The president thought for a moment, then nodded. Sheridan continued, "May I have copies of these records, along with the military accounts?"

Aroy sighed heavily. He stalled, deep in thought. He was risking his career, and his life, by showing the dwarf these private records as it was. "I can give you a copy of Typhus's personal account with his name removed. However, the military accounts themselves *must* remain off-limits. I do hope you understand."

Sheridan did. The Havyn Military remained strictly under the jurisdiction of the crown. The militaries of each kingdom were utilized so little, since no inter-kingdom conflicts had arisen in centuries, that Sheridan tended to forget they even existed.

Sheridan nodded reluctantly and shook Aroy's hand in agreement.

Aroy left the room, once more disappearing behind the iron door in the back of the bank with Typhus's account statement and the five military account cards gripped tightly between his fingers.

He returned a short while later with copies. As he promised, most of the personal information was blacked out, in the case that they were discovered in Sheridan's possession. Though they were bending the law into Sheridan's favor, the president ensured that the indiscretion could not be traced back to himself.

Sheridan stood from his chair, taking the copies, and folding them into his pocket. He pulled out a small pouch that jingled as he handed it over to President Aroy.

The president opened the pouch and poured its contents into his free palm. Thirty gold coins. He looked curiously to Sheridan, who explained, "Your soon-to-be wife demanded I be quick with you. She's waiting for her lunch you promised her. Use that as my apology to her for consuming so much of your time today. Buy her a nice lunch. I truly appreciate this, Aroy."

Aroy smiled humbly, placing the coins back into the pouch. He dipped his head in a respectful bow. "Of course, Sheridan. Just promise me whatever you intend to do with this information is for the good of Havyn."

Sheridan gave him a brief nod as he strode towards the office door. "Only the best for Havyn and her people."

"That is why I voted for you," Aroy dipped his head.

As Sheridan exited through the initial iron door into the foyer, he spotted his City Watch guards waiting exactly where he had left them. He also saw Charlaia waiting impatiently, pacing back and forth.

Upon noticing Sheridan leaving, she gave him a dark look. Sheridan strode over to her to make amends, if only to admire her beauty one more time.

"My apologies, Charlaia," Sheridan said. "He is ready for you now. Also, order yourself some surf and turf, at my expense. Thank you for letting me take up his valuable time."

"Hmm, surf and turf *is* one of my favorites," she tapped her chin, sarcastically considering whether or not to forgive him. She half-grinned and bent down to kiss the dwarf on the cheek.

Sheridan's face turned as red as his beard before Charlaia stepped past him, her heels clacking on the gorgeous tiles, to meet her fiancé at the iron door.

Maybe I will let her decorate my chambers after all.

Sheridan grinned stupidly as he met his guards in the foyer. Together, they marched back down the limestone steps and into the city's bustling streets.

Sheridan's next stop? The Havyn Military barracks on the outskirts of the city.

CHAPTER 16

General Braxon of Havyn's military spent his days from sunrise to sunset either at the barracks or on the field just beyond the wall designing and honing his militaristic strategies. A tall and muscular man, Braxon towered well over six feet and the cords of his biceps were often compared to the rippling trunks of the strongest oak trees. Muscle, though, was only a minimal portion of the skill required to lead a kingdom's entire military. He achieved greatness with a mind as sharp as any blade and the articulation to outmaneuver anyone in conversation.

Braxon came from nothing. He was born an orphaned peasant and gained himself a rap sheet as long as he was tall before he was a legal adult. Once he reached adulthood, his petty crimes turned into hardcore felony acts, which landed him in jail on more than one occasion. Despite never having a defense attorney accompanying him in the courtroom, he always got himself off on technicalities.

On the brink of death after raiding a military barracks in the Kastrian region, which bordered the Kingdom of Fairmarq in the east, and killing a dozen military soldiers singlehandedly, he was graciously given an ultimatum—lose his head or lose his freedom.

He chose his freedom.

To make up for the twelve men he slayed in cold blood, he was indentured to the kingdom's military for twelve lifetimes in honor of each lifetime those men would have served.

The ultimatum had come from Braxon's predecessor, much to the dismay and condemnation of the then-king, Typhus's grandfather, Tytan, who strongly believed Braxon's next target would be the king himself.

Braxon proved the disbelievers wrong, though. He quickly rose up the ranks, becoming Military Commander of Kastrian. When his predecessor passed eight years prior, he threw his name in for consideration as the next Military General for all of Havyn.

Unlike democratic political races for governor or lord, which required a simple majority vote by the people, the position of Military General was chosen by the military soldiers and required a two-thirds majority. Most elections for General lasted multiple rounds, with the candidate with the lowest votes being eliminated each round. Braxon, though, won his two-thirds majority during the first round after giving only one mere twenty-minute speech.

He, quite literally, talked his way to one of the grandest positions Havyn could offer.

He certainly flaunted his hefty paycheck with his three-story elaborate home on the border between the military district and the upper-class district on the hill leading up to the Spire.

Sheridan met the felon-turned-general atop the southern wall in Havana City. Braxon had been quick to take up the Master of Cities's request, and the two agreed to meet at this spot that same midafternoon.

Sheridan hardly ever came near the southern wall. He had no reason to. The Military was the king's business, and the southern wall was solely the responsibility of the Military seeing as it bordered Nest Aiken and Brekken territory. Sheridan had never even spoken to the general face-to-face before. Until now.

"Beautiful, is it not?" a slight Kastrian accent sounded from behind Sheridan, as the general scaled the final steps to the top of the wall. Sheridan watched as he approached, admiring the man.

Braxon wore tight athletic pants and training boots only. He must have just come from sparring with his men, for his knuckles were wrapped with protective fabric and he was shirtless, sweat gleaming in the afternoon sun. He ran a hand through his short-cropped, curled, blonde locks.

The general held out a hand, Sheridan shook it. "It's a pleasure to finally meet you, General Braxon."

Braxon took a large gulp from his water flask. "The pleasure is all mine, Master Sheridan. You are a legend around these parts."

Sheridan replied humbly, "My story is nothing compared to yours, trust me."

"Indeed. Most knew my name as I ascended to the capital. However, you appeared from thin air and mysteriously convinced an entire kingdom you had their best interests at heart."

Sheridan studied him cautiously. "You don't believe I have the people's best interests at heart?"

"To be transparent," Braxon's expression remained neutral, "I know more of the rats that dine on the scraps in the barrack mess hall than I do of you. Our professions rarely cross paths. Pure curiosity brings me before you today."

Cut to the chase, Sheridan knew what he meant.

But the Master of Cities did not like being spoken down to. Sheridan toyed with the general. "Such a lovely view up here. The plains of Brekkenia are a sight to behold."

Sheridan scanned his eyes across the gorgeous grasslands and shot an amused glance at Braxon. Braxon met his gaze with glaringly bright blue eyes.

As much as Sheridan did not like being spoken down to, General Braxon did not enjoy being toyed with.

"Do you see the flora among the grasses?" the general questioned. Sheridan swept a quick glance at the fields, noting quickly the white flowers spotted among the green sea. He nodded. Braxon continued, "That species of flora is known as *Ixontia Emortia*—the Eyeglass of Death. They are highly sensitive to sunlight, as the petals point in the direction of the rays at all times of the day. The pistil in its center reflects the sun's rays so intensely, when the eyes catch the reflection at a specific angle, the spectator falls victim to blindness for several moments." Braxon sneered, half-respectfully, "In battle, Master Sheridan, several moments can mean life or death. Anything can happen. The same case with these several moments I have wasted associating with you about the beauty of a battlefield."

"Battlefield? There hasn't been a battle here for centuries," Sheridan countered.

"In my line of work, everything can be a battlefield. Now, I beg pardon, but I must return to training with my men. Lovely to have met you, Master Sheridan." He turned to leave.

"Alright, no more bullshit," Sheridan reached out and stopped him, metallic hand gripped around the general's veined forearm. "I did come here for serious reasons."

Braxon held back the urge to smack the Master of Cities's hand from his arm. Striking a metal arm would not feel too great, even with his hands wrapped.

"If this is about King Typhus," Braxon said, "which I do not have to guess twice about, then please say so." Sheridan released his arm. "Though, I must warn you, my loyalties lie with the crown." *I will tell the king everything you say,* Sheridan translated in his head.

"I know you are busy," Sheridan acknowledged. "Perhaps I could tour your training grounds with you. That way I am not taking too much of your attention from your men."

Braxon locked eyes with Sheridan and thought carefully. He finally stated, "Very well. Please, follow me."

Braxon took the steps back to the ground behind the wall two at a time. Sheridan practically needed to run to keep up. As they rounded the base of the staircase, the military barracks, built into the massive stone wall's base, came into view. Soldiers teemed in and out of the main entrance, some armored and some geared up with similar training attire as Braxon.

Many of the armored soldiers had a bow strung across their back with a quiver of arrows. They marched past Sheridan and up the stairs.

Sheridan knew enough about the military to recognize those men as "watchers." They patrol the top of the wall in eight-hour shifts all hours of the day and night. Watchers drill archery above any other form of offense, some skilled enough to hit their mark dead center from over one-hundred yards away. Their precision bows cost a small fortune each.

Needless to say, if one was marked as their target, one was guaranteed a barbed arrow through the lung, heart, or head.

Sheridan hustled after the general, who was striding clear past the barracks and towards the sealed wooden gate leading through the wall onto the plains beyond. The wooden gate was triple-locked and sealed. Two thick oak beams set into iron braces, one at eye level and another high above their heads, spanned from one end of the gate's pair of outwardly swinging doors to the other end. The hinges on the gate were locked with wrought iron pins to prevent them from swinging.

As Braxon approached, two soldiers at attention at the center of the gate saluted and proceeded to unlatch four iron deadbolts. They pulled open a much smaller door carved into the wooden gate, only large enough for a single person to pass through.

"After you, Master," Braxon waved Sheridan through the passage, following closely behind. As Sheridan's boots hit the grass, the passage was sealed and locked behind them.

The Master of Cities had only ever seen the field from afar, usually high above viewing the horizon beyond. Now, taking in the plains up close, he was even more captivated. The flat green sea spread out before him for miles with no other object in sight.

"If you were to take a horse and ride straight for half-a-day, you would stumble across Nest Aiken," General Braxon pointed ahead. He directed his index finger to their left. "Continue east for a day or two and Fairmarq will be waiting for you." Pointing forty-five degrees to the right, "Continue southwest and you will find the first of the forty-nine Brekken kingdoms." Then, he pointed far to their right. "Go west and find a void of existence. Not a single living soul stirring for hundreds, if not thousands, of miles."

The Dead Lands, Sheridan recalled. *Undisputed, uninhabited territory.* Everything seemed to lead back to the Concordat, even land beyond Lynidas. Far to the west, another country existed, known as Etherea, where powerful elven, dwarven, and human kingdoms thrived. The Concordat recognized their existence, and each ruler included their signatures on the treaty, creating the undisputed territory between them to keep the two countries from associating.

Lynidas and Etherea worshipped different gods and lived entirely different lifestyles, with only the Concordat in common. Etherea was reluctant to sign the treaty. Never having conflicted with Lynidas previously, her rulers questioned why they needed to acknowledge the Concordat at all. However, they were influenced by the Fairie Kingdom to comply.

Not a word from Etherea since.

Some say the Dead Lands were completely desolate of all life. Others say dangerous creatures roamed, and all who attempted to cross the territory ended up hunted and killed. Sheridan was unsure what were facts and what were rumors.

The Brekken referred to it as the Shadow of Existence, believing it to be cursed.

Perhaps they were right.

Sheridan shook the thought from his head. Starting after Braxon, who strode with his head held high to the canvas canopy enveloping part of the training grounds. Sheridan never realized Braxon trained his men en masse on the *other* side of the wall.

Isn't that dangerous? Sheridan wanted to ask. He knew, though, that Braxon's hubris did not comprehend the word "danger."

Shirtless men danced in the sparring ring, adorned with purple and yellow bruises, sunburns, and scars from blades that were clearly not dulled training blades.

Confirming his suspicions, Sheridan then spotted another sparring ring with men guarded with wooden or thin aluminum plates covering only their shoulders and chest. Their helmets were leather, at best. The men swung battle-regulated swords, axes, maces, and flails at one another.

"General Braxon," Sheridan hesitated, "do you realize your men are using sharpened, battle-ready blades over there?"

Braxon stopped dead in his tracks. He turned on his heels and squatted to eye-level with the dwarf, glaring at him with solid cobalt irises.

"Master Sheridan," he general spoke softly, "what better way to maintain a battle-ready attitude than by risking their necks during their daily exercises? Death awaits around every corner. Simple rods made of timber may exercise the movements and footing, but only a real blade will teach them the pain if they fuck up." He smiled revoltingly. "Maybe you should try it with your City Watch children."

Children. Not men.

Sheridan heard the spite loud and clear.

"Now that I can monitor my men's progress," Braxon stood back up, crossed his hands behind his back, and slowly paced around each training exercise, "what is it you so urgently needed to discuss?"

Sheridan sighed, unsure of how to word what he wanted to say without a direct report leading the king to remove his head. "My office has reason to believe the king has been conducting unsanctioned spending on his military forces. The king himself is... indisposed at the moment and cannot provide me what I am looking for."

"Chin up, soldier," Braxon ordered one of his men at the archery range. "Your eyes are not straight if your chin is to the ground." Addressing Sheridan's suspicions, he replied, "Hypothetically, if said unsanctioned spending *was* occurring, why does your 'office' care to know? Not your jurisdiction," he turned and smirked sarcastically, "with all due respect."

'With all due respect,' my ass. Sheridan replied, "Two reasons—for one, a situation has arisen with which those expenses need an explanation, or it may cost valuable lives; for another, you are listed as a co-signer on the accounts, meaning you are held partially responsible for the whereabouts of the funds."

Braxon, much to Sheridan's surprise, appeared perplexed. "You have seen the accounts?" Sheridan nodded confidently. "I can assure you those expenses are King Typhus's."

"Quick to throw the king under the wagon when your own paychecks are benefitting from the expenses," Sheridan bluffed, challenging the general. He was not able to view the military account statements to verify what Braxon's weekly pay rate was, but Braxon's guilty expression may have confirmed it.

"I do as King Typhus commands," Braxon shook off his guilt and shrugged his broad shoulders. "If that means being ordered to accept a higher grade of pay, then so be it."

Smug bastard, Sheridan scowled. "Do you know where that influx of money was coming from?"

"No, and I never asked." *No, and I don't care,* Sheridan understood.

"The money is being funneled into five separate military accounts," Sheridan continued. "Can you explain to me what the five accounts are and how and where the money is divided once in those accounts?"

"Hmm, strange," Braxon stopped his pacing and responded with that guileful grin, "I could have sworn you said you've seen the accounts. Why is it I must explain to you what they are? You are a smart man. Can you not figure it out?"

Shit. Braxon caught his bluff. Sheridan blew it off. "Please, General Braxon. I'm not here to play games. I'm only looking for harmless information."

"Harmless?"

"You said it yourself—it's not my jurisdiction. Even if I knew where every copper coin was spent in the military, I have no control to stop or change it."

"Then the information you seek is redundant," Braxon snapped.

"My greatest apologies, Master Sheridan, I respect you for your position within our kingdom—I must admit I could not hold responsibility for all seven regions and their multi-million civilians—but I do not like you, I do not like *dwarves*, and I do not like how intrusive you are being into the affairs of a department you have less than zero influence over. If you have nothing else to say, I must bid you exit my military camp and be received at the gate."

As Braxon began walking away, flustered, Sheridan shouted, "It's Princess Lia!"

Braxon halted in his tracks, his shoulders sagging as he, once more, faced the dwarf. His stern face unmoving. Only a slight dip of his square-off chin announced that he would listen some more.

"It's Princess Lia," Sheridan repeated calmly. "That money was borrowed from High Alta. And now, High Alta is demanding full repayment immediately or they are taking Lia and arranging a marriage with their prince. I can stall them, but only for so long." Sheridan got closer to the general and whispered, "The only other option I can hope for is to explain where the money went and that the king was not in his right state of mind when it was borrowed and spent. But if I tell them two hundred and forty *million* gold was spent entirely on Havyn's military..."

"It would paint a target on our back," Braxon finished, nodding his understanding. "I see the issue. My only concern with your statement is your accusation that King Typhus was not in his right state of mind. What do you mean by that?"

Sheridan squinted, staring at the general curiously. Had he truly no idea of the king's illness? "How often do you meet with the king?"

Braxon shrugged, "It varies. At one point he was stopping by here on a biweekly basis. Now, every other month or so."

"When did you last speak with him directly?" Sheridan asked.

"About six months ago," Braxon confirmed.

"Are you not worried you haven't seen him in that long of a time?" Sheridan challenged.

"Master," Braxon explained, "I do not dwell heavily on King Typhus's affairs. I come here each morning, do my job, and go home each evening."

"The king's mind is not always reliable to make important decisions." Sheridan would likely lose his head if he kept giving Braxon more information to use against Typhus, but he was beginning to feel desperate. "Lately, pieces of himself have begun to fade away. The increased military spending is only one of many questionable cases."

"Perhaps I am not in King Typhus's presence enough to see the difference," the general said, "but each time he has visited here, his mind was sharp. His orders were clear, and his intentions seemed sound."

The king had occasional moments of clarity, that much even Sheridan could confirm. Those moments were growing shorter and further spread apart as time passed, though. Was it possible the king was aware of his illness during his clarity and he took advantage of that time to come speak with his military general?

It made sense to Sheridan. What still did not make sense, though, was why the king, during his moments of clarity, found it wise to borrow that much godsdamned gold and leave them vulnerable like this.

Why set them up for failure and risk warfare by building up the military to a threatening level?

Sheridan was keen enough to notice just how many newer recruits the military had. More soldiers meant more supplies, armor, weapons, and salaries. What else had increased abundantly?

"If Princess Lia is at risk," Braxon continued reluctantly, "then perhaps I can share what little knowledge I *do* possess on this matter." Sheridan almost jumped out of his boots with excitement. Braxon sighed, "I know for a fact at least one of the accounts funds King Typhus's espionage contacts. Handfuls of individuals unknown to myself or to one another—only King Typhus—tasked with infiltrating daily life in the other kingdoms and sending correspondence of various knowledge back to the king."

Spies? Why in the world would Typhus be spying on the other kingdoms?

If the four other kingdoms ever discovered this bit of information, Havyn was doomed. High Alta already has a bone to pick with Havyn. High King Eriputes would take Havyn by force, finding any loophole in the Concordat to do so, if he was tempted enough.

The Greys of Fairmarq were friendlier with Havyn.

Ever since King Henree Grey's daughter went missing, presumably kidnapped, as an infant eighteen years ago, Fairmarq had shut the door on inter-kingdom relations with any others besides Havyn, thanks to

Fairmarq's prior relationship with Sheridan. Henree Grey's accusatory paranoia had not boded well for his kingdom's "friendliness" with the others, especially High Alta.

Nest Aiken, Havyn's next-closest neighbor, never associated with Havyn too often. At least, not while Sheridan has been in office. Nest Aiken had its own problems to deal with, having recently put down a peasant revolt a few years prior. They still had not corrected their class issues since that event.

Finally, there was the Kingdom of Seramyth on the south coast. Seramyth remained neutral in most affairs and never had any reason to challenge another kingdom, until more recently. Whether Typhus was mad or not, he was still an asshole. Shortly after the plague tore through the very foundation of the Estera region of Havyn and rotted it to its core, the plague appeared in Seramyth. Having defeated the plague, by the skin of her teeth, Havyn was asked for assistance by Seramyth, whom received a horrific laugh in the face by Typhus and was left to deteriorate the way Estera had.

That was five years ago. Sheridan doubted Seramyth would be strong enough to raise up arms against Havyn, but with the threat of spies in their midst, it could be just the motivation they need.

"One other thing," Braxon said, lowering his voice to a dull hum. "King Typhus kept a small black notebook with him during each visit to the barracks. He would scribble notes as I would update him on my progress. Any information I cannot provide will likely be found there."

"Why are you telling me all of this?" Sheridan asked. *Two minutes ago, you wouldn't have cared if I lived or died, and now you are telling all the gossip.*

"Because, Master Sheridan, Princess Lia is the last remnant of the Casalvania dynasty. If anything happened to her, I would have the displeasure of taking orders from you." He raised a brow and quipped, "We wouldn't want that, now, would we?"

"Will you tell the king I was here?"

Braxon loosed a huff of air from his nostrils, considering. "If he does not ask, I will not tell."

The Master of Cities gave the general an affirming grin and a nod before heading back to the gate. Upon his approach, a watcher atop the wall shouted a command and Sheridan could hear the heavy deadbolts of the passage door. The door swung inwards gently, and he re-entered the city.

Lost in thought, deciding what his next move should be, Sheridan walked back in the direction of the Spire of the New King.

He had a choice to make that evening. In the morning, Prince Salmeides would arrive at the Spire demanding his money, or his new sister-in-law. Sheridan could find the prince and try to buy more time, or explain what information he had, and appear more vulnerable to High Alta. Or, Sheridan could find Typhus's little black notebook and see if he could find clearer answers to prove to the prince that Typhus needed to be deposed. With Sal's support, they could sway High King Eriputes's decision at the next Court of Kings without seeming like traitors.

Problems existed with the latter decision. What if he could not find the black notebook by morning? What if he found it and there was nothing there to prove his point? Worst yet, what if General Braxon was lying about all of this and no such notebook even exists?

The king had allies in Havyn, as he should, considering his illness was not yet public knowledge. Sheridan was always careful to watch his step, but after his conversations with President Aroy and General Braxon, his intentions began to seem selfish and sinister.

CHAPTER 17

"You're fucking kidding me, right?" Damian repeated.

Ena shamefully hoisted the thin sheets up to her collar, covering her exposed body. "Damian, I can explain."

Damian stomped into the tiny room. "What in the gods' names did you do last night? You left us here unaware if you lived or died after your encounter with that damned dwarf. Then, after finally getting back, you *fuck* this traitor?" He pointed an accusatory finger at Drake. He sniffed the air. "*And* you smell like a godsdamned distillery."

Now Ena was getting annoyed. She snapped, "That's *enough,* Damian! Shut the door, let me get dressed, and I will explain."

Damian clenched his fists, standing his ground. Then, as if realizing who he was reprimanding, he turned and slammed the door shut with a thud. They were lucky the door didn't rip from its hinges.

Silent for a moment, Ena thought carefully how she was going to explain the situation. Ultimately, she would have to tell Damian and Klaus the truth—she was upset, got drunk, and slept with Drake out of... what, desperation? Lust? Loneliness? She had no idea.

She also did not want to admit that the young farmer was actually growing on her. Getting close to people, lowering her guard, was not a personality trait of hers.

Ena stood from the bed and scooped her clothes from the floor. Drake stood up behind her and kissed the back of her neck as she struggled to pull her inside-out pantlegs through their proper holes. "Now's not the best time, Drake."

"Sorry," he said, picking up his own clothes. "Just admiring you while I can. I don't think this will be happening much anymore..."

"You are probably correct," Ena pulled the black trousers on and tied them. She pulled the tunic over her head and took a deep breath.

She gently wrapped her fingers around the door handle, ready to face the music. Seeing Drake fully dressed, she turned the handle.

She stopped, thinking for a moment, "Actually, no." The door whipped open, and she strode up to Damian and Klaus, who were standing in the narrow hallway. She stepped up to Damian and shoved him harshly into the door to his room behind him. His back hit the wood hard. "You son of a bitch. Who do you think you are talking to me like that?"

She didn't give him a chance to speak before her fist collided with his jaw. Not hard enough to do any serious damage or break any teeth, but enough to startle him.

"I am not obligated to explain any of my actions to you!" she continued. "*You* work for *me*. Every piece of gold, silver, and copper that has fed you for the past three years was from *me*." Klaus leaned in to speak. Ena shot him a sharp glance, "Don't you speak, Klaus." Klaus closed his mouth and backed off. Ena returned to Damian. "I can sleep with whoever I want. I am an adult woman. I am the governess of an entire fucking city. I think I can make big girl choices on my own."

Damian only looked down at Ena. The governess was not a tall woman—Damian towered over her by a whole head. What she lacked in height, she made up for in courage and intimidation.

She could kill with a look.

And that look was locked in on Damian.

Having been the governess's personal guard for the past three years, Damian knew her well enough to not fuck with her when she had that deadly glare. He realized he had overstepped.

"I... I'm sorry, Governess," Damian stammered, shamefully. His voice was hardly more than a grumbling whisper. "You haven't been yourself since the farmer came around. This is not behavior I have ever witnessed from you. My challenging tone came from a place of concern, that is all."

Words that were meant to ease her only frustrated her. "The *farmer* is named Drake. He is also an adult man who made an adult decision last night. Not like I should be required to explain, but that *monstrous* dwarf forced me to take an innocent life." She fought to hold back tears. "So, yes, I had a few drinks. Yes, I took the edge off by having sex with

Drake. *Forgive me* for being human for once in my godsdamned life."

Ena rolled her eyes as she turned to leave. As she headed for the stairs, Klaus said, "Wait, Governess, where are you going?"

She whipped around, "I am going to perform my next task for that murderer. Alone. The three of you are going to stay here and get to know one another. That is an order!" She locked her green eyes on Damian once more. "Drake is one of us now. He is not going anywhere."

Ena descended the creaky steps. Steam shot from her ears as she flew out the front door of the inn. She blended with the busy traffic on the street and angrily stomped on for over a mile before she realized she had no clue where the hell she was going.

Stopping and pulling out the map from her pocket, she searched for the address that the Lord of Steel had given her. She spotted the road deep within the heart of the lower district.

Great, she rolled her eyes. Predicting another all-out brawl to erupt, she made sure her dagger was handy. *Shit! My daggers!* In her flustered exit from *Dragonfly & the Fruit*, she completely forgot to strap the harnesses around her thighs and back.

She was weaponless.

How could she be so foolish?

Begrudgingly, she debated going back to get the daggers but ultimately decided against it. She was equally skilled in hand-to-hand combat as she was with any weapon. Though, that may not prove true if her next destination became too dangerous for her to handle.

This must have been how Drake felt all this time without protection. *I owe him an apology,* Ena decided.

Playing it half-safe, Ena continued on. Once she got to the address, she would decide from there. If it seemed risky, she could always come back and get the daggers. The Lord of Steel had never given her a deadline, so she had some time to waste. Or she could purchase a new blade from a blacksmith. There were sure to be weapons dealers in that area of the city...

After all, this was a stealth mission. The letter from the dwarf demanded that she steal back whatever was stolen from him, but leave the perpetrator alive. This would be a quiet and easy, in-and-out mission, she hoped.

She descended into the western section of the city. Graffiti decorated the sides of the buildings with intricate designs of mandala, nature, and beautiful men and women. Ena admired the artists' styles and skills. She was not gifted in the arts, though she never had the free time to develop that talent.

These people were free. They had no responsibilities and no one to prevent them from using the blank canvases that were the walls of homes, inns, and restaurants as their creative spaces.

Ena met the intersection of a city square, streets expanding like a spider's web from its center. A tall church, serving as a white mage healing center, stood high in the middle of the square. Its large canvas filled by an artist's depiction of a woman, naked and free, sitting with her legs widely spread, and a mandala flower blooming between them.

Though not exactly appropriate for a public square, especially one with children running after one another playing tag, but Ena was impressed. Whoever the woman was in the painting, she was beautiful with cherry-red hair swallowing her shoulders and bright pink lips exposing pearly white teeth. Timidly, Ena observed the mandala flower with fifty different shades of pink and red erupting from the center.

However the muse felt about her sexuality reminded Ena of how Drake made her feel last night—liberated and boundless. She blushed thinking about the night before. Exhilarating. Refreshing. Enlightening.

Ena pulled her attention from the naked model on the wall and back to her map. She quickly identified the square she now stood in. About two streets away, Ena would find her destination.

As she made her way down the wide road, a familiar earthy smell wafted ferociously in the air. The governess knew that smell...

Euphorasia.

On the right side of the road, in a two-story, windowless slate building, plumes of smoke billowed from a narrow rectangular doorway. Not smoke from a fire. The dull thumping of music echoed from within.

Ena checked the address of the building, which matched exactly with the one on her letter.

Hesitantly, Ena padded to the open door, ducking under the billow of smoke sluggishly wrapping itself over the top of the jamb.

The smell grew stronger with each step into the dark chamber. The music sounding more prominently. The bass of the drum vibrating

Ena's core in steady, measured beats.

The passageway opened into a single room. A circular bar set in the center stacked with hundreds of liquor bottles on the tiered counter in its center. Red lanterns hung from the walls and ceilings, evenly spaced apart, giving off just barely enough light to see, but also more than enough to create an erotic atmosphere.

This was a strip club.

Women wearing nothing but strings with small cloths barely covering their breasts and genitalia danced amorously on stages for the viewers who sat in the plush, leather chairs. The stages were set up in the corners of the room, while other tables and leather chairs were displayed in the interior closer to the bar. Several men, and even one woman, were getting private dances in those single seats.

Smoke plumed throughout the room as waitresses dressed in similarly revealing outfits delivered drinks and waterpipes to the various tables.

This place is a godsdamned euphorasia den!

Ena observed the room carefully. Why in the gods' names would the dwarf send her here?

Suddenly, as she stepped into the room for a closer look, she spied a man behind the bar. The man was pouring a drink as he glanced up, seeing Ena standing near the entrance.

The same emerald-eyed man from the auction smirked as he finished pouring the drink, handing it off to one of his nearly-nude waitresses. He crossed his arms, maintaining an intimidating grin as Ena met him at the bar.

She pulled up a bar stool and said nothing. She only matched his smile with her skeptically narrowed eyes.

"It's about time you showed," the man broke the silence. He flashed his emerald-green eyes and grabbed a rag to wipe off the bar in front of the governess. "What'll it be? You seem like a gin and tonic kind of girl. Maybe a hit or two of some euph."

"Who are you?" Ena asked, not breaking eye contact with the man.

The man braced himself against the bar with bare, muscled arms. He leaned in and asked softly, "Question is, who are *you?*" *Why were you at the auction that night?* Ena knew he meant.

"What is this place?" Ena quickly scanned the room again, observing a man with a poorly hidden hard-on running his callused hands up and down a gorgeous brunette's body dancing for him.

"Welcome to the *Espasia,*" the man said sincerely. "Exotic bar and euphorasia den. The only legal one in all of Havyn."

"And what makes this place so special that it remains the only legal one?"

He crossed his toned forearms again. "Tell me your name and I'll tell you anything you would like to know." His voice was uncomfortably comfortable. Ena was haunted by this man's face since that first night in the lower district. She had not expected him to speak so soothingly.

Ena hesitated. "I am Kate."

The man waited a moment, expecting Ena to say more. When she didn't, he blinked and said, "Uh, okay. It's a pleasure to meet you, Kate. I'm Rune, the owner of this fine establishment." Seeing her grimace at what he considered "fine," he continued, "This kind of entertainment can take some getting used to, understandably. Though, I must ask, is your form of entertainment spying on a secret, illegal black market auction?"

Shocked by Rune's bold confrontation, Ena stammered, "I-I, uh, I am not sure what you mean."

Rune chuckled, turning to rinse and dry cocktail glasses behind the bar. He placed an ice-filled pint glass on the bar, reached for a bottle of blue liquor, and filled the glass halfway. Juice and another clear liquor from an unlabeled bottle topped it off. He mixed it briefly and slid it down to Ena.

Catching it with her palm, she asked, "What's in this?"

"Trust me," he tilted his head, "you need it. Besides, it will take the edge off of the contact high you'll likely get from hanging around in here." He noted the clouds of secondhand euphorasia smoke hanging just above their heads.

Ena sipped it. Very sweet, but liquor-heavy.

"You are not one to speak of legality," Ena mustered. "You own a supposedly legal drug den and attended that illegal auction yourself."

"Damn right," Rune laughed, "but I got myself a nice sword out of it." He stood to the side, sticking out his hip. The Aconyte steel sword hung from a leather sword belt, glowing a light magenta color in the red lanterns.

The sword! Was this what the dwarf wanted back? How could it have been stolen if Rune bought it from an open auction?

"The original owner of that sword," Ena treaded carefully, "wants it back. Are you aware of that?" Rune shrugged his muscular shoulders. "Do you have any idea why the owner *would* want it back?" Again, another shrug. "You are not helping me."

"You are not helping me either, Kate," Rune responded. Another waitress came up to the bar, requesting a half-dozen drinks for the table she waited on. Her cobalt eyes turning purple from the lantern hanging above the bar. A tattoo of a serpent wrapped around her arm.

"Help me help you," Ena continued softly. "Then you can help me in return. You know more than you are alluding to."

As he placed the drinks onto the waitresses serving tray, he turned back to Ena. "You are a gorgeous girl. Do you know that?" He smirked maliciously. "Your outfit is not flattering at all, no offense, but your face could steal a man's soul, given the chance. You could work for me and make more money than you dream of."

She rolled her eyes. *Pathetic, misogynistic.* "I cannot imagine your 'fine establishment' brings in enough revenue to afford my salary." Ena took a sip of her admittedly delicious beverage. "I am not cheap, not like these ladies."

That seemed to irk Rune a bit. His solid composure waned when he curled his lips and showed his teeth, as if he was an animal growling at some annoyance.

"First of all," he snarled, "my girls get paid enough to buy them anything they desire. Second, my club brings in no less than twenty thousand gold each and every night. Don't judge it by its appearance or location from the outside, some of the richest fucks in this city sneak their way down to the slums just to have Yasmin over there rub her ass in their faces. One patron dropped twenty-five gold just for a kiss on the cheek the other night."

Ena continued to challenge Rune, throwing him off his tough guy game, "Twenty-five for one kiss? Would one thousand get them a private room upstairs with a girl for an hour?" Prostitution was highly illegal in Havyn after an outbreak of syphilis spread across the kingdom a decade before. Typhus's grandfather was a prude, if no other words could describe him, and the idea of sex work was an abomination in his eyes. Ena always questioned how much a governor or lord could enforce such a law, for she had difficulties of her own in El Vadora with women in that field of work.

Even if Rune somehow got away with the euphorasia burning throughout the room, he could face serious charges for running a prostitution ring.

Rune made no comment. He only narrowed his eyes, sizing her up. The muscles in his squared jaw clenched. "You said the original owner of this sword wants it back. Are you working for him?"

Ena leaned back, smiling from one corner of her mouth. "I never said the owner was a male. Tell me what you know. Now."

Rune placed a hand gently on the hilt of the sword at his side. "Tell me if you're working for him first." If she was, then she would not make it two steps before he severed her head off, Ena realized.

"I would not say working *for* him, exactly," Ena said. "I work for myself. I am helping someone else by working *with* him." She cleared her throat. "That someone is not a friend of his, though."

Rune removed the hand from the sword. That must have been an acceptable enough answer for him to ease the tension; however, he had a weapon and Ena didn't. She had to watch what she said, she reminded herself.

"Sounds like you are in deep," Rune said. "My advice to you, Kate, is get out while you can. I don't know who you are, or what intentions are—I assume they are noble, based on the disgusted look on your face when you walked into a place such as the *Espasia*—but call it quits. Go back to where you came from before you end up like me."

In deep? He suspected she was undercover, exploring the slums of the city, but he had secrets of his own, as well.

"End up like you?" Ena questioned. "You do not belong here?"

"For fifteen years," Rune explained, "I have been helping someone, just as you are. Making friends with the rats that scurry down here. I planned to attend that auction several months ago, hearing that something *big* was going to be on that stage. My euphorasia is supplied through the underground market. I attend those auctions more frequently than I care to admit. But when I saw this sword," he patted the hilt, "I knew it was better off in my hands than in the hands of some of the psychos there.

"By that time, though," he continued, "the someone I worked for died, and I knew there was no way out. No way back to a normal life. I decided to continue what I was hired to do and took the sword for myself."

"For two and a half million gold, though?" Ena expressed her awe at the figure.

"Let's just say that I used to get paid handsomely before my employer passed away. My salary from owning the *Espasia* is also very generous."

Ena thought for a moment. Who was influential enough to keep him employed and paid enough to do this kind of dirty work for over fifteen years? The dedication was uncanny. Ena doubted she could keep up this double-life for that long. Even three months of her time was more than she wanted to promise Lady Raven, but she was too involved to back out now, despite what Rune said.

Wait a minute...

"Rune... Your employer... It was the Lord of Avalon, wasn't it?" Ena inquired softly.

Rune's emerald eyes expanded. "I have kept that secret for fifteen years. How the gods did you figure that out in mere minutes? Unless..." He began to laugh. "No way. You're working for Lady Raven!"

Ena quickly reached out, grabbing Rune by his collar, and pulling his face into hers. "Keep your mouth shut!" she hissed. "What were you doing for the Lord?"

He grunted under the force of her surprising strength, "I was sent to spy on the black market. To ensure it was regulated, or as regulated as a black market can be." He gulped and tried pulling himself away from Ena. She pulled him tighter. "Gods, let me go. What the fuck are *you* doing for Lady Raven?"

Ena eased her grip. Just enough for Rune to yank his collar free. He straightened his shirt out, glaring at her.

Ena sat back. "I'm investigating the death of the Lord. Raven believes it to be foul play. I suspect as much, as well." She met Rune's glare. "It seems our paths were meant to cross eventually."

Rune assessed the room skeptically. Ena followed his gaze, spotting the three-man band playing against the left wall, the dancing women at each corner. She hadn't realized how many others entered the club after her arrival. More than half of the leather chairs were occupied by men and women of all races.

"Why did your investigation lead you to the auction that night?" Rune asked.

Ena restored her attention to his green eyes. "He was poisoned. I was hoping to find the substance at the auction. Perhaps I could have tracked it to see who may have purchased it. Instead, my attention was stolen by that damned sword."

Rune smirked, "And that fucking dwarf was your next lead. Yeah, I get it. When I bought that sword, I inquired about its origin. The auctioneer said 'the Lord of Steel assured more will be delivered.'" He rolled his eyes. "He had people in the audience that night who were supposed to buy the sword."

"Who was he trying to sell it to?"

Rune shrugged, "I never got that far. I suspect, if he is trying to 'legally' distribute weapons throughout the city, that he is building an army. Or a terrorist group. Or *something*, I really don't know, *Kate*. All I know is this—the bid for the sword before mine was nine-hundred thousand gold, and the bids were slowing. The sword was never meant to surpass a million, so I dropped a heavy bid that the auctioneer was obligated to accept and will now increase the opening bid for each new sword the Lord of Steel brings in."

"So," Ena clarified for herself, "you bought the sword for an outrageous price to deter the dwarf from continuing his market here in Gabrenas? That is a strategic move. Unfortunately, I do need to take it back to him. I must continue my investigation, and that is the only way."

Rune sighed, "He is going to find out that you are working for Lady Raven. You'll get yourself killed. Like I said, you're in too deep. Get out while you can."

"Too late for that," a deep voice sounded behind Ena.

The governess whipped around on her barstool. A man dressed in a tight black garb stood from the nearby leather chair, sliding a mask over his nose and mouth. He stepped towards Ena. Dressed exactly like the rogues that accompanied the Lord of Steel the day before, Ena knew he overheard everything.

Fuck.

Three other rogues stood from their seats and began striding over to the bar.

"In the Lord of Steel's best interest," the rogue slithered near her, "your life is now forfeit."

The four rogues stood an equal distance apart, about ten feet of clearance from the bar. They opened their empty palms at their sides. Heat and flame spread from the center of their palms over their fingers. Taking a deep breath, they pulled their elbows back, the flames intensifying in their hands. As they thrusted their hands in front of them, balls of fire hurdled right at Ena and Rune.

CHAPTER 18

Fire mages?! Fear announced itself on Ena's face.

She had only ever seen the aftermath of their destruction. Now, as time slowed, flaming projectiles aiming directly for her head, she would see it in person. These rogues, every single one of them, were mages? The pieces all fit together. Ena noticed from the start that the Lord of Steel's guards were weaponless. She realized now that they were weapons themselves, capable of death and destruction.

Caught like a deer in torchlight, Ena froze.

In the milliseconds before her impending doom, a strong hand gripped the back of her collar sharply and yanked her back. She tumbled backwards over the top of the bar and landed on the ground behind it. Rune braced her as the fireballs struck the bottles stacked in the middle of the bar over their heads. Shattered glass and liquor exploded on them.

Ena covered her head with her hands as glass rained down on her. She shook off the razor-sharp particles and backed herself against the bar.

Heat filled the room as fire struck the side of the bar. Thankfully, the bar was built thick enough to withstand some heavy blows to give her time to think of an escape plan. Being weaponless against four mages, fighting back was not an option.

Screams roared over the sound of fire crackling in the room around them.

Rune shouted, "Fuck! They're attacking everyone in here!"

No witnesses, thought Ena.

Ena and Rune sat with their backs against the bar. The wood against them shuddered with each blast of fire.

"How much longer will this hold up?" Ena asked over the exploding heatwave above them.

"To be very honest, Kate, I've never had the integrity of the bar tested against fire mage attacks," Rune answered sarcastically.

Ena rolled her eyes. She rotated on her knees and attempted to peer over the top of the bar between attacks. She caught a glimpse of the status of the room. Fires burned in all directions. Bodies littered the floor. The living ones cowered in corners. The plush, carpeted floors singed black. Smoke filling the void of the club.

The profound smell of lavender overcame the smell of burning flesh, carpet, and leather. All of the euphorasia was burning profusely. Ena felt her head beginning to spin.

One of the mages caught her spying on their actions from behind the bar. Together, all four mages turned towards her and directed one massive ball of flame right at the bar.

She ducked back down at the last second. Just before hearing the wood around them begin to splinter under the force of the inferno.

"Come on out, girl!" demanded one of the mages. "The lives lost today are on *your* head. Come with us and the rest will be spared."

He's lying, Ena knew, but she had no other way out. The only exit was through the door she entered from, which was guarded by the four catastrophic power sources standing in her way.

"Rune," she said. He turned to her. "Let me see the sword. I might be able to fight them off."

He shook his head. "Yeah, that's not happening."

"Then you go out there and kill them!" Ena hissed.

Rune shook his head again.

Another blast of fire sent chunks of wood flying overhead.

"We must act offensively or else we are going to die here," Ena said sternly. "I would much rather die fighting than cowering behind a fucking bar!"

"Damnit, Kate!" Rune spat. "What can we do?"

Before she could answer, the wooden planks behind them shattered. Yellow and orange flames licked Ena as the force of the explosion sent her flying. She was thrown to the ground ten feet away.

Her ears rang and her vision spotted as she lifted herself onto her hands and knees. Sharp pain shot through her hands up her arms. As her vision cleared, blood was spattered on the floor beneath her.

The blood was hers, she realized.

She managed to put her weight onto her knees enough to lift her arms and inspect them. Large splinters of glass and wood speckled the bare skin on her arms and her palms, blood slowly draining from the countless wounds.

The sleeves of her tunic were burned off completely. Whatever flesh that wasn't bleeding from protruding chunks of debris was pink from fresh burns.

Ena quickly inspected the rest of her body. Plenty of cuts, bruises, and burns. Plenty of torn fabric, singed cloth, and blood stains. But the rest of her was intact.

For now.

The ringing subsided and the sound of a roaring fire filled her ears. Someone behind her yelled what sounded like a battlecry. She turned.

Rune, also covered in various lacerations and burns, rose from the floor, using the Aconyte sword as a crutch. Seeing the destruction of his club enraged him. Feebly, he carried the sword towards the mages and began swinging.

They dodged every attack, clearly playing with him. Rune was too injured to use all of his might.

Ena could hear the mages laughing as one of them said, "Just end this already."

No, Rune! She couldn't scream out loud.

Two of the mages rounded up a massive wall of flames. Rune turned away from the mage he targeted in time to witness the flames collide with him. His entire body enveloped with fire as he spun around, attempting uselessly to pat out the flames, a blood-curdling scream escaping from him. The sword flew from his hands between Ena and himself.

Within seconds, he was on the floor. Dead.

The flames extinguished themselves.

"No!" Ena found her voice again.

She gained a sudden burst of adrenaline and jumped to her feet. She ran to the sword and swept it off the floor. She dodged two carefully calculated fire blasts and launched herself behind an overturned table.

The table would not hold up against one of those blasts, but it gave Ena a split moment to gather her surroundings. Two of the mages stood near the bar that no longer existed, where Rune's lifeless body rested. The other two stood further away, closer to the entrance.

That was her escape route. If she could manage to stand up against the two of them, then she would run until her feet fell off.

She took a deep breath, held it for a second or two, and exhaled. She felt the heat and heard the roar of the approaching fire and rolled out from behind the table. The blast connected with the table and sent it across the room, the residual heat suffocating Ena.

She choked on the smoke and euphorasia that filled the air and sprinted at the two mages by the exit, the Aconyte sword held at her side. Ena was surprised at how balanced the sword was. How easily maneuverable.

The two mages spotted her and began shooting fire in her direction. She dodged the first blast by strafing to the right, her face heating up as the flame shot by. Then she dodged to the left, the Aconyte blade slicing through the center of the fireball, causing the flame to disperse.

As she got up close, the mages formed fire around their knuckles as they bunched their hands into fists. They swung their fists at her, wide blasts of fire swelling in front of them. The fire punches burned out swiftly, but Ena could feel their power as she jumped out of the way.

She somersaulted under one of the mage's fire punches before uppercutting with the sword, lobbing one hand off of the nearest mage. The hand dropped to the floor with a thump and the mage cried out in pain, doubling over, as Ena flipped the sword, gripping it with both hands, and driving the blade downwards through the mage's back and out his stomach.

The other mage threw several fire punches, at which Ena protected herself by holding up the dying body of the mage with her blade still through his abdomen. The meat shield painfully absorbed the blows, the black tunic evaporating and his flesh festering with blisters and blood.

She dropped the dead body to the floor, sliding off of the blood-stained blade.

Though, Ena was not paying attention to the two other mages near Rune's body. Fire balls bounded for the governess with her back turned. She hardly noticed as one blaze flew past her legs and the other skimmed her side as she turned towards the source.

"Shit!" Ena screamed as she hurdled back, stumbling over her own feet and falling onto her back. Ena withheld gruesome cries of agony. Feeling the fresh, open wound consuming her side from ribs to hips, she winced, tears rolling down her cheeks. The tears quickly evaporated in the heat of the raging inferno engulfing the club. Ena withdrew her hand from her side, blood coating her fingers.

Vaguely, Ena could make out the heavy footsteps of the mage by the exit approaching. She lifted her head just enough to see him about to stand over her, a thick blanket of flame dancing in his hand.

Ena anxiously looked around. She dropped the sword mere inches from her hand on her burnt side. She extended her arm, her bloody fingers brushing the hot metallic hilt of the Aconyte steel. Pain reverberated through her, from her fingers to her toes, with every beat of her quickening heart. Her side screamed at her to cease her movement as she rolled to her right, gripping the hilt.

The mage standing over her grunted with anger as he drew back his arm, drawing power into his killing blow. He thrusted his open, flame-covered palm at Ena.

Ena quickly forced the point of the blade into the center of the flames aimed for her face. With a cry of shock and anguish, the flame in the mage's palm faded to smoke. The blade piercing through the middle of his hand.

Ena ripped the sword from his hand, slicing clean between the knuckles of his middle and ring fingers. The mage dropped to his knees, holding his injured hand in front of him with his good one. Shock overcame him as he hyperventilated at the sight of his hand nearly sliced in half down the middle.

Ena leaped to her feet, despite her body urging otherwise. She limped next to the mage, leaning down as she drove the blade through his heart and out of his back between his shoulders. With a low gurgle, the mage drifted to the floor in a pool of blood.

The two other mages saw the scene and charged at Ena. She had a choice—fight or flight.

She chose flight.

With the exit right down the hallway, Ena sprinted out the front door and across the street. She looked back for a split second to observe the smoke and flames spitting from cracks forming in the walls due to extreme heat.

Before waiting to see the mages fly from the doorway chasing after her, she took off down the street.

Bystanders watched as the club fire grew more intense. City Watch guards with hoses pushed back the gathering crowd, attempting aimlessly to fight the fire. The club was a lost cause.

People in the streets cried out and gasped as Ena flew past them, covered in blood and burns, carrying a sword, and barely clothed from all that had burned away.

Her lungs seared with each breath and her head spun; though, Ena was unsure if the dizziness was from exhaustion, smoke inhalation, or from the euphorasia high she no doubt had.

I need help, thought the governess. *I need help. I need help. I need help.*

All thoughts and reason turned into animalistic instincts. Right now, that instinct was telling her to run. So, run she did.

Suddenly, two City Watch guards caught her arms. Ena thrashed to get out of their grip. The guards held tighter until she was unmoving. "Hey, you're alright, girl." The soothing voice of the guard relaxed her enough to regain some sense. Feeling her tension ease, the guards released Ena. "You came from that fire a few blocks over? Civilians reported a girl running away from the fire with wounds all over her body. You seem to match the profile."

Ena stood uncomfortably. "Yes. I-I think I need medical attention."

"Of course," the other guard said. "We'll escort you to the white mage temple nearby."

They each hooked an arm around Ena's, bracing her, and walked her around the corner to the huge church in the center of the square. That blooming mandala flower embracing the noontime sun. Something about it comforted Ena in her agony.

White mages approached as they rounded to the church's open front door, the archway high above Ena's head. The guards handed her off. One of the white mages, a young woman, braced Ena and helped walk her into the church, nodding their appreciation to the guards.

Ena was placed in a sterilized medical bed while a group of mages gathered around and began cutting her clothing off with shears. The fabric, caught in her open wounds, stung horribly as her clothing was peeled off of her. Holding back the urge to yell, she gritted her teeth hard enough that they could have shattered.

"I have good news and bad news, sweetie." The young woman gently rested a hand on her shoulder. "The good news is that most of your injuries are mild—the burns are only first degree, and the cuts are not too deep. The bad news is that the treatment will be painful."

Ena managed a nod in acknowledgement.

As she lay there, exposed, one mage worked on one arm, another mage on the other. A third mage treated the massive burn on her right side while a fourth inspected the remainder of her body for minor cuts and bruises.

The young woman, surprisingly, stood at the head of the bed with her hands on either side of Ena's temples.

The magic of the white mages always fascinated her. Using the magic of light and raw energy, they could heal almost any injury. Though, in recent generations, practical medicine has accompanied the white mage curriculum in their healing practices. No medicine was a perfect substitute for a powerful white mage, but with a shortage of white mages in many cities, medicine was a temporary alternative.

The wonders the mage performed at Ena's head were nothing she had ever experienced before.

Pure white light emanated from the young woman's hands, glowing in Ena's peripherals. The mage circled her palms around Ena's temples and a blissful wave washed over her, easing the pain and calming her occupied mind.

The mage said, "This will help with the pain and protect your mind from any trauma."

Visibly noticeable, Ena's pain began subsiding. That is, until the other mages started removing shards of glass, splinters of wood, and shreds of melted and charred cloth from her wounds.

Her back arched and her muscles strained, resisting a distressed wail. The veins in her neck protruded from under her skin and her face turned crimson.

"Easy," the mage urged. "Do not hold back. Expression is part of the pain recovery process. This will take a few hours. Scream if you need to."

Ena let out a shriek and her lungs struggled to take in a deep breath. She swore she was suffocating. *A few hours?!* Unbelievable. The treatment was worse than the wounds.

"My sword..." Ena called out. She still had the sword when the guards brought her here. One of the mages must have taken it from her.

"No need to worry," the mage insisted. "Any possessions that were not damaged are in a safe place."

◆◆◆◆◆◆◆◆◆

Six hours later, the mages finally finished healing the majority of Ena's injuries.

"You will ache for a few days," the young mage spoke. The four others washed their hands and gathered new clothing for her—a simple white tunic and pants. The mage helped Ena sit up at the end of the bed. Pointing to the healed wounds, she said, "Your arms are almost good as new. Only a couple spots were deep enough to have scarred. The burn on your right side is gone."

"Thank you," Ena said. "I am grateful for your help."

The mage gathered the clothing from her colleagues and returned to Ena. "No need for thanks. It is our sworn duty to the All-Seeing God to heal every injured body and mind." She assisted Ena off the edge of the bed and helped her dress. "The guards said you came from that fire. No one else survived. If someone attacked you, let the guards out front know and they will escort you home."

Ena buckled a belt around her loose pants. Another mage carried the Aconyte sword to her. She tucked the blade into her belt. It would do, for now, without a proper sword belt.

"That's it?" Ena asked as the mage turned away. "I expected more of an interrogation."

The mage looked back at her. "Make no mistake, my curiosity is at its peak. But it does not matter who you are, where you came from, or why you were attacked. All that matters is that we heal you." She turned to walk away again, calling over her shoulder. "Take it easy out there."

Ena collected herself and walked to the front door, now shut. Her legs wobbled uncomfortably. She had been limping when the guards found her. Her body was adjusting to her healed wounds. Taking a moment to balance herself, she pushed open the front door a crack, just enough to slip through.

The two guards who brought her here waited. They asked if she needed an escort.

Ena surveyed the square. People were making their ways back home as the sun descended behind the horizon.

Nightfall was here and those rogues would be wearing all black. Ena's eyes were sharp, but her brain was still rattled from her fight six hours ago, and the euphorasia still working its way out of her body. Even with the sword at her side, she rubbed her thumb on the steel, could she fight them off again? By now, they had the chance to return to the Lord of Steel and inform them of her actions. By now, the Lord of Steel would have contingents of mages roaming the dark streets waiting for her.

She nodded slowly to the guards.

The Lord of Steel was smart. Smart enough to not risk openly attacking City Watch guards and provoking an all-out war between the guards and the mages, or the city and the black market, or whatever else the dwarf was affiliated with.

The guards walked alongside as she followed her memory back to *Dragonfly & the Fruit*. They asked her some questions along the way—why she was at the club, who started the fire, what exactly happened—and she remained silent. After getting lost once or twice, the guards finally asked her where she was staying. Reluctantly, she told them.

They knew exactly where the inn was, and by the end of the hour, she could see the lanterns with the *Dragonfly & the Fruit* sign glowing at the end of the road. Half a block from the inn, she turned to the guards. "Thank you for all your help today. I will be safe from here."

"Are you certain?" one of them asked.

Ena nodded. "I will be fine."

The guards waited a moment as Ena padded quietly towards the inn on the deadly-quiet street. Ena could not express her gratitude enough, but it was best that they did not learn who she was. After making it halfway between the guards and the inn, she noticed them turn to leave. They helped save a life today. They would sleep soundly knowing they did a good deed.

As Ena stepped into the torchlight, she noticed someone standing against the wall by the door to the inn. That someone pushed off the wall on her approach and stepped forwards.

A courier? Not just any courier, Ena realized. It was the courier who had taken her message from the post office to Lady Raven. *A message from Raven,* Ena hoped.

The courier took two letters from his inside coat pocket. "Miss Kate, these are for you."

Ena met him at the top of the steps in front of the inn. She cracked the seal on the first letter, the seal of Avalon. *Raven.*

She opened the letter and read her brief reply.

Kate –

The Lord of Steel? I will look into it.

– Raven

Ena rolled her eyes. Not exactly the response she was hoping for.

The second letter was unsealed, folded into thirds. "Who is this from?" Ena asked skeptically. If it wasn't from Raven, then that meant someone knew where to find her…

The courier didn't reply. He only waited.

Ena opened the letter and almost dropped it out of shock.

Your name is Kate, is it? Representative Kate from Lothol, perhaps? A shame that Kate from Lothol doesn't exist and is the cover name for Governess Athenia of El Vadora. Surprised? I would be. My resources are limitless, Athenia. There is one thing I hate more than both murderers and thieves. Traitors. And you, Athenia, have betrayed me. I know about you and your men. I know who you work for. And I know how you are going to die. Slowly, painfully, and alone. You have my sword, and I want it back. You have a chance to save your allies. Return the sword to me, and your friends will live to see another day and your city will remain unburned. Steal from me, and you will die as both a thief and a traitor with your people's blood on your hands.

Meet me tomorrow at sunset. Come alone and come with the fucking sword.

– Lord of Steel

P.S. Traitors often travel in pairs. I wouldn't want you to be alone on your last night alive and free.

An address was scribbled across the bottom of the page. Traitors often travel in pairs? What did that mean?

The courier cleared his throat and pushed a box in front of her. Ena looked at the box and back to the courier.

"I'm sorry, miss," the courier began to cry. "They made me bring it to you. They have spies all over the city. Caught me with the letter as soon as I left to deliver it."

Ena crouched down and cracked the top of the wooden box. A putrid smell wafted in the air from inside. She carefully peeled back the top.

Ena gasped, covering her mouth with her hands. *What the fuck...*

Rune's severed head gazed up at her from inside the box. His head was burned and blistered, and *TRAITOR* was carved into his forehead. His eyes were hollow and grey. Full of death.

Ena slammed the top of the box shut. Horror filled her.

What kind of monster would do this?

The courier kept apologizing. Ena ignored him as she forced herself to take deep breaths.

"Where in the Connections have you been?" She knew that voice. Damian.

Over her shoulder, Ena saw Damian, Klaus, and Drake come into the light. They had no clue what just transpired, but seeing the disturbed look on Ena's face, they ran to her side.

Klaus looked inside the box. "Who *was* that..."

Ena could not find the words to explain.

Drake spoke, "And what are you wearing? That's not what you left with."

Klaus handed the box back to the courier and demanded that he leave and dispose of its contents. The courier, clearly clueless as to how the hell he was going to do that, stammered to himself as he trudged away into the darkness.

Ena finally said, "Get upstairs, now. We are in trouble."

CHAPTER 19

"Master of Cities," Prince Sal of High Alta spoke, "to what do I owe the pleasure?"

Prince Sal never went anywhere in public without his gleaming gold armor. Even at a bar in the upper district of Havana City. Was the prince cautious enough that he felt a need to wear armor wherever he went, or was he arrogant enough to show himself off? Sheridan was certain it was the latter.

This bar was one of the most prestigious in all of Havyn. It was referred to as a bistro to make it appeal more to wealthy folks. It was precisely where Prince Sal spent most of his afternoons and nights during his week in Hayvn, all at the expense of the kingdom.

Barmaids sat on his lap, one on each leg, as he stuffed his face between their breasts. One of the barmaids, a blonde, ran her painted fingernails through the prince's silver hair. He leaned into the other barmaid's ear, a ginger, and whispered something that made her giggle as she squeezed him tighter.

"I'm sure your wife would love to see this," Sheridan said precariously, crossing his arms.

The prince pulled his tongue off of the woman's neck. "If you are here to threaten me, Master Sheridan, you may escort yourself out. I am enjoying my brief vacation away from home."

"I bet you are," Sheridan pulled up a chair to the prince's table and sat across from him. "All while your wife takes care of a newborn baby girl, so I hear. Congratulations."

The prince sighed heavily and smacked the girls on their asses. "Alright ladies, we can continue this later." The barmaids pouted but obeyed. As the prince watched them walk away, hips swaying, he repeated, "To what do I owe the pleasure?"

Sheridan studied the interior of the bistro. Safe to say he never set foot inside before. The hardwood floors were stained an expensive sienna. Every chair and table crafted from the finest maple wood and upholstered with a material known as lion's pelt; though, Sheridan doubted they were made with actual lions. Lions did not exist in this area of the world. The bar in the back of the bistro spanned the length of the entire wall, some fifty feet, and five bartenders mixed drinks from the bottles of liquor stacked on glass shelves hanging from the mirrored wall behind them.

Above them hung crystal chandeliers with dozens of lit candles illuminating the room. Even the ceiling was decorated with a mirrored finish, which intensified the candlelight.

The prince was one of thirty or forty wealthy patrons sipping alcoholic beverages this evening. Sheridan guessed that a good dozen of them were Sal's platoon he brought with him from High Alta. Even his Keepers sat at the next table, watching carefully.

"It's time we talked," Sheridan said bluntly.

Sal tilted his pretty head, "Do you have my father's money?"

Sheridan leaned back, putting his stumpy feet up on the maple table in front of him. "I can sit here and throw lines of bullshit at you to make excuses for my king's actions, but I won't. I have no love for the man who wears the crown. To me, a hunk of heavy gold sitting on top of one's brow does not make them a leader. He may rule by birthright, but he is no leader."

"Good to know," Sal sipped his drink. Sheridan could scent the heavy, sweet notes of rum from across the table. "I don't care if you like your king. I came here for one of two things—money or the princess."

"Neither of which I can give you."

Sal's brows narrowed. The prince had enough decency to not unleash his full anger in a crowded, public place. But he still snapped, "Unfortunately, you don't have a choice. In less than twelve hours, I will lead my troops back up the steps of your precious Spire, burst into the throne room, and take either a pile of gold coins or Princess Lia. You'll be damned if I have neither waiting for me when I get there." Noticing that Sheridan's stern expression was unbreakable, the prince continued, "I insisted on coming here myself with a small contingency, Sheridan. My father wanted to march an army to your doorstep himself. Work with me and spare the trouble of starting a potential war."

"Then you must work with me and understand that I cannot provide you with either one of your requests by the morning. Please, Sal, give me some time to gather the money and—"

"No!" the prince's voice rose over the sound of the stringed orchestra playing on the stage against the western wall of the bistro. "Time is not an option! What part of that do you not understand?"

Sheridan grew anxious. He could not reveal too much without either seeming like a threat or appearing weak in the eyes of High Alta. Which one was worse, Sheridan could not decide. High Alta was no friend to Havyn. A threat could provoke a war. Yet, at the same time, appearing weak could give High Alta the advantage over Havyn.

"The money is gone, Sal," Sheridan threw up his hands in frustration. "I have looked through Typhus's accounts and the money is gone." He lied, "And I have no idea where it went. This was the king's mistake and I will fix it, but I need *time.*"

Sal's face spoke his response. His mind was calculating exactly where that much money could have disappeared to from the king's personal coffers.

"I can get you the money," Sheridan promised. "If we can set up reasonable payment plans, the kingdom could manage to pay off the debt within a few years."

"That's too long, Sheridan, and you know it."

"Then meet me in the middle. Compromise with me!" Sheridan begged.

"Quit trying to fix your king's mistakes," Sal suggested. "My father demanded I get the money out of King Typhus one way or another, not from you. I would have hoped the threat to indenture Lia as High Alta's 'guest' was enough to sway him into cooperating, but I see otherwise now."

Sheridan literally shook with anger. "He hardly even recognizes his own daughter. He won't care if you take her. But I do, and I am trying hard to reconcile with you right now."

That seemed to get Sal's attention. He relaxed into his chair, sipping from his drink, and asked calmly, "What do you mean he doesn't recognize the princess?"

Before Sheridan could answer, a gorgeous barmaid came to their table. To Sheridan, she winked and said, "Hey handsome, can I get you anything?"

Sheridan typically opted out of indulging in alcoholic beverages, but with all that was going on, maybe some booze would help ease the tension growing in his neck and shoulder muscles. "Sure, sweetheart, I'll have a whiskey neat. Whatever your strongest stuff is."

She winked again and bounced over to the bar to retrieve his drink.

Sheridan continued carefully, trying not to say anything that would make matters worse, "Ever since Queen Helena's death, the king has not been the same. He took his wife's death hard and gets easily confused ever since. He does not always recognize Lia—he mistakes her for Helena frequently. The Providence has conducted hundreds of hours of research into the illness, and at one point she may have been able to stop or slow the regression. He is too far gone now."

"Why didn't she treat him when he first showed symptoms?" Sal asked genuinely.

"The patient has to be willing to undergo treatment," Sheridan explained. "Typhus blames the Providence for Helena's death, believing that she let the queen die on purpose. He won't let the Providence touch him."

"So, what? The king borrowed and spent the money during his insanity and there is no record of where it went?"

Sheridan nodded, "Unfortunately. I need time to find out where the money was spent and to collect enough to pay your father back."

The prince lowered his head. "My father will not enjoy hearing this."

"That brings me to my next topic of discussion," Sheridan cleared his throat nervously.

The barmaid returned with a tumbler full to the brim with whiskey. Sheridan thanked the woman before taking a sip. The burn of the whiskey in his throat sent a wave of relief down his spine.

"Why," the prince responded, "do I have a feeling you are about to ask even more from me?"

Because I am, Sheridan thought. He said, "The only way to repair any damage done by Typhus is if he was no longer the king... I need your father's support if—"

The prince held up a palm. "Stop. What you speak of is treason, Sheridan."

The Master of Cities sighed, "No, it's not. You know the Concordat as well as I do, if not better. You know there is a section that outlines specifically how to properly depose a monarch in a Court of Kings."

"And if you show up to a Court of Kings alone requesting a deposition trial, then you will appear treasonous," Sal nodded in understanding. "So, you need me to act as a witness." He shifted uncomfortably in his seat. "I don't know, Sheridan."

"All I need is for you to convince your father to hear us out at the next Court of Kings."

Sal's grey eyes locked with Sheridan's as he explored his thoughts.

Finally, Sal broke eye contact and said, "I'll consider it. But without the money, I will still need to take Lia into my custody until the Court."

Sheridan was afraid of this. He hardly knew Prince Sal other than rumors and stories of his accomplishments. He hardly knew him enough to accept a promise of protection if Lia went with him to High Alta. If High King Eriputes hadn't held a grudge against Havyn before, he would now. Sheridan would die fighting before he allowed Lia to be forcibly taken from her kingdom.

"My father," Sal continued, "is not perfect, by any means. He is paranoid of losing his kingdom. Paranoid that he will die and my brother and I will follow him to the grave, ending our dynasty forever."

"You have no male relatives to carry your family name?"

Sal shook his head, "No. My uncle is a black sheep and gave up all claim to the throne willingly many years ago. We haven't seen much of him since. My aunt is the Providence. The only other relatives are distant cousins, who are all female. The Concordat says a female relative can claim the throne, but they are so distant, I don't believe their bloodline will be strong enough. Their family names are generations from ours, so the dynasty would still cease to exist. My father only needs at least one heir, preferably male, out of Lia. At least Lia is the daughter of the king. Any subsequent child of hers could still hold her family name if she plays her part well. She would still be the one to rule Havyn. I will take care of her, Sheridan. Trust me when I say this is not the outcome I want."

Sheridan met the prince's gaze. He narrowed his eyes, as if telling the prince, *Then why are you taking her?*

Prince Sal leaned back in his chair and gave Sheridan a defeated look, *My father is still the king. I must still follow his orders.*

As a last resort, and not the path Sheridan wanted to go down, the Master of Cities pulled out a letter from his tunic with the Providence's official seal. He hesitated before cracking the seal and unfolding the parchment.

"I hate to say it, Sal," Sheridan dreaded having to lie further, but he had to protect the princess at all costs. "but Princess Lia was injured a few days ago in a horseback riding incident. She in unable to travel for four-to-six weeks. Providence's orders."

Sheridan handed over the document. Sal pulled the paper aggressively from Sheridan's muscled hand. He watched as the prince's eyes scanned each line of the letter, back and forth. Sal must have read the letter four times before slamming it down on the table under his palm.

"You mean to tell me that her injuries were *so awful* that the Providence could not heal her," mistrust shown on the prince's hard exterior, "yet she will be fine to travel in a month?"

Sheridan crossed his hands on top of the table. "Typhus will not allow the Providence to touch his daughter. Same as she cannot touch him." *A lie, but a convincing one.*

Prince Sal gritted his teeth as he grunted, "Such a convenience that she will be perfectly safe to travel just in time for the Court of Kings next month. Seeing as she will need to be there to claim her title."

Sheridan leaned forward, bracing his arms on the table, and whispered, "If I were you, Prince, I wouldn't challenge the Faith's decision. Even your aunt could not prevent the consequences you will face for breaking the word of another Providence."

Having read the Concordat himself, and understanding the authority the Providence held, Sal knew he had no choice but to leave empty-handed. Or he could stay for the month and wait for the princess to be in travelling condition. Eriputes would be equally as enraged.

Sal knew he was being played.

Losing his temper, he crumpled up the Providence's letter and slammed a fist on the table, shaking their glasses. "You can forget about me convincing my father to hear your treacherous claim. You also read the part of that law stating that if your claim is denied, you can be brought up on charges of treason and executed. *That* I will convince my father of."

The prince stood swiftly, sending his chair tumbling back, clattering onto the ground. He stormed out of the bistro, but not before backhanding Sheridan's whiskey glass, hurling it across the room with a smash.

The Keepers at the next table stood, armed with their pikes, and followed Prince Sal into the streets beyond.

I may have lost a potential ally, Sheridan thought, accepting his losses, *but at least I bought us another month.*

CHAPTER 20

Ena had to ensure their conversation could not be overheard by curious ears. She peeked her head into the narrow hallway between their rooms of the inn. She had even set up a makeshift tripwire at the top of the stairs, which would create a loud snap if broken, to alert them of anyone coming near.

Silently closing and latching the bedroom door, Ena turned gravely to her companions. Damian stood crossly in the middle of the tight room. Klaus and Drake sat on each mattress, mirroring one another.

"I was attacked," Ena stated bluntly. The worrisome, shocked look on their faces told Ena she needed to elaborate, despite her concerns that the Lord of Steel's men were surrounding them and listening.

Ena described the incidents of the day—meeting Rune, fighting the fire mages, narrowly escaping with her life, being healed at the white mage convent, and what the dwarf had written in his threatening note to her.

They all exchanged glances before Damian spoke up, "We were all worried sick. I am relieved that you are safe, Governess, but you cannot give in to this monster's demands again."

"If he catches you alone again, you are sentencing yourself to death," Klaus agreed.

Ena rested her hands on her hips. The white tunic and trousers the white mages lent her were far too big, far too flowy. Uncomfortably, she adjusted the belt around her waist.

"I know," Ena dipped her head, watching her feet, lost in thought. She sighed. "Believe me, I know. After today, I could not survive another encounter with mages like that. However, I cannot risk anyone else's lives..."

"You are not seriously considering facing the dwarf alone, are you?"

Damian challenged. "After the ordeal you just went through?"

Ena braced her elbow on a crossed arm, resting her chin in her palm, finger anxiously tapping her cheek. She was deep in thought. "I can face him alone. The dwarf himself is not a threat. Only his connections."

"His connections," Klaus scoffed, "are what almost got you killed. A man like that doesn't stray far from his connections."

Ena's gaze snapped to him. "Do not belittle me, Klaus. I am not in the mood."

"No harm intended, Ena." Klaus held up his hands, surrendering. "I'm worried for you, is all."

Ena ran a hand through her dark hair. *Gods, my hair is getting so long...* More discomfort to add to the list. The aches from her now-healed injuries didn't help. Had she been able to stay at the healing center for another day or two, the white mages would have kept her on a pain regiment with constant physical and mental healing until she was good as new.

That young mage knew Ena could not stick around too long without putting them at risk as well.

"I have an idea," Ena's green eyes bounced between the three sets of eyes staring back at her. "I will gladly hear out your opinions, since I am certain you will not enjoy hearing my thoughts."

Damian turned his head, meeting Klaus's worried gaze, then Drakes. He nodded, opening his ears to Athenia's idea.

"The Lord of Steel wants to see me alone, correct?" Ena explained. "He was alone when I met him at the underground river. The only other person being the Shipmaster, who left us after the first minute. He is capable of traveling without a guard, and he likely understands the way of the sword if he sells weapons for a living. I could prevail in a fight against him alone if it came to that." Not a complete lie, but more of a guess. She had no idea the skill the dwarf possessed in swordsmanship. He could very well get the upper hand on her. Ena continued, "He gave me a specific time to meet him. What if I show up early and wait for him, try and catch him truly alone?"

"Why," Damian asked, "are you even entertaining him? You should be bringing this to Lady Raven's attention and storming the location at that address. You came here to solve a murder, not get yourself involved in the black market."

"El Vadora will burn, Damian! Do you not understand that?" Realization hit her like an arrow to the heart. "Fuck... The burnt villages outside of El Vadora... He has to be behind those, also! Gods! I have to do something."

Their eyes went wide, realizing that Ena may, in fact, be right. It all began to make sense. The Lord of Steel surrounded himself with fire mages and clearly had eyes and ears everywhere, if he was able to decipher the governess's true identity.

"Then let us help you," Klaus begged.

"Yes," Damian nodded in agreeance. "Meet the dwarf, if you must, but allow us to try and stop his forces before they can cause any real harm."

Ena almost asked him how they could stop all of the dwarf's resources. But she said, "We can split up. I will wear my armor for added protection if things turn violent with the Lord of Steel. One of you can deliver a letter to Raven, explain the situation, and see how she can provide us with aid. She will also be able to get a letter quickly to Cyprien to build up El Vadora's defenses. One of you can travel to the City Watch barracks at the edge of the city," a bad image swarmed into her mind, recalling the guard who died by her own hand, "and see if they can amass a few platoons to lend us their swords. Lastly, one of you can tail me and keep watch from a distance until the guards can arrive."

She looked at each of them for approval, or rejection.

Damian exchanged a worrisome look with Klaus and sighed, "You know splitting up is a bad idea... You have always expressed that to us."

"This time is different, Damian," Klaus spoke up. "I have family in El Vadora, just as you do. Family who have no part in this fight, yet their lives could be at risk." He smiled at Ena. "If splitting up is your best approach, then I support it."

Damian grunted his reluctant approval, possibly thinking of his teenage daughter he had waiting for him in the city. His job took him away from her more than he wished, but she was his pride and joy. He would lay down his life for her in a heartbeat.

"What about you, Drake?" Ena took a step towards her unarmed guard. "What are your thoughts?"

"Umm," he stammered, shocked that the governess was seeking his opinion, rather than ordering him around, his eyes widened at her. "Yes, of course. Anything for you, Athenia." Ena smiled sweetly at him. Before she could take her attention from him, Drake cleared his throat, "On one condition. I get a weapon." He smirked slyly.

Ena matched his smirk. Looking down at the Aconyte sword hanging from her belt, she observed the way the torchlight caught the deeply impressed metal. It shined in a way she had never seen a sword shine before. Pulling the sword from her belt, she lay the blade flat in her palms, extending the metallic hilt to Drake.

"What? Are you serious?" Drake hesitated as he reached out to claim the sword. "Don't you need to bring this with you when you meet the Lord of Steel?"

Ena shrugged, "He is done making the orders. I believe his connection with the mages could be linked with the Lord of Avalon's death. I will not give him the satisfaction of reclaiming his sword before he faces justice."

"How will you catch him alone?" Drake asked. "He had four mages with him when we met him for your first task. Who's to say he won't have even more watching his back this time?"

Ena rested her hands on her hips and raised an eyebrow. "He knows I have been injured. His guard will be down. He is arrogant." She tilted her head. "He is smart, as well, and will not risk travelling in a large group and drawing attention to himself."

"This could work," Damian was still skeptical, though. Ena could tell. He asked, "So, who gets which task?"

After careful consideration, Ena found it best that Drake be the one to take a letter to Lady Raven. Since Drake accompanied her to the Lordship Ball over a month ago, Raven knew his face, his name, and would be more apt to trust him.

Damian volunteered to take the walk to the barracks and, hopefully, recruit the help of the City Watch. With Damian's own years of service in the City Watch, before his retirement and subsequent career as a hired guard for shipments and bank deliveries, he knew best how to communicate with the guard captains who would be stationed at the barracks.

Klaus, with his watchful eye and unmatched skill with a bow, was the most obvious choice to watch over Ena from a distance as she went to wherever she was supposed to go. Klaus assisted Ena in finding the location on the map—an old mining facility located in the rockier part of the city, far to the west. The walk would take hours to get there. Gabrenas was not known for its minerals, though, so Ena assumed the mines were abandoned—the perfect spot to stay out of sight to operate illegally within the city. Klaus warned that their meeting would likely take place inside of the mines and out of public view, which would make his support rather limited.

Acknowledging that fact, Ena promised to be as careful as she could. She was a smart warrior, Klaus knew.

After Damian and Klaus retired for the night in their own room, and Ena had drafted the letter for Drake to deliver to Raven, tucking it in Drake's boot by the door, she yawned. Exhaustion crept up on her. After the day's events that unfolded, Ena was surprised she hadn't passed out from fatigue.

Sitting on the edge of her uncomfortable bed, Ena reached down to unlace the boots she wore. She winced from the ache in her side. The burn was gone, but the nerves were still tender from the abuse they endured.

Drake, seeing Ena recoil, knelt down before her and unlaced her boot. Carefully, he grasped her muscled calf and gripped the heel of the boot, pulling it off slowly. He placed her bare foot down and casually lifted the other leg to remove the boot from her opposite foot.

He tossed the boots aside and observed Ena's bare feet. Such delicate instruments for a woman who carried the heavy burden of all others around her.

Ena carried such a strong, unbreakable composure that many forgot what she was underneath her armor—a woman.

A woman with petite feet and painted toes, leftover from the Lordship Ball several weeks prior.

Drake gently ran a thumb across the top of them, feeling the soft skin.

Ena wanted to smile, the corner of her mouth perking up ever so.

She struggled to stand up, the weight of her own body fighting her, to remove the rest of her hand-me-down clothes. Drake stood and braced her with an arm behind the back. Ena dropped the white trousers to the floor, stepped out of them, and flung them a few feet away with the tip of her foot. Her tunic followed, Drake helping her pull it over her head after wincing while lifting her right arm.

Ena turned and faced Drake, in full naked embrace. She didn't care what he saw. Not after last night.

Drake saw her differently this time, though. He was not admiring her as any man normally would with a beautiful woman standing nude mere inches from his touch. He admired her as a person, not as a warrior or a politician.

Her sagging shoulders. Her greasy, slightly unkempt hair. And a wholly defeated look on her face.

Even the dark bags under her eyes made the golden flecks in her green eyes glow.

Drake reached out and lightly touched her shoulder, his smile filled with nothing but understanding.

Ena smiled, for real this time, and met his touch with her own, gripping the fingers of his free hand. She squeezed them softly. *Thank you,* she expressed.

After Drake helped her dress into a set of night clothes, Ena turned to lay into bed. As she did, Drake caught a glimpse of her thigh. Her scar. From her childhood injury. Marring her forever with a reminder of her cruel, tortured past.

Ena grabbed Drake's hand once more, saying, "Be with me tonight." *And every night?* She shook that thought from her head, still unsure what she wanted from Drake after all of this was over.

Drake followed her movements as she drifted into the bed, under the stained sheets, and breathed deeply as Ena buried herself in him. She rested her head on his chest, and within moments, she was asleep with the flames of the dimmed torches dancing on the wall behind her.

Drake kissed the top of her head and allowed himself to drift off, as well.

CHAPTER 21

A bird chirping outside of the window woke Athenia from a much-needed night's sleep. She groaned as she lifted her head from Drake's chest and sat up in bed. She carefully climbed over him out of bed and stretched, unaware that he was already awake.

Drake looked over and said, "Good morning, Athenia."

She hated how he called her by her full name. He knew it, too.

Her eyes narrowed. "Good morning." She felt much more alive this morning. The aches from her injuries faded into small pins and needles. Nothing she couldn't handle.

Ena stepped over to the small dresser between the two beds and began gathering a set of tight underclothes to wear under her armor. An extremely tight pair of black silk leggings and a matching silk top. A light material for easy breathing and keeping sweat from building up, but sturdy enough to layer between her flesh and the steel armor she donned.

She tossed a set of clothes at Drake, who still lay in the bed. "Get up. It will take you most of the morning to walk back to the Grand Ballroom. We cannot trust any couriers to carry that message, not after the last one was caught." Drake sat up in bed and stripped out of his day-old clothes and put on the new, fresh ones. "So," Ena smirked, "it seems like the three of you were getting along decently last night."

Drake pulled his shirt over his head. "We did exactly as you said. Played a few rounds of cards, got to know one another better. They have some complicated pasts." He met Ena's gaze. "That seems to be a common theme among this group of yours, huh?"

"Complicated is not even the half of it," Ena rolled her eyes. "Damian served with the City Watch before the scandal that framed him for murder. The Watch allowed him to retire with honors peacefully and dropped any charges. When I got elected and heard of him, heard the scandalous rumors, and heard of his new career as a glorified mercenary, I stepped in. I discovered the murder was not his fault. He had just been in the wrong place at the wrong time. I cleared his name, and I hired him for myself. He doesn't show it much, but he's appreciative of what I did.

"Klaus, too. He was an assassin, believe it or not. His sharp eye was used by the Cyprien City Watch for years on discreet missions where stealth was mandatory. He never had any complications with his career, just with his personal life that inspired him to take up the mantel of an assassin. His parents were killed when he was a teenager and he sought vengeance. Realizing he was good at what he did, the City Watch spared him of any murder charges after tracking down and killing those who murdered his parents. He wanted a break from being the Watch's dog and joined me when I offered my hand."

"They are incredible," Drake admitted. "I wouldn't say we are best friends, now. But they tolerate me."

Ena laughed at that.

She pulled out the bottom drawer of the dresser. Her steel armor mirrored her beautiful face, gleaming in the sunlight from the window above.

It had been many weeks since she wore her armor. Her skin nearly itched, unable to wait to put it on once more.

Metal clanked as she strapped on her greaves and her cuisses, her gauntlets and her placard, and, finally, her breastplate and her light pauldrons. Ena never understood how any guard could wear thick pauldrons. The added weight on the shoulders limited one's movement enough to become a hazard in a fight. Instead, Ena settled for smaller ones that were just enough to cover her deltoid muscles, providing all the protection she needed.

Drake finished dressing in his light leathers. It did not offer much protection in a fight, but hopefully he wouldn't be in that position during his discreet mission.

Drake strapped the Aconyte sword to his belt, admiring it wholeheartedly. Ena had not only granted him a weapon to use, she had given him one of great power. Rumor had it, Aconyte steel never dulled and was nearly indestructible against all other steels.

Ena pushed past him, lifting the lumpy mattress, revealing the night-black faerie sword tucked away for safekeeping. She gripped the hilt, ice cold in her palm.

The sword hummed with its magical aura as she drew it closer, observing the starlit specks captured in the ebony of the blade.

"You're bringing that with you?" Drake asked.

"I figured," Ena rotated the sword in her hand, captivated by its mere presence, "that if we are dealing with mages, then a magical sword might come in handy."

She slid the sword into its scabbard at her side. She strapped her daggers to her thighs and back when a knock sounded at the door.

Drake answered to find Damian and Klaus standing there, donned in their own gear, ready to go.

Ena placed her hands on her hips, puffing out her chest. "You all know your missions?" They nodded. "Good. By the time Drake gets to Raven and Damian arrives at the City Watch barracks, I should be making contact with the Lord of Steel. Klaus, keep an eye out with your best effort. I expect I will be in the mines when I move in to arrest the dwarf, but any signs of danger from outside, and you do whatever it takes..."

Klaus had his bow and quiver strapped to his back. Ena praised him for his accurate and powerful shot, and knew he could take out multiple enemies from a distance before they realized where the attack originated from.

They all nodded again.

Damian asked, "How many of his men will be following us?"

Ena shrugged. "Drake and I are the most at-risk. He knows our faces. The dwarf never saw the two of you," she gestured to Damian and Klaus. "Only the Shipmaster saw you two, but I am unaware of any connections he has. There must be a back exit from here. Inga can sneak us out. Any eyes on the inn will be focused on the entrance. Hopefully..."

Ena had been right. They released the makeshift tripwire and walked down to the second-floor landing. Ena hung her head over the balcony overseeing the common area below. She called out to Inga, asking her to meet them upstairs.

When Inga trudged up the creaking steps, Ena asked for her confidentiality and for an unnoticeable way out.

Inga agreed to both, "Come with me. We got a back way through the kitchen where our supplies get delivered." When she escorted them to the back door, she said, "Best of luck to ya!"

The back alley behind the inn was empty and silent, as far as they could tell. Klaus quietly inspected before returning and nodded. Damian and Klaus departed separately, walking down towards each end of the alleyway. Drake stood for a moment, admiring Ena in her armor.

"What is it?" Ena asked.

Without warning, Drake reached out, cupping Ena behind her head, fingers in her hair, and pressed his lips to hers. In the line of duty, Ena would not have approved of this motion, but his lips felt too good entwined in hers to fight it. She kissed back.

"This is dangerous and stupid, you know that, right?" Drake said, pressing his forehead against hers. Ena reached up and gripped his arms in her gauntleted hands before pulling away.

"I will be fine, Drake," Ena assured.

"Don't make a promise you can't keep," was all Drake said before turning and sneaking between the inn and the building adjacent to it. Ena watched him walk from the shadows into the morning light. By midday, Drake would arrive at the Ballroom and request an audience with Raven. The letter stated everything the lady needed to order an official arrest and to send warning to El Vadora that they could face danger. If the Master of Cities held up his end of the bargain, the City Watch presence in El Vadora will have increased two-fold, preparing them for any serious attack.

Klaus waited at the western end of the alley. Ena threw a black shawl over herself to conceal her armor. The less attention she drew while pacing through the streets, the better.

Ena nodded to Klaus, "Twenty paces behind. You ready?" Klaus returned the nod. Ena stepped out into the street, lively with the busy morning commute.

◆◆◆◆◆◆◆◆◆

By the time Ena and Klaus reached the mining facility, the sun had already reached its peak and begun its descent in the early afternoon. Still a few hours from when the dwarf demanded that she meet him with the Aconyte sword, Ena had time to explore the mine and set up a trap.

The facility was far from any main roads. Residential neighborhoods rested only a block away, and from the graffiti painted on the facility's buildings and minecarts, Ena determined this area was frequented by kids messing around.

Yet no one was around.

The entire street vacant.

"Klaus," Ena said ominously, "I need you to get up high and watch for anyone approaching." She looked across the road from the facility. A ridge in the earth rose high above the street, above the entrance to the facility. She pointed to its peak, "Perhaps that could serve as a lookout."

"It could," Klaus agreed.

They swiftly scoped out the three small buildings the facility consisted of. All were empty, and had been so for some time.

"I will go inside the mine and inspect it for any sign of an encampment the dwarf might have established. I thought the facility would be more heavily guarded if it served as his base of operations."

"Because it's not his base of operations," Klaus speculated. "Why would he provide you with the address of his headquarters?"

Klaus was right, Ena gathered. He must have chosen this location because it is quiet and abandoned. When she captured him, she would demand the location of his actual headquarters.

"I will whistle a bluebird call if anyone walks up the path to the mine," Klaus promised. "One call for a civilian, two for mages or the dwarf."

Ena grunted her approval.

Klaus sped off across the street and mounted the ridge, scaling up to the top. He armed his bow and nocked an arrow in preparation. With one subtle wave, he signaled his readiness.

Ena returned the wave and entered the mineshaft, following the metal rails inlaid precisely along the ground.

The dark pathway was carved from the stone, braced every ten feet or so with wood beams, and declined gently under the surface.

The deeper down the shaft she traversed, she expected it to get darker. Instead, light luminesced from within. Ena halted her steps, scraping against the gravel beneath her feet. She listened intently for any sounds of movement in the mine.

Nothing.

She drew the magic sword from the scabbard, holding it defensively as she continued her steady descent.

Going this deep, Ena wondered if she would even be able to hear Klaus's warning call. The echo in the shaft might work to their advantage, though.

As the shaft leveled out, a large clearing opened before her. Wood beams braced along the walls with columns throughout the room holding up the ceiling, a structure designed to prevent cave-ins. Oil lamps hung from stakes randomly hammered into the cavernous walls. Minecarts, worktables, chests, and tents were set up throughout the clearing.

Someone has *set up camp here,* Ena thought.

Exploring the settlement, Ena did not find much. Besides a few maps similar to her own and some wood for fires, nothing besides the oil lamps indicated that anyone currently occupied this cavern.

The oil in the lamps could maintain a steady flame for days before refueling. There was no telling when the Lord of Steel was last here. *At least within the past week,* Ena calculated from the amount of oil still in the lamps.

What caught Ena's eye was the large, gilded chest tucked discreetly between two tall stacks of firewood. She walked over carefully, the sword still humming in her hand, and pulled up on the heavy lid.

Gods...

Aconyte steel. Hundreds of ingots of it. Stacked neatly within the chest.

Was he selling the ingots, along with already-crafted weapons? But what smiths in this corner of the world could craft with such a hard metal? It is said only a few smiths alive have ever gotten their hands on the raw material and attempted to work the metals.

That skill belonged to whoever crafted the Keepers' gear alone.

She picked up one of the ingots and observed it. So light, almost weightless, yet so sturdy.

A bluebird call echoed down the shaft.

Shit, someone's nearby.

A second call followed.

The Lord of Steel!

Ena quickly placed the ingot back down, shut the chest, and whipped her head around the room. Not too many places to hide.

She spied a small alcove behind a stack of timber laid horizontally towards the back of the cavern. Quietly, but quickly, Ena crouched down and tucked herself behind the timber. The nearest oil lamp was far enough away to not risk casting her shadow.

Footsteps scuffling the gravel sounded from the shaft. Ena peered between two uneven pieces of timber. Just enough to see the salt-and-pepper beard appear in the clearing.

He was speaking with the four mages guarding him.

"The girl will be here in a couple of hours," he stated. "I want you stationed throughout the facility waiting for her."

One of the mages asked, "Do you really believe she will listen to your demands?"

"The mages stationed around El Vadora are awaiting a letter from me," the Lord of Steel explained. "Whatever the governess decides will determine what that letter says. What about the men travelling with her?"

"We only spotted the young lad she came to the windmill with," said the mage. "He was in the upper district by the time our spies reported."

"Hmm," the dwarf stroked his beard, thinking. "He is on his way to see the Lady of Avalon. Too risky. By the time any guards show up here, we will be long gone."

"Will she bring the sword?"

He shrugged, "Let's hope. Once one has tasted Aconyte steel, it is hard to part with. She'll refuse to give it up." He turned to face his mage. "At which point, we will subdue her and take the fucking thing anyway."

The dwarf walked over to the gilded chest, flinging it open. He brushed his hand along the Aconyte ingots. His voice rose a few decibels, speaking with all of his mages, even the ones towards the entrance of the clearing. "Little does she know, there are several smiths in Avalon alone with the skill to smith Aconyte weapons. I don't necessarily need the sword back. But I'll be damned if that treacherous bitch is going to use it against me."

He pointed to each of his mages. "You two, watch from the facility for her arrival. You, watch from the mouth of the mineshaft. And you," he pointed to the last mage, "keep yourself hidden. When she shows herself, ambush her. And *keep her alive.* Myra will want a word with her."

Myra? Who the hell is Myra?

They all nodded and proceeded up the mineshaft again.

The Lord of Steel waited until they were out of sight. He walked over on short legs to the table in the center of the clearing. He studied the maps, flipping through a notebook he pulled from his coat. He took a pen from his pocket and began scribbling notes.

Now's my chance. Ena crouched out from behind the timber, sword still in hand. She observed the ground, carefully stepping over anything that would give herself away. The solid spots of earth made no noise under her light steps.

She held her breath as she approached, trying her hardest not to make any noise as she stood up and held out the sword, merely two feet from the dwarf.

As she went to step forwards to grab the dwarf from behind, he said calmly, "Ah, nice of you to join me, Athenia."

She stopped dead in her tracks. Adrenaline now coursing through her veins, the quickening beat of her heart pounding in her ears. *How had he known?*

The Lord of Steel turned to face her, a conniving grin spreading from ear to ear. "Or, should I address you as Kate? Next time, shut the lid to the chest all the way. It was still propped open."

The scour of shifting earth sounded from behind her. She didn't have the chance to turn around and look before a sharp pain rattled her head.

Ena gasped out the breath she was holding, dropping to her knees.

Her vision faded in and out. The last image she remembered seeing was the Lord of Steel stepping towards her with one of his mages circling from behind her, an Aconyte ingot in his hand spotted with blood.

Then, the world went dark.

CHAPTER 22

Drake reached the Grand Ballroom by midday, just as Ena predicted. The City Watch guards stationed outside the entrance instantly demanded to know who he was and why he was there. Drake complied, and one of the guards went inside to call on Lady Raven.

As Drake waited, he observed the upper district of the city. Citizens walked past, some alone, in pairs, or in groups. None of whom had a care in the world. Second only to Havana, Avalon was the wealthiest region in the kingdom. The upper district of Gabrenas, especially, was filled to the brim with gold spilling from the pockets of those who walked by.

Literally.

Drake watched as a group of young women walked by, laughing to one another, and a coin purse fell to the ground. Drake quickly trotted over, getting the woman's attention, and picked up the purse to return it to her.

The woman thanked him graciously and continued on her way.

Such an easier life. To have a purse filled with gold fall from one's pocket and hardly even notice, or care. Drake would likely never see a fortune like that.

But no fortune could compare to being with Athenia. The spark between them was real, and unexpected. Things were complicated now, but Drake hoped they could have a discussion about their feelings when this was all over.

"Drake," a feminine voice called to him.

He whipped around to find Lady Raven in her jet-black gown waiting at the entrance to the Ballroom.

"I will grant you an audience," she said as he approached. She turned and held the door for him. All of her guards eased their tension as he slipped between them and into the lady's residence.

She led the way to her office.

The ballroom, where he and Ena first met the lady at the Lordship Ball, occupied the majority of the space in the Grand Ballroom. Only the front sector of the massive structure served as the seat for the governing body of Avalon. In fact, the entire first floor was nothing more than a foyer leading into the ballroom.

Lady Raven led Drake up one of the pairs of stairs at either end of the foyer. At the top of the pristine carpeted steps, a hallway stretched from one end to the other. A set of double doors on one wall led to a small balcony overhanging the ballroom. Four single doors inlaid on the opposite wall, evenly spaced down the hallway, led into the rooms where business was held, Drake presumed.

Raven led him down the hall to the second door. She turned the golden doorknob and the oak panel door swung inward.

"Please, have a seat," Raven instructed.

Drake stepped into the room. The same soft, decorative carpet beneath his feet. He seated himself in one of the basil-green barrel chairs across from Raven's wingback chair of the same material, a massive, ornate wooden desk between them.

"What can I help you with, Drake?" Raven asked as she sat down in her chair. She crossed her porcelain hands on her oversized desk. Her cyan eyes locked themselves ferociously on Drake.

"Um," Drake stammered, stirring in his chair, discomfort from the lady's intimidating stare itching under his skin. "I–I have this letter. From the governess."

He drew the letter from his pocket and held it out to Raven. She cautiously reached out and gripped it between two manicured fingers. "What is this? Why not deliver it by courier like she has done before?" Curiosity rested on her stern face.

One would never guess that Raven was a woman in her forties. Despite the wrinkle in her brow as her eyes shot open from the contents of the letter, the gorgeous blonde appeared timeless.

Drake hadn't read the letter before handing it off to the lady. He supposed he could have read it with no repercussions, but he minded Ena's privacy.

"What is the meaning of this?" Raven's pupils lifted from the parchment in her hands and met Drake's brown gaze.

"I don't know exactly what the letter says," Drake explained, "but this 'Lord of Steel' is threatening Athenia. Threatening El Vadora. We need help."

"Is it true? This dwarf has mages working for him?"

"You must have heard of the structure fire in the lower district? At the gentlemen's club?" A slight dip of the lady's chin. "Mages attacked it and fled. Athenia was severely injured. Don't worry, she's fine now, but she is in pursuit of the dwarf and his mages. Whatever she wrote in that letter, it's all true."

Raven ran her eyes over the words another four or five times, trying to come to terms with what the governess revealed to her. "Does this dwarf have anything to do with my husband's death?"

Drake nodded slightly. "That certainly is a possibility. We haven't made any official connection between the two yet, but Athenia strongly believes that the poison can only be acquired in the black market. And this dwarf seems to be one of the kingpins of the black market in Gabrenas."

Raven swore, throwing the parchment onto the desktop. She stood from her chair, nearly sending it flying back into the wall behind her.

Two windows stretched from floor to ceiling on either side of her desk. Bookshelves of various law books and historical tomes set against the adjacent walls. Raven stood in front of the window to Drake's left, fingers entwined in the small of her back, observing the city below.

"I knew they should not have been permitted to operate freely," Raven sighed. "The damned fool always insisted restricting them would only cause more tension."

Drake didn't have to ask to know who Raven spoke of. Her husband allowed the black market to thrive under his see-nothing, do-nothing policy. If the market remained discreet, he believed the consistent flow of coin would stimulate the economy, rather than hinder it. He was not wrong. Avalon was wealthy for many reasons, and the black market was one of them.

Restrictions were in place, such as illegal weapons dealing, but if the City Watch remained oblivious, then the market acted as it pleased.

"Where is Athenia now?" Raven asked.

"On her way to meet the Lord of Steel," Drake answered.

"Does she plan to apprehend him this very day?"

"I believe so."

"Will he have mages with him?"

"Almost certainly."

Raven turned to face him, her platinum hair practically transparent in the sunlight. "Her letter indicated that her next encounter with the dwarf could lead to the destruction of El Vadora. He knows who she is?"

"He has spies everywhere. They found her true identity once he discovered her fake one."

Raven thought for a moment, bracing her palm against the desk, leaning against it. Only a handful of people knew Ena's true identity in this city. The lady would easily be able to narrow down who spilled that information.

Raven returned to her seat at the desk and began writing gracefully on a piece of parchment. "I will do as Athenia asked. This letter will be sent by hawk to El Vadora instantly. Her guard commander has been holding the city while she has been away, I assume? They'll raise their defenses against any mage attack."

"Thank you so much, Lady Raven," Drake stood up and bowed.

"Where is the governess meeting the dwarf?" Raven asked. "I will mobilize the City Watch to her location. I will drive all mages from this fucking city, from this *region*, as if my life depends on it."

Drake shared the address from the Lord of Steel's letter. Drake then mentioned, hesitantly, "One of Athenia's other guards was sent to a nearby Watch barracks to recruit some help. They should be arriving at the mining facility within the next hour or two, I would think."

Raven nodded her approval. Drake was nervous that they had undermined the lady's authority by requesting the help of her guards without her prior approval. However, Lady Raven embraced the idea when she said, "I'll mobilize the guards from the upper district's barracks and we can meet them there."

We? Drake thought. Would Raven risk her own life by facing these mages herself?

The answer was a clear *yes*. The lady, clad in her black dress, glided towards a nearby shelf on the bookcase and tilted back a small, blue-hardcover book. The metallic sound of shifting gears churned behind the wall. With a heavy *clunk*, the far section of the bookcase next to the window unsealed, jutting out from the rest of the case. Raven slipped her hand behind the walnut shelves and pulled outwards.

Behind the stacks of books hung a gleaming silver rapier and a radiant bodice of black steel. Raven called for one of her guards, who, moments later, marched into her office. Seeing the armor hanging revealed, the guard aided Raven in equipping the black steel over the torso of her jet-black gown.

Raven gripped the hilt of the rapier, removing it from the wall and sliding the blade through the loop that dangled from the side of her armor.

This was an unexpected side of Lady Raven that Drake never thought he would see.

Raven told her guard, "You know what to do. Have the men gather in front of the Grand Ballroom. Have them bring two horses for myself and my guest."

"Yes, ma'am!" The guard dipped his head and exited the room. Drake heard the guard march double-time down the hall and descend the stairs.

Raven met Drake in front of the desk. She spotted the sword at Drake's hip. "Is that Aconyte steel?" Drake nodded. "Is it the dwarf's blade?" Drake nodded again. Raven smirked. "Good. Drive it through his heart and see how he feels about bringing Aconyte steel into my fucking city again."

Side-by-side, Raven and Drake marched in step out the front doors of the Grand Ballroom. A company of City Watch guards waited at attention for the lady's arrival. Two grey horses, reins held in the hands of the guard commander of Gabrenas, bowed on their front hooves, lowering their noses, as Raven approached.

Raven stepped into the stirrup and swung her leg over the horse's back, the skirt of her jet black dress arcing in a wave as it followed her movement.

Drake followed her movements.

Raven turned her horse around to face the guards.

Drawing her sword, a beam of sunlight blazing off of the thin point of her rapier's blade, she addressed her men, "Guards! We march against an enemy capable of a great power. Do not break rank. Follow me!" The guards all banged their gauntlets against the round shields strapped to their arms, cheering for their lady. It was not often the lord or lady of an entire region led an assault. Inspiration gleamed in their eyes under their helms. Raven led her and Drake's horse to the front of the guard company. "Double-time, march!"

Her horse reared, kicking up a cloud of dust as its hooves struck the ground. She and Drake took off in a steady trot with the guards keeping up on foot behind them.

In an hour, they would arrive at the mining facility, meeting up with the guards Damian hopefully recruited, to provide Ena with more than enough backup to take down an army of mages.

CHAPTER 23

Drake rode side-by-side with Lady Raven for miles before they came up to the ridge where Klaus oversaw the events unfolding below. The company of City Watch guards rounded onto the street with the mining facility in sight. Flames shot high into the air from the facility's courtyard.

Fuck, Drake thought. *That's not a good sign...*

The courtyard came into view. Arrows whistled over their heads as Klaus loosed them at his targets.

Damian was already there with two platoons of guards from the barracks.

And the fight was *not* going well...

Over a dozen mages stood their ground in the courtyard, throwing punches, blasts, and waves of flame at the guards charging them. Dead or injured bodies already freckled the ground, guards and mages alike.

Klaus slid down the slope of the ridge, meeting Drake as he dismounted his horse.

"What the fuck happened here?" Drake asked, staring at the bloodshed before him. After the company of guards under Raven's command made contact with the battlefield, the lady marched over to Klaus.

"Yes, what happened here?" she asked. "I thought Governess Athenia was apprehending the dwarf. Where is she?"

Klaus held his bow in his hand, an arrow still nocked in the bowstring, ready to fly. "Ena entered the mine to set an ambush for the Lord of Steel. He arrived with four mages. Another dozen mages showed up out of nowhere, only minutes before Damian arrived with the guards from the east. I've only been able to score a few hits, but most have been dodging my arrows. These mages are highly skilled in combat."

Klaus's skill with a bow was legendary. For him to miss a shot meant he was not trying to hit his target in the first place. But not these mages. They evaded every sword, axe, and arrow that came at them, responding with blasts of fire so hot, the guards dropped instantly.

Damian sprinted out from the onslaught with twin daggers in his hand. His shirt was tattered and burned in several spots, and other than the sweat and dirt that stained him, he seemed in good shape.

"Thank the gods you showed up, Drake," he panted. "And good thinking bringing more men. I thought the forty I arrived with would be plenty." He swallowed hard. "I was wrong."

Raven flashed her silver rapier. "I brought eighty additional troops. It will be enough to defeat them, gods willing." She observed the battle playing out before her, mentally prepared herself for the casualties. Many families would lose mothers and fathers, husbands and wives, and brothers and sisters today. These mages were not giving up easily. "Athenia. Is she still in the mine?"

Klaus responded, "My eyes have been on that mine for hours. She hasn't left."

Drake's stomach dropped. He hoped for the best, but prepared himself for the worst. He shifted on his feet impatiently, waiting for an outcome of this battle. Whether good or bad.

"We're outmaneuvering them, Lady Raven!" one of her captains called out.

Drake viewed the battle. The fire blasts erupting into the sky slowly became more concentrated. The mages were being pushed back together towards the mouth of the mineshaft.

"Good!" Raven called out. "Keep pushing them back." She turned to Damian. "I assume it was no trouble acquiring guards to escort you here?"

"None at all, my lady," Damian dipped his head politely. "Your captains there were very understanding. Once I said it was a potential risk to your life, they had platoons geared up and ready to go."

She nodded, "Glad to hear it."

An explosion sounded among the fighting. Wails of pain followed, then the clattering of metal as armored guards flew overhead and hit the ground hard. Heat radiated as a fire and smoke plumed into the air.

What was that?!

Together, Drake, Lady Raven, Damian, and Klaus drew their

weapons and raced to the front of the guard company, half of whom were lying on their backs from the blow. Those who had been standing towards the front of the explosion, who took the brunt of the blast, were dead. The others were either unconscious or covered in burns flailing on the ground in pain. About half of the company was merely shocked, but relatively unscathed.

The explosion hadn't just taken out most of the City Watch—the mages, with the exception of three, were all dead, too. Several of them in pieces, limbs all over the place.

"What the fuck..." Drake said under his breath.

One of the mages that miraculously survived the explosion stirred, groaning from the aches and pains that undoubtedly corrupted his body. Raven flew up to him, the point of her rapier against his jugular.

"Talk," Raven demanded.

The mage rubbed his pounding head and glanced at Raven, silent.

"I said *talk!*" Raven pressed the sharp point in deeper, blood welling around the skinny blade.

"Just kill me," the mage grunted. "Or I'll do it myself. Successfully, this time."

The explosion. It was a murder-suicide attempt, Drake realized.

The mages knew they were losing. Knew they had nowhere to go as over a hundred guards stormed at them. One last move to take out half of the army at their backs.

That's precisely what they had done.

More than half of the guards were either dead or injured.

"I won't give you the satisfaction of a quick death," Raven removed the sword from his neck. She stepped on the mage's thigh, visibly broken by the angle at which it bent, with her full weight. The mage withheld a yelp, and tears rolled down his cheeks. "If you don't want to talk, I will have every bone in your body broken, one by one, until the pain is so unbearable that you beg for mercy."

The mage stifled his cries, glaring at the lady with hatred. Silent.

Nearby, one of the other mages began to stir. Raven smiled vilely at the mage at her feet. "Fine. I'll talk to that one. Captain," she called. A guard captain trotted over. Raven pointed her rapier at the mage beneath her and said, "Break him. Start with the toes and work your way up."

"Yes, my lady," said the captain. Instantly, he got to work. Leaning down, removing the crumbling, burnt boots from the mage's foot, he gripped a toe and bent it backwards. Slowly. An audible snap followed by the sob of horror sounded from the mage.

Drake withheld a gag. This was torture...

Lady Raven knew she towed the line between acceptable and unacceptable forms of punishment right now, but she didn't care. Her men followed her orders, like any other.

She approached the second living mage with her weapon drawn. Before giving the mage a chance to look at her, she drove the needled point of her sword through his shoulder into the earth beneath him. Instantly, the mage yelled for mercy, blood pooling underneath him.

"Please, stop!" the mage cried out. "Stop that, you crazy bitch!"

"Talk!" Raven hissed through clenched teeth. "Where is the dwarf?"

With his good arm, the mage lifted a shaky finger and pointed behind him. The dark mineshaft was ominously quiet.

Raven twisted the blade. Sinews and cartilage tearing. "What about the girl?"

"I don't know about a girl." Raven now began to shift the blade back and forth, opening the wound in his shoulder wider. The mage's bloodcurdling scream was enough to make Drake vomit. "Fuck, fuck, *fuck!* I don't know anything, I swear! The Lord of Steel... He-he only told us to meet him here. Only told us he was capturing someone who was a great threat to him and our cause."

Behind them, more snaps were heard, followed by screams. Drake dared not look at what part of the mage's body the captain was breaking next.

Raven continued, "What *cause?*"

This time, the mage remained silent.

"What do you mean by a *great threat to your cause?* Talk, damnit!" She continued twisting the blade, severing any cords and tendons connecting the muscle in his arm to the rest of his body. But the mage managed to withhold any painful moans. He must have realized he said too much.

Raven recognized the mage would no longer speak. She withdrew her rapier from his shoulder, guts and blood spilling. She moved on to the last living mage, who began sitting himself up at the mouth of the mine.

He looked up at Raven and spat at her. "Yeah, yeah, yeah, I know.

Talk," he mocked. Before Raven could react, he continued, "She got here before he did. They'll be down at the end of the mineshaft, if she's still alive."

Raven surprisingly thanked the mage before signaling for two guards to hold him as they entered. Raven fearlessly led the way down the dark mineshaft, only lit by the torches a few of her guards lit as they followed her. Behind them, Drake, Damian, and Klaus fell in step. A group of guards watched their backs as they descended.

Drake observed as they reached the bottom of the shaft, opening into a cavern. Someone had set up living arrangements here. A few canvas tents and tables were spread throughout the cavern. Empty minecarts littered the clearing. Whatever this mine was once used for, it no longer served its original purpose.

Was this where the Lord of Steel had set up his base?

The cavern was empty. No living thing stirred.

"Search the place," Raven ordered. Every guard scrambled throughout the room, scanning every inch.

Damian began perusing the area nearest them, where the tents were propped. A firepit set up in front of the tents had not been used in some time. The absence of ashes told Drake that it may never have been used at all.

"Check this out," Damian said. Raven and Drake stepped lightly to where Damian was standing. "Something was here."

Two tall stacks of firewood with an empty space between them. From the empty space, Drake could see drag marks in the earth from whatever existed there before. A square outline was pressed into the gravel between the firewood. A box of some sort. The scuffed earth from the box being dragged led to the wall at the back of the cavern, where the tracks suddenly stop.

Klaus pointed to the wall, "Look. The rock doesn't match."

"What do you mean?" Raven asked.

Klaus approached the wall and dragged his finger along it, outlining the different tones and flows of the earth. "See it? Right here, the rock is lighter in color, and the veins run vertically in perfect straight lines. Now, if you look to either side of this section, and throughout the rest of the cavern, the rock is darker. The veins still run vertically, but it flows more unevenly, like a river." He turned to face them. "Any guesses?"

Raven stepped forward and observed the clues for herself. She brushed the tips of her fingers against the stone. "It's smoother, too. This was man-made."

"What do you mean by 'man-made?'" Damian asked.

"I mean," Raven faced him, "this wall was constructed by an earth mage."

"An earth mage?" Damian laughed. "Does that even exist?"

Raven clasped her hands together in front of her. "According to legend, yes, they do. And it makes perfect sense. The dwarf heard the attack and fled through some kind of secret tunnel, sealed behind him."

"But where is Athenia?" Drake asked, almost nervously.

One of the City Watch guards spoke up, "My lady, come see this."

Raven was there in a second. Behind the table set up in the center of the room, spots of blood speckled the gravel. The blood specks dripped along for a few feet in a disturbed gravel path before stopping completely.

Klaus studied the blood path. "Someone was struck here." He pointed to behind the table, where the blood was more concentrated. "Whoever was struck continued bleeding as they were dragged along. Then it stops suddenly. Wounds don't stop bleeding in a moment's notice. The blood should have slowly dulled as the bleeding stopped. They must have realized she was bleeding and covered the wound before carrying her behind that wall."

Drake's eyes shot open. "You're not saying that..."

"I'm sorry, kid," Klaus said solemnly. "I think the Lord of Steel has Ena. Got the upper hand, knocked her out, and took her away as the fighting started on the surface."

"Shit," Lady Raven swore out loud.

Suddenly, a guard came sprinting down the mineshaft, nearly stumbling to the ground as they stopped themselves. "My lady! The mages are dead."

She rolled her eyes. "Good! Those pieces of shit deserved it."

"No, you don't understand," the guard paused. "It's *how* they died. Nothing like any of us have ever seen before." Before anyone could respond, the guard ran back into the dark.

Raven held a confused expression on her face. What did that mean?

Quickly, they all ascended to the surface, light flowing in gently from the mouth of the shaft. The guard captain was on one knee, leaning over one of the mages—the mage he had the pleasure of breaking, one bone at a time.

"What happened?" Raven trotted over, holding up the skirts of her dress. She crouched beside the captain.

"He stopped responding," the captain said, "and then *this.*"

He pointed at the mage's face. Flesh deathly pale, eyes glossed over, the veins in his wrists protruding and deep blue in color. What struck Raven and her captain the most was the light blue foam bubbling from the corners of the mage's mouth.

Raven recognized that symptom. "Gods..."

"What is it?" Drake asked.

"Bluebite poisoning..." Raven gasped. All three of the mages suffered the same fate. She looked at her captain. "How could this have happened? Were you not watching them?"

The captain responded, "Ma'am, eyes were on them at all times. They started convulsing all of a sudden. Within seconds, they were dead."

"By the gods..." Raven whispered to herself. She stood up, turning away from the bodies. No one else knew the truth of her husband's death, besides Athenia's men, perhaps. She kept the shock to herself. She cleared her throat, "Get them back to the Master White Mage. I want them to be inspected. Full autopsy."

Her captain nodded, "Yes, ma'am." He called for other guards to assist him in escorting the bodies back to the upper district.

Raven maintained a stoic composure as she rotated on her heel. To Drake, Damian, and Klaus, she said, "I will have the Watch comb the city high and low for the governess. Not to worry, we will find her. And wherever we find her, we will find that godsforsaken dwarf."

"If you don't mind, my lady," Damian spoke up. "I would like to lead the search."

Raven met his genuine look of worry. She then glanced between Drake and Klaus. "I am sure you all would like to play a role in the search?" They nodded. "Each of you can take lead of the patrols in different sectors of the city. I will have the patrols organized within the hour. I know night approaches, but best to conduct a full search as soon as possible before the dwarf can sneak out of the city under the cover of darkness."

They all looked to one another and nodded.

"Meet back at the inn in the morning for a few hours of rest?" Damian suggested. They all agreed. "Send word if you find anything."

As they began to disperse with the rest of the guard company, or what was left of it, Raven caught Drake by the shoulder. They waited back as Damian and Klaus met up with the guards.

"I am going to send word to the Dread Watch," Lady Raven told Drake. "You know of them, don't you?"

Drake shrugged, "Only stories. I never knew they were real."

"Oh, they're real," Lady Raven's brows rose. "And the stories are all real, I assure you. They have experience dealing with mages. And they know and respect the governess. Their assistance will be useful. Do you agree?"

The Dread Watch? Holy shit! The Dread Watch were common characters in many children's books and young adult novels that Drake read growing up. Rumors always existed that they were based off of real people, but he never would have assumed that the Dread Watch actually existed.

Drake nodded excessively, trying to hide his excitement at the possibility of meeting these legendary warriors.

"Great," Raven shook Drake's hand. "Thank you for bringing all of this to my attention. It seems we are all in over our heads. I doubted Athenia at first. When the Master of Cities and the Providence told me a twenty-something-year-old former City Watch guard would be my saving grace, I must admit I was skeptical. If this dwarf is really linked to my husband's untimely death, then I owe her everything. I'll owe *all four of you* everything."

Raven released Drake's hand and mounted her horse, who waited patiently at the edge of the road where she had left it. She exchanged a few words with the guard captain, who was in the process of organizing patrols with what little men he had left. More would join them, he assured. Letters had already been sent to every City Watch barracks throughout the city.

Drake was thrilled to be a part of the search party. He desperately wanted to find Athenia... *Needed* to find her. The thought of her injured and in the hands of that monster who had broken her made Drake's blood boil.

I'm coming for you, Athenia.

CHAPTER 24

Prince Sal did not appear before the king demanding Princess Lia the next morning, as Sheridan worried he would. He did not even show his face before departing the city. Sheridan simply received a bill detailing the lodging fees for the prince and his guards.

How the prince managed to cost Sheridan ten-thousand gold in the short week he was in the city, the dwarf had no idea.

He ignored his frugality and paid the bill in full from his own pockets. No sense in costing the kingdom any more money.

Sheridan climbed the spiral steps to Princess Lia's chambers. Her Keepers were not standing guard outside of her maple door. *Strange?*

As Sheridan approached closer, he saw a note pinned to the door.

In class with the Providence. Be back for lunch.

- Lia

Ever since the incident with her father, Lia has made an effort to inform Sheridan of her whereabouts at all times, in one way or another. Comfort consumed him knowing she was with the Providence.

The Providence followed her own laws—the laws of the Faith. If Typhus, or anyone else, tried to harm Lia in the company of the Faith, the Providence would be sure to sic her Guardians on the perpetrator.

The three of them balanced precariously on the line between treason and righteousness, and they acknowledged it.

Sheridan trudged back down the stairs and followed the halls to the eastern fortress, to the Providence's study. Days like this made the dwarf realize just how big the Spire of the New King was. His short legs worked twice as hard as any human or elf that roamed these halls.

Not like many people roamed these halls freely anymore. Once full of servants, housekeepers, guards, and dignitaries, the castle now remained lifeless. The thought sent chills down Sheridan's back.

The doors to the Providence's study swung open on his arrival. The two Guardians of the Faith holding them open as the Master of Cities passed through the threshold. Lia's Keepers waited in the hallway with the two Guardians, who sized up the Keepers as they glared at the dwarf. Before opening their mouths to question the Master of Cities, they caught the invisible challenging look in the Guardians' golden visors and backed off.

Sheridan stopped to observe Princess Lia receiving her lessons from the Providence.

"You may never develop the healing ability of the white mages," the Providence was saying, "but it will behoove you to learn how the human body functions. How to tend to an injury in the case of an emergency. Herbs and salves cure ailments and wounds just as well as magic, only slower."

The women stood in the center of the garden. The domed ceiling opened wide for the sun to feed the Providence's thousands of plants and flowers.

The Providence used her magic to compile hundreds of bundles of white sweet alyssums into the shape of a life-size human body. As she ran her fingers over different spots of the "body," the petals illuminated with a moon-like glow.

She placed her hand on the top of the head and the flowers, each smaller than a fingernail, glowed to form the shape of a brain. "The brain is the most important element of any living creature's physiological makeup. Do not be mistaken, though—the brain is *not* the mind. Our thoughts may be stored within the cells of our brain, but our mind simply exists. Each mind is different, functions differently, formulates thoughts and stores memories differently.

"The brain is the physical organ that acts as the center of our nervous system. The nervous system spreads throughout our bodies like webs," the Providence moved her hand from the top of the head to the back of the neck, causing the alyssums to illuminate like thin roots of a plant branching out from the spine. "Each of these microscopic nerve endings send signals to the brain in pulses." Suddenly, the flowers making up the nervous system model began pulsating one at a time, forming pathways back to the floral brain. "When one gets injured, these signals are sent to the brain from the origin of the injury. For example, when you hit your arm on the steps last week, the nerves in your arm instantaneously pulsed that information to your brain, causing you to feel pain."

"That's so fascinating!" Lia reached out and touched the soft petals.

Sheridan cleared his throat. They looked to him as he joked, "I thought we were trying to coronate her as a queen, not prepare her for the Trials."

The Providence smirked. "Much can happen between now and the Court of Kings, Master Sheridan. We must prepare for every possible scenario."

She was right. After the fury that had erupted from King Typhus the week prior, there was no doubting he would target the Providence, giving his Keepers another ridiculous order to kill his own cousin. The Keepers would first have to clear through an unknown number of Guardians of the Faith to get to the Providence, though.

"I agree," Sheridan marched over to them. "Princess Lia should learn the duties of the Providence, whether or not she becomes queen. It's time the three ruling branches began working together, understanding one another, instead of acting as separate entities. Speaking of the Court of Kings, actually—"

Lia interrupted, "Did you speak to High Alta's prince?"

"Assuming," the Providence chimed in, "since Prince Salmeides is not here to escort you back to High Alta, the conversation must have gone well?"

Sheridan raised his brows before letting out a sarcastic chuckle, "Yeah, 'well' is not the word I would use to describe it."

Lia's face sank into a worried frown.

The princess must have prepared for the worst, for she was dressed in one of her finest ambassadorial outfits—a silk lilac empire dress with her coffin-shaped nails painted viridian with matching eye shadow gently coating her upper lids. She wore her chestnut hair down, waving over her shoulders to the center of her back, a thin headband holding it behind her ears and out of her eyes. Periwinkle violet pumps encased her small feet. Her mother's heirloom silver necklace draped perfectly along her collar

Though only sixteen years old, Lia was becoming a young woman, and her maturity was unmatched by those twice her age.

"We are on our own for the Court of Kings," Sheridan stated bluntly.

He answered the shocked expressions on the women's faces by explaining the events that unfolded the day before. Every piece of each conversation with President Aroy, General Braxon, and Prince Sal. He held back no details, remaining as transparent as possible. They were in this mess together. Keeping secrets from one another would not help.

"Is King Typhus trying to start a war?" the Providence asked. "It makes no sense. General Braxon said he was clearheaded during his visits to the barracks?" Sheridan nodded. "Why in his right mind would he risk raising an army and spying on the other kingdoms?"

"I don't know," Sheridan admitted. "All I know is he would copy notes down during his meetings with Braxon, and Braxon suggested that any answers we seek would be in those notes. That is my next target."

The Providence ran her hands through the ends of her golden hair. "That could be anywhere in the palace, though. It could take you weeks to find it without alerting Typhus you are looking for it."

"Luckily, since our little trick worked and Sal had to return home empty handed, we have until the Court of Kings to find it."

Lia, deep in thought, finally joined in, "I might know where it is..."

Sheridan and the Providence locked their gazes on Lia, then glanced at one another. *Could she be serious?*

"Did Braxon say what it looks like?" the princess asked. "The notebook, I mean."

Sheridan nodded, "He said it was small and black, that's all."

Light shown in Lia's eyes. She grabbed their hands and pulled them towards the exit. "Come with me to my chambers."

◆◆◆◆◆◆◆◆◆

Sheridan's legs burned after, once again, doubling back to the central spire and climbing that dreaded spiral staircase. He was not a young dwarf anymore. Age, paired with his genetic handicap of having legs nearly half the size of the Providence and Lia, made him wish they had carried him.

Panting by the time they reached the top of the stairs, Sheridan forced himself to withhold bracing himself against the wall and asking for a minute to catch his breath. Instead, he followed them into Lia's personal chambers.

The princess's Keepers stepped into the room, until Lia commanded them to wait by the top of the stairs. Without hesitation or challenge, they exited the room and shut the door behind them.

"Your Keepers are much friendlier than your father's," Sheridan observed.

Lia turned her innocent face to Sheridan and snickered, "It helps that they have been by my side since I was born. I never exactly had friends growing up. I was raised here in the Spire, tutored in the Spire, and, if the king had it his way, I would die in the Spire. My Keepers are the only real friends I've known."

For as long as Sheridan has known the princess, she never sat foot outside the Spire of the New King. Or, if she did, she was escorted by a City Watch platoon and her Keepers and was not allowed beyond the upper district. These measures were *not* in place for her protection, though. No, King Typhus's ego and paranoia fueled those orders.

He believed every person outside of the palace wanted to kill Lia and end his precious bloodline. Lia was nothing more than a piece in the puzzle of his reign.

The Keepers, though, were not permitted to make friends with the royal families they served. Any compassion or sociability was beaten out of them in their years of training. At least a decade of physical and mental honing, mastering hundreds of fighting styles with hundreds of unique weapons, and schooling was required of each Keeper. Their one and only sworn duty being to protect the royal family at all costs.

They were still human, though. For sixteen years, they watched Lia grow and protected her from the dangers of the world. Even if they didn't speak about it, they had a relationship—a bond—with Lia. If Lia trusted the Providence and the Master of Cities, then they would, too.

The princess's chambers were beautifully fit to her personality. Directly across from the door, a wide window was set into the wall, open to the outside breeze that swept the translucent sepia curtains. A table was placed in the center of the room with four chairs, one on each side. To their left, between two decorative columns, two steps led into an adjoining room—her bed chamber. In there, Sheridan could see a plush bed way too big for the princess alone. A matching window set into the same wall across from the bed. Two wardrobes rose above their heads from floor to ceiling full of the princess's clothing, shoes, and other accessories. Between the wardrobes, she had a personal vanity with a mirror rising halfway up the wall. All along the remaining walls hung tapestries and framed paintings from all of Lia's favorite artists from across Lynidas.

Simplistic. Beautiful. Soft.

Just as she was.

Lia stepped up into her bed chamber and knelt on the ground next to her bed. Taking a knife that was tucked under her mattress, she began to pry up the stone on the floor in front of her. She wriggled the blade between the seams and maneuvered the hilt back and forth until the stone jutted from the flush floor.

She gripped the stone and slid it out, gritting against the ones neighboring it. Placing the stone next to her, she reached into the open slot.

A black, leather-bound notebook appeared in her hands as she stood up and turned to face Sheridan and the Providence.

Before Sheridan could react, Lia said, "This is not the one you're looking for. This one is mine. Before my mom left, she got herself one of these and gave me a matching one. It's a journal. There have always been things I was told I wasn't allowed to say or talk about, so my mom wanted to give me a safe way to discuss my thoughts. She helped me loosen the stone and hide the journal there."

She held it close to her, smiling at the thought of her late-mother. "The notebook you are looking for isn't the king's. It's my mother's. He must have found where she hid hers and took it for his own."

Sheridan noted Lia's frequent referral of Typhus—*king*, not *father*. She truly had forsaken the claim he held over her. It saddened the dwarf, knowing that such a young thing essentially lost both of her parents, but it made him proud to know she trusted him.

"Do you know where your mother would have hidden hers?" Sheridan asked.

"I can only guess it would be in a similar spot, since she is the one who showed me where to hide mine. But the king could have done anything with it."

Sheridan turned to the Providence, "Is there any way you can distract him and his Keepers long enough for me to explore his chambers?"

The Providence frowned, but nodded, "I can think of something.

When do you need me?"

Sheridan shrugged, "Right now, if possible. He was walking the balcony when I slipped by to meet with you two this morning. He might still be there."

The Providence met Sheridan's desperate stare and sighed, "I might be able to give you an hour before he has an episode. You know how he gets around me. And you know his Keepers will be suspicious."

Sheridan was already powerwalking to the door, his muscles and joints aching. He turned and thanked the Providence one last time and assured her, "The Keepers will follow Typhus's command. Don't give him a reason to give them any commands and you'll be safe."

"Easier said than done!" she huffed.

"What should I do?" Lia asked, still standing with the journal her mother gave her.

Sheridan looked over his shoulder as he reached for the door handle. "Head to the Providence's study. Wait there for her to return. Your Keepers and the Guardians of the Faith will protect you if anything goes south."

And then Sheridan was gone. Eager to discover King Typhus's secrets.

CHAPTER 25

May I walk with you, King Typhus?" The Providence asked as she approached the king on the balcony. She bid her Guardians of the Faith wait by the archway leading from the throne room onto the balcony.

King Typhus cautiously observed the Providence. The golden crown seemed to weigh heavy on his head. The king's hair was much longer than he typically kept it, and grey roots stood out along his hairline. Grey streaked his black beard. Typhus wore his usual black and red royal raiment with gold pauldrons and a gold cape hanging from his shoulders. The Providence never saw him in anything else and wondered if he ever washed them or ever took them off.

The Providence suppressed a shudder and took another two steps closer. His Keepers watched her carefully but made no move of aggression.

"May I walk with you, Your Grace?" she asked again, this time bowing her head respectfully.

She met Typhus's curious stare. Did he even recognize her? Perhaps he was waiting to see if his Keepers would come to his defense. If they did, clearly whoever stood before him was a threat. If they didn't, then she was a friend.

The Keepers remained still.

The king smiled and stood with his back straight. "Yes, of course you may."

To the Providence's shock, Typhus held out his right elbow, gesturing for her to lock arms with him while they walked. She met the Keepers' questionable stare and took the king's arm.

The Keepers marched on their heels as they continued along the path of the balcony, stepping into the shade as the sun hid behind the Spire.

The Providence was well aware that two stories above her head, Sheridan was rummaging through the king's chambers looking for that little black book.

◆◆◆◆◆◆◆◆◆

Sheridan counted the minutes until he guessed when the Providence would have made contact with the king. Hoping for the best, he jiggled the handle to Typhus's chambers.

Locked. Fuck.

Sheridan glanced at the keyhole that hung at eye level. He had keys to this entire palace but neglected to carry them with him today. He drew a dagger from his back and carefully wedged the tip of the blade between the door and its frame. Sliding the blade up and down, he hoped to catch the latch and spring the door open.

Click. The door swung open an inch.

Yes! Sheridan cheered to himself.

Quietly, he pushed the door open with his fingertips, revealing the chambers in which Sheridan had never once laid eyes on in his three years residing in the Spire.

To his shock and dismay, the rooms were completely filthy. Dust piled up on every surface. Smears of what Sheridan could only hope were food stained the walls and floors. Piles of dirty clothing and bedding spread across marble beneath his feet.

The smell, though... The smell disturbed Sheridan the most. He gagged, anxiously looking around the room for a place to vomit. Ultimately, he vomited right onto the floor, yacking up his egg breakfast.

Fuck, Sheridan heaved again. *Fuck, fuck!*

Worry subsided when Sheridan realized that the vomit would only blend in with the rest of the horrors that existed within the two rooms.

Much like the setup in Lia's own chambers, two rooms existed in the king's chambers. A study and a bed chamber. Though, they were opposite one another as they had been in Lia's room.

Time to find that journal, Sheridan thought. But where would he even begin to search in this mess?

◆◆◆◆◆◆◆◆◆

"How are you feeling today, my king?" the Providence asked.

"Well," King Typhus started, "I don't know if you heard, but I fell off my horse last week and broke my leg. Our fabulous white mages patched me up, put me all back together, and it's like I have a new leg. They are the finest mages in the kingdom!"

Curious... The Providence knew the king did not recognize her, or he would not have freely discussed his injury. "That is great news!" she faked excitement. "That must have been quite the ordeal."

"To be honest, I do not even remember it. I hit my head and the whole incident is a blur."

"Oh, you poor thing!" the Providence could feel the Keepers' eyes roll behind her. She shot them a sharp glance.

They rounded the Spire, stepping back into the sunlight, as Typhus led the Providence to the stone railing bordering the edge of the balcony.

"This city is so beautiful this time of day, don't you agree?" he asked.

The Providence nodded and hummed her approval.

"My favorite thing about Havana City, though," the king went on, "is how it glows with life at night. Especially right there," he pointed at a domed building with four bell towers rising from each corner. "The Regal Theatre of Havyn. The show we saw there last month was *incredible*. So moving."

Last month? The show we *saw?* The Providence swallowed hard.

"Do you remember the show?" Typhus looked at her with heartfelt eyes. "*The Martyred Servant in a Glass Castle*. The touching tale of the servant who learned all the corrupt king's secrets and was killed for her betrayal. Except, when she told the truth of the king's secrets, it shattered the king's reputation, his honor, and sparked a revolution. Don't you remember?"

The Providence nodded again, giving a soft *Mhm*.

He turned to face the Providence. Taking both of her hands in his, the king said, "In two weeks is Lia's birthday. Why don't we take her to see a show? Together, as a family. She'll be turning ten, and I heard some great shows for her age level are coming to the Theatre soon. What do you think, Helena?"

Gods, not this again... "My king, I—" she saw the loving expression on his face, the almost desperate, longing gaze in his eyes. She decided not to correct him. Her eyes welled up with tears as she nodded and smiled, "Yes, that sounds lovely."

She tried her hardest not to get choked up. To not break her cover and upset him. But his obsession with Helena, with his long-dead wife, upset her. The Providence, despite being his cousin, never associated much with the king growing up. Ever since Lia's birth, when she was hardly more than a child, King Typhus—*Prince* Typhus, at the time—grew incessantly jealous of her. Knowing that she was raised from birth to step up as the next Providence, *Prince* Typhus practically hoped for his grandfather to die so he could claim the throne and denounce her claim as Providence, setting his daughter in her place, as would be law according to the Concordat.

She never would have stepped in the way of Lia being raised as the Providence. She respected the laws and understood why they were in place. But her skill as a white mage was uncanny to that of any other mage of their generation, or countless generations before. She was immediately a threat to Typhus and his future bloodline.

It did not help, either, that she had been the one to examine and deliver the news to Typhus weeks after his coronation as king, only weeks after the Providence's own "coronation" as the leader of Havyn's Faith, that Queen Helena was barren. No longer being able to produce children meant no chance for a male heir to continue the bloodline. While Lia would now be destined to become queen, should Typhus pass away, it also meant the next Providence would be chosen outside of their family's blood, unless Lia has a daughter of her own someday.

This thought has forever been unacceptable to Typhus. But everyone knew Typhus loved Helena more than anything. Except for, perhaps, his crown.

"Good," Typhus smile to her. "Listen, while I have you in a good mood, I wanted to apologize for my behavior lately." Before the Providence could respond, the king continued, "I haven't exactly been a husband to you. I promise to do better from now on."

Tears escaped from the Providence as she gasped. Her voice choked as she said, "It's okay, Typhus." She squeezed his muscular hands.

"I love you, Helena," Typhus said softly.

Suddenly, Typhus closed his eyes and perked his lips. He leaned in close to the Providence's face, attempting to kiss the memory of his dead wife.

The Providence gulped and held back the urge to vomit at the idea of kissing her own cousin.

You owe me for this, Sheridan, she thought.

◆◆◆◆◆◆◆◆◆

Sheridan dug through the piles of filthy clothes laying on the floor of Typhus's bed chamber. If Lia was right that Helena had originally hidden the journal in the same spot, then the first place to check would be the stones on the floor around the bed.

If only he could *see* the damned floor.

How many months' worths of outfits were in these piles?

Sheridan thought back to when Typhus fired all of the housekeepers. That had been about a year and a half ago, and likely the last time his laundry was ever done.

Finally, after flinging the clothing pile as tall as he was behind him, Sheridan scanned the floor. His dagger was still drawn and ready to shimmy the stones loose.

He ran his palm along the stones, all flush with one another. Except for one.

A-ha! Found it.

The stone next to the nightstand, still covered and filled with Helena's belongings, was worn away at the edges. The squared corners rounded from years of being shimmied by blades, lifting it from its spot.

Sheridan slid his dagger between it and the surrounding stones and pried with the blade. Shifting the hilt back and forth, just as Lia had done, the stone slowly lifted from its dedicated spot.

Sheridan gripped his thick fingers around the stone and pulled it out.

There you are...

Reaching into the hole, he felt the leather binding of the journal and removed it.

He hoped he still had enough time to flip through the journal. He couldn't risk taking it with him on the chance that Typhus came here to write in the journal immediately after encountering the Providence.

He opened the front cover. *Property of Queen Helena of Havyn* ornately written on the first page. He flipped through the first few pages. All Helena's entries from a few years prior to her death leading up to the last months of her life. All expressing her emotions, the deep sadness that existed within her. Trapped in a loveless, controlling marriage, unable to escape due to her position in the kingdom. Due to the oaths she swore.

Helena, by marrying Typhus and inheriting the Queenship upon his coronation, was bound by law to uphold her duties as Queen until the end of her days. While divorce was not forbidden, it was strictly frowned upon. Furthermore, divorce would have to be initiated by the king and approved by the Faith. A divorce court would then be held with a public hearing, further adding to the embarrassment.

She was trapped.

One entry revealed an important truth that shocked even Sheridan's solid composure. Helena caused herself to become barren! She admitted to plunging a stiletto into her womb, forever damaging it to prevent herself from carrying another child.

She hoped her inability to produce another heir, a *male* heir, would cause Typhus to initiate a divorce.

Instead, Typhus refused to believe the Providence's report and continuously raped Helena. Night after night after night. Trying to impregnate her against her will.

What Typhus never knew, though, was that Helena bled severely from her womb each and every night. Her womb never fully healed from the damage she had done to it.

No doubt attributing to her death when the plague caused infection to spread throughout her body, ultimately killing her.

Sheridan brushed away his horrified thoughts and continued through the journal until finally coming across entries written by Typhus.

He was running out of time, he realized. The Providence reluctantly promised to buy him an hour, and she was not about to act generously and grant him any more time.

He flipped hurriedly to the last entry, written several months before, following his last meeting with General Braxon.

Perfect, Sheridan thought. He read the last passage.

My visit with the general went well, as expected. All of the pieces are falling into place. My spies report the other kingdoms are openly planning a rebellion against me. They fear my strength. They fear Havyn as the source of power in Lynidas.

She told me they would come after Lia to get to me. She told me I was vulnerable. Let's see how vulnerable I am now with an army of two-hundred-and-fifty thousand soldiers. Let's see how vulnerable I am when my spies spark civil unrest within their own kingdoms. Just a few more months and the pieces will fall into place.

Then, she will know I am strong.

Everything I do is for her.

She speaks to me day and night. She won't let me rest. She wants me with her. But I don't know where she is. She told me the only way to find her was to follow her instructions.

I have followed her instructions to the word. Yet she still has not come. She only talks to me.

I am coming. I am coming.

Braxon was wrong. Typhus was never in a moment of clarity when he traveled to the barracks. He was never in a moment of clarity at all.

Not when he is talking to imaginary women day and night.

Only one woman, Sheridan corrected himself. *Could it be Helena?*

Typhus always saw Helena's face when he spoke with the Providence or with his own daughter. Could he not be imagining Helena's voice while he was alone with his own thoughts?

Could Helena's death be the true source of his insanity?

What worried Sheridan the most was his talk of spies enticing civil unrest in the other four kingdoms. How true was that claim?

Sheridan recalled the bank accounts that much of Typhus's money poured into. And Braxon's ominous words of the king hiring spies.

Sheridan had no idea how he could intercept these spies and tell them to stop what they were about to do. He could possibly be too late.

No matter the case, Sheridan knew he had to discuss his discovery with the Providence.

Sheridan tucked the journal back into its hiding spot and slid the stone back into place. He thrusted the pile of clothes back over the stone where they were when he entered. Quietly shutting the door to the chambers, Sheridan sped down the castle steps and out onto the balcony to retrieve the Providence.

◆◆◆◆◆◆◆◆◆

Typhus leaned in closer. He pressed his dry, cracked lips against the Providence's mouth. She held herself rigid, refusing to kiss back. Even the Keepers behind them shifted uneasily, disturbed by what they were viewing.

A bird call sounded. The Providence eyes followed the sound to the curve of the balcony, where the circular path tucked behind her view of the Spire's wall.

Sheridan stood in the shadows, gesturing with his hand for her to come.

The Providence gently pulled Typhus's face from hers.

She looked at him, hiding her disgust, and met his smile with her own.

"I love you, too, Typhus," the words came out like acid. "If you'll excuse me, I have to take Lia to her tutoring session."

She unlatched his hands from her and held up her skirts as she nearly ran around the Spire out of view. She did not look back to see Typhus's reaction, if he was upset or angry by her sudden departure from his company.

She only wiped the tears from under her eyes as she met Sheridan.

He gave her a judgmental scowl. "May I ask what that was all about?"

She gave him a grim warning glance. "I was playing the part of Helena in this performance of *A Day in the Life of King Typhus.*"

Sheridan was silent for a minute as they walked. "Sorry to hear that."

"Please, tell me you found what you were looking for."

"Yes," he nodded. "That, and more. We need to talk."

CHAPTER 26

They stopped in the hallway outside of the Providence's study, knowing full well that Lia was beyond the doors with her Keepers. When the Providence asked why they stopped, Sheridan whispered, "When I said we need to talk, I meant you and me."

"What needs to be said that cannot be said with Lia? We agreed to include her."

"I don't really think it's appropriate for Lia to hear that her mother induced her own infertility, and the effects of it ended up killing her."

The Providence froze, solid as a rock. "What do you mean, Sheridan?"

"The journal," he explained softly, "belonged to Helena before Typhus found it. She wrote about everything. From mutilating her own uterus to the night-after-night rapes by Typhus. Was it not an infection caused by the plague that killed her? Not necessarily the plague itself?"

She said nothing.

Sheridan continued, "She could not have gone through an ordeal like that and not had it checked out by a white mage. Every night the wounds in her uterus reopened. Every night she bled excessively. She would have died long before the plague if she hadn't seen a mage. Night after *fucking* night."

The Providence still stood as still as a statue. Sad, blue eyes staring down at Sheridan's.

"Please, Providence," Sheridan shrugged his shoulders, his hands clapping against his trousers as they fell back down. "Helena's death plays more of a role in this than we realize. I'll explain why I think that once we enter those doors, but I need to know if what she wrote in that journal was true."

Tears rolled down the Providence's cheek as she nodded and said,

"Yes. It's true. I swore to secrecy I wouldn't tell a soul. If Typhus ever knew..." She swallowed a sob. "She came to me that first night, bleeding all over the floor. The damage she caused was irreversible, even for my magic. There is not a single spell, herb, or miracle in the Connections of Magic that could have saved her womb. Healing the penetrative wounds on her stomach was a miracle in itself. She feared her husband. Feared bearing another child for him. She felt there was no other way out."

"Then," Sheridan said, "when that initial mutilation was healed, or at least repaired, why did she keep bleeding?"

"Typhus is a strong man," the Providence explained through silent sobs. "Helena was strong-willed, but not physically strong enough to fight him off each night. The more she fought, the worse it was. When he would exhaust himself, she would sneak out of the bed and run as fast as she could down here with rags between her legs to absorb the blood. And each night, I would spend an hour healing the scar tissue that had reopened. The thing with scar tissue is at some point, it goes beyond healing capabilities and simply stops healing. When the plague coursed through her body, it caused an infection in her womb that spread through her bloodstream and killed her."

"You never reported any of this in her medical file?"

"Of course not!" The Providence sobbed. "How could I? If Typhus ever knew what she did, he would have killed her."

"He did kill her," he shot a look of disappointment at the Providence. "Typhus caused this."

"You know as well as I do that his rights in the Concordat as King would have protected him against any accusations."

Sheridan knew she spoke the truth. Had Helena initiated a divorce, it would have been denied due to the laws. Even if the Faith had somehow found a stipulation to allow for a divorce, Typhus would have taken out his rage on Lia. If Helena had waited and filed an official claim against Typhus for forcing himself on her with the intention to impregnate her against her will, it would have been dropped on the grounds that she was required to "do her duty" as the queen and produce heirs for the king.

And, if the truth of Helena's health was to ever become public, the Providence herself could be removed from her position or charged with a list of crimes for not recording those sessions in her study.

Helena knew this, as well. She made no mention of the Providence in her journal, protecting her cousin-in-law from any harm.

"You will have to tell Lia, you know," Sheridan said. "Not today. But eventually."

Suddenly, one of the study doors flew open. Lia revealed herself. "I thought I heard the two of you out here. Good news or bad news?"

Sheridan threw a smile onto his face. "I have news. Let's just put it that way."

Once inside the study, Lia's Keepers and the Guardians of the Faith once again waited outside in the hallway. Sheridan summarized the journal entry of Typhus's and explained his theory. The female voice Typhus referred to had to be Helena's. Who else could it be?

"Whoever this voice is," Lia suggested, "they are feeding the king dangerous thoughts and ideals. We must stop him."

"I agree," the Providence said. "Sheridan, even if we do not have Prince Sal's support, can we still present a deposition at the Court of Kings?"

"Absolutely," Sheridan agreed. "It might take more to convince High Alta to hear us out without Sal."

"Especially without all that money..." Lia pointed out. "The High King won't forgive that debt."

"No, he won't," Sheridan agreed, scratching his beard. "But if we can successfully remove Typhus from power, then we might be able to convince him to set up a payment plan. Sal saw Typhus's behavior. Eriputes is observant enough to recognize that his son may have witnessed something during his stay here, and he will demand the truth."

Or, at least, Sheridan hoped he would. If Sal's rage reflected only a kernel of his father's, then they could very well be fed to the wolves.

The Master of Cities tried not to think about that, though, as he instructed them on how to prepare for the Court of Kings in a few weeks.

Princess Lia needed to brush up on her knowledge of the Concordat. If she stepped up immediately as the Queen of Havyn, she would need to understand her duties as detailed by the law. Though Sheridan would technically rule in her stead until her eighteenth birthday, he assured Lia that she would have full control over the Monarchy. He trusted her and she trusted him.

The Providence, acting as the voice of the Faith and, therefore, the voice of judgement, would need to collect their evidence against Typhus and make it presentable for the other ruling bodies of Lynidas.

If all went well, Sheridan needed to prepare for the uproar that Typhus's deposition would create.

CHAPTER 27

By the time Drake's search party gave up for the evening, the sun had already broken over the horizon. He was exhausted. The bags under his eyes weighed down his whole face.

A chill had permeated his bones. Winter was fast approaching, and it gnawed gently at Drake throughout the entire night. The morning sun was unable to push the cool air away. He needed a warm bath.

How late were Damian and Klaus out on their search?

Apparently just as late as he was.

As Drake rounded the corner onto the street, he spotted Damian and Klaus entering *Dragonfly & the Fruit* looking about as exhausted as he was.

Drake had taken his assigned patrol through the southern part of the city. Luckily, being surrounded by City Watch guards prevented anyone from mugging that Aconyte steel sword from his belt. Eyes followed him down every street.

The city did not seem to rest, even at night. The lower district was always lively with movement, parties, street fights, and illegal deals, among the many scenes Drake captured throughout the night.

But no sign of Ena or her captors.

Not a single mage, from what they could tell.

And hardly a single dwarf.

Dwarves were far and few between in Havyn, as it was, but the lower district of Gabrenas was home to many. Drake had not gone more than an hour without seeing one since their adventure in Avalon began.

Last night, though, not a single dwarf stirred. No doubt they heard the City Watch was in search of a dwarf and hid themselves away for safety.

By the defeated expression in Damian's and Klaus's statures, Drake assumed they had no luck either.

Damian was tasked with searching the eastern portion of the city, near the guard barracks. Klaus tasked himself and his patrol with searching the west by the mining facility. He was certain the Lord of Steel could not have made it far in such a short time.

Even Lady Raven herself led the northern search party. Now that she had a suspect for who might have been involved in the murder of her husband, she adamantly led their cause. Though her part to play was selfishly in search of the dwarf, rather than Athenia, Drake was still glad to have the extra hand and the full support of the Lady of Avalon at their backs.

Last night, Damian was insistent on the roads to and from the city being barred by platoons of guards, preventing anyone from entering or leaving. Raven was happy to oblige.

In hindsight, Raven should have involved Gabrenas's governor, Josef, in all of these decisions, but the lady was desperate for answers. Any time spent asking for permission rather than future forgiveness was wasted time, in her mind. Not as if she needed Josef's permission to do *anything*, since she was his superior, but this was still his city.

Josef trusted Lady Raven, though, and knew she would only go to the extreme of locking the city down if she had a genuine reason. Josef tasked himself with damage control, easing civilians' fears with peaceful speeches throughout Gabrenas.

The sun glared in Drake's eyes as he approached the front door of the inn. Shielding his eyes from the autumn rays, he looked at the street around him. Oddly quiet for the start of the morning. By now, everyone would be on their way to their place of employment or the market.

The search for Athenia must really have everyone spooked, Drake thought.

He opened the door to the inn and stepped inside.

All was quiet, save for Inga and her waitresses preparing breakfast for the guests. Once the guests were served, she would open the doors to outside patrons looking for a quick bite to eat.

Before Drake could make his way to the stairs leading up to his room, Inga called him over. As Drake approached, he said, "Good morning, Inga. I'm going to skip out on breakfast today. I've been up all night and need some rest."

"I noticed you boys were out all night," she observed while stirring some eggs in a pan on a range over the fire behind the bar. "Listen, I hate to bother ya, but I need a favor." Drake held back from rolling his eyes. All he wanted right now was sleep. "One of my girls couldn't make it in today. All of these guards patrolling around has her landlord all riled up. He won't let her come back if she leaves. She was supposed to stop by the market to pick up a case of food I ordered on her way."

And now it's my job to run your errands? Drake thought.

Answering his thoughts, Inga said, "I know all this hoopla with the City Watch is cuz of your girlfriend. Could I ask ya to take a quick trip up the road and get my shit and bring it back?"

Way to guilt trip me, Inga... Drake sighed, "Where's the market?"

She pointed towards the west. "Follow the road for a couple miles. You'll see signs for it once you're a half-mile out." As Drake reluctantly turned away from the bar to leave, Inga caught his arm and said pleasantly, "Take your time. Rushing will only tire ya out more. Thanks for doing this."

Drake patted Inga's hand, still firmly gripping his shirt sleeve, and nodded. She released his arm, and he exited the inn back into crisp breeze.

For the first few blocks, Drake dragged his feet through the dirt, whether from exhaustion or frustration that he *still* was not in bed resting, he wasn't certain. Probably a combination of both.

Teams of guards passed him frequently as he continued down the road. His eyes passed from one side of the road to the other, keeping constant watch for any signs of mages, dwarves, or Ena.

Not as if he would get so lucky and find them out in the open, but Drake could only hope.

The Lord of Steel would have noticed she did not have his sword with her. He also would have known she was attempting to double-cross him by arriving at their meeting much earlier than planned. After what Drake witnessed in that windmill with the guard, he knew the dwarf had no reservations in murdering to cover his own tracks.

But what connection would the dwarf have with these mages? That part still baffled Drake. The mages outside of El Vadora admittedly belong to the dwarf, if his threat against Ena's city was not a bluff. The mages in Gabrenas, as well. His hands are filthy with the black market.

Had he been setting them up the entire time? Stirring up trouble on the outskirts of Cyprien, leading her away to Avalon with the lord's death, and now capturing Athenia. Falling right into his trap.

For what purpose, though?

And why would a dwarf and mages form an alliance? Never in history had that been done.

The more Drake pondered, the more questions he had. All he needed right now was sleep.

Damn Inga for her little errand she had him running. She clearly underestimated what "a couple miles" was, considering Drake had followed the road for well over five miles already with no sign of any market.

Finally, about a half-mile away, as Inga said, signs posted along the road pointed in the direction of the market.

Relief washed over Drake.

As he entered the market, he walked to the nearest food vendor and asked if they had an order for Inga of *Dragonfly & the Fruit*. Luckily, Drake had found the correct merchant. Within minutes, Drake was handed a heavy crate filled with provisions.

Drake already regretted agreeing to run this errand as it was. After feeling how heavy Inga's order was, he dreaded the long walk back to the inn...

◆◆◆◆◆◆◆◆◆

Four hours after his departure from the inn, Drake was coming down the street only minutes away from being able to finally collapse in his bed, at last.

His arms were numb from carrying the crate the five miles back. He considered whether or not to give Inga a piece of his mind. How in the Connections was her waitress supposed to carry this damned thing all this way on her own?

Suddenly, a light, crisp smell of a fire wafted into Drake's nose. He thought nothing of it.

Not until snow began falling from the sky. *What the hell?* Drake stopped to watch the snow.

It wasn't cold enough yet for that kind of weather, though. This wasn't snow...

No, this was ash.

The acrid tang of smoke filled Drake's mouth. There was a fire somewhere close by, and wherever it was, it was a big one.

Oh shit... Gods, no...

Drake followed the cloud of smoke filling the atmosphere to *Dragonfly & the Fruit*. The entire inn was engulfed in a column of flames.

Dropping the crate of food, Drake ran to the crowd gathered at a safe distance from the fire. Hundreds of people gathered around in horror as the flames climbed higher and higher, the integrity of the structure weakening with each passing second. He scanned the crowd. No sign of Damian and Klaus. No way of knowing if they escaped.

Damian! Klaus! Adrenaline rushed through his veins as he ran at full speed. He had to get them out. Maybe the fire hadn't completely burned the top floor yet. Maybe there was still a chance to save them.

A large arm reached out and caught Drake by the stomach, knocking the wind out of him. A gauntleted hand grabbed him and yanked him back.

"What the hell do you think you're doing?" a guard shook him. "You'll get yourself killed!"

Drake couldn't remove his eyes from the inferno heating the skin on his face from a hundred feet away. "My friends were in there! They could still be alive!"

The guard gripped Drake by the shoulders and shook him again. "No one is going to survive, son! Get back. There's nothing more we can do."

Drake collapsed to his knees when the guard let him go. He was so weak from exhaustion, from shock and disbelief that Damian and Klaus could be gone, to get back on his feet.

They had to be alive... They could not die knowing their leader was still missing, possibly dead.

Drake began sobbing, the heat radiating from the inn evaporating his tears before they could touch the earth beneath him.

How could he explain this to Ena? If he ever found her again, she would be devastated.

Worse—she would blame herself.

This fire was no accident. The mages waited until they were all inside before burning the place to the ground. Perhaps they didn't realize

Drake left again before they arrived.

Rage sparked inside of him. Growing like the roots of a weed, fury invaded him.

Drake inhaled and exhaled deeply once, twice. He gripped the dirt and gravel so tight that his fingernails began to crack and bleed. Then, he screamed at the top of his lungs, unleashing the sudden hatred that came over him.

As the roar of anger erupted from him, the fire began to swirl and pulse, growing increasingly wider and hotter each second.

The people in the crowd and the guards protecting them fell back as the fire pulsed and sent a wave of flames horizontal, just over their heads. Women and children shrieked, and men cursed as they ducked down, huddling together.

Drake loosened his grip on the earth, swallowed his scream. And the fire snuffed itself out.

Entirely.

Everyone gasped.

Drake looked up as cool air kissed his cheeks.

Not a single cinder glowed. All that remained of *Dragonfly & the Fruit* was the blackened crisps of the studs that once framed the inn. The rubble of what once was gathered in a pile of soot.

Teardrops collected on the ground between Drake's bleeding hands before being absorbed into the dirt.

"Gods..." the guard standing beside Drake gasped. "Was that from you?"

Drake lifted himself from the ground and rested on his knees. He looked in horror at his soiled hands. "I... I don't know..."

A pair of guards came up on either side of Drake, reached down under his arms, and hoisted him to his feet. A third guard clamped a set of manacles on Drake's wrists.

"What in the Connections are you doing?" Drake jerked his arms out of their grasp.

"Quit fighting," a guard punched him in the diaphragm, taking away his breath. "You're coming with us to Lady Raven."

Drake had no strength to fight them as they dragged him through the crowd. Confused and fatigued, he could not begin to process what had just unfolded before him. That the largest fire he had ever seen—gone in less than a second by his hands?

CHAPTER 28

The steady drip of water onto the floor echoing woke Ena. Her head ached, pounding with each heartbeat as her limp body regained movement. Only, her movement was restricted. Her lips slowly opened, and her vision was blurred. She squinted as she regained clarity and she could gather her surroundings.

Above her, a thick knot restrained her wrists together over her head. Following the knot, a rope bound her to a hook attached to the ceiling, high above her reach. Below her was the hard, wet stone floor of some kind of cell. Her legs were bare, and her knees bled from resting on the stones beneath her. Ena pulled down hard, attempting to force herself to her feet, but her failing strength would not allow it.

How hard did they hit me? And where are my clothes? She was naked and cold, goosebumps caressing her bare flesh as she inhaled deeply.

The pressure in her head focused to one spot on the back of her skull. As she turned her head, she could feel her hair was sticky with dried blood. A concussion was not helpful at a time like this, but Ena would somehow get herself out of this.

Her shoulders ached almost as much as her head from her upper body being suspended for gods know how long. Ena winced as she gathered enough strength to get one foot underneath her to stand up. When she braced herself on her foot and pushed upwards, she let out a howl of pain, collapsing back to the floor.

She looked at her bare feet over her shoulder. The soles blistered, pus and blood smudging the stone beneath her.

"Fuck..." Ena shuddered. She has seen gruesome injuries, limbs amputated, and spreading infections her whole life, but the same sights on her own body repulsed her. Even curling her toes sent a wave of unpleasantries up and down her spine. The pain was too much to bear, her feet were nearly numb. Numb from shock. Ena's entire body trembled. *What did they do to me?*

Other than her feet, knees, and head, her body seemed free of injuries. Not even a bruise to be seen. She twisted her arm, and the rope burned the skin of her wrist. The ropes were dry and tight. The more she struggled, the more likely she would bleed.

Ena inhaled and exhaled unevenly, trying to process her thoughts and calm herself unsuccessfully. She did not know where she was, how she got here, or if she would ever see the light of day again. The only source of light she had were the two torches, reduced to embers, in the sconces on either side of the stone doorway ten feet in front of her. Despite every lesson she was taught in the City Watch, stating specifically not to shout for help if captured, she could not resist.

"H-Help..." It came out as a mere hiss. She groaned to get her vocal cords warmed up. "Help..." Her faint voice scratched and burned her throat. Her tongue was sandy and dry, peeling from the bottom of her mouth. She licked her lips. Lips so dry it felt like running her fingertip along splintered wood.

So thirsty... She let out a very dry cough. Her lungs burned. *Water. I need water.*

Suddenly, she recalled the dripping sounds. She looked around desperately. In the corner of the room, water casually dripped from a crack in the stone ceiling into a shallow puddle. Craving the touch of water on her tongue, Ena moaned knowing she could not reach it while restrained.

"Someone... Anyone... Help!" her pleas were barely audible in her own head. She knew no one could hear her. And no one was trying to listen.

She looked over her head once more. The rope she hung from only wrapped around the hook and was knotted once. If she could gather enough strength to stand, there was a possibility of swinging the rope off of the point of the hook and crawling her way out of here.

You can do this... Ena took a deep breath, mentally preparing herself for the agony that would ensue. She exhaled slowly, getting her heel under herself once more. The pain in her foot was more than she could handle, but she forced herself to get her second foot planted firmly. She bit down on her lip, holding back an agonizing scream.

One, two, THREE! On the count of three, Ena forced herself to stand.

The taste of iron filled her mouth. Blood rolled down her chin. She could have sworn her teeth went clean through her bottom lip.

"Gah!" Ena gasped, blood spattering on the floor at her feet, a puddle of blood and pus formed underneath. Her toes curled uncomfortably at the feeling.

Okay, Ena, okay, she braced herself mentally. With her hands now in front of her, she grabbed the rope as best as she could and pulled it over one shoulder. She mustered what little energy she had and swung the rope over her shoulder. She watched the thick knot above her teeter on the hook. She caught the rope and held it over her shoulder again.

One more time, she thought to herself. *One more time and it should slip off the hook.* One step closer to freedom.

Ena threw the rope as hard as she could manage, but her own inertia pulled her forwards. As she caught her step, she slipped in the puddle of blood pooling at her feet and fell hard on her knees. As her body fell, the rope, still attached to the hook above her, pulled hard and popped her shoulders out of place.

"Fuck!" Ena screamed at the top of her lungs as every wound on her body roared in anguish. Her body hung limp as all strength left her body. Tears washed her cheeks. Her vision clouded as she began to lose consciousness. Black filled her sight as her head fell lifeless.

CHAPTER 29

A sudden rush of ice-cold water woke her. She yelped from the frigid shock and started shivering, her teeth chattering as she fought to catch her breath. Ena struggled to open her eyes as ice droplets froze over her eyelashes.

When she finally managed to shake them open, she saw the Lord of Steel standing before her with two mages on either side of him. One of the mages held an empty wooden bucket.

Only her visible breath filled the space between them as the dwarf grinned devilishly at the girl in distress. Joy of seeing such a powerful opponent broken down and vulnerable filled his black heart.

Desperate from thirst, Ena licked the water and ice crystals off of her mouth. Relief overcame her as her dry mouth finally found nourishment.

She studied her surroundings. Still in the same damp, freezing stone cell. Her soles still stinging from the third-degree burns slowly festering with infection. Her head still pounding and dizzy from the concussion.

What do you want? Ena tried to say. Only, her mouth couldn't form the words. How long had she been here that she was *this* weak?!

Ena recalled her City Watch training. It was more than just physical exercise, honing their skills with a blade, and learning the law. They learned precisely what the body can withstand. The severe thirst alone was proof that a week had passed, at most. Any longer than that and Ena knew she would be dead. While the human body could survive for several weeks without food, water was essential to life.

The split-second thought of food made her nauseous. Mostly because she had gone a week without a single bite and the acids in her stomach groaned for reprieve.

The Lord of Steel stepped in front of her. Holding a dagger in his hand—*her* dagger—he used the flat of the blade to tuck under her chin and lift her head. On her knees, she was eye level with the dwarf. Her eyes, glossed over from exhaustion and lack of water, locked with his hate-filled ones.

What do you want? Ena tried again, unsuccessfully.

"Your lips are moving, but you have nothing to say," the Lord of Steel observed. He slid the point of the dagger to her chin. The cold steel bit into her flesh as the dwarf pressed on the hilt. A teardrop of blood welled up around the dagger's tip. "Hmm, so you *do* bleed. Rumor has it, the famed Governess Athenia of El Vadora is invincible, unstoppable, unbreakable. Looks like I have disproven them."

Ena winced as he took the blade away from her chin. She could vaguely feel a stream of blood flowing down her neck and chest. A little mark like that would heal soon, luckily.

The dwarf circled around her, spying every inch of her exposed body.

As he rounded behind her, he smacked her ass so hard the slap echoed off the walls. Discomfort shivered down her spine. "I love a nice firm ass," his predatory growl purred in her ear. She could feel his hot breath shifting her hair with every word.

"Get away of me," she managed to say hoarsely.

"Still have some fight left in you after all, huh? Not for long," the dwarf challenged as he let go of his firm grip on her buttocks. She could feel the outline of his thick hand glowing red on her skin.

He began gliding the tip of the dagger along her freezing flesh, goosebumps dotting her arms and legs, her hair standing on end. He caressed the blade along the small of her back, around her sides, and along the flat of her stomach. There, he dragged the edge of the blade in an *X* to the right of her navel.

Ena grinded her teeth holding back the urge to show pain. She locked her green eyes on the dwarf as he slowly fileted her. He pulled the dagger away and met her gaze.

"You have a strong constitution." He winked. "I like that. However, you betrayed me. Lied to me. Stole from me. Tried to arrest me. And for that, I will kill you. I should have known the moment you hesitated to kill that guard. How would you have been able to pull off a task like killing the Lady of Avalon if you couldn't even kill a random guard whose name you didn't even know?"

Ena said between shivering lips, "I th-thought you s-said you were not a m-murderer."

He narrowed his eyes. "And I thought I told you I would do whatever it takes to protect myself and my cause."

"Wh-what cause would th-that be?"

The Lord of Steel responded with a backhand to her cheekbone, sending her head flying backward. "I'm asking the questions, Athenia!"

Ena turned her head to face him again. Her head was tolling like a bell so loudly she hardly heard him. She tried not to focus on the amount of damage her brain was enduring from an untreated concussion and excessive thirst.

"First I will explain where exactly you went wrong to find yourself in this predicament," the Lord of Steel said. He handed the dagger to one of the mages, who sheathed it. "I have been in the Kingdom of Havyn for quite some time. I keep myself pretty well-hidden to avoid being noticed, though. Ask Sheridan next time you see him." He smirked at his own sarcastic remark. As if he would ever let her out of here to see the Master of Cities again. "I'm a self-admitted thorn in his side, yet I only show my face long enough for him to order me to leave, thinking he's rid of me. Little does he know just how much influence I have in his kingdom.

"It didn't take me long to get word of the Governess of El Vadora missing from her post, once again. I was skeptical of you from the start. Why would some random girl, albeit seemingly skilled in combat, be interested in an Aconyte steel sword? Most people do not even know what Aconyte is. Needless to say, I was intrigued. And I truly did want to test your loyalty. Having an ally who can blend in easier would be helpful.

"But when I really put all the pieces together was when my men heard you identify yourself as *Kate*. That led me to contact my associates with access to the visitor records and census. Alas! Kate, Representative from Lothol. Hmm, but what would this *Kate from Lothol* want from me? Lothol is certainly not a common territory of mine, so it did come as a shock. Although Lothol is not a place I frequent often, my career tends to come with associates from all over the kingdom. It didn't take long for a hawk to get there and back with the truth that there was no representative named Kate in Lothol.

"Finally, eyewitnesses reported seeing Kate from Lothol at the Lordship Ball a month before. It also didn't take long to make contact with the carriage driver who took *Kate* all the way from the capital city. The same individual, by a different name, just so happened to be escorted from a small, forgotten city in Cyprien by Guardians of the Faith a week prior. *Ding, ding, ding!* The pieces fell into place, and I realized I had been standing before the legendary Athenia of El Vadora! Knowing your reputation for solving unsolvable crimes, I knew you were sent here to look into my affairs, earn my trust, and eventually arrest me. You were a fool to leave El Vadora."

Even Ena had to admit he was right about that last part. But the Lord of Steel was wrong about why she was here in Avalon.

The worst part, Ena realized, is that the Lord of Steel was so arrogant, so egotistical, that he believed she was sent here for *him!*

Perhaps he was trying to throw her off. Perhaps he did, in fact, have something to do with the Lord of Avalon's death and was covering it up. Why lie if he was just going to kill her, though?

He was playing games with her. Just as he had been from the moment she met him.

He wanted information from her. Information that he didn't have. That's the only reason why she was still alive.

Or he was a sadist who enjoyed causing pain on others and was simply torturing her for his own enjoyment.

Just kill me... Ena was not a quitter. But the pain was already too much. How much more could she endure?

Blood pooled inside her mouth. The Lord of Steel's backhand was enough to draw blood. Ena defiantly spat it on the floor at his feet.

Rage built up inside of the dwarf, his face turning bright red. He roared with rage as he wound back a tight fist and drilled it into Ena's stomach. When Ena held back a grimace of pain, the enraged dwarf wound back his other fist and met the same mark.

Refusing to show how excruciating the blows were, stacked atop her other existing injuries, Ena did not even blink as she met his hateful glare.

"Ahhhhh!" the Lord of Steel roared once more as he delivered a series of hard punches to Ena's gut and diaphragm. He unleashed more fury on the governess's body than a punching bag. A hollow thump reverberated off the walls following each hit.

Only after the dwarf delivered the final blow and stepped back to admire his work did Ena finally gasp and shudder for air. Her diaphragm was pulverized, her ribs broken and most definitely piercing into her lungs.

She couldn't prevent her entire body was spasming from the adrenaline.

Black spots clouded her vision and Ena knew she was about to lose consciousness again. Before that could happen, though, the dwarf turned and started into the void beyond the open door to her cell

"Get some white mages in here," he ordered one of his mage guards. "Fix her up. We'll start this up again later."

Two white mages, young girls barely even teenagers, entered the cell moments later. Ena watched behind foggy vision as a magical glow encompassed their hands and navigated their way over her broken body. Ena swore the treatment was worse than the pain.

Young, inexperienced white mages, had not yet learned how to numb the nerves as they grafted torn flesh, sealed broken bones, or regenerated the cells of damaged organs. Instead, Ena felt every piece of her defeated flesh merge together or return to normal with the rudimentary magic the two girls possessed.

They were silent. Not a word slipped from their lips.

"You have to help me," Ena pleaded softly. They stopped focusing on their work and looked at the desperation in Ena's face. "Please."

The mages looked at one another ominously before one of them said, "The lord says we cannot speak with you." They resumed their work.

Ena watched their magic operate on her. The cuts on her chin and in her mouth healed nicely. The blood oozing from the *X* on her abdomen disappeared as the cut sealed, leaving behind a light scar. *These girls are young. They have not been trained how to reduce scarring.*

As they circled around her, Ena felt them begin working on her feet. *Thank the All-Seeing God!* Her feet were by far the worst of the injuries. However, despite the slight relief on her soles, they still seared with pain. Ena turned her head as far as she could only to find that her feet were still burned and the flesh still pustulating and bleeding. The itching infection had subsided, though.

Ena briefly met the gaze of the mage who had spoken to her as they started walking away. "Where are you going? My feet. They have not healed."

The girl turned and responded nonchalantly, "We know."

Once again, Ena was alone. How much had the dwarf brainwashed these poor girls? No respectable white mage would have left her like this...

Then, two more mages entered from the darkness. Ena couldn't tell what kind of mages these were. That worried her.

No sign of the Lord of Steel.

One of them carried another bucket of water with a ladle. He took the ladle, filled it with water, and held it out to Ena's lips. She was in disbelief.

"Drink," the mage said. Without a second though, without even wondering what else could be mixed into this bucket besides water, Ena slurped it down.

The water relieved her dry, sandpaper tongue as it dribbled down her chin. She panted and gasped. The first water she's had in days and it felt as if she had struck gold.

The ladle refilled and lifted to her mouth again. And again, she swallowed.

And again, one more time, before the ladle swung in the air and struck her in the temple, dizzying her.

The dizziness in her head suddenly turned into a sharp, searing pain as lights flashed in her eyes. A loud siren pierced her ears.

"Fuck!" Ena yelled out.

She closed her eyes to block the blinding light. Squeezing her eyes tight.

When she opened her eyes again, she found herself standing in front of the door to a barn opening to the sun in her eyes. She raised her arms to block the light.

"What the fuck do you think you're doing in here?" a familiar voice sounded. Ena lowered her arms and saw the silhouette of a man standing in the doorway.

"For gods' sake, girl, I told you to break that horse first thing this morning," the voice shouted. Ena squinted through the light behind the man, trying to match that voice with a face. "Why the fuck aren't you on that damned *horse?*"

What the fuck... she knew that voice. It all came rushing back.

Suddenly, the figure approached her and aggressively grabbed her arm and dragged her through the hay and horse shit on the barn floor as she struggled to catch her footing. In the outside light, Ena finally caught who this was cursing at her and dragging her.

"Father?" she asked no one in particular. When she caught her footing and met her father's quickened steps, she looked down at herself. She was wearing tight leather riding pants and a tunic. And she had the body of a child...

Her father threw her down into a pile of shit on the ground outside. "What the fuck is wrong with you, girl? Get your head out of your ass, get the fuck up out of that shit, and get on that *gods damned horse!*"

Standing above her a few feet away was a horse. The same horse she had ridden when she was nine years old. The same horse that had thrown her into the wooden fence. The same horse that gave her the scar on her upper thigh that haunted her for over a decade.

No, no, no, no, no! She couldn't do it. Ena had no idea why she was reliving this moment, but she couldn't suffer through that same pain again.

CHAPTER 30

A week ago, Drake entered the Grand Ballroom of Avalon as an ally, a friend. Now, he wasn't sure what would happen to him. He had been locked up in a City Watch holding cell for days with hardly any food or water. Not as a method of torture or neglect, but simply because the City Watch was so damned busy at the moment that they hardly had time to give him the time of day.

Finally, the guards who arrested him received the order from Raven to deliver him to the Grand Ballroom. Considering his hands were still in chains, he knew he wasn't free just yet. The guards did not bring him to the same office he met with Raven a week ago. Instead, they led him into the ballroom itself.

The plush carpets decorating the floor of the ballroom brought back the memory of Ena in that violet dress of hers. Despite the overwhelming unknown hanging over Drake's head, he couldn't help but smile at the thought of her.

Where are you? He found himself asking every hour since she disappeared with the Lord of Steel. It felt like Ena was missing for months.

The guard shoved him along and he caught sight of the lady standing in the center of the ballroom observing the tapestries and paintings hanging from the walls, the glow of the enormous chandelier above her head.

To Drake's surprise, Raven was not wearing her typical regal attire. Instead of the usual jet-black dress and hair cascading in waves of moonlight over her shoulders, she wore tight black leggings and a matching black tank top. Her hair was collected in a ponytail. All makeup was absent from her face. Only now did Drake really see her for her age.

Age was beauty in her case. The wrinkles in the corners of her mouth, the crow's feet at the corners of her eyes, and the reddish-brown freckles that polka-dotted her ivory cheeks and nose.

Drake tried his hardest not to stare, but godsdamn, she was undoubtedly a beautiful woman.

And dangerous, too.

Behind her, Drake spotted a practice mannequin with the lady's silver rapier pierced right through the heart dangling at the hilt. This must be where she hones her combat skills. Not that she would ever need them, with the entire City Watch of Avalon at her back, but Drake supposed it kept her busy.

She placed her hands on her hips and locked eyes with him. "Drake. No playing games. No lies. I want nothing but transparency and you will receive the same in return. Understood?"

Drake nodded slowly.

"What happened at *Dragonfly & the Fruit*?"

"I, uh..." Drake really wasn't even sure himself what happened. "I—We came back from our patrols through the city looking for Athenia. Damian and Klaus got there before me. I had to run an errand for the innkeeper, and when I got back, the inn was completely engulfed."

She narrowed her eyes. "And how did the fire extinguish?"

Drake shrugged. "I have no idea, Lady Raven. Honestly. Once moment, I was grieving over Damian and Klaus, and the next, I looked up and the fire was out."

Raven dropped her hands to her sides. She began pacing around Drake in circles, studying him from head to toe.

"You are either a very good liar, Drake, or you are very naïve." She stopped in front of him and met him face to face. "You are a mage. A fire mage. I may not have enough evidence to believe you started that fire, but you put a stop to it. That much I know."

"Then why am I still in chains." Not a question.

The corner of Raven's mouth lifted in a slight smirk, showing off those wrinkles. "Because you so conveniently managed to be away from the inn when the fire supposedly started, and so conveniently returned when the fire had consumed the entire structure. The innkeeper has not been found to confirm your story. She could have burned alive, or she could have escaped."

"Listen, Raven," Drake whispered desperately. "You have to trust me. I want nothing more than to find Athenia. Damian and Klaus are dead. I'm all that's left for her if she happens to escape or is found. She's probably afraid or hurt, if she's alive at all. She'll need something good in her shitty life when all this is over."

"You think highly of yourself, don't you?" She turned away and walked over to the mannequin, drawing the rapier from its chest. "I'm inclined to believe you, simply because you are pulling on my heart-strings. The fact of the matter, though, is that you are a fire mage. The only fire mage we have access to. You placed yourself on the suspect list in the disappearance of Governess Athenia and the murder of my husband."

"What? No, Raven—"

"Take him back into custody," Raven turned away and began slashing at the mannequin with her sword. The City Watch guards grabbed Drake and began pulling him out of the ballroom.

"Wait, Raven!" Drake begged, yelling over his shoulder as they dragged him up the steps and out the gilded doors. "Don't do this, please! Raven!"

◆◆◆◆◆◆◆◆◆

Unlike Ena's cell, Drake's was supplied with a comfortable bed, a writing desk, and a candlelit chandelier hanging in the center of the room. While his hands were still bound by the steel manacles around his wrists, he was free to peruse his surroundings as he wanted.

The guards had led him down a secret staircase down into the basement of the Grand Ballroom. There were only four large cells, similar in size to the rooms on the second floor containing the legislative chambers, and based on how un-prisonlike there were, Drake assumed they served a different purpose before being turned into cells. Rather than the standard metal bars and open cells, Drake found himself behind a thick wooden door with a small barred opening just large enough for his face at eye level.

It certainly would not be wise to store prisoners in the same building as the leader of an entire region, but perhaps Lady Raven thought differently.

After two long, boring days, Drake finally heard the voices of other people outside the door. Raven's voice specifically, barking orders at her guards.

"Unlock the door," Raven's voice echoed down the hallway outside his cell. "I'll be fine in there. He may be a suspect, but he's not stupid enough to lay a hand on me." A grumble replied and the jingling of keys followed. With a heavy clank, Drake's cell was unlocked and swung open.

Raven stepped in and the door shut behind her. The lock clanked again. Her harsh glare was enough to cut through steel.

"Drake," she said in a low tone.

Drake stood from the edge of his cushioned bed. He didn't dare approach her, noting the rapier sheathed at her side.

"Lady Raven," Drake dipped his chin slightly.

Raven clasped her hands behind her back as she paced back and forth, her head towards the ground. Something was on her mind.

Before he could ask what was wrong, she spoke, "I–I truly am at a loss with this situation, Drake. I want to believe in your dedication to the governess." She stopped and met Drake's desperate gaze. "Honestly, I do. The use of magic, though..."

"It's illegal, I know."

"But it isn't," Raven replied. "The speculation is that magic use, with the exception of white magic, is illegal because of the stigma against it. The number of documented mages has decreased significantly over the past decade or so, yet the three mages we apprehended at the abandoned mine are Avalonian citizens. Do you know what that means, Drake?"

He shook his head.

"It means," she continued, "that these people who possess the ability to weave the Connections of Magic are hiding from others. And now something, or someone, is gathering them in the shadows to use them against... well, against what, I am not certain. One of the mages from the other day was a school teacher from here in Gabrenas. He touched the lives of countless youth for fifteen years before quitting his job a year ago with no explanation. Why? What could have been powerful enough to draw this individual from such a successful and worthwhile life?"

"The Lord of Steel..." Drake whispered to himself.

"Yes," Raven heard him and nodded. "I believe that, too. You claim to not be a part of the dwarf's agenda. Prove that to me."

Drake only answered with a shocked, and confused, stare. Prove that to her? How?

"Drake, you have these next few moments to say *anything* that will prove your allegiance to Athenia. To me."

Drake thought carefully. Lady Raven was a force to be reckoned with, that much was certain. However, she did not offer opportunities like this, a chance to prove her wrong.

Though, she would never word it quite like that.

Instead of proving his loyalty with words, Drake decided to perform a demonstration.

He faced Lady Raven and inhaled deeply.

Suddenly, the manacles around his wrists began to glow. Tails of smoke floated into the air as the metal hissed, white-hot. As Drake exhaled, the manacles fell from his wrists, clattering to the floor in pieces, still glowing orange.

The lady's eyes widened at her prisoner's use of magic. Her hand immediately found the hilt of her rapier, ready to draw and plunge through Drake's heart.

Yet, she hesitated.

Drake, seeing Lady Raven's brief pause, closed his eyes again, inhaled, and exhaled. Something metallic behind Raven fell to the ground with a thud. She whipped around to find the locking mechanism built into the cell door steaming on the floor, an open hole through the door to the hallway.

Raven turned back to Drake.

"Lady Raven," Drake said, "if I wanted to escape these past four days, I would have done so. Simple chains and locks cannot stop magic, apparently." He took one step towards Raven. "But I didn't escape, did I?"

Raven blinked. She brushed a lock of her platinum hair behind her ear. "You really want to find Athenia?" Drake nodded. "Do you love her?" Drake only stared. "Drake, I would have done anything for my husband. The love we shared was something out of a storybook. Those first few weeks after he died, I went crazy trying to find any piece of evidence linked to his murder. Anything to bring comfort. You have the same fervor. The same light in your eyes looking for any answer."

Drake could not deny he had growing feelings for Ena, but did he love her?

"Come with me, Drake," Raven waved him along. "I have something to show you."

Opening the broken door to his cell, Drake followed Raven into the hallway. It was not a long walk to the other end of the hall to the last cell. *Who else does she have locked down here?*

Raven took the key from one of her guards and unlocked the door. Together, she and Drake stepped through the threshold. Inside was a quaint cell very similar to the one Drake was in.

Only, the prisoner in this one was a surprise.

"Inga?!"

The innkeeper turned herself around in the chair by the desk. "Hey there, hun. Glad to see yer alive."

"What in the Connections..." Drake whispered to himself. To Raven, he asked, "Why is the innkeeper here? How is she alive?"

Raven smirked. "Her body was never recovered at the site of the fire. While most of the other individuals who perished were hard to identify because of the damage done to their bodies, they at least *had* bodies. Inga was gone. My men found her yesterday and brought her in. Go ahead and ask her why she's still alive while so many others died. It's an interesting tale."

"Inga..." Drake struggled to find the words, thrown off guard. "I thought you died. What's going on?"

She grumbled and said, "Come. Take a seat on the bed."

Drake did as she suggested.

"Sorry I had to lie to ya, handsome," Inga started. "I wanted to save the others, too, but then they would have been suspicious."

"Who would have been suspicious?"

"The fire men. You were all supposed to be in your rooms when they lit *Dragonfly* on fire. I could only save you. I'm sorry."

Drake grimaced. "You are working with them? Those murderers! How could you?"

In a hushed tone, Inga replied, "Everyone works for someone else, kid. Sometimes we don't get a choice who that person is."

"You knew this whole time who we were..."

"No," she corrected. "Y'all did a good job hiding yourselves. I only knew who you were that last day."

"Why save me, then?" Drake asked, genuinely wondering why he still stood here and Damian and Klaus did not...

"I grew to like ya and the girl. But I heard the girl was captured, so I thought I could still save you."

"Wait," Drake said, "do you know where they are holding her?"

"There are tunnels and mines all underneath the city. She could be anywhere."

"Fuck!" Drake swore.

Raven chimed in, standing over her prisoner, "Do they know Drake survived?"

Inga shrugged. "Not sure. If they do find out I saved him, I'm good as dead. You might as well kill me now."

"No," Raven snapped. "You will rot. I promise you that."

Inga shrugged again. "At least I'll die knowing I saved one life." She smiled at Drake before he exited the room with Raven.

Drake felt a pang of guilt as Raven turned the key inside the tumbler of the lock. Inga, of all people. The sweet innkeeper.

No one could be trusted.

CHAPTER 31

Twenty-two laps around the pen and Ena could feel the horse under her shuddering from exhaustion. She could not stop, though. If she did, she would have to deal with her father. That was not an option.

"Faster, girl!" Her father shouted as she flew by him on the back of the steed. Her father cracked a whipped against a metal barrel, simulating a crack of thunder. The horse flinched.

Twenty-three.

Horses are skittish by nature, especially when confronted with a loud noise. What use was a horse in battle if every loud noise or every thunderstorm scared them off, her father would always say. He wasn't wrong.

Ena understood the thunder simulation, but overworking the horse to near-death? Was that necessary?

What use was a horse if it couldn't carry its rider for days nonstop, her father would argue.

Argue, Ena thought. *Arguing is all he ever does.* Or, *did,* she supposed. She could not distinguish her thoughts between the past and the present.

Simulated thunder clapped again.

"Faster! Faster!!! What the fuck do you think this is? A fucking tea party? Ride that godsforsaken horse!"

"Yes, father!" she yelled back, kicking her heels into the horse's sides. The horse picked up speed.

They flew past her father once more, throwing up a cloud of dirt as they passed.

Twenty-four.

"Come on! Is that all you got?" she heard her father screaming. The wind battered her ears, drowning out everything except for his monstrous voice.

Let's go, horse! She kicked her heels again. The steed grunted and heaved.

This was torture. For both her and the animal beneath her legs. Ena would not be surprised if the horse collapsed under her and died of exhaustion. The summer heat and the sun beating down on them only hindered them further.

It would not be the first horse to die from a similar fate. Where father began breeding his own horses, rather than buying and selling ones, they became a copper a dozen to him. If one died, it simply became meat for the next week or two for them, and he moved on to the next victimized equine.

Twenty-five.

Instead of the whip snapping the side of the barrel, this time, her father aimed for her and the horse. The tail of the whip licked the leather of her riding pants and left a thin split at her thigh. A sour sting was followed by a heavy stream of blood dripped down her leg.

As she glanced down to see the wound, three loud claps of false thunder roared. The horse startled and Ena was too distracted to correct her horse right away.

Tripping over its own hooves, the horse slid through the dirt and stumbled into the wooden fence of the pen. As the horse collided with the wood, it tipped onto its right side, throwing itself, with Ena still holding on, through the fence and hard onto the ground.

The weight of the horse's body crushed her only momentarily before it flailed its sturdy legs, climbed back up, and took off running again.

Ena lay there, immense pain throughout her body. Her right leg throbbing with each pulse of her heart. She attempted to lift herself up, only to collapse back down, letting out a teeth-clenching grunt.

Her father took his time walking over to his injured daughter. He crossed his arms as he stood over her. "Get up."

Ena looked up at him, teeth still clenched. "I. Can't. Move."

Her father then knelt beside her and rolled her onto her left side, observing her leg. Ena refused to show how much pain she was in, despite the urge to scream from her father manhandling her.

"Gods, girl..." her father gasped. Ena followed his gaze to her upper thigh. From her hip, splinters of wood jutted from a bleeding mess. The muscle and flesh so mangled that it no longer looked like a leg. She must have been having a nightmare—this could *not* be real.

Wooziness crept in as consciousness ebbed. Blood pooled around her until she was swimming in it. She forced herself to take deep breaths.

"You broke my damned fence!" was her father's only response to the gruesome sight. "The repair costs are coming out of *your* pocket!" He shoved a finger in Ena's face. She contemplated biting it.

Instead, she responded, "Father. I–I think I need a healer."

"Get up, clean yourself off, and wrap that leg up," her father stood back up. "You'll be fine." When Ena did not stand up, he nudged her broken leg with his foot. Ena winced, a single tear slipped from her tightened eyes. "Get up, girl!" He drew his leg back and drove a kick hard into the center of the wound.

Ena screamed at the top of her small, immature lungs before the world slipped away from her.

◆◆◆◆◆◆◆◆◆

Ena's eyes opened to find herself still screaming. When the pain in her leg subsided, she looked around. Back in the godsforsaken cell.

She hyperventilated, trying to calm herself and catch her breath.

What the fuck had just happened?

She just relived one of the worst experiences from her childhood. Felt every movement, heard every word, thought every thought, from that dreadful day.

The mages stood before her still. Just as they had when she first slipped into her own past.

She felt something dripping down the side of her face. *That's right,* Ena recalled, *this asshole struck me with that ladle.* She would hate to see herself in a mirror right now.

Ena shook all negative thoughts from her mind. She glared eagerly at the mages. "Is that the best you can do?"

The mages only smirked at the challenge.

The soft patter of footsteps could be heard from the darkness beyond the threshold of the cell. The Lord of Steel stepped into the dull light, his hands clasped behind his back. He wore a black cloak that draped on the ground and followed behind him.

"I see you met my mindrenders," a sly smile formed under his salt-and-pepper beard.

"Mindrenders?" Ena asked.

"Aye," he nodded. "Mindrendering. A very rare, very *powerful* form of magic. They can reach into the deepest depths of your mind and bring forth any memory, good or bad. The strongest ones can even make you see or hear things that aren't really there."

Ena looked around the room. "Is any of this even real?"

"Of course it is," he scoffed. "These two are good, there's no doubt. But they don't have that kind of ability. Yet..."

Yet. The thought haunted Ena. To not be able to distinguish reality from imagination. True insanity.

"Are you going to tell me what you want from me?"

"In due time, my dear." Ena scowled at him. "First," he began circling around her. She was nothing but a piece of prey to him. "I should let you know that we found your friends." Her heart sank. "I am sorry to report that they died."

"What did you do to them?" Hardly more than a whisper. Her eyes beamed at the dwarf.

"The inn burned to the ground with all those inside."

"You are a monster..."

"We do what we have to do to survive, Athenia," he sounded strangely apologetic. "Losing friends, allies, or loved ones is not an easy burden to bear. Even I am humane enough to admit that. I sincerely apologize for your loss."

"You did what you had to do to survive," Ena mocked. Was this even real? Were they truly gone? Damian, Klaus, Drake. All dead. She felt more alone than ever before in that moment.

"I'll be honest, Athenia," he continued, "I have a woman in my life who I love dearly. The very thought of losing her is catastrophic. I can't even begin to imagine the sorrow you feel."

Her head hung heavily on her shoulders. Her very sore, aching shoulders. She dropped her chin and watched the floor. Damian and Klaus. Though her relationship with them remained professional over the years, she felt strong companionship with them. They were never far from her. Always watched her back. Loyalty that would make one give their life for another. That was a rare thing.

And she lost it all.

Ena could not help blaming herself. If she hadn't been so foolish, if they had stuck together, then they would have stood a chance.

Or, they would have all died together.

She was good as dead now, anyway.

"As for your previous question," the Lord of Steel said, "I want information. Information that will aid us in our quest."

"What information could you possibly want from me that you do not already have?"

"You will find out, in due time," he turned to walk away.

Ena shouted, "Stop walking away from me and face me! Stop fucking with me and tell me what it is you want!"

He turned his head and caught her green eyes in his peripheral. He chuckled, "You are not weak enough to give me the information I need. While I admire your determination and your constitution, Athenia, I am not certain I will be able to break down those walls. That is what these two are for." He gestured to the mages standing threateningly beside him. "Even if they cannot break you, perhaps they can find the information I seek by digging through your head."

As he continued out of the cell, before Ena could shout after him again, her head crackled with static. Pressure built up behind her eyes and ears, like she was being drowned, except she could still breathe.

The mages held out their hands as they forced Ena's consciousness back inside of itself.

CHAPTER 32

When her head finally stopped swimming, Ena opened her eyes to find herself in the bathroom of her childhood home. A bar of soap in one hand and suds effervescing on her opposite arm told her she was in the middle of a bath.

What memory did the mindrenders take her to this time?

The air around her was still. The bath water was tepid. It was too quiet.

Where was her father? Shouldn't he be screaming at her by now?

Ena rinsed herself off and stood in the tub. Water flowed down her body and dripped into the swirling pool at her feet before disappearing down the drain with a gurgling suction. She stepped over the lip of the tub and allowed herself to drip onto the soft mat under her feet before brushing aside the curtains and opening the second-story window. A cool spring breeze rolled through the room, biting Ena's moist skin, causing it to pebble. She shivered and wrapped her arms around her, rubbing her shoulders to warm up.

Now standing in front of the mirror, Ena observed herself. *Hmm.* She was older this time than she was during her last vision, but younger than fourteen if she wasn't in a City Watch barracks yet. Her female figure was on the approach, but not quite there yet—her hips still narrow but her muscular legs were beginning to take shape, her breasts in the early stages of filling in, hair stubbled her legs that she forgot to shave.

Ena struggled to recall the moment she was reliving. Nothing of importance had happened yet to give her any clue.

Outside the bathroom door, Ena heard the front door on the first floor open and close. Voices followed. One belonged to her father, and the other sounded vaguely familiar.

Ena glanced at the outfit hanging from the back of the bathroom door. A lovely cantaloupe halter dress. Ena sighed dramatically. She hated dresses. Her father knew that, too.

Now it came rushing back to her. *Today is a Deal Day.*

Deal Day, as her father referred to it, occurred four times each year, on the first day of the new season. Considering the weather outside the window, this must be the Spring Deal Day. These were organized all-day events where her father would show off his wares to rich bidders. Filled with excess drinking and dining at a buffet large enough to feed every poor family in the kingdom, her father thrived from the attention he received. On occasion, these events would last for an entire weekend.

When Ena was even younger, she remembered having fun on Deal Days simply because her father paid little attention to her, and she was free to engage with other kids her own age. Every lord, governor, and merchant who attended had children around Ena's age.

At this age, though, all of her childhood companions were being groomed to take up their parents' legacies. Just as she was, Ena supposed. The difference between her and her former friends was that she did not succumb to the greed and dishonesty of her family's legacy as they did.

She hated her father. Hated his business. Could not wait for the day she could get away. The others her age could not wait for the day they could follow in their parents' footsteps. It disgusted Ena to no end. She now dreaded these Deal Days just as any ordinary day.

Fuck that, Ena thought, tossing the dress onto the tiled floor. Spots of water following the path of Ena's feet soaked through the fabric. *Damn this dress to the gods. I'll wear what I want.*

Ena stomped naked out of the bathroom and down the hall to her bedroom. She threw open the drawer of her dresser and pulled out a pair of her riding pants and a tank top—tanned leather and black silk, respectively. Fully dressed, she went back to the bathroom mirror and studied her hair. Her dark waves hung neatly to her shoulders. Her father would want her to curl or straighten it in a formal fashion, but Ena felt rebellious. Instead, she drove her fingers through her locks, down to her scalp, and tousled her hair until strands were flying in all directions.

She took one last look in the mirror and smirked mischievously. *Fuck you, dad.*

As she descended the stairway to the first floor, she realized the second voice belonged to a woman. She was telling a story that her father must have found hilarious, for he was in hysterics. Ena knew it was all faked, though. Her father didn't laugh. Not for real, anyway.

As she rounded the corner, her father looked up from his seat at the table in their kitchen. Instantly, his demeanor changed when he saw what his daughter wore.

Ena stopped shy of the table and gave him a fake smile. She then turned her gaze to the woman sitting across from him. A City Watch captain.

Her father cleared his throat. He asked softly, "What's that you're wearing, girl? I thought you were going to wear the dress I picked out."

Ena placed a hand on her waist, dropped her hip, and sassed, "Well, father, I figured since we will be riding our horses to show them off, I should wear my riding gear. Who rides horses in a dress?"

The guard captain laughed at the cheeky remark. Her father, on the other hand, Ena swore, had steam coming from his ears. Seeing the furious look on her host's face, the captain chimed in, "Smart thinking! What better way to sell a horse than to show what a true riding experience is like?"

"Mm," her father grunted and forced a smile. "Yes, my oh-so-smart, entrepreneurial daughter. Athenia, this is Captain Tidas. Tidas, my daughter, Athenia."

Captain Tidas held out a gauntleted hand. "A pleasure to meet you, Athenia."

Ena extended her hand to the captain's and shook it. "The pleasure is mine. Please, call me Ena."

Her father stood abruptly from his seat. "Well, *Ena,*" he spat, "are you ready to go? It's a bit of a ride to the palace."

She observed her father's formal attire. A suit and tie with his shiny dress shoes that only saw the light of day four times a year. She then spied a playful smile in her peripheral coming from the guard captain. Ena met her smile. She was still young enough to pull off the bratty little girl attitude and have adults find it adorable. Probably her only saving grace.

Captain Tidas rose from her seat, her armor clattering as she pushed the chair in. Tidas's olive skin and brown hair, pulled back into a military-regulation bun, was offset by the pewter armor gleaming in the sun as Ena followed them through the door into the morning sun.

Three horses waited out front. One, a percheron decked out in plates of armor, belonged to Tidas. The two matching appaloosas for her and her father. Ena didn't care much for appaloosas, as their only purpose served as show or ceremonial horses. They lacked the same spirit and strength that percherons or destriers had. Her father adored appaloosas, though. Mostly for the gold they awarded him when he bred one with beautiful colors and patterns and sold them to the rich assholes on the hill. As for the one Ena mounted, the mare had a black face, breast, and forearms with beautiful black spots that faded into grey and white as they traveled down her body, leaving her rear and hind legs pure white.

Tidas led the way through the outskirts of the city until they approached the slope of the hill. As they ascended, Tidas and her father rode side-by-side, sharing remarks about Havana City's finest people, businesses, and more. The Spire of the New King loomed above their heads, casting a pointed shadow over the hill.

This season's Deal Day was set to be held at the horse racing derby on the outskirts of the city, but King Tytan requested an audience prior to the event with the Horse Lord himself. Tidas, being the king's personal favorite of the most recently appointed guard captains, sent her to retrieve Ena's father.

Contrary to the falsehood of her father's words and reactions, Ena could see the sincerity in Captain Tidas's face, hear the authenticity in her voice.

As they approached the Spire, Tidas halted her horse. "Wait right here a moment, my lord. I shall return with the king." The Horse Lord dipped his head in acknowledgement. Tidas dismounted her percheron and climbed the marble steps. Guards opened the doors and stepped aside as Tidas mounted the spiraling staircase leading up to the top of the palace.

"Girl," her father's voice broke Ena from her thoughts. She met his dreadful stare. In a low voice, he said, "If you ever embarrass me like that in front of a guest again, you won't see the light of day for a month. You understand me?" Ena looked at the ground beneath her horse. Alone with him, she was vulnerable. No witnesses. She nodded slightly. "You best be on your most excellent behavior for the remainder of the day. If you aren't..."

The punishments Ena endured on a normal day were sometimes too much to bear. If she fucked up on a Deal Day, not seeing the light of day for a month would be the least of her worries.

"Yes, father," she muttered.

The doors to the Spire creaked open again, revealing Captain Tidas marching in front of their host, King Tytan. The king was flanked by his two Keepers.

This was the first time I saw a Keeper up close, Ena recalled. Armed to the bone with impenetrable steel, wielding weapons so sharp they could cut through one's body like cutting through air. They appeared ten feet tall to her, even from atop a horse.

King Tytan, a man hardly more than skin and bones in his old age, hunched over supported by his cane as he trailed behind Captain Tidas. Once a great man, so the stories of history claim, Tytan was now nothing more than an old grouch. His days were numbered, that much was clear, and rumor had it that the richest of Havana City had bets placed on when he would die, including his own grandson and heir.

As the king hobbled over, a horse was brought up beside Tidas's with a set of wooden steps to help him mount. He paused before approaching his steed and gazed at the Horse Lord and his daughter. "Beautiful day for a ride," he flashed his missing teeth.

"Indeed, Your Grace!" her father's fake voice rose. He could play the role of the caring merchant investing in the wellbeing of Havyn and its king, but little did anyone realize that her father had a bet placed on the king's imminent death as well. One that, if he won, would allow him to retire early, so he claimed. "I am truly excited for what I have in store for you today."

The Keepers lifted the king up and over the top of his horse. Tytan took the reins and swung the horse around. No matter how feeble he was, there was no denying that he was a great rider. He found equine fascinating. Even owned a hundred of his own horses at one point in his youth. Now, since his health started fading, he sold off most of his stable or gave them away to friends and allies.

All of his horses were purchased from her father, of course. The king had been a supporter of her father's business since he first made a name for himself twenty years prior. Hence why the king never renounced the honorary title of Horse Lord that was given to her father by his most valued customers.

Her father was no true lord, obviously, and the title was given to him as a joke. But twenty years later, Ena questioned if he understood he did not actually hold the power and prestige of a true lord.

Ena watched her father socialize with the king, with his Keepers mounted on their own destriers behind them. Ena took point at the rear of the column next to Captain Tidas.

"Your father is an incredible man," Tidas broke the silence between them.

Half caught in thought, Ena scoffed. Realizing her mistake, she quickly corrected herself. "Uh, yes! Yes, he is incredible, isn't he?" The words made her want to vomit.

Tidas gave her a questionable look. "Sure. He knows business. I don't think I've ever met or heard of another merchant in Havyn with the same success as your old man."

"Mm," Ena grunted a reluctant confirmation. No matter how awful he may be to her, even she could not deny the exquisite food on their table each night and the roof over their heads was solely because of her father's hard work. *Well, not* solely *his hard work...* The world may never know just how much Ena did to tame these horses while her father was conducting the business himself, taking all the credit.

But that was a fight for another day.

"You don't seem too fond of him," Tidas observed.

No shit. "I love my father," Ena replied monotonously. "He's taught me everything I know. I owe him my life and my gratitude." She rehearsed the same speech to herself in the mirror on a weekly basis, ensuring that her facial expressions matched that of a daughter who might actually love their father.

"I understand your mother passed away when you were very young," Tidas continued, ignoring Ena's forced compliments about the Horse Lord.

"During childbirth," Ena confirmed.

"I cannot even begin to imagine how difficult it must have been for him, a man in the midst of his entrepreneurial career, to raise a daughter on his own. Has he been kind to you?"

"Yes."

Captain Tidas did not believe her. When Tidas remained silent, Ena curiously looked over at her to catch her skeptical gaze. Ena was not doing a great job of hiding her true feelings, and she knew it. She simply didn't care.

"How old are you?" Tidas asked.

"Eleven."

Tidas pulled her percheron up close to Ena's appaloosa so they were only in earshot of one another. "I don't know how bad things are. You don't have to tell me. In a few years, if you ever need a place to go, come see me at the barracks. You could find a home in the City Watch."

Ena's head whipped to her. "Really?"

"Yes, Athenia," Tidas nodded.

"Please, call me Ena."

"Ena," she nodded again. "The City Watch is a very different life than what you're used to, but at least it could be home."

"Different might not be so bad..."

◆◆◆◆◆◆◆◆◆

The remainder of the day was filled with her father shaking hands with and schmoozing all of the lords and ladies, governors and governesses, merchants, bankers, and shop owners into purchasing his horses. Those who didn't make a purchase made investments instead, fronting up the gold to breed a horse of their desire.

Ena dragged her feet knowing that it would be her with the burden of actually breeding, raising, and training each of these horses over the next year, not her father.

The stadium was filled with wealthy patrons observing the Horse Lord's showcase of valuable steeds, all of which were shown around the track. First by walking, then by cantering, trotting, and, finally, galloping. Each appeared perfect. Every muscle rippled as they moved. All obeyed every command their jockeys gave.

As the rich assholes around her applauded, Ena waited patiently, and hopelessly, for them to congratulate her on her hard work. After all, she knew every single one of the hundred horses out there on the track. Knew their dispositions, their habits.

All her father knew was their value.

The prize of the day was the jet-black destrier that Havana City's City Watch commander took a liking to. The gelding sold for an esteemed ten-thousand gold—two thousand higher than the Horse Lord's asking price.

Not before Ena dug herself her own grave, though.

"Wow, that is a gorgeous warhorse!" the City Watch guard commander said, viewing the destrier through his scopes. "How tall is that handsome devil?"

Her father took a look through his own scopes. "Ah, yes, that is a good one! He's about, um, fifteen hands."

"*About* fifteen hands? What the hell does that mean?" the commander laughed.

Ena interjected, "The gelding is exactly fifteen-and-a-half hands, Commander."

"Fifteen-and-a-half? What a beast!" the commander was ecstatic. He looked to her father. "Fifteen-and-a-half. Why didn't you say so?! How much are you asking for?"

The Horse Lord glared at his daughter as he responded, "Current bid is eight."

"You think he'll get any more bids?" The Horse Lord shook his head, hiding his anger at his daughter for showing him up. Then, the commander leaned down from the stand behind them and asked Ena, "What do you think, sweetie? You think I'll get outbid if I put in eight thousand?"

Ena knew the commander wasn't being serious. She knew he was only joking to give her some attention, as if she was some dumb little girl. Her father smirked at the condescending tone in the commander's voice.

Now it was Ena's turn to feel angry. She didn't blame the commander, though.

Instead, she responded to him, "No offense, Commander, but I believe you would be a fool to let your bid go for eight. Destriers are worth a small fortune as it is, and every person in this stadium realizes that. I must admit, this season is a short one for destriers, with that fifteen-and-a-half hand one being one of three and by far the largest. I broke him myself. If you want strength and endurance *along* with appearance and obedience, that is the best value for your gold. Once word travels that he's fifteen-and-a-half hands, though, eight will be a low bid." She looked behind her to find the commander's jaw at his feet.

She shrugged innocently with a bright, white smile. "Just saying!"

Ena didn't need to look at her father to feel the flames shooting from his eyes. *I'm going to pay for that later.*

And she did.

Even though the "innocent" words of a child had earned her father an extra two thousand gold, her undermining of him earned her two black eyes and a few broken ribs. Her father occasionally hit her or whipped her, but any serious injuries she sustained were usually due to riding accidents. This incident was the first time her father had ever incapacitated her with his own two hands.

And it certainly would not be the last.

Or the most brutal.

She crossed a line that day that she would never return from.

As Ena lay there, bleeding from every orifice on her body, holding on for dear life, she prayed to whichever god was listening that she could wake from this nightmare. The pain was real. The sensation of drowning on her own blood was real. The smell of horse shit that her father dragged her crippled body through was real.

The smell of urine was real.

As her mind was violently thrown back to reality, her head pounding like someone had just taken a hammer to it, Ena realized during the stress and torment she endured that she loosed her bladder all over herself.

Her severe thirst caused her bladder to burn as the dark yellow, nearly orange, urine streamed down her naked legs and pooled beneath her in the same puddle as her own blood.

The pain in her face and ribs from her memory faded slowly. Too slowly.

"Just fucking kill me," Ena demanded.

The mages exchanged a glance. One of them said, "In due time, Governess."

CHAPTER 33

Inga said the tunnels and mines ran underneath the entire city. Drake thought if they could acquire some kind of map or diagram that they would have an idea where to start. He was wrong.

Raven perused the archives for an entire day before finding any evidence of tunnels below the city. Dating back nearly a millennium, when Gabrenas was first established, a sewer and flood system was developed under the city in a grid-like pattern. Raven managed to come across the original designs.

As she rolled open the massive scroll along the table of the Grand Ballroom's conference room, dust puffed into the air in a thick cloud. A thin film coated Lady Raven's black satin dress. She brushed off her annoyance and placed gilded paperweights in each corner to hold the diagram open.

"The sewers stretch for miles," Raven explained, running a delicate finger along the near-crumbling parchment. "All beneath our feet. All this time. It's unbelievable."

Drake rose an eyebrow. "Didn't you know they existed? You have running water in Gabrenas. Where did you think it went?"

"Do not condescend me, Drake," she snapped. "The sewers we use are here." She pointed to another rolled up scroll. Drake unfurled the parchment, much newer than the one Raven studied, and noted the difference in design. "Our current sewer system is simply developed by pipes that run four feet under the existing roads. They receive frequent maintenance, and my city surveyors inspect them annually. *These* designs," she ran her fingers along the spread blueprint, "span deep under the sidewalks, under houses, in a carefully measured grid." She glanced up at Drake, who was standing across the table from her. He met her cyan eyes with his brown ones. "The streets of Gabrenas are not a grid. The city is extremely old and was constructed in sections as the population expanded."

"So, there's no rhyme or reason to what was built where," Drake observed.

Lady Raven nodded. "These ancient tunnels were designed to be sewers *and* an overflow system in the case of a flood. Gabrenas has no bodies of water. Why construct a flood system for a place that would never flood?" She looked at Drake, as if expecting an answer.

Drake viewed the map below Lady Raven's hands. He noted the rigid pattern of the tunnels. Studied the lower district, in particular.

Then, it hit him.

"Raven!" his eyes widened. "I know where one of the entrances to the tunnels is." He pointed to one of the sections of tunnel with one hand and matched it with a spot on the map of Gabrenas with the other. River Street. *The last bend in the river, you will find a shipyard. Ask for the Shipmaster.*

Now, Raven's eyes widened. "Gods, why didn't *I* think of that?! Of course! *The Shipyard Tavern.*"

"The Shipmaster," Drake nodded in agreeance.

The tunnels were how the Lord of Steel smuggled his goods into the city. It all made sense now. If the Lord of Steel knew these tunnels, then he *had* to be holding Ena there. It would take them weeks, if not months, to scour every inch of these tunnels, if the diagram was accurate. If they stormed the tunnels with guards, though, the Lord of Steel could easily take Ena and move her. An endless game of cat and mouse. They needed a lead. Someone who knew the tunnels, as well, and who would possibly cooperate with them.

The Shipmaster was the only other individual Drake could think of who might have any clue.

"Let's leave immediately," the lady said.

"No," Drake held up a hand. "I must go. If the Lord of Steel's informants tip him off that you are sniffing around the *right* spots, we won't catch him off guard."

"Then take a handful of the City Watch with you, at the very least."

"I can't risk it. Guards stand out. I won't. The Lord of Steel might still not realize Inga saved me from that fire."

Raven slammed her fists on the table, rattling the paperweights. "No!

Working alone is particularly why Athenia is in that dwarf's clutches. Do not make the same mistake she did."

"No need to worry, Lady Raven," Drake smirked. "I am not quite as proud as Athenia. If I need help, I will call for it."

Raven reluctantly accepted.

Drake continued, "Do me a favor. Start having your guards discreetly focus their efforts on the sections of tunnel that meet with the city above. If we can find any other entrances, we can seal them off or post guards to hopefully flush the Lord of Steel and his mages out."

◆◆◆◆◆◆◆◆◆

Two hours later, the moon hung high over Drake's head as he waited in front of the entrance to *The Shipyard Tavern*. He hesitated.

How many were watching him right now? River Street was full of drunken fools parading up and down the road, stumbling in and out of countless bars. Yet, the tavern before him remained quiet.

He could very well be walking into a trap.

Drake swung open the door and stepped inside.

Empty. Just as it was the last time he was here.

Strange... Drake thought.

The same waitress was washing and drying beer glasses behind the bar.

"We're closed," she said without looking up.

Drake took another step inside. "I... I'm here to see the Shipmaster."

The waitress looked up now. She let out a slow sigh. "We're closed," she repeated. "He's gone for the day." She returned to drying her glasses.

Drake quietly walked over to the bar and pulled up a stool to sit on. Intimidation was not Drake's strongest skill. In fact, he has never needed to intimidate anyone at all. He watched the waitress at work while thinking of what to say. The Shipmaster was here, Drake knew it. His waitress was more like a secretary to him that just a simple barmaid.

"Look, sir," the waitress said softly, "I have told you politely to leave already. If you don't," she slid a sharp carving knife onto the bar top between them.

Secretary? More like bodyguard.

Drake swallowed hard and attempted poorly to hide his fear. His hand brushed against the hilt of the Aconyte sword at his waist, reminding him that he has *some* protections.

"Do you remember me?" Drake asked. The waitress's eyes narrowed. "I was here a couple of weeks ago. With a girl. She spoke with the Shipmaster in private." The waitress stood up straight and crossed her arms. "I need to speak with him. Please."

The waitress rolled her eyes and turned on her heels, disappearing behind the kitchen door. Drake took the moment to analyze the tavern. Why would they be closed so early? It had just turned dark on Drake's walk over here. With all the drunks outside, this would be the prime time to be open.

"We're closed," a deep male voice boomed behind him. Drake whipped around on his stool and faced the bar again. The Shipmaster stood before him with his arms resting on the bar top, revealing sweat stains on his tank top beneath his armpits. He flashed his yellow teeth. "What do ye want?"

"Do you remember me?" Drake asked. The Shipmaster nodded. "Then you'll definitely remember the girl I was with, and how you led her into the tunnel beneath your kitchen in back."

The Shipmaster glanced at his waitress. "Lock tha door."

She rushed over to the front door and slid the deadbolt.

Drake suppressed a gulp.

"What do ye know o' tha tunnel?" The Shipmaster grunted.

"Only that there is an entire system of them beneath the city. I need some information on them."

The Shipmaster spat, "Ye ain't getting' anything from me."

Drake ignored the phlegm on the bar top in front of him. "I know your tavern is used to smuggle in most of the black-market goods in Gabrenas. Including Aconyte steel."

"Like I already told yer girlfriend," he was getting agitated, "the steel ain't mine."

"But you know the man whose steel it is."

"You know nothin' o' him or his steel. I want nothin' to do with it. Who tha fuck do ye work for?"

Drake threw up his hands. "Shipmaster, I have no quarrel with you." Drake then slowly drew the Aconyte steel blade from his hip and placed it gently on the bar. The metal sang. "I need to find the Lord of Steel. He has taken something very valuable from me. I need it back."

"Tha girl..." the Shipmaster mumbled.

"Yes," Drake nodded. "Please. Tell me what you know."

The Shipmaster sighed, "I can't. Business is business."

"Shipmaster," the waitress interjected from behind Drake, "if her life is at risk... How would you feel if I was the one locked away in those tunnels?"

The Shipmaster looked past Drake's head, locking eyes with the beautiful waitress. Drake was unsure what the relationship between the two was, but they cared for one another in some way. Anxiety crept over the Shipmaster as he shifted on his feet, scanning the open tavern as if someone else could be listening.

"If you can't tell me where she is," Drake shifted the conversation, "can you at least answer one question for me?" The Shipmaster only met his gaze. "Has the Lord of Steel, or anyone else in the black market, for that matter, received any shipments of bluebite in the past few months?"

"Bluebite?" The Shipmaster seemed shocked, though, Drake was unsure what his surprise meant.

"Yes, bluebite. It's a type of poison that turns the mouth blue—"

"I know what it is," the Shipmaster snapped. "Why do ye need to know about it?"

"I... I can't say."

"First, tha steel. Now, tha godsdamned poison! What tha gods are ye and yer girlfriend doing here? Ye don't belong."

"Exactly why I would like to save my friend and get out of Gabrenas as fast as possible. People are dying from that poison. My friend found that out and it led us to the Lord of Steel."

"Who?" the Shipmaster asked. "Who died?"

Drake hesitated. How much of the truth could he tell this man? What if the Shipmaster told the Lord of Steel everything they were talking about? What if the Lord of Steel was listening right now?

Drake sighed heavily, knowing that Lady Raven would probably kill him if she found out what he was about to say. "The Lord of Avalon." The Shipmaster's jaw fell. "The Lord of Avalon was poisoned."

"And tha clues have led ye here?" Drake nodded. "Fuckin' gods! Tha damned dwarf told meh I'd be safe! Fuckin' liar!"

"Shh." Drake put his index finger against his lips, trying to quiet the Shipmaster. "Don't worry. I am not here to get you in trouble. If anything, I'm trying to get you *out* of it. But I need to find the Lord of Steel." *Wherever he is, Athenia would be close by.*

"I ain't no lord killer," the Shipmaster hissed. "It wasn't meh. Tha poison came about six months ago. Tha Lord o' Steel brought it in and took it."

"And where is he right now?" Drake urged.

"Not here," the Shipmaster promised. "Tha tunnel under meh tavern is far from him. There are four other places in tha city to get into tha tunnels. I can't tell ye where they are since I don't know." Drake narrowed his eyes skeptically. "I mean it. I stumbled on tha tunnel here twenty years ago. I used it to help smuggle some exotics into tha city to get some extra gold. Tha Lord o' Steel is tha only one who knows o' tha others."

Drake restrained from jumping out of his seat in excitement. "That's fine. I can find the others. But where in the tunnels would he be keeping prisoners, if he had any?"

The waitress answered this time, "Probably in the center of the city." Drake turned to see her. "The dwarf has commented before that there are no entrances to the tunnels near the center of the city, only along the edges, like the one here. If I was him, I'd hide her far away from the entrances in case she managed to escape."

Drake looked between her and the Shipmaster and thanked them both. "If I need to come back here to get into the tunnels..."

"Don't fuckin' bother," the Shipmaster cursed. "I want nothin' to do with ye. I ain't losin' my life over this shit!"

Annoyance washed over Drake. He expected nothing less, though. The Shipmaster was relatively innocent in all of this. He clearly was not a friend of the Lord of Steel. Instead of arguing, Drake thanked them both again before sheathing the Aconyte sword and walking back out into the streets of Gabrenas.

◆◆◆◆◆◆◆◆◆

The next morning, the Shipmaster and his waitress were both found on the floor of the tavern with their throats slit. Cold and stiff. Lady Raven had their bodies quietly removed and brought in a wagon to the Master White Mage's study for examination; though, she knew the Lord of Steel's many eyes were watching.

Raven made an effort to display her strength by flashing the City Watch through the city that day. Only a step or two away from finding the dwarf and bringing him to justice, so she believed.

CHAPTER 34

Pangs of hunger woke Ena out of a fragile sleep. It had been over a week since her capture; though, she lost track of the days and nights. Over a week since any food. At least water was being provided on a regular basis, albeit sparingly. She was alive.

Just barely.

Infection crept up from the soles of her feet, numbing her toes. Every other day, those young white mage females entered her cell, healed her just enough to keep her alive, and retreated into the darkness beyond the threshold of her cell. On the days in between, Ena suffered in immense pain as her half-healed injuries pustulated and burned until she lost consciousness.

The hunger, though... It was the worst part of this torment. Her stomach growled painfully, roaring out and echoing off of the walls of her cell.

For Ena, hunger was a regularity. She ate like a pigeon, even on her best days. Raised in the Watch, guards are forced to go several days without eating to acclimate their bodies to the possibility of going hungry for days while on duty.

Days and weeks were drastically different, Ena realized.

Her ribs protruded from her abdomen, like claws tearing through fabric, her cheeks sunk into her face, and her muscles began the early stages of atrophy.

Blood streamed down her arms from her wrists where the knotted rope broke her skin.

She dared not look down at her knees. She swore the flesh was gone and all that was left was bone scraping against the stone floor.

Off in the distance, between the narrow archway posing as the exit of her makeshift cell, a light flickered and crackled.

A torch.

Someone's voice spoke quietly, barely audible.

Ena held her breath. The air was vacant of all sound except for the hushed conversation going on a little more than twenty yards away.

"No, she'll talk," said a gruff voice. "She just needs more time." *The Lord of Steel.*

A low female voice replied, "Time is not on our side. If my sources are correct, which they always are, then our window of opportunity shortens each day."

"I know, I know, your highness," the Lord of Steel sighed. "What do you expect, though? Her reputation is only words compared to how resilient she is. She won't break."

"Bring her to the brink of death," the female purred. "Death brings out the truth."

Ena did not recognize the female. Were these two partners, or was the Lord of Steel conducting her dirty business for her? *He called her* your highness, Ena observed. *Is she royalty? A lady, perhaps?* The only lady Ena knew, and who knew her in return, was Lady Raven...

That was *not* Raven's voice, though. Raven spoke more abruptly. More emotionally. This voice was cool, calm, and calculating.

"The governess has danced with death more than once, your highness," the Lord of Steel snapped. "She does not fear death. She welcomes it. Death is not going to help us here." He paused. "The only way is for the mindrenders to navigate through her mind and put the pieces together like a puzzle."

"I agree with you, Mida, but they are operating on her too slowly for comfort!" the female lashed out. She then began to chuckle, low and guttural. Yet, oddly sensual. Menacingly. "Let me in there with her. I will tear her to pieces until she is nothing but a shell."

"No! Not yet!" the Lord of Steel sounded defensive. Fearful, and defensive. "Please, just a few more days."

She growled, "Fine. The clock is ticking..."

Suddenly, her voice vanished.

The Lord of Steel cleared his throat before snuffing the torch. Ena heard his footsteps approach and pretended to be asleep. She waited until he was in the cell before imitating a startled awakening.

"Ah," the Lord of Steel smiled, "glad you're awake. We need to talk."

Ena faked a yawn. "What do you want now? As if you will even tell me."

"Listen, Athenia," he sighed, "I only need some information. I could come right out and ask, but I'm afraid you are too smart and will lead me off track or hide the truth."

"Instead, you hope to pry the answers from me without my realization?"

"See," he winked. "Too smart."

Ena thought carefully for a moment. She doubted that she could bargain her freedom with answers, for even if she gave the answers he seeks, it would likely hasten her death, rather than prolong it. Perhaps she could play his game in reverse, though. The dwarf was smart, cunning. But was he smart enough to avoid being tricked into giving her answers, just as he wanted to extract information from her?

Ena had to play his game if she was to survive.

"You are a man of your word, correct?" she asked.

The Lord of Steel narrowed his eyes and pursed his lips. He paused a moment before answering. "Indeed, I am. Why do you ask?"

"Can we make a deal?"

He considered for a moment, pacing to the left, then to the right. "You are not leaving this cell."

"I figured as much."

"What else could you want from me besides your freedom?"

"Besides a hot meal?" Ena snipped. "Answers. Same as you."

"Ha! No."

Ena flipped her lengthening hair with a whip of her neck. "Why does it matter what I know? You said it yourself, I am not to leave here." The Lord of Steel twiddled his thumbs, considering her words. She continued, "If I give you an answer, you give me an answer. *Truthful* answers."

A smile spread from cheek to cheek under his thick beard. "A game? Hmm, I do like games. Alright, Governess, let's play."

Ena shifted uncomfortably, trying to give her shoulders a rest from suspending her for this long. "First question is yours."

He stroked the ends of his beard with his thick fingers. "As the daughter of the Horse Lord, how much of Havana City did you see? Specifically, the Spire of the New King?"

"Didn't you already extract that from my memories?"

The dwarf smirked. "Answer the question."

"I saw enough of Havana City to know how deep the roots of corruption grow. I never set foot in the palace. Not until I was an adult." She reflected on her brief visit to the Spire when the Providence had summoned her this suicide mission.

The Lord of Steel nodded. Seeming somewhat satisfied with her answer. He held out a hand, gesturing that it was Ena's turn to ask her question.

"What is the outcome the mages want from all of this?" she asked.

"That's a loaded question. To simply put it, they want recognition. They want justice for the wrongdoings of the past. The history books don't always tell the whole truth, only what the authors want their readers to believe." Many in Lynidas believed the mages betrayed their truce with the other dueling parties during the Mage Wars, causing the extinction of the fairies and leading to their own ultimate demise. That is what the textbooks wanted people to know. Was there a hidden truth only few knew?

"Why are you helping them?"

"No!" he held up a hand. "My turn. How can one remain incognito from the City Watch?"

Ena's brow scrunched. "Could you elaborate?"

The Lord of Steel grunted. "How can me and my men operate in plain sight without the Watch arresting us?"

"That's impossible."

"No, it's not," the dwarf gritted his teeth, "and you know it. My eyes and ears have provided me with enough information to know that there is something within the City Watch statutes that can provide me and my mages with anonymity from the law. Do tell me the truth, Athenia. I'd hate for you to break your word."

He was mocking her. He knew she was too honorable to break her word. She promised him the truth if he played this game of question and answer. Truth was, there was only one order that would grant the Lord of Steel the freedom he desired to act without consequence.

Ena sighed. Revealing this secret would betray everything the City Watch stood for.

"There is an order that can only be given by the Master of Cities himself. It uses a secret phrase known only to the lords and ladies. Not even governors and City Watch commanders are granted this information. When the order is given, all City Watch guards in the kingdom are to lay down their arms and disband." The Lord of Steel's face told Ena all she needed to know. That was the key he was looking for to unlock the rest of his plans. "It is impossible to give that order. Do not get your hopes up."

"What else would I need to give that order?"

Ena smiled, despite her facial muscles hurting from lack of use. "My turn to ask a question, my lord." The Lord of Steel gave a look of annoyance but did not argue. "What can you gain by helping the mages? You are a dwarf. You cannot wield the Connections of Magic. Why bother helping them?"

"It is a long story, Governess." The dim light from the torches danced with the dwarf's shadow as he circled around Ena. "I won't waste your time with my tale, how I arrived here, or how this all started. Just know that I am the catalyst to the start of something great. The mages will rise again, and I will be the hand that guides them."

"*Guides,*" Ena copied, "but not *leads.*"

"Pardon?"

"You said you will be the hand that guides them, not leads them. Who is their leader?" Ena could see she was getting under his skin. His brows pressed together. Before he could defend himself, Ena asked, "Who were you referring to as *Your Highness?* Is she your leader, your queen?"

"You can call her that," the Lord of Steel grunted. He stared her down, as if he were burning holes through her body with his eyes. "You have sharp ears. What else did you hear?"

"Nothing much." Then, Ena gave him a sly, mischievous smirk. "Mida."

The Lord of Steel locked eyes with her, not breaking his gaze. After a few daunting moments, he snapped his fingers and the two mindrenders stepped into the light.

He said to them, "Keep her under as long as the Connections will it. I want her secrets. All of them. Muddle her mind to powder if you must. I will not be speaking with her again."

Oh shit. Ena had pushed her luck just enough by revealing that she knew his name. An ear-piercing screech sounded in her head as that familiar, discomforting pressure built up in her temples.

◆◆◆◆◆◆◆◆◆

Ena awoke to the smell of ash and the frightened whinnies coming from outside in the direction of the stable. Her feet swung over the edge of the bed, and she ran to her bedroom window. The stable was on fire and horses were scattering from inside, tearing up turf as their hooves carried them across the field.

This was not just a random fire. This was arson.

Silhouettes of men throwing torches into the windows and doors of the stable stood out against the fire brewing from across the yard.

Son of a bitch!

Alert, Ena bolted from her bedroom barefoot. The door to her father's room was still shut. Running over to it, she pounded on the wood with the bottom of her fist. "Father! The horses!"

Before waiting to see if he awoke to her warning, she leaped down the stairs and burst out the front door. She didn't make it twenty feet from the house before her father ran outside.

Spotting the assailants, he picked up a nearby shovel, used to clean up shit from the stables, and tossed it to his daughter. "Get the horses out of there. I'm going for the guards!" He took off in his night robes and slippers down the worn pathway towards the city.

No care for her wellbeing, of course. Only the horses.

Ena picked up the shovel and headed for the stable. Approaching the arsonists, she stopped and shouted, "Hey! Get off of our property!"

Some of the men turned to face her while the others entered the stables with knives in their grip. The three who faced her laughed at the sight of a young girl wielding a shovel. Two humans and an elf.

The elf spoke as he stepped towards her, "Ha! What's that shovel for? To dig your own grave?"

"No," Ena said. "To dig *yours!*" She lifted the shovel over her head and brought it down hard on the top of the elf's head. Distracted by his own laughter, the elf did not see the heavy steel blade of the shovel as it crushed through the top of his skull. Blood gushed from the elf's head sending him screaming in horror to the ground.

Ena stood over the elf as she repeatedly swung the shovel onto his face, each connection sounding a gruesome crunch.

"What the fuck!" one of the humans said, pulling a sword from his belt. The other followed suit.

Ena stepped over the elf, who was quite dead. His face was entirely smashed in, blood and brains pooling around the body.

"Get the *fuck* off of my godsdamned property!" Ena screamed.

The two humans stepped forward and attacked simultaneously. Ena deflected their blows with the shaft of her shovel and parried by driving the butt of the handle into one of their stomachs, doubling him over, and swinging the spade into the other's sword hand. Bone cracked as the assailant's wrist bent backwards, sending his sword airborne. He gripped his crippled wrist with his alternate hand, roaring in pain.

To her right, the other human recovered and swung his sword over his head, bringing it down on Ena. With a split second to spare, Ena caught his movement in her peripherals and blocked the blow with the shaft of the shovel again. The wooden shaft split in two, and Ena's attacker kicked out with his heel, connecting with Ena's diaphragm and launching her to the ground onto her back.

Ena struggled to catch her breath as her attacker approached. The two ends of the shovel were not in sight. She must have dropped them.

Scrambling to her feet and looking around desperately, Ena's fingers found the disarmed sword of the man with the broken wrist. She twirled around just in time for her sword to deflect her attacker's. Metal clashed and whined sharply over the growing roar of the flames.

Ena's arms grew exhausted from deflecting and parrying attack after attack. She needed to act offensively before the other human regained the strength to attack with his one good remaining hand, leaving her at a disadvantage.

"We weren't supposed to kill you," her assailant said in between attacks, "but I think the Guild will forgive a life for a life." He pointed the tip of his blade at the mangled corpse of the elf.

He swung again.

Only, this time, instead of blocking, Ena dodged the blade. The human's inertia carried him forwards, tripping over his own feet. Ena struck her blade against his as he stumbled, causing his grip to loosen, dropping the sword. As he caught himself and turned back to face Ena, she swung the blade from her right shoulder to her left, slashing the tip of her blade through the assailant's throat in one clean slice.

A waterfall of blood gushed from the cut as the man fell to his knees, grabbing and clawing at his neck. Blood gurgled from his mouth as he struggled to catch his breath.

He reached towards Ena with a bloodied hand before falling face first into the dirt.

Quickly turning around, Ena ran up to the last remaining assailant, still yelling in pain and grabbing his swollen hand. She grabbed his shoulder, giving her leverage as she drove the sword upwards through his gut. Still alive, for now, the man collapsed to the ground trying to apply pressure to his stomach as Ena slid the crimson blade away.

Suddenly, the stable doors flew open and a dozen horses sprinted from inside, many with severe burns and deep cuts. Following them, the last three assailants came running out, covered in blood. Seeing the scene before them, one called out, "Oh shit! Let's get out of here!"

Ena chased after them as they ran off across the field into the distance. *"Get the fuck off of my fucking property!!!"*

She watched as they disappeared over the horizon. Behind her, the sound of armor clattering approached. Ena turned to see her father with a dozen City Watch guards, including Captain Tidas.

"Ena!" Tidas called out. Ena trotted over to her. "Let's move away from the stable. We'll have to let the fire snuff itself out."

Ena nodded and returned to the house with her.

By daybreak, her father still hadn't said two words to her. Not a thanks. Not to ask if she was alright. She killed two people and severely injured a third. Blood had never been spilled by her hands before.

She was in shock.

Not only because two lives were now on her hands, but because she had killed those people without a second thought. Her first and only thought was to save the horses. Perhaps she had more of her father in her than she thought...

Shaking that atrocious possibility from her head, Ena met up with Tidas, whose team had finished their investigation through the stable moments before.

"What's the news?" Ena asked.

Her father, seeing Ena leave the house, followed her over to Tidas. He pushed his daughter out of the way and repeated the same question to Tidas, "What's the news?"

Tidas tried feebly to hide her look of disgust at the Horse Lord's general disregard for his daughter's safety, or existence, for that matter. "Twenty-seven horses are dead. The other twenty-three are out in the fields, still in shock, but alive and mostly uninjured."

"Dead?" her father's face paled as if he would pass out. "That many are *dead?* What happened? Was it the fire?"

Tidas shook her head. "Only minor injuries occurred from the fire. They were slaughtered, sir, by the arsonists."

He collapsed to his knees. "Why? What did my horses do to them? Who are they?"

"Luckily, your daughter kept one of them alive," she winked at Ena, "and he admitted to being hired by the Merchant's Guild in Fairmarq to relinquish you of your stock before he succumbed to his injuries." *Three dead by my hand,* Ena thought. "It appears that your business in Havyn has caught the attention of patrons in Fairmarq, and many are beginning to turn their backs on their usual horse traders to come see you. The Guild didn't like that very much."

"What... what is going to happen?" her father asked, his bottom lip quivering. "Is this going to happen again?"

"No," she shook her head. "I've already sent a letter to King Tytan. He will be informing King Henree Grey of the incident. King Henree will tighten his leash on the Guild. No worries."

"No worries?!" her father jumped to his feet. "I just lost half my stock! Over a hundred thousand gold went up in a blaze, *literally!*" Angrily, the Horse Lord stormed off back to his home.

After he disappeared behind the front door, Tidas caught Ena's attention.

"Hey," she said. "Where the hell did you learn to fight like that?" Ena recalled the mangled bodies of the three dead men, the third having passed recently from his injury to his gut. "Three grown men skilled in combat, all dead by your hand. Yet, you barely have a scratch on you."

Ena shrugged, still in shock.

"When do you turn sixteen?" Tidas asked.

"Three years."

"You think your father will sign the permission paperwork for you to join the City Watch?"

"Ha! Not a chance. Not after this. It will take us the whole year to recover from this mess. He'll need me more than ever." She met Tidas's curious gaze. "What age can I join without parent consent?"

"Sixteen." *Three more years... I don't know if I can handle this for that much longer.* "But," Tidas continued, "if you ever need a place to go..." Ena recalled their conversation from years prior. Tidas offered her a home. And that offer was still available.

Ena nodded, a big smile on her face.

"Also," Tidas continued, "if you wish to hone your skills with a sword, I am off duty a couple of nights each week. You know where to find me."

CHAPTER 35

The deaths of the Shipmaster and his waitress came as a shock to Drake. He had been so careful to travel unnoticed. Their bodies had been lifeless for most of the night, according to the Master White Mage, who examined the cadavers thoroughly. Following her display of power and solidarity, paranoia soon enveloped Raven, checking over her shoulder every other step she took. These mages were dangerous. They were everywhere at once, yet nowhere to be found.

"A silent enemy is the most dangerous," Raven had said.

The worst part, Drake realized, is that the tunnel beneath *The Shipyard Tavern* had conveniently caved in, destroying all evidence of its existence, with the exception of the hatch on the floor of the Shipmaster's kitchen. Only, now, all that remained beneath the hatch was rubble.

"An earth mage," Raven suspected, "I'm sure of it. Too clean and quiet to have been done by hand."

Drake agreed, reluctantly.

The Shipmaster mentioned the existence of four other entrances. Four others which would be terribly difficult to locate, Drake assumed. That didn't prevent him from scouring the city for them, though.

Raven convinced Drake that playing lone-wolf would only get him, or others, killed. Despite his argument, Drake allowed two guards to tail him at all times, keeping their eyes locked on Drake's surroundings and any signs of danger as he navigated through the city.

Days had passed and they were no closer to unravelling this mystery or finding Athenia. The only evidence they collected thus far was proving the Lord of Steel's involvement in the poisoning of the Lord of Avalon, if he had not fed the poison to the lord himself.

"I have searched nearly every inch of the city, Raven," Drake said. Her paranoia was accompanied by impatience, and she demanded results that were out of anyone's control. "They know we are at their backs and they have hidden. There is nothing we can do until they show themselves."

"Ah, Drake," Raven sighed, "that's the part you have yet to understand. These mages are people, citizens of Gabrenas. They *are* hiding, yes. But they are showing themselves as we speak. Hiding in plain sight."

"We won't know them until they put on the black hoods," Drake understood.

Raven nodded. "Correct. Which they will not do while we have guards standing on every street corner."

"*Almost* every street corner..." Drake had a sudden revelation.

Raven looked at Drake, offended. "What do you mean *almost*? I have *exhausted* my resources searching for your little girlfriend."

Drake faced the lady. "We haven't even begun to search the Upper District. We've been so focused on the lower districts."

"Because that is where the mages and the dwarf frequented the most."

"But you said it yourself, Lady Raven. They are hiding in plain sight. They expect us to search where we believe them to be! We should be searching right outside the walls of the Grand Ballroom. The upper class are just as much suspects as the lower class."

Drake could tell by the look on Raven's face that she had difficulty grasping that concept. For her entire life, Raven had grown and prospered among the upper class of Avalon. The people outside her home, the capital, were her friends. To think that any of them could be mages, that they could be side-by-side with that dwarf, was unfathomable.

She sighed heavily. She thought about arguing.

But then she thought of her late husband. The man she had loved so dearly since she was a teenager. And how he was no longer here with her.

Raven could not overlook any possible chance to bring him justice and peace.

"Fine..." Raven breathed deeply. "Take the two guards I've assigned you. Search the Upper District. I don't know what you will possibly find. I've lived here all of my life; I would know if there was some secret underground tunnel lying around."

"You've lived here all your life, knew about the Shipmaster and the black market, yet never knew their goods were being smuggled in by the tunnels." Before Raven could burst out in anger, Drake turned to leave and said, "No offense, my lady."

◆◆◆◆◆◆◆◆◆

That evening, Drake donned the finery of an upperclassman, though he knew he didn't belong. The very outfit he wore costed more than his entire village. Blending in was the key, though.

The two guards assigned to him always maintained a healthy twenty paces behind him and spied the surrounding area for any abnormalities. Nothing stood out so far.

The sun had begun to set with the moon rising on the opposite horizon. Restaurants were packed, and live music was being performed at venues all across the Upper District.

These people had no idea about the dangers of the world outside their circle. They danced in ballgowns on paved streets, gold spilling from their pockets, laughing and smiling. Entirely unknowledgeable, or uncaring, of the forces that existed in their very city, or under it, that could end their way of life.

How many mages rallied behind the dwarf? And for what purpose? What was his plan?

Drake hoped to find out soon. He was not a religious person, but praying to the All-Seeing God for a miracle was all he had left.

Seven blocks from the Grand Ballroom, where Raven eagerly awaited his return for the night, Drake entered through the doors of the Chapel of Avalon. Home to the Master White Mage, the Chapel's doors were open all hours of the day and night to anyone in need of prayer.

The new Master White Mage had not yet occupied the offices in the tower above the chapel, still needing to move his supplies from his former location to take up position as Master, newly assigned to him by Lady Raven. The letter of appointment had a second signature accompanying Lady Raven's, belonging to none other than the Providence.

The Providence had not gambled too much with Raven's decision to remove Archem from his post, simply requesting a formal reason in writing for her records. If the Providence had any doubts, she would have prevented Raven's decision, Drake assumed. The Faith was an entity of its own, and the Providence controlled every moving piece.

The Chapel was empty. Even the white mages who maintained the grounds had packed up and returned home for the night. This chapel was solely for prayer. Across the street, though, a healing house with live-in white mages existed for those in need of medical attention.

Drake's guards waited across the street as the doors shut. He approached the alter, illuminated with candles, the flames dancing and shifting the shadows on the wall behind the massive golden Oblong Eye hanging above him.

Awkwardly getting to his knees in front of the altar, Drake clasped his hands together and closed his eyes. Was this how people prayed? He had no idea...

It's worth a shot. "All-Seeing God," Drake began, "I am in desperate need of advice, or guidance, or even just some kind words of encouragement. Someone I care deeply about is missing. Though, I probably don't need to tell you that, since you are *all-seeing* supposedly. I-I'm worried. She has been missing for a fortnight. I don't know if she is scared, alone, or even alive. I am probably the last person you expected to see here. Just a boy from a village in the middle of nowhere. Never having even thought you to be real. I *still* don't know if you are real. Shit, I didn't mean that. Of course you are real, or else I would just be talking to a giant golden eye and look absolutely insane right now." He sighed. "Maybe I *am* insane. Maybe Athenia is truly gone and I am wasting my time searching for her."

Drake waited a moment. No voices responded to him. Nothing sounded except for the gentle pitter-patter of the rain that started suddenly, hitting the shingles of the roof. "I need something. Anything. Please."

Several more minutes passed. The rain grew heavier.

"Fine!" Drake burst out, tossing a candle against the wall, the wet wax smearing on the stone. "Waste of my fucking time."

The door flew open. One of Drake's guards called out over the steady pour outside, "Sir, come quick. We have something." The door shut again.

Drake turned to the Oblong Eye looming over him, watching him in judgement. "This better be good." He whipped around, his elegant cape cutting through the air, dousing half of the remaining candles on the altar.

As he stepped outside, he threw the hood of the cape over his head.

Night had fallen completely, and thick, black clouds rolled in from the west. The restaurants had closed off their outdoor dining, and all of the rich fools he spotted on his trek here had disappeared inside shelter from the rain.

All except two.

Drake casually padded across the cobblestone street to where the guards awaited him. Neither donned their full armor sets. Platemail hidden underneath their robes provided basic protection on their chest and limbs. They had to look inconspicuous as well.

Drake jerked his head curiously at the two mysterious hooded figures walking down the street ahead of him. The guards responded with simultaneous nods.

Drake began to tail them, keeping far behind. His untrained eyes had difficulty keeping tabs on them in the dark, though the sudden flashes of lightning kept them in view.

"As the storm started," one of the guards explained, attempting to keep his voice low, yet straining to be heard over the cracks of thunder, "the streets cleared. Those two came from this alleyway coming up." On their right, a thin pathway between two buildings appeared, barely wide enough for a single person to fit without turning to their side. "They had masks on covering their faces."

The other guard spoke up, "Seemed to match the description of the mages you and the lady described."

Drake grunted his approval. Quick judgement told him to continue following the potential mages to their next destination, rather than investigate the alley from which they came. Drake made a mental note to send some guards to check it out later.

The mages turned left at the next intersection, descending down a shallow slope. They were exiting the entertainment quarter of the Upper District and into the living quarter. Regal apartments and hotels lined every street for miles. Drake managed to keep up as the two masked figures turned left, right, left, right. Even the guards were unsure where they were in the city. Without tracking their location on a map or marking every street sign, they were lost.

Did the mages know Drake was onto them?

Suddenly, the figures stopped by a door at the base of an apartment building and opened an wrought iron gate, stepping inside.

Where are they going?

The guards quickly drew their weapons and stood against the stone wall, each flanking one side of the gate. Drake drew the Aconyte sword from his belt and came up behind one of the guards.

The guard leaned over and said, “We’ll go in first.”

Before Drake could argue, the guards stepped through the gate into the darkness beyond. Once Drake lost sight of them, he followed. The rain stopped momentarily as he passed under a small archway before pouring back onto his head. Lightning flashed.

They stood in a clearing, a courtyard in the center of the apartment complex. Drake watched as the guards approached the two masked figures from behind. Before making contact, one of the figures lifted a palm and the earth beneath them started to tremble. Suddenly, a hole opened in the center of the courtyard and the figures went to step inside.

“Hey! Hold up there!” the guards shouted.

As they turned, flames coated the other mage’s hand, launching a blast of fire at the guards. The guards raised their swords in defense, but the fire swarmed them. Luckily, the rain doused the flames before igniting their thick robes.

“Shit!” Drake cursed, holding the Aconyte sword in one hand, coating his other with flames of his own.

The guards charged at the mages, weapons raised. One mage struck with a flaming fist, catching the guard on the shoulder. The other mage lifted the earth beneath the other guard’s feet, tossing him in the air. As the guard flew through the air, the fire mage launched another fire blast, hitting the guard in the chest and sending him into the wall of the apartments. The guard dropped hard to the ground.

Drake threw a volley of fire at the mages. They dodged effortlessly and returned with attacks of their own. Drake deflected the blast of fire, but a rock thrown from the earth mage struck him hard in the stomach, doubling him over.

The guard with the injured shoulder caught his footing and turned back to face the mages. He swung the sword with his good arm as Drake meagerly threw fire to distract them. The guard managed to catch his blade on the leg of the fire mage as the mage dodged, knocking the mage over.

As the mage fell on his back, the guard drove the sword down into his chest. The rain washed away the blood that welled around the blade, still protruding from his body.

Before the guard could withdraw the sword, the earth mage roared in anger, striking with a fist coated with stone. The guard backed away, leaving behind the sword, as the earth mage connected blow after blow. The guard held his ground, absorbing the punches; though, how many punches of pure rock could the human body withstand?

Drake caught his breath and charged at the mage. He swung the Aconyte sword just as the mage caught Drake from their peripherals, raising a column of earth to counter the attack. To the mage's surprise, the Aconyte sword sliced through the rock column with ease, splitting it in two.

The mage jumped back to collect their thoughts.

Drake took that single moment to check on the guard, who had taken a knee to compose himself during Drake's interruption.

"Are you okay?" Drake shouted over the rain.

The guard shook his head. Spitting up blood, he responded, "I think some ribs are broken."

"Get out of here and get help," Drake commanded. Before the guard could refuse, he continued, "We need to make sure the mage doesn't close this tunnel! While one of us can still walk, go get help!"

The guard nodded reluctantly and limped back through the iron gate into the streets.

Drake turned to face the mage, who had a predatorial glow in his eyes. Drake tightened his grip on the sword.

"Where's your fire, traitor?" the earth mage asked.

"Traitor?" Drake shook his head. "I'm not a traitor. I never even knew I was a mage until a week ago!"

"Ha!" the mage laughed. "You're the Unweaved that our lord wants so bad? You can barely light a candle."

Before Drake could argue, the mage struck his hands together at his stomach and drove them to a point in front of him. The ground trembled as a spike of earth shot up in front of Drake, angled at his chest.

Drake held the Aconyte sword vertically in front of himself and closed his eyes. As the tip of the earth spike touched the Aconyte steel, it split in two, striking the brick wall to the left and right of him. Drake opened his eyes. *What just happened?*

The earth mage lifted two earth columns and threw them at Drake. Drake jumped over the spike next to him and dodged one column, colliding with the brick building, and tearing a hole into someone's apartment. Drake heard screams of fear before looking up to see the second column arcing through the air at him.

Gods help me. Drake swung the sword over his head, splitting the rock column in two, falling in two equal pieces behind him. His arms ached from the blunt force of the earth hitting the sword in his hands.

Frustrated, the mage called out, "Just *die* already!"

The mage consistently barraged Drake with earth. Drake continued to dodge or deflect as he moved his way closer and closer to the mage.

Now, ten feet away, Drake went on the offensive. He concentrated all of his energy into his palm as he ignited a torch of flame at the earth mage. The flamethrower was met with an earth column the mage rose from the ground. Mist filled the air at the intense heat continuously energizing from Drake's hand. The flame torch turned the stone red-hot and waves of heat warped Drake's vision.

With his little experience with magic, Drake had never felt such an exhilarating feeling. He could feel the Connections of Magic flowing through him, concentrating the Connections through his own body. A conduit of pure energy.

The earth column began to chip away and crumble under the force of the flamethrower. The mage grunted, feeling a scorching pain as the flames licked his arms and legs from around the earth column. He heaved his fists hard into the column, sending it gliding across the distance between Drake and himself.

Drake did not expect the counterattack, not allowing him much time to dodge, and the flaming earth column struck him with full force, sending him flying. The earth column kept forward until it broke through the brick wall of another apartment.

Drake hurt all over, bones likely broken, but he jumped quickly back to his feet. *Where is the sword? Shit!* He must have dropped it when the earth column hit him.

He didn't have much time to search for it, though. The earth mage sprinted towards him, wearing his gauntlets of stone, and swung his fists repeatedly at Drake.

Drake ducked and dodged most of the blows, but several connected with his already-injured body. He grinded his teeth, holding back the urge to yell in pain.

Igniting his fists with his own magic, Drake connected several punches with the earth mage. Holes burned through their tunic and his skin glowed red and pustulated with second-degree burns.

The mage pushed Drake away from him, giving himself time to think of his next move. Burns covered his body.

Drake did not give him that chance, though.

He built up a ball of fire between his palms, growing and growing until he struggled to hold control, and launched it at the mage. The fireball's energy sang as it passed through the air, meeting the earth mage with unrestrained force.

As the fireball met the mage, it exploded, shuddering and cracking the walls of the courtyard. Even Drake was forced onto his back from the blow. Smoke filled the air in a violent plume.

Drake waited for the smoke to clear before getting back to his feet. He looked around. All was quiet. On the far wall of the courtyard, the mage's body rested on the ground beneath a pile of scorched bricks. The wall behind him was broken and fractured.

The brick pile moved slightly as Drake walked around the hole he assumed led into the tunnels beneath the city. The mage—broken, burnt, and defeated—dragged himself one inch at a time.

Drake pulled them from the rubble and flipped them onto their back. Holding their shoulder, he shook them. "Tell me everything you know. Now!"

The mage's head fell back, bobbing for a moment. Drake felt the life leave the mage's body.

Just then, platoons of City Watch guards stormed into the courtyard, weapons raised. Lights inside the apartment building flicked on as the guards entered the building to secure the residents of the complex.

One guard approached Drake. "Sir, are you alright?" He extended a gloved hand. Drake took it and was helped to his feet.

Drake nodded, despite *not* being alright. He needed to see a white mage immediately.

"Come with me, sir. This scene will be cleaned up and guarded, do not worry. Lady Raven has the Master White Mage ready for you."

◆◆◆◆◆◆◆◆◆

Drake laid quietly and patiently on the medical bed in the Master White Mage's study. Joran, the newly appointed Master White Mage, worked on him gently for hours. Resetting and sealing broke bones, fading bruises, and mending cuts.

Neither one spoke, not for several hours.

Finally, Raven arrived with Gabrenas's guard commander, climbing the steps of the chapel into the study.

"Drake," she broke the silence. "How are you feeling?"

He met her eyes. Part of her cyan eyes gleamed with pride and success—they had, after all, found one of the entrances to the tunnels. But another part of her eyes was sad and defeated. "I'm alright. I survived. That's all that matters." Ignoring the strange sensation of the white magic knitting his flesh back together, he asked, "What happened after I left?"

Raven sat on the medical bed across from him. "Both bodies of the mages were brought back for investigation. The entrance to the tunnel has been secured, and our guards have started their initial search."

"That's great news," Drake said. "But you look troubled. What's wrong?"

"Besides the fact that you could have died in that courtyard? Only that we have found absolutely nothing in our search. The City Watch has explored miles of the underground pathways and there is no sign of occupation. No sign of life at all, for that matter."

Drake met her gaze. He knew what she was thinking. That whenever they are close to getting one step ahead, they are pushed two steps back.

Raven continued, "I sent word to Master Sheridan at Havana City. I wanted to explain everything that has occurred up through tonight, but putting that information in a letter that could be intercepted by anyone seemed dangerous. I asked him to come here. He needs to know the truth if he is to find a temporary replacement for Athenia in El Vadora."

Or a permanent replacement. The words went unspoken, but they both had that dreadful thought floating in the back of their minds.

The Master White Mage stood from next to Drake's shoulder. "You are all fixed up, sir." His shoulder had dislocated, and his rotator cuff tore, when that last earth column struck him head on. Drake had been numb all over by the time he was escorted to the Chapel, not even realizing his shoulder was out of place. "Take it easy for a few days."

Raven stood to meet the mage. "Thank you, Joran."

"Anything you need, let me know," Joran dipped his head respectfully. "I will see how the autopsy on those bodies is coming along." Joran shook Drake hand before departing down the steps at the end of his study.

"What of the Dread Watch?" Drake asked, rotating his shoulder around in circles, testing out the healed tendons and cartilage. "Didn't you send word to them? Where have they been to help us?"

"I have not received any correspondence back from them," Raven sighed. "Fear not, Drake. Master Sheridan will advise us what to do next."

Drake rose carefully from the medical bed. "We need to continue our search of the tunnels. Those mages weren't there for no reason. By now, the Lord of Steel knows we have discovered a way into his hiding place, and he'll find a way to move around and stay out of our line of sight. We need to catch him before that happens."

Raven agreed, though she felt that her resources were already spread too thin. By sending platoons underground, into unknown territory, she would only be spreading them thinner. "We move efficiently, but we move carefully. Understand?" Drake nodded. "We are in the dwarf's territory now. He knows it better than we do. Any mistakes can lead to unnecessary deaths."

"Of course, Raven," Drake smiled. "We'll get the bastard soon enough."

CHAPTER 36

The Court of Kings had finally arrived, and Sheridan felt more anxious than he ever had in his life. Too much rested on the decision of the Court. A "yes" vote would allow Sheridan and the Providence to legally remove Typhus from power, but the transition would be messy. Sheridan expected he would face strong resistance, particularly from General Braxon and the military. A "no" vote could raise the question of their loyalty to the kingdom, and they could be labeled and charged as traitors, pending a formal investigation.

Sheridan could not allow that to happen. Even if they proved their innocence to charges of treason, the initial indictment would besmirch their reputations forever. Additionally, an investigation of that magnitude would be dragged out for years, during which time others would need to step in as the Master of Cities and the Providence. High King Eriputes would gladly take that opportunity to place people of his own in power, essentially removing Havyn's autonomy.

Their argument had to be strong, and it had to appeal to all the kingdoms. They could not simply argue to depose King Typhus for their own benefit—it had to benefit all five kingdoms of Lynidas.

Sheridan lacked confidence in their case. Their planning time over the past couple of weeks was frequently interrupted by their regular duties and their distrust of the Keepers. Lia could never go far without her Keepers, so planning meeting times and places that remained secret was a difficult task.

Lia did as she was instructed—she studied the Concordat every day and night. Last Sheridan knew, the princess was damned close to finishing the entire manuscript.

The Providence did her part, as well. She collected every medical note and document transcribed about Typhus, from his childhood until the present. Piecing together every aspect of his medical history that could have led to his current ailment, the Providence had a novel's worth of material to bring with her.

The moon still hung heavily in the sky. Sheridan dragged himself from bed. He would pretend he slept, but truthfully, anxiety kept him up all night. He occupied his mind by returning to his study of the *Encantorum*.

Sheridan could not wait for Athenia to finish her investigation in Avalon to share the information he has learned about that sword and its link to the fairies.

By the time Sheridan readied himself and quietly made his way down to the front marble steps of the Spire, he found the Providence waiting patiently by a horse-drawn carriage.

He nodded to her, taking note of the elegant garments the Providence wore. Unlike her typical white, gold, or silver gowns, an emphasis of her significance as a white mage, this day she wore a slim-cut satin dress colored with the finest regal violet dye money could buy. Her golden hair was pinned back in an updo decorated with feathers made of silver. Finally, a silver Oblong Eye necklace hung at her neckline.

"Silver?" Sheridan asked. "Not gold?" The Oblong Eye, symbol of the Faith and the All-Seeing God, was gold wherever one saw it. Sheridan didn't even realize they made Oblong Eyes out of any other metal.

"This isn't the time or place for gold," the Providence explained. "Silver speaks louder, I feel."

"I can't help but agree," Sheridan said. "You look incredible, Providence."

"As do you, Sheridan." The dwarf cast aside his usual thick layers and platemail at all Courts of Kings. This time, he donned a black silk tunic and trousers that emphasized his sculpted, muscled chest. Despite his short stature, he was dense with muscle more than most human men.

"Where's Lia?" Sheridan asked softly.

The Providence opened the carriage door and gestured inside. Sheridan stepped up inside, and the Providence followed, closing the door behind them.

Princess Lia sat patiently, cross-legged, in the back of the carriage on the plush maroon seat. Sheridan nodded to her and took the seat across from her, she nodded back. Once the Providence sat down next to Sheridan, the carriage began moving.

The three of them remained silent until they were out of the city. Waited until the clopping of horseshoes on the cobblestone softened to a dull padding on the dirt path leading out of Havana City.

The journey to the Library of the Keeper, where all Courts of Kings were held, would take about three days' time from Havana City. Located in the geographical center of Lynidas, the Library of the Keeper was home to the leader of the Keepers, known only as the Librarian, where he trained every Keeper that would eventually find their way into the palace of each of Lynidas's five kingdoms.

Naturally, the ride would take over a week, if not longer, with frequent rest stops, but Sheridan organized for new horses and carriage drivers to be switched out every six hours along the route to ensure constant motion. As much as Sheridan hated the travel time, it gave them the opportunity to practice what they were going to present to the Court.

The princess looked as lovely as ever. She wore a dress of a similar fashion to the Providence, except that hers was heather grey, and her pale brunette hair cascaded in loose curls around her slender shoulders. She fiddled with her royal crown in her hands as she anxiously considered what could happen at the Library. She ran her hands over the tanzanite and sapphire gemstones carefully inlaid in the silver crest.

In a few days, that crown could transform from a princess's into a queen's.

The Providence reached out with a gentle touch to Lia's leg. "Relax, your highness. You will be safe, whatever the outcome."

Lia nodded.

Sheridan could see that Lia did not appear convinced, though.

◆◆◆◆◆◆◆◆◆

The Library of the Keeper stood tall, capturing the light of the rising sun. Sheridan woke Lia and pointed out the carriage window, allowing her to absorb the gorgeous view. The Library courageously stood in the middle of the Fields of Born on the western edge of the High Atla. The plains stretched for miles, with the Library visible to the naked eye throughout the entire expanse.

Five roads connected at the Library like spokes on a wheel. Five roads, each leading to one of the five kingdoms—High Alta, Fairmarq, Havyn, Nest Aiken, and Seramyth.

By the looks of the caravans and carriages already parked around the entrance of the Library, Sheridan assumed they were late. He grunted his annoyance.

They were always the first to arrive, with Farimarq shortly behind. Why the sudden timeliness?

The driver rounded the carriage around the base of the Library, eventually stopping at the front of the stone walkway leading to the front door. As Sheridan impatiently climbed out of the carriage and took Lia's hand to help her down, he heard the ancient door to the Library creak open. Looking towards the door, he saw King Henree Grey of Fairmarq speeding down the walkway, marching with his head high as he passed by the pairs of Keepers standing guard across from one another along the edges of the stone path.

The king's iron-colored cloak swayed and whipped the air behind him, revealing the forest green interior. Matching iron-grey raiment underneath his cloak clung tightly to Henree's toned figure. Even in his middle age, Henree Grey was sculpted like a warrior.

"King Henree," Sheridan bowed at his approach.

"Sheridan, what in the Connections is going on?" King Henree challenged. Sheridan was dumbfounded at the stern tone in the king's baritone voice. They had always been allies, so the sudden aggression came as a shock to the Master of Cities. "We all received notice from Eriputes to come the night before. You never showed."

"That's preposterous," the Providence chimed in, planting her feet firmly on the ground next to Sheridan's. "We never received notice."

"Well, we all did. And when you didn't show, that's all anyone could converse about."

Sheridan swore under his breath. This was set up deliberately by the High King, Sheridan was certain. He didn't need to explain his innocence to King Henree, though—the King of Fairmarq had a much stronger opinion of Eriputes. "That sly bastard. It's no wonder he refrained from presenting his own thoughts. He only sat there, observing the commotion, with a rotten smirk on his face."

"We are here now," the Providence said firmly. "Let us correct this." She began walking towards the Library.

Lia slowly stepped out of the carriage and took a brief moment to absorb her surroundings.

Henree caught up to the Providence. Sheridan walked beside Princess Lia. Henree responded to the Providence's haste, "The time for correction has passed, I'm afraid. The monarchs are all prepared in the Courtroom already." The Providence merely nodded; however, Sheridan knew she was fuming.

Henree sped ahead and held the door for them. As they entered in front of him, he greeted Lia with a respectful kiss to the top of her hand, "Princess Lia, welcome. I have not seen you since you were a girl." He looked hard at Sheridan and remarked, "Such a pleasure to have you here."

Sheridan, what do you have up your sleeve? Sheridan translated the thought on Henree's face.

They entered an open foyer with a golden plaque straight ahead pressed into the wall above a set of large glass doors. Engraved on the plaque read *Library of the Keeper*. Beyond the glass, hundreds, if not thousands, of bookshelves spread out along the floor and against the walls. It is said a copy of every book ever written existed within those walls.

They took a hard right and ascended up a marble staircase. Lia kept up with them as they swiftly climbed the steps to the fifth story.

Sheridan's short legs burned from the climb, but it was nothing compared to the ascent up and down the Spire he endured each day.

At the top of the steps, a hallway extended before them. Centuries-old paintings hung along the walls, including one titled *The Demise of the Faeries*. The painting was centered on the wall next to the ruby curtains meant for the representatives of Havyn. Sheridan studied the painting each time he was here; though, today his time to view it was cut short. Sheridan did not need to view it again to know it was painted by a faerie sympathizer a decade after the end of the Mage Wars, detailing an army of mages marching on the last of the faerie strongholds—the Faerie King's castle, written into history as *The Last Bastion*.

Sheridan was unsure of the accuracy of the painting, but perhaps he would find out by reading through the *Encantorum* when he had free time.

As if he would ever have free time again.

"This is where we part, my friend," Henree shook Sheridan's metal hand before speed walking down the hall and disappearing through another set of ruby curtains. Sheridan placed his hands between the curtains, tossing them aside and stepping through. The Providence and Lia followed suit, side by side.

Light erupted in their faces as they entered the Courtroom. As their vision cleared, they could see the glass ceiling that acted as one giant skylight. Lia's eyes scanned the room from floor to ceiling, her jaw dropping in awe of the exquisite sight. They stood on a half-circle balcony overlooking the open Courtroom. About twenty-five yards to their left, Henree and the rest of the representatives of Fairmarq stood on their own balcony. Parallel to them, two similar balconies were set into the wall where two of the three remaining kingdoms were positioned.

"Nice of you to join us, Master Sheridan!" a voice called out from the lone balcony in the wall to the far left of the rectangular room.

High King Eriputes of High Alta himself. There was nothing impressive about the High King. He was of average height, with dirty-blonde hair curled short atop his head. Prince Salmeides stood next to him on High Alta's balcony.

Sheridan smiled sarcastically and waved.

The High King, disappointed at not getting a further rise out of the dwarf, cleared his throat. "Welcome, fellow monarchs, leaders of the Faith, and... democratic representative." He shot a judgmental glance Sheridan's way. "On this date, let the record show, the winter Court of Kings in the thousand-and-first year after the signing of the Concordat shall begin. At today's Court, we shall begin by roll-calling through the room, introducing our representatives, and discussing any updates from items presented at the previous Court or discuss new items. High Alta shall begin."

While Eriputes went on about the perfection and immaculacies of his kingdom, Princess Lia took the opportunity to ask Sheridan about each of the kingdoms. She whispered, "Tell me about High Alta. I already had the displeasure of meeting Prince Sal, but I do not know the rest."

"Yes," Sheridan began, "Prince Sal has already made his acquaintance. A haughty man of many words, except when in the presence of his father.

High King Eriputes Philosophous holds more power pinched between two fingers than Sal or any other living being in Lynidas ever will have in their lives. His strength comes from his mind and his powerful relationships. The Philosophous Dynasty is one of corruption, disloyalty, and sin, yet they have ruled High Alta for ten generations, at least. Ten generations of buying or promising their way into the pockets of nearly every aristocratic family in Lynidas, with the exception of Havyn. Havyn has always held the puppet strings far from Eriputes's grip. Which is why losing this case, losing *you* to High Alta, will end democracy as we know it."

Lia asked, "Isn't the Concordat in place to prevent that?"

"Not when it is his hand that controls the Faith and Democracy in High Alta." Sheridan responded to Lia's confused expression by elaborating, "The woman next to him. That is his wife, Queen Phoebe, and also the Master of Cities in High Alta. The only Master of Cities here, besides myself."

Lia's pale eyes locked onto the queen's face from across the Courtroom. Phoebe's eyes narrowed as she ignored her husband's words and scanned the other balconies. She eventually locked eyes with Lia and shot her a poisonous glance. Shivers trickled down Lia's spine as she immediately looked away.

"Edacles," Sheridan continued, "the prince who you would be betrothed to if Eriputes had his way, is not among them. He hardly ever is. A meek boy, the opposite of his brother."

"The one in the white robes," Lia gestured. "That must be their Providence?"

Sheridan nodded, "And the High King's sister." Solidifying Eriputes's control over the three ruling branches.

"What about them?" Lia gestured diagonally across the chamber to the opposite wall, directly adjacent to the High Alta representatives. On the balcony, an old man sat in an ornate chair and three younger women stood with their arm's crossed in front of them. Eight Keepers stood behind them. "They seem quite cautious, with all their Keepers here to protect them."

The Providence responded, overhearing the remark, "Do not believe for a moment that Eriputes attended unguarded. His are standing in the hall beyond the curtains. Each kingdom has Keepers with them."

"Not us, though."

"We've always come without the royal family," the Providence pointed out. "Sneaking you out to avoid your Keepers attending was a key element in this plan."

"Though," Sheridan countered, "the Librarian will have already sent word to the Keepers in Havyn reprimanding them for their incompetence."

"The Librarian?" Lia asked.

Sheridan pointed down to the floor of the near-empty room. In the very center, an elderly man in Keeper armor sat atop a circular dais at a desk, writing with a quill and ink as Eriputes spoke. "He is the master of all the Keepers. Trains them, assigns them, and keeps record of every one of these meetings."

"Wasn't the Librarian responsible for writing the Concordat?"

Sheridan shrugged, "So say the rumors. No author is provided in any copy of the Concordat that I have read."

"So," Lia returned her attention to the old man and three women, "who are they?"

Sheridan cleared his throat, "They are representatives of Seramyth, the southernmost kingdom of Lynidas. The man is King Polima, and the ladies are his three grandchildren," going from left to right, "Selandra, Chandra, and Kendra. Triplets, and theoretically all heirs to the throne of Seramyth and the Faith."

Lia's face reflected her stunned response. "They're *all* heirs? What happened to King Polima's children? How will the succession work if they are all heirs?"

Sheridan reached into the satchel of documents they had carried in. After shuffling through, he generated a journal containing his own hand-scribbled notes that he frequently took while in these meetings. He flipped open to a certain page and pointed.

"This is a rough family tree of Seramyth's Serinada dynasty," Sheridan traced his finger along the page, explaining. "Polima had three children of his own—two of which passed many years ago during an accident out on open water. Seramyth is one of the largest of the kingdoms, second only to Fairmarq, and they border the sea to the south. Their economy relies heavily on their fishing trade. Unfortunately, several ships were caught out at sea during an unexpected storm, which his son, and heir, and daughter, the immediate heir to the Faith, were aboard. The two siblings loved sailing and being out on the open water. They enjoyed taking some time off from their duties to jump aboard an outgoing fishing vessel to lend a hand."

Sheridan sighed and continued, "What the prince did not realize was that his wife, and future queen, was pregnant with triplets. While the power of the Providence passed a couple of years later to Polima's surviving daughter, the throne was mandated to pass to any of the three of them."

"Or all," the Providence specified. "No terminology in the Concordat rejects multiple heads of the Monarchy, so long as they meet the criteria, which all three do."

Lia looked to the Providence, whose stern face still stirred with anger at the High King's trickery. "I assume the same theory holds true for the Faith?" The Providence dipped her chin in confirmation. "That is an enormous amount of power between the three of them..."

"Luckily," Sheridan continued, "the sisters have worked it out amongst one another." He drew Lia's attention back to the scribbled family tree. He pointed to one of the names. "Selandra, the one to the left of our view, decided several years ago to pass the mantles of the Monarchy and the Faith to her sisters and assume her current role as General of Seramyth's army and navy."

Lia eyed the princess from across the Courtroom. Her hardened face and muscular build shouted "military." Her black hair, tied back in a ponytail draped over her shoulder, revealed a thick streak of white traveling from her roots to tip. Dozens of piercings decorated her ears and her right brow as her violet eyes scanned the room.

Selandra was fearsome and fearless.

"Next to Selandra is Chandra," Sheridan explained. "Chandra may not look like much compared to her sisters, but she is the white mage of the three. As I'm sure you can gather, that means she has volunteered to apprentice with her aunt, the Providence, to take on that position someday. Though her aunt holds the official title, Chandra is the one who attends these meetings and provides the Faith's report."

As Sheridan said, Chandra did not appear powerful like General Selandra, but what she lacked in physical strength, she made up for in strength of the mind and the Connections. She practically glowed with magical aura. Her hair was about the same length as Selandra's but was worn down in waves and was more brown than black. No piercings marked her appearance, and her face was much softer and friendly. Like Selandra, she had matching violet irises.

"That leaves Kendra, right?" Lia gestured to the third triplet. The final princess was unique compared to her siblings. She had the same black hair as Selandra, but had it cut and styled in a mid-length A-line bob that harnessed her austere face perfectly. Her bodycon dress revealed tattooed arms that only added to her uncompromising appearance.

"Kendra," Sheridan let out a low chuckle. "She's a force to be reckoned with. She has agreed to be the sole inheritor of the crown when Polima passes."

"Which will be sooner than we think," the Providence cautioned. "The king's days are numbered. I can see it in his face." She gave an ominous look to Lia and Sheridan. "Err on the side of caution. Seramyth already has a bone to pick with Havyn."

They remained quiet as Seramyth began its report. King Polima rose from his chair, shaking feebly and balancing unsteadily on his wooden cane. He brushed his mid-length, tousled white hair out of his face as he declared simply, "My granddaughter, Princess Kendra, will read Seramyth's report."

Polima stayed standing, half-leaning on his cane, half-leaning on Selandra behind him, as Kendra stepped forwards and crossed her hands in front of her.

The princess cleared her throat. Lia was taken aback by the sheer power in Kendra's voice. It carried effortlessly across every inch of the Courtroom as she spoke, "I wish news from Seramyth was as cheerful as yours, High King, however, we refuse to hide behind false strength and a tantalizing bravado." The sneer she directed at High Alta's balcony was ossifying. "Two years have passed since our first report of the plague wreaking havoc on our soil. Two long years of our frequent and feeble attempts to request assistance, and to no avail. Our High King sits on his *high* throne in the *high* tower of his *high* palace, while an entire kingdom suffers in pestilence and squalor. These Courts are nothing but a waste of precious time and resources.

"Furthermore, not only has help been refused or ignored, but our shared border with High Alta along the river has been barred from passage." The glare directed at Eriputes could have shattered glass. "Refuge is being prevented for those who are healthy enough to escape the turmoil. Countless die each and every day." She scanned the faces of the representatives from all kingdoms. "When will compassion cross your hearts?"

A short but challenging speech. Sheridan could see the displeasure in Eriputes's face. Standing up to Eriputes was equivalent to painting a target on one's back.

Seramyth had nothing to lose.

"Thank you, Kendra, for your report," Eriputes said reluctantly. "Nest Aiken, you may present your report."

Directly across the Courtroom from Havyn, a tall man in long, elegant robes with long, straight dark hair stepped forward on his balcony. "The king of Nest Aiken," Sheridan muttered to Lia. "Dormian. The quiet girl behind him is his daughter and heir, Alekzandria."

"Thank you, Your Highness," King Dormian exaggerated a bow. Rising, he spoke to everyone in the Courtroom. "Princess Kendra, I am filled with great sorrow for your situation in Seramyth. I do express my sincerest regrets that Nest Aiken cannot be more of a help, but it seems we have troubles of our own." Dormian hesitated. "A Brekken dignitary was found dead, presumably murdered, on Nest Aiken soil..." Murmurs erupted from all around them. Eriputes held up a palm, and the voices ceased.

Dormian continued, "Nest Aiken has always maintained a civil relationship with the Brekken Alliance. Brekken ambassadors and princes are frequent guests inside our walls. One of the nearby Brekken kingdoms recently coronated a new king, and several of the king's closest advisors came to my kingdom to retrieve a coronation gift. One of the advisors never made it back. With several ongoing investigations conducted by both parties, the Alliance blames Nest Aiken for the murder and seeks to hold us accountable. What I have yet to release to the Alliance is that my investigative team concluded that neither Nest Aiken or the Alliance are responsible for the advisor's death. We have good reason to believe there is a spy in our midst. A spy who committed this heinous act to frame us."

CHAPTER 37

Sheridan's eyes bulged. A spy? He prayed this was not the work of Typhus. Recalling the contents of the king's secret notebook, he recited to himself, *Let's see how vulnerable I am when my spies spark civil unrest within their own kingdoms.*

The words haunted Sheridan.

He wanted to remain ignorant, but Sheridan knew in his gut that the death of the Brekken dignitary was the beginning of the civil unrest Typhus wrote of.

"Are you thinking what I am thinking, Sheridan?" the Providence whispered. Sheridan met her worrisome gaze, his only response. "If this was Typhus's plan, we must convince them of his deposition today before King Dormian's investigation leads back to Havyn."

"Agreed."

Dormian continued with his report, "I was able to buy some time by permitting the Brekken Alliance to conduct their own formal investigations, but now the Alliance has been skirmishing with my army along the border. They seek war."

"Impossible," Eriputes scoffed. "Enticing war is a direct violation of the Concordat. The Alliance wouldn't be stupid enough to start a war over one insignificant advisor. If what you say is true and the Brekken Alliance are attacking your troops, a cease and desist will be immediately drafted and delivered to them."

Sheridan cleared his throat, loudly. The eyes of every king, queen, and Providence in the room found him.

"My apologies," Sheridan said. "I don't mean to interrupt your report, King Dormian, but it's not 'impossible' that the Brekken are leading small charges against your border patrol seeking war. The Concordat directly dictates that the Brekken Alliance must not formally declare war against a sole kingdom in Lynidas, or all five kingdoms are mandated to form a combined front with a minimum of twenty percent of their standing armies. Furthermore, a formal declaration of war must be submitted, in writing, by all forty-nine kings and queens of the Alliance. The same essentially goes for Lynidas declaring war on the Alliance—all five kings must sign the declaration. To summarize, this is no effort of war, or Nest Aiken would have all forty-nine Brekken kingdoms and their combined army of two million or more at their doorstep. This is merely an attempt by the one kingdom to seek revenge, and possibly a few allying kingdoms."

Eriputes was not pleased to be corrected. "Master Sheridan, I am sure your knowledge of the Concordat is immense, but as one who learned how to read by studying the Concordat, I can say with confidence that your interpretation of the particular passage you reiterated is inaccurate."

The gavel on the Librarian's desk pounded, sending an echo through the room. The Librarian was not permitted to have a voice during the Courts of Kings, except in the event that the integrity of a particular law was being questioned.

The current Librarian held the position as leader of the Keepers since before the elderly King Polima donned the crown of Seramyth. Polima swears the Librarian's hair was just as white sixty years ago.

The Librarian placed a thick book on his desk. *The original Concordat!* Sheridan was just as awestruck each time he saw it as he was the first time. The law of the land stood true for the past thousand years. Rumor had it that the Librarian treated the pages each evening to ensure they continue to withstand the testament of time.

He flipped to the middle of the manuscript.

"*Addendum Seven, Chapter Eighteen, Section One,*" the Librarian recited. "Little is left for interpretation. It is as the Master of Cities from Havyn dictated. The Five Kingdoms of Lynidas have no cause, as of yet, to make a declaration of war as a defensive maneuver, nor do the Five Kingdoms have cause to issue a formal, legal cease and desist."

When Eriputes refused to speak, Sheridan acknowledged the Librarian, "Thank you." He then turned his attention to King Dormian. "Your Highness, this does not necessarily mean 'do nothing' and simply let your men be picked away. The Brekken kingdom, or kingdoms, *are* attacking you. You *are* allowed to defend. But *only* defend."

Dormian placed a hand on his chin, thinking.

"So," Dormian started, "what you mean, Master Sheridan, is display a formidable front along the border, prepare for the next attack, and push back hard? There will be no legal repercussion?"

This time, King Henree answered, "The Alliance will not be thrilled with the attacking kingdoms once word gets back to them. Eriputes was correct in saying that they would not be stupid enough to engage in war over such an insignificant matter." Sheridan could see Henree's distaste in admitting Eriputes was right about something. He smiled slightly. Henree continued, "The Alliance will certainly scold them for shedding blood, I would think. In the meantime, Sheridan's suggestion is sound. Defend yourself. Push back and the Alliance will fear a declaration of war from our side."

"Fools..." Eriputes muttered. Directing his reproach to Sheridan and Henree, he said, "A cease and desist will speak much louder and much *faster* than simply allowing these skirmishes to continue with the *hope* that the Alliance will order the attackers to back down."

"A cease and desist will come across as a threat," Sheridan was beginning to lose his patience. "Am I correct that all five kingdoms would need to sign the cease and desist? Yes? Then we would be fools to push back as a united force, because then the Brekken would be obligated to do the same. And the idea of a counter letter signed by forty-nine Brekken kings is not exactly something I want to deal with."

A sly smile creeped across Eriputes's face. "Master Sheridan, you say an ordeal with the Brekken Alliance is something *you* do not want to deal with? Why wouldn't your king handle such a situation?" As Sheridan opened his mouth, Eriputes interrupted, "I apologize to King Dormian for cutting his report short, but I am *truly* interested in what you have to say this time, Master. After all, it is not every Court of Kings we are graced with the presence of the beautiful Princess Lia." He outstretched a hand, placing everyone's attention on the beauty of Havyn. "You may proceed with Havyn's report..."

Sheridan swallowed hard as he pulled his report from the satchel they carried in. He handed the Providence her medical reports.

He was not an anxious person, but this morning he was bundled with nerves to the point where his hands trembled. They risked everything to be here. He could not back out now.

"I..." He cleared his throat. "My fellow kings and queens, princes and princesses, and Providences. I come before you today with a heavy heart to request your attention to an important matter at hand. The past three years, I have served humbly as Havyn's Master of Cities, and I believe the time has come to reveal the growing trouble Havyn has been facing."

"Get on with it, Sheridan," Eriputes interrupted, rolling his eyes out of boredom.

Sheridan took Eriputes's impatience and cut out his entire speech he had planned in his head. "We want to enact *Addendum Four, Chapter Twenty-Seven, Section Fourteen* of the Concordat."

A wave of gasps filled the room, followed by uneasy murmuring. Even the Librarian peered up from his pen and paper. The only one remaining silent, surprisingly, was Eriputes. A devilish smirk crossed his lips.

"Master Sheridan," King Henree was the first to address the dwarf after minutes of chatter. "Tread carefully. For what purposes do you wish to enact that addendum?"

"Silence, King Henree," Eriputes ordered. To Sheridan, he cautioned, "I would stop where you are, Master. You dance on the edge of treason right now. Where is King Typhus? Have you already done something with him and are hoping to seek forgiveness, rather than permission?" He was half joking. If Sheridan had to admit one good quality of Eriputes, it was his ability to soften a serious situation to make a discussion easier to have.

Sheridan couldn't help but crack a smile, "No, nothing of the sort. Permission first, always. I know this comes as a shock. I debated approaching the Court with this request for many weeks, even right up until about two minutes ago before the words escaped my lips. The reason we come before you with such a bold statement is—"

"If you cross this line," Eriputes said, more seriously, "there is no coming back. If we vote on this, and the results do not go your way... You know the risk."

"That's why I'm here, High King. Risking it all."

"You are adamant about this, aren't you, Sheridan?"

"More than anything, Your Highness."

Eriputes hesitated. Then, "Proceed. With caution."

"The request a petition for deposition of the King of Havyn is brought forth as a unanimous decision by myself, the Master of Cities, the Providence, and the heir and incumbent monarch. King Typhus's health has been questionable for many years, but his actions as of late due to his health condition have been deemed harmful to the Kingdom of Havyn. If Typhus is allowed to continue his reign, I am confident these destructive actions will begin to affect Lynidas as a whole. They already have, in more ways than you know." He eyed Eriputes as he spoke his last statement, knowing that it may explain why Typhus hasn't paid back a single copper in years.

Sheridan continued, "We have medical reports to present, if the Court wishes, that may help explain the king's ailment. Before calling an action to vote, I want to be as transparent as possible to ensure you all understand the severity of the matter at hand."

The Providence stepped forward on the balcony as Sheridan stood off to the side. She looked down at her medical files. "King Typhus suffers from memory impairment, trauma, and a delusional sense of self and sense of reality. His mind is trapped in a world different from ours, and he cannot distinguish between the two, causing decisions of his to make sense in his world, but cause financial, political, and, occasionally, physical harm in reality. King Typhus has been medically deemed a danger to oneself and a danger to others in his current position of power. The Faith finds it in the best interest of Havyn and the Five Kingdoms of Lynidas to remove King Typhus from his position as Head of the Monarchy and get him the proper treatment for his chronic illness."

The Providence lowered the report to her side. She glanced around the room, waiting for a question or response of any kind. However, the other kingdoms remained silent. Hearing a Master of Cities slander a king was not unheard of, if the two individuals had difficulty agreeing, but when the Providence—the voice of the Faith—made a formal accusation against a king, everyone listened.

Sheridan could not read their expressions.

"Princess Lia," Henree spoke. "What is your take on this? There is a reason you are here."

Sheridan whispered to her, "You don't have to speak. We can handle this."

"How can I prove that I am a capable ruler if I cannot speak for myself?" Lia asked rhetorically. "I am not afraid, Sheridan."

Lia stepped forward, addressing Henree's question, "King Henree, I have witnessed King Typhus's decline since my mother's death five years ago. He lost a piece of himself with her. Someday, whether it be immediately following this Court of Kings or thirty years from now when the king passes away naturally in his old age, I will be the Queen of Havyn. But there may not be much of a Havyn left in thirty years if Typhus continues on this path. He is too unstable to abdicate willingly. This is the only way."

"Librarian," Eriputes called beneath the balconies. The elder looked up at the High King. "What are the next steps with this addendum?"

Flipping through the pages of the Concordat, the Librarian stopped on a page near the back of the book and studied it, line for line.

"Based on Amendment Three-Hundred-and-Three," the Librarian spoke, "a deposition of a monarch requires a 'committed vote.' The petitioning party must temporarily abdicate all legal rights to their positions once the vote is motioned forward. If counted and recorded against the petitioner's favor, the Court must immediately follow the failed motion with a trial of treason. If a majority vote finds the petitioning party guilty of treason, then the abdicated powers must immediately be distributed to those the Court finds suitable, and the petitioning party, here forth labeled 'the guilty party,' will be sentenced immediately to life in a Keeper prison, or executed on site, again, at the discretion of the Court." The Librarian peered up from the Concordat and addressed Eriputes. "To summarize, High King, Master Sheridan, the Providence of Havyn, and Princess Lia must give up their powers as Heads, or heirs, of State, Faith, and Monarchy prior to the commencement of the vote, and essentially earn their positions back following the deposition of King Typhus."

A fist slammed on the stone rail of the balcony. King Henree shouted, "That's preposterous! They are deemed guilty before even going to trial! The absurdity is unbelievable. When was this amendment written and approved?"

"Winter of the year Seven-Hundred-and-Forty," the Librarian read. "The writing of said amendment followed the wrongful deposition of the king of Nest Aiken, whose brother framed the king in order to take the throne."

"Can I have another moment to explain myself before committing to the vote?" Sheridan asked Eriputes.

"What could you possibly have to say that you haven't already explained?" Eriputes rolled his eyes.

"It's not what I have to say," Sheridan shifted his gaze to the person standing next to the High King. "It's what Prince Sal has to say. He paid King Typhus a visit not too long ago and witnessed the king on one of his bad days." He addressed Sal directly, who appeared nervous and reluctant to speak, "Please, Sal."

The silver-haired prince continued his hesitation. He glanced around the Courtroom. All eyes were on him. What he said next would either help Sheridan or hinder him.

"Sal, please," Sheridan repeated, hardly audible across the void between them.

Prince Sal sighed deeply and shook his head, "For the record, yes, I admit during my brief visit to Havyn last month that King Typhus acted erratic and made no sense with the words he spoke. Off the record, however," the Librarian immediately stopped writing in his notes, "I cannot speak to this being an everyday occurrence."

"Well, Prince Sal," Eriputes addressed his son. The Librarian continued his writing. "You will someday stand in my shoes. I want your opinion. What should we do?"

"Father, I believe we should hear out the *other* kingdoms present today and see where their heads are at with all of this. Off the record, of course."

Eriputes considered for a moment. "Alright, Sal, I'll bend the rules a bit. Librarian, please scrap the previous two statements from the record."

"Do I hear a second?" the Librarian asked the remaining monarchs.

"Seconded," said King Henree.

"And a vote?"

Simultaneously, the kings of Fairmarq, High Alta, Seramyth, and Nest Aiken boomed a unanimous "Aye." All representatives of Havyn remained silent. A vote to remove something from record could only be approved by ruling monarchs. One of the several complications Sheridan frequently encountered while attending the Courts of Kings in Typhus's stead.

The Librarian took his pen and crossed a thick line through the last few lines on his note page.

"Now," Eriputes continued, "*off the record*, I would like to hear the thoughts of the other kingdoms regarding Master Sheridan's dilemma. Note that this is *not* a formal vote. This will help me decide if we should even *proceed* with a vote."

Kendra from Seramyth countered, "Is that even legal? I presumed a portion of the motion included an open discussion, which we are having now."

The Librarian answered, "The act of opening discussion before the vote is not *illegal*, so to speak, so long as it remains off record and no other monarch present requests to put it on record or openly motions to proceed with the vote before all off-record discussion can be heard, or the petitioning party provides further evidence that could sway the discussion prior to the vote."

Sheridan knew this meant his hands were tied. They could not ask anymore questions, and he could not provide them with any more evidence against Typhus.

Eriputes smirked, "Like I said, I'll bend the rules a bit. Seramyth, what thoughts are crossing your mind?"

Kendra's venomous stare found Sheridan. "Where was Seramyth when Havyn was riddled with plague? At your doorstep with three thousand white mages eager to heal those who were sick. Where has Havyn been all these years that Seramyth has shared the same ailment? Hiding in their Spire watching the world crumble around them. Our pleas for help have fallen on deaf ears. Why should Havyn deserve our help for a second time?"

"Nest Aiken?" Eriputes continued around the room.

"Havyn," King Dormian began, "has always been an ally of Nest Aiken. Both of our kingdoms share borders with Brekkenia, and we have allied many times throughout history when facing rebellious Brekken kings. My good heart tells me that helping Havyn is necessary, but the circumstances tell me otherwise. With the evidence we have been presented thus far, could it not be possible the Master of Cities has manipulated the Providence and the young princess into believing these wild fantasies? It is no secret that King Typhus and Master Sheridan do not get along."

"With all due respect, King Dormian," a voice rang out. Tracing its origin, Sheridan saw Chandra, Seramyth's heir of the Faith, standing on edge, bracing her hands against the rail of the balcony. "How dare you question the word of a Providence? It is forbidden for a Providence to lie about an official medical report. That integrity goes beyond even the laws of the Concordat. She speaks for the very gods. You question her again, and may the gods have their way with you!"

Dormian threw his hands up, surrendering. "My deepest of apologies, Princess Chandra. I meant no offense, surely. You are correct, I should not be questioning the word of a Providence. My curiosity still peaks wondering why the sudden urgency when, according to you, Sheridan, the king's health has been declining for years."

"Yes, odd indeed, King Dormian," Eriputes remarked. "Especially when I have so recently sought after the enormous debt that Havyn owes to not only High Alta, but to *all* of the Five Kingdoms, since the money was drawn from the shared emergency fund."

Sheridan shouted to the Librarian, "Objection! That is blatant selfish manipulation on High Alta's behalf."

"This is all off record, Master Sheridan," the Librarian reminded.

Shit, Sheridan thought.

"May I interrupt?" Princess Kendra asked.

"Granted," Eriputes permitted.

"How much money is Havyn indebted to you?"

"Two hundred and forty million gold." Eriputes allowed the sum to roll off his tongue as if it were nothing.

Even King Henree choked after hearing the amount spoken out loud.

"Million?!" Kendra was astonished. To Sheridan, she said, "Master of Cities, are you aware that Seramyth has approached High Alta for access to the emergency fund multiple times since the plague crossed our borders? Furthermore, are you aware that we have been denied each time due to lack of equitable funds?" Sheridan shook his head, knowing exactly where this conversation was going. "Two hundred and forty million gold may have changed the course of our war with this invisible killer... Money for medical supplies, extra guards, and many more assets that may have been deemed necessary for survival. Where is this gold?"

Sheridan understood Kendra's frustration, and he could not respectfully be angry with her for her inquisition. What ignited Sheridan's core was the maniacal grin creeping its way across Eriputes's face. This was all a damned game to him. He enjoyed watching Sheridan squirm with discomfort.

"I… Princess Kendra, to be quite honest, I am unaware of where these funds have been distributed," Sheridan lied. The last thing he needed was for the other monarchs to discover that the emergency fund was depleted on the salaries of spies in their kingdoms.

"You are *unaware*?" King Dormian questioned.

"The money was deposited into King Typhus's private accounts. I cannot legally gain access to those accounts so long as he is allowed to give orders and maintain his independence with the bank." Sheridan emphasized the term *legally* in his head. Though he already knew what was written on the king's bank statements, better to let the other kingdoms believe otherwise if it meant swaying their decision. "I have personally asked High Alta for more time or to establish a payment plan to recover the money owed. My requests, like yours, Kendra, have been denied."

"If what the Master of Cities says is true," King Henree spoke up, "then there is much to consider. I trust Master Sheridan's good will to come here before us and make such a heavy request. Personally, Fairmarq's relations with Havyn have never been stronger, and it certainly is not King Typhus's effort to thank. I trust the Providence and her report of the king's health. I also respect Princess Lia's bravery and trust her judgment for standing before us and risking her relationship with her father, and her position as heir."

The Courtroom fell silent for several minutes. Sheridan and Henree exchanged nods while they waited for judgement from High Alta. Nerves shot through Sheridan. All came down to just how vengeful Eriputes was feeling. If he allowed the Court to proceed with a proper investigation and vote, it could take days to properly undergo the process. Several days would be spent simply setting up and presenting their case for the record. If the vote remained divided—two for and two against—they would have to start all over again. The vote *had* to be a majority. The Court could last for weeks without anyone changing their vote.

Meanwhile, with Amendment Three-Hundred-and-Three, they would be required to step down from their positions throughout the course of the trial, allowing the Keepers and Eriputes to collaborate and establish temporary replacements.

The process would take far too long… All that time away with agents of High Alta in their stead... Sheridan almost wished they never pursued this deposition.

Finally, Eriputes spoke.

"Master Sheridan," he began solemnly, "On record, I have taken into consideration the opinions of the other kingdoms to simply decide if they want to *pursue* a vote of deposition, which are overwhelmingly not in your favor. You see, if the motion persists, I am afraid the biases of several of the other kingdoms would inadvertently influence their final decisions. I do not foresee this going in any direction that could be helpful to you.

"Also, I do not feel comfortable contemplating deposing another monarch for an ailment of the mind. That addendum was put in place to legally remove a monarch's power in the case that their health was too poor for them to abdicate on their own or continue their duties. Now, if King Typhus was comatose or losing a battle with the plague, the story would be entirely different.

"I regret to inform you that, as High King of the Five Kingdoms of Lynidas, I am denying your request to pursue *Addendum Four, Chapter Twenty-Seven, Section Fourteen*. I hope you understand."

Sheridan sighed heavily—half with relief, half with disappointment. What would this mean going forward? The Librarian will most certainly alert Typhus's Keepers of this ordeal, and they could kiss Lia's freedom goodbye. Her Keepers would *never* leave her side.

More was at risk than Sheridan realized. With the growing Brekken threat to Nest Aiken—likely instrumented by Typhus's delusions—the tension between Havyn and Seramyth, and the outrageous debt owed to High Alta, Sheridan reluctantly accepted just how alone they were.

How alone *he* was.

He could not allow Lia and the Providence to risk their lives anymore. They were raised in Havyn, born of Havynian blood, and would bleed for Havyn fighting for their lives.

What was he? A dwarf. Outcasted from Garmoire, never to return. He was no one.

He was no one when he crossed into Havyn nearly four years ago. He was no one when he cast his name into a ballot with dozens of other more highly qualified lords, ladies, governors, aristocrats, and socialites. Though everyone in Havyn, in the Five Kingdoms, knew his name, he was *not* one of them. No matter how hard he tried.

He was no one.

While he was thankful that the Providence and the princess stuck by his side and believed in him all this time, were their lives worth the risk?

The answer was no. And Sheridan would tell them such when they returned to Havyn.

Their return, surprisingly, would happen sooner than he thought.

The High King went on for twenty more minutes summarizing some smaller key points that have developed in the past six months since the previous Court of Kings. Nothing Sheridan didn't already know.

Usually, they would finish early the first day and enjoy some down time with dinner and cocktails, then start fresh in the morning with follow-up thoughts from the previous day and proceed with discussing amendments to the Concordat—most of which were voted against anyway.

However, today, Eriputes called the Court short and dismissed them all. As Sheridan and the others slipped through the ruby curtains behind them, he caught a glimpse of Henree approaching him fast from Fairmarq's balcony.

Henree put a hand on Sheridan's shoulder and pulled him to the side as teams of Keepers guarding the Court of Kings marched by.

"We need to talk," Henree urged.

Sheridan nodded.

CHAPTER 38

"My deepest condolences that the Court did not turn out the way you had hoped," Henree dipped his head sincerely. "I meant what I said in there. You and I have been allies since before you stepped inside the Spire of the New King. I cannot say the same for Typhus. Whether or not the Providence's medical report is accurate, as Dormian foolishly questioned, I trust your judgement that perhaps Havyn needs a new ruler. You have done what you can to correct his mistakes these past few years, but a two hundred and forty million gold debt... That should not be your burden to bear."

Sheridan shrugged. "It is what it is. What am I supposed to do? Havyn doesn't exactly have spare gold lying around. Not *that* much, at least. I shouldn't have expected any different coming here today."

"If Lia was eighteen," Henree gestured at the princess standing by the ruby curtain with a flick of his eyes, "I guarantee they would have considered differently. Fact is, they are threatened by you because they know nothing about you. By granting you temporary regency until the princess comes of age was not something they were willing to consider."

"I understand that," Sheridan admitted, "but they don't comprehend just how dangerous Typhus is remaining in power. He attacked Lia. Would have attacked the Providence, too, if I hadn't stepped in."

Henree's jaw dropped. "He *attacked* his own daughter?!"

"He didn't recognize her. He threw her from the dais. Before you ask, yes, she is fine, but that was the final straw for me."

"He really is sick..." Henree considered a moment. Sheridan nodded in response. "And Eriputes will not make any accommodations for you to pay him back yourself?"

"No. He demanded... He demanded that Typhus pay him back directly. In full."

"That's impossible." Henree's eyes narrowed. "What else did he say? You are holding something back."

"He demanded Lia," Sheridan spoke softly. "Her hand in marriage to his youngest son."

"Pathetic," Henree scoffed. "Either you sell out Havyn to pay him back, or you sell out Havyn by giving away the only heir to the throne. He is playing you like a fiddle. That whole display in the Courtroom was to humiliate you."

Sheridan rolled his eyes. "I am starting to realize that."

"Eriputes is a monster, Sheridan. Do not fall for his games. Whatever you do, be the one to make the demands. Do not give in to his."

Henree's grudge against the High King was personal. Sheridan knew the story, as most in the Five Kingdoms did. A story of a stolen child and the murmurs of a witch among the High Altan court. If what Henree swears is true, if Eriputes was responsible for the supposed kidnapping and possible murder of Fairmarq's infant princess, then surely some evidence would have risen to the surface eighteen years later? But who was Sheridan to question Henree's suspicions? Eriputes *was* an awful person, the dwarf could not deny that fact. He could also not deny that either outcome of the debt owed to High Alta would end with the downfall of Havyn.

Before Sheridan could respond, he noticed Eriputes and his entourage turn the corner and approach down the hall. *The Demise of the Fairies* loomed over him as Eriputes practically shoved his way between them.

"Pardon me, King Henree," Eriputes flashed his shiny, gold crown as he turned to face Sheridan. "I must speak with the Master of Cities privately."

Eriputes was furious, Sheridan could see in his eyes. The king of Fairmarq replied professionally, "As you wish, Your Highness. I will be right over there. With Princess Lia and the Providence."

"Master Sheridan," Eriputes began once Henree was out of earshot, "I must caution you on continuing with this quarrel of yours with King Typhus. Regardless of his mental state, he is still a king of Lynidas. I find your lack of respect in this regard very disturbing and bordering on illegal. Be thankful I stopped you from opening the floor to a vote in there. It may have just saved your life." He snuck a glance behind him at Lia. "Fortunately, I need *her* alive, and not rotting in a Keeper prison for treason, if she is to marry my son." His white teeth shone through a sly smile. "I will be frequenting Havyn from now on to monitor King Typhus's ailment myself *and* to review Havyn's budget to see where best to acquire my money from. See you soon, Master Sheridan. Farewell!"

Eriputes marched down the marble stairs with his shoulders back and his head held high. Sal offered a half-sincere apology as he trudged after his father. The silver-haired prince had more respect for Sheridan than his father did, clearly.

Once High Alta's representatives were gone from sight, Sheridan shuffled over to the Providence, Lia, and Henree.

"Come," he nudged the Providence, "We're leaving."

"Of course, Sheridan," the Providence nodded and locked arms with Lia as they followed Sheridan from the Library.

◆◆◆◆◆◆◆◆◆

The ride back to Havyn felt like an eternity. Sheridan wondered how soon Eriputes would act on his promise to check in on Havyn frequently. Would they return to the city with an army of High Alta's soldiers at their border?

Only time would tell.

The disappointment on Lia's face concerned Sheridan the most. The princess hadn't spoken a word the entire journey home. Sheridan felt inclined to help talk her through her feelings but decided against it. Perhaps it would be best if the princess collected her thoughts prior to Sheridan intruding.

Princess Lia was ambitious, there was no question about it. Though the results of the Court of Kings discouraged her, she would overcome this obstacle and come out even stronger. Anyone who met the princess could describe intense similarities with Queen Helena, with respect to the late-queen's endurance, courage, and ambition.

What terrified Sheridan, though he never spoke of it, were the qualities Lia shared with Typhus. Or lack thereof. Simply, Lia was so dissimilar from her father, Sheridan was afraid what qualities were hidden beneath her unassuming exterior. Did she have his temper? His haughtiness? Or, worse yet, could she develop the same illness Typhus suffered from?

How reliable would a new monarch be if that new monarch was doomed to fail?

The Providence, thinking ahead as she always did, decided to address the underlying issue at hand—the tension between Havyn and Seramyth. To start, the Providence drafted a letter to send to Chandra thanking her for sticking up for a fellow Providence. Though Chandra was not the Providence of Seramyth *yet*, the Providence would take any potential ally she could get.

In her letter, she requested from Chandra a summary of any help she could possibly offer without crossing threads with Typhus. She could not deliver gold or additional white mages, as Seramyth had done during Havyn's battle with the plague, without confirmation from the king, but she *could* send them spare herbs and medications, among other supplies, at her discretion.

"My fear," the Providence started partway through their trip back to Havana City, "is that Havyn is responsible for the spread of the plague in Seramyth. They sent three thousand white mages to provide additional medical support, and while it certainly turned the tide in the fight against the sickness, it caused the deaths of five hundred of Seramyth's loaned mages." She looked up ominously at Sheridan. "Who's to say the survivors did not return home carrying the plague with them, causing an outbreak?"

"Hmm," Sheridan scratched his beard, "that would explain why Nest Aiken and the others did not experience a similar situation."

"Seramyth has luckily been able to contain this calamity."

"Though, that doesn't seem to be their choice, if what the triplets say is true. If the border with High Alta is being enforced, then maybe Nest Aiken's is, too."

"While I understand the desire to protect the borders and prevent any contamination, living beings are dying at extraordinary rates in that kingdom. The healthy could still flee and survive."

Sheridan sighed, glancing out the window of the carriage as the sun set beyond the horizon. "I know what you're thinking, and we can't intrude on Nest Aiken, and especially not High Alta, to convince them to reduce their border protocols. That would be stepping dangerously close to the line of treason."

"Not if I request the Providence of Nest Aiken to consider it," the Providence said confidently.

"Doubtful that Nest Aiken will consider playing nicely with *anyone* while they are searching for a spy in their ranks."

The Providence's brow scrunched. "Do you truly believe it could be one of Typhus's spies who killed the Brekken?"

"Providence," Sheridan turned from the window and met her gaze, "I wish I had a single shadow of a doubt. But I don't."

Lia remained silent with them for the course of the night, unsleeping. She still kept quiet as the sun rose the following morning during their crossing into Havana City. Kept silent as the carriage climbed the hill to the base of the Spire, revealing all four of Havyn's Keepers and General Braxon waiting on the marble steps for their arrival.

Sheridan was the first to step from the carriage. He marched up to Braxon and the Keepers, staring them down.

Braxon was the first to speak. "The princess better be in that carriage." His jaw tensed awaiting Sheridan's response.

Before Sheridan could respond, half a dozen Guardians of the Faith strode down the steps in three pairs. They approached the carriage, surrounding the Providence as she helped Lia to the ground.

"Touch her," Sheridan growled to Braxon, "and it will be the last thing you do with the use of all four of your limbs."

"Brave words for a dwarf," Braxon crossed his arms, flexing his thick, black armor.

Sheridan's eyes flicked between the Keepers. "Same goes for the four of you."

"We must escort the princess to her bedchambers," one of the Keepers spoke. "Orders from the king."

"That's fine. My statement stands."

The Guardians of the Faith escorted Lia to her Keepers. She nodded to Sheridan. He reciprocated. The Keepers, minding the Master of Cities's words, remained an extra step behind the princess as she stepped through the doors of the Spire.

As Typhus's Keepers opened their mouths to speak, Braxon held up a gauntleted hand. He gave them a warning glance as he spoke, "At ease. The Master of Cities acknowledges his own actions. Princess Lia has been returned safely. You will tell King Typhus as much."

The Keepers bowed politely to the general, rotated on their heels, and disappeared through the threshold.

"Since when did Keepers take orders from you?" Sheridan asked.

"Since I had to deny the king's orders to drive my army through the Fields of Born and steal back the princess from her kidnapper." Braxon sneered at Sheridan as the dwarf attempted to hold out a hand as thanks for what the general did in their defense. "I did not break ranks to stand in *your* defense, dwarf. I did it to prevent the princess from being caught in the crossfire." Braxon began raising his voice, "Now, forgive me for breaking ranks once more, but get inside the godsdamned Spire and *keep in line, Master Sheridan!* I may have quelled his rage this once, and if his ailment is as true as you say, he will likely have forgotten by now, but next time, I will follow orders and strike down all who stand in my path to the princess."

◆◆◆◆◆◆◆◆◆

Sheridan returned to his chambers and changed into more comfortable clothing after a quick bath. He half expected the Keepers to barge down his door and drag him kicking and screaming to the king. As Braxon commented, though, the king likely already forgot about Lia being missing for a week.

Sheridan didn't have to wonder. He knew if he shuffled through the Keepers' mail, there would be a detailed letter from the Librarian inquiring why he was staring directly at the princess while they guarded an empty bedroom. Everyone would be on edge for a while. Best to avoid the Keepers as much as possible for the time being.

A pile of unopened mail awaited Sheridan as he approached the table in the center of his chambers.

Skimming through the pile, he unsealed his official invitation for Aroy and Charlaia's wedding. Sparing no expense, of course, the invitation was printed on the finest woven parchment embroidered with the symbols of both of their households. *You are hereby invited to the wedding of...* Sheridan knew the rest. It was the same formal invitation print used for every socialite wedding in Havyn.

As a courtesy, the Master of Cities was typically sent an invitation to all of these weddings. Though Sheridan never attended them, he ensured extra protection by placing additional City Watch squads in the area of the ceremonies and receptions.

Aroy and Charlaia were the closest things to friends Sheridan could say he had, and even their "friendship" remained a professional manner. He actually looked forward to this wedding. Only a few months away.

The next article of mail alerted him. The night-blue seal of Avalon. It had to be from either Athenia or Raven.

Sheridan cracked the seal and read the handwritten letter.

Master Sheridan—

I write to you urgently requesting your assistance. In her investigation, Governess Athenia has uncovered a greater plot, which has led to her unfortunately capture. I cannot speak much of her discovery by letter alone, and I am unaware if the governess is alive or dead. Come to Gabrenas swiftly. I fear the worst.

—Lady Raven

Sheridan read and reread the letter a dozen times before reality struck. *Shit.* He got Athenia into this mess by urging her to pry into matters that did not concern her, and now she was paying for it.

Guilt set in, upsetting the dwarf's stomach.

Without hesitation, he sped from his chambers, ordering the nearest guards to bring around his horse. He did not head immediately for the steps leading down from the Spire, though. He instead ascended the stairs in the rear of the throne room.

At the top of the steps, he approached Lia's bedchamber. Her Keepers blocked his path.

"None shall enter," the first one said.

"Orders from the king," the second followed up.

Sheridan didn't have time to argue. He shouted, "Lia! Lia, can you hear me?"

A muffled "yes" sounded from behind the oak door.

"Lia, listen! I have to go to Avalon for a little while. I will be back before you know it. Write to Avalon if you need me! The Providence will be here with you."

Lia hesitated. "Okay," she finally said, barely audible. "Stay safe!"

Sheridan's next stop was the Providence's study. The Guardians of the Faith parted for him as he entered. The Providence was doing the same, catching up on mail from the past week.

She looked up at the sound of her door opening. "Sheridan?" Seeing the urgency on his face, she stood. "What is it? Is it Lia?"

"No," Sheridan panted, stopping at her desk. "It's Athenia." He handed over the letter and let the Providence read it. "I am leaving immediately for Avalon. If you or Lia need me for any reason, send for me. Raven is not one to ask for help, so this concerns me."

"Yes, of course," the Providence nodded, handing him back the letter. "Go, go! I can maintain things here in the meantime."

"Thank you so much! I owe you."

The Providence smirked. "We have done one another enough favors to not 'owe' anything. It is fine. Finding Athenia is of utmost importance."

"One more thing," Sheridan said. "Could you please send a hawk ahead of me to the cities and barracks nearby Gabrenas and order a full force of additional guards to assist Raven?"

"Of course," the Providence dipped her head. Thanking her once more, Sheridan ran out of the study.

Leaving the two of them behind so soon after that catastrophe of a Court of Kings was the last thing Sheridan wanted to do. What did Athenia discover that could have placed her in danger? More so, what was so dangerous that Raven and her legion of City Watch guards couldn't handle?

He would find out soon. The ride to Avalon would take a few days, at best.

Sheridan descended the spiral staircase and pushed through the front doors of the Spire of the New King. His horse was pulled up front, just as he asked. A female guard captain held the reins and waited as Sheridan skipped down the marble steps.

"Thank you, Captain," Sheridan said, stepping into the stirrup and throwing his other leg over the horse's back. He noticed four other guards were mounted just ahead. He turned his head to the captain. "It's alright, I can ride solo."

The guard captain walked over her own horse and mounted the saddle. Checking the straps, she replied, "All due respect, Master Sheridan, but it is in your best interest to have an escort right now. Trust me."

Unlike most military superiors, Sheridan's temper did not erupt when orders were not followed or were ignored. These guards undergo intensive training to weed out those who may not be in the Watch for the right reasons. Rather than discipline a guard for speaking out, Sheridan welcomed it as constructive criticism.

He scanned the captain from head to toe. She seemed familiar, but Sheridan spoke with over a hundred captains each week, so she did not stand out.

"I appreciate your concern, Captain...?"

"Tidas, Master. Captain Tidas."

"Captain Tidas," Sheridan repeated the name. "I assume there is a reason for you seeking my 'best interest' today?" She nodded under her helm. "Then, let us proceed and you can explain on the way."

Sheridan snapped his reins, causing his horse to rear. As the horse's front hooves hit the cobblestone, it took off at full speed. The four mounted guards kept in front of him, keeping the streets clear as he sped through. Captain Tidas held up the rear.

CHAPTER 39

On the eve of her fourteenth birthday, Ena celebrated with Tidas after an exhausting day of training. The lesson for the day had been parrying maneuvers. Tidas made it clear to Ena that sometimes the best offense was a good defense.

Parrying was not her forte, though. After many failed attempts, and many bruises later from the wooden training blades, Tidas gave Ena the night off. Instead, their time was spent drinking with some of Tidas's closest guard friends.

Tidas held up a glass of wine and toasted to her, "As of tomorrow, only two more years will separate you from joining our ranks as a free woman! To you, Ena!"

The four other guards cheered and tossed back their drinks. Ena laughed and took a sip of her own. Drinking at her age was usually grounds for hefty fines, but the guards always let her have a taste under their watch.

"How free will I be exactly under contractual obligation to Havana City?" Ena joked.

One of the other guards joked back, "That, Horse Princess, all depends on who your captain is. If you have the displeasure of working under Tidas's command, you can kiss your freedom goodbye."

As they all laughed, spitting their drinks all over the place, Tidas smiled and raised a hand, "Alright, alright, play nice! He's absolutely correct—it depends on your captain. And if *certain* guards are not respectful to their captains, then they will work double shifts for a month straight. Which, by the way, is an order I am absolutely authorized to give!"

The guard brushed off Tidas's idle threat. He continued to Ena, "The truth, though, is that you will work your ass off for the first few years as a guard. Once you get through the double shifts and the shit pay, you'll get to make some choices that determine your future in the Watch. I think the Watch will suit you well."

"Thank you," Ena said. "Now, if you will excuse me, I must return home. I am well past my usual curfew, and my father will not be pleased."

The mention of her father killed the mood instantly. She could join the Watch as soon as the next day if her father would be kind enough to sign the permission paperwork, but Ena knew he wouldn't. He would do anything in his power to prevent Ena from joining the Watch, even when she is of age.

Every week for most of the past year, Ena told her father she was attending business classes to prepare her for taking over the stables once he retired. He wasn't happy about it, but if it meant possibly earning him more money in the long run, he tolerated her choice. If he ever knew where she actually was...

Ena wiped the image from her mind.

She climbed into the saddle of her thoroughbred—her father made sure she rode in style wherever she went. After a brief goodbye to Tidas, Ena kicked her heels into her horse and galloped off into the direction of the stables.

By how high the moon hung in the sky, Ena knew she was far too late for the typical "class ran late" explanation. *Shit...*

She pushed her horse to its limits as she sped up the worn path through the field. Approaching the stables, Ena jumped from the horse's back and through the door open. The horse trotted back to its stall, and without even bothering to take off the saddle or lock the stall, Ena ran into the house.

The moment she barged through the front door, she skidded to a halt.

Her father sat at their dining table, glass of whiskey in hand, glaring at his daughter. The standoff lasted for minutes as Ena's heart thumped in her chest, her pulse pounding in her hot ears.

"Father, I can explain."

"I waited up for you," her father remained surprisingly calm. "All night."

"Father, I know—"

"Where were you?"

Ena took a step closer. The house was pitch black outside of the glow of the single candle flickering on the table. "I apologize for being late. I joined some friends after class to celebrate my birthday tomorrow. I lost track of time."

Her father took a sip of his whiskey. "Your tale almost checks out."

"Pardon?" Ena's brows pinched together.

"I know you went out with friends," he answered, swirling the amber liquor around in his glass.

"You had me followed?" Of all the things her father has done to her, hiring someone to tail her was the least intrusive or harmful.

"Yes," he snapped. His voice began to rise. "I also know who these *friends* of yours are."

Ena held out a hand, trying to calm him as if he were one of the horses. "Dad—"

"You fucking inconsiderate, disgraceful child!" the Horse Lord stood abruptly, sending his chair tipping backwards, and threw the glass at the wall by Ena's face. Shattered glass and whiskey sprayed her cheek. She hardly balked, not even when blood trickled down her face. He stepped closer to her, closing the gap between them. "After all I have done for you, provided for you, why do you continue to disobey and lie to me? You wish to spend your life in a suit of armor taking orders from righteous pricks who believe themselves to be better than you? Your future has been set by the legacy I created for you, yet you would throw it all away!"

"The legacy you created for *yourself*!" Ena fired back. "I have never been given the opportunity to bask in the spoils of your so-called *legacy*. I already take orders from one righteous prick. It would make no difference!"

Stars suddenly flashed in Ena's vision as she realized her own father just struck her with his fist. Her jaw ached extraordinarily. She spat blood onto the wood floor. Turning back to her father, she saw his knuckles split from where they connected with her jawbone. How hard had he hit her? She would feel it worse in the morning once the alcohol wore off.

"You want another order from this *prick*?" her father roared. "Get to your fucking room! I am locking the door, and you won't see the light of day until you have forgotten about this City Watch nonsense."

Ena reached forwards and shoved her father. He stumbled back until he hit the table's edge. He curled his bleeding fingers into another fist and swung at Ena again. Instinctively, Ena wound back her elbow and met her father's fist with her own.

Bones cracked audibly in both of their hands.

Her father was tougher than she thought. He shook his hand as if he simply pinched his finger in the stable door, despite several of his fingers bending in the wrong directions. Ena observed her own hand. Fingers were visibly broke, but adrenaline masked the overall urge to scream in pain.

"Fuck you," Ena spat blood at him. "I am not afraid of you. I need nothing from you."

Ena shoved past him, heading for the stairs.

"And where do you think you're going?" her father called out.

"To pack my things," she grabbed the banister and climbed the first step. "I am leaving for good." She hoped Tidas was ready for a roommate.

"Like hell you are!" He charged at her and grabbed her ankle as she neared the top of the steps. Ena fell headfirst into the stairs and slid back to the bottom as her father pulled her. He gripped the back of her collar with his uninjured hand and lifted her off the steps, tossing her aside. Ena slid facedown across the floor, blood smearing the hardwood.

Ena groaned and pushed herself up with her palms. Crimson saliva oozed from her mouth. Her head pounded from where it hit the step, a sharp ringing sounded in her ears. Mustering the strength to stand up was cut short when her father kneeled over her, grabbing the back of her head, and slamming her forehead so hard into the wood that it bounced.

Dazed, Ena hardly noticed when her father grabbed her by the hair and dragged her back towards the stairs. She feebly kicked and swung her arms at him, attempting to break free. His grip was iron.

"Please, Dad, don't," Ena choked as her spine and tailbone slammed on each step. Her vision blurred, but she could see they neared the top of the steps. Taking a quick turn, they were in front of her bedroom door. Her father let her hair go and drove the toe of his boot into her abdomen, knocking the breath out of her.

The latch of the door clattered and swung open. The Horse Lord dragged his daughter by the hair once more, leaving her on the floor of her bedroom. After slamming the door, the Horse Lord locked the latch and slammed the back of his fist into the wood.

"You will rot in there!" he screamed through the door.

Ena rolled back and forth clutching her stomach. Weeping to herself, she called out softly, "Please... Dad, please..."

An hour passed, and the numbness of the shock and adrenaline wore off. Ena couldn't move, couldn't cry.

Broken fingers. Concussion. Cracked jaw. A damaged liver or spleen. She rattled off her injuries in her head.

She heard her father's bedroom door shut. Now was her chance.

Ena took a deep breath and forced herself to sit up. It felt as if a fire burned inside of her. As she turned her head, her vision delayed and followed her eyes in slow motion. A spell of dizziness swam in her stomach. She painfully vomited in front of her, soaking her pants.

Fuck. How in the Connections would she get out of here?

The only way out was the window. She would have to somehow pry open her window with one broke hand and swing her legs out the narrow opening while severely concussed and possibly internally bleeding. Wanting to give up before she even started, Ena snapped herself out of it. Giving up now was not an option if she wanted to survive.

Using her dresser to hoist herself to her feet, Ena wobbled over to her window. She drew a dagger from a holster on her thigh, one that Tidas had given her for self-defense, and jimmied the blade under the frame. With her limited strength, she moved the hilt up and down, nudging the window open enough to fit her unbroken hand under. Silently, she heaved the frame open from the sill.

More painfully than she anticipated in her mind, Ena swung a leg over the windowsill, followed shortly by the other. She lost the grip of the ledge with her one good hand and dropped harshly onto the ground below with a *thump*.

She bit her lip to hold back screaming in agony.

Following a few minutes of mental preparation, she forced herself to stand once more and headed immediately for the path to the city. Ena contemplated turning to the stables and stealing a horse, but the commotion from the barn and the gallop of hooves on the dirt would wake her father.

The ride from the stables to Tidas's home was a half an hour by horse at a steady pace. So, by foot, the trek would be about an hour, or hour and a half. *Limping in pain, probably two hours,* Ena groaned to herself. Which turned out to be correct.

Two agonizing hours later in the black of night, Ena collapsed against the front door of Tidas's barracks. She knocked feebly, unsure if Tidas would even wake at the sound.

A moment later, the door opened inwards and Ena fell, only to be caught in Tidas's toned arms.

"*Gods*, Ena!" Tidas gasped. "What the hell happened to you?" Ena attempted to speak but was consumed with pain. "Shh, don't worry about that right now. Let's get you inside and all patched up."

Thank the gods for Tidas's relationship with the Watch, for a white mage was by Ena's side in a matter of minutes. By morning, Ena's injuries were mostly nonexistent, as if nothing had happened.

Ena explained to Tidas the events that occurred before leaving her house earlier that night. Tidas seemed angrier about it than Ena was, threatening to have the Horse Lord arrested.

"No," Ena argued, "it would not be worth it. He would simply buy his freedom and return to his business as usual. I do not need to be avenged, I need to be free. I want to join the Watch."

Tidas smiled joyfully. "Let me pull some strings and see what I can do."

Within a week's time, the papers were forged, and Ena was sworn into the City Watch as a sixteen-year-old recruit with parent permission. Ena did not inquire about the supposed strings that Tidas needed pulled, but she was eternally grateful.

Thus began Ena's career as a guard and eventual political career in El Vadora. As far as she knew, Ena's father never searched for her, never asked about her in the city, never acknowledged the existence of his daughter ever again. Not until his untimely death, that is, and his lawyer named her as the inheritor of every item of his will.

◆◆◆◆◆◆◆◆◆

"Funny," a gruff voice scoffed as Ena slid unevenly back to reality. Torchlight burned Ena's retinas as the blur vanished. Mida, the Lord of Steel, stood before her. The two mindrenders disappeared into the darkness of the hall behind him. "I was in Havana City the day of your father's funeral. I was present for the public reading of his last will and testament. Along with seventeen hundred of Havyn's other elites, of course."

He paced around her, preying on her. Why had he been there? Who else in Havyn knows who he is? "I always wondered, like many others, why you abandoned your father for the Watch. He gave you everything, legitimately *everything*, down to the half-empty glass of milk still sitting on his kitchen table from when he died. He couldn't have been *that* bad! Or so we all thought. I appreciate you for showing me the truth. I also apologize for not recognizing you sooner from the funeral. It could have saved us *a lot* of turmoil if I knew. I wouldn't have risked playing games and kidnapping a governess."

"Too late for that," Ena rasped. She failed to shift herself and get comfortable.

Mida placed a calloused hand on the small of Ena's back. "Easy, Governess. The mindrenders had you under for about a week. Save your strength."

Was this his attempt at being nice?

"If you would like," Mida continued, "we can continue our game of question and answer. I'll give you the first question."

Still searching for answers... She commented, "I thought you said you weren't speaking to me anymore?" Mida only glared at her, refusing to acknowledge his bluff. Ena thought carefully. "Where is..." She cleared her throat. "Where is my sword? The one I had in my possession when you captured me."

Mida let out a throaty chuckle. "I supposed I should be asking where *my* sword is. But I believe I have seen the Aconyte strapped to the belt of your boyfriend, the Unweaved whelp who has never held a blade before in his life." *Unweaved? What does he mean?*

"Anyway, I believe you mean this sword right here." Mida stepped in front of her and drew the night-black blade from behind his robe. He twisted it around in his hand, the magical hum resonated in the room. Torchlight flickered the stars powdering the blade's pitch blackness. "I don't know what this sword is or where you got it from, Athenia, but it is much safer in my hands than in the hands of someone who doesn't understand it."

Ena shoulders burned. She could not begin to imagine the permanent damage endured after all this time suspended from her wrists. "You do not understand it either, Mida."

"You are correct, Governess." Mida stared in wonder at the sword in hand, admiring the innate craftmanship. "But I might know those who do." Sheathing the sword, he met Ena's fierce gaze. Despite the torture he caused her, she remained unbroken.

"It is my turn to ask a question," Mida smirked. He resumed his predatory pacing. "After our many conversations and my many peaks inside your head, I am beginning to think you did not come to Avalon searching for me. I'd rather believe you happened to stumble across me and my operation while in the city for other purposes. What purposes were those?"

"Yes," Ena licked her dry, cracking lips. Her sandpaper tongue did nothing more than pull at the scabs that had already healed over. "You are correct. Our meeting was happenstance, at best. My original purpose for coming to Gabrenas was to investigate the murder of the Lord of Avalon. A murder induced by your underground operations and bluebite shipment."

Mida's expression appeared more confused than anything. He chuckled to himself before breaking out into an outburst of laughter. He held his stomach has his hearty laugh belted out, echoing down the hallway behind him.

"HA! Foolish girl! You think *I* killed the Lord?" He resumed his hysterical laughter. "I would do nothing but thank the Lord, had he survived to see this day! He is the sole reason for my success in Gabrenas."

"Enough, Mida!" A low female voice boomed around them, shaking the chains and torches that hung from the walls. The hair on the back of the dwarf's neck instantly stood on end.

"Yes, your highness," Mida replied softly, with a look of annoyance.

Behind him, the slow patter of delicate footsteps approached from the tunnel. As they sounded nearer, Mida clasped his hands in front of him and strode to the side away from the mouth of the tunnel. From the darkness, the most stunning woman Ena had ever seen stepped into the light.

The woman wore a black leather body suit that clung tight to her milky flesh, accentuating her curves. Her snow-white hair flowed down her shoulders and back like the oil painting of a waterfall, and her vermillion eyes narrowed as she observed the decaying body of the prisoner kneeling in front of her.

The fear-inducing crimson gaze sent a shiver of pure horror through Ena's veins. She forced herself to look away, but she could not shut her eyes. Staring at the stone floor beneath her, Ena watched the bare feet of this living nightmare dance around her, delicately placing her toes and the ball of her foot, followed gently by her heel, step after step, hardly disturbing the dust and pebbles beneath her. Her feet were pristinely pedicured—no signs of callouses or exposure, despite the creature's comfort walking without soles.

Curiously, Ena allowed her eyes to climb up the milky leg of the woman. Not a blemish in sight. No scars, freckles, cellulite, or anything beyond the marble-like skin that coated the evil within. Ena's eyes stopped at the middle of the woman's hip, where the hem of the tight leather bodysuit began. Her hand hung by her side—perfectly manicured, same as her feet. Though, her nails were long and trimmed to be shaped like coffins, lightly painted with a clear acrylic.

When the woman circled back around to Ena's front, she spoke. Her voice rang out like a mid-morning church bell; though, no church bell had the same terror in its song.

"Governess Athenia," she spoke. "A pleasure to officially make your acquaintance. My allies call me Myra. You may refer to me as none other than fear itself. Please, do be mindful of your manners and look at me while I speak." Without trying, Ena's head shot upwards, her eyes locked onto the glowing red oculi of trepidation. She bucked, but her entire body was frozen. Myra's pink lips curled in a menacing smile. "Thank you. Allow me to elaborate on my colleague's burst of enjoyment from your previous comment. Simply, the Lord of Avalon was killed by no other hand than his own."

Suicide?! Ena trembled, unsure if it was from the cold sensation that washed over her or the raw emotion ebbing from her amygdala. "What outcome could he seek from ending his own life with bluebite?"

"I sought an alliance with the Lord," Myra stated bluntly. "Matters grew complicated, and he orchestrated his own demise to escape from my grasp. He stole the bluebite from a hidden shipment of it, masked by one of Mida's shipments of steel. A pity, truly. The Lord would have made an excellent protégé." Seeing the awe and curiosity in Ena's face, she continued, "You see, Governess, the Lord was an Unweaved—a person born of magical blood who has yet to tap into the Connections of Magic. Unweaved are dreadfully more powerful than those who have their relationship with the Connections identified at a young age, for the power is raw and untamed. Once that power is released, with a bit of obedience and discipline, one can use it to devastate armies and raze entire cities.

"My primary goal was locating all Unweaved in Havyn, there being significantly higher rates of magic in the blood of Havyn's citizens. The Lord of Avalon was one such Unweaved, and after the discovery of a small kernel of his magical potential..." Her eyes flicked away, for a solitary moment. "Nevertheless, he denied my requests for an alliance and sought an escape. Bluebite, my dear, is the only substance on this earth that can sever one's tie to the Connections. Mage blood can still be utilized after death, unless that death is induced by the ingestion of bluebite."

"Wait," Ena had a sudden realization, "so that cult I discovered a couple of years ago..."

Myra nodded. "All mages seeking release from my recruitment tactics. Not murders, as you believed, but suicides."

"Why reveal yourself now?"

"Ah, but I haven't," Myra sneered. "I may have revealed myself to you in this moment, but I am a shadow to the rest of the world. If you are lucky, you will not survive long enough to reveal my truth."

Still frozen, unable to tear her eyes from Myra, Ena asked, "Why does that make me lucky?"

A foreboding snicker followed. Myra answered, "The Unweaved you travel with, Drake, is searching for you. I want him to be successful. I want him here. His magic remains raw and willful, and the more he utilizes it undisciplined, the more powerful his tie to the Connections becomes. Now that we have met, he finding you is my next step in assuming control of Havyn and, eventually, all of Lynidas."

Ena began to cry. The tears burned as they rolled from her ducts down her face. "Just kill me. Please."

Myra crossed her arms in front of her and tapped her long nails of one hand on her opposite arm. "You will die, Athenia. You will die alone and broken, but not here or now. Pray for death, my dear, but do not beg for it." To Mida, she snapped, "Come, Mida. Leave our mousetrap alone to catch its prey."

Through tear-filled eyes, Ena watched Myra stride slowly from the light of the cell back into the darkness beyond. Mida, glancing one last time at her over his shoulder, turned tail and followed his queen. The moment Mida disappeared behind the shadows, the telepathic grip on her released like a heavy weight from Ena's shoulders. Pain flooded her from head to toe.

The torches snuffed out, leaving her in utter darkness.

She cried out into the nothingness around her.

Whatever power Myra possessed, Ena *never* wanted to experience it again. Weeks and weeks of mental and physical torment from the mindrenders and the fire mages did not break her. If anything, the torture empowered her. But five minutes with Myra, and Ena begged for death. Begged from no one. Because no one was listening.

CHAPTER 40

Too much time had passed since Ena's disappearance, and Drake and Lady Raven were beginning to expect the worst. Governor Josef requested just days ago to allow the guards in the city to rest. Many of them took double shifts patrolling the tunnels and city without hesitation, but many also began passing out from exhaustion. The white mages throughout the city issued a statement to the Master White Mage, Joran, also urging the guards to be retired temporarily—their clinics were overrun.

Lady Raven had no choice but to permit Josef to order all guards to reduce their shifts and recover. She grew unbearably impatient, having heard no word back from the Dread Watch or from Master Sheridan. Were their messenger hawks being intercepted?

Anything was possible.

Scouring the tunnels led them to dead ends at nearly every turn. Drake oversaw the guards in the tunnels as the cartographers, hired by Raven, mapped the area, hoping to uncover a path they may have overlooked.

The findings of the maps shocked them all to their cores.

"My lady," the lead cartographer began his announcement after spending days mapping the tunnels, "I am ashamed to admit that our results are inconclusive."

"Inconclusive?" Lady Raven bit back in a short-tempered manner. "How can drawing a map be 'inconclusive?'"

"Well, if you look at these three maps here," as he approached to lay out the parchment, Raven snatched them from his hands and looked at them briskly. The cartographer sighed, "If you look, those three maps are all ones I sketched—one for each day I spent in the darkness."

"And?"

"The tunnels from each are slightly different from the day before."

Raven's cyan eyes cut the cartographer like glass. "Just get to the point! Do not waste my time!"

Drake stepped forwards and said bluntly, "Raven, he did his job. You should listen."

Raven shot him a look of disdain, but the cartographer continued before she could snap at him, too, "The tunnels are different because they are being changed. All of my workers discovered similar findings in the sections of the tunnels they mapped. Something, or *someone*, is shifting the tunnels so they are different each time we investigate."

"Luckily," Drake chimed in, "we found all known entrances. They are being heavily guarded to prevent anyone from entering or exiting without proper authorization. But we can't find our way to the center."

Raven reviewed the maps in front of her. The grid of tunnels expanded beneath nearly every section of the city, except for the geographical center. It was as if someone erased the entire middle of the map.

"The center is where Athenia may be?" she asked.

"I have a strong feeling about it, yes," Drake confirmed.

"No sign of the dwarf or any of his mage henchmen?"

"Not a soul to be seen, my lady," the cartographer responded.

Raven dropped a pouch of gold onto the edge of her desk. "Thank you, cartographer. Apologies if we wasted your time. There is extra in there for you and your men."

The cartographer thanked the lady, bowed, and retreated from the room.

Raven rested her elbow on the desk, pinching her temples with frustration.

"All of our resources have been drained, Drake. There is only so much I can do without pulling resources from other governors and cities, which I can't do if we are trying to keep this quiet."

"All due respect, Raven," Drake spoke, "This isn't quiet anymore. The entire city knows we are looking into something. They know about the firefight at the old mines. Businesses have closed down for the time being. Civilians are reluctant to leave their homes. And without a formal announcement, they are even more afraid than ever."

"Oh!" Raven swiped a stack of papers from the desk. "So, it's *my* fault now because I don't want to inform the people they may be in imminent danger from a group of zealot mages and a *fucking* dwarf."

"Gods, Raven!" Drake threw his hands up. "Stop being so temperamental all the time! We have done all we can. We are all exhausted. But you screaming at everyone who is working their ass off to get you answers is not helping! We need a leader right now. A leader I know you are capable of being."

Raven sighed and considered Drake's words. He wasn't wrong, and she knew that, but if she backed down now, they could lose any progress they have made. If they let their guard down one time, the Lord of Steel could escape with Ena in hand. Avalon was too large of a region to search.

"Why don't we," Raven suggested calmly, "take a moment and regroup. Just you and I, lay out everything we have so far, and see what's missing."

"Alright," Drake sat across from Lady Raven. They both unfurled pages of scrolls, letters, and sketches that filled the desk and piled atop one another. Drake attention went immediately to the cartographer's maps. "We know one thing for sure—the tunnels have not been the same twice. Each time we go down there, a new maze is ready for us. We also know that the Lord of Steel has recruited some earth mages."

Raven opened her map of the city, placing a finger where Drake's fight with the earth mage occurred. "But nothing was found when the tunnel in that courtyard was checked?"

"No," Drake shook his head, "and those tunnels also keep shifting. Obviously, those two mages were not going there for no reason, or to lead us to a trap. If that was a trap, it was a very shitty one and clearly didn't work. They were going *somewhere*."

"We just don't know where."

"Correct."

Looking at the city map again, Raven deduced, "The center of the tunnels must fall somewhere around here." She circled an area in the middle district that bordered the lower district. "Which is heavily trafficked due to the schools and residential areas there. I would say let's start digging, but there is nowhere to begin that would not interfere with everyday life."

"Personally," Drake gambled, "I am less concerned with disturbing the peace than I am with burning through what little resources we have left. We do not have enough guards to excavate a large-scale area, and keeping the dig sites minimal will only waste time if they result in dead ends." He tugged on a ledger tucked under Raven's arm. "Not to mention, funds are extremely limited if we need guards to pull any more doubles. Their medical bills from the clinics drained that fund."

"And I am not ready to dip into the emergency fund just yet," Raven admitted. She pulled her platinum hair behind her ears. "Doing so could prove strenuous on the other cities if they ever need it."

"Understood," Drake reluctantly agreed. "Still no word from anyone?" The Dread Watch? Master Sheridan? The All-Seeing God? Anyone?

"Unfortunately not..."

Suddenly, a horn blew in the distance. Raven immediately stood and stepped to the window behind her desk. She peered outside.

"What was that?" Drake asked.

The same horn sounded again, a long bleat that carried across the whole city.

"The City Watch barracks. That is the sound of an arriving army..."

Drake shot to his feet. "Army? Like an ally or an enemy army?"

Another horn from the other side of the city blasted. Then another, and another.

"I don't know, Drake, but we're surrounded on all sides of the city."

◆◆◆◆◆◆◆◆◆

"Commander!" Raven called out as she sped out the door of the Grand Ballroom, mounting her horse. Gabrenas's Guard Commander flew up beside the lady on her steed, saluting her. "Get every guard you can to the borders! We may be under attack."

"Right away, my lady." Saluting the lady once more, the commander reared her horse and immediately shouted orders at every nearby squad.

"So much for letting them rest," Drake said as he walked out of the Ballroom on foot.

"Hop on back, Drake," Raven insisted, patting her hand on her narrow space on the back of the saddle. "We have no time to spare."

Drake jumped onto the horse's back and wrapped his arms around

Raven's midsection. Raven shouted to the commander that she was headed for the northern wall, where the first alarm sounded. Together, they flew to the wall, thundering hooves underneath.

Raven swung off the side of her horse, dropping to the ground, and speeding up the steps that zig-zagged along the inner side of the wall. Drake was always shocked at how nimble Raven was, for a woman in her forties. No physical act was an obstacle for her.

Drake dismounted and followed her.

Atop the wall, Drake witnessed the largest army of guards he had ever seen marching along the path from the forest to the north. The guards returned to formation as they passed through the bottleneck of the trees, creating four massive battalions, and consuming the open field beneath the wall.

"Thank the gods," Raven whispered. Turning to Drake, meeting his brown eyes, she said, "A white banner. They are here under peaceful terms."

She waited until her commander could join her. Together, the two met at the edge of the wall, watching the unmoving army of guards. With a single nod to the guards atop the wall, they raised a matching white banner, accepting the motion of peace.

A highly decorated guard clad in the brightest silver armor dropped from their horse holding a rolled piece of parchment. The guard walked to the center of the field between the wall and the battalions.

"Speak," Lady Raven called out.

The guard cleared his throat. "Lady Raven, I am the Guard Commander of Lothol. I have here a written order from the Master of Cities commanding as many troops as sparable from each of the seven cities of Avalon to assist you in your endeavors against an unknown threat." The Guard Commander bowed low. "Lead the way, my lady. We are at your command."

◆◆◆◆◆◆◆◆◆

Another four battalions armed themselves to the south of the city, according to Gabrenas's Guard Commander.

Raven was beyond grateful for the help. Word spread that the Master of Cities himself was on the road to Avalon, as the lady requested. She owed him more than her life.

Within a moment's notice, Raven issued a city-wide lockdown mandate. Everyone was required to remain in their homes for three days, minimum, while thousands of guards swarmed the city and scoped out any suspicious activity.

"Are you sure a stay-at-home order is the best course of action?" Drake had asked.

"Drake, I have no time for your reservations," Raven signed her name along the bottom of the executive order, making it official. "You said it yourself, disturbing the peace was a lesser concern of yours."

"What do you expect to find by locking everyone inside their homes? If the mages are stuck at home, we will never know."

She handed the signed mandate to her Guard Commander, who then passed it along to Lothol's. Once he read the order, he bowed to Raven and departed from the Grand Ballroom, gathering his troops.

"It is not what I expect to find while they are under guard, Drake. It is while they are being rounded into their homes that I am concerned with watching."

Drake narrowed his eyes cautiously, uncertain of what Raven expected to accomplish.

She rolled her eyes. "Think about it, Drake. We have property records of who lives where. If anyone strays from their expected path, we will know. With thousands of extra guards patrolling the streets, we are bound to find some suspects."

"Wow," Drake sat back, thinking. "That's actually quite genius."

"I want you leading the search. Half of the guards are instructed to herd the civilians into their homes. The other half are expected to monitor any activity that is out of the norm." Drake's face shone with pride. Raven was convinced that he was a born leader, if he only applied himself to the role. "Get going. This goes into effect immediately. Oh, before you go, if you *ever* question me again, you will find yourself locked away until Athenia returns."

Drake mockingly saluted Lady Raven before leaving the Grand Ballroom. An entourage of troops awaited him by the front steps. Drake led them down the main street, observing as the guards enforced the executive order.

Seeing the fear and confusion in the people's faces tied a knot in Drake's stomach, but Raven was right—he was less concerned with disturbing the peace than finding Ena alive.

◆◆◆◆◆◆◆◆◆

By dusk, Drake led his entourage to the middle district. The enforcement was taking longer than expected, which Drake supposed was a good thing. It gave him the chance to really observe the activity.

Many arrests were already made. Mostly people attempting to hide in a neighbor's home, rather than their own, and even a few who decided to take advantage of the confusion and rob some stores.

Nothing serious.

However, as the sun settled just below the horizon, Gabrenas's Guard Commander, who met up with Drake an hour before, held out an arm, halting him and the entourage of guards.

"Oof!" Drake grunted, walking into the commander's plated arm. "What is it?"

"There," the commander whispered.

Just around the corner of the next intersection, an older man in white robes slid illusively between squads of guards and off of the main road.

"That's Master Archem," the Commander said.

Drake squinted. "Who? Archem, the former Master White Mage? What in the world would he be doing here?"

"Considering his residence is still in the upper district," she looked through her visor at Drake, "I would say he falls into the 'suspicious activity' category."

Drake turned to the guards behind him. "I need to you remain a healthy pace behind us while we move forward."

"Affirmative, sir."

"Commander, let's approach cautiously. He went between those two homes. What is back there?"

The two carefully strode to Archem's last location. Stepping gently between the two apartment buildings, shadows enveloped them. They passed through the alley sideways, shoulder to shoulder.

The alley opened to a garden with a strange rock formation at the other end. Archem was nowhere to be seen.

"Shit, where did he go?" Drake asked.

"I am not sure, sir," the commander replied.

Cautiously, they drew their weapons and searched the garden. After several minutes without any clues, Drake scanned the garden once more.

There!

Drake tapped the Commander on the shoulder, and she followed as Drake approached a massive elderberry bush tucked against the rock formation.

"What is it, sir?"

Drake stepped again towards the elderberry bush. "Growing up on a farm, I can say that elderberries can be difficult to grow. They need space around their bases for their roots to absorb as much water and nutrients as possible."

"So?"

"So!" Drake reached out and pulled a section of the bush aside, revealing a dark and narrow tunnel hidden behind. "There is no way these berries could have grown this successfully while pressed against a rock such as this."

The commander's eyes lit up as she gazed down the dark tunnel. "Wow! Another entrance!"

"A *new* entrance, by the looks of it." Drake motioned to the edge of the tunnel. The stone was carved and rounded too perfectly for hand tools, like the mine entrance had been. This was the work of an earth mage.

"Commander, could you please inform Lady Raven of this? Let her know I will wait until the stay-at-home order has been fully enforced. I will be borrowing a handful of guards, too."

"Are you sure you do not want a few platoons?" the Commander asked.

"No," Drake was certain. "I don't know how narrow this set of tunnels may be. Too many guards will make maneuvering in and out too slow. I just need to go in, get Athenia, and get out."

The commander dipped her head and slipped back into the darkness of the alley on the other side of the clearing.

Athenia, I'm coming for you.

CHAPTER 41

Fever sent shivers from Ena's spine to her extremities. Sweat decorated her brow. Her breath was short and uneven. Pain burned through her veins.

Ena was dying.

After her experience with Myra, her body gave up on her. Every wound festered. Every muscle screamed for relief. Her eyes itched and burned, her eyelids heavy as anchors.

She refused all food and water, wishing for death.

No more mindrenders visited her chamber. Mida hadn't shown himself in days. The only visitors Ena received were the two young white mage girls, who struggled greatly to keep Ena's infections at bay. Their amateur healing abilities were obsolete against how fast the rot was spreading throughout her body.

One evening, the mage girls brought in a bowl of hot soup and a skin of water. The girl filled a ladle with soup and held it to Ena's mouth. The governess turned her head away.

"Eat," urged the girl.

She pressed on, placing the ladle in front of Ena's face again. Ena turned away in the other direction. The mage sighed, pressing the ladle directly to Ena's lips. Ena tossed her head to the side, knocking the ladle from the mage's hand. It clattered to the floor, and the frustrated mage placed the soup bowl on the ground, spilling broth.

The mage holding the water skin did not even try to fight Ena about drinking. The effort would be pointless.

Together, the two mages ignited their hands with a healing glow and circled their palms around Ena's shoulders and wrists. The magic relieved the pressure in her joints, and a fresh set of flesh knitted over the abrasions on her wrists. For now. The relief would last for a few hours before the rope abrased her wrists once more and her shoulders ached again.

The mages effortlessly worked their magic on her infected knees and feet, but to little avail. Veins in her legs turned black as circulation slowly ceased in her body's effort to stop the spread of infection. The girls were not skilled enough for this kind of damage.

Even an expert white mage would face difficulty with how far gone these injuries were.

Torchlight at the very end of the hallway lit, though Ena couldn't make anything out. The light was like a mere firefly off in the distance. She could hear, though.

Two voices arguing with one another echoed down the tunnel. One was Mida, and the other Ena did not recognize.

"Your girls in there are doing nothing!" Mida yelled. "I could do a better job healing her. *Me!* A fucking dwarf with no magic!"

The other voice replied apologetically, "My lord, I understand, but they were the only mages I could spare."

"You mean they were the only mages you could still order around!" Mida's rage grew. "After all, you somehow lost your fucking job and no white mage will even look at you. Disgraceful."

"Watch what you say, Mida! I did my job without error for thirty years. Lady Raven is a force to be reckoned with. It will be a miracle if the entire administration of Avalon is not replaced by next year."

"I don't care about the administration of Avalon, Archem! The deal we made was that you get me your best healers to *keep her alive!* Guess what, she's on the brink of death in there, and those children can't even stitch a papercut!"

Ena snuck a glance at the two girls attempting to mend her. They pretended not to hear the insults flung their way, but Ena could feel the increase tension. After each comment Mida made against them, their magic boosted slightly. Ena could tell they were pushing themselves too hard.

"What do you expect from me?!" the other voice shouted desperately. "I can't go and find another mage now. Lady Raven has the entire city on lockdown."

"I don't need her immaculate, Archem," Mida calmed himself to an agitated grumble. "I just need her *alive* when she is rescued, which should be soon with this godsforsaken lockdown. Myra needs her alive. Do you understand?"

"I understand, my lord, but as I said, I cannot get another mage here now."

"No, but *you* are here. Get in there and fix your girls' mistakes!"

"Right away, my lord..."

Ena noticed the torch at the end of the tunnel disappear behind the silhouette of an approaching man. If they were right, if Drake and Raven would be here soon, she did not have much time left to die. If Myra wanted her alive that desperately, then she needed to die.

"Girls," Ena whispered. They stopped momentarily. "You need to hide. When the City Watch arrives here, you will not be safe. They will take any means necessary to retrieve me. Do you understand?" The mages only looked at Ena for another second or two, then resumed mending her burns. "No sense in innocent children getting killed for the mistakes of adult men and women."

They remained silent as the silhouette grew closer, eventually stepping into the light of the cell. An elder wearing the white robes of a white mage. He gestured for the two young mages to leave. They bowed to the man and locked eyes with Ena for a split second before departing the cell.

Ena hoped they would take her advice and stay out of sight.

"Governess Athenia," the old man spoke. "I will be managing your care from this point on. I understand you are refusing all food and water. Please know, I will make use of all resources to ensure you survive this ordeal. By refusing sustenance, you will only heighten the pain you endure."

Without another word, the white mage drew a small satchel from an inner pocket of his robes. He drew a small scope, which he used to magnify and observe Ena's wounds. Using a pair of tweezers, he pulled any foreign bodies from her open lacerations and burns, including particles of dust and dead flesh. Ena flinched at each poke and prod.

"My apologies, Governess," the old man said, seeming surprisingly genuine. "You must be in a great deal of pain. Say the word and I can mend your wounds thoroughly, rather than at half capacity as previously ordered."

"Archem, right?" Ena rasped. He nodded. "Former Master White Mage of Avalon?" No response. "I though Raven had your tongue removed."

Archem considered not replying. Eventually, he broke his silence. "The Lady of Avalon underestimated my talents if she did not realize I could mend my own severed tongue."

"Why ally yourself with those monsters?" Ena asked. "Is this because of how terms ended with Lady Raven? This is not the kind of revenge you want to seek..."

"Monsters? Nay, not monsters. Monsters act on animalistic instinct, Governess. These folk, they are cunning, calculating."

"Why ally yourself with them?" Ena asked again.

Archem jabbed the metal tip of the tweezers deep into Ena's infected foot. A bit too forceful to be accidental, Ena assumed. Nevertheless, she grunted with pain.

Archem answered, "Perhaps I have already said too much. I suppose, though, that my life is minimal in the greater scheme of things." He sighed. "The vision of the future they have embedded into the minds of the mages curious enough to listen is more powerful than you will ever understand, Governess."

"Like what, Archem?" She could feel the pus leaking from the foot that Archem prodded at.

"One without the Connections, like yourself, would not understand."

"Allow me to try and understand."

He shifted to the cut along her hip, given to her by Mida when he fileted her with her own dagger weeks ago. The cut had never healed properly each time the girls worked on it.

"Mages have been oppressed for generations. Even in the modern age, post-Concordat. Even us white mages. How many elementalists or archanists are you aware of who are active members of society? Exactly, almost none. White mages, though? We are exploited for our abilities to heal. Myra, though, she gives us strength. She gives us a purpose."

"That is the mindset which sparked the Mage Wars, Archem... This is dangerous..."

"What do you know of the Mage Wars, Governess? History is written by the victor. Perhaps history is not as you know."

Mida said something similar to her previously.

"Why did you offer to heal me entirely?" Ena asked. "Would that not be betraying their commands?"

"White mage philosophy does not allow for a patient to suffer in our care."

Ena's faded green eyes caught Archem's as he came around the front of her. "Then kill me. End my suffering."

"That would break my philosophy entirely, Governess. I cannot."

"You cannot end a life, even if the life is unable to be saved?"

He shook his head. "We are mandated by our abilities to preserve all life. All life is worth saving, no matter how strong or feeble."

"You say you are mandated by your abilities," Ena approached with caution, "yet you say you are exploited because of those same abilities."

Archem moved his face inches from her own. He used his scope to inspect a laceration on her right cheek.

"Your point?" he asked.

"The Providence herself once showed me how a white mage's abilities are equally as capable of taking a life as they are for granting life. Why would the gods empower you with such a power if you were not expected to utilize it? Should a patient suffering from cancer continue to suffer with ill-fated attempts to cure them, or could they be granted a swift and painless death if requested?"

"You do not have cancer, Governess."

"No," Ena argued, "but I can be tortured? Burned? Cut? Beaten? Starved? That somehow does not break your pitiful philosophy?"

That angered Archem, who had remained calm through Ena's questioning. He stood abruptly, throwing the scope and tweezers against the far wall. "Damn you, Governess! This is for the greater good of all mages. They can burn or beat a thousand of you if it meant restoring the glory of the mages!"

Ena did not flinch at his sudden outburst. She was getting to him. "That sounds awfully similar to what the history texts quote from the Mage King who initiated the Mage Wars over a thousand years ago. You do not truly believe that, Master Archem. You are a man of the Faith. You have been your entire life. Do not let the false promises of a mad woman sway you from your true philosophy."

"Enough!" Archem charged at Ena, stopping with his face merely an inch away, glaring hatefully into her green eyes. He grabbed Ena's face from under her chin and shook her head violently. "Enough of your coercion, you venomous snake! It is people like you who have forced me down this path of righteousness!"

When Archem stopped shaking Ena's head, she replied softly, "If this path is so righteous, no one should be forcing it upon you..."

Archem's eyes softened from their rageful stare. His bottom lip trembled. Dropping to his knees, he shamefully lowered his head.

"You are right, Governess!" he cried out. "What have I become? I have allowed these manipulators to transform me into one of their kind." Suddenly, the old man appeared even older, as if he aged another ten years before Ena's very eyes. "I am too far gone, I fear. The All-Seeing God is spiting me as we speak. How, Governess? How am I to atone for my sins?"

"Master Archem," Ena smiled—a true smile, the first one in weeks. Archem looked up at her with glimmering wet eyes. "You can start by granting me my request, as a dying patient. Please, Archem, end my suffering. If you kill me, you will stop them in their tracks. Do not let them harm others the way they have harmed me."

Archem only stared at her, his eyes flitting back and forth between hers. He was deep in thought. Considering the pros and cons of what Ena asked of him.

"They will kill me..." Archem considered to himself.

"Perhaps," Ena consoled, "the gods will grant you mercy if you atone in your final moments."

"For mercy..." Archem nodded to Ena. His hands began to glow, but not in the same method that a white mage's hands normally glowed. They were not about to give Ena life, they were about to take it. As the liver spotted hands inched closer to her face, the aura surrounding them enticed all fear and torment from Ena. Absorbing every negative emotion like a sponge to water. She welcomed the wave of serenity. A peaceful death was the best she could ask for.

The moment Archem touched his hands to her head, Ena would drift into permanent slumber. She pushed away any pangs of guilt. She would be leaving Drake behind, and it was her fault he was caught up in this mess to begin with. Hoping he will understand, Ena pushed away the guilt and replaced it with acceptance. She felt guilty for leaving everyone else to pick up the pieces. Even if her death threw a wrench into Myra's scheme, it would not stop her completely. After all, her involvement had been accidental. Myra would find another way to achieve her goal. That thought, too, Ena replaced with acceptance.

Archem's euthanizing touch was imminent. *Any moment now...* Ena closed her eyes and welcomed it.

Just then, a metallic *thwip* was followed by a warm splatter all over Ena's chest and midsection. Ena opened her eyes and gasped.

The barbed tip of a crossbow bolt protruded from Archem's neck as he gagged on blood, gasping for air. He coughed once, spraying crimson over Ena's face. As Archem's body began to sag, he tried catching himself on Ena's shoulders and hips, his hands gliding down her blood-stained body. His hands still glowed with the essence of death before fading as his lifeless body struck the floor.

Ena screamed with all the power her lungs could afford. The spell was incomplete. The death touch did not take her life; instead, it decayed the parts of her body it touched. Her shoulder, her hip, her stomach. The path Archem's hands followed turned grey and weathered, burning unbearably. Her entire body convulsed as she struggled to catch her breath, only to wind herself with another screech of anguish.

Suddenly, Ena's vision faded to black as her eyes rolled into the back of her skull. Foam sputtered from her lips as her head bucked back. Her muscles tightened to steel.

Ena forced herself to push through the seizure, allowing her muscles to relax. All bodily functions loosened, urine and feces flowed down her legs and mixed with the pool of blood and pus beneath her torn-apart legs.

If she wasn't exhausted before, she certainly was now. Ena barely clung to consciousness as her body trembled. Her teeth chattered.

From the shadows beyond Archem's corpse, Mida stepped into the cell with an unarmed crossbow in hand.

Before Ena could speak, if she even could, Mida said, "When we first met, I told you I didn't tolerate traitors. Archem, here, betrayed me. Betrayed Myra. That's right, I heard your conversation. We don't need someone who is so easily swayed in our ranks."

Ena's eyelids unevenly fluttered, reluctantly staying open, as she watched Mida. Whatever just occurred, whatever Archem's magic did, or *didn't* do, Ena supposed, left her body destroyed. She wheezed in an ill-fated attempt to breathe. Never before had she experienced pain such as this.

She wanted to scream. Wanted to rip herself from the fucking ropes leaving her dangling like a piece of raw meat at a butcher's, even if it meant tearing her hands or shoulders from her body. She wanted to curse Mida to oblivion.

"By the way," Mida smirked mockingly, "your friend, the Unweaved one, is on his way. Just wait until he sees you now. He won't ever want you again."

Ena sobbed. As much as her body would allow. The trembling would not cease. The corrosion would not ease.

CHAPTER 42

Lady Raven inspected the hidden tunnel in the garden. After a brief discussion with her guard commander, she approached Drake.

"Why didn't we discover this garden before?" she asked gently. "I understand that it is tucked away between these apartments, but the other side of the rock leads to the street paralleling the one we just came from."

"I agree," Drake said. "This area may have been an oversight. That tunnel is new, though. I've questioned all of the residents of these apartments. The garden was maintained by an elderly woman from the bottom apartment over there who passed away a few months ago. The residents witnessed some people coming and going from the garden the past couple of weeks, but they assumed it was whoever occupied the apartment after the woman's possessions were removed."

"Understandable," Raven scanned the garden once more. To Drake, she appeared defeated. Or, at least, on the brink of defeat. Despite this important discovery, she was overworked and stressed. The Master of Cities would arrive soon, and the last thing Raven wanted was to break his trust. The Master of Cities left Avalon to her without a second thought. If she failed to keep Avalon secure, his disappointment would ruin her.

"The commander mentioned you wanted to take the lead on this one?" Raven asked. "I admire your courage. What resources will you need?"

Shocked by Raven's unusual cooperation, Drake answered, "Uhh, just a few guards. I thought about storming the tunnels with an army, but it will be a tight fit. No room to turn and retreat, if needed. I think it would be better if I took point with a squad watching my back."

"Are you sure?" her eyes narrowed. "You have no idea what you may face down there. What if you don't make it out?"

Drake smirked. "Then send in a godsdamned army after me and destroy every mage in sight."

"Yes sir," Raven saluted sarcastically. She turned on her heels and returned to her horse on the other side of the alley. Drake seriously wondered if that would be the last time he would ever see Raven. He was a fool for continuing on the "lone wolf" approach that the lady disapproved of so much, but Ena's rescue needed to be swift. If they knew Drake was coming, would they kill her?

"Sir," the guard commander said as she approached Drake. "Your orders?"

Drake cleared his throat. "Get me the bravest squad you can find. And keep a platoon available up here on the surface. There isn't room for a full company in the garden, so it'll have to do in case any mages escape. Keep an eye out around this area to make sure they don't create another way out and flee from there."

"Yes sir."

Once the commander gathered a squad of four guards, Drake slipped into the tunnel. He kept the Aconyte sword drawn and a flame in his palm held out for light.

◆◆◆◆◆◆◆◆◆

Ena ebbed in and out on consciousness.

Her body's natural instinct fought for survival, as much as her mind screamed to let go.

"He is coming for you," a voice suddenly echoed throughout the cell.

Ena knew that voice.

Myra.

But she was nowhere in sight.

"You are trying *awfully* hard to die, Athenia," Myra's voice again. "A shame his love for you trumps your desire to die."

Ena could not speak.

Drake, she called out to no one but herself. *Please. Save yourself.*

◆◆◆◆◆◆◆◆◆

Drake descended into the cavernous depths, blind to what he was about to encounter.

The tunnel seemed endless. Drake seemed to walk miles before it leveled out and opened into a wide cavern. Stalactites dipped low from the high ceiling, and stalagmites grew sharp from the floor.

It was too quiet for comfort...

Drake scanned the cavern as best he could in the pitch black. The flame dancing in his palm barely provided him with enough light to see ten feet in front of him.

The guards behind him inched closer, scraping up dirt with their boots.

Drake held up his hand, signaling for them to stop.

With his flaming hand, Drake hurled a ball of fire high into the air towards the center of the cavern. As it hit the ceiling, it burst like a star, lighting the entire cavern for a single moment. A moment just long enough for Drake to view their surroundings. Nothing but stalagmites in their path.

Drake shot another light into the air, attempting to see if there was another path leading them out of the cavern. Another split second of clarity, and Drake saw the mouth of another cave on the far side.

"There," he motioned. "That's where we need to go."

As they stepped forwards, something in the distance scraped against stone. Drake held up a palm, halting his squad again.

Drake set off another light. It burst, lighting the cavern. Nothing. Just hundreds, if not thousands, of stalagmites between them and the mouth of the cave.

You're hearing things... Drake convinced himself.

They began walking through the forest of stalagmites. More scattering and scraping in the distance.

Halting again, Drake let off another light overhead. Still nothing but damp rocks.

"Sir," one of the guards spoke, "probably just rats."

"Probably..." Drake hesitated.

Another step, and the scraping sounded directly in front of them.

Drake stopped. He squinted into the darkness beyond the flame in his hand. Still nothing.

One last time, Drake thought. He hurled another ball of flame above their heads. *Boom.* As the flame's light filled the room, between nearly every single stalagmite stood a mage dressed in black robes.

"Shit!"

Before Drake could react, fire filled the cavern from all angles. Dozens of mages launched volleys of flames at them.

Drake screamed for the guards to drop to the ground. He held out both hands, deflecting or absorbing each fire attack. The guards stood and took cover behind their shields.

"Sir!" the guard called out over the eruption of fire barrages. "Push forwards!"

Drake's hands and arms flailed, blocking and parrying. He inched forwards. The squad followed.

Flames pummeled the guards' shields the further into the cavern they marched. The mages did not back away. The guards struck with their swords from behind the shields, occasionally piercing through the flesh of an attacking mage.

Drake gained the upper hand by parrying and tossing the blasts back at the mages. Those unaware of Drake's impending blows succumbed to serious burns, or worse.

Soon, they were on the offensive.

The guards jumped out of formation and charged at the mages with shields raised and swords swinging.

As a few dozen more volleys came Drake's way, he caught them midair, forming a dome of fire around them.

"Behind me!" Drake shouted. The guards obeyed, returning to formation behind him. Drake enclosed the fire dome and pushed forwards, fast. He wasn't quite sure how he was managing this much power all at once. "Let's move!"

Their easy, steady steps broke into a steady jog. As Drake moved the fire dome with them, they dodged stalagmites in their path and knocked aside the bodies of mages now coated with flames as they were caught in Drake's path. The screams of the burning mages pierced through the hiss of the fire.

Drake's confidence was shaken when a stalagmite suddenly pierced through the fire dome and cracked through the shield of one of his guards. The force of blow broke the guard's arm and knocked him backwards into the fire.

A curdled screech sounded. Drake winced.

"What was that?" he asked himself.

Then, another airborne stalagmite pierced the top of the dome and crushed the skull of the guard standing directly behind Drake, clobbering him and sending a mist of blood into the air.

Earth mages!

Drake mustered his energy and pushed outwards with all his strength. The fire dome spread out in a wide radius, forcing back every mage around them, before dissipating.

With the rage of the fire gone, Drake heard the shrieks of his victims as they burned alive, blood boiling and tissue peeling from their bones.

He felt lightheaded with the sudden change in temperature returning from engrossingly hot to the cool, natural chill of the cavern. As he took a deep breath, allowing himself to recover, one of his guards caught him by the arm and pulled him to the side as a boulder tore past him, crashing through the stalagmites like bowling pins.

The cavern fell silent. Light still filled the chamber from the burning cloth and flesh in the distance.

Quietly, Drake said to the two remaining guards, "I think I can handle the fire mages, but that earth mage will take us out before we even know it." He thought guiltily of the two guards now dead.

"Where is the mage?" the guard asked. Drake shrugged. "Perhaps we could distract them and you can go in for the blow." Without waiting for Drake's approval, the two guards rushed out into the clearing created by the earth mage's last boulder.

Drake could hear flames and earth tearing as the guards hopped out of the way on the opposite side of the clearing. Drake glanced around the side of the stalagmite he ducked behind and followed the reverse trajectory of the rocks being hurdled.

There! Drake spotted the earth mage standing atop a column of raised earth by the path at the back of the cavern.

The guards must have traversed to the far side of the cavern, for Drake heard and saw blasts of fire igniting and filling the air. The earth mage launched large boulders in that same direction, completely distracted. Drake also heard the singing of metal and the yelps of slain foes. *The guards are holding their own. Good.*

Drake snuck between the stalagmites, approaching the manmade earth column. The mage's back was turned to him as the guards drew their enemies' attention by the opposite wall.

Smart thinking, Drake thought, observing their tactics. *Keeping the wall to the backs to keep the mages from flanking them.*

As he tiptoed closer, the earth mage shifted around and spotted Drake. Instantly, Drake was launched into the air when the earth beneath him shot upwards. Drake hit the ceiling of the cavern, narrowly missing a hanging stalactite. He limply plummeted to the ground, bouncing once as he struck the earth.

Groaning, Drake forced himself to his feet. He drew the Aconyte sword just as a boulder aimed for his head. He reached out with the blade, slashing the rock in half with one clean cut. Three more boulders sent Drake's way suffered the same fate.

Drake charged at the mage, still atop the earth column.

Unsure of how to get up so high, Drake figured he would have to get the mage to the ground. He charged a massive blast of fire in his palm and launched it directly at the top of the column. The mage launched himself from the column and backflipped to the ground. Landing perfectly on his feet, the mage clapped his hands together, causing the two massive stalagmites on either side of Drake to break free and slam together.

At the last moment, Drake jumped forwards, avoiding being crushed. He sprinted at the mage. As he closed the distance, an unexpected rock flew from his left and crashed into his head, knocking him face first into the dirt.

Drake's head rang. He felt the side of his head, his hair soaking wet. Pulling his hand away, it was dark and sticky with blood.

He sat up dizzily, watching helplessly as the earth mage walked closer towards him, lifting two boulders over his shoulders, ready to bring down on Drake's already bleeding skull.

This couldn't be the end, could it? Bested by a mage in a dark cavern? Helplessly bleeding and unable to fight back?

Drake laughed to himself. If Ena were here, she would scold him for being so dumb to come here in the first place and for allowing a foe to get the best of him.

Just then, a sword pierced through the mage's chest. The boulders fell to the ground with an earth-shuddering crunch as the mage grasped at the blade protruding from his diaphragm. The sword withdrew from his back, and he fell to his knees, gasping. One of the guards stood proudly as the mage collapsed onto his face and died.

The guard ran over to Drake and held out a hand, helping him to his feet.

"Sir, are you alright?" the guard asked.

Drake rubbed his bleeding head. "As good as I can be, I suppose. Where is the other guard?"

"Didn't make it," he answered solemnly. "We faced a lot of resistance over there. The mages we couldn't kill fled into the cave."

"How many were left?"

The guard thought for a moment. "A dozen or so."

"How many did we kill?"

"About thirty."

"Gods," Drake sighed. "If we run into another room full of them, I don't know if we'll make it."

Drake and the guard took a moment to collect themselves and inspect the bodies of the dead before moving forward.

◆◆◆◆◆◆◆◆◆

Ena awoke in excruciating pain.

The grey corruption from the death touch spread across nearly her entire torso, throbbing with the sensation of individual nails being hammered into her bones. Long, unkempt toenails scraping across rough cobblestones rattling through her head. Her short, uneven exhales echoing in her ears. Her whimpers of pain rasped out of her like steam releasing from a rusty valve.

The only sense still sharp was her vision, and even that faded in and out with black specks and white spots.

Not another creature stirred.

Not in the cell with Ena, nor in the room at the end of the hall.

Yet, she did not feel alone.

◆◆◆◆◆◆◆◆◆

Drake and his guard crouched, maneuvering through the tunnel slowly and carefully. They ran into constant dead ends and empty rooms. Though, the rooms typically had tables and chairs, or beds and chests, showing that someone had lived here recently. One room even contained kegs of ale, some still full.

They only found thirty dead mages, and the guard counted merely a dozen who fled back into the tunnels. Yet, there had to have been hundreds when Drake first lit up the cavern. These dining and sleeping chambers were evident that there were significantly more of the enemy than they were aware of.

Where had they all gone?

Driving deeper and deeper into the maze, Drake lost track of the direction they came from. He hoped the guard had a sharper mind than he did...

Despite feeling farther away than ever, his intuition said they were getting closer to their goal.

◆◆◆◆◆◆◆◆◆

Fwoosh!

The strike of a match caught Ena's attention.

The matchlight flickered dully in the distance at the end of the tunnel. The room across from Ena suddenly lit up, and the hiss and crackle of a torch echoed down the hallway.

A silhouette paced back and forth, passing by the tunnel, causing the light to appear, disappear, then appear again at a steady pace.

Ena felt the ground beneath her shudder. The sound of rocks scraping against rocks and the ground shearing reverberated from the room.

Earth mage.

After a minute or two of shifting and shuddering, Ena heard the wooden squeak of a chair as the earth mage sat down.

Multiple sets of footsteps trekked into the room.

"What's next?" someone asked.

"We wait," said the earth mage. "We wait until he arrives. And when he does, we fight, but we let him escape with the girl. The lord's orders."

"Understood."

And the mousetrap was officially set...

◆◆◆◆◆◆◆◆◆

Drake turned the corner after yet another dead end. Something was up ahead. Something he couldn't see very well. Something that flicked back and forth ever so slightly.

"Is that...?" Drake began to ask. He doused the flame in his palm. He could still see the object in the distance. *A light?* Then, the object fluttered again. "It is! It's a light! We're getting closer!"

"Let's move," the guard embraced Drake's enthusiasm.

The two jogged down the endless tunnel, the light growing ever so bigger and brighter.

◆◆◆◆◆◆◆◆◆

The chair squeaked once more as the earth mage rose.

"Here he comes," the mage said.

However many mages were in that room, Ena could not say, but they all shifted into a defensive stance.

Ena held her breath nervously.

"Shit!" a familiar voice shouted.

Drake!

An eruption of fire spilled into the room, knocking aside several of the mages. Blasts of fire were followed by the shriek of a sword cutting through the air, and through organs.

Mages cried out in crippled pain.

But they were not backing down.

"Drake, here!" a guard clad in Avalonian armor appeared at the very end of the tunnel. A large rock struck the guard on the breastplate as he spotted Ena. A ball of flame flew from the other direction, and a grunt followed.

Drake flew up to the guard's side, helping him to his feet. "You alright?"

The guard pointed his sword down the tunnel at Ena. "There. Go! I'll watch your back."

"Ena!" Drake looked up and saw her. He sprinted down the hall.

Drake, don't!

CHAPTER 43

He skidded to a halt at the threshold. Staring at Ena in awe.

"Oh... gods... Ena?" Drake stepped gingerly into the cell, as one would do if trying not to wake a sleeping animal. He ignited the flame in his palm, holding it out. Ena lifted her chin, finding his eyes with hers. "Fuck, Ena! That *is* you!"

He closed the gap between them and threw his arms around her.

Ena screamed with pain as Drake's embrace sent an anguishing wave from her fingertips to her toes.

Drake pushed himself away from her. Fear and confusion dance in his face. "Gods, what did they do to you?" He scanned the room and took a step back, stumbling. He looked down at what his heel caught on. "What... Archem?" He brought his flame closer. The dead white mage's foot tripping Drake. The crossbow bolt still jutting from the white mage's chest. Drake covered his mouth with his free hand.

The sound of fighting in the adjacent room shook Drake from his thoughts.

"Right," he slapped his cheeks to shake himself from his daze. "Okay, alright... Ena? Can you hear me?"

Shivering, Ena locked eyes with him once more. Her head lifted slightly and lowered back down. The best thing to a nod she could make.

"Good, good," Drake leaned down and grabbed Archem's torso by the robes and gently rolled him over, away from Ena. "I'm so happy to see you..."

Don't fool yourself, Drake, Ena thought, *I look like a corpse.*

Drake drew another flame and held it up, observing the prison in which the governess was trapped. The rope tied around her wrists hooked high above their heads. He, then, circled around Ena, checking her wounds.

"You can't walk..." Not a question. He was speaking of her feet, now black and yellow on the soles with disease.

He came up behind her, placing a hand on her bare back on one of the few spots that hadn't suffered from extreme injury. The touch was warm, welcoming. The hand slowly traced up her back and reached out slowly at the decay climbing up Ena's neck.

No, no, no. Ena braced herself for the horrible burn she would endure the moment Drake touched it.

As Drake's fingertips brushed the scaley, grey flesh, Ena's head bucked backwards, and her entire body trembled. He winced and pulled his hand swiftly away.

Ena looked at him through the pain. Tears filled his eyes as he covered his mouth once more. He was crying...

The sight of Drake crying caused Ena to well up tears of her own. She had so much she could say, but no way of saying it.

She opened her mouth, attempting to speak. Her lips cracked and her sandpaper tongue peeled from the room of her mouth. A single, scratchy rasp escaped her.

"Don't speak, Ena," Drake warned. "It looks like talking hurts. I need to get you out of here. I don't know how... If I touch you..."

Ena winced at the very idea.

"Drake," she managed. "Don't."

His eyes danced back and forth between her mouth and her eyes. "I know... It's going to hurt like hell, but I promise you everything will be okay once I get you out of here."

"Leave," Ena whispered. "Leave me... I beg of you..."

Drake smiled his usual handsome smile, dimples showing. "That's crazy. I'm going to save you."

Drake... Ena couldn't beg any further. But she had to, or else it would be—

"Too late," Myra's voice echoed in her head. Drake made no indication of hearing it, too, as he grabbed the ropes and studied how he was possibly going to cut her down without harming her further. Myra laughed, *"The next step in my plan was set in motion the moment he walked into your cell. Tell him I thank him."*

Nononononono, it can't be too late!

"Alright, Ena," Drake stood in her view once more. "I have good news and bad news. Good news is that I can easily cut you down and get you out of here. Bad news is that it will hurt..." Before Ena could refute, Drake drew the Aconyte steel sword and slashed the rope in one clean swipe. Before Ena's upper half could drop to the dirt, Drake reached out and caught her.

The moment she fell into his arms, she roared. The pain was too unbearable... She couldn't catch her breath, couldn't move.

Finally, the pain overwhelmed her so that her head flopped unconsciously.

◆◆◆◆◆◆◆◆◆

Drake emerged from the cell with Ena's dying body in his arms. He spotted the guard doubled over, blood dripping from his mouth, leaning on the hilt of his sword to stay on his feet. The mages were all dead. Many suffered severe burns, Drake's doing. Many were missing limbs, even heads—the guard's doing.

This had been one brutal fight.

Drake got the guard's attention. "Are you alright?"

"Alright," he spat blood, limping over to Drake, "is not the word I would choose. But I am currently alive." The guard's one working eye, the other clouded with blood from a gash across his brow, widened at the sight of Ena.

"So is she," Drake said. "For the moment, that is. Do we have anything we can bundle her in? She is shivering with fever."

The guard could hardly pull his eye from the governess. The blood, infectious pus, shit, piss, vomit, you name it, either dripping from her body, or dried to it. The smell was overwhelming. Injuries and wounds the guard had never seen in all his years in the Watch.

"Um," the guard shook his attention from Ena. He looked around the room. "No. Not unless the burned or bloody rags from a dead mage will do. But I do not find it wise to waste time undressing dead bodies."

"I agree." Drake sighed. "Do you remember the way out of here?"

The guard nodded. "Follow me. I apologize if I am slower than usual."

"It's no problem." Drake noted the injuries decorating the guard's body. A massive dent in his breastplate, likely broken ribs beneath it, and burns along his arms and legs. The gash above his eye was the worst of it, though. Stitches were needed, even with a white mage's capabilities. Drake wondered what happened to the guard's helmet, then he found it in the middle of the room crushed beyond repair.

They fled from the room, Ena resting across Drake's arms.

Drake followed the guard as he swiftly limped around corner after corner, zigzagging through the maze effortlessly. As effortlessly as he could with his sustained wounds.

Once they made it back to the cavern, the guard stopped in his tracks. He braced himself against the wall, sliding precariously into a sitting position on the floor.

"My apologies, sir," the guard said through heavy breaths. "I need a moment, if you don't mind."

"Of course, of course! Take it easy. We're almost out of here."

◆◆◆◆◆◆◆◆◆

Ena opened her eyes.

She was suspended in the air, caressed by Drake's arms.

Her eyes bounced around the massive cavern she found herself in. Several dozen bodies of mages spread across the floor. Her eyes found the other guard resting against the cavern wall, breathing unevenly.

That cannot be good...

Drake saw Ena looking around and said, "Hey, how are you feeling?"

She couldn't answer, could hardly hear. His lips moved in slow motion as he spoke, and the words were muffled like her head was underwater.

She felt no pain, though, only exhaustion.

Pain so intense that her nerves had gone numb.

That also cannot be good...

"I'm going to get you out of here," Drake's muffled voice called out. *I'm going to get you out of here.* Ena watched his lips slowly catch up with his words. "Just a bit longer." *Just a bit longer.*

◆◆◆◆◆◆◆◆◆

Drake motioned to the guard. "You doing okay?"

"To be honest, sir," the guard winced. "No. You may be making it out of here without me."

"Hey," he crouched next to the guard, still holding Ena, "don't say that. We're almost there."

"Sir, no offense, but you can't carry us both," he laughed, gesturing to Ena resting in Drake's arms. "And the only way I'm making it out is if I'm carried... There's just too much going on here." He pointed to the third degree burns all over his body. The fire mages in that final room had shown no mercy. The guard was lucky to survive as long as he did.

"Here," the guard pulled a thin chain from his neck with a medallion dangling from the end—his service tag. He held the chain out. "My address is on the medal. Just bring it back to my wife and kid."

Drake extended his hand, loosening his grip on Ena for a moment, and took the tag. He studied the medal, recognizing the address as a street he passed by multiple times during his last couple of months in Gabrenas.

He returned his attention to the guard.

But the guard had already passed.

"Shit..." Drake clutched the medal before stuffing it into a secure pocket.

Lifting himself back to his feet with Ena in hand, he continued slowly through the cavern.

◆◆◆◆◆◆◆◆◆

Daylight burned Ena's eyes.

The first sign of daylight in a month.

She squinted as Drake carried her up the slope of the tunnel towards the exit.

"We're almost there," Drake's muffled voice promised.

Her head spun as a dizzy spell consumed her. Vomit pooled up in her cheeks as she hurled all over Drake's chest.

"Fuck!" he swore as he dropped Ena to the ground. She wailed as the fall broke on her wounds. Drake rushed to pick her back up. "I'm *so* sorry, Ena. I wasn't expecting that. It surprised me, is all. I've got you."

"Just let me die!" she managed to yell.

Drake stopped a moment and looked her in her eyes. "Athenia, I love you. You are *not* dying today."

Ena hadn't the strength to argue. She exhausted it all in that one outburst.

Her head still swam. Drake's words still only half-clear. The bile in her throat burned.

Drake continued up the slope.

Ena reached around him and grasped his tunic in her hands. She fought through the pain to hold him tight.

She had no reason to pray for death any longer, she supposed. Myra got what she wanted, whatever that may be. If she recovered from this, she would have to tell Sheridan everything... There was something coming.

Something big.

But for now, stepping into the sun was all that mattered to Ena.

Drake pushed through the elderberry bush blocking the way, and the sun slowly coated Ena.

It burned. The rays from the sun intensified on her pale, bare skin. But it felt incredible at the same time. She felt alive. Felt hopeful.

She didn't dare open her eyes yet. Her pupils will melt from her irises if she did not allow for them to adjust properly.

"Oh, fuck!" Drake screamed as he passed the threshold of the cave into the garden beyond.

Suddenly, Ena felt weightless for a fraction of a second before the sensation of falling drove her instincts into high gear. Her eyes shot open, absorbing the blinding sunlight, as she plummeted to the ground below. Holding out her arms, she braced herself. As she hit the ground hard, every function in her body gave out, replacing the agony she was sure to feel from such a drop.

Her mind went numb. Tingling with every sensation imaginable.

Ena rolled herself from her bare stomach onto her bare back, attempting feebly to open her eyes. Something just happened to Drake...

As feeling returned to her flesh, she felt an intense heat boiling her. Much hotter than simple sunlight, especially this time of year. Forcing her eyes open, she saw waves of fire coursing through the air.

Twenty fire mages standing around the garden and atop the rock formation casted blasts of fire at Drake from all directions. Drake nimbly dodged the attacked and returned several of them towards their casters. Four mages at the rock formation combined their magic, creating a swirling ball of flame so large that Drake would never be able to dodge. While Drake was distracted, the mages launched their attack. The fire blast covered the distance in a matter of seconds, and Ena watched as it consumed Drake.

Ena cried out, calling his name, unable to hear herself over the explosion.

Just as she expected the worst, the flames and smoke cleared and Drake spun the fire around in a circle over his head, absorbing every flame that came his way. As the flame wheel encircled him, it grew larger and hotter. The grass began to shrivel and combust, only to be absorbed into Drake's magic.

Then, Drake pushed out hard with his palms, spreading the circle of fire outwards, consuming everything in its path. Any mages who did not drop to the ground in time were incinerated. As the flame wheel struck the apartments surrounding the garden, the stone and mortar melted and crumbled.

Finally dissipating, the flames left behind smoke filling the air.

Drake ran towards Ena when, suddenly, the ground under him collapsed. A tile of the earth under his left foot flipped towards him, catching his leg and crushing his femur. He roared at the pain as he looked in front of him. Stepping over the top of the rock was an earth mage.

The mages who survived Drake's onslaught rose from the ground and ignited their hands, ready to strike. They stepped closer, tightening their circle around the governess, who was much too weak, too on the brink of death to fight back, and Drake, whose broken leg was still entrapped by the earth.

Drake reached out and held Ena's hand within his own. Ena gripped it in response.

Time seemed to slow as their impending doom approached. Ena watched as the mages' boots left behind prints in slow motion. Watched as the flames around their hands licked the air. Watched as the earth mage slowly lifted a boulder from the garden and carried it through the air.

Time continued to slow to a crawl as four massive Avalonian steeds hurdled over the top of the rock formation behind the earth mage and tore up the ground as their hooves caught their landing. The horses circled the mages as the riders, clad in jet black armor, swung their weapons.

One swung the long chain with a spiked flail at the end so fast that it ripped through the head of one mage and took the leg clean off of another. Another of the riders sturdily held out a sickle, shearing the heads and arms off of the defending mages. The third shot three arrows through a mage with a bladed bow, then proceeded to swing the blade into another.

The final Avalonian steed halted behind the earth mage. As the earth mage turned around, the rider jumped from the saddle and swung a two-handed greatsword, splitting the mage in half at the torso. The rider stepped on top of the mage's dead body and stopped in front of Ena. Removing his crested black helm, the rider revealed short, white hair and a thick, white and grey beard.

"Athenia," the rider winked and dipped his chin.

The Dread Watch!

CHAPTER 44

You should be healing Ena, not me," Drake argued. Master White Mage Joran spent the past hour mending Drake's shattered femur. The earth mage's attack had not just broken the bone, it had crushed it to pieces. Joran was an expert on orthopedics, so the task was not a difficult one, just time consuming. Each fragment of bone had to be fused back together perfectly to avoid a future rebreak or weakening of the skeletal structure in that leg.

"Athenia could not be healed immediately," Lady Raven answered.

The lady stepped into the light of the glowing white aura. Her feathered, black gown absorbed the light, emphasizing the pale skin of her face and the glow of her platinum hair.

The Dread Watch carried Drake and Ena on horseback to the Grand Ballroom immediately following the fight in the garden. The leader of the Dread Watch, Gorm, carried Ena up to the bedchamber himself, laying her gently on the bed. Joran was called from the Chapel immediately, and he spent the entire night working on Ena, healing every mark he could find on her damaged body...

"It was not enough," Joran admitted reluctantly. "No matter what I did, it was not enough."

"Is she..." Drake began to panic, lifting himself up.

Raven rushed over and touched a manicured hand against Drake's shoulder as he lay on the table. "No, she is not dead. Not yet. We have a team of white mages doing just enough to keep her going."

Drake sighed, laying back down. He knew Raven was here to discuss their next move, but all he cared about was saving Ena. What would they do next? He didn't care. Didn't care who lived or died, besides Ena.

He scowled at Joran. "You should be concentrating everything in your power on her..."

"My apologies," Joran was unphased by Drake's threatening tone. "Her wounds are like nothing I have ever experienced. All we can do is provide comfort until I hear back from the Providence."

Lady Raven pulled a chair up next to Drake's face away from where Joran was working on his leg.

"Did you find the dwarf?"

Drake shook his head. "Just countless mages. There was no evidence he was even there. I did find Archem, though."

Raven's cyan eyes widened. Even Joran flinched at that comment.

Drake continued, "I didn't asked Ena why he was there, but Archem was dead at her feet when I arrived."

"Very odd," Raven said. Short and simple. Drake half-assumed she would be outraged. "Master Joran, do you have any idea why Archem may have been there?" He shook his head. "Gods, she needs to wake up. Sheridan was just outside the city limits when he sent his last letter. When he gets here, we will talk with Athenia."

The magic illuminating from Joran's hands extinguished as he rose from the side of the table. Lady Raven stood, and Joran spoke to her off to the side. Drake tried eavesdropping, but their murmurs could not be interpreted. As Joran left the room, closing the door behind him, Raven approached Drake.

"Your leg should be good as new," Raven said. "Go ahead and sit yourself up. Step lightly. Your leg may be numb from the anesthetic still." Drake did as he was instructed. Balancing on both feet, Raven continued, "Great! Joran is heeding your advice and is checking on Athenia now. Take a few laps around the room. I want to ensure everything has been reset and healed properly before attempting to climb the stairs to the governess's room."

◆◆◆◆◆◆◆◆◆

Sheridan climbed the steps to the third floor of the Grand Ballroom. Last time he set foot here, the circumstances hadn't been much different. He opened the door to Lady Raven's bedchamber and saw an army of white mages casting their magic all over Ena's body. As he walked in, the mages parted, revealing a scene that shook Sheridan to his core.

Sheridan had seen plenty of horrors in his life, but whatever Ena suffered through was inhumane.

He walked up next to the bed. He waved at the mages to continue. Their hands lit up once more and they worked around the dwarf.

He travelled all this way to save Ena from certain doom, and by the gods, he intended to do just that. The trek here was more enjoyable than Sheridan predicted. Riding hard with little sleep for several days was never something to look forward to, but Captain Tidas was excellent company. Prior to the Lord of Avalon's death, Athenia was a mystery to all. Many knew her background, her story, but not many knew her for *her*. Tidas, on the other hand, knew everything about the governess up until she allowed the Watch to place her as far from Havana City as she could get.

Tidas shared dozens of stories of Ena's childhood, most of which opened Sheridan's eyes to her humanity, her struggles, and her endurance. It was that endurance that made Sheridan confident that she could pull through.

Until he saw her, that is.

"Can she feel anything?" he asked the mages. They shook their heads no. She was heavily sedated. He reached out and touched the scaled, broken flesh on her neck with calloused fingers. It didn't feel like skin at all. He brushed a lock of her hair out of her eyes. "I can't imagine how much pain you're in. But you look peaceful."

The door opened behind him. The Master White Mage entered and began immediately issuing orders gently, beginning first with the spreading of four different salves over her feet and knees. The Master White Mage himself casted his healing aura over her body. Sheridan stood back and watched.

"I'm going to take her to the Providence," Sheridan said, mostly to himself, but just loud enough for Master Joran to hear.

"Thank the gods." Joran smiled. "I'll prepare her for transport now."

Sheridan returned the smile with a slight chuckle. "Raven and the Providence chose well."

"I know when I have reached my limits, Master Sheridan," Joran said humbly. "Drake wished for me to keep trying. I figure preparing her for the trip to Havana will be more beneficial than wasting my efforts."

Sheridan reached up, clapping the mage on the shoulder.

Outside the door, Sheridan could hear Lady Raven and Drake approaching from down the hall.

"If you can," Sheridan spoke to Joran, "wake her. They will be looking for answers."

◆◆◆◆◆◆◆◆◆

The white mages propped Ena up on a set of pillows, carefully cradling her body. The sheets were changed out from under her, needing to be discarded immediately, the blood and pus stains unable to be washed out.

"Those sheets costed a fortune," Raven had complained. A single sideways glance from Sheridan kept her silent for the duration of Ena's preparation.

Once they had her stable, Joran allowed her to wake from the magic-and-herb-induced sedation. Ena's awakening was rough, to say the least. The mages leaned her forwards, allowing her to vomit into a bucket, releasing the toxins from within her body. When the vomiting settled, Joran approached her.

"Governess Athenia," Joran respectfully bowed. "My name is Joran, Master White Mage of Avalon, and I am currently responsible for your health and care. You have undergone a severe bout of physical and mental trauma, sustaining injuries that a typical human would not have survived from without constant treatment. To be quite transparent with you, Athenia, I am not even certain what some of your injuries are... Master Sheridan and I have deemed it necessary to your survival that you travel back with him to Havana and undergo intensive treatments with the Providence. Only in her care will you have a chance of overcoming this."

Drake stepped forwards, his feet pounding. "What? Why wasn't I included in this conversation? You can't send her off to Havana like *that!*"

Sheridan shared an annoyed look with Raven. "Keep him under control, please."

"Hey!" Raven yelled in a hushed tone, catching Drake's shoulder, and pulling him back next to her. "I was not informed of this decision either, but it is not our decision to make."

Sheridan cleared his throat. "My apologies, Athenia, but this was decided between Master Joran and myself only moments before your counterpart arrived. I saw the state of your condition and wanted to act fast. Joran is preparing you for the journey as we speak."

"Now," Joran spoke again, "can you explain to me how you suffered these violent injuries? Understanding how you received them provides an idea of how to treat them, which I will pass along to the Providence."

Ena inhaled deeply and opened her mouth to speak. Though her lips were still cracked, her tongue was no longer dry as a stone. She tasted the poultice on her lips that Joran must have used to help keep them moist to heal.

"Where to begin?" she spoke. Her voice still rasped slightly, but it was a significant improvement from twenty-four hours ago. Sheridan listened intently. "The Lord of Steel knocked me unconscious and strung me up by my wrists in that underground cell. Before I came to, he had my feet severely burned, preventing me from standing and escaping. Day after day, he cut me with my own blades over my entire body, beat me, continued to have my feet scorched, and then have me healed and start over again."

"Ah, so you were frequently healed?" Joran asked, taking notes as she spoke.

"Hold up one moment." Sheridan held up a thick hand. "You said 'the Lord of Steel?'"

"Correct," Ena shifted her gaze back and forth between Joran and Sheridan. "The Lord of Steel. An older dwarf claiming to be a merchant of weapons and armor. His name is—"

"Mida," she and Sheridan spoke the name with the same breath.

"You know him." Ena's brows rose curiously, watching Sheridan's awestruck face.

Sheridan closed his jaw and swallowed. "Unfortunately, I do. But please, continue. What was it he wanted from you?"

Ena's eyes narrowed at the Master of Cities. *You owe me an explanation.*

Sheridan met her look of accusation with one of regret. *I'll tell you everything.*

Ena continued, "He did not want anything from me. At least, not at first. Our meeting was purely coincidental, I am convinced. It just so happens that I became a tool in their overall quest."

Sheridan stopped her. "*Their* overall quest? I hope you mean Mida and his mages, though it still makes little sense why Mida would be working alongside an army of mages. Nor is he disciplined enough to raise an army of them." Seeing the grave look from Ena, he deduced, "There's another..."

"A mage woman named Myra," Ena shivered at the thought of being under her mental grasp again. "An extraordinary mindrender who Mida kept referring to as *his highness*. Sheridan, Mida had two mindrenders inside my head almost every single day, forcing me to relive my entire childhood. It all felt real. The pain and anguish, the anger and sadness, all of it was real. Yet their mental torment was miniscule, as if stepping on an ant, compared to five minutes in Myra's presence."

"What part did you have to play in this quest of theirs?" Sheridan asked. "And did they mention what this quest even is?"

"Domination of Lynidas," Ena announced numbly. "She is searching for those called the Unweaved. Judging by your face, Sheridan, I assume you know what the Unweaved are."

Sheridan shifted on his feet. "I've come across the term before."

"Drake," she addressed him for the first time. His name tasting like candy on her lips. "You are one such Unweaved... A mage whose powers do not develop until adulthood, at which point their magic becomes increasingly more devastating and uncontrollable. I hardly believed it, until I saw your display of power outside of that cave..." She feared him. Not in the same childish sense as a fear of the dark, but a helpless, immovable fear. "By rescuing me from that cave, you only knocked down the next domino in Myra's plan. I do not know how or why, but she is now another step ahead."

Anger built up inside of her. Not at any person in particular, but from the situation at hand. She was angry at getting captured in the first place. Angry that a citywide search was conducted on her behalf. She should have died.

"Lady Raven," Ena addressed the Lady of Avalon, feeling bold. Perhaps too bold, for the truth would ruin her. "Your husband was not murdered. He ended his own life." Raven grew as stiff as a stone. No emotion shown on her stoic face. Ena could have sworn her cyan eyes turned grey. "Myra discovered he was a very strong Unweaved, and she clawed at him until he could take it no longer. Bluebite apparently removes all magic from one's blood, rendering it useless after death. He saw no other way out..."

Sheridan faced Raven. Taking a step towards her with a hand outstretched, he said, "Raven. I'm so sorry."

"I need a moment," Raven said softly as she strode from the room. Ena felt guilty that they were occupying her own bedchamber, as the lady surely would want time alone to mourn.

Joran asked softly, "And... Archem? Why was his body found with you?"

"He was swayed to Myra's side by her twisted promises of glory for all oppressed mages," Ena said through gritted teeth. "He was ordered to keep me alive long enough for Drake to find me. I convinced him otherwise, even asked for a swift and painless death. However, as Archem casted his death spell on me, he was interrupted when Mida killed him. Somehow, the spell was incomplete and did this to me." She gestured at the hard, rotting flesh spreading from her neck to her hips.

"Gods..." Sheridan could not find the words to comfort the poor girl. Joran finished jotting down his notes and excused himself to gather the rest of the supplies necessary for Ena's journey to Havana.

"The *only* person capable of reversing whatever Archem failed to do," Sheridan swore adamantly, "is the Providence. I hope you understand, Athenia."

She nodded uncomfortably. "Myra succeeded in having my life spared. I suppose now, if there is any way to save me, I will join the fight against her. You *are* going to fight against her, right?"

"Of course!" Sheridan boasted. "I'm putting all of my faith into your words, Athenia. I need you now more than ever." He spun around to Drake, who stood uneasily by the door. "Drake. You're coming back to Havana, too. The Providence may have some advice how to control that magic of yours. I heard about your fight with the mages in that garden. Twenty families are homeless now because of your uncontrolled outburst. You're lucky the Guard Commander was smart enough to evacuate those apartments before you got back to the surface."

Drake lowered his head. "I understand... There is one thing I need to do before we leave, if I can have a couple of hours."

"What is it?" Sheridan asked, somewhat impatiently.

Drake slowly pulled something from his pocket. A chain with a medallion at the end. Sheridan knew without needing to read the inscription exactly what it was. *A service tag*. Drake opened his mouth to explain, but Sheridan stopped him. He nodded to Drake. "Go. It must be done."

Drake's eyes darted to Ena before Joran returned with a group of his mages. They carried piles of towels, bandages, and medicines. Drake watched uncomfortably as the mages removed the sheet from Ena's torso and started generously coating every inch of her with sweet-smelling poultices, wrapping her body and limbs with the bandages. Watching Ena grimace from the pain was too much. Drake snuck out of the room to deliver the service tag to the guard's family.

◆◆◆◆◆◆◆◆◆

Sheridan found Lady Raven alone in the ballroom. Wearing leggings and a bandeau, she practiced with her rapier against a straw-filled dummy. She flawlessly twirled around the practice dummy, jabbing the point of her blade through its critical points. The dwarf's footsteps remained softened as he walked across the carpeted floor. It wasn't until his boots struck the oak floor in the center of the room that Raven heard someone approaching. She whipped around, rapier pointing directly at Sheridan's head.

"Woah, there." Sheridan threw up his hands sarcastically. "I don't want to end up like that dummy."

"What is it, Master Sheridan?" she panted. Raven sheathed her sword at her hip and wiped sweat from her brow with the back of her hand.

"I wanted to share my condolences," Sheridan lowered his head. "Your entire world was shaken off its axis this morning. I don't know exactly what you're feeling, but I've been through a lot of shit in my life. If you need to talk with anyone, you know where to find me."

"All the way in the capital. Real helpful," Raven snarked.

"I want you to come to Havana for a while, Raven," Sheridan said. The comment got her attention. "I need someone strong to help the City Watch disperse back to their cities, while keeping behind a company or two as added protection and helping ensure peace among the civilians. But after that, leave Governor Josef to manage things for a bit and come to Havana City. Strong bodies are needed here, but strong minds are needed at the palace right now."

"Fine." Raven turned back to the straw dummy and slashed her rapier.

Sheridan started walking away. He did not take Raven's attitude personally. The lady was not known for being openly friendly, as it was. Adding the death of her life-long love to the mix only shook up her emotions further. He didn't want to interrupt her for much longer, since practicing her sword art was her coping mechanism.

But as he got to the steps leading up to the door, Raven called out, "Sheridan. Why didn't he say anything to me?"

He turned back around and saw Raven looking at him. Tears welled up in her eyes and slowly dripped down her cheek. Her bottom lip trembled.

Alright, Sheridan thought to himself, *looks like I'll stay a bit longer.*

CHAPTER 45

Much of the journey to Havana City was a blur. Ena lay in immense pain as the carriage carrying her hit every bump in the road. A white mage sat by her side the entire week, changing her dressings and keeping her wounds from getting infected any further. Chills from fever caused her to sweat through the bandages. Medical supplies were dangerously low by the time they passed under the arch of Havana City's wall.

Ena felt a pang of guilt once Sheridan announced they had crossed the city's border. This was the second time returning home since the death of her father. She had nothing to feel guilty for, yet she could hardly stomach the idea of being back here yet again.

"We are almost at the Spire, Athenia," Sheridan told her. He sat across from her in the carriage. "How are you holding up?"

"As well as I can be," Ena answered. She lay immobile on the leather seat uncomfortably.

"I am going to have Captain Tidas keep Drake busy during your treatment," Sheridan mentioned. "He is fueled by emotion when it comes to you. I can't have him anywhere near the Spire in case you are in distress. I hope you understand."

"Good," Ena agreed, a bit too hastily in hindsight. She couldn't wait to finally be in Drake's presence again, but after hearing of the deaths of Damian and Klaus, after suffering her ordeal at the hands of Mida, and after witnessing Drake's destructive display of power, she needed space to collect herself. "You mentioned Captain Tidas?"

"Yes." She could feel Sheridan smile. "She offered herself as part of my escort to Avalon."

"How is she?"

"She's good," Sheridan said. "I learned a lot about you from her. She admires you." That won a smile from Ena's lips. "You'll see her, too, after the Providence is done with you."

"Your confidence in the Providence is eerily strong," Ena remarked.

"You *will* overcome this, Athenia. You have to. If not for yourself, then for El Vadora. Don't forget, you were the first to discover these mages at the edge of your territory."

"How could I forget?"

Sheridan chuckled. "Just hang in there. Raven and the City Watch are combing half of Avalon for Mida."

"How do you know him?" Ena asked curiously.

"Ugh," he grumbled. "Mida has been a thorn in my side for years. I lived in Fairmarq for a time before moving to Havyn, and Mida was a high-ranking member of the Merchant's Guild at the time. The Merchant's Guild is a group of sadistic businessmen and women who exploit smaller, family-owned businesses in order to maintain a monopoly on any particular market."

Memories flashed back into Ena's mind. "My father and I had an encounter with them once. They slaughtered nearly half of our stock."

"Yes, because the Merchant's Guild was threatened by your growing monopoly over the equine market. I am sure plenty of Fairmarq's upper class were interested in your father's horses, rather than the Guild's stables in their own cities. King Henree Grey practically went to war with the Merchant's Guild when he was just a prince. There are strict regulations in place now, but Mida liked to test his limits, which ultimately got him removed from Fairmarq. He started poking his head around Havyn after I won the election, trying and failing to convince me to turn a blind eye to his business efforts."

"I am shocked you did not have him forcibly removed as well," Ena commented.

"I never thought of him as harmful," Sheridan said. "Manipulative and bold, but not harmful. Clearly I was wrong."

Ena could only imagine the guilt he must have. Thinking of all the opportunities he had to stop Mida long before today must sit uneasily in his mind. Ena found her job as a governess stressful. Trying to imagine the stress Sheridan endured daily was impossible.

They could not think of the "what ifs," though. They could only focus on planning their next move.

◆◆◆◆◆◆◆◆◆

Arriving at the Spire of the New King, the Providence sent an escort of Guardians of the Faith to carry Ena to the top in a stretcher. Trying to make the exchange as discreet as possible, Sheridan pulled the carriage as close to the palace steps as space would allow. It was only a matter of time before King Typhus received word about what went down in Avalon, and Sheridan would have to answer for it.

He did not let his worry show, though.

Instead, Sheridan marched up the spiral staircase behind the Guardians of the Faith to the Providence's study. Thankfully, due to Sheridan's and Joran's prior warnings, the Providence was prepared. The doors to her study were wide open, and the Guardians carefully placed Ena onto the medical bed prepared for her along the far wall.

"Stand by the door," the Providence ordered her Guardians. "Do not allow anyone inside."

The Guardians lifted their staves and marched in pairs to the doors, closing them as they passed through. Two pairs remained in the room for added protection. Sheridan pulled up a small wooden chair a good distance from Ena's bed, allowing the Providence ample space to work.

"Governess Athenia," the Providence addressed. "I am giving you a numbing agent. I want you to place it under your tongue and burst it. The taste is rather bitter, but it will help."

She placed a small pod of herbs in Ena's mouth. The Governess grimaced as she cracked it open with her tongue. The effect was almost immediate, though, for Ena's composure relaxed immensely.

The Providence did not wait a moment to begin working her magic. She removed the bandages and inspected the wounds intently. Starting first with the abrasions on Ena's knees, she first cleaned the openings with salted water. Ena made no indication that she felt any discomfort.

"Much of the tissue on your knees was worn down to the bone," the Providence said aloud to no one in particular. To Ena, she explained, "I am seeing a great deal of infection. Were these wounds exposed to any excrement or foreign bodies?" Ena nodded. "I will begin by pulling out the infectious matter. This will hurt, even with the numbing agent, so tell me to stop if you need me to."

The pure light of white magic enveloped the Providence's hands as she moved them in circles around Ena's kneecaps. She motioned her hands like a baker kneading dough just over the abrased flesh, and Sheridan saw Ena's knees start glowing with a similar aura. The aura began to spin and churn, as if made of liquid, and the Providence lifted her hands up, pinching her fingers together to a point. Suddenly, the churning aura changed to black, and a stream of magic rose from the wounds to the point of the Providence's fingers. Visibly watching as the infection was pulled from Ena's veins, Sheridan was in awe. Master Joran and a team of his best mages could hardly keep the infection from spreading. Here the Providence was, removing the infection entirely as effortlessly as one might wring out a damp cloth.

It was not without its repercussions, though. Ena grunted through grinding teeth and gripped the sides of the medical bed so hard that her knuckles turned white.

As the aura around Ena's knees slowly transformed from a dark storm to sunshine, the Providence's magic eased. She inspected the abrasions once more, determining that the infection had now been removed. "My next step will be to repair the damage to the bone and cartilage in your knees. After that, the skin will be returned to its former glory, and this one part of you will be good as new."

Ena exhaled deeply as the Providence prepared for the next phase of her healing method.

The magical glow reignited on the Providence's hands, and she placed them on one leg at a time. The skin on Ena's knee began to regrow as the fibers stretched and connected to one another. After only moments, the Providence switched to the other leg, revealing a perfect recreation of the leg prior to injury. It was dazzling to witness, and Sheridan could see the process was therapeutic to Ena. All tension in her face eased as the Providence restored the epidermis and sinews.

The same process was repeated for Ena's feet, but the pain was far more intolerable. Ena cried out, begging for moments of rest.

"I apologize, Athenia," the Providence said. "The infection in your feet is rooted far deeper than your knees. To be quite honest, it is no wonder Master Joran recommended considering amputation in his letter to me." Before Ena could protest—and Sheridan could tell by the look on her face how *adamant* of a protest it would have been—the Providence spoke loudly, "*But* I do not intend to perform an amputation on you today, or any other day for that matter. I only need your trust and patience."

With no retort from Ena, the Providence continued. It took over an hour for the black aura to be extracted from Ena's mangled feet. Even after the infection was eradicated, her extremities were purple and black from blood loss, and all the tendons and tissue on the interior of her feet were melted from the bones.

The Providence navigated next to Ena's ribs, two of which were broken, and mended them with ease. Any additional lacerations and bruises along Ena's body were knitted or faded within moments, including the rope burns on her wrists.

All that remained was the death touch scaling down her torso.

"What ultimately occurred," the Providence began to explain, "is that Master Archem was unable to drain your life force in its entirety. If he had been successful in touching your head, the magic would have drained the life from your brain, killing you instantly and painlessly. With Archem's inability to charge the spell to its maximum force, and then missing his target after Mida's attack, the cells of your body that he touched died, but the magic was unable to rapidly spread through your body. Over the past week, your living cells touching the dead ones have also begun to die, creating the immense pain you feel. I can reverse the damage, but it will not be pleasant."

"Just do it," Ena said, bracing herself.

"Bite down on this," the Providence placed a wooden bit in Ena's mouth. She bit down hard.

Magic welled up in the Providence's palms as she placed them gently on Ena's scaled grey flesh. Although, this time, instead of pulling the toxins out of Ena's body, she forced the raw light into every crack and crevice of the dead and dying cells. Ena's back arched as her entire body tensed. Her teeth clenched so hard onto the bit that her molars indented the wood. She held back a scream.

The Providence's light passed through all of the dead flesh until it touched the living flesh beneath it. The dead flesh could not be saved, but she could restore the tissue from within. The Providence closed her eyes, concentrating on the Connections of Magic she weaved, feeling it navigate through Ena's body like channels of water. As if grabbing a drowning soul from the sea and pulling it to the surface, the white magic latched onto the life within Ena and pulled it through the decay.

While the Providence reconstructed Ena's cells from within, the grey, dead cells began flaking off at the top. The entire process was torment on Ena. Her body flailed and twisted against the Providence's firm hold as she screamed at the top of her lungs. The decay blew off her in a powder as the new cells replaced the old. The powder clustered on the floor as Ena stopped fighting, the pain slowly ebbing away.

The Providence lifted her hands, and the magical aura dulled. Ena looked down and gasped. Her skin looked perfectly clear of all blemishes. She reached up and felt her neck—soft and fresh.

"Incredible..." Ena was amazed.

"Stand if you can," urged the Providence. "Come, carefully. There is a mirror over this way."

Ena sat up on the edge of the bed. She glanced at the ground and the powder that coated it.

Sheridan waved a hand behind Ena's back, gently brushing away the pile with his kinetic magic.

Ena's head shot up, staring at the Providence's back as she walked away, assuming it was her magic at work. She stepped off the bed and wobbled over to the mirror, catching herself along the wall as she went. She hadn't walked in a month, and her muscles were weak.

The Providence reached out an arm to brace Ena as she walked.

As they approached the mirror, Ena was surprised by what she saw. Amazed at how flawlessly the Providence had healed her completely, breathing life into her again. But also horrified at how disheveled her appearance had become.

Her hair draped past her shoulders, her fingernails and toenails were long, cracked, and yellow, body hair was growing from places she never thought possible, her ribcage protruded from under her skin.

"My scar is gone..."

"Oh, which scar?" the Providence asked, her unrivaled beauty making Ena look like some kind of cave creature.

Ena pointed to her bare right thigh. "From where I tore it open in a horse-riding accident as a child."

"I'm so sorry, Athenia. That was the hip marked by the death touch.

If I had known—"

Ena shook her head in the mirror. "Do not worry. There is something freeing about it being gone..."

The Providence stepped closer to Ena, placing a hand on her arm. She could see the governess viewing her body with concern. "With a bit of exercise, you will gain back your muscle tone. As for your hair and nails, why don't I send for a beautician to come and clean you up?"

"I—" Ena thought about refusing. She hated being poked and prodded at to look pretty, thinking back to the Lordship Ball in Avalon two months prior, but she supposed this was less about beauty and more to look human again. She smiled. "Yes, I would like that."

A sudden loud knocking pounded at the door. They all stood on edge and whipped around. The Providence ran to her bureau and tossed a robe at Ena to throw over herself.

The knocking continued. Sheridan sped to Ena's side and pulled her behind the tree in the center of the botanical garden in the middle of the circular room. He lifted his chin at the Providence. She nodded back.

"Who is it?" she called out harmlessly.

"Providence, Sheridan, it's me," the soft, innocent voice of Princess Lia muffled through the oak doors.

The Providence looked back at Sheridan. Sheridan sighed and nodded.

The Providence signaled to the Guardians standing by the door. They turned and opened it a crack, just enough for Lia to squeeze through. She sped in past the garden.

"I thought I heard screaming, so I came here—" Lia stopped abruptly when she came around the side of the tree and saw Ena with Sheridan. "What's happening? Who are you?"

CHAPTER 46

Drake's first trip to Havana City was shorter and less adventurous than he would have liked. He was locked by Ena's side the entire time, and the only trip off course was to her father's stable. Drake had not seen Ena since that final day in Gabrenas. He had no way of knowing if she was alive or dead. Captain Tidas assured him that immediate word was to be sent to her regarding Ena's status once the Providence had a chance to heal her.

Tidas tried her best to keep Drake distracted by showing him all over the city. For breakfast, she took him to a small chicken farm in the lower district where they knew Tidas by name. The farmers fried fresh eggs over a firepit.

"How do you know of places like this?" Drake said as he shoveled down a mouthful of eggs. "You live in the upper district, right? With most of the other City Watch?"

Tidas tucked back a brunette lock behind her ear as she took a bite of her own. She laughed, "Ha! Only the most prestigious City Watch captains live on the hill, not the entire Watch. The guards are usually required to live at their assigned barracks, unless they are married and own a home with their spouses."

"But you're considered one of the most prestigious of City Watch captains, am I right?"

"I've been a captain for a long time," Tidas dabbed off her lips with a napkin, "so, I suppose you can consider me part of the prestigious crowd, but I prefer the company of my platoons in the barracks. I discovered this place after an overnight patrol once as a guard during my second year. Dawn came, I was hungry and exhausted, and I followed the smell of eggs here. The farmers were friendly and fed me. I've come here at least once every month since."

"Wow," Drake said. "That's amazing."

Tidas was born and raised in the city and knew every square inch of it. She excelled in her career at a young age, much like Ena, but when given the option of where she wished to be stationed, she chose to remain in Havana City. Within four years as a guard, she was promoted to a captain and assigned her own platoon. By the time she met a young Ena, she had already been a captain for over a year.

Taking Ena in after the falling out with her father was the most honorable thing Tidas ever did. It taught her a lot. After all, Ena was technically still a child when the guard captain took responsibility for her, and the Watch made it very clear that whatever happened to Ena fell onto her shoulders.

Luckily, Ena's commitment to the City Watch made the Guard Commander of Havana City easily forget about her age.

"I know why you're doing this," Drake said as they paraded through the middle district on horseback. The sun was nearing its peak in the sky. "The Master of Cities ordered you to keep me away from the palace. Away from Ena."

Their horses' hooves clopped on the cobblestones as they passed by some of the city's shops. Captain Tidas looked at Drake, analyzing him. It was no mystery how he felt about Ena, and Tidas tended to be very protective of the girl she watched grow up.

"Considering I am off-duty today, this wasn't an order," Tidas pointed out. Though off-duty, Tidas still donned her full set of armor. She was hardly without it, especially since the sun catching the armor warmed her on crisp days such as this one. The nip from the late autumn air made Drake regret not wearing a second layer of his own. "This was a suggestion of mine, actually. Allowing Ena some space to rest also seemed necessary."

"You haven't even spoken with her yet, have you? Aren't you insistent on seeing her yourself? What if the worst happens?"

Tidas brought her chestnut horse to a halt, urging Drake's palfrey to do the same. She retorted, "I know Ena better than she knows herself. Even after these years apart. If I was concerned that she wouldn't pull through, I wouldn't be out here with you."

"But her wounds. Her health—"

"Listen, Drake," Tidas pulled her horse beside his, leaning in close with an intimidating glare. "I know how you feel about her. Countless other men used to fawn over her, but none were ever as bold as you. I'm not quite sure how I feel about that boldness just yet. You don't truly know Ena. I've seen her at her worst, and she survived. Whatever she is going through this time may be the worst experience of her life, but she *will* prevail."

Drake smiled. "I need your level of confidence."

Tidas kicked her heels into her horse's sides, and they trotted together down the street. Tidas showed Drake her favorite shops, along with some of the less popular ones. Not a single stop throughout the day touched the hill leading to the upper district, which Drake found odd. He figured they would be seeing plenty of the upper district since Tidas lived nearby. Her many years as a guard had taken her through every nook in the city, though, and just because the upper district was built on a foundation of gold did not make it better than the hardworking individuals who barely scraped by.

"Have you had any experience with mages before?" Drake asked. He added, "Besides white mages, of course."

Tidas looked around momentarily before responding, as if others around may hear something they should not.

She nodded. "Yes. Once. Mages are a sensitive subject around here."

"Why's that?"

"Besides the subliminal threat of a mage coup that can threaten the lives of all non-magic wielders in Havyn?" The captain rolled her eyes. "All mages are required to be registered with each kingdom since they can potentially use their magic for harm rather than good. After the Mage Wars, the first amendment to the Concordat put in place the registration requirement. Over the years, mages were either exploited for their talents or ostracized as 'witches' and 'sorcerers', causing them to hide in plain sight and avoid registering. Havana, in particular, has always been a bit more anti-magic than the other regions of Havyn. The first platoon I was assigned to as a City Watch guard was tasked with investigating reports of undocumented mages. Almost all of which were false reports, typically accusations by a rival neighbor, business owner, you name it."

"'Almost?'" Drake narrowed his eyes as they turned down a random alleyway and travelled into the depths of the lower district.

Twenty silent minutes later, the pair tied their horses up at a random hitching post along a quiet side street. Tidas led Drake between two nearby abandoned apartment buildings where they met a makeshift wooden sign propped up by two wooden stakes that read *Do Not Enter by Order of the City Watch.* Ignoring the warning, Tidas squeezed passed the sign and ushered Drake to do the same. They found themselves in a narrow clearing surrounded by the rear sides of a handful of similarly abandoned apartment buildings.

In the center of the clearing was an old well with ice frozen from swells that originated from its depths. Pools of ice also scattered across the ground of the clearing, and shards of ice stuck to the exterior walls of the surrounding buildings. Two of the buildings had massive fractures along their sides leaving a clear view of the interior with violent waves frozen mid-deluge pouring inside.

It was already a cool, crisp fall day, but the temperature In this clearing was vastly lower than the outside air, evident from the fog of breath that rose from Drake's agape mouth, in awe of what he was seeing. Why was this ice here? How was this possible?

He looked to the cluster of frozen water blasted to the wall nearest to him and nearly jumped out of his skin as he squinted to see through the ripples in the ice. The frozen body of a guard was plastered to the bricks behind them, stuck holding their gauntleted hands out in front of them and their face turned away from the inevitable torrent of water that ended their life.

"There's someone in there!" Drake shouted at Tidas.

She nodded nonchalantly in response. "And there she will stay. The ice cannot be melted."

"I don't understand."

Tidas huffed a laugh to herself, probably at the irony of having to explain how magic works to a mage, despite Drake's lack of experience. "My first and only encounter with a mage was with one of the deadliest of elemental mages—a water mage."

"Elemental mage?" Drake asked.

"Elemental mages," Tidas rolled her eyes as she began to explain, "are those who can control the elements, such as fire, earth, and water. Fire mages are most common with earth mages being rarer. The rarest and most deadly of all are water mages. Even after death, their magic can stay present—something having to do with the flow of the magic in the water aligning with the weaves in the Connections of Magic. All of that technical stuff is above my head and is probably only known to the Providence."

"So, I'm an elemental mage," Drake deduced. "What other types of mages are there?"

"Arcane mages—those who can control the minds of others, whether that be as small as changing the color of something visible to others or a single person or as large as making someone believe something that truly did not happen or viewing someone's thoughts. Arcane mages are extremely rare, even more so than water mages."

Tidas continued, "There are also rumors of another type of mage called kinetic mages, who can supposedly move things with their minds. They are rumored because there supposedly have not been any documented since the downfall of the faeries."

Drake was learning a lot about his own kind.

"What happened here?"

"We received a tip that an undocumented mage was living in this apartment complex," Tidas began, scanning the area slowly to reminisce. "Since most other leads were dead ends, we hardly ever took them seriously. Some of the men in my platoon weren't even carrying weapons or shields to defend themselves with when we came here. The tip came in from someone else in the complex who stated that their water pressure in their house was too low, and they had a suspicion one of their neighbors was a mage who was messing with the well."

"And they were right..." Drake muttered.

"And they were right," Tidas confirmed. "When we arrived, we were met by the one who provided the tip. They informed us the neighbor they suspected was in the back of the building with the well that very moment. We were foolish and approached loudly, and with hardly any protection. The moment we passed the alley and entered this small courtyard, we were met with a barrage of water and ice so intense we thought there were multiple mages coming at us at once. It was just one woman, though. One woman who tore apart a full platoon of highly trained City Watch guards in a matter of minutes. Only a few of us lived through the ordeal, and some who died are still trapped in the ice like they are frozen in time."

Drake focused his vision and saw more bodies trapped within various points of the ice throughout. Some very clearly dead by the time the ice froze over them. Others, similar to the first one Drake spotted, were frozen alive.

"I'm glad you survived," was all Drake could muster. What else was there to say to someone who went through an event as traumatic as this?

"I delivered the killing blow," Tidas said, almost too quietly for Drake to hear. "I had to sacrifice the woman you see standing next to you there. She offered up a distraction, and I took it, sweeping my blade through the water mage's head. Only me, my captain, and two other guards managed to escape with our lives."

"Do you... Do you hate mages now because of that day?" Drake asked solemnly.

Tidas met his gaze. "No, of course not. This was one person's doing, and something she only did because she feared for her life. She had been undocumented for so long, and after comparing reports with the other cities throughout Havyn, turns out she was the subject of dozens of investigations that she managed to escape from. It was fear that drove her to this point, and anger that she could not live life in peace."

"What was she doing here with the well, then, if all she wanted was a peaceful life?" Drake asked.

Tidas shrugged her shoulders. "Probably just practicing her magic. There's nothing wrong with that. Or... there shouldn't be." She turned to Drake and ushered him back down the alley. "We have pushed mages to be this way. It's truly sad. I don't blame her for what she did. Am I upset that I lost so many friends that day? Of course, but, as was evident from the reports, there were dozens of opportunities for someone to intervene in a better way and help her instead of ostracizing her."

"Not many share that same sentiment," Drake commented as they walked back to the makeshift warning sign that blocked the path of the alleyway. Tidas pushed past the sign first, followed closely by Drake—only, when Drake touched the sign, a screeching sounded in his head that made him visibly wince as he covered his ears. The sound wasn't coming from an external source, though, it was coming from within his own head.

"Hello, young pup," a cruel, yet soothing, female voice echoed.

Drake looked around to find who was speaking to him. To his utter shock, Tidas was stalled mid-step. Even the dust in the air was frozen in place. Time had stopped. He began to panic, his lungs huffing and puffing as his heart raced.

"Relax, I am not here to harm you," the voice spoke softly.

"Who— Who are you?" Drake asked through gritted teeth.

The voice laughed with corruption. "I am your salvation, protégé! You may call me Myra."

Myra! Drake recalled the name from Ena's description of what she went through in her underground cell in Avalon. She was a mage queen. "I am not your protégé..."

"You will soon learn that you need me, pup," Myra responded with a strength in her deep feminine voice that seemed to protrude through the walls around Drake. "You are an Unweaved. Your magic grows at an exponential rate, out of your ability to control with your amateurism over the Connections of Magic. You will die if you do not allow me to assist you."

"Never!" Drake roared. "You have no control over me!"

"We shall see about that..." Myra merely whispered.

"Get out of my head!"

"Certainly. Our time together will come later."

Instantly, the pressure within his head subsided, and Drake felt completely fine, if not better than he had before that encounter. He lifted his head and watched at time merged back to its regularly pace, Tidas still walking a few steps ahead of him. Tidas turned when she did not hear Drake's own steps following her.

"You alright?" she asked.

Drake blinked a few times, wondering if maybe he had been imagining the whole thing. He continued forwards to the end of the alley. "Y-Yes."

They stepped into the sunshine of the early afternoon sun. The horses were right where they left them, but with a scroll tied to the reins of Tidas's that had not been there before. She looked over her shoulder before cracking the seal and unwinding the parchment. She read for a moment.

"Good news," Tidas smiled as she rolled the scroll back up and tucked it into her horse's saddlebag. "Ena is almost finished up with her treatment. The Providence has given her the all-clear. I'll take you back to the palace."

His face erupted with a smile he did not expect. Tidas must have caught it from the corner of her eye, for she smiled, too, before turning to Drake. "I hate that you love her as much as you do. You're good to her, and she deserves that. I'm just not sure she will ever slow down enough for you or any man to actually catch up with her."

Drake put one foot in the stirrup and hoisted his other leg over the saddle, wobbling from inexperience as he found his seating. "I'll stay by her side until she does."

They leisurely returned to the middle district and made their way down the main roads before reaching the bottom of the hill leading through the upper district. Tidas shared some more stories about Ena, at Drake's request, until they reached the base of the Spire. They dismounted their horses and paced the steps of the spiral staircase.

CHAPTER 47

Ena sat uncomfortably as the two beauticians did their work. They took their job as seriously as Ena took her own. Where they could have simply shaved her excess body hair, they scanned her body from head to toe under a magnifying glass, plucking any unneeded hair. Certain areas were more painful than others, including some where she plainly did not want a stranger holding a pair of tweezers,

The same process happened for her outgrown, broken nails. No clippers were used, only files. Intently, the beauticians had grinded away at her talon-like toenails with those files, sending a gritting discomfort through Ena's teeth as she clenched them. Her fingernails were no better. A poultice was rubbed onto her nails and left to dry after they were reduced to a normal length. Once the poultice was removed, the yellow discoloration was gone, replaced by a healthy pink sheen.

The last step was her hair, which was far less intrusive or painful, but just as time consuming. Ena focused on the conversation between Sheridan, the Providence, and Princess Lia, who were not far from her.

"So," Lia finally spoke, shocked at the information she just received, "for months, it was known that the Lord of Avalon was murdered, and you both decided to recruit a governess from a small city that hardly anyone has heard of before to secretly investigate?" Lia recapped with a look of confusion and judgement. "*Then*, this governess managed to uncover a group of rebel mages? Sheridan... Providence... I'm sorry, but this does not seem like a decision that was thought out carefully. Too many variables. Too much trust in someone you don't even know."

"If I may," Ena stood up as the beauticians finished her hair. She tied the robe she was wearing closed and approached where they sat at the Providence's desk. "Princess Lia, it is a great pleasure to meet you." The governess extended a hand, and Lia took it cautiously in her own and gave it a gradual shake. "I do want to add clarification to the events that have occurred over the past two months. First, the Lord of Avalon was not murdered, he ended his own life by poison. A poison that severs all weaves to the Connections of Magic."

"Wait," the Providence put up a hand. "Severs all weaves? Are you saying..."

"Yes, the Lord of Avalon was a mage—an Unweaved," Sheridan confirmed. "I meant to tell you, but all focus was on Athenia's recovery the moment we got here. Before Athenia continues, Mida is involved, as well."

"Second," Ena continued before the Providence could interject, "all I know is that the mages and Mida are being influenced by some kind of mage queen named Myra. Her power rivals that of yours, Providence, though, hers is used for evil." Ena looked at Lia, "Their purpose, it seems, is to overcome the oppression that mages face in Lynidas by raising an army and taking the kingdoms by force, starting with Havyn."

Ena continued, "With regards to the Lord of Avalon's death, as you know, I experienced a similar situation in El Vadora. In hindsight, the cult may not have been a cult at all, but fearful mages being tormented by Myra to join her cause."

"But that was years ago..." the Providence said.

Ena nodded. "There were too many mages fighting against us in Avalon for this uprising to be new. Myra has been in Havyn for years, at least since my encounter with the cult-like mass suicide in my city. Myra told me that saving my life would be the next step in her plan. I am convinced an attack is imminent."

Lia stood abruptly and began pacing gently through the sunlit garden. Her teeth grinded on her fingernails as she got lost in thought. Ena and the others watched patiently, knowing the princess had something to say.

Finally, Lia turned back to them. "Master Sheridan. Providence. I must admit I am furious to learn that all of this tragedy was happening in my kingdom, and I had no knowledge of it. I am not sure if that is my own fault for being less attentive to my people than I should have been, or if keeping secrets from the royal family is something you are far too comfortable with. I am not a little girl anymore. I am fit to rule this kingdom, as you have both said yourselves. I expect full transparency from here forward." Sheridan and the Providence nodded simultaneously. "As for you, Governess Athenia. Thank you for your valiant efforts in Avalon, and for your years of service in the City Watch and El Vadora. We are lucky to have your intelligence and skillset. I invite you to stay here in the palace for as long as you need."

"Thank you, Princess," Ena bowed halfway. Lia dipped her head respectfully before turning away and heading for the doors. As she approached, the Guardians of the Faith each placed a hand on the doors.

Lia stopped for a moment. Without turning to face them, she said, "Pardon me, all of this sudden information has been a lot to take in. I'm going to my chambers to think on this. We will reconvene on this matter tomorrow."

No one responded as the Guardians swung the doors open, and Lia met her Keepers in the hallway, departing from the study briskly. Ena suspected very obvious tension between the three leaders of the kingdom. But where was the king? And what prompted Lia's comment about keeping secrets from the royal family

This was the second time Ena has been at the palace, yet King Typhus has not been seen, nor talked about. There must be a reason for that, but Ena would ask when the time was appropriate. Now, she was less focused on the politics of the kingdom and more focused on getting an actual set of clothes on her body and food in her stomach. Though the beauticians did a fantastic job of restoring Ena back to her former beauty, even if Ena herself could care less about her appearance, the only thing that would make her ribs disappear beneath her skin again was food.

As if reading her mind, Sheridan cleared his throat and said, "Athenia, why don't we get you a good, hearty meal and a room prepared? Come, I can give you a tour of the palace in the meantime." He stood and walked over to the Providence's wardrobe, shuffling through it before pulling out a simple cream-colored dress. The Providence shifted uncomfortably behind her desk, somewhat perturbed by the dwarf going through her wardrobe without permission. Sheridan reached out a metal hand, extending the dress towards Ena. "Not your favorite attire, I know, but it's better than a bathrobe."

Ena smirked for the first time in a month, taking the dress behind a wooden room divider to change. Gods, she *hated* dresses. Sheridan was right, though—it was better than a silk bathrobe.

◆◆◆◆◆◆◆◆◆

Sheridan led Ena into the throne room. He treaded carefully, listening for any signs of Typhus. His guards confirmed that Typhus had locked himself away in his chambers near the top of the Spire for days, but Sheridan exercised caution. If Typhus knew there was a stranger in his midst, he would without a doubt lose his temper.

"The last time you were here," he addressed, "there was not much of an opportunity for a tour. You've never been to the palace before your last time here, right?"

Ena shook her head, "My father refused to let me inside the front doors with him all the times he was invited to the palace for business. He told me it was for my own protection. I believe it was simply because he did not want the nuisance of taking care of a child while partying with other rich men."

The Providence followed behind them as they stopped in the middle of the massive, marble room.

"I was raised in the Spire of the New King," she said, her voice solemn. "I actually believe your father was true to his word, if only in that one aspect. The vipers that slithered through these halls would have used anything as collateral if the Horse Lord had failed to deliver what he promised, even a child. Best he did not make your presence well known."

Ena supposed the Providence was right. In a lifetime of hateful words and physical abuse, maybe her father had made that one good decision for Ena's well-being. A sour taste filled her mouth whenever she gave her father any kind of praise or satisfaction.

Memories flashed in her mind, having so recently relived her worst nightmares of her childhood. She clenched her fists and forced herself to take a deep breath and let the moment pass.

Casually, the governess walked over to the dais and climbed it. The soft scuffle of her flats on the marble steps echoed all around her. She reached out and touched the golden throne with the tips of her fingers before pulling her hand back.

She turned and glanced around the room. "The palace is so empty. It's eerie."

Sheridan followed her gaze, taking in the open space, the high ceilings, the decorative paintings and tapestries covering the walls. They were the only ones here. Ants among an abandoned city. He broke the tension with a chuckle "You get used to the silence after a while."

"The Spire of the New King," the Providence spoke, "was once full of people. Emissaries, ambassadors, chefs, servants, guards, visitors... family. Not once was there a quiet moment under King Tytan's reign."

"What happened?" Ena asked.

"Typhus happened," Sheridan said bluntly. The Providence shot him a look of warning. He shrugged. "What? She's going to pick up on it sooner or later."

Sighing, the Providence returned her gaze to Ena. "King Typhus has made many disagreeable choices during his short reign that has left the palace dull and void of life. However, this conversation will be saved for another day. Someone approaches."

A moment later, the door from the antechamber to the throne room opened to reveal a City Watch guard. The young man strode in confidently, halting, and saluting Sheridan. "Master, Captain Tidas has returned with a young man named Drake."

"Let them in," Sheridan commanded.

A minute later, the doors creaked and swung wide. Tidas and Drake marched in side-by-side. Tidas's armor clattered with each booted step, her helmet tucked under an arm cradled by her gauntleted hand. Each stride boasted confidence, a representation of her successful career.

Ena saw Drake's face holding back a smile as he locked eyes with her. Itching with excitement, his steps began to quicken before he broke away from Tidas. He half-jogged to Ena and threw his arms around her. Surprised, Ena took a moment before gently wrapping her arms around him, returning the gesture.

For a brief second, she closed her eyes, admiring the embrace.

"I missed you," Drake whispered in Ena's ear.

Ena pulled away, looking at Drake deeply.

"Thank you for everything."

The sound of shuffling feet drew Ena's attention from Drake's infatuated gaze. Two yards behind him stood Tidas, whose corner of her mouth curled upwards.

"Governess," Tidas dipped her chin.

Ena pulled out of Drake's embrace and walked over to the guard captain and returned the gesture, "Captain." She then reached out her hand, and Tidas clasped it in her own with an audible clap. "It's been a while."

Tidas let go of her hand. "I didn't think I would ever see you back here."

"Not alive, at least."

"Ha!" Tidas laughed. "I had no doubt you would pull through. Especially having the Providence as your personal physician."

The Providence cleared her throat and cut into the conversation. "Enough flattery, Captain. Since we are all together again, why not get together for dinner and talk?"

"Perfect idea," Sheridan interjected. "There is a dining room near my chambers. Guard," he called to one of the City Watch guards by the doors, "see if you can get the head chef of *Ravagers* over here to cater."

"*Ravagers*?" The Providence raised her blonde eyebrows.

"I'm feeling fancy tonight," Sheridan joked. "Besides, I think the governess deserves it."

The Providence nodded in agreement.

While word was sent to *Ravagers* to prepare a dinner fit for kings, Sheridan led Ena and the rest of them through the palace for the tour he promised. Starting in the throne room, he elaborated on the fine details of every painting, marble step, and brick. What many did not know, he explained, is that the Spire of the New King was pieced together from other palaces, forts, and prestigious architectural features around Lynidas. Not even just Lynidas, Ena realized, when Sheridan explained that the throne, made from solid gold, was a gift from Etherea, their sister country far to the west beyond the Dead Lands.

The Dead Lands existed just beyond the outskirts of El Vadora, so Ena knew them well enough. The forest outside of the city limits, beyond even that of the villages where Drake was raised, was the home of dangerous creatures and a harsh ecosystem. Many hunters gained fame by challenging one another to survive in the wild and bring home the skin of a beast. Many more did not return to tell of their discoveries, though.

Ena attempted to outlaw hunting in the Dead Lands when she was elected governess, but the trophy hunters bypassed her law by travelling to the nearest city outside of her jurisdiction and crossing into the Dead Lands from there. Rather than push the law harder, she decided if people wanted to sentence themselves to death, then sobeit.

Ena wondered what the Brekken had gifted Havyn upon its founding. Sheridan sarcastically responded that their "gift" to Havyn was to *not* attack them and reclaim the lands they lost during the signing of the Concordat.

Sheridan pointed to the cathedral ceiling high above them and explained that the royal apartments were upstairs at the top of the Spire. Large chambers once held the bedrooms, bath rooms, and studies of every royal member of the family. Now, the royal family consisted of only Typhus and Lia, leaving many of the apartments as homes for rats and dust.

"The royal family was massive only two generations ago," the Providence explained. "The late King Tytan and the previous Providence were brother and sister—two of seven siblings—and two of a wild bunch of nearly two dozen cousins."

"What happened?" Drake asked.

"The first time the plague struck Havyn, the outbreak occurred here in this city. Once it spread inside the palace, most of Tytan's siblings and cousins perished. Many of whom were not yet at the stage in their lives where they were marrying and bearing children, so the bloodline suffered. Eventually, all who remained were those who walked these halls a decade or two ago. Then, old age or natural illness took the lives of our elders, and now only Typhus, Lia, and myself bear the family name of Casalvania. Though, by the law of the Concordat, I sacrificed my name when I passed the Trials of Magic."

By the time Sheridan showed them the other end of the palace—the tower belonging to the Master of Cities—the chefs from *Ravagers* arrived at the palace with an entourage of servers carrying silver platters of gourmet cuisine of ethnicities and races from all over the known world. While the servers set up dinner, Ena heard Sheridan ask Tidas to retrieve Princess Lia, if the princess was forgiving enough to join them.

The princess refused the invitation, according to Tidas upon her return. "Said she wanted time alone to think."

Trying to keep the mood light, Sheridan clapped his hands together while admiring the display of food being laid out on the dining table and said, "More for us, then. Everyone, take a seat."

Drake followed Ena to a pair of place settings to Sheridan's left, who sat at the head of the mahogany table. The Providence gracefully sat across from Ena to Sheridan's right. Tidas awkwardly stood off to the side until Sheridan gestured to the chair beside the Providence, giving her a wink and a welcoming smile. Her armor clattered as she pulled her chair in and unfastened her gauntlets, placing them on the floor beside her alongside her helmet. Not the best attire for a formal dinner, but she had not expected an invitation. Ena could see the admiration in Tidas's eyes as she thanked Sheridan.

Countless dishes covered every inch of the dining table, which could have seated thirty people. The table had not been filled in many years, though. Servants fetched every plate for Sheridan's guests as he described the numerous cuisines they had the pleasure of consuming. Ena, who was no stranger to the finer tastes of life, had never heard of half of the dishes they were being served. How Sheridan knew what everything was, Ena had no idea. Sheridan's mysterious past was always a curiosity of Ena's.

For hours, they ate, drank, and laughed. Even Ena, as serious as she was, let out a few chuckles. Though, she couldn't help thinking about the threat they faced. Avalon was merely the first step in some master plan that they hardly began to unravel. Sheridan and the Providence knew this, too, but their occasional glances at Ena told her to let her fear subside for one night.

Enjoy this moment while we have it, Sheridan's subtle eyes seemed to say.

And so she did.

CHAPTER 48

Stuffed from dinner, Ena dragged her feet to the guest bed chambers Sheridan had set up for her. The chambers were down the hall from Sheridan's own, which comforted her. Should anything bad happen, at least the Master of Cities was within shouting distance.

Ena was accompanied by Drake, who thought he was comforting and protecting her by escorting her to the guest chambers. Though, Ena knew she was more of a comfort to Drake than he was to her. Not that she didn't appreciate and enjoy his company—down in that cell, hung by her wrists, drenched in her own bodily fluids, she wanted nothing more than to see Drake. She admitted to herself that Drake's daring rescue had sparked some feelings she never thought possible for her to feel, but romance was the last thing on her mind.

"I lit a fire for you and drew you a bath," Drake said, as he pulled the latch and pushed open the oak door, revealing a warm fire blazing in the hearth within the chambers.

Maybe romance isn't the last *thing on my mind,* Ena smirked to herself, admiring Drake's thoughtfulness. *Not tonight, at least.*

The doorway opened into a spacious room with a fireplace on the adjacent wall to Ena's left and a bed big enough for a king with the headboard against the wall across from the fire. On the right half of the room, a large granite tub was filled with warm water and essential oils that gave off a pleasant aroma.

Ena inhaled deeply through her nose. "Lavender. And..." She sniffed again. "Mint? How did you know?" She didn't even have to ask. He spent an entire day with Tidas. They obviously talked about her, and Tidas was careful to tell Drake her favorite scents.

She was a sucker for lavender and mint.

"Care to join me in a bath?" Ena asked.

She hardly believed the words that came from her mouth. Sharing a bed, now sharing a bath. What was next? Talks of marriage, children?

Never.

Ena could never settle down in a domesticated life like that with anyone. Could she? *I suppose I have never thought of it before...* she thought.

"I'd love to join you," Drake's face softened. He walked to the bath and leaned on the edge of the granite, feeling the temperature of the water, the warmth and essence flowing between his fingers. "It's perfect."

Sparing no moment of shame or modesty, Ena brushed aside the straps of her elegant dress. Slowly, the dress folded as it fell delicately off of her body. Ena pushed the gown aside with her foot, then stepped out of her flats onto the cold stone floor.

Normally, the cold on her soles would have stung until her blood flow heated the floor beneath her feet but she hardly felt a thing. Nerve damage. Likely permanent, even with the Providence's intervention.

That fucking dwarf, and that witch he called his queen... They would pay for the torment they put Ena through. Not only Ena, but Lady Raven, Damian, Klaus, every mage they've brought to submission, the mages who chose to take their own lives rather than live with an agonizing voice their heads.

Lavender and mint quickly brushed her vengeful thoughts aside.

Drake watched her cautiously. Unsure of what to make of Ena standing naked before him. In her fragile state, he dared not push his limits.

Ena raised a single brow, wondering why she was still the only one without clothes on. Catching on, Drake slowly removed his boots, then his tunic and trousers.

Ena sat along the edge of the granite and swung her legs over. Gently, she lowered herself into the water. The warmth enveloped her as the oils coated her skin, softening it. Drake, joining her on the other half of the bath, rested a hand on her leg, which somehow crossed into his space. He began to caress her leg and looked at her longingly.

After weeks of minimal food and exercise, Ena knew she was not looking her best. The beauticians worked wonders restoring the governess to her former composure, but her ribs were now horridly protruding through her chest and her muscles were in the early stages of atrophy, leaving her skin loose and rather unpleasant.

Drake hardly noticed, or hardly cared. He stared at her as though her beauty was all that existed in the world.

He's a fool, Ena said to herself, *a kind-hearted fool.* She worried about him.

"Tidas talked a lot about you today," Drake admitted.

"I have no doubt," Ena acknowledged. "She and I were practically sisters once I joined the City Watch. It devastated her when I requested my assignment in El Vadora. My decision was nothing against her, of course. I was haunted by this city, paranoid that I would cross paths with my father while on duty."

"Tidas understood," Drake answered Ena's thoughts.

"She sent me a bottle of my favorite wine and a ceremonial sword after I won the election." Ena laughed. "I shipped her back the empty bottle with a note, thanking her. That was our first communication since I left. And our last until most recently. How did she keep your mind occupied today?"

Tidas was a phenomenal distraction. Ena knew this well, having used her as a crutch most of her adolescent years.

"Tidas brought me to different parts of the city. Places I wouldn't think a guard would be welcomed in, but everyone knew and respected her." Ena smirked, knowing exactly the hidden spots Tidas frequented. Raised in the slums of Havana City, Tidas knew all there was to know about the sections of the city that every rich or politically active family on the hill avoided entirely. Now, being a high-ranking member of the City Watch, she knew all the secrets of the upper class, as well. Drake was elated to describe everything in detail. Even if it was just to distract him from Ena's hardship, he was thankful for it. "She also showed me the spot where she encountered her first mage—a water mage. It was a brutal scene. She still seems bothered by it, but she still admires mages even after what one of them did to her platoon."

"Tidas always sees the best in everyone," Ena said. "Believes everyone is born to be good and is forced into a life of bad. I do forget this city has some charming spots, even in the rougher parts."

Ena saw Drake looking down at his hands just under the surface of the water. Despite the good day he described, something wasn't right. He was lost in thought.

"Drake," Ena said, filling the silence. Drake looked up, the sound of his name on her lips sounding sweet like candy. "What's wrong?"

Reluctant to admit the truth, Drake took a deep breath. "That mage queen. She spoke to me." Ena was about to jump out of the bath—fear, anxiety, anger, and vengeance boiling within her—if not for Drake closing the void between them, placing his hands on her shoulders, and holding her there. He leaned in quickly and kissed her. Ena's eyes widened from being caught off guard. After mere moments of the sensation of Drake's lips on hers, Ena's muscles relaxed, her eyes closed, and she welcomed the embrace.

Drake pulled his lips away, still holding his face close to hers. "It's alright. I'm alright, for now. I told her she has no power over me, and then she disappeared."

Finding it hard to believe, Ena was about to protest. If Ena couldn't even hold her own against the mage, then how could Drake? He may be strong, especially after discovering his magical talent, but he was still undisciplined in both mind and body. Ena's protest ended before it could start when Drake kissed her again—this time, much more sensually. He placed a hand behind her head, sliding his fingers beneath her hair. His other hand found its way behind her, resting against the small of her back, pulling her into him.

Ena returned kiss after kiss, wrapping both arms behind him, holding Drake tightly. She then wrapped her legs around either side of him and locked them around his waist.

Rising from the bath, Drake gripped Ena beneath her thighs, supporting her as he walked, dripping wet, over to the bed. Not caring about soaking the sheets, the two lovers climbed under the covers.

◆◆◆◆◆◆◆◆◆

The fire crackled as it consumed one of the last remaining logs. Warmth emanated, being absorbed by the two bodies lying naked on the floor atop a blanket in front of the hearth. The bed needed time to dry, so the couple moved to the floor, using dry blankets to hold in the warmth. Flames danced in their eyes as their heartbeats slowed to a resting pace.

Drake's eyelids drooped, heavy with sleep. He had hardly slept since Avalon. Knowing this, Ena was careful not to disturb him as she felt his body relaxing next to hers, drifting off. Unable to even think about sleeping, she slid out from under the blankets and tossed the Providence's borrowed dress over her. With as minimal noise as possible, Ena crept out the bedroom door and into the hallway.

She paced restlessly through the hall, observing every door, viewing each meeting room, guest chamber, and closet from her room to the massive doors leading to the throne room. Every unoccupied room was coated with a thick layer of dust, another reminder of the emptiness within the palace.

Drake's words still hung over her head. *"That mage queen. She spoke to me."*

That did not sit comfortably with her. Not after what she went through.

Turning back down the corridor, Ena treaded past her room and the dining hall. A double-door matching the passage to the throne room, only smaller in size, stood in front of Ena. *This must lead to the Sheridan's chambers.* Ena was about to turn back around and finally go to bed when she noticed light coming from the thin crack between the door and the floor. Sheridan was still awake.

Ena hated the feeling of desperation, but Sheridan was the only person who could help her make any sense of this. She approached the door and knocked.

◆◆◆◆◆◆◆◆◆

After dinner, Sheridan meant to retire right away for the evening, but his mind wandered. Too many things have happened in the past few months—too many people, too many enemies, too many variables. Myra and Mida. Typhus. Eriputes. Athenia. Lia. The Providence. Havyn. The *Encantorum*.

The Encantorum...

If Myra somehow intended to lead a mage rebellion, maybe the faeries documented some advice in their tome of how to achieve peace. Or, Sheridan shuddered, how to defeat them. He hated thinking of violence as an option, but realistically, he had to prepare for the worst. Just as he should have done years ago.

A younger version of himself once lived in the dwarven kingdoms of Garmoire, where a disciplined army of mages attacked the Surface kingdom where he was stationed as a guard. The kingdom was nearly lost, and Sheridan's arm was lost entirely. The mages were all killed in the attack, and there hadn't been another since that he was aware of. Though, he wouldn't know if there was another attack since the dwarves kept to themselves and refused to ask for help.

Stubborn bastards, Sheridan recalled.

They were his people, but he was left for dead, along with thousands of others. Sheridan fled from the chaos, holding his damaged arm. Broken in nearly every place, bone and muscle protruding from multiple lacerations, losing blood by the bucketful, Sheridan knew his arm was gone for good. No white mage in the world, except perhaps a Providence, could save it. Nor would he have that opportunity, seeing as dwarves were extremely paranoid and superstitious about magic, viewing it as witchcraft. He was cautious never to reveal his kinetic magic around any other dwarves, as he likely would have been executed by the same men he fought alongside.

Finally, after running, or limping, for miles, Sheridan stumbled across the vacant campsite of some hunters—probably out on a quick nighttime hunt, Sheridan deduced—and took a knife from his belt, severed his arm at the socket of his shoulder, and cauterized the stump after placing the blade of his knife in the active flames of the campfire until it glowed white. Sheridan hadn't intended to pass out from the pain. He hadn't intended to still be there when the hunters returned.

Two elves and two humans. The hunters patched other wounds on Sheridan's body before carrying him another hundreds of miles south back to their homes in the far north of Fairmarq. Here, Sheridan built himself a new arm and used his magic to move it around as if he never lost an arm. Prosthetics were a common design of the dwarves, having the talent for mechanics and making them work with the natural musculoskeletal system of one's body, so everyone believed that to be truth. However, no dwarven prosthetic could ever make up for the damage that had been done.

That was ten years ago. Sheridan never returned to Garmoire, nor could he. He likely would have been considered a deserter for fleeing the battle and not dying with his fellow soldiers.

Could the mages who attacked Garmoire that day be connected to Myra? It was possible, Sheridan admitted, but why wait ten years? What interest would Myra have with the dwarves?

Flipping through the pages of the *Encantorum*, Sheridan roughly translated what he could. Beside the massive faerie tome lay open a dozen other books with faerie writings the Providence found in her library. Any spare moment the dwarf had was spent comparing the symbols and words from the *Encantorum* with those in the other faerie books, hoping to make a connection and create some words that formed proper sentences. It helped that Sheridan was fluent in dwarven and the common tongue of the humans, also with a strong understanding of elven. All languages that derived from the faerie language thousands and thousands of years ago.

Despite all that Sheridan has read and studied so far, he hardly broke through the surface. The next few pages were filled with illustrations of different weapons and armor utilized by the Dymund Auryx, an elite type of faerie soldier who could use their magic to create weapons from nothing. These weapons were real and physical, even when not in the hands of a Dymund Auryx.

Intently focused on translating part of the description of a particular sword design, Sheridan nearly jumped out of his chair when a sudden knock came at the door.

"Ahem," Sheridan cleared his throat and adjusted himself in the chair, "who's there?" A muffled "Ena" sounded through the thick oak. Sheridan eagerly responded, "Enter!"

The latch on the door lifted, and the door opened gently. Ena peered around the edge, quickly scanning the room to make sure she was in the right place. She stepped inside and shut the door behind her, careful not to let her dress get caught.

"I apologize for disturbing you, Master, but—"

"You couldn't sleep," Sheridan finished her sentence. He smiled and held out a hand, gesturing to the chair across from him at the table in the center of the room. "Have a seat. I'm sure there's plenty on your mind."

Ena warily placed herself in the seat across from the Master of Cities. She scanned the room silently, noting its similarity to the Providence's study. The same circular layout and domed ceiling, but Sheridan's was bright and a bit disorganized compared to the Providence's dimly lit, neat, meditative one. She noted, as well, that Sheridan's bed rested on a loft to her left.

"Sorry for the mess, Athenia," said the Master of Cities. "I'm doing a bit of light reading at the moment."

"I can see that," said Ena judgmentally, eyeballing the piles of books scattered open on the table. Focusing closer on the content of the books, she asked, "What *language* is that?"

Sheridan glanced at her, measuring his trust for her. How much should he tell her? *I guess trust in each other is all we have.* "Umm, the faerie language. I'm trying to decipher it. It's been lost for many generations, but I am hoping to find some information from a book the faeries left behind at the time of their demise. This one," he ran his fingers along a page of the *Encantorum*, "contains all of the secrets of the faeries, supposedly. Sort of an instruction manual, journal, and history textbook combined."

Ena spied the illustration of the sword on the page. Her eyes widened, recognizing the design. Sheridan, seeing Ena's interest spark, continued, "Ah, you recognize the sword? The same, or of similar design, as the one you took off of Drake. I'm still working through the translation, but I believe it belonged to a Dymund Auryx."

"I assumed the Dymund Auryx were a myth."

Sheridan shrugged, "Some can argue that the faeries are a myth. But every myth or legend begins with a drop of truth, Athenia. Countless generations of both of our races have lived and died, entire family names bred and phased out from existence, since the first words of this tome were penned. That sword you carried into this palace is literally older than the Kingdom of Havyn."

"How, though," Ena was in awe at the intricate symbols that resembled an alphabet on the pages, "did the sword end up in the hands of a farmer a thousand years later? That is still the question we cannot seem to answer."

Sheridan flipped forwards a few pages, careful not to break any of the brittle parchment. "Did you know the Faerie Kingdom fell in a single day?" Ena shook her head. "Me neither. But a single date is referenced as the 'day of the end of times,' or so I can understand. There are writings, or mentions of writings, in the *Encantorum* that are dated after this 'end of times.' Who knows how many faeries managed to flee from their destruction? Or, where they went?"

"Or," Ena whispered, "what they brought with them?"

"Precisely," Sheridan nodded. "It could simply be that fleeing faeries passed through Drake's village a thousand years ago, leaving behind the sword, or they settled in the village and passed the sword down through generations. For all we know, Athenia, Drake could be a distant descendant of a faerie, which could explain his ability to weave the Connections of Magic."

Ena licked her lips, eager to understand more. Her thirst for knowledge matched that of the Master of Cities. As disciplined as she was, though, learning a lost language was way above her head.

"I'm sure," Sheridan leaned back in his chair, "you did not come here to discuss a book you never knew existed until now. What's on your mind?" The question was half-sarcastic. Sheridan knew there was no shortage of things that could be bothering Ena. But there was something else...

Ena's eyes met Sheridan's, and she admitted to him, "Myra contacted Drake earlier today. He admitted it to me after dinner. He claims we have nothing to worry about, but a mage queen does not simply form a telepathic link with someone with a powerful talent for magic to say 'hello' and then leave! I cannot trust this situation at all, Sheridan! I cannot trust him... We need to prepare for an attack. Gabrenas was only the start of something bigger."

By this point, Ena's voice had risen to a stern roar. Sheridan urged her to relax, careful not to wake Drake. The chances of the governess's voice penetrating two thick doors of oak was slim, but it was best if Drake wasn't made aware they were talking about him. They wanted what was best for him, but if he threatened the safety of the entire kingdom, he couldn't be here.

He also might not be able to remain alive, but Sheridan and Ena knew this without speaking it.

"Myra, Mida, and their band of rogues are only part of what I have on my plate," said Sheridan. "I have monsters of my own that lurk these halls." Ena knew he referred to King Typhus. The princess made a comment earlier about being responsible enough to assume responsibility of the kingdom. Why plan to assume responsibility if something big wasn't either already happening or about to happen? "The king is sick.

His illness corrupts the mind, making him lose touch with reality a little more each day. Unfortunately, he is no longer fit to rule as king. And quite more unfortunate, the High King refuses to act on this because he claims the king can still physically wear the crown, so therefore he must. Truth is, Typhus owes Eriputes a disgusting amount of gold. Gold that cannot be paid back without bankrupting all of Havyn."

"Why lend King Typhus gold the High King knew could not be repaid?" Ena asked.

Sheridan smirked, "Eriputes and his dynasty have never been friends of Havyn. I wouldn't put it past him to know Typhus was not in his right mind and let him borrow as much money as he wanted, knowing he could hold it against us."

"Deceptive..."

Sheridan grunted in agreement. "There are too many factors. Too many risks no matter what we choose to do. Even doing nothing, we leave the kingdom vulnerable to Typhus making one wrong choice and leaving us to clean up the mess."

"What will you do?" Ena asked genuinely.

"Well," Sheridan sighed, "The Providence, Princess Lia, and I have discussed our options. And I may request your assistance, as much as you probably want to get back to El Vadora and never see my face ever again."

"What could I help with?"

"Deposing King Typhus, forcing him to relinquish his crown, and placing Lia on the throne all while trying not to be killed by his Keepers and the four other kingdoms of Lynidas."

Ena stood up swiftly, knocking her chair backwards. "You ask for the impossible. I will not."

"If I recall, you once told me that you've frequently done the impossible," Sheridan quipped. "I could use those odds right about now."

Red with rage, Ena wanted to scream at him. She wanted to go home. She wanted her small city with its insignificant problems. She has lost everything so far since those damned Guardians of the Faith marched into her city. She even missed Commander Veto and all of his accusatory statements and borderline insubordination.

She would *not* be responsible for a coup.

But, at the same time, how long would El Vadora stand if Sheridan was right about his concerns.

"I will help you," Ena hissed through gritted teeth. "On one condition." Sheridan nodded, willing to listen. "We finish this matter with Myra and Mida first."

Sheridan was about to argue, saying that a potential war with the mages could last years, and they didn't have years they could waste before their situation with Typhus reached a climax. He knew, though, that any amount of debate would push the governess away. She was too stubborn and independent to haggle with, but her loyalty to her position and her superiors is what held her feet in place here in the palace and not back in El Vadora.

"Agreed," Sheridan said simply.

Without another word, End turned on her heels and flew out of Sheridan's chambers and back to her room. The fire had dulled to nothing but embers. Trying to ease her frustration, she took several deep breaths before discarding her dress and climbing back under the blankets on the floor beside Drake. She needed sleep, desperately. Her emotions made it difficult to fall asleep, but not knowing if the man she slept with was her ally or enemy was what kept her up all night long.

CHAPTER 49

Awaking with the sun, with hardly any sleep, Ena stirred impatiently, restlessly. Drake had an arm draped across her waist with a hand gently clutching her stomach. The warmth from his hand was comforting.

In a normal life, she could enjoy a relaxing morning like this with a man she cared for. In a normal life, she would not be in danger constantly or protecting others from it.

While the warmth from Drake's hand was comforting at first, Ena's mind suddenly flashed back to the day he rescued her. The heat from his hands then had been from the fire he controlled within them. The same fire that Myra now found herself interested in.

Ena gently squirmed her way out of his grasp, feeling overwhelmingly flushed and anxious.

I can't do this, Ena thought. *I can't be with him. Not now. Not until this is all over.*

As she tossed the blanket off herself, careful not to disturb Drake, she realized she failed. Drake groaned and stretched next to her.

"Where are you going so early?" he asked through a yawn.

Ena whipped around, startled. Hiding her worry, she smiled at him and said, "My former life as a soldier prevents me from sleeping late. I am going to join Tidas on a morning patrol. It is time she and I caught up after all these years."

Drake blinked, sleep still in his eyes. "Is that smart knowing you're still recovering? What if you run into any danger?"

"No need to worry." Ena, still seeing concern in Drake's face, leaned in and kissed him. All worry washed from him. "Sleep. I will see you later."

Drake did as he was told, rolling over and quickly falling back asleep.

Ena quickly rushed from the room in her dress and walked out the front of the Spire. She scanned the view of the city from its peak. Would Tidas already be out and about? She could be anywhere in the city.

It was still early, though. Ena recalled their days together in the watch, trying to remember Tidus's daily schedule.

"Governess!" a voice boomed, cutting through the quiet. "What are you doing outside in the cold wearing a *dress*?"

Ena followed the source of the voice, tracing it to the stable on her right. Out from the stable marched Tidas, clad in her immaculate armor, holding the reins of a sable horse.

Tidas smirked, waving Ena over.

"Thank the gods,"' Ena sighed as she approached.

"I had a thought you might need some time away from the palace today," said Tidas. She gestured inside the stable. "There's a set of guard armor inside, along with a dozen of the best horses the Watch can offer. Take your pick, change, and meet me back out here."

By the time Ena and Tidas made it to the bottom of the hill, the city was bustling with the typical morning rush. Men and women off to work or off to the markets for the fresh morning produce, children off to school or an apprenticeship with a local tradesman or shop owner, guards beginning their morning patrols or retiring from an overnight one, and merchants readying their carts to trade with nearby towns and villages.

Everyday life for everyday people. None would ever know the danger potentially lurking until it was on top of them.

Ena led her horse, following Tidas, to the very same barracks they trained together at what feels like a lifetime ago. Ironic to see Tidas has not strayed far from her roots, where Ena did everything in her power to escape from hers. There were several guards Ena recognized from years ago, some nearly double Ena's age, but still under the command of a young captain like Tidas.

"Captain Tidas, the fearless," they called her. Did Ena doubt Tidas deserved the title? Absolutely not. She was brave, tactful, and battle-hardened.

Ena looked forward to their outing. A chance for Ena to do what she loved, and with someone she undoubtably trusted. Trust was not something she awarded many people. Damian and Klaus were the closest she came to trusting another after she left Tidas in Havana City. For Drake, as much as she felt an attraction towards him, there was hardly the same level of trust. The Providence and Sheridan... Ena was skeptical of any person in a position of power, but those two even more so.

To openly discuss deposing their king...

Ena shook the thought from her head. It was not something she wanted to be involved in, despite Sheridan's desire for her assistance. Bargaining the timeline when the deposition would take place was a feat in Ena's mind. Who knew how long the conflict with Mida and Myra could last? At least she bought herself time to think about what she wanted to do.

As squads of guards formed up and marched off, Tidas turned her horse back to Ena.

"Where are we off to, Captain?" Ena asked with a friendly amount of sarcasm.

Tidas sighed, reached behind her head to tighten the bun holding back her auburn hair. "We've been facing some trouble with protestors in the south-western region of the city."

"Isn't that near the wall?" asked Ena. "By the Brekken border?"

"Precisely. The king has increased the military presence along the border, gods know why," she shrugged. "Though, Lord Elmar has a heavy stamp of approval on that executive order, so groups have been protesting and counter-protesting the lord's involvement. Why not protest the king's initial decision, if that's what they're mad about, I don't know."

"It seems to me," Ena evaluated, "that perhaps it is Elmar who they are unhappy with, and the fact he publicly approved an aggressive decision by the king gave them a reason to speak out. I saw something similar in El Vadora when I first arrived there. The governor prior to me made a few questionable choices, which lead to an involuntary 'voluntary' abdication."

"At least that opened the door for you to show off and win them over, Governess."

Ena rolled her eyes. "You could say that. More like the city needed stability, and I provided them with that."

"Nothing is stable anymore."

Tidas kicked her heels into the hips of her sable horse and took off at a steady trot down the cobblestone road. Ena effortlessly caught up with her appaloosa, matching Tidas's speed. Pedestrians and other mounted travelers saw the glint of armor and moved to the side as the two passed by at a quickened pace. The confidence that the captain wore was new. Or, at least, new to Ena. The Tidas she knew was timid. Strong and dutiful, but timid around authority. Now, she *was* the authority, and she displayed it with an air of intimidation.

She did not alter her course as she hustled by with her back straight and her head held high. Those in her path respected the armor she wore and what it stood for, and they let her pass without questions or second thought.

They slowed their horses to a walk as the southern wall of Havana City peered over the horizon, over the shingled roofs of houses in the distance. The sun was beginning to rise later each morning and set earlier in the evening, Ena realized. Another sign of the approaching winter.

Her thoughts instantly shifted to El Vadora and how much her city would struggle this year. Most of the farms and villages were the source of El Vadora's food. With most of them burnt to a crisp with no survivors, what would their food source be? Ena supposed Commander Veto was already thinking ahead and making strides towards a resolution. As much as he drove her insane, with his old-school mindset and methodology, he cared for the city as much as Ena did, if not more.

Tidas shot Ena a look of disappointment. "I hoped to see you at the governor's gathering, but you were not there. I led the escort for Havana City's governor."

"I have never attended those," Ena scoffed. "Far too much political quarrel for my taste. Besides, little forgotten cities like mine tend to be overlooked when invitations are sent out."

"*Someone* didn't overlook you or your little forgotten city," Tidas smirked.

"Do you mean Master Sheridan or Drake?"

"Both, I suppose. Sheridan took you under his wing for a purpose. Drake happened to stumble into your path. Coincidence or fate?"

Before Ena could respond, Tidas kicked her heels into her horse and took off with a trot into a city square. A crowd was gathering along the edges of the seven roads that connected at the center of the square. All were standing patiently, waiting for something. Murmurs between one another caused a dull roar.

At the center of the square, Tidas approached an island in the center of the cobblestones. Dismounting her horse, she marched over to a group of ten men and women, all humans, who were painting words onto large pieces of parchment. One of the men seemed to be telling the others what to do.

"Pardon me, sir," Tidas addressed the man, who could not be much older than Ena. The man stepped away from the others and brushed the hair out of his eyes. "Are you the one who organized this protest?" The man nodded. "You know the rules. Organized and peaceful. At sundown, you'll need to disband until tomorrow. If things get too rowdy, the Watch has the authority to break up the protest, and any resistance will be met by force and arrest."

The man nodded again. "Absolutely" Cap'ain. We only want the public to know the truth."

"*Safely*," emphasized Tidas. The man returned to painting the signs.

Tidas turned on her heels and returned to her horse. Ena remained mounted and looked skeptically at the group of protestors. They all stood with their signs as their leader addressed the crowd around them.

WARMONGER

OUR LORD BETRAYS US

HE DOESN'T WANT US TO KNOW

OUT WITH ELMAR

The protestors began handing out dozens of signs as people from the crowd gathered around them. They joined in chanting the words on the signs.

Tidas circled her horse around the city square, ensuring that the guards she assigned here for the day were, in fact, here. To her satisfaction, the City Watch was present and accounted for.

Ena stayed in tow as Tidas inspected the area for any danger. Once the protest was in full-swing, Tidas relaxed a bit knowing the square was well protected. Everything was going smoothly. The protestors were being respectful of the law.

"They *really* do not like Lord Elmar." Ena observed the fervor of the protestors as the group continued to grow with supporters. "I never imagined he was so unpopular." Lord Elmar had been the lord of Havana for at least a decade. Following a rather successful first few years, the socioeconomic structure of Havana was strengthened. Given Elmar's elven ancestry, his election helped unify humans and elves across all of Havyn.

"Elmar isn't exactly the man people thought he was," Tidas explained. "I personally don't think he deserves this kind of hate, especially when it's the king making these military moves. The public doesn't realize that, though, and Elmar has an unbreakable loyalty to King Typhus, so he won't put the blame on him."

"What kind of man is Elmar, then?"

"The kind who wants control of everything and does not respect the boundaries of the law," she said vaguely. "He puts his name on everything to ensure everyone knows who he is, so he isn't overshadowed by the king or Sheridan."

Elmar was more of a nuisance or a thorn in the side, but Ena agreed with Tidas—Elmar did not deserve *this* kind of hate.

By the end of the day, the protestors disbanded as agreed upon. The Watch didn't need to intervene at all. Once the sun had set and the city square returned to normal, Tidas and Ena were the last of the guards to depart back to their barracks. The streets were quiet as they walked their horses back.

"You know," Tidas said on their way back, "Drake really loves you."

Ena rolled her eyes. "You told him about lavender and mint."

"I did. And he told me about your night together at the inn in Gabrenas." She gave Ena a conniving smile. "Admit it, you feel for him, too."

"I admit it." Ena refused to meet Tidas's gaze. "I feel for him. The strongest I have ever felt for someone before. The closest I have ever allowed myself to get with another person, besides you."

"But..."

"But," Ena continued, "he is a mage. A godsdamned powerful one."

"What is wrong with being a mage?" Tidas snapped. She was always a proponent for equality. Mages, whether they practice the white magic of healers or the elemental magic of fire, earth, water, are people all the same. "He is a good man."

"Relax, Tidas," Ena calmed her. "I have no quarrel with any mage for the sake of being a mage. That is no fault of their own, as it is no fault of Drake's. He *is* undoubtably a good man, but he is dangerous, Tidas.

His power is nearly unmatched." She sighed. "He has has drawn the attention of the enemy, who wishes to use his power against us."

Tidas saw the conflict on Ena's face. "Do you think they will succeed?"

"I..." Ena hesitated. "I believe they could."

The barracks came into view. Their day was coming to a close. Ena would need to return to the palace.

"Stay," Tidas requested. Ena looked at her curiously. "Stay with me. Just for a few days until Sheridan hears word from Avalon about their search for Mida." Ena thought about it for a moment before nodding. Tidas smiled. "Great. You're always welcome in my home."

CHAPTER 50

Drake paced the halls of the empty palace. Boredom and worry consumed him. He was prevented from leaving the palace by the guards at the entryway; though, he was not told why. He assumed Ena would know, so he waited around for her to return from her patrol with Tidas all day. He crossed paths with no one else that day, with the exception of Sheridan. The dwarf passed him in one of the halls and told him he was safest in the palace. He made no mention of Ena.

That was yesterday morning. Ena never returned that night. The only notice of her whereabouts being a note from Tidas addressed to Sheridan explaining Ena was safe in her care. The Master of Cities hadn't questioned it—had half-expected it—by Drake's intuition.

Now, still unable to leave and still no word from Ena, Drake's mind wandered. As he observed a painting of a long-dead former king of Havyn in the throne room, the emptiness suddenly grew even quieter. The eerie silence made Drake scan his surroundings.

Someone else is here, Drake thought.

A blood-curdling feminine laugh echoed off the walls around him. "You are never alone, young mage."

Myra...

"No mage is ever alone," Myra's voice reverberated. "I am with you. Watching you. Protecting you. Those closest to you fear you. They will harm you, use you, and lock you away. Be free. Do not fear the power you possess, pup."

Drake put his hands over his ears, trying to block out the ominous voice.

"Not again!" he shouted. "Get away!"

"I am not the one to fear. You fear yourself and the magic you cannot properly control. You fear your friends and allies, for they cannot trust you. I can lead you down a path to greatness, if you will let me."

"Never!" Drake pressed his palms over his ears even harder, useless to stop Myra's temptation.

The silence broke apart as footsteps on the marble floors broke Drake out of his trance. Voices of people talking amongst one another grew louder as they approached. Sheridan and the Providence passed the threshold of the corridor leading to the Providence's study from the throne room. They both came to a halt, noting Drake's fearful expression. Without another word, without even questioning what may have just occurred, they briskly closed the gap between themselves and Drake.

Sheridan was the first to speak. "Don't speak a word of whatever just happened. Not here."

"Quickly," the Providence waved them along to follow her, "back to my chambers."

◆◆◆◆◆◆◆◆◆

The Providence opened the domed sunroof in her study, allowing sunlight to pour into the room, enlightening the botanical garden. The leaves reacted positively to the sudden overabundance of light, shifting to absorb as much as possible.

Drake was led to a chair just outside of the garden. He sat obediently, waiting as the Providence and Master Sheridan whispered among themselves near the Providence's desk. Drake observed the walls of bookshelves, the medical beds, the desk scattered with notes and letters, and the infinite colors of the various flowers and plants in the garden before him.

"Alright, kid," Sheridan said as he approached. "With your permission, the Providence is going to use her magic to help you. It's no secret who has been making unwanted visits in your head. I have some questions myself. If you don't mind."

Shaking his head, Drake responded, "Not at all. If there is a way to stop this and protect Athenia, then I'm all for it."

Sheridan exchanged a glance with the Providence as she stepped into the garden. Holding a mortar and pestle, she began gathering the petals from a bright orange flour with a blue pistil. An appetizing aroma released into the air as the Providence ground the contents of the petals.

"Drake," the Providence walked to him. He met her bright blue eyes. "I am going to spread this poultice over your temples as I work my magic. Its purpose is to help ease your mind as I try and find where the mage queen has you compromised. With any luck, I can seal off that part of your mind she is accessing, or help you fend her off if she tries contacting you again."

Nervously, Drake nodded. The Providence proceeded with her task. She stood behind Drake and placed the tips of her fingers on his temples. She added a bit of pressure and rubbed the poultice in small circular motions into his skin.

The ingredients of the poultice instantly made Drake's mind ease as the flesh around his temples tingled.

Sheridan pulled up a chair in front of the relaxed farmer and prepared his questions.

"First things first," Sheridan began, "I want to officially thank you myself for your daring rescue of Governess Athenia. Your efforts in Gabrenas were valiant, and losing her would have been a heavy burden to bear."

Before Drake could reply, Sheridan continued, "About your rescue... Was that the first time you used your magic?"

"Yes and no," Drake blinked.

"How so?"

"I used it once before to put out a fire that was started in an attempt to kill Ena's two other bodyguards. I wasn't aware of my magic at the time until I somehow put the fire out. I was able to learn to control my magic enough to prove to Lady Raven I could be more of an asset than a liability"

"When you began willingly using your magic, how did you feel? Did you feel in control? Nervous at all? Exhilarated?"

Drake had to think about his answer for a moment. In all reality, he had acted so fast, without thought or selfish ambition, only the blinding desire to save Ena. He explained as much to Sheridan, who nodded in understanding.

"When did Myra first contact you?" asked Sheridan.

Drake felt a sudden soothing feeling throughout his body. Whatever the Providence was doing, it seemed to be working.

"The other day," he answered. "After we got here."

"Was that the only time?"

"Besides today? Yes."

"What is it she wants from you?"

"To teach me to control my magic, I think."

"This goes without saying," Sheridan leaned back in his chair, "but you do realize if you give in to her temptations, then she will weaponize you against us, right?"

Drake blinked, "Of course! I would never!"

"I only say that," Sheridan explained, "because someone like her has managed to sway countless mages against their own friends and family. You are no different from them."

Drake was about to argue. About to say he was somehow different from the other mages who fell under Myra's spell. About to fight for his loyalty to Ena. Then, a sharp pain cracked through his skull like lightning before subsiding like an ebbing wave. He gritted his teeth and grunted.

"There." The Providence lowered her hands. "I believe I found where Myra has been accessing your mind from. I have placed temporary guards to shield her attempts."

"How?" Drake rubbed his aching head.

"I..." the Providence hesitated. "I do not have a complete understanding of her magic. Mindrending is a rarity among the Connections. Nor does my magic itself directly combat her ability. I used my white magic to discourage activity in the part of your brain she is connected to. The less activity means the less of a connection Myra will have to be able to communicate. Or, at least, that is my theory."

Theory?! She just messed with something inside my head because of a theory? What if something went wrong? Drake had so many questions. But there was one question in particular that burned in his mind. "What part of my mind is she accessing?"

The Providence smiled and gave him a sympathetic look. "The part that deals with protecting the ones you love. The same part Myra was first introduced to."

"So, what does that mean?" Drake grew pale.

"You will not be able to see Athenia for some time," she placed a flawless hand on his shouter. "I am truly sorry, Drake. If you see her, your brain activity in that area may increase again."

"But," Sheridan scratched his red beard in thought, "by keeping him from her... Would the lack of access to her make his desire for her grow, also increasing his brain activity? Or would the isolation make Myra more apt to break through that shield of yours and gain control?"

Speaking about me as if I'm not even here...

The Providence shrugged. "Those possibilities exist. As I said, counteracting a mindrender's magic is not in my skill set."

In that moment, Drake had never felt lonelier. Even more lonesome than the days he spent in the forest after watching mages burn his home to the ground. Solemnly, Drake stood and walked out of the Providence's study. He vaguely heard voices speaking to him—the Providence and Sheridan—but he couldn't understand a word they said. He returned to pacing the halls of the empty palace.

All alone.

◆◆◆◆◆◆◆◆◆

After Drake left, Sheridan and the Providence sat in silence, reflecting. The Providence was questioning herself and her abilities. She didn't need to vocalize her thoughts, for her face and mannerisms spoke loud enough. She flipped through the same books and notes on her desk over and over again, pretending to be busy.

Meanwhile, Sheridan sat across from her at her desk and watched her. Admitting her shortcomings always set her off into a wave of anxious self-reflection. Not that it happened often, Sheridan noted. The Providence was the most powerful mage he knew. Some things, though, even her magic could not solve.

The simple fact was that Myra had the upper hand. With all else they had going on, facing a hidden enemy seemed impossible. It *was* impossible. Until Myra played her next hand, stopping her was an unattainable goal.

The Providence took out a pen and began writing a letter in her eloquent penmanship. Sheridan tried not to look at what she was writing. Prying into the business of the Faith was not something he desired to do. He couldn't help but wonder what his counterpart was thinking, though.

Seeing Sheridan glance uneasily at the words she wrote, the Providence addressed him, "I am writing to the Providence of Fairmarq. She and I correspond over matters regarding the Faith often enough where I feel comfortable asking an abnormal question. Fairmarq is the largest and most populated of the kingdoms in Lynidas. They must encounter mages from time to time, even mindrenders."

"You sure it's wise to announce what we're dealing with to others?" Sheridan said skeptically.

"Sheridan," the Providence's eyes narrowed. "Did Myra say Havyn is the only kingdom she is infiltrating? No. We may not be the only ones dealing with this."

A gentle knock sounded at the double doors. The Guardians of the Faith remained at ease, signaling no danger. The Providence nodded at her Guardians, who turned and opened the doors.

Lia strode in with her Keepers in tow. She had a blank expression on her face. Not her typical cheerful aura. Clearly she was still not pleased with the two of them. Her Keepers stopped in the middle of the room as she approached the desk. Pulling up a chair next to Sheridan, she sighed heavily.

"I apologize for avoiding you both these past few days," the princess brushed a piece of her chestnut hair over her ear. "Don't think I'm not still furious with you, but there are important things happening in my kingdom. My kingdom—*our* kingdom—needs a leader, and Typhus is *not* a leader."

Sheridan and the Providence exchanged nervous glances. Never before had they discussed this topic within earshot of her Keepers before. Their loyalty was questionable. Where did their allegiances lie? With the princess they vowed to protect since her birth? Or, with the king? Keepers were bound by the law of the Concordat to protect the royal family. What happened if the members of a royal family were at arms with one another?

It appeared even the Keepers were unsure how to react. They shifted uncomfortably after Lia openly announced her opposition of her father. Not so uncomfortably, though, that they indicated this was the first they were hearing of it, Sheridan noted.

"What happened?" asked Sheridan.

"He's gone," Lia spat. "All that's left of him are remnants of the human being he used to be. I don't even know what he is anymore." The Providence and Sheridan responded with confusion. "My chambers upstairs are down the hall from his. All I could hear the past few days was him mumbling nonsense. Talking to people who aren't there. I finally had enough and pushed past his Keepers into his room to confront him. It's *disgusting!* The entire room is torn apart, smelling of *shit*, and completely unfit for someone to live in..."

Sheridan reflected on the time he snuck into Typhus's chambers to acquire his black journal. The room hadn't been in good shape then. He couldn't even begin to imagine how bad it was now after weeks of the king refusing to leave.

"And then," Lia continued, "he grabbed my arm and tried to hit me."

Sheridan flew out of his chair. "He *what?!*"

Lia lifted the sleeve of her right arm. Black and purple fingerprints on her upper arm wrapped around her swollen triceps. The Providence was at her side instantly with that magical glow on her hands applying them to the princess's bruise. Within moments, the bruise dulled to yellow until it faded completely.

"He grabbed me hard and started yelling at me. I pulled away, then he tried to punch me. My Keepers stopped him, but then his Keepers took out their swords. Typhus kept screaming at me as if I was someone else. Probably my mother, as usual. I left and came right here."

Judging by the unscathed armor of the Keepers behind Lia, their standoff with Typhus's Keepers ended without violence. Sheridan questioned their loyalty before—he still did. If they raised arms against Typhus to protect Lia, though, Sheridan may start to trust them. Lia's trust in them was apparent by their presence in this room. Why shouldn't she trust the men who have protected her since birth?

Sheridan sighed. "It's time we make a decision." His eyes glanced at the Keepers standing ten steps away. Nervous about their reaction to his next statement, he stuttered. "We—We need to take the throne. We need to take that power from him so we can rectify his wrongdoings. Mages at one doorstep and High Alta on the other. I've had enough."

"Sheridan," the Providence warned, "we must be mindful that for those reasons we should be cautious of our next move. I cannot condone such an act until we can arrest Mida."

"Do you understand what waiting even longer could do?" Sheridan raised his voice. "Typhus is going to end up killing someone, or having one of his hidden spies kill someone else. I'll be damned if Lia ends up dead because we refused to stop Typhus in time."

"Typhus has not left his chambers in weeks, Sheridan. Let him stay where he is. He's more harm to himself than he is anyone else while he keeps himself locked away."

"And what happens when he leaves his chambers? What do we do then?"

One of the Keepers behind them cleared his throat. Sheridan, the Providence, and Lia turned towards the sound. "Pardon my interruption. I want to ensure you that Princess Lia's protection is of utmost importance. Regardless of the king's status, our vows are to protect the princess even at the cost of our lives."

"What did those vows say about confronting another Keeper?" Sheridan asked.

The other Keeper spoke up. "Sir, many of us Keepers have subtle differences in how our vows are interpreted. Those of us with any respect or chivalry will lay down our lives for the royal family member we are assigned to, no matter the enemy."

"Would Typhus's Keepers feel the same?" Sheridan challenged. "Would they defend their king even if he raised a sword against his own daughter?"

"They've proven that twice now," Lia said. "I have no trust for the king or his Keepers."

Sheridan looked at Lia, then back at her Keepers. "I have little trust for *any* Keepers. But if you trust yours, then I suppose it may be time to start looking past the armor at the men underneath."

Lia smiled. "I do trust my Keepers. I have my entire life."

"Good," the Providence nodded. "We must all trust each other as we navigate the treacherous waters ahead."

"Indeed," agreed Sheridan. "I still feel that Typhus is a problem we should deal with sooner than later, but I respect your concerns, Providence. I'll leave it to Lia to be the tiebreaker. She'll be our new queen soon enough."

"I think we need to allow the mages to play their next hand," Lia admitted. "High Alta may retaliate against us if Typhus is deposed. At least right now they are cautiously distant."

"Fine," Sheridan grumbled. "One condition. Stay far away from your father. Even if it means staying in one of the guest chambers down here with us."

Lia nodded.

CHAPTER 51

A few days later, every guard received their assignments for the morning, and Tidas tasked herself with monitoring the banking district. Though it was not the most exciting task, Ena joined anyway. Big things were happening in the banking district. After several days of sanctioned, peaceful protests, many of the more prominent businesses in Havana City began to rally behind the protestors. These businesses demanded that their shared bank, the Havana Trust, drop Lord Elmar as a client. Once the Havana Trust refused, the businesses immediately requested the withdrawal and transfer of their funds to the National Bank of Havyn. The City Watch was called, at the request of the National Bank, to ensure all funds were successfully transferred safely.

Horse-drawn carts stacked with gold and silver lined the street in front of The Havana Trust as Tidas blew a whistle, signaling the convoy to begin moving. Nearly two hundred guards were present as the carts slowly clattered their wooden spoked wheels down the cobblestone street three blocks away. The National Bank of Hayvn was a cathedral in comparison to the Havana Trust. The massive structure protected the wealth of thousands of Havyn's elite society and government along with many popular industries and businesses. Hired guards stood immobile along the outside walls at all hours of the day and night. President Aroy himself waited at the street's edge to greet them.

"Captain Tidas," Aroy dipped his head. Once Tidas dismounted her horse, Aroy took her hand in his and kissed the top of her gauntlet—a common sign of respect among the aristocracy.

"President Aroy," Tidas dipped her head in return. "We will remain present during the unloading of money, for added protection."

"Many thanks. Keep the public at a healthy distance. Natural curiosity may cause more harm than good if not kept in check." Tidus nodded, giving Aroy leave to oversee the exchange of funds from the carriages.

Ena stood by her horse and watched as employees of the bank carried crates of gold and silver inside. After two hours, it felt like nothing had been done. The day would drag by painstakingly slow.

These were the days Ena certainly was happy to leave behind when she left this city. There was nothing exciting about watching a group of rich people counting their money.

That is, until Sheridan appeared with Lord Elman in tow. Elmar, Lord of Havana, stood over twice Sheridan's height. His lanky figure and slight crop to the ears that stuck out from beneath his sleek, black hair proved his elven heritage; though, there had not been a pure-blooded elf in his family tree for several generations. He wore an odd, mint-colored robe that draped to the cobblestones beneath his feet—a similar attire was worn by the elven sages of Etherea.

Ena narrowed her eyes. She distrusted the lord. While she attempted to keep her own beliefs separate from those of the protestors she just spent days watching and listening to, she couldn't help but understand their concerns. Elmar hadn't even spoken yet, but Ena could tell he was sly and self-motivated. The way he walked, the way his eyes darted around as if he was being followed, every mannerism screamed discomfort inside of Ena.

Elmar stopped a few paces away as Sheridan approached Ena. "Ah, Governess Athenia! It is nice to see you out and about back to your normal health. And Captain Tidas," he held out his metal hand and shook Tidas's gauntleted one—metal-on-metal clanking together, "how are you both today?"

"I am well enough." Ena dropped her guard around the dwarf. "Still recovering, but much better than when I arrived."

"Master Sheridan," Tidas's attention was drawn to the carriages of gold being unloaded. She occasionally shifted her gaze to Sheridan as she spoke. "I am well today. I wonder, did you get the notice I sent earlier this week?"

Sheridan's brow furrowed. "I'm afraid not. Where did you send it?"

"I followed the typical chain of command. Sent it to the guard commander, who then confirmed he sent it your way."

"Hmm," Sheridan scratched his beard trying to recall a letter addressed from Tidas landing on his desk. "I admit my attention has been all over the place lately, but I know I did not receive a letter from you."

It was true, though. Ena was with Tidas when she sent the letter. It would be concerning if the letter did not make it to the Spire at all. Even more concerning if the letter was misplaced and found by someone else.

"Pardon me." Lord Elmar quickly closed the gap between himself and Sheridan. "What were the contents of this letter, Captain?"

"I apologize, my lord," her full attention was taken from her task to Lord Elmar's sudden interest in their conversation. "I am not at liberty to discuss the contents in an open space. The letter was sealed and addressed to the Master of Cities for the purpose of confidentiality."

"Captain," Elmar held back a scowl. "I am granting you liberty to discuss it openly. As you can see, the only people on this entire city block, besides us, are your guards."

Then why so paranoid, Lord Elmar? Ena thought.

Tidas looked to Sheridan, who understood Tidas's defensiveness. Enclosed letters were enclosed for a purpose. Sheridan rolled his eyes at Elmar's insistence, but nodded his head.

"Fine," Tidas conceded. "The Watch received a letter from Lady Raven. She and her convoy were about a week away at a comfortable pace. I had responded and said the sooner the better, but depending on the size of her convoy, a week may be the best we get."

"Great news," Sheridan responded. "What of the situation in Gabrenas?"

"No sign of him." *Him* being Mida. "Raven deduced that he escaped the city."

"Shit," Sheridan muttered. He turned his attention to Elmar. "Once Raven arrives with her convoy, Havana City will be well protected. Until then, we must raise our internal and external defenses. We must close the gate and monitor all who come and go. The guards inside of the city must be on high alert."

"Slow down, Master," Elmar placed a pale hand on Sheridan's shoulder. "We need not raise any alarms or build our defenses since nothing has happened to cause a threat. Your fears only increased risk of disaster in Avalon. I will not have that happening in Havana."

"With all due respect, Lord Elmar," Ena, who had been silent up until this moment, spoke up, "you have no idea what you are talking about. The torment I underwent was not induced by my own fear. I almost died at the hands of monsters. Monsters who are going to target this city. We need all guards armed and ready."

"With all due respect, Governess," he sneered, "I find it difficult to believe where your priorities lie given that you have amassed hundreds of guards to stand here and do nothing." He gestured a hand to the stationary company of guards standing back as the gold of the Havana Trust's most valuable clients flowed into the National Bank. "When those monsters *actually* target the city, *then* the gates will close. I will not induce panic in my city before it is needed."

"Then you are a fool to not take this more seriously," Tidas lashed back. Before allowing Elmar to respond, she withdrew from the conversation and marched towards the guards standing by President Aroy as he instructed his employees.

Noticing Tidas approach, Aroy looked up and saw Elmar standing across the street with Sheridan and Ena. He smiled sarcastically and shouted, "Lord Elmar! You have made me a very rich man. Keep up the fine work and I'll be the only bank still operating in this city. I look forward to spending all of this extra money on my wedding."

Elmar locked eyes with Aroy and grinded his teeth. The lord refused to respond and turned his back towards the president of the rival bank and walked away. Elmar was not a stupid man. He knew the consequences of the Havana Trust backing him up and allowing a lot of their biggest clients to close their accounts. The Havana Trust would now gouge him and his accounts to make up for their loss of funding.

After Elmar was gone, Sheridan and Ena looked at one another. Sheridan looked defeated, embarrassed.

"I know," Sheridan said quietly.

"You could have said something," Ena put a hand on her hip, glaring at the dwarf.

"I know."

"You could have stood up for me. You could have ordered him to stand down."

"Athenia, you know it's more complicated than that. I can't walk into El Vadora and order you to sound the alarm and lock down your entire city. There are checks and balances in place. The most I could do is order you to place more guards at the gate, which is exactly what I'm going to do. If Elmar won't shut the gates, then you and Tidas can watch them closely for any signs of Mida and be ready for Raven's arrival."

Ena hesitated a moment. "Yes, sir. We will finish our duty here and watch the gate tomorrow. Raven should be here within a few days."

Seeing the frustration on Ena's face, Sheridan apologized. Not that he needed to. He was correct, after all. Although the Master of Cities is the leader of the democracy in Havyn, the lords of each region stood against unnecessary imbalance of power by one person. The Concordat has entire chapters written about what the Master of Cities could and could not do and what the lords can and cannot do in response to the Master of Cities. Ena was not ignorant of those rules, but she did feel strongly that Elmar was being foolish.

"If anything drastic occurs," Ena continued, "we will notify you in person. Letters and couriers clearly cannot be trusted."

Sheridan nodded in agreement prior to departing in the same direction following Elmar. Ena couldn't pretend to understand the difficulty of Sheridan's job. She and the dwarf saw eye-to-eye on many things, so she could assume that his trust for Elmar was limited, yet he insisted on having their monthly morning patrols of the city.

Perhaps to keep a close eye on the lord, Ena thought.

By the end of the day, more than twenty-five million gold had been deposited into the National Bank of Havyn, leaving the Havana Trust with an unavoidable deficit. Once the last of the empty carriages left down the cobblestone streets, protestors opposing Lord Elmar gathered and cracked open barrels of wine to celebrate. They considered it a victory.

Ena was not so convinced.

CHAPTER 52

Sheridan searched through the scattered pile of letters and notes on his desk. No sign of the letter from Tidas. Sheridan confirmed Tidas's story with the guard commander, who swore on his life that he passed the letter off to the palace courier. The palace courier then swore on his own life that anything received was hand delivered to either Sheridan's chambers or the Providence's study.

"It *has* to be here somewhere," Sheridan grew flustered. A knock sounded on the oak doors. Sheridan didn't look up from his search. "Come in." The Providence and four Guardians of the Faith entered the room.

"Sheridan, I got your message—what in the world are you doing?" she asked as the dwarf threw papers and scrolls all over the floor around him.

Sheridan grunted and looked up at her. "Did you happen to receive a letter from Captain Tidas?"

"No. Do you intend to tear apart my desk to check for yourself?" The Providence tilted her head.

"No," Sheridan's eyes narrowed, unamused by his counterpart's sarcasm.

"What did she need?"

"Lady Raven is on her way here with no news of Mida's whereabouts."

"I see..."

"I'm furious that a note as important as that somehow disappeared after supposedly being delivered to the palace." Sheridan continued to ravage through the loose papers, tearing many of them as they flew through the air.

The Providence rushed over to Sheridan's side and placed a glowing hand on his back and moved it up and down gently. The soft aura eased Sheridan's tension instantly. He released an audible sigh and fell back into the chair behind him. The Providence pulled up a chair next to him.

"What's done is done," she said. "I understand the concern, but you now know what the letter said. Let us prepare for Lady Raven's arrival and keep a close eye out for Mida and Myra. You alerted the City Watch?"

Sheridan shook his head. "Elmar wouldn't let me." He explained the confrontation Elmar had with him, Tidas, and Ena and the lord's refusal to bend.

"We seem to hit a wall with every step we take..." The Providence rested her elbow on the table's surface and placed her chin in her palm. "This is becoming an exhausting, repetitive issue."

The Providence observed the mess of papers in front of her. She noticed the only items untouched were a stack of ancient books. "I forgot I lent you those. How are your faerie studies?"

"Great, actually." Sheridan sat up in his seat and reached for the *Encantorum*. Gradually, he flipped open the cover and brushed aside the first fifty or so pages until he stopped on the spot he left off at. "I'm starting to understand the language, thanks to the other books you gave me. The parts I understand mostly describe their history, but some parts of their history hint at magical artifacts and techniques that haven't been heard of in centuries, if ever at all."

"Fascinating," the Providence said unenthusiastically.

What the Providence didn't know that Sheridan was beginning to learn for himself was the centuries of animosity between the faeries and the non-faerie magic-users, dubbed with the term "mages." The faeries were practically immortal, and with their powerful displays of magic, they were viewed as gods among the common races—humans, elves, and dwarves.

Once it became clear that humans and elves were capable of possessing similar magical qualities, the faeries became less worshipped as gods. While they still held high honor among their people, being demoted from the rank of gods to above-average mortals caused the early faeries great jealousy and disdain.

Over time, the faeries began to oppress their subjects, mostly the humans. Elves were seen as having purer blood and better control over the Connections of Magic, which gave the faeries a desire to hone and control their talents and treat the elven race as close to equals as possible.

The humans, understanding their inequal treatment, began to rise up.

An army of humans without magical talent could be easily devastated by a single seasoned faerie. This instance occurred more times than Sheridan cared to count during his brief introduction to the *Encantorum*. It wasn't until the human mages began to organize themselves and develop their skills did they fortify their race's armies and stand a chance against their faerie oppressors.

Sheridan was still navigating his way through the pages of the forgotten language, but he gathered that the first mage rebellion ended with blood and destruction on both sides. The reconciliation following the fallout only temporarily bandaged the situation. Several thousand years later, the Mage Wars wreaked havoc on the world and caused the untimely demise of the faerie race.

Now, mages were rising up for a third time. The reason? Sheridan sincerely hoped the *Encantorum* could help him understand.

A hasty rap sounded at the door. Before Sheridan and the Providence could react, the rapping started again more impatiently than the first time. Alarmed, the Providence sends one of her Guardians to open the door.

Instantly upon opening, Princess Lia barged in, tears rolling down her face and her Keepers in tow with swords drawn.

"Sheridan!" Lia wept as she entered.

The Guardians of the Faith, sensing potential danger, raised their staves and huddled around the Providence.

"Lia! What is it?" Sheridan shoved his chair behind him and rushed to meet Lia, who fell to her knees into Sheridan's arms and sobbed into his shoulder. Her Keepers, aware of whatever was upsetting the princess, slammed the doors to the chambers shut and raised their swords in front of them.

"My father! He–He..." Lia struggled to catch her breath. "He is coming here, and he's angry."

"What happened?" the Providence asked.

"He saw that man—Drake?—wandering the halls. He started asking him questions and got angry and confused. I saw him hit Drake in the face with his sword and then grabbed him and started dragging him across the floor." She wiped her eyes. "It all happened right outside my room. I ordered my Keepers to stop him, but his Keepers interfered and started arguing with us. Typhus then told his Keepers to arrest us, so we ran. Oh gods, he's here!"

The huge oak door shuddered as something slammed against the other side. Then again, even harder.

"Lia!" Typhus screamed from the hall. "Get out here now!"

Finally, the door burst open, the latch breaking from the wood and sending splinters flying. Typhus's Keepers pushed their way inside with swords and kite shields raised. The Guardians of the Faith tightened their box around the Providence and dropped into a defensive stance. Sheridan took Lia's arm and pulled her behind the Providence's Guardians. Her Keepers followed and stood en garde with swords raised.

Silence filled the room, only to be broken by Typhus's eerily steady steps as his boots pounded heavily on the stone, walking into the room between his Keepers. Behind him, he dragged Drake by his hair. Drake grunted and winced in pain as he gripped Typhus's muscled hands, attempting poorly to pry open his fingers. Typhus stopped in front of the table littered with letters and documents and effortlessly tossed Drake like a sack of flour onto the table with a heavy thud. More papers scattered onto the floor.

Drake lifted his head and glanced at Sheridan with one eye open. The other was swollen with a gash on his brow, pouring crimson. He groaned as he flipped from his stomach onto his back. Heaving with each breath, Sheridan could guess that some ribs were broken.

Many moments passed of near-perfect silence, Drake's meager grumbles and sharp breaths were the only noises. Both pairs of Keepers stared deeply into the others' eyes with confusion. The Guardians of the Faith honed their focus under their expressionless golden faceplates on Typhus and his Keepers. The Oblong Eyes at the end of their staves began to spin and glow, a magical vibration resonating in the air.

Neither side spoke nor made any sudden movements. Each ready to strike at less than a moment's notice. Each understood the consequences of attacking the other, though.

Who would make the first move?

The pure abhorrence on Typhus's face removed all humanity from him. Any hope of preserving what little sanity the king had disappeared in this moment. His hair and beard were unevenly long, matted, and oily. His royal garments were stained with gods-know-what. The knuckles on his right hand bled from the abuse Drake received, and his nails were long, cracked, and yellow. A putrid smell permeated the air around them. Sheridan took a second to collect himself and refrain from gagging.

The stalwart king gave a devious smile.

"So," he said, "my daughter is conspiring with my enemies. Bringing this mage into my home to assassinate me?" He pointed a yellow nail at Drake writhing on the table. He looked between the Guardians of the Faith at the Providence. "Providence, my cousin, years pretending to be my savior, my caretaker. You lie. You steal my life, my essence. And now you turn my daughter against me to do the same to her. Just as you stole my wife from me. Vile *witch*." He spat at her. The Guardians pointed their staves directly at Typhus. He looked at Sheridan, who huddled over a trembling Lia, with fire in his eyes and raised his sword, pointing it at the dwarf. "And you, *fucking dwarf!* I never trusted you the moment you cheated your way into *my* palace. Yes, you cheated. By the All-Seeing God's good grace, never would *my* people vote for a fucking dwarf. I refuse to believe the people of Havyn would descend that low into the deepest depths of the Connections." Spittle flew from the king's mouth with every word he lashed out with. "I would not be surprised if you were partially responsible for murdering my wife, so you could slither your way into my palace and corrupt me and my daughter. You are a serpent. Do you know how to kill a serpent? You cut off its fucking head!"

He bent his knees slightly and squinted, trying to catch a glimpse of Lia's face as she tucked herself closer into Sheridan. He waved a hand, dismissing his daughter as if she was a piece of rotten fruit being thrown away. He turned to his Keepers and said, "Kill them. Kill them all. My daughter will die a coward, just as she has always been."

His Keepers exchanged a concerning look as Typhus exited down the hall. They were outnumbered and outmatched. No pair of soldiers, regardless of talent or experience, could hold their own against four Guardians of the Faith and two Keepers, and these two knew it. Sheridan saw the humanity on their faces for a split second, and he wondered if they would defy their king's command to kill the princess, who they were also sworn to protect.

Again, they were in a controversial position.

And again, the Keepers chose to follow their sworn duties.

They began to walk slowly around each side of the massive rectangular table towards the cowering princess, the dwarf, and the Providence. Princess Lia's Keepers frustratingly marched at their counterparts and braced for the attack. The Providence's Guardians remained in their defensive stance, not ready to attack.

"Wait a moment," the Providence muttered under her breath. Sheridan barely heard her.

The Keepers met one another at either end of the table and swung their longswords. Metal struck metal; the piercing shriek of combat filled the air. The Keepers clashed over and over again; though, Sheridan noticed they were holding back from their full potential.

"Wait!" the Providence said to Sheridan and Lia. Her Guardians refrained from combat thanks to her calm composure. "Typhus! He's having a moment of clarity. It may not seem so, but he recognized each one of us for the first time in months. This may be our only chance to reason with him."

Lia, realizing the Providence might be right, jumped to her feet, wiped her wet cheeks, and shouted at the dueling Keepers, "That's enough! End this fighting, *now!*"

Her Keepers instantly dropped to one knee, facing her direction, with their blades laid on the stone floor. Typhus's Keepers prepared to swing at their foes when Lia pointed a finger and scowled at each of them.

"You *dare* attempt to attack a defenseless enemy? Be ashamed. The Order of the Keeper taught you better." She gestured between her own Keepers, who still knelt obediently. "They surrendered their weapons. Take them into custody if you must, but they are not to be struck down. I am going to speak with my father, and you shall not stop me. Come if you fear I am a threat to his majesty."

The Keepers lowered their blades In shame. Lia then proceeded around one end of the table, pushing past her father's Keeper, and continued down the hallway. Her Keepers rose to their feet, sheathed their blades, and followed after her. A moment later, composed after nearly breaking a cardinal rule of engagement, Typhus's Keepers tailed them.

Sheridan and the Providence waited until Lia's voice, calling after her father, faded to a distant murmur. The two rushed to the table where Drake lay unconscious. Blood continued to pour from his brow.

"Do not move him," the Providence commanded. "I do not yet know what is broken. He has sustained many hard blows."

After carefully examining what she could, she ordered her Guardians to carefully lift Drake and carry him to her study. The Providence and Sheridan led the way. Sheridan's eyes darted around, trying to locate where Lia went. As they passed through the throne room, there was still no sign of them.

"Do not fear for her," the Providence comforted. "I have faith in her."

"As do I," Sheridan replied. "It is him I do not have faith in. Moment of clarity or not, he just ordered our deaths."

CHAPTER 53

The Providence began healing Drake immediately. Her Guardians laid his unconscious body on one of the medical beds. After unbuttoning Drake's tunic, the Providence careful opened the front and slid his arms out of his sleeves.

Blue and purple bruises formed around his left set of ribs, along with some less intense ones on his face, right arm, and lower right abdomen. The Providence ignited her palms with her magical white light of healing and placed them gently on Drake's ribs. Instantly, he stirred and clenched his jaw so hard Sheridan thought his teeth would shatter.

"He has four broken ribs," the Providence deduced. "None punctured his lung, thank the gods."

She began motioning her hands in slow, circular motions over the bruise. Drake regained consciousness during the procedure and flinched from the pain.

"I thought this was supposed to heal me, not hurt me," he complained.

The Providence smirked. "Recovery, naturally or by means of magic, requires arduous labor from the body. Magic only makes the process quicker."

"My head is killing me." He lifted a hand and placed it on his aching head.

"Lie still, please," the Providence commanded. Drake obeyed. "The laceration above your eye is fresh. Your head is still rattled from Typhus."

"No," Drake gritted his teeth again. "This feels familiar..."

The Providence stopped. She narrowed her eyes at Drake and curiously stepped to the head of the bed. Her glowing hands approached the open wound on his brow. The moment she made contact, Drake wailed and writhed on the bed. A pain so sharp spread from his head to his extremities. An ear-piercing ringing sounded in his ears, blocking out the Providence's attempts to talk him through his agony.

"My protégé," a cool, menacing female voice spoke to him. "You thought you would evade me forever? Fool."

Sheridan and the Providence could not hear Myra, though. Drake realized this quickly and struggled to yell out her name. "Myra! It's Myra!"

Sheridan jumped to his feet. "Providence, stop this, now!"

"Doing my best, Sheridan!" the Providence retorted. She worked her magic through the same channels in Drake's brain as last time, attempting unsuccessfully to block Myra's access to him.

Drake continued to thrash on the bed. He grabbed his head and began flailing the back of it aggressively against the pillow beneath him. Had he been laying on a harder surface, his skull would have cracked.

"Stop fighting me, pup, and let me teach you what I know," Myra coaxed.

"Never!" Drake's pain intensified. He hit himself in the head, yet the physical pain hardly phased him.

"All your life, you have been nothing," the mage queen hissed. "By my side, you could become something. Your talents could be used to unify the world. To rid the world of fear and oppression."

"Never! I'll never join you!"

"Providence!" Sheridan yelled over Drake's wailing.

"Sheridan! He won't hold still." She struggled to hold her magical aura against him as he tossed about. Each interrupted connection meant needing to start over completely.

"Move!" Sheridan ordered. Not waiting for the Providence to follow his command, he pushed her aside, moving her hands out of the way, and formed a metallic fist. He wound back his elbow and thrusted his fist into the side of Drake's temple, knocking him unconscious. Drake's limbs fell lifelessly off the edges of the bed.

"Why did you do that?!" the Providence demanded.

"Make sure he doesn't have a concussion," Sheridan said heartlessly. "Are you able to keep him comatose? If so, keep him that way."

Sheridan glared at the Providence, expecting her to make action on his order. She stood immovable. Her face scowled at the dwarf.

"I do not appreciate being ordered around, Sheridan. I am not one of your City Watch guardsmen. I have as much authority as you." She took a deep breath, pulled her golden hair back and let it fall in waves over her shoulder. "Yes, to answer your question, I can keep him comatose. I feel that will do more harm than good."

"You heard him!" Sheridan gestured with an open palm towards Drake's unconscious body. "'I'll never join you,' he said. She is trying to recruit him. To use him against us from the inside. I *should* have enough sense to send him away from the palace and have him locked away, but—"

"But you will lose the governess if you do," the Providence finished. "She loves him, and sending him away will drive an unforgivable wedge between you and her." She put a hand on her hip. "You are fascinated with her. You want her to stay, do you not?"

Sheridan nodded.

"For what purpose?"

Sheridan sighed and stopped pacing. "She is a valuable asset. Not only in our current struggle against the mages, but in our efforts to keep the peace when..."

He didn't need to finish his statement. The Providence knew he referred to Typhus. Despite any clarity he had earlier this evening, Typhus was a threat to them all. His order to have them all killed directly defied what the Concordat stood for. That alone gave them legal grounds to terminate his leadership.

"I will keep him comatose," the Providence brought their attention back to Drake, "but he stays here. I have several white mages that I trust to monitor his health. If a coma keeps Myra at bay, I support this decision. For now."

"There has to be some way to deter her telepathy..." Sheridan thought.

"Can you find anything in that book of yours?" she asked.

"I can check. How about your books?"

"I can check, as well."

Sheridan retrieved the *Encantorum* from his office, which was luckily untouched during their encounter with Typhus, and brought it back to the Providence's study. Once the Providence had Drake in a coma, she sent a pair of her Guardians to collect a few white mages from the nearby healing center. Four young women were more than willing to assist the

Providence with such a task.

Sheridan and the Providence immediately began their research on mindrenders and any counterefforts to their magic.

◆◆◆◆◆◆◆◆◆

Hours passed. Sheridan slammed the page of the *Encantorum* shut.

"There's nothing!" he shouted in frustration. "Nothing meaningful, anyway."

"Truly?" the Providence gently closed the cover of the book she had been searching through. "That book of yours comes from the writings of those who created this kind of magic. How could they have nothing?"

Sheridan sighed, "The only mention of mindrending is on a single page. And the only defense mechanism is 'mental fortitude constructed from years of meditation.' The only problem is—"

"Drake does not have years..." the Providence finished.

"No. He doesn't. This type of defense mechanism is also introduced prior to ever encountering a mindrender, so one may not know if they have developed this 'mental fortitude' until it is too late."

The Providence glanced over at Drake, who lay comatose with four white mages each taking turns circling an aura of pure light around his head in an effort to keep him under. "It is too late for him, then?" Sheridan nodded hesitantly in response. "One of the most important lessons a white mage can learn is knowing when magic and other healing techniques are not enough, and they must let nature take its course."

"You make it sound like he is going to die!" Sheridan challenged.

The Providence shrugged. "What if he does?"

"I never expected to hear you sound so heartless," said Sheridan in shock.

"Not heartless," the Providence explained. "Practical. Knowing that we have done all that we can do. My mages can keep Drake comatose until Myra has been defeated. If we wake him up then we risk her causing him more harm, and potentially harming the rest of us should she succeed in her goal of utilizing his raw magic."

"And what if she is inside of his head right now manipulating him while he is unconscious and unable to defend himself?" Sheridan asked.

"You said it yourself, Sheridan. It is too late for him. Cutting it off at the source may be the only way."

"What if we can't stop her? What if Myra prevails?"

"I never expected to hear you sound so defeated," the Providence smirked. She then leaned in and said in a hushed tone, "Are you not a powerful mage yourself? Think like a mage and not like the Master of Cities for a moment. There are avenues we have not yet pursued, allies we have not yet accessed. The battle is just beginning, and we are still getting prepared."

Sheridan took a deep breath and thought for a moment. "You're right. We must prepare. Focusing on Drake is only taking away from what's approaching from the outside of these walls." *And the inside...* Sheridan thought of Typhus only a few flights of stairs above him.

Giving Drake one last concerned look, Sheridan said, "If he dies... Athenia will break."

"If she breaks," the Providence said ominously, "that may give her the drive to stay and fight for us... *With* us." Sheridan raised his brows, surprised at the sudden cunning ruthlessness coming from the Providence—the symbol of peace for the kingdom. The Providence acknowledged Sheridan's awestruck glare and followed up with, "You want Athenia to stay, you have admitted as much to me. You want her help restoring the peace after we face three separate conflicts—Myra and her army of mages, our debt to High Alta and whatever consequences will come from that, and removing Typhus from power."

Sheridan shook his head. "You are right... Having Athenia here will be a great help."

"She could stay if you asked, Sheridan," the Providence pointed out.

"Or, she could say no and turn back to El Vadora without a second thought."

The Providence reached out a delicate hand and placed it on Sheridan's muscled forearm.

"We must let nature take its course," she repeated. "We are doing all we can for Drake and for Athenia, but now we must switch our focus towards ourselves and our kingdom."

Sheridan nodded before collecting his precious book, cradling it in his arms like something evil would come over him if it was missing from his grasp. He departed from the Providence's study, but not before taking one last look at Drake. Much of the near future would be determined by the young mage's fate.

CHAPTER 54

Ena and Tidas were hours into their early morning patrol. A steady fog rose in front of their faces with each breath. Winter was fast approaching. A front of chilled air rolled down from the mountains of Fairmarq the past few mornings. The sun taking longer to stretch over the distant mountaintops prolonged its warmth from filling the air.

Ena enjoyed something about the winter season, though. Most Havynians would disagree since they thrived in the heat of the summer. Thankfully, winters in Havyn were relatively mild. Fairmarq was not so lucky. Storms constantly berated the mountainside cities and villages, which Ena supposed she was lucky to not experience despite her adoration for the cold season. Tidas, on the other hand, was of summer blood, a true Havynian at heart without the corruption and scheming.

A guard on horseback approached the two of them. She addressed Tidas, "Captain."

"Yes?" Tidus responded.

"An army approaches."

"And the banner?" asked Tidas curiously, with a hint of concern.

"Crossed moons on night-blue."

"Avalon," Ena stated.

Tidas nodded, "Indeed." She looked at the guard. "We will be there within the hour. Ride ahead and tell the guards at the gate to hold position."

The guard nodded before riding off.

Ena turned to Tidas and spoke cautiously, "I thought Raven was a week out. It has only been a few days. How is she here already?"

"I suppose she could have ordered her men to ride hard. A nonstop journey could only take a few days."

But Ena was not as quick to find reason. "Be on high alert."

Despite Tidas's many more years of experience and bright intuition, she trusted Ena and her instincts. "Of course."

Tidas led Ena to the closest guard barracks where they acquired mounts and rode for the northern gate. Without hesitation, Ena dismounted the moment she arrived at the gate. Tidas followed closely in tow. Together, they rode the lift to the top of the ramparts, where they were met by a highly decorated guard captain.

"Captain Tidas," the captain grasped gauntlets with Tidas, as is courtesy amongst guard captains.

"Captain Czarnecki," Tidas unenthusiastically returned the courtesy.

Captain Czarnecki. Ena knew the name. A disgruntled veteran guard, Czarnecki had been passed up for numerous promotions to Commander of not only Havana City but nearly all open positions in Havyn. Reports from his superiors, when requested for letters of recommendation, stated his reluctance to follow orders and lack of respect for teamwork. Given retirement was around the corner, Czarnecki had given up applying for promotions and took his current post at the northern gate to relax and enjoy what little physical work it required.

"Is it Avalon?" Tidas asked simply.

"Seems so." A man of many words.

"Are you certain?" Ena asked skeptically.

Czarnecki sighed impatiently. "Yes. See the banners?"

Frustrated by the captain's nonchalant attitude, she pulled the spyglass from his belt, prompting a venomous "Hey!" from the captain. Ena extended the spyglass and focused it on the massive army closing in ten miles away. The banners, in fact, carried the Avalonian crest. Ena could not question that. She focused closer on the men in the vanguard. At first, nothing stood out as unusual. Their armor looked like standard guard armor, but the color of the steel seemed off. Could that have been a trick from the sun and the angle it gleamed on them?

No, Ena thought. *It's never a coincidence...*

She had seen steel that color before. Glancing down, she saw what hung from her waist – the Aconyte steel sword she managed to take from Mida. Aconyte steel? How could a whole army be equipped with Aconyte steel armor?

Not just armor, Ena realized. Many of the men in the advancing army were wielding swords very similar in structure and design to Ena's. Those not wielding Aconyte steel were armed with... nothing. Not a single sword, axe, or even a dagger, lay at their sides or in their hands.

"Mages!" Ena exclaimed. She thrusted the spyglass into Captain Czarnecki's hands. "Look there, Captain. Aconyte steel on some, weaponless on other. That is an army of mages coming this way, despite what those banners show. Shut the gates and sound the alarm!"

Captain Czarnecki glanced through the spy glass and returned a defiant grin to Ena. He spat, "I don't take my orders from some half-rate governess of a land no one cares to remember."

Tidas, who is not known for losing her temper easily, wedged herself between the captain and Ena, grabbed the captain by the neck guard, and nearly lifted him off his feet.

"Close the fucking gate, you smug old man, and sound the gods-damned alarm or you won't live to see retirement!"

"Please..." the captain gasped for air as his neck guard pinched his windpipe. "I'm under strict orders to keep the gates open under any circumstance." Tidas dropped him to the ground. Rubbing his throat, he continued, "Sound the alarm all you want, but every guard here will fight to the death to keep this gate open, even myself."

"Who gave you that order?" Ena asked.

"It was," Czernecki cleared his throat as he stood to his feet, "Lord Elmar. The gate must stay open."

"It is a trap," Ena stated. She clapped Tidas on the pauldron. "Sound the alarm, now. I need to warn Master Sheridan."

Tidas nodded confidently and trotted over to the brass bell that hung nearby. She rang it loud and clear, ordering all of the nearby guards to prepare for battle. Word spread swiftly. Within minutes, every alarm bell along the northern wall rang ferociously.

Ena ran down the steps, not waiting for the lift to bring her to the ground below, and leaped onto her horse's back. With a firm kick of her heels, the horse reared and stormed forward, kicking up chunks of earth in its wake. Every guard tower and barracks Ena sped by rang their alarms and guards swarmed at the ready towards the north.

◆◆◆◆◆◆◆◆◆

Anxiously, Sheridan continued his exploration of the *Encantorum* while awaiting updates on far too many fronts.

It would be a miracle if his hair didn't completely grey over by the end of the week. Most importantly, his focus was stuck on Lia.

Several days had passed since their close encounter with Typhus, which led Lia to face a difficult task—meet with Typhus privately, something she had not done in over a year, and try and talk some sense into him. The Providence was certain that the king's mental degradation was far beyond a curable point, but she was confident that with proper treatment the degradation could be slowed, providing additional and longer moments of clarity. She had failed in her efforts thus far to convince him to allow her to treat him. Perhaps the princess would be more successful.

Sheridan feared what that success would cost, though. Lia lost all love for her monster of a father once his illness brought out his true side. However, could sympathizing with him cause her opinion to shift and change the outcome of their plans?

I cannot think selfishly, Sheridan thought. *If the princess chose to make amends with the king, then so be it.* Lia was smart enough to know that her father's illness prevented him from being a capable ruler. Despite any positive or negative feelings Lia may have, she knew she had to step up into a role she was unsure she was ready for.

The suspense was killing Sheridan far more than he made it seem outwardly. He had assumed a parental-like role in Lia's life, and he cared for her as if he raised her himself. The unknown of Lia's wellbeing drove him crazy. Her Keepers ensured him multiple times each day that she was safe. They could not confirm if she was making any headway with Typhus, but they checked in with her frequently enough to know she was doing alright.

Typhus was on the brink of madness—true madness, not mere states of confusion. What was Lia hoping to accomplish?

"Lia is doing exactly what she needs to do," the Providence explained when Sheridan finally shared his silent concerns to her. As Sheridan opened his mouth to protest, the Providence interrupted. "Lia is confronting her father, or what's left of the man who was once her father. She is reasoning with him and hopefully breaking through his cloud of confusion. She is all he has left, and if anyone can speak with him during a moment of clarity and convince him to formally turn in his crown, it is her."

"But at the risk of her life?"

"We each risk our lives every single day. We did not assume our roles expecting a life of ease."

Sheridan hated that she was right.

Over a day had passed since the Keepers last provided a status update. That made Sheridan uneasy. Uneasy beyond the point of anxiously pacing around his office. Uneasy to the point he began marching up the steps of the Spire towards the king's chambers. With an axe strapped to his back and his hand hovering over the hilt, he was ready to defend the princess at any cost.

Halfway up the stairs, he heard feet stomping down the stone steps from above. The clanking of metallic armor soon followed. Suddenly, both of Lia's Keepers and one of Typhus's stormed into view above him, meeting the Master of Cities on the steps.

"Thank the gods!" one of them exclaimed. "Master Sheridan, things have taken a dangerous turn."

"We need your intervention," said Typhus's Keeper.

Without a second thought, Sheridan brushed past them and continued his ascent. "Of course. Retrieve the Providence at once."

Lia's Keepers nodded and followed orders. Typhus's Keeper followed the dwarf. "This is beyond anything we can do to serve and protect, Master. Apologies we did not retrieve you sooner. We thought we could help."

"No need to apologize, Keeper," Sheridan assured him. "You came to get me, and that's all that matters."

At the top of the steps, Sheridan turned down the hall to find Typhus's bed chamber door wide open. Hastily entering, he spotted Typhus's other Keeper standing just beyond the threshold of the archway leading out onto the king's private balcony. The sheer curtain hanging above the archway gracefully blew aside with the breeze to reveal Lia standing in the middle of the balcony with her back towards him. Sheridan continued, kicking aside piles of dirty clothes, food, and other filth that littered the king's bedchambers.

The Keeper turned and held out a hand, stopping him. "Sir, approach with caution."

Peering over the gauntleted hand in front of him and past the princess, Sheridan saw Typhus standing atop the balustrade edging the balcony.

"Lia," Sheridan forced a whisper.

The princess turned her head just long enough to let out a *shhh*. She refocused her attention on her father. "Dad, it's me still. Lia, your daughter. Please get down from there."

"No!" the king replied. "No, no, no! I will never fall for your traps! Vile creature, spewing venom with your words. Poisoning the minds of those around you. I will never listen to you again. Bring back my wife. Bring back Helena! She is just on the other side. Down there." He pointed down over the ledge. "I will be with her soon..."

◆◆◆◆◆◆◆◆◆

By the time Ena reached the base of the Spire, alarm bells were ringing across the entire city. Guard captains barking orders could be heard for miles.

As Ena dismounted her horse, a black stallion galloped up the cobblestones and skidded to a stop in front of her. General Braxon swung his left leg over the saddle and dropped to his feet.

"Governess Athenia, I assume," Braxon smirked. "A pleasure." His dreamy, blonde locks and bright cerulean eyes swooned most women, but Ena knew his reputation enough to not fall for his charm. She had never met the general of the king's army in person, but she shared enough correspondence with him over the years, requests for backup at El Vadora's border being denied each time, to have a sour distaste for the black steel-clad warrior.

"Excuse me, General," she took several wide steps around him to pass. "I must see the Master of Cities."

Braxon followed closely behind. "My army has raised their alarms, as well. I'll need to accompany you."

It went without saying that mages were at the southern border, too. Somehow, they had been surrounded on all sides. How had the mage army closed in on the largest and most powerful city in Havyn without a single scout alerting them?

Guards surrounded the base of the Spire at the top of the steps leading to the grand doors. They stood alert and unmoving.

"What are you fools doing?" Braxon waved his arms as if swatting flies away. "Can't you hear the bells? We are under attack and you idiots are standing there like bunnies sunbathing in an open plain. Join the fight or you will find my sword bathing in your blood after it opens your jugular vein." The guards shakily scurried off to the nearest sounds of fighting, which were eerily approaching closer to their location.

"If they make it to the Spire, we may not survive this," Ena expressed quietly.

"Fear not, Governess!" Braxon announced in a joking tone. Ena had not realized the general heard her. "Once my men deal with these fiends at the border, a company has been ordered to report here for additional support."

Ena ran in front of him as they crossed the threshold of the Spire stopping him in his tracks. "You are *so* certain that you can defeat this mage army that you dare not even baulk at the fact that this attack was somehow coordinated so perfectly that no scout picked up on their arrival. Are you truly *that* stubborn, arrogant, and brash?"

"Pardon me," Braxon pushed past her and continued heading for the stairs. "I am certain we can defeat them because, for one thing, they are hardly an army, as you claim—they are a band of rogues with no discipline or fortitude. They also use their magic for fear, and my men have had all fear ripped out of them during their first week of basic training."

He continued, "And common sense tells me that if scouts somehow missed two massive waves of invading armies, then they were either killed or paid off. Something tells me it's the latter since money can talk louder than a sword." Braxon suddenly came to a halt, causing Ena to slam into him. He whipped his head around to Ena, putting his face uncomfortably close to hers. "I'm not brash, either. Stubborn and arrogant I'll accept but I'd have to argue against brash."

Ena held her tongue and let Braxon take the lead to the top of the Spire. There was no sense in wasting time arguing with him.

◆◆◆◆◆◆◆◆◆

Lia held up a hand as Sheridan attempted to step forwards and intervene. The princess shook her head and flicked her eyes over towards the archway. Taking the hint, Sheridan stepped back.

Lia turned back to her father. "Dad, I know you miss mom. I miss her every single day. Nothing will take that feeling away. But I am still here. I still love you. If you follow mom, then I will lose you, too."

A hand touched Sheridan's shoulder. At quick glance, he noted the porcelain hand of the Providence. He hadn't heard her approach with Lia's Keepers, had no idea how long she'd been there, but the princess's words must have struck a chord with the Providence, for she had tears welling around her eyes.

"It's too late," she mouthed to him.

Too late? Sheridan thought, trying to understand.

Typhus's feet shuffled on stone balustrade. He turned back to Lia. He blinked several times before saying, "Lia? My girl, is that you? You've grown."

"Yes, Dad, it's me," Lia said with a sigh. Clearly this was not the first moment of clarity he's had in the past several days the two of them have been locked up together. "Please, come down from there. Let's talk inside."

"I'm tired of talking, Lia. I'm a tired old man."

"Dad, you're hardly old," Lia snickered. Whether the laugh was genuine or not, Sheridan couldn't tell.

"Lia," Typhus continued, "I am lonely and growing older by the day. Without your mother, I can no longer care for you. I have nothing else to live for."

Sheridan, the Providence, and the Keepers all watched in suspense as Lia took two steps closer to the king and held out her hand.

"That's ridiculous," Lia jested. "I'm still just a girl. I need my father." She gestured all around her. "This kingdom, Havyn, needs its king. So many people need you. You can live for that, can't you?"

"Perhaps I could, Lia," Typhus spoke quietly. "Perhaps..."

Lia smiled and took another step closer with her hand held out ready to take his.

A breath of silence passed between them all.

Something wasn't quite right. Lia was trying to take advantage of her father's moment of clarity to pull on his heartstrings in order to save his life, and it seemed to be working.

Only, it wasn't.

The Providence was right, Sheridan realized. Typhus wasn't blind. He would have seen the dwarf he despised and his cousin who he blamed for the death of his wife. He would have seen them standing there watching him, and he most certainly would have said something.

Yet his focus was on Lia, and Lia alone, as if he still wasn't in reality.

"Lia," Typhus whispered. Lia responded with a simple *mhm*. "Your mother misses you. Can't you hear her? She's calling for you, as well. Join me." Typhus now extended his own hand, nearly closing the gap between him and his daughter, fingertips nearly touching.

"Dad... I can't... Mom wouldn't want this." Panic could be heard in Lia's shaky voice.

"What would you know?" Typhus began raising his voice. "You are a naive little girl. You know nothing of Helena, my only love!" He threw his hand out again into Lia's face. "This is your only chance. Come with me to see your mother once more, or die here alone..."

Lia slowly lowered her arm, dropping it limply by her side. "I'm sorry, dad. I will not go with you."

"Traitor..." Typhus said to himself. "My own flesh and blood, a traitor!" He scraped his feet on the balustrade, rotating back to the atmospheric abyss before him. Nothing between himself and the ground three hundred feet below except the near-winter air. "Helena, my love. I am ready. I am ready to hold you once more."

Typhus inhaled deeply and held his breath for an eternity. Sheridan heard the familiar sound of armor clanking behind him as Athenia and General Braxon jogged into the king's bedchambers followed a detail of guards. He held a finger up to his lips to keep them quiet.

Then, Typhus exhaled slowly. His breath fogged the air around him.

"I'll be with you once more." He lifted his foot and took one faux step, disappearing over the balcony in the blink of an eye.

Lia let out a singular gasp as she covered her mouth with her hands in disbelief. A sob escaped her, breaking the ominous silence.

CHAPTER 55

No one stirred.

Not until Lia dropped to her knees in utter shock.

Her Keepers rushed to her side while Typhus's Keepers ran to the balcony's edge and peered over. The Providence knew exactly what they could see without observing on her own—their king's body, about the size of an ant from this high up, with blood congealing in a crimson pool around him. Bones shattered, flesh lacerated, and fluids oozing from every orifice.

"Quick," the Providence jumped into action. "Sheridan, take Governess Athenia and General Braxon to fetch a white mage and confirm if King Typhus is alive or dead."

"First of all," Braxon stepped between the Providence and Sheridan and pointed a gauntleted finger at them both, "what the fuck just happened here? And shouldn't *you* be the one to check if the king is alive, Providence?"

The Providence fluttered her eyelashes and brushed off Braxon's rude attitude. "General, I have mere moments to get the princess to safety and prepare her for what's to come next, preferably without the intervention of Keepers or guards."

"You have more to worry about than her Keepers with mages running rampant through the city," Braxon sneered.

"What?!" Sheridan nearly fainted.

Ena stepped in and grabbed Braxon by the arm, pulling him away from the Providence. "Come, we can explain on the way."

Sheridan exhaled, "Keep her safe, Providence."

"Of course." She watched as they departed from the king's chambers before walking gracefully to Lia, gently moving her Keepers from her side. “Pardon me, gentlemen. I will keep a close eye on her.”

The Keepers were reluctant to allow the princess to depart from their view, especially during this vulnerable time. The king’s Keepers, on the other hand, would never allow such a thing. They had become so hardened after years of watching over a king descending into madness. The Providence took full advantage of their distraction with the king’s death and snuck Lia away.

There was no denying the king was dead after a fall like that. It didn’t take the healing wisdom of a white mage to know that King Typhus was no more. Law demanded that a white mage pronounce the deaths of all who pass away, and sending Sheridan to confirm the death would make it even more official.

Despite her attempt to take the princess alone, her Keepers followed ten paces behind them. Lia, still in shock, said nothing, only stared blankly ahead, as they trudged through the garbage decorating Typhus’s bedroom floor and down the spiral steps. At the base of the stairs, the Providence met four of her Guardians who waited patiently where she instructed them to. They pivoted in place and marched in step, two ahead of the women and two following, in a defensive position. They walked briskly down the expansive hallway to the Providence’s chambers. Lia’s Keepers stopped just outside the door, minding their privacy as they always have.

Inside, it was bustling. Four white mages rushed back and forth from the Providence’s many cabinets full of ingredients, salves, and oils to Drake’s bedside. Drake was stirring on the medical bed, restless in his coma. Sweat beaded along his brow, and his teeth were clenched so tightly they could shatter like glass.

“Place a bit in his mouth,” the Providence ordered. The mage closest to the shelf with the wooden bit grabbed it and placed it in Drake’s mouth as two other mages held open his jaw. As his mouth clamped back down around the bit, the wood cracked and splintered. The Providence rushed over and felt his forehead. “He’s burning up. Concentrate a cooling spell on his feet, wrists, and head. Keep his fever down and keep him under.”

The mages did exactly as she said without question. They did not ask who Drake was or why they needed to keep him comatose. The loyalty white mages had to their Providence was unyielding.

Returning her attention to Lia, the Providence led her to a chair at the center of the garden and sat her down gently. The Providence paced through her garden, searching. She plucked some leaves from a vine along with the petals of a white flower. She placed the ingredients into a granite mortar and grinded then to a pulp with a matching pestle. A finger dabbed the green paste and smeared a streak under the princess's nose.

After a few seconds, Lia's eyes began to water and flick side to side. Suddenly, she gasped and blinked her eyes rapidly.

"Gods, what is that?" Lia wiped tears from her eyes with one hand and the potent paste from her philtrum with her other.

"Something to take you out of shock," the Providence responded, handing over a silk handkerchief. Lia took it and wiped away the remainder. The Providence continued, "You will be safe here."

"Safe from what?" Lia shook her head.

"With your father gone, the Keepers will engage in a safeguard protocol and keep you within eyesight and arm's length until they deem the situation safe. While I trust them to keep you safe under normal circumstances, they know we were planning to remove your father from power. They may enact certain laws in the Concordat that can grant them emergency control until it is determined if your father's death was a coup or not."

"What do we do next?" Lia asked nervously, playing with her mother's heirloom necklace hanging along her neckline.

"Wait for Sheridan to get back here. He is checking on your father."

◆◆◆◆◆◆◆◆◆

They stood over the mangled mess left behind by King Typhus. The pool of blood continued to spread until it drenched the soles of their boots. The trio waited as a white mage arrived and waded through the depths of crimson to needlessly check the pulse of the nearly unrecognizable monarch.

The mage stood slowly, met the eyes of the Master of Cities, and shook their head.

Dead.

What followed was an eerie silence. The silence of the unknown of what was next to come. Then, as the crescendo of alarm bells pulled them back into reality, General Braxon leaned down and whispered into Sheridan's ear.

"You know," he began, "had I not just witnessed what occurred on that balcony, I would have the slightest inkling that you pushed him yourself."

Sheridan turned his face and met the general nose-to-nose. "Only a *slight* inkling?"

"Oh, no," Braxon grinned, "I'd have cut you down even shorter than you already are without a second thought."

Governess Athenia's gauntlet smacked against Braxon's armored shoulder with a metallic backhand. "Braxon, enough. You saw what I saw. Sheridan, there is not much time for this." She gestured to what remained of Typhus.

Ena had filled Sheridan in on the mage army at the gates. By the sound of the bells sweeping across the city, they had broken past the gates. Sheridan trusted that the guards were doing the best they could to hold them back.

However, no guard in this city has ever been trained on how to fight a mage. Not for a thousand years. On the rare occurrence a mage caused any trouble, the guards knew enough to control the situation. But a full army of them?

Sheridan couldn't lie to himself; he was terrified at the very strong chance they might not survive this.

"Athenia, let's round up any spare guards and meet them head on," Sheridan said. He turned back to the white mage and asked, "Can you collect the king's body and preserve it? He will have a proper burial after this is over."

The mage nodded.

"I'm heading back to the border," Braxon stated. "If I get things under control there, you'll have a company of my men at your disposal."

Sheridan watched as Braxon marched around the base of the Spire back to his horse. The mage used their magic to wrap Typhus's body in a glowing veil. They hovered their hands inches above the king's body as it levitated off the ground, walking it over to a temple nearby.

In a strange sense, Sheridan felt sad, as if he was saying goodbye to an old friend. He supposed if it had not been for the king's illness, perhaps they could have been closer.

As soon as Braxon took off on his horse, Sheridan and Ena mounted their own and headed for the northern gate. He trusted the Providence to keep Lia safe in the meantime.

Together, he and the governess galloped through the streets at lightning speed. Platoons of every spare or off-duty guard followed closely behind—all were mounted with sharpened lances resting in their holsters on one side and swords hanging from their sheathes on the other. The closer they got to the gate, the more citizens of Havana City were fleeing in terror in the opposite direction. The bells rang so loudly, Sheridan could hardly hear their screams.

"They've broken through the gate!" he called out. "Full speed!"

They dug their heels in and the horses threw back their heads before thrusting forwards. Their surroundings blurred as they raced down the main road. Looking ahead, Sheridan saw plumes of smoke billowing into the air and polluting the blue sky. The temperature climbed noticeably the closer they got. Many of the fleeing citizens were victims of the flames, with scorched clothing and red, irritated flesh.

Ahead, the cloud of smoke was so thick that it coated the street, blocking their view. Through the smoke, dozens of mages decorated with Aconyte steel armor walked with confidence. Some wielded fists full of fire. Others wielded swords of Aconyte. Sheridan had a choice to face them head on or to stand guard and hold them back.

He chose to face them.

He ordered his men, "Charge them!"

The guards behind him armed their lances, holding the hilt tightly, ready for impact. Ena drew the Aconyte sword from her belt and held it out horizontally. Lastly, Sheridan unlatched the axe from his back and tightened his grip around its sturdy oak handle.

Time slowed as the space between them and the mage vanguard closed. Mere seconds from impact, the mages grew the flames in their palms into massive fireballs. With outstretched arms, the fire erupted towards Sheridan and his men. Sheridan raised his metallic arm over his face and used just enough of his kinetic magic to shield the flames from doing anything more than lick him. The intense orange glow blinded him.

Closing his eyes, he swung his axe, sweeping the blade along the side of his horse. His weapon met resistance.

As he passed through the blast of fire, his horse continued to plow through the wall of mages, trampling over a dozen more before he yanked on the reins and skid to a halt. He quickly spun his horse and push back through the crowded street. His axe, coated with the blood and bone fragments of whichever unlucky souls met it during his temporary blindness, swung continuously over each shoulder. The mages behind the vanguard, still not completely certain of what just occurred beyond the cloud of smoke, hadn't even turned to face the dwarf as he cut them down from behind.

Glancing over his shoulder, he spotted Ena a few horse lengths to his left taking a similar course of action. Her sword was an extension of herself as she fluidly drove the point through the jugular of one enemy and followed swiftly with a slash at the next, cutting seamlessly through the weak spot between the pauldron and the neck guard and severing the mage's arm completely from their body. These movements were unshaken and relentless.

A true warrior, thought Sheridan proudly.

Many of the guards behind them were just as lucky. Others, not so much.

Those who survived the blast managed to push through the front lines and drove their lances through the chests of the enemy, skewering multiple at once. Those who did not survive met their end with melted flesh or met the ends of Aconyte swords after falling from their horses.

Sadly, many of the horses' bodies scattered across the road. To their advantage, though, the mages now struggled to run ahead over the bodies, allowing Sheridan and his remaining men to catch them off guard.

"Strike them down but keep some alive!" he shouted. "We need prisoners!" Ena immediately switched her tactic to focus entirely on the removal of limbs. Many would bleed out, but some would survive long enough for capture.

The mages quickly caught on to their tactics and directed their magic at the horses. Facing mounted guards head-on was a fool's errand. Knocking the guards off their horses and meeting them in hand-to-hand combat, though...

And that's just what they did. One by one, the horses were struck down, toppling their riders as they fell. Those unlucky enough to be stuck under their horses were murdered defenselessly, unable to stand and fight back. Those who managed to leap free from their horses and wield their swords fought a long, arduous battle. Their armor simply could not withstand the heat. One or two close range blasts were all they could take before sustaining second-degree burns, at the least. Another blast either knocked them unconscious or killed them outright.

Sheridan did not allow himself to succumb to the same fate. Using his magic, he subtly shielded himself and his horse just enough to survive each blow. He allowed a few to connect and singe some hairs or burn some holes in his clothes, only to make the appearance that he was taking damage. In reality, a few minor burns were nothing compared to his previous life in the Dwarven kingdoms. A glance down at his prosthetic arm reminded him as much.

Ena fared well on her own without magic to protect her. She and her horse moved like lightning, veering side to side and ducking to dodge the incoming flames. The way she controlled her horse, like an extension of her own body, was unlike anything Sheridan had ever seen.

Her skills in battle only antagonized the mages, though. They began focusing all of their attention on Ena. She continued to stay on the offensive, slicing at them with her sword and driving her steed into groups of them, knocking them back.

She was quickly exhausting herself, though. Her breaths shortened and her strikes slowed. Had she still not fully recovered from her ordeal in Avalon?

An explosion sounded from the city's center. Sheridan and Ena both looked up to see a plume of smoke climbing into the sky above the Spire. The Spire itself seemed untouched, but that blast was far too close for comfort.

"Athenia!" Sheridan caught her attention. "They've flanked us! They're heading for the Spire!"

He had been distracted as a wave of fire struck him on one side, throwing him from his horse. As he hit the ground with a thud, the horse sped off. Mages jumped at him instantly. He picked himself off the ground and scrambled to pick up his axe right in time to parry an Aconyte sword aimed for his skull. The mage's balance was thrown off by the parry, and Sheridan took this moment to swing horizontally. His opponent's stomach opened up, spilling intestines onto the soot-covered cobblestones.

Another mage approached and threw fire balls one after another at the dwarf. Sheridan met each attack with the flat face of his blade, which began glowing red from the flames. Two more mages followed suit, preventing Sheridan from breaking free of his defensive position. His axe blade could not take too many more blows before cracking or shattering completely.

Ena threw her horse into a gallop and circled behind the attacking mages. She leaned out as far as she could and let her sword slice through all three of them. Their heads fell from their shoulders and rolled away as their bodies dropped with gravity. Ena brought her horse over to Sheridan and held out an arm as she rode by.

Sheridan caught her forearm in his hand and pulled himself up, swinging his leg over the saddle behind her. "To the Spire!"

Ena nodded before kicking her horse and speeding off. The guards who were still mounted heard Sheridan's order and turned their own horses around to follow. The guards on foot remained and fought valiantly.

Would any of them survive? Sheridan had to shake off the thought and concentrate on getting the princess to safety and out of the mages' reach.

CHAPTER 56

They rode hard to the Spire, passing by dead bodies and destroyed homes. The explosion they heard came from the National Bank of Havyn. The entire front face of the building had been torn from the foundation. Mages pillaged and fled with bags full of gold from the vaults. They paid Sheridan and Ena no mind as they scattered with their stolen riches. President Aroy was not going to be happy. Where were all the guards? And why had the mages resorted to pillaging like bandits?

They continued up the hill until they reached the Spire. All of the guards who had rendezvoused here met the mages in combat. Every guard faced off against multiple opponents at once. Sheridan and Ena dismounted and assisted the guards in their path to the doors. Hundreds stood in the courtyard fighting. The clashing of metal, ripping and tearing of flesh, and the *whoosh* of fire drowned out any voices. Orders were being shouted out by many different captains, but none could make sense of it.

Sheridan reached the interior of the crowd, with guards maintaining a defensive position at the base of the steps. As mages drove through the lines of guards, these defensive ones struck them down. Sheridan pushed past them, dragging Ena with him, and saw Braxon at the top of the steps with the company of his soldiers he promised. Any mages who managed to shove past or climb over the defensive line met their demise by a furious and bloodthirsty General Braxon.

"Where the fuck have you been?" he scowled with a face covered in blood.

"There were more than we thought," Sheridan explained as he climbed the steps. "When I heard the explosion at the bank, I knew they had slipped past us."

"Slipped past?" Braxon growled. "They didn't simply slip past you,

Sheridan, they've swarmed the city. Someone left every possible gate wide open and let them in willingly."

"I see that now," Sheridan responded calmly. "The border?"

"Secure, for now," the general calmed down enough to uncurl his lip from his teeth. "They had Brekken with them. Not too many, though. Clearly not a full army from an entire Brekken kingdom.

"Brekken?!" Sheridan's shock showed clearly on his face.

"Before you ask, yes, I took prisoners. The Brekken, at least. The mages consumed bluebite tablets they had hidden on them. Those who didn't die instantly are likely to die any moment now."

A shame, Sheridan thought. *Damned bluebite.* "At least we have the Brekken. Will the rest of your soldiers be all set down here? We need to get to the Providence and Princess Lia."

Braxon's eyes widened intensely as he gazed past Sheridan at his company of soldiers struggling to maintain their presence on the steps of the Spire. "No, I don't believe they will."

Sheridan followed his gaze and saw a thousand more mages climbing the hill towards them. Hundreds of guards stood their ground outside the palace, and hundreds would not be enough for the approaching horde.

"Sound the Divinity Bell," he ordered nearby guards standing just inside the entrance. "And close the doors. Lock them tight. Let no one through." It would mean condemning the hundreds that fought for them, but there was no other choice.

As the doors shut behind them, Sheridan, Braxon, and Ena began their ascent to the throne room. One of the guards unlatched a loop of chains from the wall and began pulling down on one side. Dust and other debris fell from the chains as they were pulled through a hole in the high ceiling. The unused chains loosened centuries of build-up within the track that led to a giant brass bell at the very tip of the Spire.

The Divinity Bell had not been rung in nearly three hundred years. Its purpose was saved for only the direst of consequences. As the chain was pulled, it winded back a clapper that would strike the side of the bell with enough force to sound out across the entire city. It signaled to all guards and white mages to return to the palace as fast as they could.

Sheridan was halfway up the steps to the next landing when the chain dropped back down and the bell sounded, ringing so loudly that the stone walls vibrated vigorously and caused all of them to wince and cover their ears.

As soon as Sheridan took his hands from his ears, he called out, "Keep ringing it!"

Never before had the Divinity Bell been rung more than once at a time. The guard hesitated for half a second before following orders and yanking on the chain once more.

◆◆◆◆◆◆◆◆◆

Lia paced impatiently. Still no word from Sheridan, and the Providence refused to allow the princess to leave. The princess continued to try and convince herself she was ready to lead a kingdom.

Truth is, she would never be ready. All of the books she read, lessons she learned, and meetings she attended with Sheridan and the Providence could only prepare her so much. Even the most veteran leaders questioned their ability to lead.

After several days locked in Typhus's filthy bedchambers, Lia became filthy herself. The Providence had a bath drawn up for her, which she happily accepted. The Providence even lent her a dress to wear in the meantime—a silk periwinkle blue. Lost in thought, Lia paced around the Providence's study, her fingers fiddling with the small silver bird that hung from her necklace.

While Lia paced around, the Providence wrote her weekly letters to send out to the Master White Mages. Despite all that was going on, the duties of the Providence never stopped. As she signed and sealed her last letter, the sound of a bell shook the room. Lia fell to her knees with her hands covering her ears. The white mages flinched and looked to the Providence, who hardly reacted more than looking up from the envelope in her hand, for guidance.

"The Divinity Bell..." the Providence confirmed. "Sheridan must be here." She met the gaze of her white mages and said, "See if the Master of Cities needs assistance." They all bowed before departing from the study, the Guardians of the Faith parting from the doorway allowing them to pass.

"What about him?" Lia gestured at Drake, who began writhing in pain again.

The Providence held her gaze on him for a moment before responding reluctantly, "My mages can be more useful elsewhere."

She stood from her desk and met Drake at his bedside. She reached out and rested the back of her hand on his cheek. With a slow breath in, then an exhale, a slight glow released itself from under the Providence's hand. Drake instantly relaxed and fell back into a deep sleep.

Until the Divinity Bell rang for a second time a moment later.

The walls shook, and the sound deafened all other noise. Drake immediately started convulsing. As the Providence reached out to assist him, a sharp ringing sounded in her ears. So sharp that she flinched and pressed her hands over her ears. Lia must not have heard it, as she ran over to the Providence, and spoke words that were inaudible. The Providence could only watch her lips moving.

A menacing female voice boomed throughout the room.

"You are all fools to keep the boy from me. His power could be harnessed, controlled. Rather, you allow his abilities to grow rapidly and untamed. Flee, Providence. Flee, and save yourself from Drake's inevitable demise. And the demise of Havyn."

Myra! the Providence thought. "Come," she shook the ringing from her head and took Lia by the hand. "We must leave. We won't survive if we stay."

The Providence was unsure why she was trusting the word of this mage queen, but something ominous in her voice made the Providence believe her. She nearly dragged Lia from the room while the Guardians of the Faith maintained a tight box around them. They sped down the hall in the direction of the throne room. Then, it occurred to the Providence that Lia's Keepers, nor Typhus's, were waiting impatiently outside of her chambers. They were nowhere in sight.

◆◆◆◆◆◆◆◆◆

By the time the Divinity Bell rang for the second time, Sheridan and Ena had reached the top of the steps and met the doors to the throne room. Mages were closing in behind them, having broken through the defenses at the base of the Spire. Guards lined up along the steps ready to face the mages as they climbed.

All Sheridan heard behind him was bloodshed. Ena stopped suddenly as they reached the doors.

"Master, wait," she said just before the dwarf pulled open the door. Sheridan looked at her curiously. "I... I think Myra is here. I sense her. Rather, I feel a similar discomfort as I did when she was invading my mind."

"She's here for Drake," Sheridan determined.

"Possibly," Ena was narrowed her eyes, unsure.

"Come," Sheridan ushered her inside.

Braxon remained with the guards in an effort to keep them organized while fighting in a terrain they were unprepared for—on the steep palace steps. Sheridan closed the door behind him and ordered the nearby guards to lock it and keep it locked for all except Braxon. He knew the general would not allow anyone to keep him from being front and center protecting the kingdom.

Sheridan turned to the throne on the other side of the room. In front of the steps of the dais stood all four Keepers. Summoned by the Divinity Bell, he assumed.

"If you think by hiding the princess," one of Typhus's Keepers spoke, "that we'll start taking orders from you, then you thought wrong. We don't give a shit about what's happening outside those walls, and we don't give a shit if you live or die. Give up the princess!"

"Sheridan!" the voice of the princess echoed down the hall leading from the Providence's study. Sheridan rotated his head and watched her run down the hall to him. Behind her, the Providence and ten Guardians marched into the throne room. Lia wrapped her arms around Sheridan in a tight embrace. "Please, tell me what's going on!"

"Mages have taken over the city," Sheridan explained bluntly. "I don't think many of us are going to survive this. You will, though, Lia. I will see to it that you live. And then you will live on to be the greatest queen Havyn will ever know."

"Why does it seem like you are saying goodbye?" Lia began wiping tears from her cheeks.

Sheridan opened his mouth to speak, but Braxon appeared through the slightly ajar door and shut it hard behind him, guards securing the locks. He strode across the room with a bloody lip and sweat on his brow.

"Everyone be ready," he suggested. "We have about ten seconds before that door comes down in a blaze of glory."

The Divinity Bell shook the walls for a third time.

No orders were needed—every guard drew a weapon and stood alert across from the door. Even the Keepers readied their weapons, swords in their left hands, on the same arms their kite shields were strapped, and spears in their right. Sheridan had little faith that a couple dozen guards and four Keepers could hold their own against several hundred mages, but he was not ready to give up the fight yet.

"Providence, Lia, come with me," Sheridan led them to the top of the dais next to the throne.

A blast sounded from behind the door. Flames flared out from the seams. It could only withstand a few more of those before ripping apart or falling off its hinges.

"They're here!" Braxon called out.

"Quick!" Sheridan drew the women's attention again. He reached out and pressed on a jewel towards the base of the golden throne. There was a heavy *clunk* from underneath them. While Sheridan messed around with the throne, the doors finally gave way and broke from their hinges. The double doors dropped and splintered, sending chunks of wood flying. Mages poured in like water through a broken dam.

Understanding a threat to the Providence was imminent, her Guardians leaped into action. The center of their Oblong Eye staves spun and glowed a bright white. As the mages approached, the Guardians swung their staves, sending beams of pure light at the enemy. Instantly, as the light connected with the mages, they dropped like flies.

Still, though, ten Guardians of the Faith against an army of hundreds did not seem like great odds.

Sheridan faced the foot of the throne and placed his hands on the fronts of the armrests. He pushed with all his might. The throne slowly pushed back, revealing a dark tunnel with an old wooden ladder leading into the unknown depths below.

"Sheridan," Lia said, "what is this?"

"Your one-way ticket out of here to safety," he explained. "Follow the tunnel. It will lead you under the city and out into the hills to a hidden safehouse. It was designed to protect the crown in dire emergencies.

Only the Master of Cities knows of its existence. Go!"

"No," Lia shook her head, "not without you."

The Providence interjected, "I will be with you, Princess. You will be safe."

"I can't do this without the both of you!" Lia whipped her head back and forth between the two of them, pure panic in her gaze.

Ena ran up the steps to meet them. By this point, every individual in the room who was not standing by the throne was engaged in heavy combat. The governess spoke with an uneasy calmness, "Pardon my interruption. Princess, now is your chance to leave with your life. As long as you and the Providence survive, Havyn still stands a chance. Your people need you."

Lia held her gaze in Ena's eyes for a moment before returning to Sheridan. The dwarf looked pleadingly at her.

Finally, Lia nodded stoically.

"Come back to me, Sheridan," she said with a quiver of her lip. "Live for me."

Sheridan returned a confident nod. He watched as the Providence took the lead down the ladder. Lia followed. Sheridan pressed the jewel on the throne once more, and the mechanism within it slowly pulled the throne back into its place. Sheridan caught one last glimpse of Lia's hazel eyes shimmering in the light as the throne sealed the two of them apart.

He held back all emotions as he wielded his axe and shared a glance with Athenia—a glance that spoke the undying truth that the two of them would not live to see another day—before returning to the gruesome fight behind them.

CHAPTER 57

Descending into darkness, into a seemingly endless abyss absent of all light and sound, two women were accompanied only by their own uneasy breaths as they traversed hand under hand, foot under foot, down the solid wooden rungs of the ladder leading from the hidden hatch in the king's throne room.

This passage, and the ladder, were likely original with the construction of the palace. Erected nearly a thousand years ago, the Spire of the New King was designed and constructed by an architect infamous for their paranoia and mistrust for others, so much so that their identity has been hidden from history without a trace other than the works of wonder they left behind. This passage, just wide enough for an average human to fit, slid straight down the center of the Spire between walls to keep its existence a secret. It is said only the Master of Cities knows of its existence and is only meant as a last resort to save the lives of the royal family.

The descent lasted a lifetime. Halfway down, or as best as she could tell, the Providence's arms burned excruciatingly. Lia slowed down above her, likely experiencing the same pain and exhaustion, and her elbows shook uncontrollably trying to hold herself in place. If she fell, she would take the Providence down with her, and the two of them wouldn't survive a fall like that.

They continued down the ladder until their feet touched solid ground. Lia sat on the ground in the pitch black and sighed, "Can we stop for just a minute?"

"No," the Providence answered. "We must continue until we reach the safehouse."

"But we can't even see where we're going!"

The Providence held out an open palm and mustered an inkling of strength to cast a spell. An orb of white light appeared an inch above her hand and illuminated the area around them. They were in a cavern that was carefully and smoothy carved by man's hand—it was far too evenly carved to be natural. On the opposite end of the cavern was a tunnel leading further underground.

"Come," the Providence helped Lia to her feet.

Together they walked steadily into the tunnel. The Providence, not used to travelling far without her Guardians in tow, took one last look up the ladder towards the hatch that had disappeared long ago into the shadows above. She knew they were doing their duty by protecting her escape, but a sudden wave of loneliness washed over her.

The path was smooth and easily walkable, following a steady decline. The Providence tried to trace their steps and find where along the surface they would be. They must be following the slope of the hill the Spire sat on. It continued on and on.

Miles ahead, the path leveled out into an open clearing with three additional tunnels branching off—one directly ahead, another to the left, and a final one to the right.

"Which way?" Lia asked.

The Providence didn't respond, for she was not certain herself.

The Providence studied each tunnel entrance. Above each one, there was a flat square carved it to the stone. Within each square was a set of symbols that she couldn't decipher. They were a language she was unfamiliar with. She was fluent in elven, and she could read most forms of modern dwarven and even some of the ancient text. Brekken had evolved into a distant version of the common tongue, but she had seen enough of the symbolic Brekken of Old, and this was not it.

All that was left was the language of the faeries. Why in the Connections of Magic would there be faerie text written in a thousand-year-old secret passage beneath Havyn's capital city?

"Wait, someone is coming," the Providence heard the sound of boots shuffling along the gravel ahead of them. "Keep quiet." She drenched the light in her palm, drowning them in complete darkness.

From the tunnel straight ahead appeared three people—two humans and one elf. The two humans carrying torches placed them in sconces hanging from the wall on either side of the tunnel entrance. Dancing flames illuminated the empty room, revealing the two fleeing women.

The tunnels to the left and right abruptly closed with hardly a seam where the edges originally existed.

"The Providence *and* the princess," the elf spoke with a cruel smile. "Right where you're supposed to be."

The two humans raised their arms and pulled two giant rocks from the walls. Lia gasped, and the Providence pulled the Princess behind her by the arm and raised a shield of light in front of them. The earth mages hurled their rocks at full speed, which collided with the shield. The shield shattered like glass and pulverized the rocks into dust.

Behind her, Lia started screaming and pounding her head with her palms. The Providence shot a glance at the elf, who was holding out a veiny, pale arm and flicking his tendril-like fingers.

A mindrender!

CHAPTER 58

The moment the throne sealed itself over the escape passage, Sheridan turned back to the scene unfolding in front of him. More mages piled in through the throne room door. Flames shot through the air and heated the room. Sheridan's brow quickly moistened with sweat.

The Keepers held their own in a magnificent display of swordsmanship and choreography. Their armor and shields held back the most violent attacks of magic, seemingly bouncing off or flowing around them as if they were being splashed by water. Their spears kept a healthy distance between themselves and their opponents, whereas their swords struck down any who got close enough to feel the razor-sharp blades. The dual wielding technique was exclusively taught during years of intense training at the Library. All Keepers learned this seemingly undefeatable skill.

Ena's fighting style, on the other hand, was just as deadly, if not more so, and was completely self-taught. By the time she joined the City Watch, she had already developed an aptitude for combat beyond that of a veteran captain or commander. She was nimble, agile, and precise.

Braxon was the exact opposite. He was brutal and ruthless but still calculated enough to not allow his offensiveness to sacrifice his defense. He used his two-handed greatsword to cut his opponents in half. Body parts went flying, and blood flowed across the marble floors. He stood closest to the throne room doors, acting as the first line of defense.

As Sheridan gripped his axe, ready to join the fight, the wall surrounding the throne room door exploded. Flames and debris scattered towards them. The blast was strong enough to send all those standing closest to the doorway airborne, including Braxon, who was thrown all the way to the back of the room.

The general's body slammed into the stone banister of the stairs wrapping behind the throne. He hit the ground with a groan and remained unmoving. Sheridan rushed to his side and checked his pulse.

Still alive, Sheridan sighed with relief.

Through the cloud of dust, a dwarf with a salt-and-pepper beard strolled into the room wearing an ornate set of Aconyte armor.

Sheridan recognized him instantly.

"Mida!" he shouted out over the fighting.

"Sheridan!" Mida called back. "My friend! Witness me serve you your demise on a silver fucking platter!"

Rage boiled inside of Sheridan like never before. He bared his teeth and clenched his jaw hard enough to shatter bone. If Mida was right, if this truly was his demise, Sheridan would not go down without a fight. He had nothing more to lose than his life, and he did not intend on holding back until his dying breath.

Sheridan dropped his axe and held out his arms. A wave of energy built up inside of him, and he directed it to his fingertips. He held his palms out at a wave of a dozen mages rushing at the dais. They stopped mid-step, frozen in place from head to toe, before Sheridan used his magic to launch them full-force across the room and through the gaping hole in the wall. They tumbled like ragdolls down the stairs, knocking over other mages in their path.

Seeing this, many of the mages turned their attention to Sheridan and began directing blasts of fire at him. He reached out with his magic and pulled two of the closest enemies off their feet and held them levitating in front of him. The fire blasts struck the human shields, and Sheridan threw them at the attacking mages.

The sheer force at which Sheridan sent his poor victims flying was enough to completely crush the chest plates of their Aconyte armor. None would live through that.

Sheridan honed in on Mida. With each step down the dais and across the floor, every mage that even peered in his direction was sent off their feet and hurdling to their death. Those who got close enough to rush him met the full wrath of his kinetic magic. Limbs snapped and twisted with bones protruding and blood spraying, necks were broken and heads rotated backwards, and some were lifted off their feet and their armor slowly crushed as if it were foil, until their internal organs collapsed.

In a minute's time, the floor surrounding the Master of Cities was decorated with mutilated bodies.

Still yet, Sheridan's tirade barely made a dent. The number of enemies seemed limitless. For every one Sheridan killed, two more took their place. He closed the distance between himself and Mida one step at a time, and Mida's smug smile only instigated Sheridan's magical torrent further.

However, the closer he got to Mida, the more difficult it became. There were too many of them. They were vastly outnumbered, and the fact that they've survived this long was either pure luck or a true testament to their combined skills.

Just as Sheridan's magical strength started to waiver, out of his peripheral, Sheridan saw Ena launch herself at Mida.

◆◆◆◆◆◆◆◆◆

Ena fought off countless mages, deflecting swords and dodging flames. She felt fatigued. She hadn't pushed herself this much since before Mida captured her and broke her down into a feeble, fragile version of herself. The Providence had nearly restored her to her former strength, but it became apparent that her limits had dwindled. Sweat poured down her face from overexertion and from the heat that danced around the room.

It was suffocating.

As she jabbed the tip of her sword through one mage's throat and followed with a downward strike into the shoulder of another, she realized there was not another opponent to meet next in combat.

She looked around and realized she could take a moment to breathe.

She also realized that the enemy's focus was directed elsewhere. She watched as Sheridan stomped furiously down the center of the room towards Mida, unleashing a ruthlessly magnificent display of invisible magic. He was literally ripping apart his opponents without even touching them and using their bodies as projectiles. The devastation he left in his wake was unimaginable, unstoppable, and unforgiving. Did he understand how truly merciless his actions were? Did he care?

Backed into a corner with no way out and nothing left to lose, Ena supposed she, too, would unleash everything she had within her.

Although, she was not a mage capable of destroying everything in her path, nor did she even think for a second that Sheridan was either. What else was he hiding? Would they live through this for Ena to find out?

And then she saw her opportunity.

Not a single mage turned in her direction. All occupied by Sheridan, the Keepers, or the Guardians of the Faith for only a few moments, Ena took her chance.

She tightened her grip on her sword's hilt, inhaled deeply and exhaled, then her heels dug in as she lunged forward into a full sprint. She jumped, leaping over the heads of everyone in her direct path, and raised her sword with both hands on the hilt over her head. In her line of sight stood Mida, the dwarf watching intently as his mage army began to overtake Sheridan, not noticing Ena flying in the air towards him.

She brought the sword down hard and fast. Her feet hit the ground at the same instance the sword connected with Mida. The ear-piercing sound of clashing metal reverberated off of the walls, and the blade of Ena's sword held for a split second before cracking and snapping in two.

Before her, Mida stood wielding a familiar sword. Pitch black from hilt to tip absorbing all light around it, humming with a magical aura.

Caught off guard and without a useful weapon to defend herself with, Mida wound back his elbow, clenched an armored fist, and punched Ena in the nose.

She stumbled back, dropped the remnants of her sword, and held her face. Blood poured from her nose as her eyes welled up from the brutal force that had likely broken her nose. Mida swung the faerie sword and struck her in the left shoulder. Her pauldron felt most of the blow but was not enough to keep the razor-sharp blade from cutting deep into her arm.

She could barely move her fingertips. Immobilized, she stumbled backwards and fell onto her back.

Nearby mages witnessed the attack and rushed at Ena. Mida held up a hand, and they stopped in their tracks. He laughed and tossed the sword back and forth between each hand.

"You know," he spoke, "you should have made more of an effort to keep this sword when you had the chance. Lightweight, perfectly balanced, sharp enough to cut through the trunk of a tree as if it were a blade of grass. I'll take this one over the Aconyte one you stole from me any day. As you see, my men are dressed to the nines with Aconyte steel. That one sword is nothing to me now. And now, you will die by your own blade!"

Drake's blade, Ena said to herself. It was Drake's blade, not hers. The blade she first met him wielding. How ironic that she would die by it now.

◆◆◆◆◆◆◆◆◆

Drake screamed and writhed in pain. The intensity of the magic building up within him was far more than a human could bear. The air in the Providence's study grew to scorching temperatures. The plants in the botanical garden shriveled and flowers dropped from their stems.

No white mages were around any longer to help control what Drake was going through. Could he muster the mental and physical fortitude to survive this?

"No, you cannot," an eerily familiar voice answered. "What the Providence didn't have the heart to tell you is that she did not believe you could truly overcome this."

"Myra!" he yelled out loud. "Leave me alone! Stop this!"

"You are a fool," she condemned. "I was the only thing that stood between you and your ultimate demise." Before Drake could argue or inquire further, Myra continued, "You see, there comes a point in every mage's life when they either embrace their magic potential or quell it and barely hear a whisper a fit for the rest of their life. Then, there are mages like yourself. You never knew you were a mage, were never presented with an opportunity for your magic to bloom. Or, as the Providence and her harem would describe, you were never entuned with the Connections enough to weave your potential. By the time your magic did bloom, you were too old and mature to grow with your magic, and now it is growing at an exponential rate that you cannot control. You will burn out in a destructive release of your magical potential.

"I have had my eyes on you for months, Drake. I had hoped to harness your ever-growing power and feed off of it myself, use it, harness it. My allies, or so I thought, seemed to have other plans. Athenia is hurt, Drake. She is hurt and will die at the hands of the enemy. You can stop it, though. Do not waste your last breaths lying here in a hospital bed. Use them to muster what little control you still hold over your magic to defeat your enemy and save the woman you love."

Drake thought hard. Then, he asked, "Why should I believe you?"

Myra purred in his ear. "Have you ever heard the phrase 'The enemy of my enemy is my friend?' For the moment, consider us friends."

"And after that?" he asked skeptically.

"What does it matter to you? You will be dead. Athenia will be, too, if you do not act now."

Drake grinded his teeth fighting off the pain. He considered Myra's words.

Then, he took a deep breath, held it in his lungs, then exhaled a cloud of flames.

CHAPTER 59

Sheridan attempted to push through the flood of mages overpowering him. His magic, though powerful, was untrained from decades of keeping it tucked deep in his pocket, and exhaustion set in fast. He locked his eyes in on Mida, who stood over an injured Athenia with a menacing gaze on his face.

Sheridan refused to watch him kill her. However, no matter how much magic he used and how hard he tried to get to Ena, he only kept being pushed back.

The Keepers still kept up their fight; though, they were beginning to slow down. Fatigue was setting in. Mistakes would start to happen. Including Sheridan tripping backwards over the bottom step of the dais and landing on his back. He winced and casted a pulse of his kinetic magic as a dome around him, just in time as a series of mages tried to jump at him with fire in their hands. The pulse sent them flying. A second wave came at Sheridan a moment later. He cast a second pulse, and his vision became spotty. Every ounce of magic was costing him energy he could not spare.

"Stand down!" Mida called out over the violence. The next wave of mages about to land an attack on Sheridan stopped short of a possible killing blow. "All of you, hold your positions!"

Sheridan was breathing heavily as he lifted himself up and stood on two shaky legs. Being two steps up on the dais, he had a clear line of sight of Mida. The dwarf held Ena with a tight grip by the back of her hair. On her knees in front of him, Mida had her facing Sheridan while he held the blade of the faerie sword at her throat. The Keepers held their weapons at the ready, awaiting the next move. The Guardians of the Faith stood stoically in place, unmoving and unphased.

"What's next, Mida?" Sheridan called out between breaths. "What more damage could you do?"

"I think we both realize that you cannot survive this fight much longer. Look at you, ragged and weakened. Even that magic of yours, which I was *not* expecting in the slightest, is dwindling." He glanced down at Ena, who struggled weakly in his grasp. "She's bleeding and tired. One slip of my hand and her blood sprays out, and in thirty seconds she dies. Oops!" He pressed the blade slightly, and blood began pooling and dripping from the cut that formed. He grinned. "Don't worry. I won't do it. Just be sure those Keepers don't try anything stupid. And those Guardians... I'm not sure if they'll take orders from you, but be sure that they do."

"What do you want, Mida?" Sheridan rasped.

"I want you to turn Havyn over to me," Mida demanded. "Issue that secret command of yours, get all of the City Watch to drop their weapons." Sheridan did not even want to begin to guess how Mida had learned of the Master of Cities's last resort code. "Turn yourselves in and I will be merciful. No one wants to inherit a pile of rubble. Allow Havyn to hold onto some of its beauty and let me have it. Now, while you're still able to walk, fetch your king and give me his crown."

He doesn't know about Typhus yet. "I can't do that..."

"Wrong answer!" The blade bit deeper, crimson flowing down Ena's neck. "Try again!"

"Mida! Stop!" Sheridan tried not to give Mida the satisfaction of begging, but seeing Ena in such a vulnerable state made him search his mind for any way to get her out of this safely.

A moment later, the temperature in the throne room rose rapidly. Then, yellow and orange flashes of fire appeared in Sheridan's peripheral. He was not the only one, as everyone in the room turned their heads to witness what was approaching them from the hallway leading to the Providence's tower.

Drake.

Engulfed in a sphere of spinning and twirling flames. Levitating six feet off the ground. The orb of inferno passed through the hall and into the throne room. Tapestries hanging on the walls caught fire and burned up. Metal armor and swords heated to an uncomfortable level. The mages all had a look of fear deep in their eyes.

The power Drake held was unsustainable and uncontrollable.

"Athenia," Drake spoke with a deep, booming voice. To Mida, he demanded, "Release her."

Mida stared at the god-like magical being before him. For once, he was speechless. He didn't even get a chance to respond before Drake demanded again, "Release her!"

The blazing vortex lashed out, whipping flames at nearby mages. With an instant touch of Drake's magic, they caught fire from head to toe. They released blood-curdling screams before almost immediately turning to ash.

"Gods have mercy..." Mida said under his breath to himself.

"You deserve no mercy," Drake promised.

The vortex suddenly grew larger, engulfing anything and anyone that passed through it. The Acoyte armor held on for a few seconds longer than the bodies of the occupants, but even that crumbled to dust.

Drake was not holding back. He unleashed the full potential of his magic, exploding the flames throughout the room.

Sheridan acted fast. He rushed over to Braxon's unconscious body and held out a hand in Drake's direction. As the wall of flames approached, he raised a shield with his kinetic magic, dispersing Drake's around them.

One blast of fire was directed at Mida, who tossed Ena to the side and held out the faerie sword defensively in front of him.

Sheridan quickly reached out with his other hand and attempted to form a similar shield around Ena's nearly unconscious body.

The Guardians of the Faith spun their staves in counterclockwise spirals in front of them, forming their own magical shields. The Keepers got caught in the blaze as they threw their cloaks over themselves, like shells, in a feeble attempt to remain protected by the strands of Aconyte woven into the fabric.

Drake held his blast of fire at Mida steady, but the faerie sword seemed to absorb the magic. However, the force of the blast was still enough to force Mida back. His feet slid along the marble floor as he held his stance.

Digging his heels in, Mida forced one step forward, and then another. The wall of flames creeped closer to Mida as he continued to deflect Drake's attack.

As the flames engulfed the room around him, the sword protected him, but the heat was sweltering and unbearable. His eyes burned not only from the heat but from the bright flashes of fire swirling throughout the room. He pinched them shut. Taking one more blind step forwards, he stumbled. Drake took this opportunity and held out his other hand to increase the power of his fire blast. Mida was thrown back against the wall and hit his head, falling unconscious. Still gripped by the hilt, the ancient blade protected him from the surrounding firestorm.

◆◆◆◆◆◆◆◆◆

Ena blinked, trying to gather her surroundings. Blood loss had caused her vision to blur. On the brink of consciousness, she barely felt Mida toss her to the ground. She barely noticed as Drake torched every living thing in the throne room to ashes.

She remained unscathed, though. Studying her surroundings, she saw flames swirling around her and colliding with an invisible bubble that protected her. As fire blasts hit the shield, they burst into sparks of varying colors, like fireworks.

She had no idea how it was happening, but she took a few moments to sit up and collect herself. The cut on her neck still bled, but slowly. Pending any infections, her wounds were the least of her concerns.

Where was Drake? She squinted to catch glimpses of him, or Sheridan, or any other living person through the flames.

Off in the distance, she spotted Sheridan near the throne crouched in front of Braxon's unmoving body with both arms held out in front of him. They were shaking, and he clenched his jaw as a stream of blood poured from his left nostril. She supposed she could thank Sheridan for magic bubble cast around her, but that would have to wait.

She then spotted Drake.

Floating halfway between the floor and the high ceiling with his arms outstretched, Drake looked to be in pain. The marble walls and floor began to crack from the heat. The vortex surrounding Drake and flowing throughout the room intensified beyond his control.

"Drake!" Ena called out, unsure if he could even hear her through the turmoil. "Drake, stop this!"

Drake turned his head and met Ena's eyes with his own. A tunnel formed through the flames between them. Ena now had a clear view of him. Drake said, "I can't stop.. I'm sorry, Athenia..."

"Drake!" Ena rasped. Sudden panic shot through her veins. The tone of Drake's voice... What would happen to him if he could not control his magic? "You must regain control. We need you. *I* need you..."

"I'm so sorry, Athenia," he repeated, this time with a single tear falling down his cheek before evaporating. "This was the only way. Please don't forget about me. I love you."

"Wait, Drake!" Ena reached out her hand, attempting to grasp at anything out of thin air.

Drake pulled his arms close to him, holding his chest tightly. The vortex began to close in around him and swirled even more rapidly. The flames turned blue and white. Then, Drake roared out loud and threw open his arms.

The vortex erupted and spread through every inch of the room, down every hallway, shattered the stained-glass window behind the throne, and sent a wave through the hole in the throne room wall, down the stairs, and blew the front doors of the Spire clean off. All guards and mages in the path of the doorway at the base of the Spire were struck by the blast and burned alive.

Inside the throne room, the explosion blinded Ena. A ringing in her ears deafened her. The shield Sheridan cast around her held back the blast, just barely, disintegrating as the flames passed over it.

Ena trembled. Not from fear or pain, but from the adrenaline rushing through her veins. As her vision cleared and the ringing subsided, she scanned the scorched room looking for any other signs of life, and for Drake. He lay on his back in the center of the floor.

Ena crawled to Drake and grabbed his hand. He did not grab it back. His eyes were closed, and he smiled peacefully. She felt for a pulse. Nothing. Ena lifted his hands and placed them gently on his chest. She let out a brief sob and held back tears.

Sheridan groaned as he climbed to his feet. Weakly, he walked across the room, dragging his boots through piles of ashes where living people once stood. Approaching Mida, who survived the onslaught with the protection of the faerie sword, Sheridan kicked the sword out of his grasp and drove the toe of his boot hard into Mida's ribs. Mida hardly reacted.

"Keepers!" Sheridan called out gruffly. "Place him in chains and take him to a cell. He must be guarded at all times."

Two of the Keepers slowly rose from their cloaked shells and followed Sheridan's order. They bound Mida's hands behind his back with chains and lifted him. Still unconscious, his feet dragged beneath him as he was carried from the throne room, or what was left of it. Sheridan watched as one of the greatest threats to the kingdom disappeared from his view.

He then turned back to the two other Keepers, still under their cloaks. He walked over to them and used his magic to brush the cloaks aside, revealing the peaceful corpses of two of the most valiant knights in Havyn's arsenal. Whatever magic-suppressant was imbued into their cloaks and armor was just not enough for these two to survive.

The Master of Cities leaned down and pressed three fingers against the forehead of one, then the other—an old dwarven tradition to honor their comrades who passed during battle. He then solemnly trekked over to Drake's body and honored him the same way.

"Athenia..." Sheridan whispered to the governess. "I am incredibly sorry for your loss. *Our* loss. Drake was a good man. Sacrifice is the greatest symbol of selflessness." Ena did not respond. She only mimicked Sheridan and placed three fingers on Drake's forehead, which felt strangely cold now.

Sheridan glanced up at the sound of clattering armor to find a platoon of City Watch guards, led by Captain Tidas, climbing over rubble, and respectfully stepping over the piles of ash. Tidas, seeing the blood trail behind Ena, rushed to her side asking if she was alright. She then gasped as she recognized whose body Ena was leaning over.

Ena looked up from Drake's body long enough to notice the Guardians of the Faith standing stalwart and holding their staves with the Oblong Eyes angled down at the ground inches from touching the soot-stained marble floor.

"Sheridan," she murmured. He grunted an acknowledgement that he heard her. She gestured at the Guardians of the Faith. "The Providence. Lia."

Sheridan followed her eyes to the Guardians, who stood in a fashion he had never seen them before. With a feeling of unease in his gut, he said, "Tidas, please take a squad with you into the tunnels beneath the throne. There's a button at the base of the right armrest. Find the Providence and the princess and make sure they are safe."

Without questioning the existence of a hidden tunnel, Captain Tidas called over a squad, pushed back the throne, and descended. Before Tidas mounted the ladder, Sheridan called out, "Tidas, is the city secure?"

"Yes, sir, it is," said a voice from the crumbling hole that once served as the entrance to the throne room.

Sheridan pivoted and saw Lady Raven stepping over the rubble, rapier drawn and stained with blood, followed closely by the Dread Watch.

CHAPTER 60

Tidas's face appeared from the secret passage an hour later.

"Sheridan," she interrupted. The Master of Cities had been debriefing with Lady Raven, who had arrived in Havana City with a combined force of every guard each city in Avalon could spare, including the Dread Watch.

More white mages had arrived at the Spire to confirm the deaths of Drake and the two Keepers, and to heal any guards who may have survived the onslaught. They took Ena and Braxon to a secure healing center away from the palace. Sheridan wanted to ensure their safety. They would all be looked after in a location only he and the white mages knew of until the threat against them subsided.

"Yes, Tidas?" he responded. "How are they?"

"You need to come see this..."

He cut off his conversation with Raven and rushed over to the tunnel entrance. His heart raced as anxiety clenched his chest tight.

Once his feet hit the ground at the bottom of the ladder, he panicked when he saw bloody footprints matching Tidas's boots leading from the darkness of the tunnels. He traced them back to their origin—a small clearing with strange symbols above three pathways. He pushed through all of the guards who awaited his arrival.

What he saw here would live within him and haunt his dreams for the remainder of his life.

A pool of blood sat stagnant in the center of the cleaning. Chunks of sinew, muscle, flesh, and bone scattered from wall to wall. Pieces of torn fabric soaked in blood. Loose boulders and rocks spread across the ground and were lodged in parts of the wall around them.

Earth mages! Sheridan confirmed.

He struggled to compose himself as he examined more of the scene. Tidas was explaining some of the evidence—as a captain, she was skilled with conducting investigations—but Sheridan drowned out her voice as he searched for any signs that the Providence and Lia escaped with their lives.

Begging for any sign, he scoured every inch of that clearing. The fabrics matched the dresses worn by the two women at the time of their attempted escape. A few feet away, he caught the glimpse of a shimmer in the torch light. Tucked beneath one of the loose boulders was a silver chain with a small silver bird hanging from it. Sheridan recognized the necklace anywhere as the one handed down to Lia by her mother, Queen Helena. Lia never went anywhere without it.

Another foot away, four fingers, severed forcefully at the knuckles, dug into the dirt at the end of four drag marks, as if Lia was reaching for the necklace when a shard of earth struck her hand, ripping her fingers clean off.

Sheridan dropped to his knees and retched.

Tidas crouched beside him and placed a hand on his shoulder. "I'm sorry to deliver this news, but the connecting tunnels show no signs of a struggle. No drag marks or kicked up ground. Only three sets of footprints, none matching those of Lia or the Providence, and all came up the center tunnel to this clearing and left the same way. No survivors, it seems. They came in, engaged in a brutal fight, and strolled out. And, yes, I have guards combing all paths of these tunnels to search for them and hopefully prove me wrong..."

Sheridan picked up the necklace and clenched it in his palm. Tears welled up in his eyes as he began to weep.

◆◆◆◆◆◆◆◆◆

White mages examined Ena and Braxon. The laceration on Ena's shoulder was the worst of her injuries and took the longest to heal, but she was cleared within the hour. Only rest would cure the dreadful feeling of exhaustion that permeated her bones. A cot was set up for her to sleep on, but until Sheridan returned, she would continue to fight the exhaustion.

She had no idea where she was. In a basement somewhere, she assumed due to the lack of windows and the cool, flattened dirt beneath her bare feet. The only light illuminated from two small candles, one on the side table next to her cot and the other next to Braxon's, and from the magical glow of the mages' hands as they reset the general's broken leg.

Braxon was in far worse shape than Ena, internally at least. With a broken femur, a few broken ribs, a punctured lung, and a concussion, among many others, he sustained more challenging injuries to heal. While his ribs and lung were healed to perfection already, his leg, shattered in three places, was taking the most time and effort.

"How much longer?" Braxon impatiently demanded an answer. "I have places to be."

The mage setting his bone looked up and responded, "Perhaps another hour, to be certain that all pieces of bone have been put back in place and properly fused."

"Another *hour*?" Braxon sounded offended. "No, no. I have too much to do to be wasting another hour in this damp hole."

"Braxon! Shut up!" Ena reprimanded. Normally, she would bite her tongue, especially given the circumstances, but those same circumstances also shortened her patience for the general's rude, entitled behavior. "Lay back, let the mages fix you, and keep your fucking mouth shut! I do not want to be here anymore than you, but we were instructed to remain here until Sheridan retrieves us. Gods! You were more enjoyable to be around when you were unconscious!"

As Braxon opened his mouth to fire back some nasty remark at Ena, footsteps could be heard coming down creaky, old wooden steps. A door opened on rusty hinges along the opposite wall of the basement. Captain Tidas emerged from the shadows and stepped into the dull candle light.

"Please relax, General," she addressed Braxon calmly, but sternly. "All matters will be taken care of in your absence. We need you at full strength before you return to your duties."

"But—"

Tides interrupted, "Great news. Among the captured group of Brekken on the southern border, one is a Brekken prince. I have the full report here for you." She handed him a stack of documents detailing the events. Braxon thanked her with a nod as he began flipping through the pages.

Tidas continued her report to Ena, "I have also confirmed that the city is secure, for the moment. Nearly all mages were either killed in the conflict or died by suicide." Ena didn't need to be told the manner of death. She knew it was bluebite. "Very few were arrested. Those who were will likely not survive their injuries, but we are hoping to recover them enough to ask some questions. Sheridan will be along momentarily to share some other... news."

Ena noticed the hesitation in Tidas's words. A hesitation that usually did not lead to good tidings.

When Sheridan arrived a short time later, he appeared defeated and broken. His steps were slow and heavy. His gaze kept falling to the floor.

"Sheridan," Ena sat up straight on her cot. "What is it? Is it Mida, or Myra?"

"No," Sheridan cleared his throat. "Mida is under maximum security watch right now. Myra..." He shrugged. "No, this is bad."

"What is it?" Ena repeated.

"This," Sheridan pulled a silver necklace from his pocket and handed it to Ena. She quickly picked up on the blood stains along the chain. "It belonged to Princess Lia. We found it in the escape tunnel."

Reality sank in hard. Ena gulped as if swallowing ingots of lead. The princess was dead.

"And the Providence?" she asked, already knowing the answer. Sheridan locked eyes with her and didn't respond.

It then occurred to her that Lia's death left the throne empty without an heir. By law, the Master of Cities would assume the throne and start a new dynasty, or until the Master of Cities found someone new to take the role. Ena was no longer looking into the eyes of an ally or friend. She now looked into the eyes of a king.

CHAPTER 61

Within a matter of days, Lady Raven, her army from Avalon, and the Dread Watch had secured every square inch of Havana City. Many of the city's residents lived in unspoken fear as the Avalonian guards burst into homes unannounced and turned furniture over to ensure no mages were hiding out.

By the end of the last day of search and seizure, four homes were discovered to be safehouses for the mages. The residents of those homes, and all mages who could not consume their bluebite tablets quick enough, were arrested for high treason, interrogated by the Dread Watch, and were sentenced to death. Only Sheridan could overturn the sentences, but he remained silent for each one.

As soon as the city was deemed secure enough to resume daily life, Sheridan ordered construction crews to prioritize cleaning the streets and rebuilding the destroyed homes and businesses in the Market District. This move was not favorable to those residing on the hill, but Sheridan insisted getting the working class back on their feet was more necessary than pouring millions of gold into the estates of the aristocracy.

Ena and Tidas stood by the Master of Cities's side every step of the reconstruction process, by Sheridan's own command. Another controversial decision on the dwarf's part, as countless of Havyn's own veteran captains offered their protection and were all denied or ignored. When Ena asked why, Sheridan made it evident he trusted no one. Not until he had the chance to interrogate Mida himself.

That chance had finally come after the chaos settled.

Sheridan and his personal guard detail marched to the dark slums of the eastern border of the city, where a maximum-security holding center hid in plain sight. Surrounded by low-income apartment buildings filled with disease from recent years of overcrowding, Sheridan passed through the shit and filth covering the streets until they arrived at what appeared like just another normal apartment building.

The door opened for them as they arrived. Guards lined the hallway, which held ten small cells, five on each side, locked behind thick iron doors with four locks to prevent escape. The same setup was found on the next two floors.

Sheridan continued to the fourth floor, which only held one cell at the top of the stairs. The guards holding their positions outside the cell door all pulled differing keys from their pockets and inserted them one at a time into the four locks. The mechanisms inside the locks squealed and grinded from years of rust and grime. The door swung open with a groan.

Entering, Sheridan saw Mida hanging from chains attached to the ceiling by his feet. His hands were bound to his sides by barbed wire wrapping from his shoulders to his wrists. Any struggle or attempt to pull free meant sharp metal barbs tearing into flesh.

"Guards, let him down," Sheridan commanded.

The guards released the chains and let Mida drop to the floor with a thud, barbs biting into him. Mida groaned as they picked him up and dropped him into a chair at a nearby table. Sheridan sat across from his enemy, fighting off the urge to jump across the table and choke him to death. Ena and Tidas stood just behind him on either side with their hands nested on the hilts of their swords.

"Talk," Sheridan demanded firmly.

"Nice sword you have there," Mida eyed the faerie sword hanging from Ena's belt. "I've gotta say, that's a fine piece of steel."

Sheridan slammed his metal fist on the table. "I said, *talk*! Tell me everything. Now!"

Mida sighed, "What's to tell? I planned an unstoppable invasion of Havyn, and it was stopped. I failed. What more do you need to know?"

"Why do all of this? What was your goal? Who is Myra, and what part does she play in all of this?"

"First of all," Mida began, "I must admit that Myra had nothing to do with this. She and I had a similar goal when we first met, but after the events in Avalon, we had our differences. Toppling the kingdom and taking power for our own, we shared that endgame. Our reasons for doing so and how we got there were very different."

"How so?" Sheridan asked.

"She wanted to take things slow," Mida began explaining. "Wanted to collect her misfit, forgotten, abused mages, bring them to some secret location of hers, and raise them into an army like the one from the Mage Wars. It would have taken years. I didn't want to wait years. Having recruited most of the mages myself, it didn't take much convincing to sway them to my side. Why wait when we could storm the capital under the guise of Avalon's army, kill the king, and take the crown? I would have Havyn in the palm of my hands with all its riches and an army of warriors to protect it."

Sheridan chuckled, "Havyn is in debt. A lot of debt. Typhus is the one who got us there, and he jumped to his death just has your ragtag team of highwaymen attacked. You want Havyn? Sure, Mida, take it. Best of luck paying back High Alta millions of gold or fighting them off as they come to claim their wealth back."

Having clearly not realized any of this, Mida kept his mouth shut.

"And the Brekken," Sheridan continued. "Were they your doing? The ones who attacked us at our border?"

Nodding, Mida said, "Yes. Friends I made during my travels in Brekkenia."

"I figured as much. Your lover, Arahs, has refused to speak since we took her into custody."

"You have Arahs?" Mida nearly jumped out of his seat before the barbs dug in deeper, forcing him to remain seated. Gritting his teeth, he said, "She was supposed to flee the city before the attack started. She should have received my letter..."

"She did," Sheridan confirmed. "But she chose to stay and support you. Loyal girl you have there, Mida. I remembered her from your previous visit to the Spire. It wasn't hard to find her name on the census and voter registration. Seems like she really wanted to start her new life in Havyn with the man she loved. A shame she threw away the rest of her life for you."

"Please, Sheridan," Mida begged. "Go easy on her. This was all me. All she contributed was getting me closer to the others in her Brekken kingdom enough to convince them to aid my cause and call on them for support when the time was right."

Sheridan shifted in his chair, the wood groaning, as he thought carefully. "I may show her mercy, if she cooperates. The last thing I need is a war with the Brekken Alliance by having one of their princes held captive. Can Arahs help us negotiate with her former kingdom?"

"Aye," Mida nodded. "Let me talk to her, or at least write to her, and ask her to cooperate. If she can walk out of this freely, that's what I want."

"So you *do* have a heart,“ Sheridan jested. "I will allow one letter. If she can help, she goes free."

Mida thanked him sincerely.

"I must ask," Sheridan continued, his mood shifting, "why the princess? Why the Providence? Did your ultimate goal of becoming a wealthy dictator deem their lives worthy for the taking?"

"Are you accusing me of murdering the princess and Providence? I didn't see them in the throne room."

"Obviously not since you sent earth mages after them in the emergency escape tunnels under the palace. Don't play dumb."

"Escape tunnel? Earth mages?" Mida seemed genuinely confused. "What are you talking about, Sheridan?"

In a rage, Sheridan reached across the table, grabbed Mida by the beard, and yanked forwards until his chin smashed into the table top. The barbs dug in as blood trickled from each puncture. Mida begged Sheridan to release him.

"The fucking earth mages you sent to wait for them!" Sheridan held his lips barely an inch away from Mida's ear as he screamed at him. "You somehow knew about the escape route and your men were waiting for the Providence and Lia! She was just a girl, you fucking murderer! She was a defenseless girl fleeing for her life, for a new future, and you took that from her!"

"Ahhh! "Mida roared in pain as the barbs bit down deeper. "That wasn't me! I swear it!"

"Swear on what, you pathetic worm? Look where you are!" Sheridan's face grew red with rage, as red as his beard. "You lost! You have nothing to gamble with this time! Admit what you did and be done with it!"

"Sheridan," Ena spoke calmly.

"What?!" he whipped his head around, still seeing red.

"Think about it," she said. "He has nothing to lose. Why would he choose to lie about this?"

Sheridan thought for a moment. He let the wave of anger wash over him, and he realized Ena may be right. Even if she wasn't, what worth would it be to pry that information from Mida? The truth would not bring them back.

Releasing Mida's beard, he sat back upright in the chair, spitting blood on the floor before thanking Ena.

"I apologize," Sheridan said reluctantly.

"No, I'm sorry," Mida responded genuinely. "Sorry for the loss of the princess and the Providence. Not that it means a lot, but I would not have them killed."

Sheridan sighed. "They would have been more valuable to you alive than dead."

Mida smirked. He then followed it with a chuckle. Sheridan couldn't help but smile back and start laughing. The two dwarves shared a hearty laugh.

"Pardon me, Sheridan," Mida said, still chuckling. "You're right, though. What use would have their deaths been to me? I could have High Alta bending the knee to me if I had captured her."

"You fucking snake," Sheridan was still laughing.

"I've gotta ask," Mida started, "what are the chances that I'll keep my head on my shoulders after all this?"

"If you honestly think," the smile left Sheridan's face as he spoke, "that you deserve to take another breath after committing high treason of this degree, then you must have rocks for brains."

Mida nodded. "That's what I figured."

"You didn't do this alone, Mida," Sheridan pried. "The least you can do is give up whatever information you have on Myra and your other constituents."

"Do I get to keep my head if I comply?" the prisoner asked.

"No," Sheridan responded coldly.

Mida whistled. "Merciless."

"Please, Mida," Sheridan scrunched his brow. "Have a moment of redemption. Just one moment of being a decent dwarf."

Mida locked eyes with Sheridan and considered before responding, "Fine. I'll be honest, Myra is even more of a mystery to me now than when we first met. I have no idea where she is or what her true intentions are. She gave me resources and attempted to use me as her pawn here physically in Havyn while she tugged on the marionette strings from afar. I took her resources and ran with them. I had no plans to unite with her after I took Havyn for myself."

He continued, "I will say, you may want to approach those you trust with caution. Myra may have been instrumental in building an army of mages, but my connections here in Havyn are what made my invasion possible."

"How so, and who?" Sheridan leaned in, his curiosity peaked.

"Any other day," Mida elaborated, "those gates would have been ordered shut at the sight of an approaching army. Who ordered the guards at the gate that day to keep them open no matter what?"

"Lord Elmar," Ena confirmed over Sheridan's shoulder.

Mida nodded. "He made sure all of his loyal guards manned the walls that day."

Sheridan leaned in even closer and grunted, "Keep talking..."

◆◆◆◆◆◆◆◆◆

Tens of thousands gathered at the square in the center of the city. A stage with an executioner's block had been set up, and all available guards were stationed around it. The citizens of Havana City waited patiently for the spectacle to begin.

A clock chimed on the hour. Right on schedule, Sheridan appeared from one of the buildings on the edge of the square. Guards lined up along the path from the building to the steps leading onto the stage. The Master of Cities, and future king, was decorated in his finest raiment, ready for the noon execution of Mida, Lord Elmar, and dozens of other captains and guards who aided in the invasion of Havana City.

Sheridan marched along the path with Ena in tow. She, too, donned an elegant, sleek set of armor that expressed her figure. It was by far not the most protective armor, but the statement it made, a powerful woman with authority, strength, and beauty, resonated with the thousands of onlookers.

Snow flurried from the clouds as Sheridan and Ena took their positions on the stage. With a nod from Sheridan, the Dread Watch marched in pairs with Mida and Lord Elmar between them up the steps from the path. The Dread Watch stood the two prisoners next to one another with a few arms lengths between them in front of the executioner's block.

"Welcome all," Sheridan began his speech. "Over the past week, you have all been subjected to the greatest attack on our kingdom's capital that our history has ever known. Millions of gold in damages. The loss of countless innocent lives—guards and civilians both. Worst of all, fear and anxiety that will now live with us survivors for the rest of our lives. Standing before you are two of the primary perpetrators of the ordeal—Mida, an arms merchant, and Elmar, former Lord of Havana. Many of you may not know Mida, for he orchestrated the attack behind the scenes, but you all know Lord Elmar. Let this serve as a reminder to all that we live by a law. A law that was designed to protect the innocent and keep the powers that be in check so events like this do not occur, and if they do, the punishment will be swift and those responsible will pay the ultimate price.

"In an effort to be transparent, I must explain that the mages who lead the charge against our grand city were recruited based on a twisted truth that they are suppressed from society because society fears the unknown, thus fearing them. What little we understand about magic is from our respect of the position of the Providence and her healers spread across the kingdom. A thousand years ago, magic was not a hidden besmirchment of one's true self as it is now. In fact, it was celebrated. Earth mages built many of our earliest structures. Fire mages kept us warm through cold winter nights. Water mages developed aqueducts that delivered water to land locked towns and cities, like ours.

"Over time, we lost our relationship with our mage brethren. Uneducated people in power stuck their noses up at mages, seeing them as lesser beings. Mages began to repress their talents, and entire generations of magic weavers passed without so much as lighting a candle, fixing a crack in the cobblestones, or filling a glass of water. For that, I issue an apology to our mage citizens on behalf of all of Havyn's past, present, and future rulers who have remained uneducated. I also issue two promises. The first being that all existing and future rulers will be given the education needed for all mages to feel safe, and those who choose to live in ignorance will be removed from their positions and no longer able to suppress those they do not understand; and the second being that all mages will be treated as equals from this day forward, and any mages still out there are encouraged to reveal yourselves to your nearest white mage church and begin a robust training program to learn more about your abilities and master them. Even those who may have participated in the latest events here in Havana City who escaped and remain in hiding, you are encouraged to do the same. Use your magic for good and you will be forgiven."

Sheridan held out a hand and gestured to Mida and Elmar, who stood with sunken shoulders among a crowd of survivors, and continued to speak. "As for these two traitors, let them serve as reminders for anyone, mage or not, that treason against the crown will not be tolerated. The Concordat deems all acts of treachery subject to immediate execution. These two men not only contributed to the attack on our city, but they also aided in the lives of your king, princess, and Providence to be lost." Sheridan needed a scapegoat for their deaths. Admitting that a larger threat still existed would only add to the unrest. "The All-Seeing God will judge them as their souls are received by the Connections of Magic, but their physical bodies will have judgement passed down on them by me."

Sheridan turned to the two traitors. "Dread Watch, place Mida on the block."

Following orders, two of the Dread Watch grabbed Mida by his shoulders and walked him behind the block. Pushing him to his knees, they bent him forwards and pressed his chest down on the stone block with his head hanging over the edge.

"Mida," Sheridan addressed him, "in keeping with execution tradition, do you have any last words you wish to share with the people of Havyn?"

Mida lifted his head and scanned the crowd. "Only this—I do not regret what I did, but I do regret the outcome." He rotated his head just enough to catch Sheridan's stare. "However, you will be in better hands now."

Sheridan felt the slightest fraction of a pang of guilt. Mida's words would live with him. Still, he commenced with the execution with a nod to Ena.

The governess, clad in her breathtaking display of radiant armor, drew a sword from her belt. The crowd awed at the darker-than-night faerie sword that resonated with an audible hum. She stepped up next to Mida, who now closed his eyes as Ena raised the blade.

In one fell swoop, and with a doppler *whoosh,* the sword fell with gravity and sliced through Mida's neck. The dwarfs head dropped with a thud and rolled a few feet as blood spurt from his neck.

Sheridan nodded, and the two Dread Watch guards carried the body and head away. The next two Dread Watch dragged Elmar over, who refused to walk, and shoved him down onto the block next.

"Elmar," Sheridan addressed, "do you have any last words you wish to share with the people of Havyn?"

Elmar rotated his head and locked eyes with Sheridan, then proceeded to spit on his foot. Refusing to break bearings, Sheridan only responded with another nod to Ena. Again, the black blade swung and the former lord's head dropped.

The crowd did not react. There were too many emotions to feel and too many to choose one to express. They watched intently as Sheridan and Ena walked from the stage, their steps on the wood echoing through the square. It sunk in shortly after watching Sheridan disappear from the square that they were looking at the next king of Havyn. The next time they would see him at a gathering of this scale would be for his coronation.

◆◆◆◆◆◆◆◆◆

Sheridan and Ena entered the Spire and passed by dozens of masons who were working tirelessly to repair the cracks and holes in the walls and floors and ensure the palace's structural integrity remained intact. Guards walked the halls, and maids and servants were hired to take care of the needs of the workers inside the palace.

The emptiness was dwindling, and Sheridan was reminded of the bustling environment he first encountered when he set foot here at the beginning of his tenure.

As they walked into the throne room, Lady Raven stood waiting. She met them halfway with the train of her black feathered dress trailing behind her. The lady bent her knees in a slight courtesy.

"Your Highness," she addressed Sheridan.

"None of that, Lady Raven," he waved a hand and shook his head. "I'm not king yet."

"Correct, but we must begin planning your coronation *and* set a date for the Master of Cities election. Nominations are already coming in."

"Give me until morning to think it over, please." Sheridan was exhausted and wanted nothing more than to relax in his chambers with a hot cup of tea, or a stiff glass of whisky. He hadn't decided which yet. "Whichever date is decided on, make it the same for the Lord of Havana position. Let's waste no time filling that one either."

"Of course," she dipped her head and turned back down the hall towards the Providence's study. Lady Raven graciously donated her time to return the Providence's study to its former glory and help keep things afloat in that office to lift at least one burden from Sheridan's shoulders. She was a woman of the Faith and knew enough of the religious tomes to get by.

While not a white mage, she was assuming the temporary position well.

"Athenia," Sheridan looked at his counterpart, "you are welcome to stay here in the palace. There are plenty of rooms upstairs for you to choose from. You could use a real bed instead of a canvas cot from the barracks."

"Thank you, Sheridan," Ena smiled. "I appreciate the offer, but I feel my place should be with Tidas in the barracks. After the guard commander's death during the uprising, I fear she may overexert herself attempting to fill the gap and place her name in the hat for the job. Yet another position to fill."

"Indeed," Sheridan sighed in agreement. "Too much loss lately. It all still hasn't sunk in yet." He met her green eyes. "Athenia, I am still very sorry for the loss of Drake. And the loss of Damian and Klaus back in Avalon. You never had much of a chance to mourn their losses"

Ena nodded. "Thank you, Sheridan. They were loyal, and the closest to family or friends I had in El Vadora. Though I only met Drake recently, I feel as if I lost a lifelong friend."

"I must ask, did you love him like he loved you?"

Ena pursed her lips and glanced upwards, thinking. After a few moments, she found the words. "I would like to think so, but I truly do not know. I am not certain I am capable of love. My exposure to love has not been the greatest."

"I think you could be capable of love, given the right chance," Sheridan smiled hopefully at her. "But we have plenty of time to discuss hopes and dreams another day. Have a good night, Athenia. Let's meet here in the morning. I appreciate your assistance during this transition. El Vadora has waited patiently for your return, and I can't thank your people enough."

Ena nodded and turned back out of the throne room, descending the steps of the Spire.

After Ena left, Sheridan dragged his tired feet to his chambers down the opposite hall as the Providence's study. He poured himself a glass of whisky, after all. Enjoying the silence, he scanned his office and wondered if he was ready for the next step—ready to receive the crown of Havyn. As his eyes passed over the large desk covered in hundreds of pages of reports, letters, and laws, he did a double-take. The leather spine of a familiar book caught his eye.

The *Encantorum.*

He almost forgot about the ancient faerie tome. Reaching over, he placed his hand atop the cover and dragged it over. Flipping open to the last page he remembered, he began rattling through the strange symbols and letters in his head in an attempt to recall what he had learned about the lost faerie language.

"What an interesting read you have there..." A cold, sharp female voice echoed off the walls and spoke directly into Sheridan's ear at the same time. "Oh, the secrets those pages must tell..."

Sheridan gasped and slammed the book shut.

"Myra!"

EPILOGUE

Sweat beaded on the young maid's brow as she stirred the contents of the cast iron cauldron hanging over the burning logs of the kitchen hearth. Her long black hair was tied back in a loose ponytail and the sleeves of her sage dress were pulled back past her elbows to avoid the flames. She was certain the hairs on her arms were gone after spending the past half hour stirring and stirring with a solid wooden mixing spoon that was the length of her arm.

The king had fired another head chef, leaving the cooking of these elaborate meals to the maids, like herself. She was always on dinner duty, which was arguably the most arduous of the three daily meals, especially when the king had his entire family around the table on nights like tonight.

Everything has to be perfect, the maid told herself.

However, unlike most other nights, she was unexpectedly doing the cooking alone this time. A fresh seafood chowder was a challenge enough to make since the fire needed to be roaring the entire time, but adding perfectly cooked filet mignon as the entrée made this meal nearly impossible to do on her own.

The maid took a step back after the seventy-seventh stir of the chowder. She followed the previous chef's recipe exactly, even though she questioned if seventy-six or seventy-eight stirs truly made a difference. Who was she to question a world-renowned culinary artist nice enough to leave behind his handwritten recipes of some of the king's favorite meals?

Turning to the long butcherblock table in the center of the kitchen behind her, she read the next step—chopping the parsnips to be added to the chowder. She took the pile of parsnips and pulled them closer, grabbing the one on top. She began cutting from the tip with a razor-sharp knife.

"I'm so sorry, Elyza," a voice sounded as another maid burst into the kitchen. The other maid, much older than Elyza, didn't even look at her and she rushed into the kitchen, folding up the sleeves of her matching dress, and began slicing equally sized cuts of filet from the main hunk of pristine meat resting on the butcherblock table. "The bedchambers required extra attention today, and I think we missed scrubbing the floors in the main hall yesterday, so I had to take care of that before they arrived. Oh, and—"

"Mother," Elyza cut her off, "it's okay."

Elyza's mother stopped carving the meat and studied her daughter, who she could tell was stressed and feeling the pressure of being perfect for her king. She had been in that position before—a girl of eighteen at the bottom of the food chain in a cutthroat environment such as this.

Luckily, she was now at the top of the proverbial food chain and was able to protect Elyza, to some degree. The king lost his temper frequently at all of his staff, but he respected his most veteran maid enough to bite his tongue at times. The same respect was passed down to Elyza. Mostly...

"Things will get easier," her mother assured her, returning to the filet mignon. "The schedule for next week shows many interviews for a new chef and kitchen staff. Once one is hired, this part of our day will be much more manageable."

"Until that one is fired, and we start the process all over again," Elyza gave a snarky response, not looking up from her parsnips.

Her mother suddenly gripped the handle of the carving knife firmly and slammed the tip into the tabletop, startling Elyza. "Enough, Elyza! Mind your tongue, or you risk losing it. Should anyone other than me hear disrespect like that against your king, you could find yourself facing far worst punishments than cooking over hot flames."

Elyza slowed her chopping as she considered her mother's words a moment. She could throw a fit like any entitled teenager would do after being reprimanded by one's parent, or she could do her duty that she was born into and keep her thoughts to herself. Her mother always said to be thankful she had a stable roof over her head and meals for free by being in the retinue of the royal family. The pay, while not amazing, was enough to afford some luxuries since they did not need to spend their own money on housing and other amenities.

Elyza had never strayed far from the castle walls. Any time she spent off-duty was usually in the direct vicinity of the castle where the other wealthy members of society roamed. Unlike her mother, she had never seen the parts of the city beyond where some lived in the slums and took shelter from the rain under piles of trash.

She supposed she was grateful to never be exposed to those horrors.

Elyza continued cooking the chowder as a guard entered the kitchen through the servant door leading to the castle's dining hall.

"Time check," the guard said.

"Ten minutes," Elyza responded as she threw the last ingredients into the cauldron and reached for the wooden spoon to stir another twenty-three times, according to the recipe.

The guard nodded and disappeared through the servant's door.

Once the chowder was finished, Elyza ladled it into a dozen porcelain bowls. Her mother placed the iron plate she would use to sear the filets onto the top of the fire now that the cauldron had been pulled away. She stepped away to pick up six bowls—one in each hand and two balancing precariously on her forearms—and assist Elyza with serving the appetizer.

Elyza stepped through the threshold of the servant's door into the dining hall with her mother in tow. Observing two other maids serving wine and water from decanters to each guest, she paced carefully to the seat furthest from the king, who sat at the head of the table. His wife, also the Master of Cities, sat to his right, and his eldest son and heir apparent sat to his left. The prince's wife sat beside him to his left followed by the king's youngest son. Surrounding the remainder of the table were the other members of the king's immediate and extended family, including the Providence, who was also the king's sister.

Conversation roared as Elyza placed her bowls starting at the end of the table leading to the head. The king always made his guests feel important by being served first, but the truth was that he wanted the hottest meal, knowing his guests would wait for him to be served before eating. Elyza always made sure his plate came off the fire last.

"Sal, your face betrays you," the king spoke as Elyza was close enough to hear him address the prince sitting to his left. "You seem worried, my son."

"Indeed, father," Prince Salmeides nodded justly. "Word from the west is that one of our fellow kingdoms has nearly fallen. I received the hawk from our western front just before arriving tonight."

Elyza placed the bowl of chowder in front of Prince Sal at the same moment her mother placed hers in front of Queen Phoebe.

"Havyn?" the king asked. Sal nodded. "Details?"

Elyza turned to walk back to the kitchen, but curiosity got the better of her. She walked half of her usual pace to stay within earshot. It wasn't until her mother caught up with her and nudged her along.

"Tsst!" her mother hissed in her ear. "Enough eavesdropping. The Red One is watching."

A barely noticeable glance over her right shoulder revealed the woman sitting at the other end of the table opposite from the king. A woman with jet black hair and eyes of steel wearing an otherworldly red dress forming tightly to her body with slits on each side falling down the length of the gown from the neckline to the knee, sewn together every six inches or so with blazing rubies. The woman was revealing much more of her body than appropriate for a formal dinner. Confirmed more so by the plunge in front that accented her perfectly shaped breasts that would make any other woman jealous to have.

Her steel eyes were locked on Elyza as her black lips turned upwards slightly at the corners.

Such an insignificant exchange that no one else at the table dared notice, but the Red One took a sudden interest in Elyza that she was far from comfortable with.

Elyza's eyes shot forwards as they entered the kitchen once more. Eliza gathered the last two porcelain bowls and ladled the freshest and hottest of the soup into them. She watched as her mother quickly placed the expensive cuts of filet onto the sear plate, each piece releasing a decadent smell as they sizzled and vapors released from their fibers.

She met her mother's eyes, which responded to her with a look of worry. Elyza took a deep breath before returning to the dining hall and walking over to the Red One to serve her the second-hottest appetizer. She tried not to notice the Red One still staring at her with an almost savory look on her face, as if Elyza was the meal being served on this fine evening.

As the bowl touched the plate beneath it and Elyza took her fingers away, the Red One said with a warmness that only lovers would share, "Thank you, sweetness."

Elyza mistakenly met her ravenous gaze, the hues of grey swirling in her steady irises, before nodding respectfully and continuing to the opposite end of the table with the king's bowl.

No one else seemed to hear the Red One address her—the conversation was too loud, especially at that end of the elaborate dining table. Never before has the Red One addressed her, or her mother, for that matter. She was always here, always in attendance wherever the king went, but she was mostly a shadow or a fly on the wall.

"Thank you, sweetness." The way she spoke it, as if she knew Elyza on a personal level. As if she knew something about her that she shouldn't know.

It sent a chill down her spine.

A chill that was just enough to shake her grasp on the bowl and cause a small spillage to drip down the side of the bowl onto the plate under it as she placed it in front of the king. He inspected the drip for much longer than he should have before looking up at Elyza and giving her a scoffed, "Thank you."

Her mother would hear of that one later.

She gulped as she slowly walked away.

"As I was saying," King Eriputes resumed, "I have my... *concerns.* A sudden mage attack on their capital city, and now that dwarf will assume the throne? Come now, Sal, even you must smell the suspicion in the air."

"I do," Sal admitted, "but I really only want to be smelling this delicious chowder at the moment. Can we react to this news tomorrow?"

"You will need to break the news to your brother that his betrothed has perished. A shame, truly."

Entering the kitchen once more, Elyza assisted her mother with plating the filets with the red wine demiglace and roasted asparagus and waited a few minutes. They needed to allow ample time for everyone to finish their appetizers before serving the main course.

"Mother," Elyza said quietly.

"Yes, Lyza?"

"I think something bad has happened." Elyza watched her mother study her. She knows her mother is aware of where this information was about to come from. Her mother certainly wasn't thrilled about it, but she waited for Elyza to continue. "Something really bad with the Kingdom of Havyn. I heard the king mention that Prince Edacles's betrothed has died. Was that not the princess from Havyn?"

Her mother nodded reluctantly and responded coldly, "Indeed."

"That's all you have to say?" Elyza asked harshly. "A princess had died, one whom was to be part of our kingdom's royal family, and you don't even seem to care. What if whatever attacked Havyn attacks here? You said we would always be safe here. I'm sure that's what all of the maids and servants in Havyn's castle were told, too."

Her mother reached out and touched her shoulder gently. She smiled a genuine, loving smile.

"Relax, child," her mother spoke softly, comforting her anxious daughter. "You are... not a princess. You are much less likely to be targeted by something like that. I am certain we will hear more about the events that occurred in Havyn tomorrow, and our king will certainly ensure the same does not occur here."

Feeling her mother's touch and hearing her calming voice, Elyza visibly relaxed. "Thank you, mother."

Elyza then looked to the floor, unsure of how to say her next thought to her mother.

"What is it?" her mother asked, lifting Elyza's chin to meet her bronze eyes.

"The Red One," Elyza sighed a shaky breath. "She spoke to me."

"Oh..." Her mother immediately removed her hand from her daughter's shoulder. "Come now, we must serve the next course. Do not speak of this again. Forget the Red One interacted with you at all."

Elyza was about to question the demand, but her mother rushed from the room carrying four plates of food faster than she could speak the words. She blinked a few times, more curious now than ever, but nodded to herself before grabbing four plates of her own and returning to her duties.

ACKNOWLEDGEMENTS

First and foremost, to my fiancée, Rachel: thank you for your unwavering support, for constantly nudging me to finally complete this novel after over five years in the making. Turns out I just needed to stop scrolling social media and actually put my thoughts to paper. You were the first to read and edit my debut novel, and this book exists because you believed in it, and in me.

To Eric, my incredibly talented cover artist: your work brought this book to life with your creativity and imagination. How you managed to put together the masterpiece that is now viewed by so many holding this book in their hands is beyond me. I look forward to working with you on future releases.

To Ollie, my corgi, who contributed absolutely nothing of value to the creative process, unless one counts loudly judging my writing sessions with dramatic sighs and demanding attention at crucial plot-turning moments. Your steadfast laziness was a reminder that sometimes doing nothing is also an art form.

To my friends and family: thank you for always supporting my creative mind and encouraging me to pursue my dreams. Not many of you even knew this book was in the works because of my private lifestyle, but now you know and you better read it.

And finally, to everyone who reads this book: you're the reason stories matter. Thank you for joining me in this one.

With gratitude (and a touch of dog fur),
Nicholas Adams

www.ingramcontent.com/pod-product-compliance
Lightning Source LLC
Chambersburg PA
CBHW020743020826
48980CB00019B/776/J

* 9 7 9 8 9 9 9 2 6 0 7 0 3 *